THYRZA

THYRZA
A TALE

George Gissing

Edited with an introduction by
JACOB KORG
Department of English,
University of Washington

Rutherford . Madison . Teaneck
Fairleigh Dickinson University Press

First American edition published 1974 by:
ASSOCIATED UNIVERSITY PRESSES, INC.
Cranbury, New Jersey 08512

'Thyrza. A Tale'
First published in three-volumes, 1887 by Smith, Elder,
London

First one-volume edition published in 1891 by Smith, Elder,
London

Introduction, notes etc. © Jacob Korg 1974

Library of Congress Catalogue Number 74-500
ISBN 0-8386-1544-9

Typesetting by Campbell Graphics Ltd., Newcastle upon Tyne
Printed in England by Redwood Press Limited, Trowbridge
Bound by Cedric Chivers Limited, Portway, Bath

Contents

v

Bibliographical Note

The holograph manuscript of *Thyrza*, in the Huntington Library, San Marino, California, consists of 321 pages, with page 53 missing. The title page, with its Greek motto, is also lacking. The manuscript shows a few revisions and numerous cancellations, most of them only a few words or phrases long. In several instances more extensive corrections appear to have been made by cutting and pasting.

The first edition of 500 copies in three volumes, was published by Smith, Elder, London, in April, 1887.

The second edition, published in one volume in June, 1891, contained numerous minor revisions and cuts. Gissing eliminated passages of character-analysis, dialogue and authorial comment, either because they repeated points made elsewhere, were not relevant to the story, or interfered with objectivity. This revision is examined in "The Revision of Thyrza" by C.J. Francis, *The Gissing Newsletter,* October, 1971.

Several later editions were brought out by Smith, Elder and other publishers, including one with an introduction by Morley Roberts published by Nash and Grayson in 1927 and issued in America by Dutton.

A Russian translation of *Thyrza* appeared serially in the periodical *Vsemirnaia Biblioteka*, St. Petersburg, from December, 1891 to July 1892, and was then published in book form. A French translation appeared in 1928, and an Italian one in 1939.

This edition reproduces the one-volume edition of *Thyrza* published in 1892 by Smith, Elder.

Bibliographical Note

Introduction

When he published his first novel, *Workers in the Dawn* (1880), George Gissing declared that he was committed to the familiar task of the social novelist, that of arousing the public to an awareness of the condition of the poor. But for him, as for many other members of the middle class, the poor were a problem of conscience as much as a social problem, and his novels, like most Victorian novels of working class life, were primarily expressions of a sense of personal responsibility. He was, at heart, an individualist, and felt that he could not occupy himself with the literature and learning he cared for while masses of the urban population suffered from want. But because he soon became convinced that real reform was impossible, he was forced to shift to new attitudes toward poverty and the poor which enabled him to gain freedom of conscience in the face of continuing social evils. He began to regard poverty as a normal rather than a pathological condition, to observe that virtue and happiness existed among the poor, and to feel that improvement, if it was possible at all, would be brought about by practical measures, not acts of conscience. The expression of attitudes of this kind entailed the emergence of a new strain of social fiction.

As P.J. Keating has shown in *The Working Classes in Victorian Fiction,* the English social novelists before Gissing were generally moved by a spirit of moral indignation, and approached their subjects with powerful prejudices of one kind or another. While they may have had the best of intentions, they usually failed to perceive the truth that Henry Mayhew made plain on every page of his pioneering work of social investigation, *London Labour and the London Poor*: that the poor were unexceptional members of the human family whose peculiar habits, customs and opinions, were imposed upon them by their way of life. Keating observes: '. . .' there are few English novels which deal with working-class characters in a working-class environment in the same sense as there are novels about the middle or upper classes ... novels which treat of the working class as being composed of ordinary human beings who experience the range of feelings and emotions, social aspirations and physical relationships that it is the special province of the novelist to explore.' *Thyrza* is one of those novels. Instead of exploiting the poor for polemical purposes, it examines their way of life with respectful curiosity and even affection. But it is far from complacent, for Gissing goes beyond accounts of daily life to create an intense and painful consciousness of the sense of moral obligation the slums impose upon society, and of the spiritual conflicts poverty is bound to engender.

Gissing's novels characteristically attack the remedies proposed for social disorders as vigorously as the disorders themselves. As he rejected the reforming ideas of the nineteenth century. one after another, his novels became a sustained denial that anything could really be done to improve the nature of society. *Workers in the Dawn* is critical of revolutionary fervour and religion, *Demos* (1886) opposes socialism, *The Nether World* (1889) exposes the ineffectiveness of philanthropy. The principle of reform attacked in *Thyrza* is liberal education. Gissing's opposition to it is perhaps surprising, for he loved learning himself, and the happiest hours of his troubled life were those he spent with books. But he thought of study as a personal resource, not an instrument of social reform, and undertakes in *Thyrza* to show why it could not fulfil the idealistic expectations so often attached to it.

Because most of the sympathetic people in *Thyrza* are bookish or studious, the plan of its hero, Walter Egremont, for improving the spiritual condition of working men through lectures on literature seems, at first, to be less wildly implausible than it might otherwise appear to be. Even before Matthew Arnold's campaign on behalf of 'the best that has

been thought and said,' the idea that learning had a human-
izing influence was commonplace and literature is associated
with morality in Shelley's *Defence of Poetry,* (not published
until 1840). Gissing felt his own learning to be not only a
source of joy but a positive moral force within himself, and
one of his main criticisms of Richard Mutimer, the socialist
leader of *Demos,* and of working people generally was that
they lacked the imaginativeness and sensitivity which are
cultivated by the study of literature. When Edmund Gosse, in
an article written after Tennyson's death in 1892, expressed
doubt that the famous poet had been really popular among
working people, Gissing wrote to him to agree emphatically.
He felt that the indifference of ordinary people to works of
the imagination went far to explain the moral deficiencies he
saw in them.

The setting of the first chapter of *Thyrza,* the Newthorpes'
house at Ullswater, is Gissing's ideal environment, a placid
retreat in beautiful natural surroundings which is overflowing
with books. When Annabel goes down to the lake, she takes a
book with her, and when she asks Egremont what his recent
activities have been, he thinks she is sufficiently answered by
the reply 'Reading.' There is no irony whatever in the report
Mrs. Ormonde makes in a later chapter about Annabel: 'She is
deep in Virgil and Dante—what more could you wish her?' At
one point Gilbert Grail is interrupted at home by a visitor. 'A
volume lent by Egremont lay before him, and he was making
notes from it.' In Gissing's view, what Grail is doing is the
most fulfilling of human activities, and all other felicities are
merely conditions for making reading and study more
pleasant. 'Books, books, and time to use them, and a hearth
about which love is busy—what more can you offer son of man
than these?'

Thyrza also shows that intellectual cultivation is, as Newman
described it, a personal satisfaction, an end in itself, not a way
of solving practical problems or a sure path to happiness; it
may, in fact, exact a heavy price from those who turn to it.
When he is in the grip of his infatuation with Thyrza,
Egremont realizes that his learning is of no help to him in
coping with his despondency, and concludes that 'His

philosophy was a sham, a spinning of cobwebs for idle hours
when the heart is restful and the brain seeks to be amused. He
had no more strength to bear the torture of an inassuageable
desire than any foolish fellow who knew not the name of
culture.' It is obvious in fact, that Egremont's education and
sensitivity are responsible for his distress, for making him
capable of desires that more limited natures are spared. Gilbert
Grail, the studious workman, is an even more pitiable victim of
intellectual enlightenment. Realizing that his long hours of
work and his physical weakness will never allow him fully to
possess the knowledge he has glimpsed in his reading, he feels
that he is 'ever on the mere threshold of the promised land,
hopeless of admission,' and envies his fellow-workers whose
ignorance allows them to enjoy whatever pleasures their
narrow lives bring them.

Through the failure of Egremont's lectures, Gissing
sceptically attacks one of the most pervasive reforming ideas
of the nineteenth century—the theory that education, by
perfecting human beings, can ultimately perfect society itself.
'Let us reform our schools,' wrote Ruskin in Unto this Last in
1860, 'and we shall find little reform needed in our prisons.'
Whatever the personal advantages of education might be,
Thyrza leaves no doubt that it cannot solve social problems.
Egremont, who never really believed that it could, and entered
upon his experiment with only the most modest expectations,
learns, from his experience in America, that great social good
can be achieved without learning.

Thyrza herself becomes the subject of an educational
experiment like the one in Shaw's Pygmalion as Mrs. Ormonde
decides that her potentialities must be cultivated. But it is
significant that the landscape of Eastbourne and the sea are
stronger influences than her formal regime of music and
sewing. In fact, the special attention Gissing gives to
description throughout Thyrza has the effect of suggesting
that physical experience makes a more vital impression upon
the mind than intellectual effort, that the senses and feelings
may have more to do with shaping the spirit than Virgilian
dactyls.

The evocation of specific feelings through external detail is
not new to Gissing's technique, but it is used with new

purposefulness and discrimination. He creates the 'unutterable dreariness' of a summer Sunday afternoon in Lambeth through a well-chosen series of varied details. 'Few pedestrians were abroad; the greater part of the male population of Lambeth slumbered after the baked joint and the flagon of ale yet here and there a man in his shirt-sleeves leaned forth despondently from a window or sat in view within, dozing over the Sunday paper.' It is the same atmosphere of urban *ennui* that is found in T.S. Eliot's early poems, and Gissing's anticipation of one of the striking images in *The Love Song of J. Alfred Prufrock,* the 'lonely men in shirt-sleeves,' calls attention to the fact that *Thyrza* often emphasizes the relation between externals and feelings in a way that corresponds with Eliot's doctrine of the objective correlative, offering details that are not only equivalents to feelings, but instruments for forming them. After he has been invited to take charge of Egremont's library, Gilbert Grail walks out on Lambeth Bridge, and the various sights and sounds of the night over the river become a counterpart of his sense of elation: 'Some power he did not understand had brought him here as to the place where he could best realise this great joy that had befallen him.' But he is still in love with Thyrza, and lonely. Hence, he feels the cold of the wind and moves to the Embankment, where he hears the footsteps of a policeman and sees a pair of lovers on a bench; the carefully selected details are just enough to formulate the nature of the pain that comes into his eyes.

Gissing depends on this language of external experience again in conveying the profound change which takes place in Thyrza when she visits Eastbourne and sees the sea for the first time. 'You and I cannot remember the moment when the sense of infinity first came upon us,' he says in introducing his heroine's awakening to a new range of feeling. Through Eastbourne, with its comfortable surroundings, fine natural setting, pleasant people and music, her emotions are opened, and she becomes capable of loving Egremont. But externals can speak in another way as well. When Annabel and Egremont stand on the shore in the novel's last conversation, they look out on a scene whose extraordinary beauty and variety stand as a reproach to their own limited, unimaginative efforts to lead lives of passion. 'We have both missed something,' says Annabel, as if repeating the message of the landscape itself, 'something that will never again be offered us.' And when the two have agreed to a marriage based on only a moderate love, Egremont asks whether they shall go up to Beachy Head, but Annabel replies, 'No higher.'

This participation of daily sights and sounds in the life of feeling raises doubts about Egremont's and Grail's conviction that study is the only path to spiritual fulfillment. In a sentence that appears in the first edition of *Thyrza,* but was later eliminated, the studious Annabel herself entertains suspicions of this kind. Gissing describes her looking about at beautiful natural scenery with a book lying unread in her lap, and observes that 'it was often a doubt with her whether time spent in such seeming idleness was not in truth more gainful than that wherein she bent over her books.' The fact that Annabel is sitting on the shore of Wordsworth's Ullswater at this moment suggests that Gissing means to evoke thoughts of the debate of 'Expostulation and Reply' and 'The Tables Turned' where Matthew's friend urges him to:

  Close up those barren leaves;
  Come forth and bring with you a heart
  That watches and receives.

But he cut the sentence from later editions, no doubt because he felt that it conceded too much to 'wise passiveness.'

II

If *Thyrza* resembles Gissing's earlier novels in seeing social reform as futile, it differs from them in softening his principle that poverty crushes the finer instincts, rendering the poor incapable of true humanity. Gissing was no dogmatist on the relation of character and environment, and there are exceptions to his rule in all his novels, but in *Thyrza* for the first time he offers a variety of temperament and morality among the slum characters that he had perceived before only in middle class people. Mrs. Gandle, the proprietor of the restaurant where Thyrza works, is a member of the grasping petit-bourgeoisie in a desperately poor neighbourhood, and she is abysmally vulgar both in speech and character, yet her kindness and concern save Thyrza and lead to her reunion with

Mrs. Ormonde. Thyrza herself is far less convincing. Her virtues are not those of a working girl, but of a potential lady; she is one of those proletarian protagonists who are, as P.J. Keating observes, really middle class ladies or gentlemen in disguise. It is in Gissing's treatment of the moderately virtuous proletarians, Lydia, Luke Ackroyd and Gilbert Grail that we see a new attitude of sober respect without sentimentality; he takes them seriously without patronizing them, and treats them as distinct human beings, not mere examples of social injustice.

Evil, in *Thyrza* is not a property of human nature, but of the universe itself. Its most virtuous people come to nothing, or are forced to accept circumstances unworthy of them. In a letter to his sister Ellen dated May 14, 1887, in which he speculated on the response reviewers might have toward *Thyrza* Gissing wrote: '... all my work is profoundly pessimistic as far as mood goes.' The pessimism of *Thyrza* is the same feeling that led Gissing to observe, in an entry made in his Commonplace Book, that while he enjoyed seeing a puppy playing, he did not take the same pleasure in a baby, for 'I am oppressed by the thought of the anxiety it is costing in the present, & of the miseries that inevitably lie before it.' Human beings, Gissing felt, are marked for unhappiness. *Thyrza* is filled with a sense of the waste of human potentialities in the struggles or pointless pleasures of the slums, in futile efforts to change society, and also in the passages of private life, where people somehow fail to find the right relationship with each other. His heroine is young, sweet and innocent, but nevertheless of a 'subtly morbid physiognomy;' her innate sensitivity makes her suffer disproportionately from ordinary disagreements, she appreciates small refinements in daily behaviour, and is restless within the routine that her sister and neighbours accept. As she falls in love with a man above her station, fulfils her ambition of seeing the sea, and is lifted out of her narrow life and educated by Mrs. Ormonde, we sense that her imaginative spirit is approaching a threatening encounter with circumstances. The authentic love she feels for Egremont separates her from Grail, and ennobles her in a way that ultimately makes her unsuitable for Egremont himself, who is coarsened and disillusioned by his experience in America.

Thyrza herself is too fanciful and idealized a character to carry the weight of Gissing's conviction that adverse circumstances inevitably defeat the best in human nature. But Gilbert Grail, whom she at first intends to marry, is presented with a sympathy and authority that make him the most vital embodiment of the book's pessimism. He lives under conditions that the average working man would find pleasant enough, but is made wretched by his passion for books and a longing for an ideal love that he knows he can never satisfy. His unhappiness, Gissing tells us, is intensified by the fact that he is too old for illusions, and is forced to confront his situation realistically. When Egremont chooses him to manage the library he intends to establish in Lambeth and Thyrza agrees to be his wife, he feels that his life has been miraculously transformed. Hence, the knowledge that Thyrza has deserted him because of her love for Egremont, comes as a final confirmation of what he had always expected his life to be—an endless nightmare of toil and loneliness. Grail's breakdown in turn leads Egremont to feel that he has been cut off from the one friend and the one cause that have made his own life worthwhile, and that his effort to help the poor and the generosity of spirit that motivated it have been repudiated.

Love is not merely the familiar obligatory ingredient of nineteenth-century fiction in *Thyrza*, but a means of universalizing the sense of futility attached to its social problems. All of its numerous lovers, with the exception of Lydia Trent, the heroine's sister, suffer from hopeless infatuations which poison their lives, spread destructive influences around them, and end in frustration. On the other hand, those who love on lower terms, seeking no more than convenience and comradeship, have little trouble in finding satisfaction. Through love Gissing's characters directly experience the hostility of the universe to human aspirations. In love, as in society, the best impulses and highest expectations are defeated, while pragmatic and even venal motivations meet with a measure of acceptance, Within this framework, Gissing finds that the nature of success, as well as that of failure, is a reason for despair.

It might be objected that the lovers of *Thyrza* are the victims of their own extravagant romanticism, and that their disappointments are caused, not by the nature of things, but by their own unrealistic expectations. The fact is, however, that the conception of love found in *Thyrza*, excessive and idealistic as it may seem to be, is not an artificial fancy conjured up to prettify the novel, but one of Gissing's own firmest convictions. He thought of love as a communion that involved the spirit fully, and married lower-class women who were no more than generally congenial because he felt that his poverty would never allow him to find a wife capable of this sort of relationship. The intense misery he suffered with both of his wives did not destroy his romantic notion of the possibilities of love.

His enduring idealism emerges clearly and disquietingly in the letters he wrote to Gabrielle Fleury more than ten years after he had written *Thyrza*. In them we find Gissing, a man of forty who had already been twice married, writing to the woman he loved: 'I have no words to utter the sense of worship with which I think of your pure and noble nature . . .' (August, 1898), p. 29). 'Your beauty, beloved, is of the soul, and your soul is in harmony with all the lovely things that nature shows us.' (August 10, 1898, p. 39). Gissing was perfectly aware that he regarded Gabrielle as the embodiment of a preconceived image: 'Let me sketch the woman whom, for so many years, I have vainly imagined. I saw her, to begin with, a much nobler being than myself; I saw her, before all, a true woman, endowed with every grace of mind and heart which is characteristically feminine. Her face represented my own ideal of personal beauty . . . she had very gentle eyes, eloquent of sympathy, bright with intelligence . . . her voice was soft and varied, always musical. Then she was capable of passion . . . Her mind was open to the world of art . . . Where was I likely to meet with such a woman? I had given up all hope. Yet today I know her, and I love her . . .' (August 5, 1898, p. 31).

Gissing was eventually united with Gabrielle, but the characters in *Thyrza* to whom he assigned this ideal passion experience it only as a painful affliction. Egremont is divided from Thyrza by the barrier of class. It is his love for her that alienates her fiance, Grail, who is his chief lieutenant among the working men, and forces Egremont to flee the temptation of marrying her and go to America, where he eventually becomes too sensible to pursue his extravagant hopes any further. Thyrza's love for Egremont does not close the gap between them; she pines for him uselessly, and her sudden unmotivated death demonstrates the hostility of the universe toward natures like hers, which can love with pure devotion. At one point in the story, when Egremont is concerned about harm coming to Thyrza, Gissing observes, 'Love from of old has had a comrade superstition.' To love is to become a victim of irrationality. But it is nevertheless an expression of the finest in human nature, and when Gissing briefly fell in love with a Wakefield girl in 1890, he gave her, not his most recent novel, but the one in which he expressed his idealism about love, *Thyrza.*

Gissing's sense of the vulnerability of high ideals seems romantic enough, but its real source is the tragic vision of life projected in Greek literature. Though he was a novelist of modern life and social problems, Gissing was also a devoted student of the literature and civilization of antiquity. He had learned to love the Greek and Latin authors in school, and spent a good part of his imaginative life re-reading them and re-living their historical periods. As his travel book, *By the Ionian Sea* shows, his visits to Greece and Italy were really journeys to the past, where he could feel himself to be in the same world as Homer, Virgil and Horace. The first book set on the shelves of the working men's library Egremont begins in Lambeth is the eight-volume Milman edition of Gibbon's *Decline and Fall of the Roman Empire,* and it is put into place soberly and ritualistically, one volume at a time, by Thyrza herself. Gissing himself had this set; it had been given to him as a prize for classical studies when he was at college.

While he was writing *Thyrza,* Gissing urged his sister Ellen, in a letter dated July 31, 1886, to continue her reading of Homer and other authors, and added: 'With me it is a constant aim to bring the present and the past near to each other, to remove the distance which seems to separate Hellas from Lambeth. It can be done, by grasping firmly enough the meanings of human nature.' What Hellas and Lambeth can have in common in terms of human nature is suggested by the epigraph which appeared on the title page of the first edition of *Thyrza,* a quotation from Theocritus which Gissing translated, in a later letter to Ellen, as saying: 'But we heroes are mortal, and being mortals, of mortals let us sing.' *Thyrza,* in its broadest dimensions, tells of 'heroes' and their mortal limitations. It presents contemporary life as a spectacle resembling the tragic vision of the Greeks, in which the aspirations of men are doomed by forces beyond their understanding or control. Gissing meant to adapt the traditional pattern of tragedy to modern life by taking common, rather than exceptional people as his protagonists and by embodying the fates they contend against in social forces and circumstances, rather than the will of the gods.

This intention is perhaps more clearly felt in *Thyrza* than in any of his earlier novels because its main figures, Thyrza, Egremont and Grail are presented with genuine sympathy and admiration. The pathos of their failures to achieve high ambitions is accompanied by the ironic successes of lower desires, just as the victory of Creon combines with the defeat of Antigone in defining the nature of Sophocles' cosmos. Dalmaine, the unscrupulous politician, marries the girl he wants and makes his mark by proposing factory reform, without displaying any nobility of character. Thyrza loses the man she passionately loves, and dies, but the more practical Totty Nancarrow marries Bunce because she feels kindliness and good will toward him, and receives an inheritance for doing so. Egremont's failure to marry Thyrza is a failure of character; Annabel, to whom he proposes at the end of the novel, tells him plainly that her love will not do for him what Thyrza's love might have done, and the marriage he contemplates is clearly to be an arrangement of convenience rather than a spiritual union.

In *Thyrza* things are so arranged that gross and practical motivations prosper and even have benign results, while noble and imaginative ones are destructive. One of Gissing's clear-minded minor characters expresses contempt for Egremont and his sincere desire to do good, and continues: 'Who are the real social reformers? The men who don't care a scrap for the people, but take up ideas because they can make capital out of them. It isn't idealists who do the work of the world, but the hard-headed, practical, selfish men . . . Nothing solid has ever been gained in this world that wasn't pursued out of self-interest.' Ultimately, Egremont himself is compelled to admit the truth of this. While he is in America, he learns about the case of Cornelius Vanderbilt: 'Personally he was a disgusting brute; ignorant, base, a boor in his manner, a blackguard in his language ... Yet the man was a great philanthropist ...' and the industries he built up did immense good by employing great numbers of workmen. 'What is the state of a world,' asks Egremont, 'in which such a man can do such good by such means?' The answer, it is clear, is that it is a world without justice, an insight that leads Egremont to feel ashamed of his former idealism, and to turn his back on generosity and good works. This is the change that makes him less noble in spirit than Thyrza, and when Mrs. Ormonde senses it, she suggests that he is no longer worthy of her.

In spite of Gissing's intention of including Lambeth in the lofty tragic vision of Hellas, the reader of *Thyrza* is likely to feel that it is pessimistic rather than tragic. Gissing himself seems to have been aware that his novel did not achieve the emotional range he had originally planned for it. Very soon after it was published, and in spite of some enthusiastic early responses and a favourable review in the *Athenaeum,* he wrote to Ellen that it was less powerful than its predecessor. 'It will be a long time before I do anything better than *Demos* artistically.' He felt that he had succeeded better in the novel that dramatized the deficiencies of working people than in the one that depicted their virtues. In fact, *Thyrza* exposes the weakness of Gissing's belief in the possibility of virtue at any social level. Egremont's lectures and Mrs. Ormonde's home for poor little girls are mere routine philanthropies, bloodlessly presented. Gissing's words for the qualities he admires—nobility, passion, idealism, refinement—sprinkle the pages of *Thyrza,* but they are limp and futile, carrying little conviction. In a reproach that echoes the epigraph from Theocritus, Mrs. Ormonde says to Egremont: 'Your idealism is often noble, but never heroic.'

Gissing never arranges a decisive test between the idealist and his fate as Conrad does in a novel where a similar issue is confronted in a totally different environment, *Lord Jim.* In Conrad's novel, the practical determination that Gissing presents as the selfish motivation of Dalmaine and Cornelius Vanderbilt is dramatized in the quiet heroism of the French lieutenant, who stays with the dangerously disabled ship because it is his duty, and the weak good intentions of Egremont become the far more aggressive romantic ambitions of Jim. With both young men, the question of their moral dedication becomes a question of response to 'opportunity.' In accepting the death he deserves for failing to keep faith with himself, Jim grasps the 'opportunity, which like an Eastern bride, had come veiled to his side.' But Egremont misses his chance to claim his bride, and Annabel, seeing the dead Thyrza's picture, tells him, 'There was your one great opportunity, and you let it pass.' Egremont lacks the conviction to immerse himself in 'the destructive element' of romantic idealism, proving the truth of Stein's view that 'Man is amazing . . . but he is not a masterpiece.'

Acknowledging this, Gissing remains unwilling to blame the failure of high motives on the weakness of his idealists rather than on the malignity of the nature of things. He still clings, though without much conviction, to the belief that one must continue 'To strive, to seek, to find, and not to yield,' even in a universe hostile to such efforts. No one in *Thyrza* asks, as Biffen does in Gissing's later novel, *New Grub Street:* 'What right have we to make ourselves and others miserable for the sake of an obstinate idealism?' In *Thyrza* the call to noble action persists, but because those who hear it are weak or corruptible, the novel not only falls short of tragedy, but verges on the pathetic. It does not exhibit the grandeur of effort that exalts itself in striving against the resistance of the absolute, but rather the sorrow of lives that imperfect conditions have rendered vain and purposeless.

THYRZA

THYRZA

A TALE

BY

GEORGE GISSING

AUTHOR OF 'DEMOS' 'THE NETHER WORLD' ETC.

A NEW EDITION

LONDON

SMITH, ELDER, & CO., 15 WATERLOO PLACE

1892

CONTENTS

THYRZA

———◆———

CHAPTER I

AMONG THE HILLS

There were three at the breakfast-table—Mr. Newthorpe, his daughter Annabel, and their visitor (Annabel's cousin), Miss Paula Tyrrell. It was a small, low, soberly-furnished room, the walls covered with carelessly-hung etchings and water-colours, and with photographs which were doubtless memen-toes of travel; dwarf bookcases held overflowings from the library; volumes in disorder, clearly more for use than orna-ment. The casements were open to let in the air of a July morning. Between the thickets of the garden the eye caught glimpses of sun-smitten lake and sheer hillside; for the house stood on the shore of Ullswater.

Of the three breakfasting, Miss Tyrrell was certainly the one whose presence would least allow itself to be overlooked. Her appetite was hearty, but it scarcely interfered with the free flow of her airy talk, which was independent of remark or reply from her companions. Though it was not apparent in her demeanour, this young lady was suffering under a calamity; her second 'season' had been ruined at its very culmination by a ludicrous *contretemps* in the shape of an attack of measles. Just when she flattered herself that she had never looked so lovely, an instrument of destiny embraced her in the shape of an affectionate child, and lo! she was a fright. Her constitution had soon thrown off the evil thing, but Mrs. Tyrrell decreed her banishment for a time to the remote dwelling of her literary uncle. Once more Paula was lovely, and yet one could scarcely say that the worst was over,

B

seeing that she was constrained to pass summer days within view of Helvellyn when she might have been in Piccadilly.

Mr. Newthorpe seldom interrupted his niece's monologue, but his eye often rested upon her, seemingly in good-natured speculation, and he bent his head acquiescingly when she put in a quick 'Don't you think so?' after a running series of comments on some matter which smacked exceedingly of the town. He was not more than five-and-forty, yet had thin, grizzled hair, and a sallow face with lines of trouble deeply scored upon it. His costume was very careless—indeed, all but slovenly—and his attitude in the chair showed, if not weakness of body, at all events physical indolence.

Some word that fell from Paula prompted him to ask:

'I wonder where Egremont is?'

Annabel, who had been sunk in thought, looked up with a smile. She was about to say something, but her cousin replied rapidly:

'Oh, Mr. Egremont is in London—at least, he was a month ago.'

'Not much of a guarantee that he is there now,' Mr. Newthorpe rejoined.

'I'll drop him a line and see,' said Paula. 'I meant to do so yesterday, but forgot. I'll write and tell him to send me a full account of himself. Isn't it too bad that people don't write to me? Everybody forgets you when you're out of town in the season. Now you'll see I shan't have a single letter again this morning; it is the cruellest thing!'

'But you had a letter yesterday, Paula,' Annabel remarked.

'A letter? Oh, from mamma; that doesn't count. A letter isn't a letter unless you feel anxious to see what's in it. I know exactly all that mamma will say, from beginning to end, before I open the envelope. Not a scrap of news, and with her opportunities, too! But I can count on Mr. Egremont for at least four sides—well, three.'

'But surely he is not a source of news?' said her uncle with surprise.

'Why not? He can be very jolly when he likes, and I know he'll write a nice letter if I ask him to. You can't think how much he's improved just lately. He was down at the Ditchleys' when we were there in February; he and I had ever such a time one day when the others were out hunting. Mamma won't let me hunt; isn't it too bad of her? He didn't speak a single serious word all the morning, and just think how dry he used to be ! Of course he can be dry enough still when he gets with people like Mrs. Adams and Clara Carr, but I hope to break him of the habit entirely.'

She glanced at Annabel, and laughed merrily before raising her cup to her lips. Mr. Newthorpe just cast a rapid eye over his daughter's face ; Annabel wore a look of quiet amusement.

'Has he been here since then ? ' Paula inquired, tapping a second egg. ' We lost sight of him for two or three months, and of course he always makes a mystery of his wanderings.'

' We saw him last in October,' her uncle answered, ' when he had just returned from America.'

'He said he was going to Australia next. By-the-by, what's his address ? Something, Russell Street. Don't you know ? '

' No idea,' he replied, smiling.

' Never mind. I'll send the letter to Mrs. Ormonde ; she always knows where he is, and I believe she's the only one that does.'

When the meal came to an end Mr. Newthorpe went, as usual, to his study. Miss Tyrrell, also as usual, prepared for three hours of letter-writing. Annabel, after a brief consultation with Mrs. Martin, the housekeeper, would ordinarily have sat down to study in the morning room. She laid open a book on the table, but then lingered between that and the windows. At length she took a volume of a lighter kind—in both senses—and, finding her garden hat in the hall, went forth.

She was something less than twenty, and bore herself with grace perchance a little too sober for her years. Her head was wont to droop thoughtfully, and her step measured itself to the grave music of a mind which knew the influence of mountain solitude. But her health was complete ; she could row for long stretches, and on occasion fatigued her father in rambles over moor and fell. Face and figure were matched in mature beauty ; she had dark hair, braided above the forehead on each side, and large dark eyes which regarded you with a pure intelligence, disconcerting if your word uttered less than sincerity.

When her mother died Annabel was sixteen. Three months after that event Mr. Newthorpe left London for his country

house, which neither he nor his daughter had since quitted.
He had views of his own on the subject of London life as it
affects young ladies. By nature a student, he had wedded a
woman who became something not far removed from a
fashionable beauty. It was a passionate attachment on both
sides at first, and to the end he loved his wife with the love
which can deny nothing. The consequence was that the
years of his prime were wasted, and the intellectual promise
of his youth found no fulfilment. Another year and Annabel
would have entered the social mill; she had beauty enough
to achieve distinction, and the means of the family were
ample to enshrine her. But she never 'came out.' No one
would at first believe that Mr. Newthorpe's retreat was final;
no one save a close friend or two who understood what his
life had been, and how he dreaded for his daughter the temp-
tations which had warped her mother's womanhood. 'In
any case,' wrote Mrs. Tyrrell, his sister-in-law, when a year
and a half had gone by, 'you will of course let me have
Annabel shortly. I pray you to remember that she is turned
seventeen. You surely won't deprive her of every pleasure
and every advantage?' And the recluse made answer: 'If
bolts and shackles were needful I would use them mercilessly
rather than allow my girl to enter your Middlesex pande-
monium. Happily, the fetters of her reason suffice. She is
growing into a woman, and by the blessing of the gods her
soul shall be blown through and through with the free air of
heaven whilst yet the elements in her are blending to their
final shape.' Mrs. Tyrrell raised her eyebrows, and shook
her head, and talked sadly of 'poor Annabel,' who was buried
alive.

She walked down to a familiar spot by the lake, where a
rustic bench was set under shadowing leafage; in front two
skiffs were moored on the strand. The sky was billowy with
slow-travelling shapes of whiteness; a warm wind broke
murmuring wavelets along the pebbly margin. The opposite
slopes glassed themselves in the deep dark water—Swarth
Fell, Hallin Fell, Place Fell—one after the other; above the
southern bend of the lake rose noble summits, softly touched
with mist which the sun was fast dispelling. The sweetness
of summer was in the air. So quiet was it that every wing-
rustle in the brake, every whisper of leaf to leaf, made a distinct small voice; a sheep-dog barking over at Howtown
seemed close at hand.

This morning Annabel had no inclination to read, yet her face was not expressive of the calm reflection which was her habit. She opened the book upon her lap and glanced down a page or two, but without interest. At length external things were wholly lost to her, and she gazed across the water with continuance of solemn vision. Her face was almost austere in this mood which had come upon her.

Someone was descending the path which led from the high road; it was a step too heavy for Paula's, too rapid to be Mr. Newthorpe's. Annabel turned her head and saw a young man, perhaps of seven-and-twenty, dressed in a light walking-suit, with a small wallet hanging from his shoulder and a stick in his hand. At sight of her he took off his cap and approached her bare-headed.

'I saw from a quarter of a mile away,' he said, 'that someone was sitting here, and I came down on the chance that it might be you.'

She rose with a very slight show of surprise, and returned his greeting with calm friendliness.

'We were speaking of you at breakfast. My cousin couldn't tell us for certain whether you were in England, though she knew you were in London a month ago.'

'Miss Tyrrell is with you?' he asked, as if it were very unexpected.

'But didn't you know? She has been ill, and they sent her to us to recruit.'

'Ah! I have been in Jersey for a month; I have heard nothing.'

'You were able to tear yourself from London in mid-season?'

'But when was I a devotee of the Season, Miss Newthorpe?'

'We hear you progress in civilisation.'

'Well, I hope so. I've had a month of steady reading, and feel better for it. I took a big chest of books to Jersey. But I hope Miss Tyrrell is better?'

'Quite herself again. Shall we walk up to the house?'

'I have broken in upon your reading.'

She exhibited the volume; it was Ruskin's 'Sesame and Lilies.'

'Ah! you got it; and like it?'

'On the whole.'

'That is disappointing.'

Annabel was silent, then spoke of another matter as they walked up from the lake.

This Mr. Egremont had not the look of a man who finds his joy in the life of Society. His clean-shaven face was rather bony, and its lines expressed independence of character; his forehead was broad, his eyes glanced quickly and searchingly, or widened themselves into an absent gazing which revealed the imaginative temperament. His habitual cast of countenance was meditative, with a tendency to sadness. In talk he readily became vivacious; his short sentences, delivered with a very clear and conciliating enunciation, seemed to indicate energy. It was a peculiarity that he very rarely smiled, or perhaps I should say that he had the faculty of smiling only with his eyes. At such moments his look was very winning, very frank in its appeal to sympathy, and compelled one to like him. Yet, at another time, his aspect could be shrewdly critical; it was so when Annabel fell short of enthusiasm in speaking of the book he had recommended to her when last at Ullswater. Probably he was not without his share of scepticism. For all that, it was the visage of an idealist.

Annabel led him into the house and to the study door, at which she knocked; then she stood aside for him to enter before her. Mr. Newthorpe was writing; he looked up absently, but light gathered in his eyes as he recognised the visitor.

'So here you are! We talked of you this morning. How have you come?'

'On foot from Pooley Bridge.'

They clasped hands, then Egremont looked behind him; but Annabel had closed the door and was gone.

She went up to the room in which Paula sat scribbling letters.

'Ten minutes more!' exclaimed that young lady. 'I'm just finishing a note to mamma—so dutiful!

'Have you written to Mr. Egremont?

Paula nodded and laughed.

'He is downstairs.'

Paula started, looking incredulous.

'Really, Bell?'

'He has just walked over from Pooley Bridge.'

'Oh, Bell, do tell me! Have those horrid measles left any trace? I really can't discover any, but of course one hasn't good eyes for one's own little speckles. Well, at all events, everybody hasn't forgotten me. But do look at me, Bell.'

Her cousin regarded her with conscientious gravity.

'I see no trace whatever; indeed, I should say you are looking better than you ever did.'

'Now that's awfully kind of you. And you don't pay compliments, either. Shall I go down? Did you tell him where I was?'

Had Annabel been disposed to dainty feminine malice, here was an opportunity indeed. But she looked at Paula with simple curiosity, seeming for a moment to lose herself. The other had to repeat her question.

'I mentioned that you were in the house,' she replied. 'He is talking with father.'

Paula moved to the door, but suddenly paused and turned.

'Now I wonder what thought you have in your serious head?' she said, merrily. 'It's only my fun, you know.'

Annabel nodded, smiling.

'But it is only my fun. Say you believe me. I shall be cross with you if you put on that look.'

They went into the morning room. Annabel stood at the window; her companion flitted about, catching glimpses of herself in reflecting surfaces. In five minutes the study door opened, and men's voices drew near.

Egremont met Miss Tyrrell with the manner of an old acquaintance, but unsmiling.

'I am fortunate enough to see you well again without having known of your illness,' he said.

'You didn't know that I was ill?'

Paula looked at him dubiously. He explained, and in doing so quite dispelled the girl's illusion that he was come on her account. When she remained silent, he said:

'You must pity the people in London.'

'Certainly I do. I'm learning to keep my temper and to talk wisely. I know nobody in London who could teach me to do either the one or the other.'

'Well, I suppose you'll go out till luncheon-time?' said Mr. Newthorpe. 'Egremont wants to have a pull. You'll excuse an old man.'

They left the house, and for an hour drank the breath of the hillsides. Paula was at first taciturn very unlike herself;

she dabbled her fingers over the boat-side, and any light remark that she made was addressed to her cousin. Annabel exerted herself to converse, chiefly telling of the excursions that had been made with Paula during the past week.

'What have you been doing in Jersey?' Paula asked of Egremont, presently. Her tone was indifferent, a little condescending.

'Reading.'

'Novels?'

'No.'

'And where are you going next?'

'I shall live in London. My travels are over, I think.'

'We have heard that too often,' said Annabel. 'Did you ever calculate how many miles you have travelled since you left Oxford?'

'I have been a restless fellow,' he admitted, regarding her with quiet scrutiny, 'but I dare say some profit has come of my wanderings. However, it's time to set to work.'

'Work!' asked Paula in surprise. 'What sork of work?'

'Local preacher's.'

Paula moved her lips discontentedly.

'That is your way of telling me to mind my own business. Don't you find the sun dreadfully hot, Annabel? Do please row into a shady place, Mr. Egremont.'

His way of handling the oars showed that he was no stranger to exercise of this kind. His frame, though a trifle meagre, was well set. By degrees a preoccupation which had been manifest in him gave way under the influence of the sky, and when it was time to approach the landing-place he had fallen into a mood of cheerful talk—light with Paula, with Annabel more earnest. His eyes often passed from one to the other of the faces opposite him, with unmarked observation; frequently he fixed his gaze on the remoter hills in brief musing.

Mr. Newthorpe had come down to the water to meet them; he had a newspaper in his hand.

'Your friend Dalmaine is eloquent on education,' he said, with a humorous twitching of the eyebrows.

'Yes, he knows his House,' Egremont replied. 'You observe the construction of his speech. After well-sounding periods on the elevation of the working classes, he casually throws out the hint that employers of labour will do wisely to increase the intelligence of their hands in view of foreign competition. Of course that is the root of the matter; but Dalmaine knows better than to begin with crude truths.'

In the meanwhile the boat was drawn up and the chain locked. The girls walked on in advance; Egremont continued to speak of Mr. Dalmaine, a rising politician, whose acquaintance he had made on the voyage home from New York.

'One of the few sincere things I ever heard from his lips was a remark he made on trade-unions. "Let them combine by all means," he said; "it's a fair fight." There you have the man; it seems to him mere common sense to regard his factory hands as his enemies. A fair fight! What a politico-economical idea of fairness!'

He spoke with scorn, his eyes flashing and his nostrils trembling. Mr. Newthorpe kept a quiet smile—sympathetic, yet critical.

Annabel sought her father for a word apart before lunch.

'How long will Mr. Egremont stay?' she asked, apparently speaking in her quality of house-mistress.

'A day or two,' was the reply. 'We'll drive over to Pooley Bridge for his bag this afternoon; he left it at the hotel.'

'What has he on his mind?' she continued, smiling.

'Some idealistic project. He has only given me a hint. I dare say we shall hear all about it to-night.'

CHAPTER II

THE IDEALIST

WHEN Egremont began his acquaintance with the Newthorpes he was an Oxford undergraduate. A close friendship had sprung up between him and a young man named Ormonde, and at the latter's home he met Mr. Newthorpe, who, from the first, regarded him with interest. A year after Mrs. Newthorpe's death Egremont was invited to visit the house at Ullswater; since then he had twice spent a week there. This personal intercourse was slight to have resulted in so much intimacy, but he had kept up a frequent correspondence with Mr. Newthorpe from various parts of the world, and common friends aided the stability of the relation.

He was the only son of a man who had made a fortune by

the manufacture of oil-cloth. His father began life as a house-painter, then became an oil merchant in a small way, and at length married a tradesman's daughter, who brought him a moderate capital just when he needed it for an enterprise promising greatly. In a short time he had established the firm of Egremont & Pollard, with extensive works in Lambeth. His wife died before him; his son received a liberal education, and in early manhood found himself, as far as he knew, without a living relative, but with ample means of independence. Young Walter Egremont retained an interest in the business, but had no intention of devoting himself to a commercial life. At the University he had made alliances with men of standing, in the academical sense, and likewise with some whose place in the world relieved them from the necessity of establishing a claim to intellect. In this way society was opened to him, and his personal qualities won for him a great measure of regard from those whom he most desired to please.

Somebody had called him 'the Idealist,' and the name adhered to him. At two-and-twenty he published a volume of poems, obviously derived from study of Shelley, but marked with a certain freshness of impersonal aspiration which was pleasant enough. They had the note of sincerity rather than the true poetical promise. The book had no successor. Having found this utterance for his fervour, Egremont began a series of ramblings over sea, in search, he said, of himself. The object seemed to evade him; he returned to England from time to time, always in appearance more restless, but always overflowing with ideas, for which he had the readiest store of enthusiastic words. He was able to talk of himself without conveying the least impression of egotism to those who were in sympathy with his intellectual point of view; he was accused of conceit only by a few who were jealous of him or were too conventional to appreciate his character. With women he was a favourite, and their society was his greatest pleasure; yet, in spite of his fervid temperament—in appearance fervid, at all events—he never seemed to fall in love. Some there were who said that the self he went so far to discover would prove to have a female form. Perhaps there was truth in this; perhaps he sought, whether consciously or no, the ideal woman. None of those with whom he companioned had a charge of light wooing to bring against him, though one or two would not have held it a misfortune if they had tempted him to forget his speculations and declare that he had reached his goal. But his striving always seemed to be for something remote from the world about him. His capacity for warm feeling, itself undeniable, was never dissociated from that impersonal zeal which was the characteristic of his expressions in verse. In fact, he had written no love-poem.

Annabel and her father observed a change in him since his last visit. This was the first time that he had come without an express invitation, and they gathered from his speech that he had at length found some definite object for his energies. His friends had for a long time been asking what he meant to do with his life. It did not appear that he purposed literary effort, though it seemed the natural outlet for his eager thought; and of the career of politics he at all times spoke with contempt. Was he one of the men, never so common as nowadays, who spend their existence in canvassing the possibilities that lie before them and delay action till they find that the will is paralysed? One did not readily set Egremont in that class, principally, no doubt, because he was so free from the offensive forms of self-consciousness which are wont to stamp such men. The pity of it, too, if talents like his were suffered to rust unused; the very genuineness of his idealism made one believe in him and look with confidence to his future.

Having dined, all went forth to enjoy the evening upon the lawn. The men smoked; Annabel had her little table with tea and coffee. Paula had brought out a magazine, and affected to read. Annabel noticed, however, that a page was very seldom turned.

'Have you seen Mrs. Ormonde lately?' Mr. Newthorpe asked of Egremont.

'I spent a day at Eastbourne before going to Jersey.'

'She has promised to come to us in the autumn,' said Annabel; 'but she seems to have such a difficulty in leaving her Home. Had she many children about her when you were there?'

'Ten or twelve.'

'Do they all come from London?' asked Annabel.

'Yes. She has relations with sundry hospitals and the like. By-the-by, she told me one remarkable story. A short time ago, out of eight children that were in the house only one could read—a little girl of ten—and this one regularly received letters from home. Now there came for her what seemed to be a small story-paper, or something of the kind, in a wrapper.   Mrs. Ormonde gave it her without asking any questions, and, in the course of the morning, happening to see her reading it, she went to look what the paper was.   It proved to be an anti-Christian periodical, and on the front page stood a woodcut offered as a burlesque illustration of some Biblical incident.   " Father always brings it home and gives it me to read," said the child.   " It makes me laugh ! " '

' Probably she knew nothing of the real meaning of it all,' said Mr. Newthorpe.

' On the contrary, she understood the tendency of the paper surprisingly well ; her father had explained everything to the family.'

' One of the interesting results of popular education,' remarked Mr. Newthorpe philosophically.   ' It is inevitable.'

' What did Mrs. Ormonde do ? ' Annabel asked.

' It was a difficult point.   No good would have been done by endeavouring to set the child against her father ; she would be home again in a fortnight.   So Mrs. Ormonde simply asked if she might have the paper when it was done with, and, having got possession, threw it into the fire with vast satisfaction.   Happily it didn't come again.'

' What a gross being that father must be ! ' Annabel exclaimed.

' Gross enough,' Egremont replied, ' yet I shouldn't wonder if he had brains above the average in his class.   A mere brute wouldn't do a thing of that kind ; ten to one he honestly believed that he was benefiting the girl ; educating her out of superstition.'

' But why should the poor people be left to such ugly-minded teachers ? ' Annabel exclaimed.   ' Surely those influences may be opposed ? '

' I doubt whether they can be,' said her father.   ' The one insuperable difficulty lies in the fact that we have no power greater than commercial enterprise.   Nowadays nothing will succeed save on the commercial basis ; from church to public-house the principle applies.   There is no way of spreading popular literature save on terms of supply and demand.   Take the Education Act.   It was devised and carried simply for the reason indicated by Egremont's friend Dalmaine ; a more intelligent type of workmen is demanded that our manufacturers may keep pace with those of other countries.   Well, there is a demand for comic illustrations of the Bible, and the demand is met ; the paper exists because

it pays. An organ of culture for the people who enjoy bur-
lesquing the Bible couldn't possibly be made to pay.'

' But is there no one who would undertake such work
without hope of recompense in money ? We are not all mere
tradespeople.'

' I have an idea for a beginning of such work, Miss Newthorpe,' said Egremont, in a voice rather lower than hitherto.
' I came here because I wanted to talk it over.'

Annabel met his look for a moment, expressing all the
friendly interest which she felt. Mr. Newthorpe, who had
been pacing on the grass, came to a seat. He placed himself next to Paula. She glanced at him, and he said kindly:

' You are quite sure you don't feel cold ? '

' I dare say I'd better go in,' she replied, checking a little
sigh as she closed her magazine.

' No, no, don't go, Paula ! ' urged her cousin, rising.
' You shall have a shawl, dear ; I'll get it.'

' It is very warm,' put in Egremont. ' There surely can't
be any danger in sitting till it grows dark.'

This little fuss about her soothed Paula for a while.

' Oh, I don't want to go,' she said. ' I feel I'm getting
very serious and wise, listening to such talk. Now we shall
hear, I suppose, what you mean by your " local preacher " ? '

Annabel brought a shawl and placed it carefully about
the girl's shoulders. Then she said to her father :

' Let me sit next to Paula, please.'

The change of seats was effected. Annabel secretly took
one of her cousin's hands and held it. Paula seemed to
regard a distant object in the garden.

There was silence for a few moments. The evening
was profoundly calm. A spirit of solemn loveliness brooded
upon the hills, glorious with sunset. The gnats hummed,
rising and falling in myriad crowds about the motionless
leaves. A spring which fell from a rock at the foot of the
garden babbled poetry of the twilight.

' I hope it is something very practicable,' Annabel resumed, looking with expectancy at Egremont.

' I will have your opinion on that. I believe it to be
practical enough ; at all events, it is a scheme of very modest
dimensions. That story of the child and her paper fixed
certain thoughts that had been floating about in my mind.
You know that I have long enough tried to find work, but I
have been misled by the common tendency of the time.

Those who want to be of social usefulness for the most part attack the lowest stratum. It seems like going to the heart of the problem, of course, and any one who has means finds there the hope of readiest result—material result. But I think that the really practical task is the most neglected, just because it does not appear so pressing. With the mud at the bottom of society we can practically do nothing; only the vast changes to be wrought by time will cleanse that foulness, by destroying the monstrous wrong which produces it. What I should like to attempt would be the spiritual education of the upper artisan and mechanic class. At present they are all but wholly in the hands of men who can do them nothing but harm—journalists, socialists, vulgar propagators of what is called freethought. These all work against culture, yet here is the field really waiting for the right tillage. I often have in mind one or two of the men at our factory in Lambeth. They are well-conducted and intelligent fellows, but, save for a vague curiosity, I should say they live without conscious aim beyond that of keeping their families in comfort. They have no religion, a matter of course; they talk incessantly of politics, knowing nothing better; but they are very far above the gross multitude. I believe such men as these have a great part to play in social development—that, in fact, *they* may become the great social reformers, working on those above them—the froth of society—no less than on those below.'

He had laid down his half-finished cigar, and, having begun in a scrupulously moderate tone, insensibly warmed to the idealist fervour. His face became more mobile, his eyes gave forth all their light, his voice was musically modulated as he proceeded in his demonstration. He addressed himself to Annabel, perhaps unconscious of doing so exclusively.

Mr. Newthorpe muttered something of assent. Paula was listening intently, but as one who hears of strange, far-off things, very difficult of realisation.

'Now suppose one took a handful of such typical men,' Egremont went on, 'and tried to inspire them with a moral ideal. At present they have nothing of the kind, but they own the instincts of decency, and that is much. I would make use of the tendency to association, which is so strong among them. They have numberless benefit clubs; they stand together resolutely to help each other in time of need and to exact terms from their employers—the fair fight, as the worthy Member for Vauxhall calls it. Well, why shouldn't they band for moral and intellectual purposes ? I would have a sort of freemasonry, which had nothing to do with eating and drinking, or with the dispensing of charity ; it should be wholly concerned with spiritual advancement. These men cannot become rich, and so are free from one kind of danger; they are not likely to fall into privation ; they have a certain amount of leisure. If one could only stir a few of them to enthusiasm for an ideal of life ! Suppose one could teach them to feel the purpose of such a book as " Sesame and Lilies," which you only moderately care for, Miss New-thorpe——'

'Not so ! ' Annabel broke in, involuntarily. 'I think it very beautiful and very noble.'

'What book is that ? ' asked Paula with curiosity.

'I'll give it to you to read, Paula,' her cousin replied.

Egremont continued :

'The work of people who labour in the abominable quarters of the town would be absurdly insignificant in com-parison with what these men might do. The vulgar influence of half-taught revolutionists, social and religious, might be counteracted; an incalculable change for good might be made on the borders of the social inferno, and would spread. But it can only be done by personal influence. The man must have an ideal himself before he can create it in others. I don't know that I am strong enough for such an undertaking, but I feel the desire to try, and I mean to try. What do you think of it ? '

'Thinking it so clearly must be half doing it,' said Annabel.

Egremont replied to her with a clear regard.

'But the details,' Mr. Newthorpe remarked. 'Are you going to make Lambeth your field ? '

'Yes, Lambeth. I have a natural connection with the place, and my name may be of some service to me there ; I don't think it is of evil odour with the workmen. My project is to begin with lectures. Reserve your judgment ; I have no intention of standing forth as an apostle; all I mean to do at first is to offer a free course of lectures on a period of English literature. I shall not throw open my doors to all and sun-dry, but specially invite a certain small number of men, whom I shall be at some pains to choose. We have at the works a foreman named Bower ; I have known him, in a way, for years, and I believe he is an intelligent man. Him I shall make use of, telling him nothing of my wider aims, but simply getting him to discover for me the dozen or so of men who would be likely to care for my lectures. By-the-by, the man of whom I was speaking, the father of Mrs. Ormonde's patient, lives in Lambeth; I shall certainly make an effort to draw him into the net!'

'I shall be curious to hear more of him,' said Mr. Newthorpe. 'And you use English literature to tune the minds of your hearers?'

'That is my thought. I have spent my month in Jersey in preparing a couple of introductory lectures. It seems to me that if I can get them to understand what is meant by love of literature, pure and simple, without a thought of political or social purpose—especially without a thought of cash profit, which is so disastrously blended with what little knowledge they acquire—I shall be on the way to founding my club of social reformers. I shall be most careful not to alarm them with hints that I mean more than I say. Here are certain interesting English books; let us see what they are about, who wrote them, and why they are deemed excellent. That is our position. These men must get on a friendly footing with me. Little by little I shall talk with them more familiarly, try to understand each one. Success depends upon my personal influence. I may find that it is inadequate, yet I have hope. Naturally, I have points of contact with the working class which are lacking to most educated men; a little chance, and I should myself have been a mechanic or something of the kind. This may make itself felt; I believe it will.'

Night was falling. The last hue of sunset had died from the swarth hills, and in the east were pale points of starlight.

'I think you and I must go in, Paula,' said Annabel, when there had been silence for a little.

Paula rose without speaking, but as she was about to enter the house she turned back and said to Egremont:

'I get tired so soon, being so much in the open air. I'd better say good-night.'

Her uncle, when he held her hand, stroked it affectionately. He often laughed at the child's manifold follies, but her prettiness and the *naïveté* which sweetened her inbred artificiality had won his liking. Much as it would have astonished Paula had she known it, his feeling was for the most part one of pity.

'I suppose you'll go out again?' Paula said to her cousin as they entered the drawing-room.

'No; I shall read a little and then go to bed.' She added, with a laugh, 'They will sit late in the study, no doubt, with their cigars and steaming glasses.'

Paula moved restlessly about the room for a few minutes; then from the door she gave a 'good-night,' and disappeared without further ceremony.

The two men came in very shortly. Egremont entered the drawing-room alone, and began to turn over books on the table. Then Annabel rose.

'It promises for another fine day to-morrow,' she said. 'I must get father away for a ramble. Do you think he looks well?'

'Better than he did last autumn, I think.'

'I must go and say good-night to him. Will you come to the study?'

He followed in silence, and Annabel took her leave of both.

The morning broke clear. It was decided to spend the greater part of the day on the hills. Paula rode; the others drove to a point whence their ramble was to begin. Annabel enjoyed walking. Very soon her being seemed to set itself to more spirited music; the veil of reflection fell from her face, and she began to talk light-heartedly.

Paula behaved with singularity. At breakfast she had been very silent, a most unusual thing, and during the day she kept an air of reserve, a sort of dignity which was amusing. Mr. Newthorpe walked beside her pony, and adapted himself to her favourite conversation, which was always of the town and Society.

Once Annabel came up with a spray of mountain saxifrage.

'Isn't it lovely, Paula?' she said. 'Do look at the petals.'

'Very nice,' was the reply, 'but it's too small to be of any use.'

There was no more talk of Egremont's projects. Books and friends and the delights of the upland scenery gave matter enough for conversation. Not long after noon the sky began to cloud, and almost as soon as the party reached home again there was beginning of rain. They spent the evening in the drawing-room. Paula was persuaded to sing, which she did prettily, though still without her native vivacity. Again she retired early.

After breakfast on the morrow it still rained, though not without promise of clearing.

'You'll excuse me till lunch,' Paula said to Annabel and Egremont, when they rose from the table. 'I have a great deal of correspondence to see to.'

'Correspondence' was a new word. Usually she said, 'I have an awful heap of letters to write.' Her dignity of the former day was still preserved.

Having dismissed her household duties, Annabel went to the morning room and sat down to her books. She was reading Virgil. For a quarter of an hour it cost her a repetition of efforts to fix her attention, but her resolve was at length successful. Then Egremont came in.

'Do I disturb you?' he said, noticing her studious attitude.

'You can give me a little help, if you will. I can't make out that line.'

She gave him one copy and herself opened another. It led to their reading some fifty lines together.

'Oh, why have we girls to get our knowledge so late and with such labour!' Annabel exclaimed at length. 'You learn Greek and Latin when you are children; it ought to be the same with us. I am impatient; I want to read straight on.'

'You very soon will,' he replied absently. Then, having glanced at the windows, which were suddenly illumined with a broad slant of sunlight, he asked: 'Will you come out? It will be delightful after the rain.'

Annabel was humming over dactylics. She put her book aside with reluctance.

'I'll go and ask my cousin.'

Egremont averted his face. Annabel went up to Paula's room, knocked, and entered. From a bustling sound within, it appeared likely that Miss Tyrrell's business-like attitude at the table had been suddenly assumed.

'Will you come out, Paula? The rain is over and gone.'

'Not now.'

'Mr. Egremont wishes to go for a walk. Couldn't you come?'

'Please beg Mr. Egremont to excuse me. I am tired after yesterday, dear.'

When her cousin had withdrawn Paula went to the window. In a few minutes she saw Egremont and Annabel go forth and stroll from the garden towards the lake. Then she reseated herself, and sat biting her pen.

The two walked lingeringly by the water's edge. They spoke of trifles. When they were some distance from the house, Egremont said :

' So you see I have at last found my work. If you thought of me at all, I dare say my life seemed to you a very useless one, and little likely to lead to anything.'

' No, I had not that thought, Mr. Egremont,' she answered simply. 'I felt sure that you were preparing yourself for something worthy.'

' I hope that is the meaning of these years that have gone so quickly. But it was not conscious preparation. It has often seemed to me that in travelling and gaining experience I was doing all that life demanded of me. Few men can be more disposed to idle dreaming than I am. And even now I keep asking myself whether this, too, is only a moment of idealism, which will go by and leave me with less practical energy than ever. Every such project undertaken and abandoned is a weight upon a man's will. If I fail in perseverance my fate will be decided.'

' I feel assured that you will not fail. You could not speak as you did last night and yet allow yourself to falter in purpose when the task was once begun. What success may await you we cannot say ; the work will certainly be very difficult. Will it not ask a lifetime ? '

' No less, if it is to have any lasting result.'

' Be glad, then. What happier thing can befall one than to have one's life consecrated to a worthy end ! '

He walked on in silence, then regarded her.

' Such words in such a voice would make any man strong. Yet I would ask more from you. There is one thing I need to feel full confidence in myself, and that is a woman's love. I have known for a long time whose love it was that I must try to win. Can you give me what I ask ? '

The smile which touched his lips so seldom was on them now. He showed no agitation, but the light of his eyes was very vivid as they read her expression. Annabel had stayed her steps ; for a moment she looked troubled. His words were not unanticipated, but the answer with which she was prepared was more difficult to utter than she had thought it would be. It was the first time that a man had spoken to her thus, and though in theory such a situation had always seemed to her very simple, she could not now preserve her calm as she wished. She felt the warmth of her blood, and could not at once command her wonted voice. But when at length she succeeded in meeting his look steadily her thought grew clear again.

'I cannot give you that, Mr. Egremont.'

As his eyes fell, she hastened to add :

'I think of you often. I feel glad to know you, and to share in your interest. But this is no more than the friendship which many people have for you—quite different from the feeling which you say would aid you. I have never known that.'

He was gazing across the lake. The melancholy always lurking in the thoughtfulness of his face had become predominant. Yet he turned to her with the smile once more.

'Those last words must be my hope. To have your friendship is much. Perhaps some day I may win more.'

'I think,' she said, with a sincerity which proved how far she was from emotion, 'that you will meet another woman whose sympathy will be far more to you than mine.'

'Then I must have slight knowledge of myself. I have known you for seven years, and, though you were a child when we first spoke to each other, I foresaw then what I tell you now. Every woman that I meet I compare with you ; and if I imagine the ideal woman she has your face and your mind. I should have spoken when I was here last autumn, but I felt that I had no right to ask you to share my life as long as it remained so valueless. You see'—he smiled—'how I have grown in my own esteem. I suppose that is always the first effect of a purpose strongly conceived. Or should it be just the opposite, and have I only given you a proof that I snatch at rewards before doing the least thing to merit them ? '

Something in these last sentences jarred upon her, and gave her courage to speak a thought which had often come to her in connection with Egremont.

'I think that a woman does not reason in that way if her deepest feelings are pledged. If I were able to go with you and share your life I shouldn't think I was rewarding you, but that you were offering me a great happiness. It is my loss that I can only watch you from a distance.'

The words moved him. It was not with conscious insincerity that he spoke of his love and his intellectual aims as interdependent, yet he knew that Annabel revealed the truer mind.

'And my desire is for the happiness of your love!' he exclaimed. 'Forget that pedantry—always my fault. I cannot feel sure that my other motives will keep their force, but I know that this desire will be only stronger in me as time goes on.'

Yet when she kept silence the habit of his thought again uttered itself.

'I shall pursue this work that I have undertaken, because, loving you, I dare not fall below the highest life of which I am capable. I know that you can see into my nature with those clear eyes of yours. I could not love you if I did not feel that you were far above me. I shall never be worthy of you, but I shall never cease in my striving to become so.'

The quickening of her blood, which at first troubled her, had long since subsided. She could now listen to him, and think of her reply almost with coldness. There was an unreality in the situation which made her anxious to bring the dialogue to an end.

'I have all faith in you,' she said. 'I hope—I feel assured—that something will come of your work; but it will only be so if you pursue it for its own sake.'

The simple truth of this caused him to droop his eyes again with a sense of shame. He grew impatient with himself. Had he no plain, touching words in which to express his very real love—words such as every man can summon when he pleads for this greatest boon? Yet his shame heightened the reverence in which he held her; passion of the intellect breathed in his next words.

'If you cannot love me with your heart, in your mind you can be one with me. You feel the great and the beautiful things of life. There is no littleness in your nature. In reading with you just now I saw that your delight in poetry was as spirit-deep as my own; your voice had the true music, and your cheeks warmed with sympathy. You do not deny me the right to claim so much kinship with you. I, too, love all that is rare and noble, however in myself I fall below such ideals. Say that you admit me as something more than the friend of the everyday world! Look for once straight into my eyes and know me!'

There was no doubtful ring in this; Annabel felt the

chords of her being smitten to music.   She held her hand to
him.

'You are my very near friend, and my life is richer for
your influence.'

'I may come and see you again before very long, when I
have something to tell you?'

'You know that our house always welcomes you.'

He released her hand, and they walked homewards.   The
sky was again overcast.   A fresh gust came from the fell-side
and bore with it drops of rain.

'We must hasten,' Annabel said, in a changed voice.
'Look at that magnificent cloud by the sun!'

'Isn't the rain sweet here?' she continued, anxious to
re-establish the quiet, natural tone between them.   'I like
the perfume and the taste of it.   I remember how mournful
the rain used to be in London streets.'

They regained the house.   Annabel passed quickly upstairs.   Egremont remained standing in the porch, looking
forth upon the garden.   His reverie was broken by a voice.

'How gloomy the rain is here!   One doesn't mind it in
London; there's always something to do and somewhere
to go.'

It was Paula.   Egremont could not help showing amusement.

'Do you stay much longer?' he asked.

'I don't know.'

She spoke with indifference, keeping her eyes averted.

'I must catch the mail at Penrith this evening,' he said.
'I'm afraid it will be a wet drive.'

'You're going, are you?   Not to Jersey again, I hope?'

'Why not?'

'It seems to make people very dull.   I shall warn all my
friends against it.'

She hummed an air and left him.

Late in the afternoon Egremont took leave of his friends.
Mr. Newthorpe went out into the rain, and at the last moment
shook hands with him heartily.   Annabel stood at the window
and smiled farewell.

The wheels splashed along the road; rain fell in torrents.
Egremont presently looked back from the carriage window.
The house was already out of view, and the summits of the
circling hills were wreathed with cloud.

CHAPTER III

A CORNER OF LAMBETH

A WORKING MAN, one Gilbert Grail, was spending an hour of his Saturday afternoon in Westminster Abbey. At five o'clock the sky still pulsed with heat; black shadows were sharp-edged upon the yellow pavement. Between the bridges of Westminster and Lambeth the river was a colourless gleam; but in the Sanctuary evening had fallen. Above the cool twilight of the aisles floated a golden mist; and the echo of a footfall hushed itself among the tombs.

He was a man past youth, but of less than middle age, with meagre limbs and shoulders, a little bent. His clothing was rough but decent; his small and white hands gave evidence of occupation which was not rudely laborious. He had a large head, thickly covered with dark hair, which, with his moustache and beard, heightened the wanness of his complexion. A massive forehead, deep-set eyes, thin, straight nose, large lips constantly drawn inwards, made a physiognomy impressive rather than pleasing. The cast of thought was upon it; of thought eager and self-tormenting; the mark of a spirit ever straining after something unattainable. At moments when he found satisfaction in reading the legend on some monument his eyes grew placid and his beetling brows smoothed themselves; but the haunter within would not be forgotten, and, as if at a sudden recollection, he dropped his eyes in a troubled way, and moved onwards brooding. In those brief intervals of peace his countenance expressed an absorbing reverence, a profound humility. The same was evident in his bearing; he walked as softly as possible and avoided treading upon a sculptured name.

When he passed out into the sunny street, he stood for an instant with a hand veiling his eyes, as if the sudden light were too strong. Then he looked hither and thither with absent gaze, and at length bent his steps in the direction of Westminster Bridge. On the south side of the river he descended the stairs to the Albert Embankment and walked along by St. Thomas's Hospital.

Presently he overtook a man who was reading as he

walked, a second book being held under his arm. It was a
young workman of three- or four-and-twenty, tall, of wiry
frame, square-shouldered, upright. Grail grasped his shoulder
in a friendly way, asking:

'What now?'

'Well, it's tempted eighteenpence out of my pocket,' was
the other's reply, as he gave the volume to be examined.
'I've wanted a book on electricity for some time.'

He spoke with a slight North of England accent. His
name was Luke Ackroyd; he had come to London as a lad,
and was now a work-fellow of Grail's. There was rough
comeliness in his face and plenty of intelligence, something
at the same time not quite satisfactory if one looked for
strength of character; he smiled readily and had eyes which
told of quick but unsteady thought; a mouth, too, which
expressed a good deal of self-will and probably a strain of
sensuality. His manner was hearty, his look frank to a
fault and full of sensibility.

'I found it at the shop by Westminster Bridge,' he continued. 'You ought to go and have a look there to-night.
I saw one or two things pretty cheap that I thought were in
your way.'

'What's the other?' Grail inquired, returning the work
on electricity, which he had glanced through without show
of much interest.

'Oh, this belongs to Jo Bunce,' Ackroyd replied, laughing.
'He's just lent it me.'

It was a collection of antitheistic discourses; the titles,
which were startling to the eye, sufficiently indicated the scope
and quality of the matter. Grail found even less satisfaction
in this than in the other volume.

'A man must have a good deal of time to spare,' he said,
with a smile, 'if he spends it on stuff of that kind.'

'Oh, I don't know about that. You don't need it, but
there's plenty of people that do.'

'And that's the kind of thing Bunce gives his children to
read, eh?'

'Yes; he's bringing them up on it. He's made them learn
a secularist's creed, and hears them say it every night.'

'Well, I'm old-fashioned in such matters,' said Grail, not
caring to pursue the discussion. 'I'd a good deal rather hear
children say the ordinary prayer.'

Ackroyd laughed.

Have you heard any talk,' he asked presently, ' about lectures by a Mr. Egremont ? He's a son of Bower's old governor.'

' No, what lectures ? '

' Bower tells me he's a young fellow just come from Oxford or Cambridge, and he's going to give some free lectures here in Lambeth.

' Political ? '

' No. Something to do with literature.'

Ackroyd broke into another laugh—louder this time, and contemptuous.

' Sops to the dog that's beginning to show his teeth ! ' he exclaimed. ' It shows you what's coming. The capitalists are beginning to look about and ask what they can do to keep the people quiet. Lectures on literature ! Fools ! As if that wasn't just the way to remind us of what we've missed in the way of education. It's the best joke you could hit on. Let him lecture away ; he'll do more than he thinks.'

' Where does he give them ? ' Grail inquired.

' He hasn't begun yet. Bower seems to be going round to get men to hear him. Do you think you'd like to go ? '

' It depends what sort of a man he is.'

' A conceited young fool, I expect.'

Grail smiled.

In such conversation they passed the Archbishop's Palace ; then, from the foot of Lambeth Bridge, turned into a district of small houses and multifarious workshops. Presently they entered Paradise Street.

The name is less descriptive than it might be. Poor dwellings, mean and cheerless, are interspersed with factories and one or two small shops ; a public-house is prominent, and a railway arch breaks the perspective of the thoroughfare midway. The street at that time —in the year '80—began by the side of a graveyard, no longer used, and associated in the minds of those who dwelt around it with numberless burials in a dire season of cholera. The space has since been converted into a flower-garden, open to the children of the neighbourhood, and in summer time the bright flower-beds enhance the ignoble baldness of the by-way.

When they had nearly reached the railway arch Ackroyd stopped.

' I'm just going in to Bower's shop,' he said ; ' I've got a message for poor old Boddy.'

Boddy ?

'You know of him from the Trent girls, don't you?'

'Yes, yes,' Grail answered, nodding. He seemed about to add something, but checked himself, and, with a 'good-bye,' went his way.

Ackroyd turned his steps to a little shop close by. It was of the kind known as the 'small general;' over the door stood the name of the proprietor—'Bower'—and on the woodwork along the top of the windows was painted in characters of faded red: 'The Little Shop with the Large Heart.' Little it certainly was, and large of heart if the term could be made to signify an abundant stock. The interior was so packed with an indescribable variety of merchandise that there was scarcely space for more than two customers between door and counter. From an inner room came the sound of a violin, playing a lively air.

When the young man stepped through the doorway he was at once encompassed with the strangest blend of odours; every article in the shop—groceries of all kinds, pastry, cooked meat, bloaters, newspapers, petty haberdashery, firewood, fruit, soap—seemed to exhale its essence distressfully under the heat; impossible that anything sold here should preserve its native savour. The air swarmed with flies, spite of the dread example of thousands that lay extinct on sheets of smeared newspaper. On the counter, among other things, was a perspiring yellow mass, retailed under the name of butter; its destiny hovered between avoirdupois and the measure of capacity. A literature of advertisements hung around; ginger-beer, blacking, blue, &c., with a certain 'Samaritan salve,' proclaimed themselves in many-coloured letters. One descried, too, a scrubby but significant little card, which bore the address of a loan office.

The music issued from the parlour behind the shop; it ceased as Ackroyd approached the counter, and at the sound of his footsteps appeared Mrs. Bower. She was a stout woman of middle age, red of face, much given to laughter, wholesomely vulgar. At four o'clock every afternoon she laid aside her sober garments of the working day and came forth in an evening costume which was the admiration and envy of Paradise Street. Popular from a certain wordy goodhumour which she always had at command, she derived from this evening garb a social superiority which friends and neighbours, whether they would or no were constrained to recognise. She was deemed a well-to-do woman, and as such—Paradise Street held it axiomatic—might reasonably adorn herself for the respect of those to whom she sold miscellaneous pennyworths. She did not depend upon the business. Her husband, as we already know, was a foreman at Egremont & Pollard's oilcloth manufactory; they were known to have money laid by. You saw in her face that life had been smooth with her from the beginning. She wore a purple dress with a yellow fichu, in which was fixed a large silver brooch; on her head was a small lace cap. Her hands were enormous, and very red. As she came into the shop, she mopped her forehead with a handkerchief; perspiration streamed from every pore.

'What a man you are for keepin' yourself cool, Mr. Hackroyd!' she exclaimed; 'it's like a breath o' fresh air to look at you, I'm sure. If this kind o' weather goes on there won't be much left o' me. I'm a-goin' like the butter.'

'It's warmish, that's true,' said Luke, when she had finished her laugh. 'I heard Mr. Boddy playing in there, and I've got a message for him.'

'Come in and sit down. He's just practisin' a new piece for his club to-night.'

Ackroyd advanced into the parlour. The table was spread for tea, and at the tray sat Mrs. Bower s daughter, Mary. She was a girl of nineteen, sparely made, and rather plain-featured, yet with a thoughtful, interesting face. Her smile was brief, and always passed into an expression of melancholy, which in its turn did not last long; for the most part she seemed occupied with thoughts which lay on the borderland between reflection and anxiety. Her dress was remarkably plain, contrasting with her mother's, and her hair was arranged in the simplest way.

In a round-backed chair at a distance from the table sat an old man with a wooden leg, a fiddle on his knee. His face was parchmenty, his cheeks sunken, his lips compressed into a long, straight line; his small grey eyes had an anxious look, yet were ever ready to twinkle into a smile. He wore a suit of black, preserved from sheer decay by a needle too evidently unskilled. Wrapped about a scarcely visible collar was a broad black neckcloth of the antique fashion; his one shoe was cobbled into shapelessness. Mr. Boddy's spirit had proved more durable than his garments. Often hard set to earn the few shillings a week that sufficed to him, he kept up a long-standing reputation for joviality, and, with the aid of his fiddle, made himself welcome at many a festive gathering in Lambeth.

'Give Mr. Hackroyd a cup o' tea, Mary,' said Mrs. Bower. 'How you pore men go about your work days like this is more than I can understand. I haven't life enough in me to drive away a fly as settles on my nose. It's all very well for you to laugh, Mr. Boddy. There's good in everything, if we only see it, and you may thank the trouble you've had as it's kep' your flesh down.'

Ackroyd addressed the old man.

'There's a friend of mine in Newport Street would be glad to have you do a little job for him, Mr. Boddy. Two or three chairs, I think.'

Mr. Boddy held forth his stumpy, wrinkled hand.

'Give us a friendly grip, Mr. Ackroyd! There's never a friend in this world but the man as finds you work; that's the philosophy as has come o' my three-score-and-nine years. What's the name and address? I'll be round the first thing on Monday morning.'

The information was given.

'You just make a note o' that in your head, Mary, my dear,' the old man continued. ''Taint very likely I'll forget, but my memory do play me a trick now and then. Ask me about things as happened fifty years ago, and I'll serve you as well as the almanack. It's the same with my eyes. I used to be near-sighted, and now I'll read you the sign-board across the street easier than that big bill on the wall.'

He raised his violin, and struck out with spirit 'The March of the Men of Harlech.'

'That's the toon as always goes with me on my way to work,' he said, with a laugh. 'It keeps up my courage; this old timber o' mine stumps time on the pavement, and I feel I'm good for something yet. If only the hand'll keep steady! Firm enough yet, eh, Mr. Ackroyd?'

He swept the bow through a few ringing chords.

'Firm enough,' said Luke, 'and a fine tone, too. I suppose the older the fiddle is the better it gets?'

'Ah, 'taint like these fingers. Old Jo Racket played this instrument more than sixty years ago; so far back I can answer for it. You remember Jo, Mrs. Bower, ma'am? Yes, yes, you can just remember him; you was a little 'un when he'd use to crawl round from the work'us of a Sunday to the

"Green Man." When he went into the 'Ouse he give the fiddle to Mat Trent, Lyddy and Thyrza's father, Mr. Ackroyd. Ah, talk of a player! You should a' heard what Mat could do with this 'ere instrument. What do *you* say, Mrs. Bower, ma'am?'

'He was a good player, was Mr. Trent; but not better than somebody else we know of, eh, Mr. Hackroyd?'

'Now don't you go pervertin' my judgment with flattery, ma'am,' said the old man, looking pleased for all that. 'Matthew Trent was Matthew Trent, an' Lambeth 'll never know another like him. He was made o' music! When did you hear any man with a tenor voice like his? He made songs, too, Mr. Ackroyd—words, music, an' all. Why, Thyrza sings one of 'em still.'

'But how does she remember it?' Ackroyd asked with much interest. 'He died when she was a baby.'

'Yes, yes, she don't remember it of her father. It was me as taught her it, to be sure, as I did most o' the other songs she knows.'

'But she wasn't a baby either,' put in Mrs. Bower. 'She was four years; an' Lydia was four years older.'

'Four years an' two months,' said Mr. Boddy, nodding with a laugh. 'Let's be ac'rate, Mrs. Bower, ma'am. Thirteen year ago next fourteenth o' December, Mr. Ackroyd. There's a deal happened since then. On that day I had my shop in the Cut, and I had two legs like other mortals. Things wasn't doing so bad with me. Why, it's like yesterday to remember. My wife she come a-runnin' into the shop just before dinner-time. "There's a boiler busted at Walton's," she says, "an' they say as Mr. Trent's killed." It was Walton's, the pump-maker's, in Ground Street.'

'It's Simpson & Thomas's now,' remarked Mrs. Bower. 'Why, where Jim Caudle works, you know, Mr. Hackroyd.'

Luke nodded, knowing the circumstance. The whole story was familiar to him, indeed; but Mr. Boddy talked on in an old man's way for pleasure in the past.

'So it is, so it is. Me an' my wife took the little 'uns to the 'Orspital. He knew 'em, did poor Mat, but he couldn't speak. What a face he had! Thyrza was frighted and cried; Lyddy just held on hard to my hand, but she didn't cry. I don't remember to a' seen Lyddy cry more than two or three times in my life; she always hid away for that, when she couldn't help herself, bless her!'

'Lydia grows more an' more like her father,' said Mrs. Bower.

'She does, ma'am, she does. I used to say as she was like him, when she sat in my shop of a night and watched the people in and out. Her eyes was so bright-looking, just like Mat's. Eh, there wasn't much as the little 'un didn't see. One day—how my wife did laugh!—she looks at me for a long time, an' then she says: "How is it, Mr. Boddy," she says, " as you've got one eyelid lower than the other?" It's true as I have a bit of a droop in the right eye, but it's not so much as any one 'ud notice it at once. I can hear her say that as if it was in this room. An' she stood before me, a little thing that high. I didn't think she'd be so tall. She growed wonderful from twelve to sixteen. It's me has to look up to her now.'

A customer entered the shop, and Mrs. Bower went out.

'I don't think Thyrza's as much a favourite with any one as her sister,' said Ackroyd, looking at Mary Bower, who had been silent all this time.

'Oh, I like her very much,' was the reply. But there's something—— I don't think she's as easy to understand as Lydia. Still, I shouldn't wonder if she pleases some people more.'

Mary dropped her eyes as she spoke, and smiled gently. Ackroyd tapped with his foot.

'That's Totty Nancarrow,' said Mrs. Bower, reappearing from the shop. 'What a girl that is, to be sure! She's for all the world like a lad put into petticoats. I should think there's a-goin' to be a feast over in Newport Street. A tin o' sardines, four bottles o' ginger-beer, two pound o' seed cake, an' two pots o' raspberry! Eh, she's a queer 'un! I can't think where she gets her money from either.'

'It's a pity to see Thyrza going about with her so much,' said Mary, gravely.

'Why, I can't say as I know any real harm of her,' said her mother, ' unless it is as she's a Catholic.'

'Totty Nancarrow a Catholic!' exclaimed Ackroyd. 'Why, I never knew that.'

'Her mother was Irish, you see, an' I don't suppose as her father thought much about religion. I dessay there's some good people Catholics, but I can't say as I take much to them I know.'

Mary's face was expressing lively feeling.

How can they be really good, mother, when their religion lets them do wrong, if only they'll go and confess it to the priest? I wouldn't trust anybody as was a Catholic. I don't think the religion ought to be allowed.'

Here was evidently a subject which had power to draw Mary from her wonted reticence. Her quiet eyes gleamed all at once with indignation.

Ackroyd laughed with good-natured ridicule.

'Nay,' he said, 'the time's gone by for that kind of thing, Miss Bower. You wouldn't have us begin religious persecution again?'

'I don't want to persecute anybody,' the girl answered; 'but I wouldn't let them be misled by a bad and false religion.'

On any other subject Mary would have expressed her opinion with diffidence; not on this.

'I don't want to be rude, Miss Mary,' Luke rejoined, ' but what right have you to say that their religion's any worse or falser than your own?'

'Everybody knows that it is—that cares about religion at all,' Mary replied with coldness and, in the last words, a significant severity.

'It's the faith, Mary, my dear,' interposed Mr. Boddy, 'the faith's the great thing. I don't suppose as form matters so much.'

The girl gave the old man a brief, offended glance, and drew into herself.

'Well,' said Mrs. Bower, 'that's one way o' lookin' at it ; but I can't see neither as there's much good in believin' what isn't true.'

'That's to the point, Mrs. Bower,' said Ackroyd with a smile.

There was a footstep in the shop—firm, yet light and quick—then a girl's face showed itself at the parlour door. It was a face which atoned for lack of regular features by the bright intelligence and the warmth of heart that shone in its smile of greeting. A fair broad forehead lay above well-arched brows ; the eyes below were large and shrewdly observant, with laughter and kindness blent in their dark depths. The cheeks were warm with health ; the lips and chin were strong, yet marked with refinement ; they told of independence, of fervid instincts ; perhaps of a temper a little apt to be impatient. It was not an imaginative countenance, yet

alive with thought and feeling—all, one felt, ready at the
moment's need—the kind of face which becomes the light
and joy of home, the bliss of children, the unfailing support
of a man's courage. Her hair was cut short and crisped
itself above her neck; her hat of black straw and dark dress
were those of a work-girl—poor, yet, in their lack of adornment, suiting well with the active, helpful impression which
her look produced.

'Here's Mary an' Mr. Hackroyd fallin' out again, Lydia,'
said Mrs. Bower.

'What about now?' Lydia asked, coming in and seating
herself. Her eyes passed quickly over Ackroyd's face and
rested on that of the old man with much kindness.

'Oh, the hold talk—about religion.'

'I think it 'ud be better if they left that alone,' she
replied, glancing at Mary.

'You're right, Miss Trent,' said Luke. 'It's about the
most unprofitable thing anyone can argue about.'

'Have you had your tea?' Mrs. Bower asked of Lydia.

'No; but I mustn't stop to have any, thank you, Mrs.
Bower. Thyrza 'll think I'm never coming home. I only
looked in just to ask Mary to come and have tea with us to-
morrow.'

Ackroyd rose to depart.

'If I see Holmes I'll tell him you'll look in on Monday,
Mr. Boddy.'

'Thank you, Mr. Ackroyd, thank you; no fear but I'll be
there, sir.'

He nodded a leave-taking and went.

'Some work, grandad?' Lydia asked, moving to sit by
Mr. Boddy.

'Yes, my dear; the thing as keeps the world a-goin'.
How's the little 'un?'

'Why, I don't think she seems very well. I didn't want
her to go to work this morning, but she couldn't make up
her mind to stay at home. The hot weather makes her
restless.'

'It's dreadful tryin'!' sighed Mrs. Bower.

'But I really mustn't stay, and that's the truth.' She
rose from her chair. 'Where do you think I've been, Mary?
Mrs. Isaacs sent round this morning to ask if I could give
her a bit of help. She's going to Margate on Monday, and
there we've been all the afternoon trimming new hats for

herself and the girls. She's given me a shilling, and I'm sure it wasn't worth half that, all I did. You'll come to-morrow, Mary?'

'I will if—you know what?'

'Now did you ever know such a girl!' Lydia exclaimed, looking round at the others. 'You understand what she means, Mrs. Bower?'

'I dare say I do, my dear.'

'But I can't promise, Mary. I don't like to leave Thyrza always.'

'I don't see why she shouldn't come too,' said Mary.

Lydia shook her head.

'Well, you come at four o'clock, at all events, and we'll see all about it. Good-bye, grandad.'

She hurried away, throwing back a bright look as she passed into the shop.

Paradise Street runs at right angles into Lambeth Walk. As Lydia approached this point, she saw that Ackroyd stood there, apparently waiting for her. He was turning over the leaves of one of his books, but kept glancing towards her as she drew near. He wished to speak, and she stopped.

'Do you think,' he said, with diffidence, 'that your sister would come out to-morrow after tea?'

Lydia kept her eyes down.

'I don't know, Mr. Ackroyd,' she answered. 'I'll ask her; I don't think she's going anywhere.'

'It won't be like last Sunday?'

'She really didn't feel well. And I can't promise, you know, Mr. Ackroyd.'

She met his eyes for an instant, then looked along the street. There was a faint smile on her lips, with just a sus-picion of some trouble.

'But you *will* ask her?'

'Yes, I will.'

She added in a lower voice, and with constraint:

'I'm afraid she won't go by herself.'

'Then come with her. Do! Will you?'

'If she asks me to, I will.'

Lydia moved as if to leave him, but he followed.

'Miss Trent, you'll say a word for me sometimes?'

She raised her eyes again and replied quickly:

'I never say nothing against you, Mr. Ackroyd.'

D

'Thank you. Then I'll be at the end of the Walk at six
o'clock, shall I ?'

She nodded, and walked quickly on. Ackroyd turned
back into Paradise Street. His cheeks were a trifle flushed,
and he kept making nervous movements with his head. So
busy were his thoughts that he unconsciously passed the door
of the house in which he lived, and had to turn when the
roar of a train passing over the archway reminded him where
he was.

CHAPTER IV

THYRZA SINGS

LYDIA, too, betrayed some disturbance of thought as she
pursued her way. Her face was graver than before: once or
twice her lips moved as if she were speaking to herself.

After going a short distance along Lambeth Walk, she
turned off into a street which began unpromisingly between
low-built and poverty-stained houses, but soon bettered in
appearance. Its name is Walnut Tree Walk. For the most
part it consists of old dwellings, which probably were the
houses of people above the working class in days when Lambeth's squalor was confined within narrower limits. The
doors are framed with dark wood, and have hanging porches.
At the end of the street is a glimpse of trees growing in
Kennington Road.

To one of these houses Lydia admitted herself with a
latch-key; she ascended to the top floor and entered a room
in the front. It was sparely furnished, but with a certain
cleanly comfort. A bed stood in one corner; in another, a
small washhand-stand; between them a low chest of drawers
with a looking-glass upon it. The rest was arranged for day
use; a cupboard kept out of sight household utensils and
food. Being immediately under the roof, the room was much
heated after long hours of sunshine. From the open window
came a heavy scent of mignonette.

Thyrza had laid the table for tea, and was sitting idly.
It was not easy to recognise her as Lydia's sister; if you
searched her features the sisterhood was there, but the type
of countenance was so subtly modified, so refined, as to
become beauty of rare suggestiveness. She was of pale com-

plexion, and had golden hair; it was plaited in one braid,
which fell to her waist. Like Lydia's, her eyes were large
and full of light; every line of the face was delicate, har-
monious, sweet; each thought that passed through her mind
reflected itself in a change of expression, produced one knew
not how, one phase melting into another like flitting lights
upon a stream in woodland. It was a subtly morbid physiognomy, and impressed one with a sense of vague trouble.
There was none of the spontaneous pleasure in life which
gave Lydia's face such wholesome brightness; no impulse of
activity, no resolve; all tended to preoccupation, to emotional
reverie. She had not yet completed her seventeenth year,
and there was still something of childhood in her movements.
Her form was slight, graceful, and of lower stature than her
sister's. She wore a dress of small-patterned print, with a
broad collar of cheap lace.

'It was too hot to light a fire,' she said, rising as Lydia
entered. 'Mrs. Jarmey says she'll give us water for the
tea.'

'I hoped you'd be having yours,' Lydia replied. 'It's
nearly six o'clock. I'll take the tea-pot down, dear.'

When they were seated at the table, Lydia drew from her
pocket a shilling and held it up laughingly.

'That from Mrs. Isaacs?' her sister asked.

'Yes. Not bad for Saturday afternoon, is it? Now I
must take my boots to be done. If it began to rain I should
be in a nice fix; I haven't a sole to walk on.'

'I just looked in at Mrs. Bower's as I passed,' she continued presently. 'Mr. Ackroyd was there. He'd come to tell
grandad of some work. That was kind of him, wasn't it?'

Thyrza assented absently.

'Is Mary coming to tea to-morrow?' she asked.

'Yes. At least she said she would if I'd go to chapel
with her afterwards. She won't be satisfied till she gets me
there every Sunday.'

'How tiresome, Lyddy!'

'But there's somebody wants you to go out as well. You
know who.'

'You mean Mr. Ackroyd?'

'Yes. He met me when I came out of Mrs. Bower's,
and asked me if I thought you would.'

Thyrza was silent for a little, then she said:

'I can't go with him alone, Lyddy. I don't mind if you go too.'

'But that's just what he doesn't want,' said her sister, with a smile which was not quite natural.

Thyrza averted her eyes, and began to speak of something else. The meal was quickly over, then Lydia took up some sewing. Thyrza went to the window and stood for a while looking at the people that passed, but presently she seated herself, and fell into the brooding which her sister's entrance had interrupted. Lydia also was quieter than usual; her eyes often wandered from her work to Thyrza. At last she leaned forward and said:

'What are you thinking of, Blue-eyes?'

Thyrza drew a deep sigh.

'I don't know, Lyddy. It's so hot, I don't feel able to do anything.'

'But you're always thinking and thinking. What is it that troubles you?'

'I feel dull.'

'Why don't you like to go out with Mr. Ackroyd?' Lydia asked.

'Why do you so much want me to, Lyddy?'

'Because he thinks a great deal of you, and it would be nice if you got to like him.'

'But I shan't, never;—I know I shan't.'

'Why not, dear?'

'I don't *dislike* him, but he mustn't get to think it's any thing else. I'll go out with him if you'll go as well,' she added, fixing her eyes on Lydia's.

The latter bent to pick up a reel of cotton.

'We'll see when to-morrow comes,' she said.

Silence again fell between them, whilst Lydia's fingers worked rapidly. The evening drew on. Thyrza took her chair to the window, leaned upon the sill, and looked up at the reddening sky. The windows of the other houses were all open; here and there women talked from them with friends across the street. People were going backwards and forwards with bags and baskets, on the business of Saturday evening; in the distance sounded the noise of the market in Lambeth Walk.

Shortly after eight o'clock Lydia said:

'I'll just go round with my boots, and get something for dinner to-morrow.'

'I'll come with you,' Thyrza said. 'I can't bear to sit here any longer.'

They went forth, and were soon in the midst of the market. Lambeth Walk is a long, narrow street, and at this hour was so thronged with people that an occasional vehicle with difficulty made slow passage. On the outer edges of the pavement, in front of the busy shops, were rows of booths, stalls, and barrows, whereon meat, vegetables, fish, and household requirements of indescribable variety were exposed for sale. The vendors vied with one another in uproarious advertisement of their goods. In vociferation the butchers doubtless excelled; their ' Lovely, lovely, lovely ! ' and their reiterated ' Buy, buy, buy ! ' rang clangorous above the hoarse roaring of coster-mongers and the din of those who clattered pots and pans. Here and there meat was being sold by Dutch auction, a brisk business. Umbrellas, articles of clothing, quack medicines, were disposed of in the same way, giving occasion for much coarse humour. The market-night is the sole out-of-door amusement regularly at hand for London working people, the only one, in truth, for which they show any real capacity. Everywhere was laughter and interchange of good-fellowship. Women sauntered the length of the street and back again for the pleasure of picking out the best and cheapest bundle of rhubarb, or lettuce, the biggest and hardest cabbage, the most appetising rasher ; they compared notes, and bantered each other on purchases. The hot air reeked with odours. From stalls where whelks were sold rose the pungency of vinegar; decaying vegetables trodden under foot blended their putridness with the musty smell of second-hand garments ; the grocers' shops were aromatic ; above all was distinguishable the acrid exhalation from the shops where fried fish and potatoes hissed in boiling grease. There Lambeth's supper was preparing, to be eaten on the spot, or taken away wrapped in newspaper. Stewed eels and baked meat pies were discoverable through the steam of other windows, but the fried fish and potatoes appealed irresistibly to the palate through the nostrils, and stood first in popularity.

The people were of the very various classes which subdivide the great proletarian order. Children of the gutter and sexless haunters of the street corner elbowed comfortable artisans and their wives ; there were bareheaded hoidens from the obscurest courts, and work-girls whose self-respect was proof against all the squalor and vileness hourly surrounding them. Of the women, whatsoever their appearance, the great majority carried babies. Wives, themselves scarcely past childhood, balanced shawl-enveloped bantlings against heavy market-baskets. Little girls of nine or ten were going from stall to stall, making purchases with the confidence and acumen of old housekeepers ; slight fear that they would fail to get their money's worth. Children, too, had the business of sale upon their hands : ragged urchins went about with blocks of salt, importuning the marketers, and dishevelled girls carried bundles of assorted vegetables, crying, ' A penny all the lot ! A penny the 'ole lot ! '

The public-houses were full. Through the gaping doors you saw a tightly-packed crowd of men, women, and children, drinking at the bar or waiting to have their jugs filled, tobacco smoke wreathing above their heads. With few exceptions the frequenters of the Walk turned into the public-house as a natural incident of the evening's business. The women with the babies grew thirsty in the hot, foul air of the street, and invited each other to refreshment of varying strength, chatting the while of their most intimate affairs, the eternal ' says I,' ' says he,' ' says she,' of vulgar converse. They stood indifferently by the side of liquor-sodden creatures whose look was pollution. Companies of girls, neatly dressed and as far from depravity as possible, called for their glasses of small beer, and came forth again with merriment in treble key.

When the sisters had done their business at the boot-maker's, and were considering what their purchase should be for Sunday's dinner, Thyrza caught sight of Totty Nancarrow entering a shop. At once she said : ' I won't be late back, Lyddy. I'm just going to walk a little way with Totty.'

Lydia's face showed annoyance.

' Where is she ? ' she asked, looking back.

' In the butcher's just there.'

' Don't go to-night, Thyrza. I'd rather you didn't.'

' I promise I won't be late. Only half an hour.'

She waved her hand and ran off, of a sudden changed to cheerfulness. Totty received her in the shop with a friendly laugh. Mrs. Bower's description of Miss Nancarrow as a lad in petticoats was not inapt, yet she was by no means heavy or awkward. She had a lithe, shapely figure, and her features much resembled those of a fairly good-looking boy. Her attire showed little care for personal adornment, but it suited her, because it suggested bodily activity. She wore a plain, tight-fitting grey gown, a small straw hat of the brimless kind, and a white linen collar about her neck. Totty was nineteen; no girl in Lambeth relished life with so much determination, yet to all appearance so harmlessly. Her independence was complete; for five years she had been parentless and had lived alone.

Thyrza was attracted to her by this air of freedom and joyousness which distinguished Totty. It was a character wholly unlike her own, and her imaginative thought discerned in it something of an ideal; her own timidity and her tendency to languor found a refreshing antidote in the other's breezy carelessness. Impurity of mind would have repelled her, and there was no trace of it in Totty. Yet Lydia took very ill this recently-grown companionship, holding her friend Mary Bower's view of the girl's character. Her prejudice was enhanced by the jealous care with which, from the time of her own childhood, she had been accustomed to watch over her sister. Already there had been trouble between Thyrza and her on this account. In spite of the unalterable love which united them, their points of unlikeness not seldom brought about debates which Lydia's quick temper sometimes aggravated to a quarrel.

So Lydia finished her marketing and turned homewards with a perturbed mind. But the other two walked, with gossip and laughter, to Totty's lodgings, which were in Newport Street, an offshoot of Paradise Street.

'I'm going with Annie West to a friendly lead,' Totty said; 'will you come with us?'

Thyrza hesitated. The entertainment known as a 'friendly lead' is always held at a public-house, and she knew that Lydia would seriously disapprove of her going to such a place. Yet she had even a physical need of change, of recreation. Whilst she discussed the matter anxiously with herself they entered the house and went up to Totty's room. The house was very small, and had a close, musty smell, as if no fresh air ever got into it. Totty's chamber was a poor, bare little retreat, with low, cracked, grimy ceiling, and one scrap of carpet on the floor, just by the diminutive bed. On a table lay the provisions she had that afternoon brought in from Mrs. Bower's. On the mantel-piece was a small card, whereon was printed an announcement of the friendly lead; at the head stood the name of a public-house, with that of its proprietor; then followed: 'A meeting will take place at the above on Saturday evening, August 2, for the benefit of Bill Mennie, the well-known barber of George Street, who has been laid up through breaking of his leg, and is quite unable to follow his employment at present. We the undersigned, knowing him to be thoroughly respected and a good supporter of these meetings, they trust you will come forward on this occasion, and give him that support he so richly deserve, this being his first appeal.—Chairman:—Count Bismark. Vice: —Dick Perkins. Assisted by' (here was a long list, mostly of nicknames) 'Little Arthur, Flash Bob, Young Brummy, Lardy, Bumper, Old Tacks, Jo at Thomson's, Short-pipe Tommy, Boy Dick, Chaffy Sam Coppock,' and others equally suggestive.

Whilst Thyrza perused this, Totty was singing a merry song.

'I've had ten shillin's sent me to-day,' she said.

'Who by?'

'An old uncle of mine, 'cause it's my birthday to-morrow. He's a rum old fellow. About two years ago he came and asked me if I'd go and live with him and my aunt, and be made a lady of. Honest, he did! He keeps a shop in Tottenham Court Road. He and father 'd quarrelled, and he never come near when father died, and I had to look out for myself. Now, he'd like to make a lady of me; he'll wait a long time till he gets the chance!'

'But wouldn't it be nice, Totty?' Thyrza asked, doubtfully.

'I'd sooner live in my own way, thank you. Fancy me havin' to sit proper at a table, afraid to eat an' drink! What's the use o' livin', if you don't enjoy yourself?'

They were interrupted by a knock at the door, followed by the appearance of Annie West, a less wholesome-looking girl than Totty, but equally vivacious.

'Well, will you come to the "Prince Albert," Thyrza?' Totty asked.

'I can't stay long,' was the answer; 'but I'll go for a little while.'

The house of entertainment was at no great distance. They passed through the bar and up into a room on the first floor, where a miscellaneous assembly was just gathering. Down the middle was a long table, with benches beside it, and a round-backed chair at each end; other seats were ranged

along the walls. At the upper end of the room an arrangement of dirty red hangings—in the form of a canopy, sur-
mounted by a lion and unicorn, of pasteboard—showed that
festive meetings were regularly held here. Round about were
pictures of hunting incidents, of racehorses, of politicians and
pugilists, interspersed with advertisements of beverages. A
piano occupied one corner.

The chairman was already in his place ; on the table before
him was a soup-plate, into which each visitor threw a contribution on arriving. Seated on the benches were a number of
men, women, and girls, all with pewters or glasses before
them, and the air was thickening with smoke of pipes. The
beneficiary of the evening, a portly person with a face of high
satisfaction, sat near the chairman, and by him were two girls
of decent appearance, his daughters. The president puffed at
a churchwarden and exchanged genial banter with those who
came up to deposit offerings. Mr Dick Perkins, the Vice, was
encouraging a spirit of conviviality at the other end. A few
minutes after Thyrza and her companions had entered, a youth
of the seediest appearance struck introductory chords on the
piano, and started off at high pressure with a selection of
popular melodies. The room by degrees grew full. Then
the chairman rose, and with jocular remarks announced the
first song.

Totty had several acquaintances present, male and female ;
her laughter frequently sounded above the hubbub of voices.
Thyrza, who had declined to have anything to drink, shrank
into as little space as possible ; she was nervous and self-re-
proachful, yet the singing and the uproar gave her a certain
pleasure. There was nothing in the talk around her and the
songs that were sung that made it a shame for her to be
present. Plebeian good-humour does not often degenerate
into brutality at meetings of this kind until a late hour of the
evening. The girls who sat with glasses of beer before them,
and carried on primitive flirtations with their neighbours,
were honest wage-earners of factory and workshop, well able
to make themselves respected. If they lacked refinement,
natural or acquired, it was not their fault ; toil was behind
them and before, the hours of rest were few, suffering and lack
of bread might at any moment come upon them. They had
all thrown their hard-earned pence into the soup-plate gladly
and kindly ; now they enjoyed themselves.

The chairman excited enthusiasm by announcement of a

song by Mr. Sam Coppock—known to the company as ' Chaffy
Sem.' Sam was a young man who clearly had no small
opinion of himself; he wore a bright-blue necktie, and had a
geranium flower in his button-hole; his hair was cut as short
as scissors could make it, and as he stood regarding the
assembly he twisted the ends of a scarcely visible moustache.
When he fixed a round glass in one eye and perked his head
with a burlesque of aristocratic bearing, the laughter and
applause were deafening.

' He's a warm 'un, is Sem ! ' was the delighted comment
on all hands.

The pianist made discursive prelude, then Mr. Coppock
gave forth a ditty of the most sentimental character, telling
of the disappearance of a young lady to whom he was devoted.
The burden, in which all bore a part, ran thus :

> We trecked 'er little footprints in the snayoo,
> We trecked 'er little footprints in the snayoo,
> I shall ne'er forget the d'y
> When Jenny lost her w'y,
> And we trecked 'er little footprints in the snayoo !

It was known that the singer had thoughts of cultivating
his talent and of appearing on the music-hall stage ; it was
not unlikely that he might some day become ' the great Sam.'
A second song was called for and granted ; a third—but Mr.
Coppock intimated that it did not become him to keep other
talent in the background. The chairman made a humorous
speech, informing the company that their friend would stand
forth again later in the evening. Mr. Dick Perkins was at
present about to oblige.

The Vice was a frisky little man. He began with what is
known as ' patter,' then gave melodious account of a romantic
meeting with a damsel whom he had seen only once to lose
sight of for ever. And the refrain was :

> She wore a lov-e-lie bonnet
> With fruit end flowers upon it,
> End she dwelt in the henvirons of 'Ol-lo-w'y !

As yet only men had sung ; solicitation had failed with such
of the girls as were known to be musically given. Yet an
earnest prayer from the chairman succeeded at length in overcoming the diffidence of one. She was a pale, unhealthy
thing, and wore an ugly-shaped hat with a gruesome green
feather ; she sang with her eyes down, and in a voice which

did not lack a certain sweetness. The ballad was of spring-time and the country and love.

> Underneath the May-tree blossoms
> Oft we've wandered, you and I,
> Listening to the mill-stream's whisper,
> Like a stream soft-gliding by.

The girl had a drunken mother, and spent a month or two of every year in the hospital, for her day's work overtaxed her strength. She was one of those fated toilers, to struggle on as long as any one would employ her, then to fall among the forgotten wretched. And she sang of May-bloom and love; of love that had never come near her and that she would never know; sang, with her eyes upon the beer-stained table, in a public-house amid the backways of Lambeth.

Totty Nancarrow was whispering to Thyrza:

'Sing something, old girl! Why shouldn't you?'

Annie West was also at hand, urging the same.

'Let 'em hear some real singing, Thyrza. There's a dear.'

Thyrza was in sore trouble. Music, if it were but a street organ, always stirred her heart and made her eager for the joy of song. She had never known what it was to sing before a number of people; the prospect of applause tempted her. Yet she had scarcely the courage, and the thought of Lydia's grief and anger—for Lydia would surely hear of it—was keenly present.

'It's getting late,' she replied nervously. 'I can't stay; I can't sing to-night.'

Only one or two people in the room knew her by sight, but Totty had led to its being passed from one to another that she was a good singer. The landlord of the house happened to be in the room; he came and spoke to her.

'You don't remember me, Miss Trent, but I knew your father well enough, and I knew you when you was a little 'un. In those days I had the "Green Man" in the Cut; your father often enough gave us a toon on his fiddle. A rare good fiddler he was, too! Give us a song now, for old times' sake.'

Thyrza found herself preparing, in spite of herself. She trembled violently, and her heart beat with a strange pain. She heard the chairman shout her name; the sound made her face burn.

'Oh, what shall I sing?' she whispered distractedly to Totty, whilst all eyes were turned to regard her.

'Sing " A Penny for your thoughts."

It was the one song she knew of her father's making, a half-mirthful, half-pathetic little piece in the form of a dialogue between husband and wife, a true expression of the life of working folk, which only a man who was more than half a poet could have shaped.

The seedy youth at the piano was equal to any demand for accompaniment; Totty hummed the air to him, and he had his chords ready without delay.

Thyrza raised her face and began to sing. Yes, it was different enough from anything that had come before; her pure sweet tones touched the hearers profoundly; not a foot stirred. At the second verse she had grown in confidence, and rose more boldly to the upper notes. At the end she was singing her best—better than she had ever sung at home, better than she thought she could sing. The applause that followed was tumultuous. By this time much beer had been consumed; the audience was in a mood for enjoying good things.

'That's something like, old girl!' cried Totty, clapping her on the back. 'Have a drink out of my glass. It's only ginger-beer; it can't hurt you. This is jolly! Ain't it a lark to be alive?'

The pale-faced girl who had sung of May-blossoms looked across the table with eyes in which jealousy strove against admiration. There were remarks aside between the men with regard to Thyrza's personal appearance.

She must sing again. They were not going to be left with hungry ears after a song like that. Thyrza still suffered from the sense that she was doing wrong, but the praise was so sweet to her; sweeter, she thought, than anything she had ever known. She longed to repeat her triumph.

Totty named another song; the faint resistance was overcome, and again the room hushed itself, every hearer spellbound. It was a voice well worthy of cultivation, excellent in compass, with rare sweet power. Again the rapturous applause, and again the demand for more. Another! she should not refuse them. Only one more and they would be content. And a third time she sang; a third time was borne upwards on clamour.

'Totty, I *must* go,' she whispered. 'What's the time?'

'It's only just after ten,' was the reply. 'You'll soon run home.'

'After ten? Oh, I must go at once!'

She left her place, and as quickly as possible made her way through the crowd. Just at the door she saw a face that she recognised, but a feeling of faintness was creeping upon her, and she could think of nothing but the desire to breathe fresh air. Already she was on the stairs, but her strength suddenly failed; she felt herself falling, felt herself strongly seized, then lost consciousness.

She came to herself in a few minutes in the bar-parlour; the landlady was attending to her, and the door had been shut against intruders. Her first recognition was of Luke Ackroyd.

'Don't say anything,' she murmured, looking at him imploringly. 'Don't tell Lyddy.'

'Not I,' replied Ackroyd. 'Just drink a drop and you'll be all right. I'll see you home. You feel better, don't you?'

Yes, she felt better, though her head ached miserably. Soon she was able to walk, and longed to hasten away. The landlady let her out by the private door, and Ackroyd went with her.

'Will you take my arm?' he said, speaking very gently, and looking into her face with eloquent eyes. 'I'm rare and glad I happened to be there. I heard you singing from downstairs, and I asked, Who in the world's that? I know now what Mr. Boddy means when he talks so about your voice. Won't you take my arm, Miss Trent?'

'I feel quite well again, thank you,' she replied. 'I'd no business to be there, Mr. Ackroyd. Lyddy 'll be very angry; she can't help hearing.'

'No, no! she won't be angry. You tell her at once. You were with Totty Nancarrow, I suppose? Oh, it'll be all right. But of course it isn't the kind of place for you, Miss Trent.'

She kept silence. They were walking through a quiet street where the only light came from the gas-lamps. Ackroyd presently looked again into her face.

'Will you come out to-morrow?' he asked, softly.

'Not to-morrow, Mr. Ackroyd.' She added: 'If I did I couldn't come alone. It is better to tell you at once, isn't it? I don't mind with my sister, because then we just go like friends; but I don't want to have people think anything else.'

'Then come with your sister. We *are* friends, aren't we? I can wait for something else.'

'But you mustn't, Mr. Ackroyd. It'll never come. I mean it; I shall never alter my mind. I have a reason.'

'What reason?' he asked, standing still.

She looked away.

'I mean that—that I couldn't never marry you.'

'Don't say that! You don't know what I felt when I heard you singing. Have you heard any harm against me, Thyrza? I haven't always been as steady a fellow as I ought to be, but that was before I came to know you. It's no good, whatever you say—I can't give up hope. Why, a man 'ud do anything for half a kind word from you. Thyrza (he lowered his voice), there isn't anyone else, is there?'

She was silent.

'You don't mean that? Good God! I don't know what'll become of me if I think of that. The only thing I care to live for is the hope of having you for my wife.'

'But you mustn't hope, Mr. Ackroyd. You'll find some-one much better for you than me. But I can't stop. It's so late, and my head aches so. Do let me go, please.'

He made an effort over himself. The nearest lamp showed him that she was very pale.

'Only one word, Thyrza. Is there really any one else?'

'No; but that doesn't alter it.'

She walked quickly on. Ackroyd, with a great sigh of relief, went on by her side. They came out into Lambeth Walk, where the market was as noisy as ever; the shops lit up, the stalls flaring with naphtha lamps, the odour of fried fish everywhere predominant. He led her through the crowd and a short distance into her own street. Then she gave him her hand and said: 'Good-night, Mr. Ackroyd. Thank you for bringing me back. You'll be friends with me and Lyddy?'

'You'll come out with her to-morrow?'

'I can't promise. Good-night!'

CHAPTER V

A LAND OF TWILIGHT

It happened that Mrs. Jarmey, the landlady of the house in which the sisters lived, had business in the neighbourhood of the 'Prince Albert,' and chanced to exchange a word with an acquaintance who had just come away after hearing Thyrza sing. Returning home, she found Lydia at the door, anxiously and impatiently waiting for Thyrza's appearance. The news, of course, was at once communicated, with moral reflections, wherein Mrs. Jarmey excelled. Not five minutes later, and whilst the two were still talking in the passage, the front door opened, and Thyrza came in. Lydia turned and went upstairs.

Thyrza, entering the room, sought her sister's face ; it had an angry look. For a moment Lydia did not speak ; the other, laying aside her hat, said : 'I'm sorry I'm so late, Lyddy.'

' Where have you been ? ' her sister asked, in a voice which strove to command itself.

Thyrza could not tell the whole truth at once, though she knew it would have to be confessed eventually ; indeed, whether or no discovery came from other sources, all would eventually be told of her own free will. She might fear at the moment, but in the end kept no secret from Lydia.

' I've been about with Totty,' she said, averting her face as she drew off her cotton gloves.

' Yes, you have ! You've been singing at a public-house.'

Lydia was too upset to note the paleness of Thyrza's face, which at another moment would have elicited anxious question. She was deeply hurt that Thyrza made so little account of her wishes ; jealous of the influence of Totty Nancarrow ; stirred with apprehensions as powerful as a mother's. On the other hand, it was Thyrza's nature to shrink into coldness before angry words. She suffered intensely when the voice which was of wont so affectionate turned to severity, but she could not excuse herself till the storm was over. And it was most often from the elder girl that the first words of recon-cilement came.

'That's your Totty Nancarrow,' Lydia went on, with no check upon her tongue. 'Didn't I tell you what 'ud come of going about with her? What next, I should like to know! If you go on and sing in a public-house, I don't know what you won't do. I shall never trust you out by yourself again. You shan't go out at night at all, that's about it!'

'You've no right to speak to me like that, Lydia,' Thyrza replied, with indignation. The excitement and the fainting-fit had strung her nerves painfully; and, for all her repentance, the echo of applause was still very sweet in her ears. This vehement reproach caused a little injury to her pride. 'It doesn't depend on you whether I go out or not. I'm not a child, and I can take care of myself. I haven't done nothing wrong.'

'You have—and you know you have! You knew I shouldn't have let you go near such a place. You know how I've begged you not to go with Totty Nancarrow, and how you've promised me you wouldn't be led into no harm. I shall never be able to trust you again. You *are* only a child! You show it! And in future you'll do as I tell you!'

Thyrza caught up her hat.

'I'm not going to stop here whilst you're in such a bad temper,' she said, in a trembling voice; 'you'll find that isn't the way to make me do as you wish.'

She stepped to the door. Lydia, frightened, sprang forward and barred the way.

'Go and sit down, Thyrza!'

'Let me go! What right have you to stop me?'

Then both were silent. At the same moment they became aware that a common incident of Saturday night was occurring in the street below. A half-tipsy man and a nagging woman had got thus far on their way home, the wife's shrill tongue running over every scale of scurrility and striking every note of ingenious malice. The man was at length worked to a pitch of frenzy, and then—thud, thud, mingled with objurgations and shrill night-piercing yells. Fury little short of mur-derous was familiar enough to dwellers in this region, but that woman's bell-clapper tongue had struck shame into Lydia. She could not speak another angry word.

'Thyrza, take your hat off,' she said quietly, moving away a little from the door. Her cheeks burned, and she quivered in the subsidence of her temper.

Her sister did not obey, but, unable to stand longer, she

went to a chair at a distance. The uproar in the street continued for a quarter of an hour, then by degrees passed on, the voice of the woman shrieking foul abuse till remoteness stifled it. Lydia forced herself to keep silence from good or ill; it was no use speaking the thoughts she had till morning. Thyrza sat with her eyes fixed on vacancy; she was so miserable, her heart had sunk so low, that tears would have come had she not forced them back. More than once of late she had known this mood, in which life lay about her barren and weary. She was very young to suffer that oppression of the world-worn; it was the penalty she paid for her birthright of heart and mind.

By midnight they were lying side by side, but no 'good-night' had passed between them. When Thyrza's gentle breathing told that she slept, Lydia still lay with open eyes, watching the flicker of the street lamp upon the ceiling, hearing the sounds that came of mirth or brutality in streets near and far. She did not suffer in the same way as her sister; as soon as she had gently touched Thyrza's unconscious hand love came upon her with its warm solace; but her trouble was deep, and she looked into the future with many doubts.

The past she could scarcely deem other than happy, though a stranger would have thought it sad enough. Her mother she well remembered—a face pale and sweet, like Thyrza's: the eyes that have their sad beauty from foresight of death. Her father lived only a year longer, then she and the little one passed into the charge of Mr. Boddy, who was paid a certain small sum by Trent's employers, in consideration of the death by accident. Then came the commencement of Mr. Boddy's misfortunes; his shop and house were burnt down, he lost his limb in an endeavour to save his property, he lost his wife in consequence of the shock. Dreary things for the memory, yet they did not weigh upon Lydia; she was so happily endowed that her mind selected and dwelt on sunny hours, on kind looks and words which her strong heart cherished unassailably, on the mutual charities which sorrow had begotten rather than on the sorrow itself. Above all, the growing love of her dear one, of her to whom she was both mother and sister, had strengthened her against every trouble. Yet of late this strongest passion of her life had become a source of grave anxieties, as often as circumstance caused her to look beyond her contentment. Thyrza was so beautiful, and, it seemed to her, so weak; always dreaming of something

E

beyond and above the life which was her lot; so deficient in the practical qualities which that life demanded. At moments Lydia saw her responsibility in a light which alarmed her.

They worked at a felt-hat factory, as ' trimmers; ' that is to say, they finished hats by sewing in the lining, putting on the bands, and the like. In the busy season they could average together wages of about a pound a week; at dull times they earned less, and very occasionally had to support themselves for a week or two without employment. Since the age of fourteen Lydia herself had received help from no one; from sixteen she had lived in lodgings with Thyrza, independent. Mr. Boddy was then no longer able to do more than supply his own needs, for things had grown worse with him from year to year. Lydia occasionally found jobs for her free hours, and she had never yet wanted. She was strong, her health had scarcely ever given her a day's uneasiness; there never came to her a fear lest bread should fail. But Thyrza could not take life as she did. It was not enough for that imaginative nature to toil drearily day after day, and year after year, just for the sake of earning a livelihood. In a month she would be seventeen; it was too true, as she had said to-night, that she was no longer a child. What might happen if the elder sister's influence came to an end? Thyrza loved her: how Lydia would have laughed at anyone who hinted that the love could ever weaken! But it was not a guard against every danger.

It was inevitable that Lydia should have hoped that her sister might marry early. And one man she knew in whom —she scarcely could have told you why—her confidence was so strong that she would freely have entrusted him with Thyrza's fate. Thyrza could not bring herself to think of him as a husband. It was with Ackroyd that Lydia's thoughts were busy as she lay wakeful. Before to-night she had not pondered so continuously on what she knew of him. For some two years he had been an acquaintance, through the Bowers, and she had felt glad when it was plain that he sought Thyrza's society. ' Yes,' she had said to herself, ' I like him, and feel that he is to be relied upon.' Stories, to be sure, had reached her ears; something of an over-fondness for conviviality; but she had confidence. To-night she seemed called upon to review all her impressions. Why? Nothing new had happened. She longed for sleep, but it only came when dawn was white upon the blind.

When it was time to rise, neither spoke. Lydia prepared

the breakfast as usual—it seemed quite natural that she should do nearly all the work of the home—and they sat down to it cheerlessly.

Since daybreak a mist had crept over the sky; it thinned the sunlight to a suffusion of grey and gold. Within the house there was the silence of Sunday morning; the street was still, save for the jodeling of a milkman as he wheeled his clattering cans from house to house. In that London on the other side of Thames, known to these girls with scarcely less of vagueness than to simple dwellers in country towns, the autumn-like air was foretaste of holiday; the martyrs of the Season and they who do the world's cleaner work knew that rest was near, spoke at breakfast of the shore and the mountain. Even to Lydia, weary after her short sleep and unwontedly dejected, there came a wish that it were possible to quit the streets for but one day, and sit somewhere apart under the open sky. It was not often that so fantastic a dream visited her.

In dressing, Thyrza had left her hair unbraided. Lydia always did that for her. When the table was cleared, the former took up a story-paper which she bought every week, and made a show of reading. Lydia went about her accustomed tasks.

Presently she took a brush and comb and went behind her sister's chair. She began to unloosen the rough coils in which the golden hair was pinned together. It was always a joy to her to bathe her hands in the warm, soft torrent. With delicate care she combed out every intricacy, and brushed the ordered tresses till the light gleamed on their smooth surface; then with skilful fingers she wove the braid, tying it with a blue ribbon so that the ends hung loose. The task completed, it was her custom to bend over the little head and snatch an inverted kiss, always a moment of laughter. This morning she omitted that; she was moving sadly away, when she noticed that the face turned a little, a very little.

'Isn't it right?' she asked, keeping her eyes down.

'I think so—it doesn't matter.'

She drew near again, as if to inspect her work. Perhaps there was a slight lack of smoothness over the temple; she touched the spot with her fingers.

'Why are you so unkind to me, Thyrza?'

The words had come involuntarily; the voice shook as they were spoken.

' I don't mean to be, Lyddy—you know I don't.'

' But you do things that you know 'll make me angry. I'm quick-tempered, and I couldn't bear to think of you going to that place ; I ought to have spoke in a different way.'

' Who told you I'd been singing ? '

' Mrs. Jarmey. I'm very glad she did ; it doesn't seem any harm to you, Thyrza, but it does to me. Dear, have you ever sung at such places before ? '

Thyrza shook her head.

' Will you promise me never to go there again ? '

' I don't want to go. But I get no harm. They were very pleased with my singing. Annie West was there, and several other girls. Why do you make so much of it, Lyddy ? '

' Because I'm older than you, Thyrza ; and if you'll only trust me, and do as I wish, you'll see some day that I was right. I know you're a good girl ; I don't think a wrong thought ever came into your head. It isn't that, it's because you can't go about the streets and into public-houses without hearing bad things and seeing bad people. I want to keep you away from everything that isn't homelike and quiet. I want you to love me more than anyone else ! '

' I do, Lyddy ! I do, dear ! It's only that I——'

' What——? '

' I don't know how it is. I'm discontented. There's never any change. How can you be so happy day after day ? I love to be with you, but— if we could go and live somewhere else ! I should like to see a new place. I've been reading there about the seaside ; what it must be like ! I want to know things. You don't understand me ? '

' I think I do. I felt a little the same when I heard Mrs. Isaacs and her daughter talking about Margate yesterday. But we shall be better off some day, see if we aren't ! Try your best not to think about those things. Suppose you ask Mr. Grail to lend you a book to read ? I met Mrs. Grail downstairs last night, and she asked if we'd go down and have tea to-day. I can't, because Mary's coming, but you might. And I'm sure he'd lend you something nice if you asked him.'

' I don't think I durst. He always sits so quiet, and he's such a queer man.'

' Yes, he is rather queer, but he speaks very kind.'

' I'll see. But you mustn't speak so cross to me if I do wrong, Lyddy. I felt as if I should like to go away, some time when you didn't know. I did, really ! '

Lydia gazed at her anxiously.

'I don't think you'd ever have the heart to do that, Thyrza,' she said, in a low voice.

'No,' she shook her head, smiling. 'I couldn't do without you. And now kiss me properly, like you always do.'

Lydia stood behind the chair again, and the laughing caress was exchanged.

'I should stay,' Thyrza went on, 'if it was only to have you do my hair. I do so like to feel your soft hands!'

'Soft hands! Great coarse things. Just look!'

She took one of Thyrza's, and held it beside her own. The difference was noticeable enough; Lydia's was not ill-shapen, but there were marks on it of all the rough household work which she had never permitted her sister to do. Thyrza's was delicate, supple, beautiful in its kind as her face.

'I don't care!' she said laughing. 'It's a good, soft, sleepy hand.'

'Sleepy, child!'

'I mean it always makes me feel dozy when it's doing my hair.'

There was no more cloud between them. The morning passed on with sisterly talk. Lydia had wisely refrained from exacting promises; she hoped to resume the subject before long—together with another that was in her mind. Thyrza, too, had something to speak of, but could not bring herself to it as yet.

Though it was so hot, they had to keep a small fire for cooking the dinner. This meal consisted of a small piece of steak, chosen from the odds and ends thrown together on the front of a butcher's shop, and a few potatoes. It was not always they had meat; yet they never went hungry, and, in comparing herself with others she knew, it· sometimes made Lydia a little unhappy to think how well she lived.

Then began the unutterable dreariness of a Sunday afternoon. From the lower part of the house sounded the notes of a concertina; it was Mr. Jarmey who played. He had the habit of doing so whilst half asleep, between dinner and tea. With impartiality he passed from strains of popular hymnody to the familiar ditties of the music hall, lavishing on each an excess of sentiment. He shook pathetically on top notes and languished on final chords. A dolorous music!

The milkman came along the street. He was followed by a woman who wailed 'wa-ater-creases!' Then the concertina

once more possessed the stillness. Few pedestrians were
abroad; the greater part of the male population of Lambeth
slumbered after the baked joint and flagon of ale. Yet here
and there a man in his shirt-sleeves leaned forth despondently
from a window or sat in view within, dozing over the Sunday
paper.

A rattling of light wheels drew near, and a nasal voice
cried ' 'Okey-pokey! 'Okey-'okey-'okey! Penny a lump!'
It was the man who sold ice-cream. He came to a stop, and
half a dozen boys gathered about his truck. The delicacy
was dispensed to them in little green and yellow glasses, from
which they extracted it with their tongues. The vendor remained for a few minutes, then on again with his ' 'Okey-
'okey-'okey!' sung through the nose.

Next came a sound of distressful voices, whining the dis-
cords of a mendicant psalm. A man, a woman, and two
small children crawled along the street; their eyes surveyed
the upper windows. All were ragged and filthy; the elders
bore the unmistakable brand of the gin-shop, and the children
were visaged like debased monkeys. Occasionally a copper
fell to them, in return for which the choragus exclaimed
' Gord bless yer! '

Thyrza sat in her usual place by the window, now reading
for a few minutes, now dreaming. Lydia had some stockings
to be darned ; she became at length so silent that her sister
turned to look at her. Her head had dropped forward. She
slumbered for a few minutes, then started to consciousness
again, and laughed when she saw Thyrza regarding her.

' I suppose Mary'll be here directly?' she said. ' I'd better
put this work out of sight.' And as she began to spread the
cloth, she asked: ' What'll you do whilst we're at chapel,
Thyrza ? '

' I think I'll go and have tea with Mrs. Grail; then I'll
see if I dare ask for a book.'

' You've made up your mind not to go out ? '

' There was something I wanted to tell you. I met Mr.
Ackroyd as I was coming home last night. I told him I
couldn't come out alone, and I said I couldn't be sure whether
you'd come or not.'

' But what a pity! ' returned Lydia. ' You knew I was
going to chapel. I'm afraid he'll wait for us.'

' Yes, but I somehow didn't like to say we wouldn't go at
all. What time is he going to be there ? '

' He said at six o'clock.'

' Would you mind just running out and telling him ? Perhaps you'll be going past with Mary, not long after ? '

' That's a nice job you give me ! ' remarked Lydia, with a half smile.

' But I know you don't mind it, Lyddy. It isn't the first thing you've done for me.'

It was said with so much *naïveté* that Lydia could not but laugh.

' I should like it much better if you'd go yourself,' she replied. ' But I'm afraid it's no good asking.'

' Not a bit ! And, Lyddy, I told Mr. Ackroyd that it would always be the same. He understands now.'

The other made no reply.

' You won't be cross about it ? '

' No, dear ; there's nothing to be cross about. But I'm very sorry.'

The explanation passed in a tone of less earnestness than either would have anticipated. They did not look at each other, and they dismissed the subject as soon as possible. Then came two rings at the house-bell, signifying the arrival of their visitor.

Mary Bower and Lydia had been close friends for four or five years, yet they had few obvious points of similarity, and their differences were marked enough. The latter increased ; for Mary attached herself more closely to religious observances, whilst Lydia continued to declare with native frankness that she could not feel it incumbent upon her to give grave attention to such matters. Mary grieved over this attitude in one whose goodness of heart she could not call in question ; it troubled her as an inconsequence in nature ; she cherished a purpose of converting Lydia, and had even brought herself to the point of hoping that some sorrow might befall her friend —nothing of too sad a nature, but still a grief which might turn her thoughts inward. Yet, had anything of the kind come to pass, Mary would have been the first to hasten with consolation.

Thyrza went downstairs, and the two gossiped as tea was made ready. Mary had already heard of the incident at the ' Prince Albert ; ' such a piece of news could not be long in reaching Mrs. Bower's. She wished to speak of it, yet was in uncertainty whether Lydia had already been told. The latter was the first to bring forward the subject.

'It's quite certain she oughtn't to make a friend of that girl Totty,' Mary said, with decision. 'You must insist that it is stopped, Lydia.'

'I shan't do any good that way,' replied the other, shaking her head. 'I lost my temper last night, like a silly, and of course only harm came of it.'

'But there's no need to lose your temper. You must tell her she's *not* to speak to the girl again, and there's an end of it!'

'Thyrza's too old for that, dear. I must lead her by kindness, or I can't lead her at all. I don't think, though, she'll ever do such a thing as that again I know what a temptation it was; she does sing so sweetly. But she won't do it again now she knows how I think about it.'

Mary appeared doubtful. Given a suggestion of iniquity, and it was her instinct rather to fear than to hope. Secretly she had no real liking for Thyrza; something in that complex nature repelled her. As she herself had said : 'Thyrza was not easy to understand,' but she did understand that the girl's essential motives were of a kind radically at enmity with her own. Thyrza, it seemed to her, was worldly in the most hopeless way.

'You'll be sorry for it if you're not firm,' she remarked.

Lydia made no direct reply, but after a moment's musing she said :

'If only she could think of Mr. Ackroyd!'

She had not yet spoken so plainly of this to Mary; the latter was surprised by the despondency of her tone.

'But I thought they were often together?'

'She's only been out with him when I went as well, and last night she told him it was no use.'

'Well, I can't say I'm sorry to hear that,' Mary replied with the air of one who spoke an unpleasant truth.

'Why not, Mary?'

'I think he's likely to do her every bit as much harm as Totty Nancarrow.'

'What *do* you mean, Mary?' There was a touch of indignation in Lydia's voice. 'What harm can Mr. Ackroyd do to Thyrza?'

'Not the kind of harm you're thinking of, dear. But if I had a sister I know I shouldn't like to see her marry Mr. Ackroyd. He's got no religion, and what's more he's always talking against religion. Father says he made a speech last week at that place in Westminster Bridge Road where the Atheists have their meetings. I don't deny there's something nice about him, but I wouldn't trust a man of that kind.'

Lydia delayed her words a little. She kept her eyes on the table; her forehead was knitted.

'I can't help what he thinks about religion,' she replied at length, with firmness. 'He's a good man, I'm quite sure of that.'

'Lydia, he can't be good if he does his best to ruin people's souls.'

'I don't know anything about that, Mary. Whatever he says, he says because he believes it and thinks it right. Why, there's Mr. Grail thinks in the same way, I believe; at all events, he never goes to church or chapel. And he's a friend of Mr. Ackroyd's.'

'But we don't know anything about Mr. Grail.'

'We don't know much, but it's quite enough to talk to him for a few minutes to know he's a man that wouldn't say or do anything wrong.'

'He must be a wonderful man, Lydia.'

These Sunday conversations were always fruitful of trouble. Mary was prepared by her morning and afternoon exercises to be more aggressive and uncompromising than usual. But the present difficulty appeared a graver one than any that had yet risen between them. Lydia had never spoken in the tone which marked her rejoinder:

'Really, Mary, it's as if you couldn't put faith in no one! You know I don't feel the same as you do about religion and such things, and I don't suppose I ever shall. When I like people, I like them; I can't ask what they believe and what they don't believe. We'd better not talk about it any more.'

Mary's face assumed rather a hard look.

'Just as you like, my dear,' she said.

There ensued an awkward silence, which Lydia at length broke by speech on some wholly different subject. Mary with difficulty adapted herself to the change; tea was finished rather uncomfortably.

It was six o'clock. Lydia, hearing the hour strike, knew that Ackroyd would be waiting at the end of Walnut Tree Walk. She was absent-minded, halting between a desire to go at once, and tell him that they could not come, and a disinclination not perhaps very clearly explained. The minutes

went on. It seemed to be decided for her that he should
learn the truth by their failure to join him.

Church bells began to sound. Mary rose and put on her
hat, then, taking up the devotional books she had with her,
offered her hand as if to say good-bye.

'But,' said Lydia in surprise, 'I'm going with you.'

'I didn't suppose you would,' the other returned quietly.
'But haven't you had tea with me?'

Mary had not now to learn that her friend held a promise inviolable; her surprise would have been great if Lydia
had allowed her to go forth alone. She smiled.

'Will there be nice singing?' Lydia asked, as she prepared herself quickly. 'I do really like the singing, at all
events, Mary.'

The other shook her head, sadly.

They left the house and turned towards Kennington Road.
Before Lydia had gone half a dozen steps she saw that Ackroyd was waiting at the end of the street. She felt a pang of
self-reproach; it was wrong of her to have allowed him to
stand in miserable uncertainty all this time; she ought to
have gone out at six o'clock. In a low voice she said to her
companion:

'There's Mr. Ackroyd. I want just to speak a word to
him. If you'll go on when we get up, I'll soon overtake you.'

Mary acquiesced in silence. Lydia, approaching, saw disappointment on the young man's face. He raised his hat to
her—an unwonted attention in these parts—and she gave
him her hand.

'I'm going to chapel,' she said playfully.

He had a sudden hope.

'Then your sister'll come out?'

'No, Mr. Ackroyd; she can't to-night. She's having tea
with Mrs. Grail.'

He looked down the street. Lydia was impelled to say
earnestly:

'Some time, perhaps! Thyrza is very young yet, Mr.
Ackroyd. She thinks of such different things.'

'What does she think of?' he asked, rather gloomily.

'I mean she—she must get older and know you better.
Good-bye! Mary Bower is waiting for me.'

She ran on, and Ackroyd sauntered away without a glance
after her.

CHAPTER VI

DISINHERITED

WHEN Thyrza left the two at tea and went downstairs, she knocked at the door of the front parlour on the ground floor. The room which she entered was but dimly lighted; thick curtains encroached upon each side of the narrow window, which was also shadowed above by a vallance with long tassels, whilst in front of it stood a table with a great pot of flowering musk. The atmosphere was close; with the odour of the plant blended the musty air which comes from old and neglected furniture. Mrs. Grail, Gilbert Grail's mother, was an old lady with an unusual dislike for the upset of house-hold cleaning, and as her son's prejudice, like that of most men, tended in the same direction, this sitting-room, which they used in common, had known little disturbance since they entered it a year and a half ago. Formerly they had occupied a house in Battersea ; it was given up on the death of Gilbert's sister, and these lodgings taken in Walnut Tree Walk.

A prominent object in the room was a bookcase, some six feet high, quite full of books, most of them of shabby exterior. They were Gilbert's purchases at second-hand stalls during the past fifteen years. Their variety indicated a mind of liberal intelligence. Works of history and biography pre-dominated, but poetry and fiction were also represented on the shelves. Odd volumes of expensive publications looked forth plaintively here and there, and many periodical issues stood unbound.

Another case, a small one with glass doors, contained literature of another order—some thirty volumes which had belonged to Gilbert's father, and were now his mother's peculiar study. They were translations of sundry works of Swedenborg, and productions put forth by the Church of the New Jerusalem. Mrs. Grail was a member of that church. She occasionally visited a meeting-place in Brixton, but for the most part was satisfied with conning the treatises of the mystic, by preference that on 'Heaven and Hell,' which she

read in the first English edition, an old copy in boards, much
worn.

She was a smooth-faced, gentle-mannered woman, not
without dignity as she rose to receive Thyrza and guided her
to a comfortable seat. Her voice was habitually subdued to
the limit of audibleness; she spoke with precision, and in
language very free from vulgarisms either of thought or phrase.
Her taste had always been for a home-keeping life; she
dreaded gossipers, and only left the house when it was absolutely necessary, then going forth closely veiled. With the
landlady she held no more intercourse than arose from the
weekly payment of rent; the other lodgers in the house only
saw her by chance on rare occasions. Her son left home and
returned with much regularity, he also seeming to desire
privacy above all things. Mrs. Jarmey had at first been disposed to take this reserve somewhat ill. When she knocked at
Mrs. Grail's door on some paltry excuse for seeing the inside
of the room, and found that the old lady exchanged brief
words with her on the threshold, she wondered who these
people might be who thought themselves too good for wonted
neighbourship. In time, however, her feeling changed, and
she gave everybody to understand that her ground-floor lodgers
were of the highest respectability, inmates such as did not
fall to the lot of every landlady.

Gilbert was surprised when, of her own motion, his mother
made overtures to the sisters who lived at the top of the
house. Neither Lydia nor Thyrza was at first disposed to
respond very warmly; they agreed that the old lady was
doubtless very respectable, but, at the same time, decidedly
queer in her way of speaking. But during the past few
months they had overcome this reluctance, and were now on
a certain footing of intimacy with Mrs. Grail, who made it no
secret that she took great interest in Thyrza. Thyrza always
entered the sitting-room with a feeling of awe. The dim light,
the old lady's low voice, above all, the books—in her eyes a
remarkable library—impressed her strongly. If Grail himself
were present, he was invariably reading; Thyrza held him
profoundly learned, a judgment confirmed by his mother's
way of speaking of him. For Mrs. Grail regarded her son
with distinct reverence. He, in turn, was tenderly respectful
to her; they did not know what it was to exchange an unkind or an impatient word.

Thyrza liked especially to have tea here on Sunday. The

appointments of the table seemed to her luxurious, for the tea-service was uniform and of pretty, old-fashioned pattern, and simple little dainties of a kind new to her were generally forthcoming. Moreover, from her entrance to her leave-taking, she was flattered by the pleasantest attentions. The only other table at which she sometimes sat as a guest was Mrs. Bower's; between the shopkeeper's gross good-nature and the well-mannered kindness of Mrs. Grail there was a broad distinction, and Thyrza was very ready to appreciate it. For she was sensible of refinements; num berless little personal delicacies distinguished her from the average girl of her class, and even from Lydia. The meals which she and her sister took in their own room might be ever so poor; they were always served with a modest grace which perhaps would not have marked them if it had de-pended upon Lydia alone. In this respect, as in many others, Thyrza had repaid her sister's devotion with subtle influences tending to a comely life.

Once, when she had gone down alone to have tea, she said to Lydia on her return. 'Downstairs they treat me as if I was a lady,' and it was spoken with the simple satisfaction which was one of her charming traits.

Till quite lately Gilbert had scarcely conversed with her at all. When he broke his habitual silence he addressed him-self to Lydia; if he did speak to the younger girl it was with studied courtesy and kindness, but he seemed unable to overcome a sort of shyness with which she had troubled him since the beginning of their acquaintance. It was noticeable in his manner this evening when he shook hands with a murmured word or two. Thyrza, however, appeared a little less timid than usual; she just met his look, and in a ques-tioning way which he could not understand at the time. The truth was, Thyrza wondered whether he had heard of her escapade of the night before; she tried to read his expression, searching for any hint of disapproval.

The easy chair was always given to her when she entered So seldom she sat on anything easier than the stiff cane-bottomed seats of her own room that this always seemed luxurious. By degrees she had permitted herself to lean back in it. She did so want Lyddy to know what it was like to sit in that chair; but it had never yet been possible to effect an exchange. It might have offended Mrs. Grail, a thing on no account to be risked.

'Lyddy has Mary Bower to tea,' she said on her arrival this evening. 'They're going to chapel. You don't mind me coming alone, Mrs. Grail?'

'You're never anything but welcome, my dear,' murmured the old lady, pressing the little hand in both her own.

Tea was soon ready. Mrs. Grail talked with pleasant continuousness, as usual. She had fallen upon reminiscences, and spoke of Lambeth as she had known it when a girl; it was her birthplace, and through life she had never strayed far away. She regarded the growth of population, the crowding of mean houses where open spaces used to be, the whole change of times in fact, as deplorable. One would have fancied from her descriptions that the Lambeth of sixty years ago was a delightful rustic village.

After tea Thyrza resumed the low chair and folded her hands, full of contentment. Mrs. Grail took the tea-things from the room and was absent about a quarter of an hour. Thyrza, left alone with the man who for her embodied so many mysteries, let her eyes stray over the bookshelves. She felt it very unlikely that any book there would be within the compass of her understanding; doubtless they dealt with the secrets of learning—the strange, high things for which her awed imagination had no name. Gilbert had seated himself in a shadowed corner; his face was bent downwards. Just when Thyrza was about to put some timid question with regard to the books, he looked at her and said:

'Do you ever go to Westminster Abbey?'

The intellectual hunger of his face was softened; he did not smile, but kept a mild gravity of expression which showed that he had a pleasure in the girl's proximity. When he had spoken he stroked his forehead with the tips of his fingers, a nervous action.

'I've never been inside, Thyrza made answer. 'What is there to see?'

'It's the place, you know, where great men have been buried for hundreds of years. I should like, if I could, to spend a little time there every day.'

'Can you see the graves?' Thyrza asked.

'Yes, many. And on the stones you read who they were that lie there. There are the graves of kings, and of men much greater than kings.'

'Greater than kings! Who were they, Mr. Grail?'

She had rested her elbow on the arm of the chair, and her

fingers just touched her chin. She regarded him with a gaze of deep curiosity.

'Men who wrote books,' he answered, with a slight smile.

Thyrza dropped her eyes. In her thought of books it had never occurred to her that any special interest could attach to the people who wrote them ; indeed, she had perhaps never asked herself how printed matter came into existence. Even among the crowd of average readers we know how commonly a book will be run through without a glance at its title-page.

Gilbert continued :

'I always come away from the Abbey with fresh courage. If I'm tired and out of spirits, I go there, and it makes me feel as if I daren't waste a minute of the time when I'm free to try and learn something.'

It was a strange impulse that made him speak in this way to an untaught child. With those who were far more likely to understand him he was the most reticent of men.

'But you know a great deal, Mr. Grail,' Thyrza said with surprise, looking again at the bookshelves.

'You mustn't think that. I had very little teaching when I was a lad, and ever since I've had very little either of time or means to teach myself. If I only knew those few books well, it would be something, but there are some of them I've never got to yet.'

'Those *few* books ! ' Thyrza exclaimed. 'But I never thought anybody had so many, before I came into this room.

'I should like you to see the library at the British Museum. Every book that is published in England is sent there. There's a large room where people sit and study any book they like, all day long, and day after day. Think what a life that must be ! '

'Those are rich people, I suppose,' Thyrza remarked. 'They haven't to work for their living.'

'Not rich, all of them. But they haven't to work with their hands.'

He became silent. In his last words there was a little bitterness. Thyrza glanced at him ; he seemed to have forgotten her presence, and his face had the wonted look of trouble kept under.

Then Mrs. Grail returned. She sat down near Thyrza, and, after a little more of her pleasant talk, said, turning to her son :

'Could you find something to read us, Gilbert ? '

He thought for a moment, then reached down a book of biographies, writing of a popular colour, not above Thyrza's understanding. It contained a life of Sir Thomas More, or rather a pleasant story founded upon his life, with much about his daughter Margaret.

'Yes, that'll do nicely,' was Mrs. Grail's opinion.

He began with a word or two of explanation to Thyrza, then entered upon the narrative. As soon as the proposal was made, Thyrza's face had lighted up with pleasure; she listened intently, leaning a little forward in her chair, her hands folded together. Gilbert, if he raised his eyes from the page, did not look at her. Mrs. Grail interrupted once or twice with a question or a comment. The reading was good; Gilbert's voice gave life to description and conversation, and supplied an interest even where the writer was in danger of growing dull.

When the end was reached, Thyrza recovered herself with the sigh which follows strained attention. But she was not in a mood to begin conversation again; her mind had got something to work upon, it would keep her awake far into the night with a succession of half-realised pictures. What a world was that of which a glimpse had been given her! Here, indeed, was something remote from her tedious life. Her brain was full of vague glories, of the figures of kings and queens, of courtiers and fair ladies, of things nobly said and done; and her heart throbbed with indignation at wrongs greater than any she had ever imagined. When it had all happened she knew not; surely very long ago! But the names she knew, Chelsea, Lambeth, the Tower—these gave a curiously fantastic reality to the fairy tale. And one thing she saw with uttermost distinctness: that boat going down the stream of Thames, and the dear, dreadful head dropped into it from the arch above. She would go and stand on the bridge and think of it.

Ah, she must tell Lyddy all that! Better still, she must read it to her. She found courage to say:

'Could you spare that book, Mr. Grail? Could you lend it me for a day or two? I'd be very careful with it.'

'I shall be very glad to lend it you,' Gilbert answered. His voice changed somehow from that in which he usually spoke.

She received it from him and held it on her lap with both hands. She would not look into it till alone in her room; and, having secured it, she did not wish to stay longer.

' Going already ? ' Mrs. Grail said, seeing her rise.

' Lyddy 'll be back very soon,' was the reply. ' I think I'd better go now.'

She shook hands with both of them, and they heard her run up the thin-carpeted stairs.

Mother and son sat in silence for some minutes. Gilbert had taken another book, and seemed to be absorbed in it; Mrs. Grail had a face of meditation. Occasionally she looked upwards, as though on the track of some memory which she strove to make clear.

' Gilbert,' she began at length, suggestively.

He raised his eyes and regarded her in an absent way.

' I've been trying for a long time to remember what that child's face reminded me of. Every time I see her, I make sure I've seen someone like her before, and now I think I've got it.'

Gilbert was used to a stream of amusing fancifulness in his mother; analysis and resemblances were dear to her; possibly the Biblical theories which she had imbibed were in some degree answerable for the characteristic.

' And who does she remind you of ? ' he asked.

' Of somebody whose name I can't think of. You remember the school in Lambeth Road where Lizzie used to go ? '

She referred to a time five-and-twenty years gone by, when Gilbert's sister was a child. He nodded.

' It was Mrs. Green's school, you know, and soon after Lizzie began to go, there was an assistant teacher taken on. Now can you think what her name was ? You must remember that Lizzie used to walk home along with her almost every day. Miss——, Miss——. Oh, dear me, what *was* that name ? '

Gilbert smiled and shook his head.

' I can't help you, mother. I don't even remember any such thing.'

' What a poor memory you have in ordinary things, Gilbert! I wonder at it, with your mind for study.'

' But what's the connection ? '

' Why, Thyrza has got her very face. It's just come to me. I'm sure that was her mother.'

' But how impossible that you should have that woman's face still in your mind ! ' Gilbert protested, good-humouredly.

' My dear, don't be so hasty. It's as clear to me as if

F

Lizzie had just come in and said, "Miss Denny brought me home." Why, there *is* the name! It fell from my tongue! To be sure; Miss Denny! A pale, sad-looking little thing, she was. Often and often I've been at the window and seen her coming along the street hand in hand with your sister. Now I'll ask Thyrza if her mother's name wasn't Denny, and if she didn't teach at Mrs. Green's school. Depend upon it, I'm right, Gilbert!'

Gilbert still smiled very incredulously.

'It'll be a marvellous thing if it turns out to be true,' he said.

'Oh, but I have a wonderful memory for faces. I always used to think there was something very good in that teacher's look. I don't think I ever spoke to her, though she went backwards and forwards past our house in Brook Street for nearly two years. Then I didn't see her any more. Depend upon it, she went away to be married. Lizzie had left a little before that. Oh yes, it explains why I seemed to know Thyrza the first time I saw her.'

Mrs. Grail was profoundly satisfied. Again a short silence ensued.

'How nicely they keep themselves!' she resumed, half to herself. 'I'm sure Lydia's one of the most careful girls I ever knew. But Thyrza's my favourite. How she enjoyed your reading, Gilbert!'

He nodded, but kept his attention on the book. His mother just glanced at him, and presently continued:

'I do hope she won't be spoilt. She *is* very pretty, isn't she? But they're not girls for going out much, I can see. And Thyrza's always glad when I ask her to come and have tea with us. I suppose they haven't many friends.'

It was quite against Mrs. Grail's wont to interrupt thus when her son had settled down to read. Gilbert averted his eyes from the page, and, after reflecting a little, said :

'Ackroyd knows them.'

His mother looked at him closely. He seemed to be absorbed again.

'Does he speak to you about them, Gilbert?'

'He's mentioned them once or twice.'

'Perhaps that's why Lydia goes out to chapel,' the old lady said, with a smile.

'No, I don't think so.'

The reply was so abrupt, so nearly impatient, that Mrs.

Grail made an end of her remarks. In a little while she too began to read.

They had supper at nine; at ten o'clock Mrs. Grail kissed her son's forehead and bade him good-night, adding, ' Don't sit long, my dear.' Every night she took leave of him with the same words, and they were not needless. Gilbert too often forgot the progress of time, and spent in study the hours which were demanded for sleep.

His daily employment was at a large candle and soap factory. By such work he had earned his living for more than twenty years. As a boy, he had begun with wages of four shillings a week, his task being to trim with a knife the rough edges of tablets of soap just stamped out. By degrees he had risen to a weekly income of forty shillings, occasion-ally increased by pay for overtime. Beyond this he was not likely to get. Men younger than he had passed him, attaining the position of foreman and the like; some had earned money by inventions which they put at the service of their employers; but Gilbert could hope for nothing more than the standing of a trustworthy mechanic, who, as long as he keeps his strength, can count on daily bread. His heart was not in his work; it would have been strange if he had thriven by an industry which was only a weariness to him.

His hours were from six in the morning to seven at night. Ah, that terrible rising at five o'clock, when it seemed at first as if he must fall back again in sheer anguish of fatigue, when his eyeballs throbbed to the light and the lids were as if weighted with iron, when the bitterness of the day before him was like poison in his heart ! He could not live as his fellow-workmen did, coming home to satisfy his hunger and spend a couple of hours in recreation, then to well-earned sleep. Every minute of freedom, of time in which he was no longer a machine but a thinking and desiring man, he held precious as fine gold. How could he yield to heaviness and sleep, when books lay open before him, and Knowledge, the goddess of his worship, whispered wondrous promises ? To Gilbert, a printed page was as the fountain of life; he loved literature passionately, and hungered to know the history of man's mind through all the ages. This distinguished him markedly from the not uncommon working man who zealously pursues some chosen branch of study. Such men ordinarily take up subjects of practical bearing; physical science is wont to be their field ; or if they study history it is from the point of view of current politics. Taste for literature pure and simple, and disinterested love of historical search, are the rarest things among the self-taught; naturally so, seeing how seldom they come of anything but academical tillage of the right soil. The average man of education is fond of literature because the environment of his growth has made such fondness a second nature. Gilbert had conceived his passion by mere grace. It had developed in him slowly. At twenty years he was a young fellow of seemingly rather sluggish character, without social tendencies, without the common ambitions of his class, much given to absence of mind. About that time he came across one of the volumes of the elder D'Israeli, and, behold, he had found himself. Reading of things utterly unknown to him, he was inspired with strange delights; a mysterious fascination drew him on amid names which were only a sound; a great desire was born in him, and its object was seen in every volume that met his eye. Had he then been given means and leisure, he would have become at the least a man of noteworthy learning. No such good fortune awaited him. Daily his thirteen hours went to the manufacture of candles, and the evening leisure, with one free day in the week, was all he could ever hope for.

At five-and-twenty he had a grave illness. Insufficient rest and ceaseless trouble of spirit brought him to death's door. For a long time it seemed as if he must content himself with earning his bread. He had no right to call upon others to bear the burden of his needs. His brother, a steady hard-headed mechanic, who was doing well in the Midlands and had just married, spoke to him with uncompromising common sense; if he chose to incapacitate himself, he must not look to his relatives to support him. Silently Gilbert acquiesced; silently he went back to the factory, and, when he came home of nights, sat with eyes gazing blankly before him. His mother lived with him, she and his sister; the latter went out to work; all were dependent upon the wages of the week. Nearly a year went by, during which Gilbert did not open a book. It was easier for him, he said, not to read at all than to measure his reading by the demands of his bodily weakness. He would have sold his handful of books, sold them in sheer bitterness of mind, but this his mother interfered to prevent.

But he could not live so. There was now a danger that the shadow of misery would darken into madness, Little by little he resumed his studious habits, yet with prudence. At thirty his bodily strength seemed to have consolidated itself; if he now and then exceeded the allotted hours at night, he did not feel the same evil results as formerly. His sister was a very dear companion to him ; she had his own tastes in a simpler form, and woman's tact enabled her to draw him into the repose of congenial talk when she and her mother were troubled by signs of overwork in him. He purchased a book as often as he could reconcile himself to the outlay, and his knowledge grew, though he seemed to himself ever on the mere threshold of the promised land, hopeless of admission.

Then came his sister's death, and the removal from Battersea back to Lambeth. Henceforth it would be seldomer than ever that he could devote a shilling to the enrichment of his shelves. When both he and Lizzie earned wages, the future did not give much trouble, but now all providence was demanded. His brother in the Midlands made contribution towards the mother's support, but Henry had a family of his own, and it was only right that Gilbert should bear the greater charge. Gilbert was nearing five-and-thirty.

By nature he was a lonely man. Amusement such as his world offered had always been savourless to him, and he had never sought familiar fellowship beyond his home. Even there it often happened that for days he kept silence ; he would eat his meal when he came from work, then take his book to a corner, and be mute, answering any needful question with a gesture or the briefest word. At such times his face had the lines of age ; you would have deemed him a man weighed upon by some vast sorrow. And was he not? His life was speeding by ; already the best years were gone, the years of youth and force and hope—nay, hope he could not be said to have known, unless it were for a short space when first the purpose of his being dawned upon consciousness ; and the end of that had been bitter enough. The purpose he knew was frustrated. The ' Might have been,' which is ' also called No more, Too late, Farewell,' often stared him in the eyes with those unchanging orbs of ghastliness, chilling the flow of his blood and making life the cruellest of mockeries. Yet he was not driven to that kind of resentment which makes the revolutionary spirit. His personality was essentially that of a student ; conservative instincts were stronger in him than the misery which accused his fortune. A touch of creative genius, and you had the man whose song would lead battle against the hoary

iniquities of the world. That was denied him; he could only
eat his own heart in despair, his protest against the outrage
of fate a desolate silence.

A lonely man, yet a tender one. The capacity of love was
not less in him than the capacity of knowledge. Yet herein
too he was wronged by circumstance. In youth an extreme
shyness held him from intercourse with all women save his
mother and his sister; he was conscious of his lack of ease in
dialogue, of an awkwardness of manner and an unattractive-
ness of person. On summer evenings, when other young
fellows were ready enough in finding companions for their
walk, Gilbert would stray alone in the quietest streets until
he tired himself, then go home and brood over fruitless
longings. In love, as afterwards in study, he had his ideal;
sometimes he would catch a glimpse of some face in the street
at night, and would walk on with the feeling that his happiness
had passed him—if only he could have turned and pursued it!
In all women he had supreme faith; that one woman whom
his heart imagined was a pure and noble creature, with
measureless aspiration, womanhood glorified in her to the
type of the upward striving soul—she did not come to him;
his life remained chaste and lonely.

Neither had he friends. There were at all times good
fellows to be found among those with whom he worked, but
again his shyness held him apart, and indeed he felt that
intercourse with them would afford him but brief satisfaction.
Occasionally some man more thoughtful than the rest would
be drawn to him by curiosity, but, finding himself met with
so much reserve, involuntary in Gilbert, would become
doubtful and turn elsewhither for sympathy. Yet in this
respect Grail improved as time went on; as his character
ripened, he was readier to gossip now and then of common
things with average associates. He knew, however, that he
was not much liked, and this naturally gave a certain coldness
to his behaviour. Perhaps the very first man for whom he
found himself entertaining something like warmth of kindness
was Luke Ackroyd. Ackroyd came to the factory shortly
after Gilbert had gone to live in Walnut Tree Walk, and in
the course of a few weeks the two had got into the habit
of walking their common way homewards together. As might
have been anticipated, it was a character very unlike his
own which had at length attached Gilbert. To begin with,
Ackroyd was pronounced in radicalism, was aggressive and at

times noisy; then, he was far from possessing Grail's moral
stability, and did not care to conceal his ways of amusing
himself; lastly, his intellectual tastes were of the scientific
order. Yet Gilbert from the first liked him; he felt that there
was no little good in the fellow, if only it could be fostered at
the expense of his weaker characteristics. Yet those very
weaknesses had much to do with his amiability. This they
had in common: both aspired to something that fortune had
denied them. Ackroyd had his idea of a social revolution, and,
though it seemed doubtful whether he was exactly the man
to claim a larger sphere for the energies of his class, his
thought often had genuine nobleness, clearly recognisable by
Gilbert. Ackroyd had brain-power above the average, and it
was his right to strive for a better lot than the candle-factory
could assure him. So Grail listened with a smile of much
indulgence to the young fellow's fuming against the order of
things, and if he now and then put in a critical remark was
not sorry to have it scornfully swept aside with a flood of
vehement words. He felt, perchance, that a share of such
vigour might have made his own existence more fruitful.

    This was Gilbert Grail at the time with which we are now
concerned. His mother believed that she had discovered in
him something of a new mood of late, a tendency to quiet
cheerfulness, and she attributed it in part to the healthfulness
of intercourse with a friend; partly she assigned to it another
reason. But her assumption did not receive much proof from
Gilbert's demeanour when left alone in the sitting-room this
Sunday night. Since Thyrza's departure, he had in truth
only made pretence of reading, and now that his mother was
gone, he let the book fall from his hands. His countenance
was fixed in a supreme sadness, his lips were tightly closed,
and at times moved, as if in the suppression of pain. Hope-
lessness in youth, unless it be justified by some direst ruin of
the future, is wont to touch us either with impatience or with
a comforting sense that reaction is at hand; in a man of
middle age it moves us with pure pathos. The sight of
Gilbert as he sat thus motionless would have brought tears
to kindly eyes. The past was a burden on his memory, the
future lay before him like a long road over which he must
wearily toil—the goal, frustration. To-night he could not
forget himself in the thoughts of other men. It was one of
the dread hours, which at intervals came upon him, when the
veil was lifted from the face of destiny, and he was bidden

gaze himself into despair. At such times he would gladly have changed beings with the idlest and emptiest of his fellow-workmen; their life might be ignoble, but it had abundance of enjoyment. To him there came no joy, nor ever would. Only when he lay in his last sleep would it truly be said of him that he rested.

At twelve o'clock he rose; he had no longing for sleep, but in five hours the new week would have begun, and he must face it with what bodily strength he might. Before entering his bedroom, which was next to the house-door, he went to the house-door and opened it quietly. A soft rain was falling. Leaving the door ajar, he stepped out into the street and looked up to the top windows. There was no light behind the blinds. As if satisfied, he went back into the house and to his room.

The factory was at so short a distance from Walnut Tree Walk that Gilbert was able to come home for breakfast and dinner. When he entered at mid-day on Monday, his mother pointed to a letter on the mantel-piece. He examined the address, and was at a loss to recognise the writing.

'Who's this from, I wonder?' he said, as he opened the envelope.

He found a short letter, and a printed slip which looked like a circular. The former ran thus:

'Sir,—I am about to deliver a course of evening lectures on a period of English Literature in a room which I have taken for the purpose, No. — High Street, Lambeth. I desire to have a small audience, not more than twenty, consisting of working men who belong to Lambeth. Attendance will be at my invitation, of course without any kind of charge. You have been mentioned to me as one likely to be interested in the subject I propose to deal with. I permit myself to send you a printed syllabus of the course, and to say that it will give me great pleasure if you are able to attend. I should like to arrange for two lectures weekly, each of an hour's duration; the days I leave undecided, also the hour, as I wish to adapt these to the convenience of my hearers. If you feel inclined to give thought to the matter, will you meet me at the lecture-room at eight o'clock on the evening of Sunday, August 16, when we could discuss details? The lectures themselves had better, I should think, begin with the month of September.

'Reply to this is unnecessary; I hope to have the pleasure

of meeting you on the 16th.—Believe me to be yours very truly,

'WALTER EGREMONT.'

'Ah, this is what Ackroyd was speaking of on Saturday,' Gilbert remarked, holding the letter to his mother. 'I wonder what it means.'

'Who is this Mr. Egremont?' asked Mrs. Grail.

'He belongs to the firm of Egremont & Pollard, so Ackroyd tells me. You know that big factory in Westminster Bridge Road—where they make oil-cloth.'

Gilbert was perusing the printed syllabus; it interested him, and he kept it by his plate when he sat down to dinner.

'Do you think of going?' his mother inquired.

'Well, I should like to, if the lectures are good. I suppose he's a young fellow fresh from college. He may have something to say, and he may be only conceited; there's no knowing. Still, I don't dislike the way he writes. Yes, I think I shall go and have a look at him, at all events.'

Gilbert finished his meal and walked back to the factory. Groups of men were standing about in the sunshine, waiting for the bell to ring; some talked and joked, some amused themselves with horse-play. The narrow street was redolent with oleaginous matter; the clothing of the men was penetrated with the same nauseous odour.

At a little distance from the factory, Ackroyd was sitting on a door-step, smoking a pipe. Grail took a seat beside him and drew from his pocket the letter he had just received.

'I've got one of them, too,' Luke observed with small show of interest. There was an unaccustomed gloom on his face; he puffed at his pipe rather sullenly.

'Who has told him our names and addresses?' Gilbert asked.

'Bower, no doubt.'

'But how comes Bower to know anything about me?'

'Oh, I've mentioned you sometimes.'

'Well, do you think of going?'

'No, I shan't go. It isn't at all in my line.'

Gilbert became silent.

'Something the matter?' he asked presently, as his companion puffed on in the same gloomy way.

'A bit of a headache, that's all.'

His tone was unusual. Gilbert fixed his eyes on the pavement.

'It's easy enough to see what it means,' Ackroyd continued after a moment, referring to Egremont's invitation. 'We shall be having an election before long, and he's going to stand for Vauxhall. This is one way of making himself known.'

'If I thought that,' said the other, musingly, 'I shouldn't go near the place.'

'What else can it be?'

'I don't know anything about the man, but he may have an idea that he's doing good.'

'If so, *that's* quite enough to prevent me from going. What the devil do I want with his help? Can't I read about English literature for myself?'

'Well, I can't say that I have that feeling. A lecture may be a good deal of use, if the man knows his subject well. But,' he added, smiling, 'I suppose you object to him and his position?'

'Of course I do. What business has the fellow to have so much time that he doesn't know what to do with it?'

'He might use it worse, anyhow.'

'I don't know about that. I'd rather he'd get a bad name, then it 'ud be easier to abuse him, and he'd be more good in the end.'

Their eyes met. Gilbert's had a humorous expression, and Ackroyd laughed in an unmirthful way. The factory bell rang; Gilbert rose and waited for the other to accompany him. But Luke, after a struggle to his feet, said suddenly:

'Work be hanged! I've had enough of it; I feel Mondayish, as we used to say in Lancashire.'

'Aren't you coming, then?'

'No, I'll go and get drunk instead.'

'Come on, old man. No good in getting drunk.'

'Maybe I won't; but I can't go back to work to-day. So long!'

With which vernacular leave-taking, he turned and strolled away. The bell was clanging its last strokes; Gilbert hurried to the door, and once more merged his humanity in the wage-earning machine.

Two days later, as he sat over his evening meal, Gilbert noticed that his mother had something to say. She cast frequent glances at him; her pursed lips seemed to await an opportune moment.

'Well, mother, what is it?' he said presently, with his wonted look of kindness. By living so long together and in such close intercourse the two had grown skilled in the reading of each other's faces.

'My dear,' she replied, with something of solemnity, 'I was perfectly right. Miss Denny *was* those girls' mother.'

'Nonsense!'

'But there's no doubt about it. I've asked Thyrza. She knows that was her mother's name, and she knows that her mother was a teacher.'

'In that case I've nothing more to say. You're a wonderful old lady, as I've often told you.'

'I have a good memory, Gilbert. You can't think how pleased I am that I found out that. I feel more interest in them than ever. And the child seemed so pleased too! She could scarcely believe that I'd known her mother before she was born. She wants me to tell her and her sister all I can remember. Now, isn't it nice?'

Gilbert smiled, but made no further remark. The evening silence set in.

CHAPTER VII

THE WORK IN PROGRESS

On the sheltered side of Eastbourne, just at the springing of the downs as you climb towards Beachy Head, is a spacious and heavy-looking stone house, with pillared porch, oriel windows on the ground floor of the front, and a square turret rising above the fine row of chestnuts which flanks the road. It was built some forty years ago, its only neighbours then being a few rustic cottages; recently there has sprung up a suburb of comely red-brick houses, linking it with the visitors' quarter of Eastbourne. The builder and first proprietor, a gentleman whose dignity derived from Mark Lane, called the house Odessa Lodge; at his death it passed by purchase into the hands of people to whom this name seemed something worse than inappropriate, and the abode was henceforth known as The Chestnuts.

One morning early in November, three months after the date of that letter which he addressed to Gilbert Grail and other working men of Lambeth, our friend Egremont arrived from town at Eastbourne station and was conveyed thence by fly to the house of which I speak. He inquired for Mrs.

Ormonde. That lady was not within, but would shortly return from her morning drive. Egremont followed the servant
to the library and prepared to wait.

The room was handsomely furnished and more than
passably supplied with books, which inspection showed to be
not only such as one expects to find in the library of a country
house, but to a great extent works of very modern issue, arguing in their possessor the catholicity of taste which our time
encourages. The solid books which form the substratum of
every collection were brought together by Mr. Brook Ormonde,
in the first instance at his house in Devonshire Square; when
failing health compelled him to leave London, the town establishment was broken up, and until his death, three years
later, the family resided wholly at The Chestnuts. During
those years the library grew appreciably, for the son of the
house, Horace Ormonde, had just come forth from the academic curriculum with a vast appetite for literature. His
mother, moreover, was of the women who read. Whilst Mr.
Ormonde was taking a lingering farewell of the world and its
concerns, these two active minds were busy with the fire-new
thought of the scientific and humanitarian age. Walter
Egremont was then a frequent visitor of the house; he and
Horace talked many a summer night into dawn over the problems which nowadays succeed measles and scarlatina as a
form of youthful complaint. But Horace Ormonde had even
a shorter span of life before him than his invalid father he
was drowned in bathing, and it was Egremont who had to take
the news up to The Chestnuts. A few months later, there
was another funeral from the house. Mrs. Ormonde remained
alone.

It was in this room that Egremont had waited for the
mother's coming, that morning when he returned companionless from the beach. He was then but two-and-twenty; his
task was as terrible as a man can be called upon to perform.
Mrs. Ormonde had the strength to remember that; she shed
no tears, uttered no lamentations. When, after a few questions, she was going silently from the room, Walter, his own
eyes blinded, caught her hand and pressed it passionately in
both his own. She was the woman whom he reverenced
above all others, worshipping her with that pure devotion
which young men such as he are wont to feel for some gracious
lady much their elder. At that moment he would have given
his own life to the sea could he by so doing have brought her

back the son who would never return. Such moments do not come often to the best of us, perhaps in very truth do not repeat themselves. Egremont never entered the library without having that impulse of uttermost unselfishness brought back vividly to his thoughts; on that account he liked the room, and gladly spent a quiet half-hour in it.

In a little less than that Mrs. Ormonde returned from her breathing of the sea air. At the door she was told of Egremont's arrival, and with a look of pleased expectancy she went at once to the library.

Egremont rose from the fireside, and advanced with the quiet confidence with which one greets only the dearest friends.

'So the sunshine has brought you,' she said, holding his hand for a moment. 'We had a terrible storm in the night, and the morning is very sweet after it. Had you arrived a very little sooner, you would have been in time to drive with me.'

She was one of those women who have no need to soften their voice when they would express kindness. Her clear and firm, yet sweet, tones uttered with perfection a nature very richly and tenderly endowed. During the past five years she had aged in appearance; the grief which she would not expose had drawn its lines upon her features, and something too of imperfect health was visible there. But her gaze was the same as ever, large, benevolent, intellectual. In her presence Egremont always felt a well-being, a peace of mind, which gave to his own look its pleasantest quality. Of friends she was still, and would ever be, the dearest to him. The thought of her approval was always active with him when he made plans for fruitful work; he could not have come before her with a consciousness of ignoble fault weighing upon his mind.

She passed upstairs, and he followed more slowly. Behind the first landing was a small conservatory; and there, amid evergreens, sat two children whose appearance would have surprised a chance visitor knowing nothing of the house and its mistress. They obviously came from some very poor working-class home; their clothing was of the plainest possible, and, save that they were very clean and in perfect order, they might have been sitting on a doorstep in a London back street. Mrs. Ormonde had thrown a kind word to them in hurrying by. At the sight of Egremont they hushed their renewed talk and turned shamefaced looks to the ground.

He went on to the drawing-room, where there was the same comfort and elegance as in the library. Almost immediately Mrs. Ormonde joined him.

'So you want news!' she said, with her own smile, always a little sad, always mingling tenderness with reserve on the firm lips. 'Really, I told you everything essential in my letter. Annabel is in admirable health, both of body and mind. She is deep in Virgil and Dante—what more could you wish her? Her father, I am sorry to say, is not altogether well. Indeed, I was guilty of doing my best to get him to London for the winter.'

'Ah! That is something of which your letter made no mention.'

'No, for I didn't succeed. At least, he shook his head very persistently.'

'I heartily wish you had succeeded. Couldn't you get help from Annabel—Miss Newthorpe?'

'Never mind; let it be Annabel between us,' said Mrs. Ormonde, seating herself near the fire. 'I tried to, but she was not fervent. All the same, it is just possible, I think, that they may come. Mr. Newthorpe needs society, however content he may believe himself. Annabel, to my surprise, does really seem independent of such aids. How wonderfully she has grown since I saw her two years ago! No, no, I don't mean physically—though that is also true—but how her mind has grown! Even her letters hadn't quite prepared me for what I found.'

Egremont was leaning on the back of a chair, his hands folded together. He kept silence, and Mrs. Ormonde, with a glance at him, added:

'But she is something less than human at present. Probably that will last for another year or so.'

'Less than human?'

'Abstract, impersonal. With the exception of her father, you were the only living person of whom she voluntarily spoke to me.'

'She spoke of me?'

'Very naturally. Your accounts of Lambeth affairs interest her deeply, though again in rather too—what shall we call it?—too theoretical a way. But that comes of her inexperience.'

'Still she at least speaks of me.'

Mrs. Ormonde could have made a discouraging rejoinder.

She said nothing for a moment, her eyes fixed on the fire. Then:

'But now for your own news.'

'What I have is unsatisfactory. A week ago the class suffered a secession. You remember my description of Ackroyd?'

'Ackroyd? The young man of critical aspect?'

'The same. He has now missed two lectures, and I don't think he'll come again.'

'Have you spoken to Bower about him?'

'No. The fact is, my impressions of Bower have continued to grow unfavourable. Plainly, he cares next to nothing for the lectures. There is a curious pomposity about him, too, which grates upon me. I shouldn't have been at all sorry if he had been the seceder; he's bored terribly, I know, yet he naturally feels bound to keep his place. But I'm very sorry that Ackroyd has gone; he has brains, and I wanted to get to know him. I shall not give him up; I must persuade him to come and have a talk with me.'

'What of Mr. Grail?'

'Ah, Grail is faithful. Yes, Grail is the man of them all; that I am sure of. I am going to ask him to stay after the lecture to-morrow. I haven't spoken privately with him yet. But I think I can begin now to establish nearer relations with two or three of them. I have been lecturing for just a couple of months; they ought to know something of me by this time, On the whole, I think I am succeeding. But if there is one of them on whom I found great hopes, it is Grail. The first time I saw him, I knew what a distinction there was between him and the others. He seems to be a friend of Ackroyd's, too; I must try to get at Ackroyd by means of him.'

'Is he—Grail, I mean—a married man?'

'I really don't know. Yet I should think so. I shouldn't be surprised if he were unhappily married. Certainly there is some great trouble in his life. Sometimes he looks terribly worn, quite ill.'

'And Mr. Bunce?' she asked, with a look of peculiar interest.

'Poor Bunce is also a good deal of a mystery to me. He, too, always looks more or less miserable, and I'm afraid his interest is not very absorbing. Still, he takes notes, and now and then even puts an intelligent question.'

'He has not attacked you on the subject of religion yet

'Oh, no ! We still have that question to fight out. But of course I must know him very well before I approach it. I think he bears me goodwill ; I caught him looking at me with a curious sort of cordiality the other night.'

'I must have that little girl of his down again,' Mrs. Ormonde said. 'I wonder whether she still reads that insufferable publication. By-the-by, I found you had told them the story at Ullswater.'

'Yes. It came up à propos of my scheme.'

A gong sounded down below.

'Twelve o'clock!' remarked Mrs. Ormonde. 'My birds are going to their dinner—poor little town sparrows! We'll let them get settled, then go and have a peep at them—shall we ?'

'Yes, I should like to see them—and,' he added pleasantly, 'to see the look on your face when you watch them.'

'I have much to thank them for, Walter,' she said, earnestly. 'They brighten many an hour when I should be unhappy.'

Presently Mrs. Ormonde led the way downstairs and to the rear of the house. A room formerly devoted to billiards had been converted into a homely but very bright refectory ; it was hung round with cheerful pictures, and before each of the two windows stood a large aquarium, full of water-plants and fishes. At the table were seated seven little girls, of ages from eight to thirteen, all poorly clad, yet all looking remarkably joyous, and eating with much evidence of appetite. At the head of the table was a woman of middle age and motherly aspect—Mrs. Mapper. She had the superintendence of the convalescents whom the lady of the house received and sent back to their homes in London better physically and morally than they had ever been in their lives before. The children did not notice that Mrs. Ormonde and her companion had entered ; they were chatting gaily over their meal. Now and then one of them drew a gentle word of correction from Mrs. Mapper, but on the whole they needed no rebuke. Those who had been longest in the house speedily instructed new arrivals in the behaviour they had learned to deem becoming. A girl waited at table. On that subject Mrs. Ormonde had amusing stories to relate ; how more than one servant had regretfully but firmly declined to wait upon little ragamuffins (female, too), and how one in particular had explained that she made no objection to doing it only because she regarded it as a religious penance.

Egremont had his pleasure in regarding her face, nobly beautiful as she moved her eyes from one to another of her poor little pensioners. She had said at first that it would be impossible ever again to live in this house, when she quitted it for a time after her husband's death. How could she pass through the barren rooms, how dwell within sight and sound of the treacherous waves which had taken her dearest? It was a royal thought which converted the sad dwelling into a home for those whose reawakening laughter would chide despondency from beneath the roof, whose happiness would ease the heavy heart and make memory a sacred solace. She had her abounding reward, and such as only the greatly loving may attain to.

They withdrew without having excited attention; Mrs. Mapper saw them, but Mrs. Ormonde made sign to her to say nothing.

'Two are upstairs, I'm sorry to say,' she remarked as they went back to the drawing-room. 'They have obstinate colds; I keep them under the bed-clothes. The difficulty these poor things have in getting rid of a cold! With many of them I believe such a condition is chronic; it goes on, I suppose, until they die of it.'

They talked together till luncheon time. Egremont led the conversation back to Ullswater, where Mrs. Ormonde had just spent a fortnight.

'I think I must go and see them at Christmas,' he said, 'if they don't come south.'

The other considered.

'Don't go so soon,' she said at length.

'So soon? It will be six mortal months.'

'Be advised.'

Egremont sighed and left the subject.

'Tell me what you have been doing of late,' Mrs. Ormonde resumed, 'apart from your lectures.'

'Very little of which any account can be rendered. I read a good deal, and occasionally come across an acquaintance.'

'Have you seen the Tyrrells since they returned?'

'No. I had an invitation to dine with them the other day, but excused myself.'

'On what grounds?'

'I mean to see less of people in general.'

Mrs. Ormonde regarded him.

'I hope,' she said, 'that you will pursue no such idea.

You mean, of course, that your Lambeth work is to be absorbing.   Let it be so, but don't fall into the mistake of making it your burden.   You are not one of those who can work in solitude.'

'I am getting a distaste for ordinary society.'

'Then I beg of you to resist the mood.   Go into society freely.   You are in danger as soon as you begin to neglect it.'

'I, individually ? '

'Yes.'   She smiled at the deprecating look he turned on her.   'Let me be your moral physician.   Already I notice that you fall short of perfect health : the refusal of that invitation is a symptom.   Pray give faith to what I say ; if any one knows you, I think it is I.'

He kept silence.   Mrs. Ormonde continued :

'I hear that the Tyrrells have made the acquaintance of Mr. Dalmaine.   Paula mentions him in a letter.'

'Ha !   With enthusiasm probably ? '

'No.   They met him somewhere in Switzerland.   He gave them the benefit of his experience on the education question.'

'Of course.   Well, I am prejudiced against the man, as you know.

'He is a force.   It looks as if we should hear a good deal of him in the future.'

'Doubtless.   The incarnate ideal of British philistinism is sure to have a career before him.'

The lady laughed.

Early in the afternoon Egremont took leave of his friend and returned to London.   It was his habit when in England, to run down to Eastbourne in this way about once a month.

Since the death of his father, his home had been represented by rooms in Great Russell Street.   He chose them on account of their proximity to the British Museum ; at that time he believed himself destined to produce some monumental work of erudition : the subject had not defined itself, but his thoughts were then busy with the origins of Christianity, and it seemed to him that a study of certain Oriental literatures would be fruitful of results.   Characteristically, he must establish himself at the very doors of the great Library.   His Oriental researches, as we know, were speedily abandoned, but the rooms in Great Russell Street still kept their tenant. They were far from an ideal abode, indifferently furnished, with draughty doors and smoky chimneys, and the rent was exorbitant ; the landlady, who speedily gauged her lodger's character, had already made a small competency out of him. Even during long absences abroad Egremont retained the domicile; at each return he said to himself that he must really find quarters at once more reputable and more homelike, but the thought of removing his books, of dealing with new people, deterred him from the actual step. In fact, he was indifferent as to where or how he lived; all he asked was the possibility of privacy. The ugliness of his surroundings did not trouble him, for he paid no attention to them. Some day he would have a beautiful home, but what use in thinking of that till he had someone to share it with him? This was a mere *pied à terre*; it housed his body and left his mind free.

The real home which he remembered was a house looking upon Clapham Common. His father dwelt there for the last fifteen years of his life; his mother died there, shortly after the removal from the small house in Newington where she went to live upon her marriage. With much tenderness Egremont thought of the clear-headed and warm-hearted man whose life-long toil had made such provision for the son he loved. Uneducated, homely, narrow enough in much of his thinking, the manufacturer of oil-cloth must have had singular possibilities in his nature to renew himself in a youth so apt for modern culture as Walter was; thinking back in his maturity, the latter remembered many a noteworthy trait in his father, and wished the old man could have lived yet a few more years to see his son's work really beginning. And Egremont often felt lonely. Possibly he had relatives living, but he knew of none; in any case they could not now be of real account to him. The country of his birth was far behind him; how far, he had recognised since he began his lecturing in Lambeth. None the less, he at times knew home-sickness: not seldom there seemed to be a gap between him and the people born to refinement who were his associates, his friends. That phase of feeling was rather strong in him just now; disguising itself in the form of sundry plausible motives, it had induced him to decline Mrs. Tyrrell's invitation, and was fostering his temporary distaste for the society in which he had always found much pleasure. What if in strictness he belonged to neither sphere? What if his life were to be a struggle between inherited sympathies and the affinities of his intellect? All the better, perchance, for his prospect of usefulness; he stood

as a mediator between two sections of society. But for his
private happiness, how?

He spent this evening very idly, sometimes pacing his
large, uncomfortable room, sometimes endeavouring to read
one or other of certain volumes new from the circulating
library. Of late he had passed many such evenings, for it
was very seldom that any one came to see him, and for the
amusements of the town he had no inclination. He was
thinking much of Annabel; he could not imagine her other
than calm, intellectual; he could not hear her voice uttering
passionate words. A great change must come over her before
her reserved maidenliness could soften to such sweet humility.

And he had no faith in his power so to change her.

The next day was Thursday. This and Sunday were his
lecture days; his class met at half-past eight. Precisely at
that hour he reached a small doorway in High Street, Lambeth, and ascended a flight of stairs to a room which he had
furnished as he deemed most suitable. Several rows of school-
desks faced a high desk at which he stood to lecture. The
walls were washed in distemper, the boarding of the floor was
uncovered, the two windows were hidden with plain shutters.
The room had formerly been used for purposes of storage by
a glass and china merchant; below was the workshop of a
saddler, which explained the pervading odour of leather.

A little group of men stood in conversation near the fire;
on Egremont's appearance they seated themselves at the desks,
each producing a note-book which he laid open before him.
Thus ranged they were seen to be eight in number. Out of
fourteen to whom invitations were addressed, nine had presented themselves at the preliminary meeting; one, we know,
had since proved unfaithful. Egremont looked round for
Ackroyd on entering, but the young man was not here.

On the front bench were two men whom as yet you know
only by name. Mr. Bower was clearly distinguishable by his
personal importance and the *ennui*, not to be disguised, with
which he listened to the opening sentences of the lecture. He
leaned against the desk behind him, and carefully sharpened
the point of his pencil. He was a large man with a spade-
shaped beard; his forehead was narrow, and owed its appearance of height to incipient baldness; his eyes were small and
shrewd. He habitually donned his suit of black for these
meetings. At the works, where he held a foreman's position,
he was in good repute: for years he had proved himself skil-

ful, steady, abundantly respectful to his employers. In private
life he enjoyed the fame of a petty capitalist; since his
marriage, thirty years ago, he and his wife had made it the end
of their existence to put by money, with the result that his
obsequiousness when at work was balanced by the blustering
independence of his leisure hours. The man was a fair
instance of the way in which prosperity affects the average
proletarian; all his better qualities—honesty, perseverance,
sobriety—took an ignoble colour from the essential vulgarity
of his nature, which would never have so offensively declared
itself if ill fortune had kept him anxious about his daily bread.
Formerly Egremont had been impressed by his intelligent
manner; closer observation had proved to him of how little
worth this intelligence was, in its subordination to a paltry
character. Bower regarded himself as the originator of this
course of lectures; through all his obsequiousness it was easy
to see that he deemed his co-operation indispensable to the
success of the project. At first, as was natural, Egremont had
sometimes seemed to address words specially to him; of late he
had purposely avoided doing so, and Bower began to feel that
his services lacked recognition.

The other, of whom there has been casual mention, was
Joseph Bunce. Of spare frame and with hollow cheeks which
suggested insufficiency of diet, he yet had far more of manli-
ness in his appearance than the portly Bower. You divined
in him independence enough, and of worthier origin than that
which secretly inflated his neighbour. His features were at
first sight by no means pleasing; their coarseness was undeniable, but familiarity revealed a sensitive significance in the
irregular nose, the prominent lips, the small chin and long
throat. Egremont had now and then caught a light in his
eyes which was warranty for more than his rough tongue could
shape into words. He often appeared to have a difficulty in
following the lecture; would shrug nervously, and knit his
brows and mutter. Whenever he noticed that, Egremont
would pause a little and repeat in simpler form what he had
been saying, with the satisfactory result that Bunce showed a
clearer face and jotted something on his dirty note-book with
his stumpy pencil.

Gilbert Grail we know. It was impossible not to remark
him as the one who followed with most consecutive understanding, even if his countenance had not declared him of
higher grade than any of those among whom he sat. It had

needed only the first ten minutes of the first lecture to put him
at his ease with regard to Egremont's claims to stand forward
as a teacher ; the preliminary meeting, indeed, had removed
the suspicions suggested by Ackroyd.   To him these evenings
were pure enjoyment. He delighted in this subject, and had
an inexpressible pleasure in listening continuously to the
speech of a cultivated man. Had the note-books of the class
been examined (Egremont had strongly advised their use),
Gilbert's jottings would probably have alone been found of
substantial value, seeing that he alone possessed the mental
habit necessary for the practice. Bunce's would doubtless
have come next, though at a long distance ; a Carlylean editor
might have disengaged from them many a rudely forcible scrap
of comment. Bower's pages would have smelt of the day-book.
It was to Grail that Egremont mentally directed the best
things he had to say ; not seldom he was repaid by the quick
gleam of sympathy on that grave interesting face.

The remaining five hearers were average artisans of the
inquiring type; they followed with perseverance, though at
times one or the other would furtively regard his watch or
allow his eyes to stray about the room. They had made a
bargain, and were bent on honourably carrying out their share
in it. But Egremont already began to doubt whether he was
really fixing anything in their thoughts. How were they likely
to serve him for the greater purpose whereto this instruction
was only preliminary ? When he looked forward to that, he
had to fix his eyes on Grail and forget the others. He was
beginning to regret that the choice of those to whom his invitations were sent had depended upon Bower; another man
might have aided him more effectually. Yet the fact was that
Bower's selection had been a remarkably good one. It would
have been difficult to assemble nine Lambeth workmen of
higher aggregate intellect than those who responded to the
summons; it would have been, on the other hand, the easiest
thing to find nine with not a man of them available for anything more than futile wrangling over politics or religion.
Egremont would know this some day ; he was yet young in
social reform.

And the lectures ? It is not too much to say that they were
good. Egremont had capacity for teaching ; with his education, had he been without resources, he would probably have
chosen an academic career, and have done service in it.
There was nothing deep in his style of narrative and criticism,

and here depth was not wanted; sufficient that he was per-
spicuous and energetic. He loved the things of which he
spoke, and he had the power of presenting to others his reason
for loving them. Not one in five hundred men inexperienced
in such work could have held the ears of the class as he did
for the first two or three evenings. It was impossible for
them to mistake his spirit—ardent, disinterested, aspiring ;
impossible not to feel something of a respondent impulse.
That familiarity should diminish the effect of his speech was
only to be anticipated. He was preaching a religion, but one
that could find no acceptance as such with eight out of nine
who heard him. Common minds are not kept at high-interest
mark for long together by exhibition of the merely beautiful,
however persuasively it be set forth.

He had chosen the Elizabethan period, and he led up to it
by the kind of introduction which he felt would be necessary.
Trusting himself more after the first fortnight, he ceased to
write out his lectures verbatim ; free utterance was an advantage to himself and his audience. He read at large from his
authors ; to expect the men to do this for themselves—even
had the books been within their reach—would have been too
much, and without such illustration the lectures were vain.
This reading brought him face to face with his main difficulty :
how to create in men a sense which they do not possess. The
working man does not read, in the strict sense of the word;
fiction has little interest for him, and of poetry he has no com-
prehension whatever ; your artisan of brains can study, but he
cannot read. Egremont was under no illusion on this point ;
he knew well that the loveliest lyric would appeal to a man
like Bower no more than an unintelligible demonstration of
science. Was it impossible to bestow this sense of intellectual
beauty ? With what earnestness he made the endeavour !
He took sweet passages of prose and verse, and read them with
all the feeling and skill he could command. ' Do you yield to
that ? ' he said within himself as he looked from face to face.
' Are your ears hopelessly sealed, your minds immutably
earthen ? ' Grail—Oh yes, Grail had the right intelligence in
his eyes ; but Ackroyd, but Bunce ? Ackroyd thought of the
meaning of the words ; no more. Poor Bunce had darkling
throes of mind, but struggled with desperate nervousness and
could not be at ease till the straightforward talk began again.
And Bower ?—Nay, there goes more to this matter than mere
enthusiasm in a teacher. Who had instructed Gilbert Grail

to discern the grace of the written word ? On the other hand, it was doubtful whether Walter Egremont, left to himself in the home of his good plain father, would have felt what now he did. The soil was there, but how much do we not owe to tillage ! Read what Egremont on one occasion read to these men:

' " He beginneth not with obscure definitions, which must blur the margent with interpretations and load the memory with doubtfulness : but he cometh to you with words set in delightful proportion, either accompanied with or prepared for the well-enchanting skill of music ; and with a tale forsooth he cometh unto you—with a tale which holdeth children from play, and old men from the chimney-corner." '

What were *that* to you, save for the glow of memory fed with incense of the poets ?—save for innumerable dear associations, only possible to the instructed, which make the finer part of your intellectual being? Walter was attempting too much, and soon became painfully conscious of it.

He came to the dramatists, and human interest thenceforth helped him. He could read well, and a scene from those giants of the prime had efficiency even with Bower. Hope revived in the lecturer.

To-night he was less happy than usual, for what reason he could not himself understand. His thoughts wandered, sometimes to Eastbourne, sometimes to Ullswater ; yet he was speaking of Shakespeare. Bower was more owl-eyed than usual ; the five doubtful hearers obviously felt the time long. Only Grail gave an unfailing ear. Egremont closed with a sense of depression.

Would Bower come and pester him with fatuous questions and remarks ? No ; Bower turned away and reached his hat from the peg. The doubtful five took down their hats and followed the portly man from the room. Bunce was talking with Grail, pointing with dirty forefinger to something in his dirty note-book. But he, too, speedily moved to the hat-pegs. Grail was also going, when Egremont said :

' Could you spare me five minutes, Mr. Grail ; I should like to speak to you.'

CHAPTER VIII

A CLASP OF HANDS

GRAIL approached the desk with pleasure. Egremont observed it, and met his trusty auditor with the eye-smile which made his face so agreeable.

'I am sorry to see that Mr. Ackroyd no longer sits by you,' he began. 'Has he deserted us?'

Gilbert hesitated, but spoke at length with his natural directness.

'I'm afraid so, sir.'

'He has lost his interest in the subject?'

'It's not exactly the bent of his mind. He only came at my persuasion to begin with. He takes more to science than literature.'

'Ah, I should have thought that. But I wish he could have still spared me the two hours a week. I felt much interest in him; it's a disappointment to lose him so unexpectedly. I'm sure he has a head for our matters as well as for science.'

Grail was about to speak, but checked himself. An inquiring glance persuaded him to say:

'He's much taken up with politics just now. They don't leave the mind very quiet.'

'Politics? I regret more than ever that he's gone.'

Egremont moved away from the desk at which he had been standing, and seated himself on the end of a bench which came out opposite the fire-place.

'Come and sit down for a minute, will you, Mr. Grail?' he said.

Gilbert silently took possession of the end of the next bench.

'Is there no persuading him back? Do you think he would come and have a talk with me? I do wish he would; I believe we could understand each other. You see him occasionally?'

'Every day. We work together.'

'Would you ask him to come and have a chat with me here some evening?'

'I shall be glad to, sir.'

'Pray persuade him to. Any evening he likes. Perhaps next Sunday after the lecture would do? Tell him to bring his pipe and have a smoke with me here before the fire.'

Grail smiled, and undertook to deliver the invitation.

'But there are other things I wished to speak of to you,' Egremont continued. 'Do you think it would be any advantage if I brought books for the members of the class to take away and use at their leisure? Shakespeare, of course, you can all lay hands on, but the other Elizabethan authors are not so readily found. For instance, there's a Marlowe on the desk; would you care to take him away with you?'

'Thank you very much, sir,' was the reply, 'but I've got Marlowe. I picked up a second-hand copy a year or two ago.'

'You have him! Ah, that's good!'

Egremont was surprised, but remembered that it would not be very courteous to express such feeling. After surprise came new warmth of interest in the man. He began to speak of Marlowe with delight, and in a moment he and Grail were on a footing of intimacy.

'But there are other books perhaps you haven't come across yet. I shall be overjoyed if you'll let me be of use to you in that way. Have you access to any library?'

'No, I haven't. I've often felt the want of it.'

Egremont fell into musing for a moment. He looked up with an idea in his eyes.

'Wouldn't it be an excellent thing if one could establish a lending library in Lambeth?'

Grail might have excusably replied that it would be a yet more excellent thing if those disposed to use such an institution had time granted them to do so; but with the young man's keen look fixed upon him, he had other thoughts.

'It would be a great thing!' he replied, with subdued feeling. He seldom allowed his stronger emotions to find high utterance; that moderated voice was symbol of the suppression to which his life had trained itself.

'A free library,' Egremont went on, 'with a good reading-room.'

It was an extension of his scheme, and delighted him with its prospect of possibilities. It would be preparing the ground upon which he and his adherents might subsequently work. Could he undertake to found a library at his own expense? It was not beyond his means, at all events a beginning on a moderate scale. His eyes sparkled, as they always did when a thought burst blossom-like within him.

'Mr. Grail, I have a mind to try if I can't work on that idea.'

Gilbert was stirred. This interchange of words had strengthened his personal liking for Egremont, and his own idealism took fire from that of the other. He regarded the young man with admiration and with noble envy. To be able to devise such things and straightway say 'It shall be done!' How blest beyond all utterance was the man to whom fortune had given such power! He reverenced Egremont profoundly. It was the man's nature to worship, to bend with singleness of heart before whatsoever seemed to him high and beautiful.

'Yes,' the latter continued, 'I will think it out. We might begin with a moderate supply of books; we might find some building that would do at first; a real library could be built when the people had begun to appreciate what was offered them. Better, no doubt, if they would tax themselves for the purpose, but they have burdens enough.'

'They won't give a farthing towards a library,' said Grail, ' until they know its value; and that they can't do until they have learnt it from books.'

'True. We'll break the circle.'

He pondered again, then added cheerfully:

'I say *we*. I mean you and the others who come to my lecture. I want, if possible, to make this class permanent, to make it the beginning of a society for purposes I have in my mind. I must tell you something of this, for I know you will feel with me, Mr. Grail.'

The reply was a look of quiet trust. Egremont had not thought to get so far as this to-night, but Grail's personality wrought upon him, even as his on Grail. He felt a desire to open his mind, as he had done that evening in the garden by Ullswater. This man was of those whom he would benefit, but, if he mistook not, far unlike the crowd; Grail could understand as few of his class could be expected to.

'To form a society, a club, let us say. Not at all like the ordinary clubs. There are plenty of places where men can meet to talk about what ought to be done for the working class; my idea is to bring the working class to talk of what it can do for itself. And not how it can claim its material rights, how to get better wages, shorter hours, more decent homes. With all those demands I sympathise as thoroughly as any man ; but those things are coming, and it seems to me that it's time to ask what working men are going to do with such advantages when they've got them. Now, my hope is to get a few men to see—what you, I know, see clearly enough—that life, to be worthy of the name, must be first and foremost concerned with the things of the heart and mind. Yet everything in our time favours the opposite. The struggle for existence is so hard that we grow more and more material : the tendency is to regard it as the end of life to make money. If there's time to think of higher things, well and good ; if not, it doesn't matter much. Well, we have to earn money ; it is a necessary evil ; but let us think as little about it as we may. Our social state, in short, has converted the means of life into its end.'

He paused, and Gilbert looked hearty agreement.

' That puts into a sentence,' he said, ' what I have thought through many an hour of work.'

' Well, now, we know there's no lack of schemes for re-forming society. Most of them seek to change its spirit by change of institutions. But surely it is plain enough that re-form of institutions can only come as the natural result of a change in men's minds. Those who preach revolution to the disinherited masses give no thought to this. It's a hard and a bad thing to live under an oppressive system ; don't think that I speak lightly of the miseries which must drive many a man to frenzy, till he heeds nothing so long as the present curse is attacked. I know perfectly well that for thousands of the poorest there is no possibility of a life guided by thought and feeling of a higher kind until they are lifted out of the mire. But if one faces the question with a grave purpose of doing good that will endure, practical considerations must out-weigh one's anger. There is no way of lifting those poor people out of the mire ; if their children's children tread on firm ground it will be the most we can hope for. But there *is* a class of working people that can and should aim at a state of mind far above that which now contents them. It is my view that our only hope of social progress lies in the possibility of this class being stirred to effort. The tendency of their present education—a misapplication of the word—must be counteracted. They must be taught to value supremely quite other attainments than those which help them to earn higher wages. Well, there is my thought. I wish to communicate it to men who have a care for more than food and clothing, and who will exert themselves to influence those about them.'

Grail gazed at the fire ; the earnest words wrought in him.

' If that were possible ! ' he murmured.

' Tell me,' the other resumed, quickly, ' how many of the serious people whom you know in Lambeth ever go to a place of worship ? '

Gilbert turned his eyes inquiringly, suspiciously. Was Egremont about to preach a pietistic revival ?

' I have very few acquaintances,' he answered, ' but I know that religion has no hold upon intelligent working men in London.'

' That is the admission I wanted. For good or for evil, it has passed ; no one will ever restore it. And yet it is a religious spirit that we must seek to revive. Dogma will no longer help us. Pure love of moral and intellectual beauty must take its place.'

Gilbert smiled at a thought which came to him.

' The working man's Bible,' he said, ' is his Sunday newspaper.'

' And what does he get out of it ? The newspaper is the very voice of all that is worst in our civilisation. If ever there is in one column a pretence of higher teaching, it is made laughable by the base tendency of all the rest. The newspaper has supplanted the book ; every gross-minded scribbler who gets a square inch of space in the morning journal has a more respectful hearing than Shakespeare. These writers are tradesmen, and with all their power they cry up the spirit of trade. Till the influence of the newspaper declines—the newspaper as we now know it—our state will grow worse.'

Grail was silent. Egremont had worked himself to a fervour which showed itself in his unsteady hands and tremulous lips.

' I had not meant to speak of this yet,' he continued. ' I hoped to surround myself with a few friends who would gradually get to know my views, and perhaps think they were worth something. I have obeyed an impulse in opening my mind to you ; I feel that you think with me. Will you join me as a friend, and work on with me for the founding of such a society as I have described ? '

' I will, Mr. Egremont,' was the clear-voiced answer.

Walter put forth his hand, and it was grasped firmly. In this moment he was equal to his ambition, unwavering, exalted, the pure idealist. Grail, too, forgot his private troubles, and tasted the strong air of the heights which it is granted us so seldom and for so brief a season to tread. There was almost colour in his cheeks, and his deep-set eyes had a light as of dawn.

'We have much yet to talk of,' said Egremont, as he rose, 'but it gets late and I mustn't keep you longer. Will you come here some evening when there is no lecture and let us turn over our ideas together? I shall begin at once to think of the library. It will make a centre for us, won't it? And remember Ackroyd. You are intimate with him?'

'We think very differently of many things,' said Grail, 'but I like him. We work together.'

'We mustn't lose him. He has the bright look of a man who could do much if he were really moved. Persuade him to come and see me on Sunday night.'

They shook hands again, and Grail took his departure. Egremont still stood for a few minutes before the fire; then he extinguished the gas, locked the door behind him, and went forth into the street singing to himself.

Gilbert turned into Paradise Street, which was close at hand. He had decided to call and ask for Ackroyd on his way home. The latter had not been at work that day, and was perhaps ailing; for some time he had seemed out of sorts. Intercourse between them was not as constant as formerly. Grail explained this as due to Ackroyd's disturbed mood, another result of which was seen in his ceasing to attend the lecture; yet in Gilbert also there was something which tended to weaken the intimacy. He knew well enough what this was, and strove against it, but not with great success.

Ackroyd lived with his married sister, who let half her house to lodgers. When Gilbert knocked at the door, it was she who opened. Mrs. Poole was a buxom young woman with a complexion which suggested continual activity within range of the kitchen fire; her sleeves were always rolled up to her elbow, and at whatever moment surprised she wore an apron which seemed just washed and ironed. She knew not weariness, nor discomfort, nor discontent, and her flow of words suggested a safety valve letting off superfluous energy.

'That Mr. Grail?' she said, peering out into the darkness. 'You've come to look after that great good-for-nothing of a brother of mine, I'll be bound! Come downstairs, and I'll tell him you're here. You may well wonder what's become of him. Ill! Not he, indeed! No more ill than I am. It's only his laziness. He wants a good shaking, that's about the truth of it, Mr. Grail.'

She led him down into the kitchen. A low clothes-horse, covered with fresh-smelling, gently-steaming linen, stood before a great glowing fire. A baby lay awake in a swinging cot just under the protruding leaf of the table, and a little girl of three was sitting in night-dress and shawl on a stool in a warm corner.

'Yes, you may well stare,' resumed Mrs. Poole, noticing Grail's glance at the children. 'A quarter past ten and neither one of 'em shut an eye yet, nor won't do till their father comes home, not if it's twelve o'clock. You dare to laugh, Miss!' she cried to the little one on the stool, with mock wrath. 'The idea of having to fetch you out o' bed just for peace and quietness. And that young man there'— she pointed to the cradle; 'there's about as much sleep in him as there is in that eight-day clock! You rascal, you!'

Like her brother, she had the northern accent still lingering in her speech; it suited with her brisk, hearty ways. Whilst speaking, she had partly moved the horse from the fire and placed a round-backed chair for the visitor in a position which would have answered tolerably had she meant to roast him.

'He's in the sulks, that's what he is,' she continued, returning to the subject of Luke. 'I suppose you know all about it, Mr. Grail?'

Gilbert seated himself, and Mrs. Poole, pretending to arrange the linen, stood just before him, with a sly smile.

'I'm not sure that I do,' he replied, avoiding her look.

She lowered her voice.

'The idea of a great lad going on like he does! Why, it's the young lady that lives in your house—Miss Trent, you know, I don't know her myself; no doubt she's wonderful pretty and all the rest of it, but I'm that sick and tired of hearing about her! My husband's out a great deal at night, of course, and Luke comes and sits here hours by the clock, just where you are, right in my way. I don't mean you're in my way; I'm talking of times when I'm busy. Well, there he sits; and sometimes he'll be that low it's enough to make a body strangle herself with her apron-string. Other times he'll talk, talk, talk: and it's all Thyrza Trent, Thyrza Trent, till the name makes my ears jingle. This afternoon I couldn't put up with it, so I told him he was a great big baby to go on as he does. Then we had some snappy words, and he went off to his bedroom and wouldn't have any tea. But really and truly, I don't know what'll come to him. He says he'll take to drinking, and he does a deal too much o' that as it is. And to think of him losing days from his work! Now do just tell him not to be a fool, Mr. Grail.'

With difficulty Gilbert found an opportunity to put in a word.

' But is there something wrong between them ? ' he asked with a forced smile.

' Wrong ? Why, doesn't he talk about it to you ? '

' No. I used to hear just a word or two, but there's been no mention of her for a long time.'

' You may think yourself lucky then, that's all *I* can say. Why, she wouldn't have anything to say to him. And I don't see what he's got to complain of; he admits she told him from the first she didn't care a bit for him. As if there wasn't plenty of other lasses! Luke was always such a softy about 'em; but I never knew him have such a turn as this. I'll just go and tell him you're here.'

' Perhaps he's gone to bed.'

' Not he. He sits in the cold half the night, just to make people sorry for him. He doesn't get much pity from me, the silly fellow.'

She ran up the stairs. Grail, as soon as she was gone, fell into a reverie. It did not seem a pleasant one.

In a few minutes Mrs. Poole was heard returning ; behind her came a heavier foot. Ackroyd certainly looked far from well, but had assumed a gay air, which he exaggerated.

' Come to see if I've hanged myself, old man ? Not quite so bad as that yet. I've had the toothache and the headache and Lord knows what. Now I feel hungry ; we'll have some supper together. Give me a jug, Maggie, and I'll get some beer.'

' You sit down,' she replied. 'I'll run out and fetch it.'

' Why, what's the good of a jug like that ! ' he roared, watching her. ' A gallon or so won't be a drop too much for me.'

He flung himself into a chair and stretched his legs.

' Been to the lecture ? ' he asked, as his sister left the room.

'Yes,' Gilbert replied, his wonted quietness contrasting with the other's noise. 'Mr. Egremont's been asking me about you. He's disappointed that you've left him.'

'Can't help it. I held out as long as I could. It isn't my line. Besides, nothing's my line just now. So you had a talk with him, eh?'

'Yes, a talk I shan't forget. There are not many men like Mr. Egremont.'

Gilbert had it on his lips to speak of the library project, but a doubt as to whether he might not be betraying confidence checked him.

'He wants you to go and see him at the lecture-room,' he continued, 'either on Sunday after the lecture, or any evening that suits you. Will you go?'

Luke shook his head.

'No. What's the good?'

'I wish you would, Ackroyd,' said Gilbert, bending forward and speaking with earnestness. 'You'd be glad of it afterwards. He said I was to ask you to go and have a smoke with him by the fire; you needn't be afraid of a sermon, you see. Besides, you know he isn't that kind of man.'

'No, I shan't go, old man,' returned the other, with resolution. 'I liked his lectures well enough, as far as they went, but they're not the kind of thing to suit me nowadays. If I go and talk to him, I'm bound to go to the lectures. What's the good? What's the good of anything?'

Gilbert became silent. The little girl on the stool, who had been moving restlessly, suddenly said:

'Uncle, take me on your lap.'

'Why, of course I will, little un!' Luke replied with a sudden affectionateness one would not have expected of him. 'Give me a kiss. Who's that sitting there, eh?'

'Dono.'

'Nonsense! Say: Mr. Grail.'

In the midst of this, Mrs. Poole reappeared with the jug foaming.

'Oh, indeed! So *that's* where you are!' she exclaimed with her vivacious emphasis, looking at the child. 'A nice thing for you to be nursed at this hour o' night!—Now just one glass, Mr. Grail. It's a bitter night; just a glass to walk on.'

Gilbert pleased her by drinking what she offered. Ackroyd had recommenced his uproarious mirthfulness.

H

' I wish you could persuade your brother to go to the lectures again, Mrs. Poole,' said Gilbert. ' He misses a great deal.'

' And he'll miss a good deal more,' she replied, ' if he doesn't soon come to his senses. Nay, it's no good o' me talking ! He used to be a sensible lad—that is, he could be if he liked.'

Gilbert gave his hand for leave-taking.

' I still hope you'll go on Sunday night,' he said seriously.

Ackroyd shook his head again, then tossed the child into the air and began singing. He did not offer to accompany Grail up to the door.

CHAPTER IX

A GOLDEN PROSPECT

IT wanted a week to Christmas. For many days the weather had been as bad as it can be even in London. Windows glimmered at noon with the sickly ray of gas or lamp; the roads were trodden into viscid foulness ; all night the drop-pings of a pestilent rain were doleful upon the roof, and only the change from a black to a yellow sky told that the sun was risen. No wonder Thyrza was ailing.

It was nothing serious. The inevitable cold had clung to her and become feverish ; it was necessary for her to stay at home for a day or two. Lydia made her hours of work as short as possible, hastening to get back to her sister. But fortunately there was a friend always at hand ; Mrs. Grail could not have been more anxious about a child of her own. Her tendance was of the kind which inspires trust; Lydia, always fretting herself into the extreme of nervousness if her dear one lost for a day the wonted health, was thankful she had not to depend on Mrs. Jarmey's offices.

Thyrza had spent a day in bed, but could now sit by the fire ; her chair came from the Grails' parlour, and was the very one which had always seemed to her so comfortable. Her wish that Lyddy should sit in it had at length been gratified.

It was seven o'clock on Friday evening. The table was drawn near to Thyrza's chair, and Thyrza was engaged in counting out silver coins, which she took from a capacious old purse. Lydia leaned on the table opposite.

'Twenty-four, twenty-five, twenty-six! I'm sure I saw a very nice overcoat marked twenty-five shillings, not long ago; but we can't buy one without knowing grandad's measure.'

'Oh, but you know it near enough, I think.'

'Near enough! But I want it to look nice. I wonder whether I could take a measure without him knowing it? If I could manage to get behind him and just measure across the shoulders, I think that 'ud do.'

Thyrza laughed.

'Go now. He's sure to be sitting with the Bowers. Take the tape and try.'

'No, I'll take a bit of string; then he wouldn't think anything if he saw it.'

Lydia put on her hat and jacket.

'I'll be back as soon as ever I can. Play with the money like a good baby. You're sure you're quite warm?'

Thyrza was wrapped in a large shawl, which hooded over her head. Lydia had taken incredible pains to stop every possible draught at door and window. A cheerful fire threw its glow upon the invalid's face.

'I'm like a toast. Just look up at the shop next to Mrs. Isaac's, Lyddy. There was a sort of brownish coat, with laps over the pockets; it was hanging just by the door. We must get a few more shillings if it makes all the difference, mustn't we?'

'We'll see. Good-bye, Blue-eyes.'

Lydia went her way. For a wonder, there was no fog to-night, but the street lamps glistened on wet pavements, and vehicles as they rattled along sent mud-volleys to either side. In passing through Lambeth Walk, Lydia stopped at the clothing shop of which Thyrza had spoken. The particular brownish coat had seemingly been carried off by a purchaser, but she was glad to notice one or two second-hand garments of very respectable appearance which came within the sum at her command. She passed on into Paradise Street and entered Mrs. Bower's shop.

In the parlour the portly Mr. Bower stood with his back to the fire; he was speaking oracularly, and, at Lydia's entrance, looked up with some annoyance at being interrupted. Mr. Boddy sat in his accustomed corner. Mrs. Bower, arrayed in the grandeur suitable to a winter evening, was condescending to sew.

'Mary out?' Lydia asked, as she looked round.

'Yes, my dear,' replied Mrs. Bower, with a sigh of resignation. 'She's at a prayer meetin', as per us'l. That's the third night this blessed week. I 'old with goin' to chapel, but like everything else it ought to be done in moderation. Mary's gettin' beyond everything. I don't believe in makin' such a fuss o' religion ; you can be religious in your mind without sayin' prayers an' singin' 'ymns all the week long. There's the Sunday for that, an' I can't see as it's pleasin' to God neither to do so much of it at other times. Now suppose I give somebody credit in the shop, on the understandin' as they come an' pay their bill once a week reg'lar ; do you think I should like to have 'em lookin' in two or three times every day an' cryin' out : " Oh, Mrs. Bower, ma'am, I don't forget as I owe you so and so much ; be sure I shall come an' pay on Saturday ! " If they did that, I should precious soon begin to think there was something wrong, else they'd 'old their tongues an' leave it to be understood as they was honest. Why, an' it's every bit the same with religion ! '

Mr. Boddy listened gravely to this, and had the air of probing the suggested analogy. He had a bad cold, poor old man, and for the moment it made him look as if he indulged too freely in ardent beverages ; his nose was red and his eyes were watery.

'How's the little un, my dear ? ' he asked, as Lydia took a seat by him.

'Oh, she's much better, grandad. Mrs. Grail is so kind to her, you wouldn't believe. She'll be all right again by Monday, I think.'

'Mrs. Grail's kind to her, is she ? ' remarked Mr. Bower. Why, you're getting great friends with the Grails, Miss Lydia.'

'Yes, we really are.'

'And do you see much of Grail himself ? '

'No, not much. We sometimes have tea with them both.'

'Ah, you do ? He's a very decent, quiet fellow, is Grail. I dare say he tells you something about Egremont now and then ? '

Mr. Bower put the question in a casual way ; in truth, it was designed to elicit information which he much desired. He knew that for some time Grail had been on a new footing with the lecturer, that the two often remained together after the class had dispersed ; it was a privilege which he regarded disapprovingly, because it lessened his own dignity in the eyes of the other men. He wondered what the subject of these private conversations might be; there had seemed to him something of mystery in Grail's manner when he was plied with a friendly inquiry or two.

'I've heard him speak of the lectures,' said Lydia. 'He says he enjoys them very much.'

'To be sure. Yes, they're very fair lectures, very fair, in their way. I don't know as I've cared quite so much for 'em lately as I did at first. I've felt he was falling off a little. I gave him a hint a few weeks ago; just told him in a quiet way as I thought he was going too far into things that weren't very interesting, but he didn't seem quite to see it. It's always the way with young men of his kind; when you give them a bit of advice, it makes them obstinate. Well, he'll see when he begins again after Christmas. Thomas and Linwood are giving it up, and I shall be rather surprised if Johnson holds out for another course.'

'But I suppose you'll go, Mr. Bower?' said Lydia.

Bower stuck his forefingers into his waistcoat pockets, held his head as one who muses, clicked with his tongue.

'I shall see,' he replied, with a judicial air. 'I don't like to give the young feller up. You see, I may say as it was me put him on the idea. We had a lot of talk about one thing and another one day at the works, and a hint of mine set him off. I should like to make the lectures successful; I believe they're a good thing, if they are properly carried out. I'm a believer in education. It's the educated men as get on in the world. Teach a man to use his brains and he'll soon be worth double wages. But Egremont must keep up to the mark if he's to have my support. I shall have to have a word or two with him before he begins again. By-the-by, I passed him in Kennington Road just now; I wonder what he's doing about here at this time. Been to the works, perhaps.'

Whilst the portly man thus delivered himself, Lydia let her arm rest on Mr. Boddy's shoulder. It was a caress which he sometimes received from her; he looked round at her affectionately, then continued to pay attention to the weighty words which fell from Mr. Bower. Mrs. Bower, who was less impressed by her husband's utterances, bent over her sewing. In this way Lydia was able craftily to secure the measurement she needed. And having got this, she was anxious to be back with Thyrza.

' I suppose it's no use waiting for Mary,' she said, rising.

' I don't suppose she'll be back not before nine o'clock,' Mrs. Bower replied. ' Did you want her partic'lar ? '

' Oh no, it'll do any time.'

' Whilst I think of it,' said Mrs. Bower, letting her sewing fall upon her lap and settling the upper part of her stout body in an attitude of dignity ; ' you and your sister 'll come an' eat your Christmas dinner with us ? '

Lydia cast down her eyes.

' It's very kind of you, Mrs. Bower, but I'm sure I don't know whether Thyrza 'll be well enough. I must be very careful of her for a time.'

' Well, well, you'll see. It'll only be a quiet little fam'ly dinner this year. You'll know there's places kep' for you.'

Lydia again expressed her thanks, then took leave. As she left the shop, she heard Mr. Bower's voice again raised in impressive oratory.

On entering the house in Walnut Tree Walk, she found Mrs. Grail just descending the stairs. The old lady never spoke above her breath at such casual meetings outside her own door.

' Come in for a minute,' she whispered.

Lydia followed her into the parlour. Gilbert was settled for the evening at the table. A volume lent by Egremont lay before him, and he was making notes from it. At Lydia's entrance he rose and spoke a word, then resumed his reading.

' I've just taken Thyrza a little morsel of jelly I made this afternoon,' Mrs. Grail said, apart to the girl. ' I'm sure she looks better to-night.'

' How good you are, Mrs. Grail ! Yes, she does look better, but I couldn't have believed a day or two 'ud have made her so weak. I shan't let her go out before Christmas.'

' No, I don't think you ought, my dear.'

As Mrs. Grail spoke, the knocker of the house-door sounded an unusual summons, a rat-tat, not loud indeed, but distinct from the knocks wont to be heard here.

' Mr. and Mrs. Jarmey are both out,' said Lydia. ' They're gone to the theatre. Perhaps it's for you, Mrs. Grail ? '

' No, that's not at all likely.'

' I'll go.'

Lydia opened. A gentleman stood without ; he inquired in a pleasant voice if Mr. Grail was at home.

'I think so,' Lydia said. 'Will you please wait a minute?'

She hurried back to the parlour.

'It's a gentleman wants to see Mr. Grail,' she whispered, with the momentary excitement which any little out-of-the-way occurrence produces in those who live a life void of surprises. And she glanced at Gilbert, who had heard what she said. He rose:

'I wonder whether it's Mr. Egremont! Thank you, Miss Trent; I'll go to the door.'

Lydia escaped up the stairs. Gilbert went out into the passage, and his surmise was confirmed. Egremont was there, sheltering himself under an umbrella from rain which was once more beginning to fall.

'Could I have a word with you?' he said, with friendly freedom. 'I should have written, but I had to pass so near——'

'I'm very glad. Will you come in?'

It was the first time that Egremont had been at the house. Gilbert conducted him into the parlour, and took from him his hat and umbrella.

'This is my mother,' he said. 'Mr. Egremont, mother; you'll be glad to see him.'

The old lady regarded Walter with courteous curiosity, and bowed to him. A few friendly words were exchanged, then Egremont said to Grail:

'If you hadn't been in, I should have left a message, asking you to meet me to-morrow afternoon.'

Mrs. Grail was about to leave the room; Egremont begged her to remain.

'It's only a piece of news concerning our library scheme. I think I've found a building that will suit us. Do you know a school in Brook Street, connected with a Wesleyan Chapel somewhere about here?'

Gilbert said that he knew it; his mother also murmured recognition.

'It'll be to let at the end of next quarter: they're building themselves a larger place. I heard about it this afternoon, and as I was told that evening classes are held there, I thought I'd come and have a look at the place to-night. At last it is something like what we want. Could you meet me there, say at three, to-morrow afternoon, so that we could see it together in daylight—if daylight be granted us?'

Grail expressed his readiness.

'You were reading,' Walter went on, with a glance at the table. 'I mustn't waste your time.'

He rose, but Gilbert said:

'I should be glad if you could stay a few minutes. Perhaps you haven't time?'

'Oh yes. What are you busy with?'

Half an hour's talk followed, of course mainly of books. Egremont looked over the volumes on the shelves; those who love such topics will know how readily gossip spun itself from that centre. He was pleased with Grail's home; it was very much as he had liked to picture it since he had known that Gilbert lived with his mother. Mrs. Grail sat and listened to all that was said, a placid smile on her smooth face. At length Egremont declared that he was consuming his friend's evening.

'Perhaps you'll let me come some other night?' he said, as he took up his hat. 'I know very few people indeed who care to talk of these things in the way I like.'

Gilbert came back from the door with a look of pleasure.

'Now, isn't he a fine fellow, mother? I'm so glad you've seen him.'

'He seems a very pleasant young man indeed,' Mrs. Grail replied. 'He's not quite the picture I'd made of him, but his way of speaking makes you like him from the very first.'

'I never heard him say a word yet that didn't sound genuine,' Gilbert added. 'He speaks what he thinks, and you won't find many men who make you feel that. And he has a mind; I wish you could hear one of his lectures; he speaks in just the same easy running way, and constantly says things one would be glad to remember. They don't understand him, Bower, and Bunce, and the others; they don't *feel* his words as they ought to. I'm afraid he'll only have two or three when he begins again.'

Mrs. Grail turned presently to a different topic.

'Would you believe, Gilbert!' she murmured. 'Those two girls have saved up more than a pound to buy that poor old Mr. Boddy a top-coat for Christmas. When I went up with the jelly, Thyrza had the money out on the table; she told me as a great secret what it was for. Kind-hearted things they are, both of them.'

Gilbert assented silently. His mother seldom elicited a word from him on the subject of the sisters.

On the following afternoon, Gilbert and Egremont met at the appointed place just as three was striking. Already night had begun to close in, a sad wind moaned about the streets, and the cold grey of the sky was patched about with dim shifting black clouds. Egremont was full of cheeriness as he shook hands.

'What a wonderful people we are,' he exclaimed, 'to have developed even so much civilisation in a climate such as this!'

The school building which they were about to inspect stood at the junction of two streets, which consisted chiefly of dwellings. In the nature of things it was ugly. Three steps led up to the narrow entrance, which, as well as the windows on the ground floor, was surrounded with a wholly inappropriate pointed arch. Iron railings ran along the two sides which abutted upon pavements, and by the door was a tall iron support for a lamp; probably it had never been put to its use. There was only one upper storey, and the roof was crowned with a small stack of hideous metal chimneys.

'We must go round to the caretaker's house,' said Egremont, when they had cast their eyes over the face of the edifice.

The way was by a narrow passage between the school itself and the whitewashed side of an adjacent house; this led them into a small paved yard, upon which looked the windows of the caretaker's dwelling, which was the rear portion of the school building. A knock at the door brought a very dirty and very asthmatical old woman, who appeared to resent their visit. When Egremont expressed his desire to go over the school, she muttered querulously what was understood to be an invitation to enter. Followed by Gilbert, Egremont was conducted along a pitch-dark passage.

'Mind the steps!' snarled their guide.

Egremont had already stumbled over an ascent of two when the warning was given, but at the same moment a door was thrown open, giving a view of the main schoolroom.

''Tain't swep' out yet,' remarked the old woman. 'I couldn't tell as nobody was a-comin'. You can complain to them if you like; I'm used to it from all sorts, an' 'taint for much longer, praise goodness! Though there's nothink before me but the parish when the time does come.'

Egremont glanced at the strange creature in surprise, but it seemed better to say nothing. He began to speak of the aspects of the room with his companion.

The place was cheerless beyond description. In a large grate the last embers of a fire were darkening; the air was chill, and, looking up to the ceiling, one saw floating scraps of mist which had somehow come in from the street. The lower half of each window was guarded with lattice-work of thin wire; the windows themselves were grimy, and would have made it dusk within even on a clear day. The whitewash of the ceiling was dark and much cracked. Benches and desks covered half the floor. There were black-boards and other mechanical appliances for teaching, and on the walls hung maps and diagrams.

'The walls seem quite dry,' observed Walter, 'which is a great point.'

They laid their palms against the plaster. The old woman stood with one hand pressed against her bosom, the other behind her back; her head was bent; she seemed to pay no kind of attention to what was said.

'There's room here for some thousands of volumes,' Egremont said, moving to one of the windows. 'It will serve tolerably as a reading-room, too. Nothing like as large as it ought to be, of course, but we must be content to feel our way to better things.'

Gilbert nodded. In spite of his companion's resolute cheerfulness, he felt a distressing dejection creep upon him as he stood in the cold, darkening room. He could not feel the interest and hope which hitherto this project had inspired him with. The figure of the old caretaker impressed him painfully. For any movement she made she might have been asleep; the regular sound of her heavy breathing was quite audible, and vapour rose from her lips upon the air.

'What do you think?' Egremont asked, when Grail remained mute.

'I should think it will do very well. What is there up-stairs?'

'Two class-rooms. We should use those for lectures. Let us go up.'

The old woman walked before them to a door opposite that by which they had entered. They found themselves in a small vestibule, out of which, on one hand, a door led into a cloak-room, while on the other ascended a flight of stone stairs.

There was nothing noticeable in the rooms above ; the windows here were also very dirty, and mist floated below the ceilings.

The caretaker had remained below, contenting herself with indicating the way.

'You seem disappointed,' Walter said. He himself had ceased to talk, he felt cold and uncomfortable.

'No, no, indeed I'm not,' Grail hastened to reply. 'I think it is as good a place as you could have found.'

'We don't see it under very inspiriting conditions. Fire and light and comfortable furniture would make a wonderful difference, even on a day like this.'

Gilbert reproached himself for taking so coldly his friend's generous zeal.

'And books still more,' he replied, 'The room below will be a grand sight with shelves all round the walls.'

'Well, I must make further inquiries, but I think the place will suit us.'

They descended, their footsteps ringing on the stone and echoing up to the roof. The old woman still stood at the foot of the stairs, her head bent, the hand against her side.

'Will you go out here,' she asked, 'or do you want to see anythink else ? '

'I should like to see the back part again,' Egremont replied.

She led them across the schoolroom, through the dark passage, and into a small room which had the distant semblance of a parlour. Here she lit a lamp; then, without speaking, guided them over the house, of which she appeared to be the only inhabitant. There were seven rooms ; only three of them contained any furniture. Then they all returned to the comfortless parlour.

'Your chest is bad,' Egremont remarked, looking curiously at the woman.

'Yes, I dessay it is,' was the ungracious reply.

'Well, I don't think we need trouble you any more at present, but I shall probably have to come again in a day or two.'

'I dessay you'll find me here.'

'And feeling better, I hope. The weather gives you much trouble, no doubt.'

He held half a crown to her. She regarded it, clasped it in the hand which was against her bosom, and at length dropped a curtsey, though without speaking.

'What a poor crabbed old creature!' Egremont exclaimed, as they walked away. 'I should feel relieved if I knew that she went off at once to the warmth of the public-house opposite.'

'Yes, she hasn't a very cheerful home.'

'Oh, but it can be made a very different house. It has fallen into such neglect. Wait till spring sunshine and the paperhangers invade the place.'

They issued into a main street, and after a little further talk, shook hands and parted.

That night, and through the Sunday that followed, Gilbert continued to suffer even more than his wont from mental dreariness; Mrs. Grail was unable to draw him into conversation.

About four o'clock she said:

'May I ask Lydia and Thyrza to come and have tea with us, Gilbert?'

He looked up absently.

'But they were here last Sunday.'

'Yes, my dear, but I think they like to come, and I'm sure I like to have them.'

'Let us leave it till next Sunday, mother. You don't mind? I feel I must be alone to-night.'

It was a most unusual thing for Gilbert to offer opposition when his mother had expressed a desire for anything. Mrs. Grail at once said:

'I dare say you're right, my dear. Next Sunday 'll be better.'

The next morning he went to his work through a fog so dense that it was with difficulty he followed the familiar way. Lamps were mere lurid blotches in the foul air, perceptible only when close at hand; the footfall of invisible men and women hurrying to factories made a muffled, ghastly sound; harsh bells summoned through the darkness, the voice of pitiless taskmasters to whom all was indifferent save the hour of toil. Gilbert was racked with headache. Bodily suffering made him as void of intellectual desire as the meanest labourer then going forth to earn bread; he longed for nothing more than to lie down and lose consciousness of the burden of life.

Then came Christmas Eve. The weather had changed; to-night there was frost in the air, and the light of stars made a shimmer upon the black vault. Gilbert always gave this season to companionship with his mother. About seven o'clock they were talking quietly together of memories light and grave, of Gilbert's boyhood, of his sister who was dead, of his father who was dead. Then came a pause, whilst both were silently busy with the irrecoverable past.

Mrs. Grail broke the silence to say:

'You're a lonely man, Gilbert.'

'Why no, not lonely, mother. I might be, but for you.'

'Yes, you're lonely, my dear. It's poor company that I can give you. I should like to see you with a happier look on your face before I die.'

Gilbert had no reply ready.

'You think too poorly of yourself,' his mother resumed, ' and you always have done. But there's people have a better judgment of you. Haven't you thought that somebody looks always very pleased when you read or talk, and sits very quiet when you've nothing to say, and always says good-night to you so prettily?'

'Mother, mother, don't speak like that! I've thought nothing of the kind. Put that out of your head; never speak of it again.'

His voice was not untender, but very grave. The lines of his face hardened. Mrs. Grail glanced at him timidly, and became mute.

A loud double knock told that the postman had delivered a letter at the house. Whilst the two still sat in silence Mrs. Jarmey tapped at their door and said:

'A letter for you, Mr. Grail.'

'From Mr. Egremont,' said Gilbert, as he resumed his seat and opened the envelope. 'More about the library I expect.'

He read to himself.

'My dear Grail,—I have decided to take the school building on a lease of seven years, after again carefully examining it and finding it still to my mind. It will be free at the end of March. By that time I hope to have sketched out something of a rudimentary catalogue, and before summer the library should be open.

'I asked you to come and look over this place with me because I had a project in my mind with reference to the library which concerns yourself. I lay it before you in a letter, that you may think it over quietly and reply at your leisure. I wish to offer you the position of librarian: I am sure I could not find anyone better suited for the post, and certainly there is no man whom I should like so well to see occupying it. I propose that the salary be a hundred pounds a year, with free tenancy of the dwelling-house at present so dolorously occupied—I am sure it can be made a comfortable abode—and of course, gas and fuel. I should make arrangements for the necessary cleaning, &c., with some person of the neighbourhood ; your own duties would be solely those of librarian and reading-room superintendent.

'The library should be open, I think, from ten to ten, for I want to lose no possibility of usefulness. If one loafer be tempted to come in and read, the day's object is gained. These hours are, of course, too long for you alone ; I would provide you with an assistant, so that you could assure for yourself, let us say, four hours free out of the twelve. But details would be easily arranged between us. By-the-by, Sunday must *not* be a day of closing ; to make it so would be to deprive ourselves of the greatest opportunity. Your freedom for one entire day in the week should be guaranteed.

'I offer this because I should like to have you working with me, and because I believe that such work would be more to your taste than that in which you are now occupied. It would, moreover, leave you a good deal of time for study ; we are not likely to be overwhelmed with readers and borrowers during the daytime. But you will consider the proposal precisely as you would do if it came from a stranger, and will accept or reject it as you see fit.

'I leave town to-day for about a week. Will you write to me at the end of that time ?—Always yours, my dear Grail,
                                                    'WALTER EGREMONT.'

Mrs. Grail showed no curiosity about the letter ; the subject of the interrupted conversation held her musing. When Gilbert had folded the sheets, and, in the manner of one who receives few letters, returned it to its envelope, he said :

'Yes, it's about the library. He's taken the house for seven years.'

His mother murmured an expression of interest. For another minute the clock on the mantel-piece ticked loud ; then Gilbert rose, and without saying anything, went out.

He entered his bedroom. The darkness was complete, but he moved with the certainty of habit to a chair by the head of the bed, and there seated himself. Presently he felt a painful surging in his throat, then a gush of warm tears forced its way to his eyes. It cost him a great effort to resist the tendency to sob aloud. He was hot and cold alternately, and trembled as though a fever were coming upon him.

In a quarter of an hour he lit the candle, and, after a glance at himself in the glass, bathed his face. Then he took down his overcoat from the door, and put it on. His hat, too, he took, and went to the parlour.

'I have to go out, mother,' he said, standing at the door. 'I'll be back by supper-time.'

'Very well, my dear,' was the quiet reply.

He walked out to the edge of the pavement, and stood a moment, as if in doubt as to his direction. Then he looked at the upper windows of the house, as we saw him do one night half a year ago. There was a light this time in the sisters' room.

He turned towards Lambeth Walk. The market of Christmas Eve was flaring and clamorous; the odours of burning naphtha and fried fish were pungent on the wind. He walked a short distance among the crowd, then found the noise oppressive and turned into a by-way. As he did so, a street organ began to play in front of a public-house close by. Grail drew near; there were children forming a dance, and he stood to watch them.

Do you know that music of the obscure ways, to which children dance? Not if you have only heard it ground to your ears' affliction beneath your windows in the square. To hear it aright you must stand in the darkness of such a by-street as this, and for the moment be at one with those who dwell around, in the blear-eyed houses, in the dim burrows of poverty, in the unmapped haunts of the semi-human. Then you will know the significance of that vulgar clanging of melody; a pathos of which you did not dream will touch you, and therein the secret of hidden London will be half revealed. The life of men who toil without hope, yet with the hunger of an unshaped desire; of women in whom the sweetness of their sex is perishing under labour and misery; the laugh, the song of the girl who strives to enjoy her year or two of youthful vigour, knowing the darkness of the years to come; the careless defiance of the youth who feels his blood and revolts against the lot which would tame it; all that is purely human in these darkened multitudes speaks to you as you listen. It is the half-conscious striving of a nature which knows not what it would attain, which deforms a true thought by gross expression, which clutches at the beautiful and soils it with foul hands.

The children were dirty and ragged, several of them bare-footed, nearly all bare-headed, but they danced with noisy merriment. One there was, a little girl, on crutches; incapable of taking a partner, she stumped round and round, circling upon the pavement, till giddiness came upon her and she had to fall back and lean against the wall, laughing aloud at her weakness. Gilbert stepped up to her, and put a penny into her hand ; then, before she had recovered from her surprise, passed onwards.

He came out at length by Lambeth parish church, which looks upon the river ; the bells were ringing a harsh peal of four notes, unchangingly repeated. Thence he went forward on to Lambeth Bridge.

Unsightliest of all bridges crossing Thames, the red hue of its iron superstructure, which in daylight only enhances the meanness of its appearance, at night invests it with a certain grim severity ; the archway, with its bolted metal plates, its wire-woven cables, over-glimmered with the yellow-ness of the gas-lamps which it supports, might be the entrance to some fastness of ignoble misery. The road is narrow, and after nightfall has but little traffic.

Gilbert walked as far as the middle of the bridge, then leaned upon the parapet and looked northwards. The tide was running out ; it swept darkly onwards to the span of Westminster Bridge, whose crescent of lights it repeated in long unsteady rays. Along the base of the Houses of Parliament the few sparse lamps contrasted with the line of bright-ness on the Embankment opposite. The Houses themselves rose grandly in obscure magnitude ; the clock-tower beaconed with two red circles against the black sky, the greater tower stood night-clad, and between them were the dim pinnacles, multiplied in shadowy grace. Farther away Gilbert could just discern a low, grey shape, that resting-place of poets and of kings which to look upon filled his heart with worship.

In front of the Embankment, a few yards out into the stream, was moored a string of barges ; between them and the shore the reflected lamp-light made one unbroken breadth of radiance, blackening the mid-current. From that the eye rose to St. Thomas's Hospital, spreading block after block, its

windows telling of the manifold woe within. Nearer was the
Archbishop's Palace, dark, lifeless ; the roofs were defined
against a sky made lurid by the streets of Lambeth. On the
pier below signalled two crimson lights.

The church bells kept up their clangorous discord, softened
at times by the wind. A steamboat came fretting up the
stream ; when it had passed under the bridge, its spreading
track caught the reflected gleams and flung them away to die
on unsearchable depths. Then issued from beneath a barge
with set sail, making way with wind and tide ; in silence it
moved onwards, its sail dark and ghastly, till the further bridge
swallowed it.

The bells ceased. Gilbert bent his head and listened to the
rush of the water, voiceful, mysterious. Sometimes he had
stood there and wished that the dread tide could whelm him.
His mood was far other now ; some power he did not understand had brought him here as to the place where he could
best realise this great joy that had befallen him.

But the wind blew piercingly, and when at length he moved
from the parapet, he found that his arms were quite numb ;
doubtless he had stood longer than he thought. Instead of
returning by the direct way, he walked along the Embankment. It was all but deserted ; the tread of a policeman
echoed from the distance. But in spite of the bitter sky, two
people were sitting together on one of the benches—a young
man and a work-girl; they were speaking scarcely above a
whisper. Gilbert averted his face as he passed them, and for
the moment his eyes had their pain-stricken look.

Issuing into Westminster Bridge Road, he found himself
once more amid a throng. And before he had gone far he
recognised a figure that walked just ahead of him. It was
Ackroyd ; he was accompanied by a girl of whom Gilbert had
no knowledge—Miss Totty Nancarrow. They were talking in
a merry, careless way : Ackroyd smoked a cigar, and Totty
walked with her usual independence, with that swaying of the
haunches and swing of the hands with palm turned outwards
which is characteristic of the London work-girl. Her laugh
now and then rose to a high note ; her companion threw back
his head and joined in the mirth. Clearly Ackroyd was in a
way to recover his spirits.

At the junction of two ways they stopped. Gilbert stopped
too, for he did not care to pass them and be recognised. He
crossed the road, and from the other side watched them as

I

they stood talking. Now they were taking leave of each other. Ackroyd appeared to hold the girl's hand longer than she liked; when she struggled to get away, he suddenly bent forward and snatched a kiss. With a gesture of indignation she escaped from him.

Gilbert had a desire to join Ackroyd, now that the latter was alone. But as he began to recross the street, the young man moved on and turned into a public-house. Gilbert again stopped, and, disregarding the crowds about him, lost himself in thought. He determined at length to go his way.

Mrs. Grail had supper ready, with some mince pies of her own making.

'Each lot I make,' she said, as they sat down, 'I say to myself they'll be the last.'

'No, no, mother; we shall eat a good many together yet,' Gilbert replied, cheerily. The wind had brought a touch of colour to his cheeks and made his eyes glisten.

'Have you taken any upstairs?' he asked presently.

'No, my dear. Do you think I may?'

'Oh, I should think so.'

The old lady looked at him and grew thoughtful.

There was no work to rise to on the morrow. With a clear conscience Gilbert could sit on into the still hours which were so precious to him. And again, before going to rest, he stepped quietly from the house to look at the upper windows.

CHAPTER X

TEMPTING FORTUNE

THYRZA continued to be far from well. The day-long darkness encouraged her natural tendency to sad dreaming. When alone, in Lydia's absence at the work-room, she sometimes had fits of weeping; it was a relief to shed tears. She could have given no explanation of the sufferings which found this outlet; her heart lay under a cold weight, that was all she knew.

Lydia pursued her course with the usual method and contentment, yet, in these days just before Christmas, with a perceptible falling off in the animation which was the note of her character. Perhaps she too was affected by the weather;

perhaps she was anxious about Thyrza ; one would have said, however, that she had some trouble distinct from these.

On Christmas Eve she ran round to Paradise Street, to make arrangements for the next day. Evidently it would not be wise for Thyrza to leave home ; that being the case, it was decided that Mr. Boddy should come and have tea with the girls in their own room. Lydia talked over these things with Mary in the kitchen below the shop, where odours of Christmas fare were already rife. The parlour was full of noisy people, amid whom Mr. Bower was holding weighty discourse ; the friends had gone below for privacy.

'So I shall keep the coat till he comes, Lydia said. 'I know Thyrza would like to see his poor old face when he puts it on. And you might come round yourself, Mary, just for an hour.'

'I'll see if I can.'

'I suppose you'll have people at night ? '

'I don't know, I'm sure. I'd much rather come and sit with you, but mother may want me.'

Lydia asked :

'Has Mr. Ackroyd been here lately ? '

'I haven't seen him. I hope not.'

'Why do you say that, Mary ? ' asked Lydia impatiently.

'I only say what I think, dear.'

Lydia for once succeeded in choosing wiser silence. But that look which had no place upon her fair, open countenance came for a moment, a passing darkness which might be forecast of unhappy things.

At four o'clock on the following afternoon—this Christmas fell on a Friday—everything was ready in Walnut Tree Walk for Mr. Boddy's arrival. The overcoat, purchased by Lydia after a vast amount of comparing and selecting, of deciding and rejecting and redeciding, was carefully hidden, to be produced at a suitable moment. The bitter coldness of the day gladdened the girls now that they knew the old man would go away well wrapped up. This coat had furnished a subject for many an hour of talk between them, and now as they waited they amused themselves with anticipation of what Mr. Boddy would say, what he would think, how joyfully he would throw aside that one overcoat he did possess—a garment really too far gone, and with no pretence of warmth in it. Thyrza introduced a note of sadness by asking :

'What 'll happen, Lyddy, if he gets that he can't earn anything?'

'I sometimes think of that,' Lydia replied gravely. 'We couldn't expect the Bowers to keep him there if he couldn't pay his rent. But I always hope that we shall be able to find what he needs. It isn't much, poor grandad! And you see we can always manage to save something, Thyrza.'

'But it wouldn't be enough—nothing like enough for a room and meals, Lyddy.'

'Oh, we shall find a way! Perhaps'—she laughed—'we shall have more money some day.'

Two rings at the bell on the lower landing announced their visitor's arrival. Lydia ran downstairs and returned with the old man, whose face was very red from the raw air. He had a muffler wrapped about his neck, but the veteran overcoat was left behind, for the simple reason that Mr. Boddy felt he looked more respectable without it. His threadbare black suit had been subjected to vigorous brushing, with a little exercise of the needle here and there. A pair of woollen gloves, long kept for occasions of ceremony, were the most substantial article of clothing that he wore. A baize bag, of which Lydia had relieved him, contained his violin.

'I thought you'd maybe like a little music, my dear,' he said as he kissed Thyrza. 'It's cheerin' when you don't feel quite the thing. I doubt you can't sing though.'

'Oh, the cold's all gone,' replied Thyrza. 'We'll see, after tea.'

They made much of him, and it must have been very sweet to the poor old fellow to be so affectionately tended by these whom he loved as his own children.

Mary Bower came not long after tea, then Mr. Boddy took out his violin from the bag and played all the favourite old tunes, those which brought back their childhood to the two girls. To please Mary, Lydia asked for a hymn-tune, one she had grown fond of in chapel. Mary began to sing it, so Lydia got her hymn-book and asked Thyrza to sing with them. The air was a sweet one, and Thyrza's voice gave it touching beauty as she sang soft and low. Other hymns followed; Mary Bower fell into her gentler mood and showed how pleasant she could be when nothing irritated her susceptibilities. The hours passed quickly to nine o'clock, then Mary said it was time for her to go.

'Do you want to stay a little longer, Mr. Boddy,' she said, ' or will you go home with me ? '

'I'd rather walk home in good company than alone, Miss Mary,' he replied. 'I call it walking, but it's only a stump-stump.'

'But it would be worse if you couldn't walk at all,' Mary said.

'Right, my dear, as you always are. I've no call to grumble. It's a bad habit as grows on me, I fear. If Lyddy 'ud only tell me of it, both together you might do me good. But Lyddy treats me like a spoilt child. It's her old way.'

'Mary shall take us both in hand,' said Lydia. 'She shall cure me of my sharp temper and you of grumbling, grandad ; and I know which 'll be the hardest job ! '

Laughing with kindly mirth, the old man drew on his woollen gloves and took up his hat and the violin-bag. Then he offered to say good-bye.

'But you're forgetting your top-coat, grandad,' said Lydia.

'I didn't come in it, my dear.'

'What's that, then ? I'm sure we don't wear such things.'

She pointed to a chair, on which Thyrza had just artfully spread the gift. Mr. Boddy looked in a puzzled way ; had he really come in his coat and forgotten it ? He drew nearer.

'That's no coat o' mine, Lyddy,' he said.

Thyrza broke into a laugh.

'Why, whose is it, then ? ' she exclaimed. 'Don't play tricks, grandad ; put it on at once ! '

'Now come, come ; you're keeping Mary waiting,' said Lydia, catching up the coat and holding it ready.

Then Mr. Boddy understood. He looked from Lydia to Thyrza with dimmed eyes.

'I've a good mind never to speak to either of you again,' he said in a tremulous voice. 'As if you hadn't need enough of your money ! Lyddy, Lyddy ! And you're as bad, Thyrza ; a grown-up woman like you, you ought to teach your sister better. Why there ; it's no good ; I don't know what to say to you. Now what do you think of this, Mary ? '

Lydia still held up the coat, and at length persuaded the old man to don it. The effect upon his appearance was remarkable ; conscious of it, he held himself more upright and stumped to the little square of looking-glass to try and re- gard himself. Here he furtively brushed a hand over his eyes.

'I'm ready, Mary, my dear; I'm ready! It's no good saying anything to girls like these. Good-bye, Lyddy; good-bye, Thyrza. May you have a many happy Christmas, children! This isn't the first as you've made a happy one for me.'

Lydia went down to the door and watched the two till they were lost in darkness. Then she returned to her sister with a sigh of gladness. For the moment she had no trouble of her own.

Upon days of festival, kept in howsoever quiet and pure a spirit, there of necessity follows depression; all mirth is unnatural to the reflective mind, and even the unconscious suffer a mysterious penalty when they have wrested one whole day from fate. On the Saturday Lydia had no work to go to, and the hours dragged. In the course of the morning she went out to make some purchases. She was passing Mrs. Bower's without intention of entering, when Mary appeared in the doorway and beckoned her. Mrs. Bower was out; Mary had been left in charge of the shop.

'You were asking me about Mr. Ackroyd,' she said, when they had gone into the parlour. 'Would you like to know something I heard about him last night?'

Lydia knew that it was something disagreeable; Mary's air of discharging a duty sufficiently proved that.

'What is it?' she asked coldly.

'They were talking about him here when I came back last night. He's begun to go about with that girl Totty Nancarrow.'

Lydia cast down her eyes. Mary keeping silence, she said:

'Well, what if he has?'

'I think it's right you should know, on Thyrza's account.'

'Thyrza has nothing to do with Mr. Ackroyd; you know that, Mary.'

'But there's something else. He's begun to drink, Lydia. Mr. Raggles saw him in a public-house somewhere last night, and he was quite tipsy.'

Lydia said nothing. She held a market bag before her, and her white knuckles proved how tightly she clutched the handles.

'You remember what I once said,' Mary continued. There was absolutely no malice in her tone, but mere satisfaction in proving that the premises whence her conclusions had been drawn were undeniably sound. She was actuated neither by personal dislike of Ackroyd nor by jealousy; but she could not resist this temptation of illustrating her principles by such a noteworthy instance. 'Now wasn't I right, Lydia?'

Lydia looked up with hot cheeks.

'I don't believe it!' she said vehemently. 'Who's Mr. Raggles? How do you know he tells the truth?—And what is it to me, whether it's true or not?'

'You were so sure that it made no difference what any one believed, Lydia,' said the other, with calm persistency.

'And I say the same still, and I always will say it? You're *glad* when anybody speaks against Mr. Ackroyd, and you'd believe them, whatever they said. I'll never go to chapel again with you, Mary, as long as I live! You're unkind, and it's your chapel-going that makes you so! You'd no business to call me in to tell me things of this kind. After to-day, please don't mention Mr. Ackroyd's name; you know nothing at all about him.'

Without waiting for a reply she left the parlour and went on her way. Mary was rather pale, but she felt convinced of the truth of what she had reported, and she had done her plain duty in drawing the lesson. Whether Lydia would acknowledge that seemed doubtful. The outburst of anger confirmed Mary in strange suspicions which had for some time lurked in her mind.

On Sunday evening Lydia dressed as if to go to chapel, and left the house at the usual hour. She had heard nothing from Mary Bower, and her resentment was yet warm. She did not like to tell Thyrza what had happened, but went out to spend the time as best she could.

Almost as soon as her sister was gone Thyrza paid a little attention to her dress and went downstairs. She knocked at the Grails' parlour; it was Gilbert's voice that answered.

'Isn't Mrs. Grail in?' she asked timidly, looking about the room.

'Yes, she's in, Miss Trent, but she doesn't feel very well. She went to lie down after tea.'

'Oh, I'm sorry.'

She hesitated, just within the door.

'Would you like to go to her room?' Gilbert asked.

'Perhap's she's asleep; I mustn't disturb her. Would you lend me another book, Mr. Grail?'

'Oh, yes! Will you come and choose one?'

She closed the door and went forward to the bookcase, on

her way glancing at Gilbert's face, to see whether he was annoyed at her disturbing him. It was scarcely that, yet unmistakably his countenance was troubled. This made Thyrza nervous ; she did not look at him again for a few moments, but carried her eyes along the shelves. Poor little one, the titles were no help to her. Gilbert knew that well enough, but he was watching her by stealth, and forgot to speak.

'What do you think would do for me, Mr. Grail ? ' she said at length. ' It mustn't be anything very hard, you know.'

Saying that, she met his eyes. There was a smile in them, and one so reassuring, so—she knew not what—that she was tempted to add :

' You know best what I want. I shall trust you.'

Something shook the man from head to foot. The words which came from him were involuntary ; he heard them as if another had spoken.

' You trust me ? You believe that I would do my best to please you ? '

Thyrza felt a strangeness in his words, but replied to them with a frank smile :

' I think so, Mr. Grail.'

He was holding his hand to her ; mechanically she gave hers. But in the doing it she became frightened ; his face had altered, it was as if he suffered a horrible pain. Then she heard :

' Will you trust your life to me, Thyrza ? '

It was like a flash, dazzling her brain. Never in her idlest moment had she strayed into a thought of this. He had always seemed to her comparatively an old man, and his gravity would in itself have prevented her from viewing him as a possible suitor. He seemed so buried in his books ; he was so unlike the men who had troubled her with attentions hitherto. Yet he held her hand, and surely his words could have but one meaning.

Gilbert saw how disconcerted, how almost shocked, she was.

' I didn't mean to say that at once,' he continued hurriedly, releasing her hand. ' I've been too hasty. You didn't expect that. It isn't fair to you. Will you sit down ? '

He still spoke without guidance of his tongue. He was impelled by a vast tenderness ; the startled look on her face made him reproach himself ; he sought to soothe her, and was incoherent, awkward. As if in implicit obedience, she moved to a chair. He stood gazing at her, and the love which had at length burst from the dark depths seized upon all his being.

'Mr. Grail——'

She began, but her voice failed. She looked at him, and he was smitten to the heart to see that there were tears in her eyes.

'If it gives you pain,' he said in a low voice, drawing near to her, 'forget that I said anything. I wouldn't for my life make you feel unhappy.'

Thyrza smiled through her tears. She saw how gentle his expression had become; his voice touched her. The reverence which she had always felt for him grew warmer under his gaze, till it was almost the affection of a child for a father.

'But should I be the right kind of wife for you, Mr. Grail?' she asked, with a strange simplicity and diffidence. 'I know so little.'

'Can you think of being my wife?' he said, in tones that shook with restrained emotion. 'I am so much older than you, but you are the first for whom I have ever felt love. And'—here he tried to smile—'it is very sure that I shall love you as long as I live.'

Her breast heaved; she held out both her hands to him and said quickly:

'Yes, I will marry you, Mr. Grail. I will try my best to be a good wife to you.'

He stood as if doubting. Both her hands were together in his; he searched her blue eyes, and their depths rendered to him a sweetness and purity before which his heart bowed in worship. Then he leaned forward and kissed her forehead.

Thyrza reddened and kept her eyes down.

'May I go now?' she said, when, after kissing her hands, he had released them at the first feeling that they were being drawn away.

'If you wish to, Thyrza.'

'I'll stay if you like, Mr. Grail, but—I think——'

She had risen. The warmth would not pass from her cheeks, and the sensation prevented her from looking up; she desired to escape and be alone.

'Will you come down and speak to mother in the morning?' Gilbert said, relieving her from the necessity of adding more. 'She will have something to tell you.'

'Yes, I'll come. Good-night, Mr. Grail.'

Both had forgotten the book that was to have been selected. Thyrza gave her hand as she always did when taking leave of him, save that she could not meet his eyes. He held it a little longer than usual, then saw her turn and leave the room hurriedly.

An hour later, when Mrs. Grail came into the parlour, Gilbert drew from its envelope and handed to her the letter he had received from Egremont on Christmas Eve. She read it, and turned round to him with astonishment.

'Why didn't you tell me this, child? Well now, if I didn't *think* there was something that night! Have you answered? Oh no, you're not to answer for a week.'

'What's your advice?'

'Eh, how that reminds me of your father!' the old lady exclaimed. 'I've heard him speak just with that voice and that look many a time. Well, well, my dear, it's only waiting, you see; something comes soon or late to those that deserve it. I'm glad I've lived to see this, Gilbert.'

He said, when they had talked of it for a few minutes:

'Will you show this to Thyrza to-morrow morning?'

She fixed her eyes on him, over the top of her spectacles, keenly.

'To be sure I will. Yes, yes, of course I will.'

'She's been here for a few minutes since tea. I told her if she'd come down in the morning you'd have something to tell her.'

'She's been here? But why didn't you call me?- I must go up and speak.'

'Not to-night, mother. It was better that you weren't here. I had something to say to her—something I wanted to say before she heard of this. Now she has a right to know.'

Lydia returned shortly after eight o'clock. She had walked about aimlessly for an hour and a half, avoiding the places where she was likely to meet anyone she knew. She was chilled and wretched.

Thyrza said nothing till her sister had taken off her hat and jacket and seated herself.

'When did you see Mr. Ackroyd last?' she inquired.

'I'm sure I don't know,' was the reply. 'I passed him in the Walk about a week ago.'

' But, I mean, when did you speak to him ? '

' Oh, not for a long time,' said Lydia, smoothing the hair upon her forehead. ' Why ? '

' He seems to have forgotten all about me, Lyddy.'

The other looked down into the speaker's face with eyes that were almost startled.

' Why do you say that, dear ? '

' Do you think he has ? '

' He may have done,' replied Lydia, averting her eyes. ' I don't know. You said you wanted him to, Thyrza.'

' Yes, I did—in that way. But I asked him to be friends with us. I don't see why he should keep away from us altogether.'

' But it's only what you had to expect,' said Lydia, rather coldly. In a moment, however, she had altered her voice to add : ' He couldn't be friends with us in the way you mean, dear. Have you been thinking about him ? '

She showed some anxiety.

' Yes,' said Thyrza, ' I often think about him—but not because I'm sorry for what I did. I shall never be sorry for that. Shall I tell you why ? It's something you'd never guess if you tried all night. You could no more guess it than you could—I don't know what ! '

Lydia looked inquiringly.

' Put your arm round me and have a nice face. As soon as you'd gone to chapel, I thought I'd go down and ask Mr. Grail to lend me a book. I went and knocked at the door, and Mr. Grail was there alone. And he asked me to come and choose a book, and we began to talk, and—Lyddy, he asked me if I'd be his wife.'

Lydia's astonishment was for the instant little less than that which had fallen upon Thyrza when she felt her hand in Grail's. Her larger experience, however, speedily brought her to the right point of view; in less time than it would have taken her to express surprise, her wits had arranged a number of little incidents which remained in her memory, and had reviewed them all in the light of this disclosure. This was the meaning of Mr. Grail's reticence, of his apparent coldness at times. Surely she was very dull never to have surmised it. Yet he was so much older than Thyrza ; he was so confirmed a student ; no, she had never suspected this feeling.

All this in a flash of consciousness, whilst she pressed her sister closer to her side. Then :

'And what did you say, dear?'

'I said I would, Lyddy.'

The elder sister became very grave. She bit first her lower, then her upper lip.

'You said that at once, Thyrza?'

'Yes. I felt I must.'

'You felt you must?'

Thyrza could but inadequately explain what she meant by this. The words involved a truth, but one of which she had no conscious perception. Gilbert Grail was a man of strong personality, and in no previous moment of life had his being so uttered itself in look and word as when involuntarily he revealed his love. More, the vehemence of his feeling went forth in that subtle influence with which forcible natures are able to affect now an individual, now a crowd. Thyrza was very susceptible of such impression; the love which had become all-potent in Gilbert's heart sensibly moved her own. Ackroyd had had no power to touch her so; his ardour had never appealed to her imagination with such constraining reality. Grail was the first to make her conscious of the meaning of passion. It was not passion which rose within her to reply to his, but the childlike security in which she had hitherto lived was at an end; love was henceforth to be the preoccupation of her soul.

She answered her sister:

'I couldn't refuse him. He said he should love me as long as he lived, and I felt that it was true. He didn't try to persuade me, Lyddy. When I showed how surprised I was, he spoke very kindly, and wanted me to have time to think.'

'But, dearest, you say you were surprised. You hadn't thought of such a thing—I'm sure I hadn't. How could you say "yes" at once?'

'But have I done wrong, Lyddy?'

Lydia was again busy with conjecture, in woman's way rapidly reading secrets by help of memory and intuition. She connected this event with what Mary Bower had reported to her of Ackroyd. If it were indeed true that Ackroyd no longer made pretence of loyalty to his old love, would not Grail's knowledge of that change account for his sudden abandonment of disguise? The two were friends; Grail might well have shrunk from entering into rivalry with the younger man. She felt a convincing clearness in this. Then it was true that Ackroyd had begun to show an interest in Totty Nancarrow;

is was true, she added bitterly, connecting it closely with the other fact, that he haunted public-houses. Something of that habit she had heard formerly, but thought of it as long abandoned. How would he hear of Thyrza's having pledged herself! Assuredly he had not forgotten her. She knew him; he could not forget so lightly; it was Thyrza's disregard that had driven him into folly.

Her sister was repeating the question.

'Oh, why couldn't you feel in the same way to—to the other, Thyrza?' burst from Lydia. 'He loved you and he still loves you. Why didn't you try to feel for him? You don't love Mr. Grail.'

Thyrza drew a little apart.

'I feel I shall be glad to be his wife,' she said firmly. 'I felt I must say "yes," and I don't think I shall ever be sorry. I could *never* have said "yes" to Mr. Ackroyd, Lyddy!' She sprang forward and held her sister again. 'You know why I couldn't! You can't keep secrets from me, though you could from any one else. You know why I could never have wished to marry him!'

They held each other in that unity of perfect love which had hallowed so many moments of their lives. Lydia's face was hidden. But at length she raised it, to ask solemnly:

'It was not because you thought this that you promised Mr. Grail?'

'No, no, no!'

'Blue-eyes, nobody 'll ever love me but you. And I don't think I shall ever have a sad minute if I see that you're happy. I do hope you've done right.'

'I'm sure I have, Lyddy. You must tell Mary to-morrow. And grandad—think how surprised they'll be! Of course, everybody'll know soon. I shall go to work to-morrow, you know; I'm quite well again. And Lyddy, when I'm Mrs. Grail, of course, Mr. Ackroyd 'll come and see us.'

Lydia made no reply to this. She could not tell what had happened between herself and Mary Bower, and the mention of Ackroyd's name was now a distress to her. She moved from her seat, saying that it was long past supper-time.

Thyrza went down to see Mrs. Grail next morning just before setting out for work. The piece of news was communicated to her, and she hastened with it to her sister. But Gilbert had requested that they would as yet speak of it to no one; it was better to wait till Mr. Egremont had himself made the fact known among the members of his class. Lydia was much impressed with Gilbert's behaviour in keeping that good fortune a secret in the interview with Thyrza. It heightened her already high opinion of him, and encouraged her to look forward with hope. Yet hope would not come without much bidding; doubts and anxieties knocked only too freely at her heart.

One evening Lydia, returning from making a purchase for Mrs. Grail, met Ackroyd. It was at the Kennington Road end of Walnut Tree Walk. He seemed to be waiting. He raised his hat; Lydia bent her head and walked past; but a quick step sounded behind her.

'Miss Trent! Will you stop a minute?'

She turned. Luke held out his hand.

'It's a long time since we spoke a word,' he said, with friendliness. 'But we're not always going to pass each other like that, are we?'

Lydia smiled; it was all she could do. She did not know for certain that he had yet heard the news.

'I want you,' he continued 'to give your sister my good wishes. Will you?'

'Yes, I will, Mr. Ackroyd.'

'Grail came and told me all about it. It wasn't pleasant to hear, but he's a good fellow and I'm not surprised at his luck. I haven't felt I wanted to quarrel with him, and I think better of myself for that. And yet it means a good deal to me —more than you think, I dare say.'

'You'll soon forget it, Mr. Ackroyd,' Lydia said, in a clear, steady voice.

'Well, you ll see if I do. I'm one of the unlucky fellows that can never show what they feel. It all comes out in the wrong way. It doesn't matter much now.'

Lydia had a feeling that this was not wholly sincere. He seemed to take a pleasure in representing himself as luckless. Combined with what she had heard, it helped her to say:

'A man doesn't suffer much from these things. You'll soon be cheerful again. Good-bye, Mr. Ackroyd.'

She did not wait for anything more from him.

CHAPTER XI

A MAN WITH A FUTURE

MR. DALMAINE first turned his attention to politics at the time when the question of popular education was to the front in British politics. It was an excellent opportunity for would-be legislators conscious of rhetorical gifts and only waiting for some safe, simple subject whereon to exercise them. Both safe and simple was the topic which all and sundry were then called upon to discuss ; it was impossible not to have views on education (have we not all been educated ?), and delightfully easy to support them by prophecy. Never had the vaticinating style of oratory a greater vogue. Never was a richer occasion for the utterance of wisdom such as recommends itself to the British public.

Mr. Dalmaine understood the tastes and habits of that public as well as most men of his standing. After one abortive attempt to enter Parliament, he gained his seat for Vauxhall at the election of 1874, and from the day of his success he steadily applied himself to the political profession. He was then two-and-thirty ; for twelve years he had been actively engaged in commerce and now held the position of senior partner in a firm owning several factories in Lambeth. Such a training was valuable ; politics he viewed as business on a larger scale, and business, the larger its scale the better, was his one enthusiasm. His education had not been liberal ; he saw that that made no difference, and wisely pursued the bent of his positive mind where another man might have wasted his time in the attempt to gain culture. He saw that his was the age of the practical. Let who would be an idealist, the practical man in the end got all that was worth having.

He worked. You might have seen him, for instance, in his study one Sunday morning in the January which the story has now reached ; a glance at him showed that he was no idler in fields of art or erudition ; blue-books were heaped about him, books bound in law calf lay open near his hand, newspapers monopolised one table. He was interested in all that concerns the industrial population of Great Britain ; he was making that subject his speciality ; he meant to link his name with factory Acts, with education Acts, with Acts for the better housing of the work-folk, with what not of the kind. And the single working man for whom he veritably cared one jot was Mr. James Dalmaine.

He was rather a good-looking fellow, a well-built, sound, red-bearded Englishman. His ears were not quite so close against his head as they should be; his lips might have had a more urbane expression; his hand might have been a trifle less weighty; but when he stood up with his back to the fire and looked musingly along the cornice of the room, one felt that his appearance on a platform would conciliate those right-thinking electors who desire that Parliament should represent the comely, beef-fed British breed. He was fairly well-to-do, though some held that he had speculated a little rashly of late; he felt very strongly, however, that his pedestal must be yet more solid before he could claim the confidence of his countrymen with the completeness that he desired. Of late he had given thought to a particular scheme, and not at all a disagreeable one, for enhancing his social, and therefore political, credit. He was thinking of her—the scheme, I would say—at present.

These chambers of his were in Westminster; they were spacious, convenient; he had received deputations from his constituents here. Lambeth was only just over the water; he liked to be near, for it was one of his hobbies, one of the very few that he allowed himself, to keep thoroughly cognisant of the affairs of his borough—which, as you are aware, includes the district of Lambeth—even of its petty affairs. Some day, he said to himself, he would in this way overlook Great Britain—would have her statistics at his finger-ends, would change here, confirm there, guide everywhere. In the meantime he satisfied himself with this section. He knew what was going on in workmen's clubs, in places of amusement, in the market streets. There is a pleasure in surveying from a height the doing and driving of ordinary mortals; a member for Vauxhall studying his borough in this spirit naturally comes to feel himself a sort of Grand Duke.

It was one o'clock. There came a knock at the door, followed by the appearance of a middle-aged man who silently proclaimed himself a secretary. This was Mr. Tasker; he had served Mr. Dalmaine thus for three years, prior to which he had been employed as a clerk at the works in Lambeth. Mr. Dalmaine first had his attention drawn to Tasker eight or nine years before, by an instance of singular shrewdness in the latter's discharge of his duties. From that day he kept his eye on him—took opportunities of advancing him. Tasker was born with a love of politics and with a genius for detail ; Mr. Dalmaine discovered all this, and, when the due season came, raised him to the dignity of his private scribe. Tasker regarded his employer as his earthly Providence, was devoted to him, served him admirably. It was the one instance of Mr. Dalmaine's having interested himself in an individual ; he had no thought of anything but his own profit in doing so, but none the less he had made a mortal happy. You observe the beneficence that lies in practicality.

Before going to luncheon on a Sunday it was Mr. Dalmaine's practice to talk of things in general with his secretary. To-day, among other questions, he asked, with a meaning smile :

' What of young Egremont's lectures ? Has he recommenced ? '

' The first of the new course is to-night,' replied Mr. Tasker, who sat bending a paper-cutter over his leg. Mr. Dalmaine, knowing his secretary, encouraged him to be on easy terms. In truth, he had a liking for Tasker. Partly it reciprocated the other's feeling, no doubt ; and then one generally looks with indulgence on a man whom one has discovered and developed.

' Does he go on with his literature ? '

' No. The title is, " Thoughts for the Present." '

Mr. Dalmaine leaned back and laughed. It was a hearty laugh.

' I foresaw it, I foresaw it ! And how many hearers has he ? '

' Six only.'

' To be sure.'

' But there is something more. Mr. Egremont is going to present Lambeth with a free public library. He has taken a building.'

' A fact ? How do you know that, Tasker ? '

' I heard it at the club last night. He has informed the members of his class.'

' Ha ! He is really going to bleed himself to prove his sincerity ? '

They discussed the subject a little longer. Then Mr.

K

Dalmaine dictated a letter or two that he wished to have off his mind, and after that bade Tasker good-day.

At half-past four in the afternoon he drove up to a house at Lancaster Gate, where he had recently been a not infrequent visitor. The servant preceded him with becoming stateliness to the drawing-room, and announced his name in the hearing of three ladies, who were pleasantly chatting in the aroma of tea. The eldest of them was Mrs. Tyrrell; her companions were Miss Tyrrell and a young married lady paying a call.

Mrs. Tyrrell was one of those excellently preserved matrons who testify to the wholesome placidity of woman's life in wealthy English homes. Her existence had taken for granted the perfection of the universe ; probably she had never thought of a problem which did not solve itself for the pleasant trouble of stating it in refined terms, and certainly it had never occurred to her that social propriety was distinguishable from the Absolute Good. She was not a dull woman, and the opposite of an unfeeling one, but her wits and her heart had both been so subdued to the social code, that it was very difficult for her to entertain seriously any mode of thought or action for which she could not recall a respectable precedent. By nature she was indulgent, of mild disposition, of sunny intelligence ; so endowed, circumstances had bidden her regard it as the end of her being to respect conventions, to check her native impulse if ever it went counter to the opinion of Society, to use her intellect for the sole purpose of discovering how far it was permitted to be used. And she was a happy woman, had always been a happy woman. She had known a little trouble in relation to her favourite sister's marriage with Mr. Newthorpe, for she foresaw that it could not turn out very well, and she had been obliged to censure her sister for excessive devotion to the pleasures of Society ; it grieved her, on the other hand, to think of her poor niece being brought up in a way so utterly opposed to all the traditions. But these were only little ripples on the smooth flowing surface. You knew that she would never be smitten down with a great sorrow : she was of those whom Fate must needs respect, so gracefully and sweetly do they accept happiness as their right.

Mr. Dalmaine joined these ladies with the manner of the sturdy Briton who would make himself agreeable yet dreads the *petit maître*. His voice would have been better if a little more subdued ; he seated himself with perhaps rather more of ease than of grace; but on the whole Society would have let him pass muster as a well-bred man.

'You are interested in all that concerns your constituency, Mr. Dalmaine,' said Mrs. Tyrrell; 'we were speaking of Mr. Egremont's plan of founding a library in Lambeth. You have heard of it?'

'Oh yes.'

'Do you think it will be a good thing?'

'I am very doubtful. One doesn't like to speak unkindly of such admirable intentions, but I really think that in this he is working on a wrong principle. I so strongly object to *giving* anything when it's in the power of people to win it for themselves with a little wholesome exertion. Now, there's the Free Library Act; if the people of Lambeth really want a library, let them tax themselves and adopt the statutory scheme. Sincerely, I believe that Mr. Egremont will do more harm than good. We must avoid anything that tends to pauperise the working classes.'

'How amusing!' exclaimed Paula. 'It's almost word for word what mamma's just been saying.'

Paula was dressed in the prettiest of tea-gowns; she looked the most exquisite of conservatory flowers. Her smile to Mr. Dalmaine was very gracious.

'That really is how I felt,' said Mrs. Tyrrell. 'But Mr. Egremont will never be persuaded of that. He *is* so whole-hearted in his desire to help these poor people, yet, I'm afraid, so very, very unpractical.'

The young married lady observed:

'Oh, no one ought *ever* to interfere with philanthropy unless they have a *very* practical scheme. Canon Brougham was *so* emphatic on that point this morning. So *much* harm may be done, when we mean everything for the best.'

'Yes, I feel that very strongly,' said Dalmaine, his masculine accent more masculine than ever after the plaintive piping. 'I even fear that Mr. Egremont is doing wrong in making his lectures free. We may be sure they are well worth paying to hear, and it's an axiom in all dealing with the working class that they will never value anything that they don't pay for.'

'Oh, but Mr. Dalmaine,' protested Paula, 'you couldn't ask Mr. Egremont to take money at the door!'

'It sounds shocking, Miss Tyrrell, but if Mr. Egremont stands before them as a teacher, he ought to charge for his lessons. I assure you they would put a far higher value on his lectures. I grieve to hear that his class has fallen off. I could have foreseen that. The basis is not sound. To put it in plain, even coarse, language, all social reform must be undertaken on strictly commercial principles.'

' How I should like to hear you say that to Mr. Egremont! ' remarked Paula. ' Oh, his face ! '

'Mr. Egremont is an idealist,' said Mrs. Tyrrell, smiling.

'Surely the very *last* kind of person to attempt social reform ! ' exclaimed the young married lady.

The conversation drew off into other channels. Mr. Dalmaine was supplied with the clearest opinions on every topic, and he had a way of delivering them which was most effective with persons of Mrs. Tyrrell's composition. In everything he affected sobriety. If he had to express a severe judgment, it was done with gentlemanly regret. If he commended anything, he did so with a judicial air. In fact, it would not have been easy to imagine Mr. Dalmaine speaking with an outburst of natural fervour on any topic whatsoever. His view was the view of common sense, and he enunciated the barrenest convictions in a tone which would have suited profound originality.

A week later there was a dinner party at the Tyrrells, and Egremont was among the bidden. He had persisted in his tendency to hold aloof from general society, in spite of many warnings from Mrs. Ormonde, but he could not, short of ingratitude, wholly absent himself from his friends at Lancaster Gate. Mrs. Tyrrell was no exception to the rule in her attitude to Egremont ; as did all matronly ladies, she held him in very warm liking, and sincerely hoped that a young man so admirably fitted for the refinements of social life would in time get rid of his extravagant idealism. A little of that was graceful ; Society was beginning to view it with favour when confined within the proper bounds ; but to carry it into act, and waste one's life in wholly unpractical—nay, in positively harmful—enterprise was a sad thing. She had reasoned with him, but he showed himself so perverted in his sense of the fitness of things that the task had to be abandoned as hopeless. And yet the good lady liked him. She had hoped, and not so long ago, that he might some day desire to stand in a nearer relation to her than that of a friend, but herein again she felt that her wish was growing futile. Paula indulged in hints with reference to her cousin Annabel, and

Mrs. Tyrrell began to fear that the strangely educated girl might be the cause of Walter's extreme aberrations.

Egremont arrived early on the evening of the dinner. Only one guest had preceded him. With Mrs. Tyrrell and Paula were Mr. Tyrrell and the son of the house, Mr. John, the Jack Tyrrell of sundry convivial clubs in town. Mr. Tyrrell senior was a high-coloured jovial gentleman of three score, great in finance, practical to the backbone, yet with wit and tact which put him at ease with all manner of men, even with social reformers. These latter amused him vastly; he failed to see that the world needed any reforming whatever, at all events beyond that which is constitutionally provided for in the proceedings of the British Parliament. He had great wealth; he fared sumptuously every day; things shone to him in a rosy after-dinner light. Not a gross or a selfish man, for he was as good-natured as he was contented, and gave very freely of his substance; it was simply his part in the world to enjoy the product of other men's labour and to set an example of glorious self-satisfaction. Egremont, in certain moods, had tried to despise Mr. Tyrrell, but he never quite succeeded. Nor indeed was the man contemptible. Had you told him with frank conviction that you deemed him a poor sort of phenomenon, he would have shaken the ceiling with laughter and have admired you for your plain-speaking. For there was a large and generous vigour about him, and adverse criticism could only heighten his satisfaction in his own stability.

Something of the cold dignity in which she had taken refuge at Ullswater was still to be remarked in Paula's manner as she received Egremont. She held her charming head erect, and let her eyelids droop a little, and the few words which she addressed to him were rather absently spoken. With others, as they arrived, she was sportively intimate. Her bearing had gained a little in maturity during the past half year, but it was still with a blending of *naïveté* and capricious affectation that she wrought her spell. Her dress was a miracle, and inseparably a part of her; it was impossible to picture her in any serious situation, so entirely was she a child of luxury and frivolous concern. Exquisite as an artistic product of Society, she affected the imagination not so much by her personal charm as through the perfume of luxury which breathed about her. Egremont, with his radical tendencies of thought, found himself marvelling as he regarded her; what a life was hers! Compare it with that of some

little work-girl in Lambeth, such as he saw in the street—
what spaces between those two worlds! Was it possible that
this dainty creation, this thing of material omnipotence, would
suffer decay of her sweetness and in the end die? The
reason took her side and revolted against law ; it would be an
outrage if time or mischance laid hold upon her.

Yet there was something in Paula which he did not
recognise. Since she could formulate desires, few had found
impression on her lips which were not at once gratified ; an
exception caused her at first rather astonishment than impatience. Such astonishment fell upon her when she understood that Egremont's coming to Ullswater was not on her
account. In truth, she wished it had been, and from that
moment the fates were kind enough to notice Paula's poor
little existence, and bid her remember she was mortal. She
took the admonition ill, and certainly it was impertinent from
her point of view. She had slight philosophy, but out of that
disappointment Paula by degrees drew an understanding that
she had had a glimpse of a strange world, that something of
moment had been at stake.

Egremont, standing in the rear of a chatting group, had all
but dreamed himself into oblivion of the present when he heard
loud announcement of ' Mr. Dalmaine.' It was some time since
he had met the Member for Vauxhall. Looking upon the
politician's well-knit frame, his well-coloured face with its expression of shrewd earnestness, he for a moment seemed to
himself to shrink into insignificance. After sitting opposite
Dalmaine for an hour at the dinner-table, he was able to regard the man again in what he deemed a true light. But the
impression made upon one by an object suddenly presented
when the thought is busy with far other things will as a rule
embody much essential truth. As a force, Egremont would
not have weighed in the scale against Dalmaine. Putting
himself in conscious opposition to such a man, he had but his
due in a sense of nullity.

Mr. Tyrrell was kind to him in the assignment of a partner.
A pretty, gentle, receptive maiden, anxious to show interest in
things of the mind—with such a one Walter was at his best,
because his simplest and happiest. He put away thought of
Lambeth—which in truth was beginning to trouble his mind
like a fixed idea—and talked much as he would have done a
couple of years ago, with bright intelligence, with natural
enjoyment of the hour. It was greatly his charm in such con-

versation that had made him a favourite with pleasant people of the world. In withdrawing himself from the sphere of these amenities he was opposing the free growth of his character, which in consequence suffered. He was cognisant of that; he knew that he was more himself to-night than he had been for some months. But the fixed idea waited in the background.

When the ladies were gone, he saw Dalmaine rise and come round the table towards him.

'I'm glad to see you again,' Dalmaine began, depositing his wine-glass and refilling it. 'Pray tell me something about your lectures. You have resumed since Christmas, I think?'

Egremont had no mind to speak of these things. It cost him an effort to find an answer.

'Yes, I still have a few hearers.'

And at once he was angry with himself for falling into this confession of failure. Dalmaine was the last man before whom he would affect humility.

'I am sure,' observed the politician, 'everyone who has the good of the working classes at heart must feel indebted to you. It's so very seldom that men of culture care to address audiences of that kind. Yet it must be the most effectual way of reaching the people. You address them on English Literature, I think?'

Egremont did not care to explain that he had now a broader subject. He murmured an affirmative. Dalmaine had hoped to elicit some of the 'Thoughts for the Present,' and felt disappointment.

'An excellent choice, it seems to me,' he continued, making his glass revolve on the table-cloth. 'They are much too ignorant of the best wealth of their country. They have so few inducements to read the great historians, for instance. If you can bring them to do so, you make them more capable citizens, abler to form a judgment on the questions of the day.

Egremont smiled.

'My one aim,' he remarked, 'is to persuade them to forget that there are such things as questions of the day.'

Dalmaine also smiled, and with a slight involuntary curling of the lip.

'Ah, I remember our discussions on the Atlantic. I scarcely thought you would apply those ideas in their—their fulness, when you began practical work. You surely will admit that, in a time when their interests are engaging so much attention, working men should—for instance—go to the polls with intelligent preparation.'

'I'd rather they didn't go to the polls at all,' Walter replied. He knew that this was exaggeration, but it pleased him to exaggerate. He enjoyed the effect on the honourable member's broad countenance.

'Come, come!' said Dalmaine, laughing with appearance of entering into the joke. 'At that rate, English freedom would soon be at an end. One might as well abolish newspapers.'

'In my opinion, the one greatest boon that could be granted the working class. I do my best to dissuade them from the reading of newspapers.'

Dalmaine turned the whole matter into a jest. Secretly he believed that Egremont was poking contemptuous fun at him, but it was his principle to receive everything with good-humour. They drew apart again, each feeling more strongly than ever the instinctive opposition between their elements. It amounted to a reciprocal dislike, an irritation provoked by each other's presence. Dalmaine was beginning to suspect Egremont of some scheme too deep for his fathoming ; it was easier for him to believe anything, than that idealism pure and simple was at the bottom of such behaviour. Walter, on the other hand, viewed the politician's personality with something more than contempt. Dalmaine embodied those forces of philistinism, that essence of the vulgar creed, which Egremont had undertaken to attack, and which, as he already felt, were likely to yield as little before his efforts as a stone wall under the blow of a naked hand. Two such would do well to keep apart.

On returning to the drawing-room, Egremont kept watch for a vacant place by Paula. Presently he was able to move to her side. She spread her fan upon her lap, and, ruffling its edge of white fur, said negligently :

'So you decided to waste an evening, Mr. Egremont.'

'I decided to have an evening of rest and enjoyment.'

'I suppose you are working dreadfully hard. When do you open your library ? '

'Scarcely in less than four or five months.'

'And will you stand at the counter and give out books, like the young men at Mudie's ? '

'Sometimes, I dare say. But I have found a librarian.'

' Who is he ? '

'A working man in Lambeth. One of the most sympathetic natures I have ever met ; a man who might have gone on all his life making candles—that is how things are arranged.'

' Making candles ? What a funny change of occupation ! And you really think you are doing good in that disagreeable place ? '

' I can only hope.'

'You are quite sure you are not doing harm ? '

' Does it seem to you that I am ? '

Paula assumed an air of wisdom.

' Of course I have no right to speak of such things, but it is my opinion that you are destroying their sense of self-respect. I don't think they ought to have things *given* them ; they should be encouraged to help themselves.'

He examined her face. It was obvious that this profound sentiment had not taken birth in Paula's charming little head, and he guessed from whom she had derived it.

' I have no doubt Mr. Dalmaine would agree with you,' he said, smiling. ' I believe I have heard him say something of the kind.'

' I'm glad to hear it. Mr. Dalmaine is an authority in such matters.'

' And I, the very reverse of one ? '

' Well, I really do think, Mr. Egremont, that you are taking up things for which you are not—not exactly suited, you know.'

She said it with the prettiest air of patronage, looking at him for a moment, then, as usual, letting her eyes wander about the room.

' Miss Tyrrell,' he replied, with gravity that was half genuine, ' tell me for what I *am* exactly suited, and you will do me a vast kindness.'

She reflected.

' Oh, there are lots of things you do very nicely indeed. I've seen you play croquet beautifully. But I've always thought it a pity you weren't a clergyman.'

Walter laughed.

' Well, a local preacher is next to it.'

Both were at once carried back to the evening at Ullswater. Paula kept silence ; her eyes were directed towards Dalmaine, who almost at the same moment looked towards her. She played with her fan.

'You know that my uncle has been ill?' she said.

'No, I have heard nothing of that.'

Paula looked surprised.

'Don't you hear from—from them?'

'I have a letter from Mr. Newthorpe very occasionally But surely the illness has not been serious?'

'Mamma heard this morning about it. I don't know what's been the matter. I shouldn't wonder if they come to London before long.'

Egremont shortly changed his place, and saw that Dalmaine took the vacant seat by Paula. The two seemed to get on very well together. Paula was evidently exerting herself to be charming; Dalmaine was doing his best to trifle.

He sought more information from Mrs. Tyrrell regarding Mr. Newthorpe. She seemed to fear that her brother-in-law might have been in more danger than Annabel in her letter admitted.

'They certainly must come south,' she said. 'They are having a terrible winter, and it has evidently tried Mr. Newthorpe beyond his strength. You have influence with him, I believe, Mr. Egremont. Pray join me in my efforts to bring them both back to civilisation.'

'I fear my influence will effect nothing if yours fails,' said Walter. 'But Mr. Newthorpe should certainly not risk his health.'

He next had a chat with Mr. John Tyrrell, junior. Paula's brother was two-and-twenty, a frankly sensual youth, of admirable temper, great in turf matters, with a genius for conviviality. Jack's health was perfect, for he had his father's habit of enjoying life without excess, and his stamina allowed a wide limit to the term moderation. Like the rest of his family, he had the secret of conciliating goodwill; there was no humbug in him, and one respected him as a fine specimen of the young male developed at enormous expense. For Egremont he had a certain reverence: a man who habitually thought was clearly, he admitted, of a higher grade than himself, and he had no objection whatever to proclaim his own inferiority. Egremont, talking with him, was half disposed to envy Jack Tyrrell. What a simple thing life was with limitless cash, a perfect digestion, and good-humour in the place of brains!

His room seemed very cold and lonely when he got back to it shortly before midnight. The fire had been let out; the books round the walls had a musty appearance; there was stale tobacco in the air. He paced the floor, thinking of Annabel, wondering whether she would soon be in London, longing to see her. And before he went to bed, he wrote a letter to Mr. Newthorpe, expressing the anxiety with which he had heard of his illness. Of himself he said little; the few words that came to his pen concerning the Lambeth crusade were rather lifeless.

He was being talked of meanwhile in the Tyrrells' drawing-room. The last guests being gone, there was chat for a few minutes between the members of the family.

'Egremont isn't looking quite up to the mark,' said Mr. Tyrrell, as he stood before the fire, hands in pockets.

'I thought the same,' said his wife. 'He seems worried. What a deplorable thing it is, to think that he will spend large sums of money on this library scheme!'

Mr. Tyrrell made inarticulate noises, and at length laughed.

'He must amuse himself in his own way.'

'But after all, papa,' said Paula, whose advocacy went much by the rule of contraries, 'it must be a good thing to give people books to read. I dare say it prevents them from going to the public-house.'

'Shouldn't wonder if it does, Paula,' he replied, with a benevolent gaze.

'Then what's your objection?'

'I don't object to the library in particular. It's only that Egremont isn't the man to do these kind of things. It is to be hoped that he'll get tired of it, and find something more in his line.'

'What *is* his line?'

'Ah, that's the question! Very likely he hasn't one at all. It seems to me there's a good many young fellows in that case nowadays. They have education, they have money, and they don't know what the deuce to do with either one or the other. They're a cut above you, Mr. Jack; it isn't enough for them to live and enjoy themselves. So they get it into their heads that they're called upon to reform the world—a nice handy little job, that'll keep them going. The girls, I notice, are beginning to have the same craze. I shouldn't wonder if Paula gets an idea that she'll be a hospital-nurse, or go district-visiting in Bethnal Green.'

'I certainly should if I thought it would amuse me,' said Paula. 'But why shouldn't Mr. Egremont do work of this kind? He's in earnest; he doesn't only do it for fun.'

'Of course he's in earnest, and there's the absurdity of it. Social reform, pooh! Why, who are the real social reformers? The men who don't care a scrap for the people, but take up ideas because they can make capital out of them. It isn't idealists who do the work of the world, but the hard-headed, practical, selfish men. A big employer of labour 'll do more good in a day, just because he sees profit 'll come of it, than all the mooning philanthropists in a hundred years. Nothing solid has ever been gained in this world that wasn't pursued out of self-interest. Look at Dalmaine. How much do you think he cares for the factory-hands he's always talking about? But he'll do them many a good turn; he'll make many a life easier; and just because it's his business to do so, because it's the way of advancing himself. He aims at being Home Secretary one of these days, and I shouldn't wonder if he is. There's your real social reformer. Egremont's an amateur, a dilettante. In many ways he's worth a hundred of Dalmaine, but Dalmaine will benefit the world, and it's well if Egremont doesn't do harm.'

In all which it is not impossible that Mr. John Tyrrell hit the nail on the head. Much satisfied with his little oration, he went off to don a jacket and enjoy a cigar by his smoking-room fire.

A couple of days later, Mr. Dalmaine called at the house before luncheon. After speaking with Mrs. Tyrrell, he had a private interview with Paula. The event was referred to in a letter Paula addressed to her cousin Annabel in the course of the ensuing week.

'Dear Bell,—We are much relieved by your letter. It is of course impossible to stay among those mountains for the rest of the winter; I hope uncle will very soon be well enough to come south. The plan of living at Eastbourne for a time is no doubt a good one. You'll have Mrs. Ormonde to talk to. She is very nice, though I've generally found her a little serious: but then she's like you in that. I think it's a pity people trouble themselves about things that only make them gloomy.

'I have a little piece of news for you. It really looks as if I was going to be married. In fact, I've said I would be, and I think it likely I shall keep my word. My name will be Mrs. Dalmaine. Don't you remember Mr. Egremont speaking of Mr. Dalmaine and calling him names? From that moment I made up my mind that he must be a very nice man, and when we made his acquaintance I found that I wasn't so far wrong. You see, poor Mr. Egremont so hates everything and everybody that's practical. Now I'm practical, as you know, so it's right I should marry a practical man. Papa has the highest opinion of Mr. Dalmaine's abilities ; he thinks he has a great future in politics. Wouldn't it be delightful if one's husband really became Prime Minister or something of the kind !

'Do you know, it really *is* a pity that Mr. Egremont is going on in this way ! He's going to spend enormous sums of money in establishing a library in Lambeth. It's very good of him, of course, but we are all so sure it's a mistake. Shall I tell you *my own* view ? Mr. Egremont is an idealist, and idealists are *not* the people to do serious work of this kind. The real social reformers are the hard-headed, practical men, who at heart care only for their own advancement. If you think, I'm sure you'll find this is true. You see that I am beginning to occupy myself with serious questions. It will be necessary in the wife of an active politician. But if you *could* hint to Mr. Egremont that he is going shockingly astray ! He dined with us the other night, and doesn't look at all well. I am so afraid lest he is doing all this just because you tell him to. Is it so ?

'But I have fifty other letters to write. My best love to uncle ; tell him to get well as quickly as possible. I wonder that dreadful lonely place hasn't killed you both. I shall be *so* glad to see you again, for I do really like you, Bell, and I know you are awfully wise and good. Think of me sometimes and hope that I shall be happy.—Yours affectionately,

'PAULA TYRRELL.'

CHAPTER XII

LIGHTS AND SHADOWS

EGREMONT'S face, it was true, showed that things were not
altogether well with him. It was not ill-health, but mental
restlessness, which expressed itself in the lines of his forehead and the diminished brightness of his eyes. During the
last two months of the year he had felt a constant need of
help, and help such as would alone stead him he could not
find.

It was no mere failing of purpose. He prepared his lectures
as thoroughly as ever, and delivered them with no less zeal
than in the first weeks ; indeed, if anything, his energy grew,
for, since his nearer acquaintance with Gilbert Grail, the
latter's face before him was always an incentive. There was
much to discourage him. More than half his class fell from
lukewarmness to patent indifference ; they would probably present themselves until the end of the course, but it was little
likely that they would recommence with him after Christmas.
He was obliged to recognise the utter absence of idealism from
all save Grail—unless Bunce might be credited with glimmer-
ings of the true light. Yet intellectually he held himself on
firm ground. To have discovered one man such as Grail was
compensation for failure with many others, and the project of
the library was at all times a vista of hope. But Egremont
was not of those who can live on altruism. His life of loneliness irked him, irked him as never yet. The dawn was a
recurrence of weariness; the long nights were cold and blank.

The old unrest, which he had believed at an end when
once 'the task of his life' was discovered, troubled him
through many a cloud-enveloped day. Had he been free, it
would have driven him on new travels. Yet that was no
longer a real resource. He did not desire to see other lands, but
to make a home in his own. And no home was promised him.
The longer he kept apart from Annabel, the dimmer did the
vision of her become ; he held it a sign that he himself was
seldom if ever in her mind. Did he still love her ? Rather
he would have said that there lay in him great faculty of love,
which Annabel, if she willed it, could at a moment bring into

life; she, he believed, in preference to any woman he had known. It was not passion, and the consciousness that it was not, often depressed him. One of his ideals was that of a passion nurtured to be the crowning glory of life. He did not love Annabel in that way; would that he could have done!

This purely personal distress could not but affect his work. A month before the end of the year he came to the resolve to choose a new subject for the succeeding course of lectures. Forgetting all the sound arguments by which he had been led to prefer the simple teaching of a straightforward subject to any more ambitious prophecy, he was now impelled to think out a series of discourses on—well, on things in general. He got hold of the title, 'Thoughts for the Present,' and the temptation to make use of it proved too great. English literature did not hold the average proletarian mind. It had served him to make an acquaintance with a little group of men; now he must address them in a bolder way, reveal to them his personality. Had he not always contemplated such revelation in the end? Yes, when he found his class fit for it. But he was growing impatient with this slow progress— if indeed it could be called progress at all. He would strike a more significant note.

Walter was in danger, as you very well understand. There is no need at this time of day to remind ourselves of teachers who have fallen into the fatal springe of aposto-licism. Men would so fain be prophets, when once they have a fellow mortal by the ear. Egremont could have exposed this risk to you as well as any, yet he deliberately ignored it in his own case—no great novelty that. 'Have I not some-thing veritably to say? Are not thoughts of and for the present surging in my mind? Whereto have we language if not for the purpose of uttering the soul within us?' So he fell to work on his introductory lecture, and for a few days had peace—nay, lived in enthusiasm once more.

His week of absence at Christmas, of which we have heard, was spent again in Jersey. To the roaring music of the Channel breakers he built up his towers and battlements of prophecy. More, he wrote a poem, and for a day wondered whether it might be well to read it to his audience as preface. A friendly sprite whispered in his ear, and saved him from too utter folly. The sprite had not yet forsaken him; woe to him if ever it should! He wrapped the poem in a letter to Mr. Newthorpe, and had a very pleasant reply, written, as he after-

wards heard, only a day or two before Mr. Newthorpe fell ill.
Annabel sent her message ; ' the verses were noble, and pure
as the sea-foam.'

On returning to town, he sent a note to Grail, asking him
to come in the evening to Great Russell Street, or, if that were
inconvenient, to appoint a time for a meeting in Walnut Tree
Walk. Gilbert accepted the invitation, and came for the first
time to Egremont's rooms.

Things were not ill with him, Gilbert Grail. You saw in
the man's visage that he had put off ten years of haggard life.
His dark, deep eyes spoke their meanings with the ardour of
soul's joy ; his cheeks seemed to have filled out, his brows to
have smoothed. It was joy of the purest and manliest. His
life had sailed like some battered, dun-coloured vessel into a
fair harbour of sunlight and blue, and hands were busy giving
to it a brave new aspect. He could scarce think of all his
happiness at once ; the coming release from a hateful drudgery,
and the coming day which would put Thyrza's hand in his,
would not go into one perspective. Sometimes he would all
but forget the one in thinking of the other. Now let the early
mornings be dark and chill as they would, let the sky lower in
its muddy gloom, let weariness of the flesh do its worst—those
two days were approaching. Why, was he not yet young ?
What are five-and-thirty years behind one, when bliss unutterable beckons forward ? It should all be forgotten, that
grimy past poisoned through and through with the stench of
candles. Books, books, and time to use them, and a hearth
about which love is busy—what more can you offer son of man
than these ?

He had written his acceptance, had endeavoured to write
his thanks. The words were ineffectual.

Egremont received him in his study with gladness. This
man had impressed him powerfully, was winning an ever
larger place in his affection. He welcomed him as he would
have done an old friend, for whose coming he had looked with
impatience.

' Do you smoke ? ' he asked.

No, Gilbert did not smoke. The money he formerly spent
on this had long been saved for the purchase of books.
Egremont's after-dinner coffee had to suffice to make cheer.
It was a little time before Grail could speak freely. He had
suffered from nervousness in undertaking this visit, and his
relief at the simplicity of Egremont's rooms, by allowing him

to think of what he wished to say, caused him to seem absent.

'I've already begun to jot down lists of obvious books,' Egremont said. 'I have a good general catalogue here, and I mean to go through it carefully.'

Gilbert was at length able to speak his thought.

'I ought to have said far more than I did in my letter, Mr. Egremont. I tried to thank you, but I felt I might as well have left it alone. I don't know whether you have any idea what this change will mean to me. It's more than saving my life, it's giving me a new one such as I never dared to hope for.'

'I'm right glad to hear it!' Walter replied, with his kindest look. 'It comes to make up to me for some little disappointment in other things. I'm afraid the lectures have been of very slight use.'

'I don't think that. I don't think any of the class 'll forget them. It's likely they'll have their best effect in a little time ; the men 'll think back upon them. Now Bunce has got much out of them, I believe.'

'Ah, Bunce ! Yes, I hoped something from him. By-the-by, he is rather a violent enemy of Christianity, I think ?'

'I've heard so. I don't know him myself, except for meeting him at the lectures. Yes, I've heard he's sometimes almost mad about religious subjects.'

Egremont told the story about Bunce's child, which he had had from Mrs. Ormonde. And this led him on to speak of his purpose in this new course of lectures. After describing his plan :

'And that matter of religion is one I wish to speak of most earnestly. I think I can put forward a few ideas which will help a man like Bunce. He wants to be made to see the attitude of a man who retains no dogma, and yet is far more a friend than an enemy of Christianity. I think that lecture shall come first.'

He had not yet made ready his syllabus. As before, he meant to send it to those whose names were upon his list. His first evening would be at the beginning of February.

'I shall try with Ackroyd again,' he said. 'Perhaps the subject this time will seem more attractive to him.'

Gilbert looked grave.

'I'm anxious about Ackroyd,' he replied. 'He's had private trouble lately, and I begin to be afraid it's driving him into

L

the wrong road. He isn't one that can easily be persuaded.
I wish you might succeed in bringing him to the lectures.'

Egremont tried to speak hopefully, but in secret he felt that
his power over men was not that which draws them from the
way of evil and turns them to light. For that is needed more
than love of the beautiful. For a moment he mused in misgiving over his ' Thoughts for the Present.'

They began to talk of those details in the library scheme
which Egremont had left for subsequent discussion.

' As soon as the premises are in my hands,' he said, ' I shall
have the house thoroughly repaired. I should like you to see
then if any alteration can be made which would add to your
comfort. As soon as the place can be made ready, it will be
yours to take possession of. That should be certainly by the
end of April. Shall you be free to leave your present occupation then ? '

' I can at any time. But I am glad to have a date fixed.
I'm going to be married then.'

It was said with a curious diffidence which brought a smile
to the hearer's face. Egremont was surprised at the intelligence, glad at the same time.

' That is good news,' he said. ' Of course I had thought of
you living with your mother. This will be better still. Your
future wife must, of course, examine the house; no doubt
she'll be a far better judge than you of what needs doing.
When you are back from your honeymoon we shall go to work
together on arranging books. That'll be a rare time ! We
shall throw up our arms, like Dominie Sampson, and cry
" Prodigious ! " '

He grew mirthful, indulging the boyish humour which, as
a reaction from his accustomed lonely silence, came upon him
when he had a sympathetic companion. To Gilbert this was
a new phase of Egremont's character ; he, sober in happiness,
answered the young man's merriment with an expressive
smile.

Grail had merely mentioned the fact of his intended
marriage. When he was alone, Egremont wondered much
within himself what kind of woman such a man might have
chosen to share his life. Had he contemplated marriage for
some time, and been prevented from it by stress of circumstances ? It was not easy to picture the suitable partner for
Grail. Clearly she must be another than the thriftless, shift-
less creature too common in working-class homes. Yet it was

not likely that he had met with any one who could share his inner life. Had he, following the example of many a prudent man, chosen a good, quiet, modest woman, whose first and last anxiety would be to keep his home in order and see that he lacked no comfort within her province to bestow? It was probable. She would no doubt be past youth; suppose her thirty. She would have a face which pleased by its homely goodness; she would speak in a gentle voice, waiting upon superior wisdom.

A few days before that appointed for the first lecture of this new course, Egremont received a letter of which the address surprised him. It bore the Penrith post-mark; the writing must be Annabel's. He had very recently written to Mr. Newthorpe, who was not yet well enough to attempt the journey southwards; this reply by another hand might signify ill news. And that proved to be the case. Annabel wrote:

'Dear Mr. Egremont,—Father desires me to answer your very kind letter of a week ago. He has delayed, hoping from day to day to be able to write himself. I grieve to say that he is suffering more than at any time in the last month. I am very anxious, full of trouble. Mrs. Tyrrell wishes to come to me, and I am writing by this post to say that I shall be very glad of her presence. Our doctors say there is absolutely no ground for fear, and gladly I give them my faith; but it tortures me to see my dear father so overcome with pain. The world seems to me very dark, and life a dreadful penalty.

'We read with the greatest interest of what you are doing and hoping. I cannot tell you how we rejoiced in the happiness of Mr. Grail. That is a glorious thing that you have done. I trust his marriage may be a very happy one. When we are at Eastbourne and father is well again, we must come to see your library and no less your librarian. Do not be discouraged if your lectures seem to fail of immediate results. Surely good work will have fruit, and very likely in ways of which you will never know.

'The Tyrrells will have constant news of father, and I am sure will gladly send it on to you.—I am, dear Mr. Egremont yours sincerely,

'ANNABEL NEWTHORPE.'

It was the first letter he had received from Annabel. For some days he kept it close at hand, and looked over it frequently; then it was laid away with care, not again to be read until the passing of years had given it both a sadder and a dearer significance.

CHAPTER XIII

THYRZA SINGS AGAIN

Egremont had a fear that he might seem ungrateful to the man Bower. It was Bower to whom he had gone for help when he first sought to gather an audience, and on the whole the help had been effectual. Yet Bower had not borne the test of nearer acquaintance; Egremont soon knew the vulgarity of his nature, and had much difficulty in sustaining the show of friendly intercourse with him. One evening in mid-February, he called the portly man to speak with him after lecture, and, with what geniality he could, explained to him the details of his library project and told whom he had chosen for librarian. Bower professed himself highly satisfied with everything, and, as usual, affected Egremont disagreeably with his subservience. The latter was not surprised to find that Grail had kept silence on the subject; but it was time now for the arrangements to be made public.

From the lecture-room, Mr. Bower went to a club where he was wont to relax himself of evenings; here he discussed the library question with such acquaintances as were at hand. He reached home just after the closing of the shop. Mary was gone to bed. Mrs. Bower had just finished her supper, and was musing over the second half of her accustomed pint of ale. Her husband threw himself into a chair, with an exclamation of scornful disgust.

'What's wrong now?' asked Mrs. Bower.

'Well, I don't know what *you'll* call it, but *I* call it the damnedest bit of sneaking behaviour as I ever knew! He's given the librarianship to that fellow Grail. There's the 'ouse at the back for him to live in, and rent free, no doubt; and there's a good lumping salary, *that* you may go bail. Now what do you think o' that job?'

'And him not as much as offerin' it to you!'

'Not so much as offerin' it! How many 'ud he have got to hear his lectures without me, I'd like to know! I shouldn't have taken it; no, of course I shouldn't; it wouldn't a' suited me to take a librarianship. But it was his bounden duty to give me the first offer. I never thought he'd make one of *us* librarian ; if it had been some stranger, I shouldn't have made so much of it. But to give it to Grail in that sneaking, underhanded way ! Why, I'd be ashamed o' myself. I've a rare good mind never to go near his lectures again.'

' You'd better go,' said Mrs. Bower, prudently. ' He might pay you out at the works. It 'ud be a trick just like him, after this.'

' I'll think about it,' returned the other, with dignity, sitting upright, and gathering his broad beard into his hand.

' Why, there now ! ' cried his wife, struck with a sudden thought. ' If that doesn't explain something ! Depend upon it—*depend* upon it—that's how Grail got Thyrza Trent to engage herself to him ! He'll a' known it for some time, Grail will a' done. He's a mean fellow, or he'd never a' gone and set her against Mr. Ackroyd, as it's easy to see he did. He'll a' told her about the 'ouse and the salary, of course he will ! If I didn't think there was something queer in that job ! '

Mr. Bower saw at once how highly probable this was.

' And that is why they've put on such hairs, her an' Lydia,' Mrs. Bower pursued. ' It's all very well for Mary to pretend as there's nothing altered. It's my belief Mary's got to know more than she'll tell, and Lydia's quarrelled with her about it. It's easy enough to see as they *have* fell out. Lydia ain't been to chapel since Christmas, an' you know yourself it was just before Christmas as Egremont went to the 'ouse to see Mr. Grail. If she'd been a bit sharper, she'd never a' told Mary that. I ain't surprised at Thyrza doin' of under-handed things; I've never liked her over-much. But I thought better of Lydia.'

' I've not quarrelled with *them*,' said Mr. Bower, magnani-mously. ' And girls must look out for themselves, and do the best for themselves they can. But that soft-spoken, sneaking Hegremont ! You should a' seen him when he had the cheek to tell me about it ; you'd a' thought he was going to give me a five-pound note.'

' Now, you'll see,' said Mrs. Bower, ' they'll take off old Boddy to live with them.'

' So much the better. He can't earn his living much longer, and who was to pay us for his lodging and keep, I'd like to know ? '

Thus did the worthy pair link together conjectural cause and effect, on principles which their habit of mind dictated.

On one point Mrs. Bower was right. Mary and Lydia had not come together since the former's triumph over her friend. Lydia still visited the shop to see Mr. Boddy, but generally at the times when Mary was away at prayer-meetings.

There was no sign that she suffered at all, the good Lyddy; the trouble of those days before Christmas was lost in the anticipation of the great change that was soon to come upon her sister's life. To that she had resolved to look forward cheerfully; the better she came to know Gilbert, the warmer grew her affection for him. They were made to be friends; in both were the same absolute honesty of character, the same silent depths of tenderness, the same stern self-respect. Brother and sister henceforth, with the bond of a common love which time, whether it brought joy or sorrow, could but knit closer.

From the first there was, of course, an understanding that the marriage should take place as soon as the house was ready for Gilbert's tenancy. Thyrza went secretly and examined the dwelling from the outside, more than once. That Lydia would come and live there went without saying. She pretended to oppose this plan at first; said she must be independent.

'Very well,' said Thyrza, crossing her hands on her lap, 'then I shan't be married at all, Lyddy, and Mr. Grail had better be told at once.'

There was laughing, and there were kind words.

'I don't think you ought still to call him Mr. Grail,' said Lydia.

'Gilbert? I shall have to say it to myself for a few days. Still, it's a nice name, isn't it?'

Yes, that point needed no discussion; where Thyrza abode, there abode Lydia, until—but sadness lay that way. Mrs. Grail was equally clear as to the arrangements concerning herself; she would keep two rooms and continue to live in Walnut Tree Walk. Thyrza thought this would be unkindness to the old lady, but Mrs. Grail had a store of wisdom and was resolute. In practice, she said, she would not at all feel the loneliness; she could often be at the house, and it had occurred to her that her son in the Midlands would be glad to send one of his two girls to live with her for, say, half a year

at a time. Gilbert understood the good sense of this disposition.

The weather continued doleful, until at length, in the last
week of February, there came a sudden change. A rioting
east wind fell upon the murky vapours of the lower sky, broke
up the leaguer of rain and darkness, and through one spring-
heralding day drove silver fleece over deeps of clear, cold blue.
The streets were swept of mire; eaves ceased to distil their
sooty rheum; even in the back-ways of Lambeth there was
a sunny gleam on windows and a clear ring in all the sounds
of life.

It was Saturday. Between Egremont and Grail it had
been decided that the latter should to-day take Thyrza to
inspect the house. Egremont had gained the surly compliance of the caretaker—the most liberal treatment made no
difference in the strange old woman's moroseness—and Grail,
promising himself pleasure from Thyrza's surprise, said
nothing more than that he wished to see her at three in the
afternoon.

The sisters did not come home together from their work.
Lydia had an engagement with Mrs. Isaacs, of whom we have
heard, and went to snatch a pretence of a dinner in a little
shop to which she resorted when there was need. Thyrza,
leaving the work-room at half-past one, did not take the direct
way to Walnut Tree Walk; the sun and the keen air filled
her with a spirit of glad life, and a thought that it would be
nice to see how her future home looked under the bright sky
came to her temptingly. The distance was not great; she
soon came to Brook Street and, with some timidity, turned
up the narrow passage, meaning to get a glimpse of the house
and run away again. But just as she reached the entrance to
the rear-yard, she found herself face to face with someone
whom she at once knew for the caretaker whom Gilbert had
described to her. The old woman's eye held her. She was
half frightened, yet in a moment found words.

'Please,' she said—it seemed to her the only way of
explaining her intrusion—'is there any one in the school
now?'

The old woman examined her, coldly, searchingly.

'No, there ain't,' she replied. 'Is it you as is a-goin' to
live here?'

This was something like witchcraft to Thyrza.

'Yes, I am,' fell from her lips.

'All right. You can go in and look about. I ain't got nothink to hide away.'

Thyrza was in astonishment, and a little afraid. Yet she dearly wished to see the interior of the house. The old woman turned, and she followed her.

'There ain't no need for me to go draggin' about with you,' said the caretaker, when they were within the door. 'I've plenty o' work o' my own to see to.'

'May I look into the rooms, then?'

'Didn't I say as you could? What need o' so many words?'

Thyrza hesitated; but, the old creature having begun to beat a door-mat, she resolved to go forward boldly. She peeped into all the cheerless chambers, then returned to the door.

'Don't you want to see the school-rooms?' the old woman asked. 'Go along that passage, and mind the step at the end.'

Thyrza was bolder now. The aspect of the house had not depressed her, for she knew that it was to be thoroughly repaired and furnished, and she was predisposed to like everything she saw. It would be her home, hers and Lyddy's; the dignity of occupying a whole house would have compensated for many little discomforts. Thanking the old woman for her direction she went along the dark passage, and came into the large school-room. And this was to be filled with books! She looked at the maps and diagrams for a few moments; though it was so bright a day, the place still kept much of its chill and gloom. Gilbert had told her of the rooms up above, and she thought she might as well complete her knowledge of the building by seeing them. At the first landing on the staircase she came to a window by which the sun streamed in brilliantly: the rays gladdened her. It was nice that the old woman had remained behind; the sense of being quite alone, together with the sudden radiance, affected her with a desire to utter her happiness, and as she went on she sang in a sweet undertone, sang without words, pure music of her heart.

In one of the two rooms above, Egremont happened to be taking certain measurements. Impatient to get his plans completed in detail, he had resolved to come for half an hour on this same day which had been appointed for Grail's visit. Curious as he was to see the woman whom Grail was about to marry—as yet he knew nothing more of her than her casually learnt name—delicacy prevented him from using the opportunity this afternoon would give; the two were to arrive at three o'clock, and long before that time he would have finished his measuring and be gone. And now he was making his last notes, when the sound of as sweet a voice as he had ever heard made him pause and listen. The singer was approaching; her voice grew a little louder, though still in the undertone of one who sings but half consciously. He caught a light footstep, then the door was pushed open.

His hand fell. Even such a face as this would he have desired for her whose voice had such a charm. Her dress told him her position; the greater was his wonder at the features, which seemed to him of faultless delicacy—more than that, of beauty which appealed to him as never beauty had yet. Thyrza stood in alarm; the murmur had died instantly upon her lips, and for a moment she met his gaze with directness. Then her eyes fell; her cheeks recovered with interest the blood which they had lost. She turned to retreat.

But Egremont stepped rapidly forward, saying the first words that came to him.

'Pray don't let me be in your way! I'm this moment going—this moment.'

From her singing, he concluded that she was accustomed to be here. Thyrza again met his look. She guessed who this must be. The kindness of his face as he stood before her caused her to speak the words she was thinking:

'Are you Mr. Egremont, sir?'

Then she was shocked at her boldness; she did not see the smile with which he replied:

'Yes, that is my name.'

'I am Miss Trent. Perhaps you have—perhaps Mr. Grail has told you——'

This, Miss Trent? This, Gilbert Grail's wife? His astonishment scarcely allowed him to relieve her promptly.

'Oh then, we already know each other, by name at least. You have come to look at the building. Mr. Grail is downstairs?'

'No, sir. I came in alone. I thought I should like to see——'

'Of course. You have been over the house?'

He wondered rather at her coming alone, but supposed that Grail was withheld by some business.

'Yes, sir,' she answered.

'I'm afraid you think it doesn't look very promising. But I'm sure we can do a great deal to improve it.'

'I think it's very nice,' Thyrza said, not at all out of politeness, but because she did indeed think so.

'I will do my best to make it so, as soon as it is vacant. These two rooms,' he added, loth to take leave at once, 'we shall use for lectures. Have you been into the other one?'

He led the way, taking up his hat from the desk. Thyrza was overcoming her timidity. All she had ever heard of Egremont prepared her to find him full of gentleness and courtesy and good-humour; already she thought that far too little had been said in his praise. His singular smile occupied her imagination; she wished to keep her eyes on his face, for the pleasure of following its changes. Indeed, like her own, his features were very mobile, and the various emotions now stirring within him animated his look. She kept at a little distance from him, and listened with the keenest interest to all he said. When he paused, after telling her the number of books he had decided to begin with, she said:

'Mr. Grail does so look forward to it. I'm sure nothing could have made him so happy.'

Egremont was pleased with a note of sincerity, of self-forgetfulness in these words. He replied:

'I am very glad. I know he'll be at home among books. Are you fond of reading?'

'Yes, sir. Mr. Grail lends me books, and explains what I don't understand.'

'No doubt you will find plenty of time.'

'Yes, sir. I shan't go to work then. But of course there'll be the house to look after.'

Egremont glanced towards the windows and murmured an assent. Thyrza moved a little nearer the door.

'I think I'll go, now I've seen everything.'

'I am going myself.'

She preceded him down the stairs. He watched her ungloved hand touch place after place on the railing, watched her slightly bent head with its long braid of gold and the knot of blue ribbon. At the turning to the lower flight, he caught a glimpse of her profile, and felt that he would not readily forget its perfectness. At the foot he asked:

'Do you wish to pass through the house? If not, this door is open.'

'I'll go this way, sir.'

She just raised her face.

'Good-bye, Miss Trent,' he said, offering his hand.

'Good-bye, sir.'

Then he opened the door for her. After standing for a few moments in the vestibule, he went to speak a word to the caretaker.

Thyrza walked home, looking neither to right nor to left. There was a little spot of colour on each cheek which would not melt away. Reaching the room upstairs, she sat down without taking off her things. She ought to have prepared her dinner, but did not think of it, and at length she was startled by hearing a clock strike three.

She ran down to the Grails' room. Gilbert and his mother had just finished their meal. The latter gossiped for a moment, then went out.

'I want you to go somewhere with me,' Gilbert said.

'Yes, I'm quite ready ; but——'

'But——'

'I have something to tell you, Gilbert. I wonder whether you'll be cross.'

'When was I cross last, Thyrza ?'

'No, but I'm not sure whether I ought to have done something. As I was coming home, I thought I'd walk past the house. When I got there, I thought I'd just go up the passage and look. And that old woman met me, and asked me if it was me that was going to live there. How *did* she know ?'

Gilbert laughed.

'That's more than I can tell.'

'But that isn't all. She said I might go in and look about if I liked. And I thought I would—did I do wrong ?'

She saw a shade of disappointment on his face. But he said :

'Not at all. Did you go over all the rooms ?'

'Yes. But there's something else. I went into those school-rooms upstairs, never thinking there was any one there, because the old woman told me there wasn't. But there *was* —and it was Mr. Egremont.'

'Really ? Did he knew who you were ?'

'I told him, Gilbert.'

He laughed again, and there was a look of pride in his eyes.

'Well, there's nothing very dreadful yet. And did he speak nicely?'

'Yes, very nicely. And when I went away, he shook hands.'

'It's a very queer thing that you happened to go just to-day. That's exactly where I meant to take you this afternoon. I'm rather disappointed.'

'I'm very sorry. But couldn't I go with you again? We shall be alone this time: Mr. Egremont said he was just going.'

'It won't tire you?'

'Oh, but I should like to go! I made up my mind which'll be Lyddy's room. I wonder whether you'll guess the same.'

'Come along, then!'

CHAPTER XIV

MISTS

PAULA TYRRELL was married at Easter. Convenience dictated this speed—in other words, Paula resolved to commence the season as Mrs. Dalmaine and in a house of her own. Mr. Dalmaine had pointed out the advantage of using the Easter recess. As there was scarcely time to select and make ready an abode for permanence, it was decided to take a house in Kensington, which friends of the Tyrrells desired to let for the year.

Annabel was not present at the wedding. It was the second week in March before Mr. Newthorpe felt able to leave Ullswater, and Annabel had little mind to leave him for such a purpose immediately after their establishment at Eastbourne. Indeed, she would rather not have attended the wedding under any circumstances.

Her father had been gravely ill. There was organic disease, and there was what is vaguely called nervous breakdown; it was too clear that Mr. Newthorpe must count upon very moderate activity either of mind or body henceforth. He himself was not quite unprepared for this collapse; he accepted it with genial pessimism. Fate had said that his life was to result in nothing—nothing, that is, from the point of view of his early aspirations. Yet there was Annabel, and in her the memory of his life's passion. As he lay in silence through the days when spring combated with winter, he learned acquiescence; after all, he was among the happier of men, for he could look back upon a few days of great joy, and forward without ignoble anxiety.

He felt that the abandonment of Ullswater was final, yet would not say so to Annabel. Mrs. Ormonde had made ready a house at a short distance from her own, and here the two would live at all events into the summer; beyond that, all must hinge on circumstances. They broke the journey for a couple of days in London, staying with their relatives. During those days Paula behaved very prettily, A certain affection had grown up between her and her uncle whilst she was at Ullswater, and the meeting under these dolefully changed conditions touched her best feelings. Yet with her cousin she was reserved ; her behaviour did not bear out the evidence of latent tenderness and admiration contained in that letter of hers which we saw. Annabel had looked for something more. Just now she was longing for affection and sympathy, and Paula was the only girl friend she had. But Paula would only speak of Mr. Dalmaine and, absurdest thing, of politics. Annabel retired into herself. She was glad to reach at length the quiet house by the sea, glad to be near Mrs. Ormonde.

The circumstances of Annabel's early life had worked happily with her inherited disposition. Her father, had he been free to choose, would have planned her training differently, but in all likelihood with less advantage than she derived from the compromise between her parents. Though at the time of her mother's death she still waited for formal recognition as a member of Society, being but sixteen, she was of riper growth than the majority of young ladies who in that season were being led forth for review and to perfect themselves in arts of civilisation. From her mother she had learnt, directly or indirectly, much of that little world which deems the greater world its satellite ; from her father she received love of knowledge and reverence for the nobler modes of life. She was marked by a happy balance of character ; all that came to her from without she seemed naturally to assimilate in due proportions ; her tastes were those of an imaginative temper, tending to joyousness but susceptible of grave impressions. She relished books, yet never allowed them to hold her from bodily exercise ; she knew the happiness of solitude, yet could render welcomest companionship ;

at one time she conversed earnestly with those older and
wiser than herself, at another she was the willing play-
mate of laughing girls. She was loved by those who could
by no possibility have loved one another, and in turn she
seemed to discover with sure insight what there was of strength
and beauty in the most diverse characters. With this breadth
of sympathy she developed a self-consciousness of the kind to
which most women never attain ; habitually studying herself,
and making comparison of herself with others, she cultivated
her understanding and her emotions simultaneously.

Her time of serious study only began when she exchanged
London for the mountain solitude. Henceforth her father's
influence exerted itself freely, and Annabel had just reached
the age for profiting most by it. Her bringing up between a
brilliant drawing-room and a well-stocked library had preserved her from the two dangers to which English girls of the
free-born class are mainly exposed : she escaped Puritanism,
yet was equally withheld from frivolous worldliness. But it
was well that this balance, admirably maintained thus far,
should not be submitted to the risks of such a life as awaited
her, if there had come no change of conditions. She would
be a beautiful woman, and was not unaware of it; her social
instincts, which Society would straightway do its best to abuse,
might outweigh her spiritual tendencies. But a year of life by
Ullswater consolidated her womanhood. She bent herself to
books with eagerness. The shock of sorrow compelled her to
muse on problems which as yet she had either not realised, or
had solved in the light of tradition, childwise. Her mind was
ripe for those modern processes of thought which hitherto
had only been implicit in her education.

To her father Annabel's companionship was invaluable.
She repaid richly out of the abundance of her youthful life
that anxious guidance which he gave to her thoughts. Her
loving tact sweetened for him many an hour which would else
have been spent in profitless brooding : when the signs of
which she had become aware warned her that he needed to
be drawn from himself, she was always ready with her bright
converse, her priceless sympathy. Without her he would
seldom have exerted himself to wander far from the house,
but Annabel could at any time lead him over hill and valley
by pretending that she had need of a holiday. Their communion was of a kind not frequently existing between father
and daughter ; fellowship in study made them mental com-

rades, and respect for each other's intellectual powers was added to their natural love. What did they not discuss? From classical archæology to the fire-new theories of the day in art and science, something of all passed at one time or another under their scrutiny.

Yet there was the limit imposed by fine feeling. Mr. Newthorpe never tried to pass the sacred bound which parts a father's province from that of a mother. There was much in the girl's heart that he would gladly have read, yet could not until she should of herself reveal it to him. For instance, they did not very often speak of Egremont. When a letter arrived from him, Mr. Newthorpe always gave it to Annabel to read ; at other times that was a subject on which he spoke only when she introduced it. After Walter's departure there had been one conversation between them in which Annabel told what had come to pass ; she went so far as to speak of a certain trouble she had on Paula's account.

'I think you must use your philosophy with regard to Paula,' her father replied. 'Of course I know nothing of the circumstances, but,' he smiled not unkindly, ' the child I think I know pretty well. Don't be troubled. I have confidence in Egremont.'

' I have the same feeling in truth, father,' Annabel said, ' and—I feel nothing more than that.'

' Then let it rest, dear. I certainly have no desire to lose you.'

So much between them. Thereafter, both spoke of Egremont, when at all, in an unconstrained way. Annabel showed frank interest in all that concerned him, but, as far as Mr. Newthorpe could discern, nothing more than the interest of friendliness. As the months went on, he discerned no change. Her life was as cheerful and as steadily industrious as ever ; nothing betrayed unsettlement of the thought. If her father by chance entered the room where she studied, he found her bent over books, her face beautiful in calm zeal.

The first grave symptoms of illness in her father opened a new chapter of Annabel's life. It was time to lay aside books for a little ; the fated scheme of her existence required at this point new experiences. The student's habit does not readily reconcile itself to demands for practical energy and endurance, and when the first strain of fear-stricken love was relaxed, Annabel fell for a few days into grievous weakness of despon-

dency; summoned from her study to all the miseries of a
sick-room, it was mere nervous force that failed her.   When
her father had his relapse, she was able to face the demand
upon her more sternly.   But the trial through which she was
passing was a severe one.   With the invalid she could keep a
bright face, and make her presence, as ever, a blessing to him.
Alone, she cared no longer for her books, nor for the beauty
that was about her home.   You remember that passage in her
letter to Egremont : ' The world seems to me very dark, and
life a dreadful penalty.'   She could have uttered much on that
text to one from whom she had had no secret.

One day, when Mr. Newthorpe was again recovering
strength, there came a letter from Mrs. Tyrrell which announced
the date of Paula's marriage.   Annabel received the letter to
read.   As she was sitting with her father a little later, he said,
with a return of his humorous mood :

' I wonder on what footing Egremont will be in the new
household ? '

' I suppose,' Annabel replied, ' his acquaintance with Mr.
Dalmaine will continue to be of the slightest.'

He paused a little, then, quietly :

' I am glad of this marriage.'

Annabel said nothing.

' It proves,' he continued, ' that we did well in not thinking
too gravely of a certain incident.'

Annabel led the conversation away.   She had singular
thoughts on this subject.   Paula's letter, first announcing the
engagement, made mention of Egremont in a curious way;
and it was at least a strange hap that Paula should be about
to marry the man against whom Egremont had expressed
such an antipathy.

Her father said no more, but Annabel had a new care for
her dark mood to feed upon.   She felt that the words ' I am
glad of this marriage' concerned herself.   They meant that
her father was glad of the removal of what was perchance one
barrier between Egremont and herself.   And in these long
weeks in which she was anguished by the spectacle of suffering, it had become her first desire to be of comfort to the
sufferer.   Her ideal of a placid life was shattered ; the things
which availed her formerly now seemed weak to rely upon.
In so dark a world, what guidance was there save by the hand
of love ?

With Egremont she was in full intellectual sympathy, and

the thought of becoming his wife had no painful associations : but could she bring herself to abandon that ideal of love which had developed with her own development ? Must she relin- quish the hope of a great passion, and t ke the hand of a man whom she merely liked and respected ? It was a question she must decide, for Walter, when they again met, might again seek to win her. The idealism which she derived from her father would not allow her yet to regard life as a compromise, which women are so skilled in doing practically, though the better part in them to the end revolts. Yet who was she, that life should bestow its highest blessing upon her ?

When at the Tyrrells' house in London, she feared lest Egremont should come. Mrs. Tyrrell spoke much of him the first evening, lamenting that he had so withdrawn himself from his friends. But he did not come.

At Eastbourne, Mr. Newthorpe's health began to improve. Even in a week the change was very marked. He seemed to have taken a resolve to restore the old order of things by force of will. Doubtless his conversations with Mrs. Ormonde about Annabel were an incentive to effort; relieved from the weight of suffering, he could see that the girl was not herself. On Paula's marriage day, he said, in the course of conversation with Annabel :

' Your aunt desires very much to have you with her for a part of the season. What do you think of it ? Would you care to go up in May ? '

Annabel did not at once reject the idea.

' It is my opinion that you need some such change,' her father continued. ' The last quarter of a year has done you harm. In a month I hope to be sound enough.'

' I will think of it,' she said. And there the subject rested.

The town was secretly attracting her. The odour of the Tyrrells' house had exercised a certain seduction. Though she saw but one or two old acquaintances there, the dining- room, the drawing-room, brought the past vividly back to her. She was not so wholly alien to her mother's blood that the stage-life of the world was without appeal to her, and circum- stances were favourable to a revival of that element in her character which I touched upon when speaking of her growth out of childhood. It is a common piece of observation that studious gravity in youth is succeeded by a desire for action and enjoyment. Annabel's disposition to study did not return,

M

though quietness was once more restored to her surroundings
And thus, though the settlement at Eastbourne seemed a
relief, she soon found that it did not effect all she hoped.
Her father began to take up his books again, though in
a desultory, half-hearted way. Annabel could not do even
that. A portion of each day she spent with Mrs. Ormonde;
often she walked by herself on the shore; a book was seldom
in her hand.

Two or three days before the end of March, Mr. Newthorpe
spoke of Egremont.

'I should like to see him. May I ask him to come and
spend a day with us, Annabel?'

'Do by all means, father,' she answered. 'Mrs. Ormonde
heard from him yesterday. He came into possession of his
library-building the other day.'

'I will write, then.'

This was Monday; on Wednesday morning Egremont
came. The nine months or so which had passed since these
three met had made an appreciable change in all of them.
When Egremont entered the room where father and daughter
were expecting him, he was first of all shocked at the wasting
and ageing of Mr. Newthorpe's face, then surprised at the
difference he found in Annabel—this, too, of a kind that
troubled him. He thought her less beautiful than she had
been. With no picture of her to aid him, he had for long
periods been unable to make her face really present to his
mind's eye—one of the sources of his painful debates with himself. When it came, as faces do, at unanticipated moments,
he saw her as she looked in walking back with him from the
lake-side, when she declared that the taste of the rain was
sweet. Is it not the best of life, that involuntary flash of
memory upon instants of the eager past? better than present
joy, in which there is ever a core of disappointment; better,
far better, than hope, which cannot warm without burning.
Annabel was surpassingly beautiful as he knew her in that brief
vision. Beautiful she still was, but it was as if a new type of
loveliness had come between her and his admiration; he
could regard her without emotion. The journey from London
had been one incessant anticipation, tormented with doubt.
Would her presence conquer him royally, assure her dominion.
convert his intellectual fealty to passionate desire? He regarded her without emotion.

Yet Annabel was not so calm as she wished to be. Only

by force of will could she exchange greetings without evidence of more than friendly pleasure. This irritated her, for up to an hour ago she had said that his coming would in no way disturb her. When, after an hour's talk, she left her father and the guest together, and went up to her room, the first feeling she acknowledged to herself was one of disappointment. Egremont had changed, and not, she thought, for the better. He had lost something—perchance that freshness of purpose which had become him so well. He seemed to talk of his undertakings less spontaneously, and in a tone—she could not quite say what it was, but his tone perhaps suggested the least little lack of sincerity. And her agitation when he entered the room ? It had meant nothing, nothing. Her nerves were weak, that was all.

She wished she could shed tears. There was no cause for it, surely none, save a physical need. Such a feeling was very strange to her.

They had luncheon ; then, as his custom was, Mr. Newthorpe went apart to rest for a couple of hours. Mrs. Ormonde was coming to dine ; the hour of the meal would be early, to allow of Egremont's return to town. In the meantime the latter obtained Annabel's consent to a walk. They took the road ascending to Beachy Head.

' You still have opportunity of climbing,' Egremont said.

' On a modest scale. But I am not regretting the mountains. The sea, I think, is more to me at present.'

They were not quite at ease together. Conversation turned about small things, and was frequently broken. The day was not very bright, and mist spoiled the view landwards. The sea was at ebb, and sluggish.

Annabel of her own accord reverted to Lambeth.

' You must have had many pleasures arising from your work,' she said, ' but one above all I envy you. I mean that of helping poor Mr. Grail so well.'

' Yes, that is a real happiness,' he answered, thoughtfully. ' The idea of making him librarian came to me almost at the same moment as that of establishing the library. I didn't know then all that it would mean to him. I was fortunate in meeting that man, one out of thousands.'

' He must be deeply grateful to you.'

' We are good friends. I respect him more than I can tell you. I don't think you could find a man, in whatever position, of more sterling character. His love of knowledge touches me as something ideal. It is monstrous to think that he might have spent all his life in that candle factory.'

Annabel reflected for a moment. Then a look of pleasure lighted her face, and she spoke with a revival of the animation which had used to appeal so strongly to his sympathies.

'See what one can do! You become a sort of providence to a man. Indeed, you change his fate; you give him a new commencement of life. What a strange thought that is? Do you feel it as I do?'

'Quite, I think. And can you understand that it has sometimes shamed me? Just because I happen to have money I can do this! Isn't it a poor sordid world? Not one man, but perhaps a hundred, could be raised into a new existence by what in my hands is mere superfluity of means. Doesn't such a thought make life a great foolish game? Suppose me saying, "Here is a thousand pounds; shall I buy a yacht to play with, or—shall I lift a living man's soul out of darkness into light?"'

He broke off and laughed bitterly. Annabel glanced at him. She noticed that thoughts of this cast were now frequent in his mind, though formerly they had been strange to him. He used to face problems with simple directness, in the positive spirit or with an idealist's enthusiasm; now he leaned to scepticism, though it was his endeavour to conceal the tendency. She was struck with the likeness of this change in him to that which she herself was suffering; yet it did not touch her sympathies, and she was anxious forthwith to avoid coincidence with him.

'You yourself offer the answer to that,' she replied. 'The very fact that you have exerted such power, never mind by what means, puts you in a relation to that man which is anything but idle or foolish. Isn't it rather a great and moving thing that one can be a source of such vast blessing to another? Money is only the accident. It is the kindness, the human feeling, that has to be considered. You show what the world might be, if all men were human. If I could do one act like that, Mr. Egremont, I should cry with gratitude!'

He looked at her, and found the Annabel of his memory. With the exception of Mrs. Ormonde, he knew no woman who spoke thus from heart and intellect at once. The fervour of his admiration was rekindled.

'It is to you one should come for strength,' he said, 'when the world weighs too heavily.'

Annabel was sober again.

' Do you often go and see him at his house ? ' she asked, speaking of Grail.

' I am going on Friday night. I have not been since that one occasion which I mentioned in a letter to Mr. Newthorpe. I had to write to him yesterday about the repair of the house he is going to live in, and in his reply this morning he asked me to come for an hour's talk.'

' You were curious, father told me, about the wife he had chosen. Have you seen her yet ? '

' Yes. She is quite a young girl.'

He was looking at a far-off sail, and as he replied his eyes kept the same direction. Annabel asked no further question. Egremont laughed before he spoke again.

' How absurdly one conjectures about unknown people ! I suppose it was natural to think of Grail marrying someone not quite young and very grave.'

' But I hope she is grave enough to be his fitting companion ? '

He opened his lips, but altered the words he was about to speak.

' I only saw her for a few minutes—a chance meeting. She impressed me favourably.'

They walked in a leisurely way for about half an hour, then turned. Mists were creeping westward over Pevensey, and the afternoon air was growing chill. There was no sound from the sea, which was divided lengthwise into two tracts of different hue, that near the land a pale green, that which spread to the horizon a cold grey.

Nothing passed between them which could recall their last day together, nothing beyond that one exclamation of Egremont's, which Annabel hardly appeared to notice. Neither desired to prolong the conversation. Yet neither had ever more desired heart-sympathy than now.

Annabel said to herself : ' It is over.' She was spared anxious self-searching. The currents of their lives were slowly but surely carrying them apart from each other. When she came into the drawing-room to offer tea, her face was brighter, as if she had experienced some relief.

Mrs. Ormonde had not seen Egremont for some six weeks. The tone of the one or two letters she had received from him did not reassure her against misgivings excited at his latest visit. To her he wrote far more truly than to Mr. Newthorpe, and she knew, what the others did not, that he was anything but satisfied with the course he had taken since Christmas in his lecturing. 'After Easter,' was her advice, 'return to your plain instruction. It is more fruitful of profit both to your hearers and to yourself.' But Egremont had begun to doubt whether after Easter he should lecture at all.

'Mr. Bunce's little girl is coming to me again,' she said, in the talk before dinner. 'You know the poor little thing has been in hospital for three wreks?'

'I haven't heard of it,' Egremont replied. 'I'm sorry that I haven't really come to know Bunce. I had a short talk with him a month ago, and he told me then that his children were well. But he is so reticent that I have feared to try further to get his confidence.'

'Why, Bunce is the aggressive atheist, isn't he?' said Mr. Newthorpe.

Mrs. Ormonde smiled and nodded.

'I fear he is a man of misfortunes,' she said. 'My friend at the hospital tells me that his wife was small comfort to him whilst she lived. She left him three young children to look after, and the eldest of them—she is about nine—is always ill. There seems to be no one to tend them whilst their father is at work.'

'Who will bring the child here?' Egremont asked.

'She came by herself last time. But I hear she is still very weak; perhaps someone will have to be sent from the hospital.'

During dinner, the library was discussed. Egremont reported that workmen were already busy in the school-rooms and in Grail's house.

'I'm in correspondence,' he said, 'with a man I knew some years ago, a scientific fellow, who has heard somehow of my undertakings, and wrote asking if he might help by means of natural science. Perhaps it might be well to begin a course of that kind in one of the rooms. It would appeal far more to the Lambeth men than what I am able to offer.'

This project passed under review, then Egremont himself led the talk to widely different things, and thereafter resisted any tendency it showed to return upon his special affairs. Annabel was rather silent.

An hour after dinner, Egremont had to depart to catch his train. He took leave of his friends very quietly.

'We shall come and see the library as soon as it is open,' said Mr. Newthorpe.

Egremont smiled merely.

Mr. Newthorpe remarked that Egremont seemed disappointed with the results of his work.

'I should uncommonly like to hear one of these new lectures,' he said. 'I expect there's plenty of sound matter in them. My fear is lest they are over the heads of his audience.'

'I fear,' said Mrs. Ormonde, 'it is waste both of his time and that of the men. But the library will cheer him; there is something solid, at all events.'

'Yes, that can scarcely fail of results.'

'I think most of Mr. Grail,' put in Annabel.

'A true woman,' said Mrs. Ormonde, with a smile. 'Certainly, let the individual come before the crowd.'

And all agreed that in Gilbert Grail was the best result hitherto of Egremont's work.

CHAPTER XV

A SECOND VISIT TO WALNUT TREE WALK

THE man of reserve betrays happiness by disposition for companionship. Surprised that the world all at once looks so bright to his own eyes, he desires to learn how others view it. The unhappy man is intensely subjective: his own impressions are so inburnt that those of others seem to him unimportant—nay, impertinent. And what is so bitter as the spectacle of alien joy when one's own heart is waste!

Gilbert Grail was no longer the silent and lonely man that he had been. The one with whom he had formed something like a friendship had gone apart; in the nature of things Ackroyd and he could never again associate as formerly, though when need was they spoke without show of estrangement; but others whom he had been wont to hold at a distance by his irresponsiveness were now of interest to him, and, after the first surprise at the change in him, they met his quiet advances in a friendly way. Among his acquaintances there were, of course, few fitted to be in any sense his associates. Two, however, he induced to attend Egremont's lectures, thus raising the number of the audience to eight. These recruits were not enthusiastic over ' Thoughts for the Present ; ' one of them persevered to the end of the course, the other made an excuse for absenting himself after two evenings.

Gilbert held seriously in mind the pledge he had given to Egremont to work for the spread of humane principles. One of those with whom he often spoke of these matters was Bunce—himself a man made hard to approach by rude experiences. Bunce was a locksmith ; some twelve years ago he had had a little workshop of his own, but a disastrous marriage brought him back to the position of a journeyman, and at present he was as often out of work as not. Happily his wife was dead ; he found it a hard task to keep his three children. The truth was that his domestic miseries had, when at their height, driven him to the public-house, and only by dint of struggles which no soul save his own was aware of was he gradually recovering self-confidence and the trust of employers. His attendance at Egremont's lectures was part of the cure. Though it was often hard to go out at night and leave his little ones, he did so that his resolve might not suffer. He and they lived in one room, in the same house which sheltered Miss Totty Nancarrow.

On the evening which Egremont spent at Eastbourne, Grail came across Bunce on the way home from the factory. They resumed a discussion interrupted a day or two before, and, as they passed the end of Newport Street, Bunce asked his companion to enter for the purpose of looking at a certain paper in which he had found what seemed to him cogent arguments. They went up the dark musty staircase, and entered the room opposite to Totty's.

' Hollo ! ' Bunce cried, finding no light. ' What's up ? Nellie ! Jack ! '

It was usual, since the eldest child was at the hospital, for the landlady to come and light a lamp for the two little ones when it grew dusk. Bunce had an exaggerated fear of giving trouble, and only sheer necessity had compelled him to request this small service.

' They'll be downstairs, I suppose,' he muttered, striking a match.

The hungry room had no occupants. On the floor lay a skeleton doll, a toy tambourine, a whipping-top, and a wried tin whistle. There was one bedstead, and a bed made up on a mattress laid on the floor. On a round clothless table stood two plates, one with a piece of bread and butter remaining, and two cups and saucers. The fire had died out.

A shrill voice was calling from below stairs.

'Mr. Bunce! Mr. Bunce! Your children is gone out with Miss Nancarrow as far as the butcher's. They won't be more than five minutes, I was to say, if you came in.'

'Thank you, Mrs. Ladds,' Bunce replied briefly.

He came in and closed the door.

'That's a new thing,' he said, as if doubtful whether to be satisfied or not. 'I hope she won't begin taking 'em about. Still, she isn't a bad lot, that girl. Do you know anything of her?'

'Why, yes. I've heard of her often from Miss Trent. Isn't she a good deal with Ackroyd?'

'Can't say. She's not a bad lot. She's going to take my Bessie down to Eastbourne at the end of the week.'

'But why don't you go yourself? It would do you good.'

Bunce shrugged his shoulders.

'No, I can't go myself. Just for the child's sake, I have to put up with that kind of thing, but I don't like it. It's charity, after all, and I couldn't face those people at the home.'

'What home is it?' Grail asked. He knew, but out of delicacy wished the explanation to come from Bunce.

'I don't know as it has any name. It seems to be in connection with the Children's Hospital. The matron, or whatever you call her, is a Mrs. Ormonde.'

'Oh, I know about her!' Gilbert exclaimed. 'She's a friend of Mr. Egremont's. He's spoken of her once or twice to me. You needn't be afraid of meeting *her*. She's a lady who has given up her own house for this purpose: as good a woman, I believe, as lives.'

'Well,' said Bunce, doggedly, 'I'm thankful to her, but I can't face her. What's this, I'd like to know?'

His eye caught something that looked like a small pamphlet lying near the fireplace. He stooped to pick it up.

'If they're beginning to throw my papers about——'

The sudden silence caused Gilbert to look at him. Bunce was not a well-favoured man, but ordinarily a rugged honesty helped the misfortunes of his features, a sort of good-humour, too, which seemed unable to find free play. But of a sudden his face had become ferocious, startling in its exasperated surprise, its savage wrath. His eyes glared blood-shot, his teeth were uncovered, his jaws protruded as if in an animal impulse to rend.

'How's this got here?' he almost roared. 'Who brings things o' this kind into my room? Who's put this into my children's hands?'

'What on earth is it?' Gilbert asked in amazement.

'What is it? Look at that! Look at that, I say! If this is the landlady's work, I'll find a new room this very night!'

Gilbert tried to take the paper, but Bunce's hand, which trembled violently, held it with such a grip that there was no getting possession of it. With difficulty Grail perceived that it was a religious tract.

'Why, there's no great harm done,' he said. 'The children can't read, can they?'

'Jack can! The boy can! I'm teaching him myself.'

He raved. The sight of that propagandist document affected him, to use the old simile, as scarlet does a bull. Gilbert knew the man's prejudices, but, in his own more cultured mind, could not have conceived such frenzy of hatred as this piece of Christian doctrine excited in Bunce. For five minutes the poor fellow was possessed; sweat covered his face; he was shaken as if by bodily anguish. He read scraps aloud, commenting on them with scornful violence. Last of all he flung the paper to the ground and trampled it into shreds. Gilbert had at first difficulty in refraining from laughter; then he sat down and waited with some impatience for the storm to spend itself.

'Come, come, Bunce,' he said, when he could make himself heard, 'remember Mr. Egremont's lecture on those things. I think pretty much as you do about Christianity—about the dogmas, that is; but we've no need to fear it in this way. Let's take what good there is in it, and have nothing to do with the foolish parts.'

Bunce seated himself, exhausted. Not a few among the intelligent artisans of our time are filled with that spirit of hatred against all things Christian; in him it had become a mania. Egremont's eirenicon had been a hard saying to him; he had tried to think it over, because of his respect for the teacher, but as yet it had resulted in no sobering. His mind was not sufficiently prepared for lessons of wisdom; had Egremont witnessed this scene, he might well have groaned in spirit over the ineffectualness of his prophesying.

Gilbert spoke with earnestness. To him his friend's teaching had come as true and refreshing, and he could not lose such an opportunity as this of pushing on the work. He insisted on the beauty there was in the Christian legend, on its profound spiritual significance, on the poverty of all religious schemes which man had devised to replace it.

'We want no religion!' cried Bunce angrily. 'It's been the curse of the world. Look at the Inquisition! Look at the religious wars! Look at the Jesuits!'

He was primed with such historic instances out of books and pamphlets spread broadcast by the contemporary apostles of 'free thought.' Of history proper he of course knew nothing, but these splinters of quasi-historic evidence had run deep into his flesh. Despise him, if you like, but try to understand him. It was his very humaneness which brought him to this pass; recitals of old savagery had poisoned his blood, and the 'spirit of the age' churned his crude acquisitions into a witch's cauldron. Academic sweetness and light was a feeble antidote to offer him.

Gilbert soothed his companion for the time. He knew where to stop, and promised himself to find a fitter season for pursuing the same subject. Just as he had reverted to the topic of conversation which brought him here, there came a knock at the door.

'Come in!' growled Bunce.

Totty Nancarrow appeared. One of her hands led a little fellow of seven, a bright lad, munching a 'treacle-stick;' the other, a little girl a year younger, who exclaimed as she entered:

'Been a walk with Miss Nanco!'

'We've been to the butcher's with Miss Nancarrow, father,' declared the boy, consciously improving on his sister's report.

Totty had drawn back a step at the sight of Grail. He and she knew each other by sight, but had not yet exchanged words.

'I found them in the dark, Mr. Bunce,' she said, half laughing. 'Mrs. Ladds was out, and couldn't get back in time to light the lamp for them. I hope you don't mind. I thought a little bit of a walk 'ud do them good.'

Bunce always softened at the sight of his little ones.

'I'm much obliged to you, Miss Nancarrow,' he said.

'Miss Nanco bought me sweets,' remarked little Nelly, when her father had drawn her between his knees. And she exhibited a half-sucked lollipop. Her brother hid away his own delicacy, feeling all at once that it compromised his masculine superiority.

'Then I'm very angry with Miss Nanco,' replied Bunce. 'I hope she'll never do anything o' the kind again.'

Totty laughed and drew back into the passage. Thence she said:

'Could I speak to you a minute, Mr. Bunce?'

He went out to her, and half closed the door behind him. Totty led him a step or two down the stairs, then whispered:

'I'm so sorry, Mr. Bunce, but I find I can't very well go on Saturday. But I've just seen Miss Trent, the one that's going to marry Mr. Grail, you know; and she says she'd be only too glad to go, that is if Mr. Grail 'll let her, and she's quite sure he will. Would you ask Mr. Grail? Thyrza—that's Miss Trent, I mean—was so anxious; she's never been to the seaside. Will you just ask him?'

'Oh yes, I will.'

'I'm sorry I've had to draw back, Mr. Bunce, after offering——'

'It don't matter a bit, Miss Nancarrow. Miss Trent 'll do just as well, if she really don't mind the trouble.'

'Trouble! Why, she'd give anything to go! Please get Mr. Grail to let her.'

Bunce returned to his room and closed the door. Gilbert had taken Nelly on his knee, and was satisfying her by tasting the remnant of lollipop.

'I say, Jack!' cried the father, his eye again catching sight of the bruised tract on the floor. 'Who brought that here?'

'I did, father,' answered the youngster stoutly, though he saw displeasure in his father's face.

'Where did you get it, eh?' was asked sharply.

'A lady gave it me at the door.'

'Then I'd thank ladies to mind their own business. And you never take anything else at the door; do you understand that, Jack?'

'Yes, father.'

Bunce turned to Gilbert, who was waiting to depart.

'Miss Nancarrow tells me she can't go to Eastbourne on Saturday. But she says Miss Trent's very anxious to go instead of her. What do you think of it?'

Grail reflected. The plan pleased him on the whole,

though he had just a doubt whether Thyrza ought to travel by herself.

'I see no reason why she shouldn't,' he said. 'It'll be a pleasure to her, and I shall be glad to have her do you the kindness.'

'Then could I see her before Saturday?'

'Come in to-morrow night, will you?'

The second course of lectures was at an end. Egremont had only delivered one a week since Christmas, and even so it cost him no little effort to spread his 'Thoughts for the Present' over the three months. Latterly he had blended a good deal of historical disquisition with his prophecy: the result was to himself profoundly unsatisfactory. He sighed with relief as he dismissed his poor little audience for the last time. For the future he had made no promises, beyond saying that in his library-building there were two rooms which were to be devoted to lectures. The library itself was now his chief care. This was something solid; it would re-establish him in his self-confidence.

Yes; 'Thoughts for the Present' had been a failure.

The first lecture was far away the best. It dealt with Religion. Addressed to an audience ready for such philosophical views, it would have met with a flattering reception. Egremont's point of view was, strictly, the æsthetic; he aimed at replacing religious enthusiasm, as commonly understood, by æsthetic. The loveliness of the Christian legend—from that he started. He dealt with the New Testament very much as he had formerly dealt with the Elizabethan poets. He would have no appeal to the vulgar by aggressive rationalists. Let rationalism filter down in the course of time; the vulgar were not prepared for it as yet. It was bad that they should be superstitious, but worse, far worse, that they should be brutally irreverent, and brutal irreverence inevitably came of atheism preached at the street corner. The men who preached it were themselves the very last to guide human souls; they were of coarsest fibre, without a note of music in them, fit only for the world's grosser purposes. And they presumed to attack the ministry of Christ! It was good, all that he had to say on that point, the better that it made two or three of his hearers feel a little sore and indignant. Yet, as a whole, the lecture appealed to but one of the audience. Gilbert Grail heard it with emotion, and carried it away in his heart. To the others it was little more than the sounding of brass and the tinkling of cymbals.

To-night—Friday—he was going to Grail's. Of course no ceremonious preparation was necessary, yet he wasted a couple of hours previous to his time for setting forth. He could not apply himself to anything; he paced his room. Indeed, he had paced his room much of late. Week by week he seemed to have grown more unsettled in mind. He had said to himself that all would be well when he had seen Annabel. He had seen her, and his trouble was graver than before,

At the hour when Egremont set out for Lambeth Lydia was busy dressing her sister's hair. Perhaps such a thing had never happened before, as that Thyrza's hair should have needed doing twice in one day. She had begged it this evening.

'You won't mind, Lyddy? I feel it's rough, and I think I ought to look nice—don't you?'

'You're a vain little thing!'

'I don't think I am, Lyddy. It's only natural.'

A moment or two, and Thyrza said:

'Lyddy, I think you ought to come down as well.'

'I've told you that I shan't, so do have done!'

'Well, dear, it's only because I want you to see Mr. Egremont.'

'I've seen him, and that's enough. If you're going to be a lady and make friends with grand people, that's no reason why I should.'

'You'll have to some day.'

'I don't think I shall,' said Lydia, as she began the braiding. 'You and me are very different, dear. I shall go on in my own way. Do keep still! How am I to tie this ribbon?'

'Kiss me, Lyddy! Say that you love me!'

'I don't think I shall.'

'Lyddy, dear.'

It was said so gravely that Lydia, having finished her task, came round before the chair and looked in her sister's face.

'What?'

'I think I should die if I hadn't someone to love me.'

'I don't think you'll ever want that, Thyrza.'

The other drew a profound sigh, so profound that it left her bosom trembling. And for a few moments she sat in a dream.

Then she proceeded to change her dress and make ready for her formal appearance downstairs on the occasion of Egremont's visit. She had never been so anxious to look well. Lydia affected much impatience with her, but in truth was profoundly happy in her sister's happiness. She looked often at the beautiful face, and thought how proud Gilbert must be.

' Do you think I ought to shake hands with Mr. Egremont ? ' Thyrza asked.

' If he offers to, you must,' was Lydia's opinion. ' But not if he doesn't.'

' He did when he said good-bye at the school.'

Before long they heard the expected double knock at the house-door. They had left their own door ajar that they might not miss this signal. Thyrza sprang to the head of the stairs and listened. She heard Gilbert admit his visitor, and she heard the latter's voice. It was now a month since the meeting at the school, but the voice sounded so exactly as she expected that it brought back every detail of that often-recalled interview, and made her heart throb with excitement.

She was now to wait a whole quarter of an hour.

' Sit down and read,' said Lydia, who had herself begun to sew in the usual methodical way.

Thyrza pretended to obey. For two minutes she sat still, then asked how they were to know when a quarter of an hour had passed.

' I'll tell you,' said the other. ' Sit quiet, there's a good baby, and I'll buy you a cake next time we go out.'

Thyrza drew in her breath—and somehow the time was lived through.

' Now I think you may go,' Lydia said.

Thyrza seemed to have become indifferent. She turned over a page of her book, and at length rose very slowly. Lydia watched her askance ; she thought she saw signs of timidity. But Thyrza presently moved to the door and went downstairs with her lightest step.

Gilbert had told her not to knock. Her hand was on the knob some moments before she ventured to turn it. She heard Egremont laughing—his natural laugh which was so attractive—and then there fell a silence. She entered.

No, Gilbert had not seated his visitor in the easy chair; that must be reserved for someone of more importance. Egremont rose with a look of pleasure.

'You know Miss Trent already?' Gilbert said to him.

Thyrza drew near. She did not hear very distinctly what Egremont was saying, but certainly he was offering to shake hands. Then Gilbert placed the easy chair in a convenient position, and she did her best to sit as she always did. Her manner was not awkward—it was impossible for her to be awkward—but she was afraid of saying something that 'wasn't grammar,' and to Egremont's agreeable remarks she replied shortly. Yet even this only gave her an air of shyness which was itself a grace. When Grail had entered into the conversation she was able to collect herself.

Gilbert said presently : ' Miss Trent is going to take Bunce's child to Eastbourne to-morrow, to Mrs. Ormonde's.'

'Indeed!' Egremont exclaimed. ' I was there on Wednesday and heard that the child was coming. But this arrangement hadn't been made then, I think?'

'No. Somebody else was to have gone, but she has found she can't.'

'You will be glad to know Mrs. Ormonde, I'm sure,' Egremont said to Thyrza.

'And I'm glad to go to the seaside,' Thyrza returned. 'I've never seen the sea.'

'Haven't you? How I wish I could have your enjoyment of to-morrow, then!'

Mrs. Grail was knitting. She said: 'I think you have voyaged a great deal, sir?'

It led to talk of travel. Egremont was drawn into stories of East and West. Ah, how good it was to get out of the circle of social prophecy! It was like breathing the very mid-Atlantic sky to talk gaily and freely of things wherein no theory was involved, which left aside every ideal save that of joyous living. Thyrza listened. He—he before her—had trodden lands whereof the names were to her like echoes from fairy tales; he had passed days and nights on the bosom of the great sea, which she looked forward to beholding almost with fear; he had seen it in tempest, and the laughing descriptions he gave of vast green rolling mountains made to her inward sight an awful reality.

'You never thought of going to one of the Colonies?' Egremont asked of Gilbert.

'Yes, years ago,' was the reply, in the tone of a man who sees the trouble of life behind him. 'I think at one time my mother rather despised me because I couldn't make up my mind to go and seek my fortune.'

'I never despised you, my dear,' said the old lady, 'but that was when some friends of ours were sending wonderful news from Australia, sir, and I believe I did half try to persuade Gilbert to go. His health was very bad, and I thought it might have done him good in all ways.'

'By-the-by,' remarked Gilbert, 'Ackroyd talks of going to Canada.'

'Ackroyd?' said Egremont. 'I'm not surprised to hear that.'

Thyrza had looked at Gilbert anxiously.

'Who told you that?' she asked.

'He told me himself, Thyrza, last night.'

She saw that Egremont was gazing at her; her eyes fell, and she became silent.

Egremont, in the course of the talk, wondered at his position in this little room. He knew that it was one of very few houses in Lambeth in which he could have been at his ease; perhaps there was not another. It seemed to him that he had thrown off a great deal that was artificial in behaviour and in habits of speech, that he had reverted to that self which came to him from his parents, and he felt better for the change. The air of simplicity in the room and its occupants was healthful; of natural refinement there was abundance, only affectation was missing. Would it have been a hardship if his father had failed to amass money, and he had grown up in such a home as this? He knew well enough that by going, say, next door he could pass into a domestic sphere of a very different kind, to the midst of a life compact of mean slavery, of ignorance, of grossness. This was enormously the exception. But his own home would have been not unlike this. Poverty could not have taken away his birthright of brains, and perhaps some such piece of luck might have fallen to him as had now to Gilbert Grail. Perhaps, too—why not, indeed!—he would have known Thyrza Trent. Certainly he would have seen her by chance here or there in Lambeth, and he—the young workman he might have been—assuredly would not have let her pass and forget her. Why, in that case, perchance he might have——

He had lost himself for a moment. Thyrza was standing

before him with a cup of tea : he noticed that the cup shook a little in the saucer.

'Will you have some tea, sir ? ' she said.

Mrs. Grail had been perturbed somewhat on the question of refreshments. Gilbert decided that to offer a cup of tea would be the best thing ; Egremont, he knew, dined late, and would not want anything to eat.

'Thank you, Miss Trent.'

She brought him sugar and milk. This was quite her own idea. 'Some people don't take sugar, some don't take milk ; so you ought to let them help themselves to such things.' He took both. She noticed his hand, how shapely it was, how beautiful the finger-nails were. And then he looked at her with a smile of thanks, not more than of thanks. Could any-one convey thanks more graciously ?

'I hope,' Egremont said, turning to Gilbert as he stirred his tea, 'that we shall get our first books on the shelves by the first day of next month.'

Grail made no reply, and all were silent for a little.

The visitor did not remain much longer. To the end he was animated in his talk, making his friends feel as much at their ease as he was himself. When he was about to depart, he said to Thyrza :

'I hope you will have a fine day to-morrow. There is promise of it.'

'Oh, I think it'll be fine,' she replied. 'It would be too cruel if it wasn't ! '

Surely—thought Egremont as he smiled—to you if to any one the sky should show a glad face. How many a time thereafter did he think of those words—'It would be too cruel ! ' She could not believe that fortune would be unkind to her ; she had faith in the undiscovered day.

CHAPTER XVI

SEA MUSIC

RETURNING to the upper room, Thyrza sat down as if she were very tired.

'No, I don't want anything to eat,' she said to Lydia. 'I shall go to bed at once. We must be up very early in the morning.'

Still she made no preparations. Her mirth and excitement were at an end. Her eyelids drooped heavily, and one of her hands hung down by the side of the chair. Lydia showed no extreme desire for an account of the proceedings below. Yes, Thyrza said, she had enjoyed herself. And presently:

'Mr. Egremont says he wants to begin putting up the books by the first of May.'

'Did he say when the house would be ready?'

Thyrza shook her head. Then:

'He told us about foreign countries. He's been everywhere.'

'Gilbert told me he had been to America.'

'Lyddy, is Canada the same as America?'

'I believe it is,' said the other doubtfully. 'I think it is a part. America's a very big country, you know.'

'What do you think Gilbert says? He says Mr. Ackroyd told him last night that he was going to Canada.'

Lydia gave no sign of special interest.

'Is he?'

'I don't think he means it.'

'Perhaps he'll take Totty Nancarrow with him,' remarked Lydia, with a scarcely noticeable touch of irony.

The other did not reply, but she looked pained. Then Lydia declared that she too was weary. They talked little more, though it was a long time before either got to sleep.

Thyrza saw Grail in the breakfast hour next morning, and received his advice for the day. Bunce had already conveyed the little box of Bessie's clothing to the hospital; thence Thyrza and the child would go in a cab to Victoria.

She was at the hospital by nine o'clock. Bessie, a weakly, coughing child, who seemingly had but a short term of suffering before her, was at first very reticent with Thyrza, but when they were seated together in the train at Victoria, she brightened in the expectation of renewing her experiences of Mrs. Ormonde's home, and at length talked freely. Bessie was very old; she had long known the difficulties of a pinched home, and of her own ailments she spoke with a curious gravity as little child-like as could be.

'It's my chest as is weak,' she said. 'The nurse says it'll get stronger as I get older, but it's my belief that it's just the other way about. You never had a weak chest, had you, Miss

Trent ? You haven't that look. I dessay you're always well ;
I shouldn't mind if I was the same.' She laughed, and made
herself cough. ' I can't see why everybody shouldn't be well.
Father says the world's made wrong, and it seems to me that's
the truth. Perhaps it looks different to you, Miss Trent.'

' You had better call me Thyrza, Bessie. That's my
name.'

' Is it ? Well, I don't mind, if *you* don't. I never knew
anybody called Thyrza. But I dessay it's a lady's name.
You're a lady, ain't you ? '

' No, I'm not a lady. I go to work with Miss Nancarrow.
You know her ? '

' I can't say as I know her. She lives in the next room to
us, but we don't often speak. But I remember now ; I've seen
you on the stairs.'

' Miss Nancarrow has made friends with your brother and
sister whilst you've been in the hospital.'

' Have she now ! They didn't tell me about that when
they come to see me last time. I suppose things is all upside
down. By rights I'd ought to have gone home for a day or
two, just to see that the room was clean. Mrs. Larrop comes
in wunst a week, you know, she's a charwoman. But I haven't
much trust in her ; she's such a one for cat-licking. The
children do make such a mess ; I always tell them they'd
think twice about coming in with dirty shoes if only they had
the cleaning to see after.'

Then she began to talk of Mrs. Ormonde, and Thyrza
encouraged her to tell all she could about that lady.

' I tell you what, Thyrza,' said Bessie, confidentially, ' when
Nelly gets old enough to keep things straight and look after
father, do you know what I shall do ? I mean to go to Mrs.
Ormonde and ask to be took on for a housemaid. That's just
what 'ud suit me. My chest ain't so bad when I'm there, and
I'd rather be one of Mrs. Ormonde's servants than work
anywhere else. But then I perhaps shan't live long enough
for that. It's a great thing for carrying people off, is a weak
chest.'

Both grew excited as the train neared their destination.
Bessie recalled the stations, and here and there an object by
the way. It was Thyrza who felt herself the child.

The train entered the station. Bessie had her head at the
window. She drew it back, exclaiming :

' There's Mrs. Ormonde ! See, Thyrza ! the lady in black ! '

Thyrza looked timidly; that lady's face encouraged her. Mrs. Ormonde had seen Bessie, and was soon at the carriage door.

'So here you are again!' was her kindly greeting. 'Why, Bessie, you must have been spending all your time in growing!'

She kissed the child, whose thin face was coloured with pleasure.

'This is Miss Trent, mum,' said Bessie, pointing to her companion, who had descended to the platform. 'She's been so kind as to take care of me.'

Mrs. Ormonde turned quickly round.

'Miss Trent?' She viewed the girl with surprise which she found it impossible to conceal at once. Then she said to Thyrza: 'Are you the young lady of whom I have heard as Mr. Grail's friend?'

'Yes, ma'am,' Thyrza replied modestly.

'Then how glad I am to see you! Come, let us get Bessie's box taken to the carriage.'

Mrs. Ormonde was not of those philanthropists who, in the midst of their well-doing, are preoccupied with the necessity of preserving the distinction between classes. She always fetched the children from the station in her own unpretending carriage. Her business was to make them happy, as the first step to making them well, and whilst they were with her she was their mother. There are plenty of people successfully engaged in reminding the poor of the station to which Providence has called them: the insignificant few who indulge a reckless warmth of heart really cannot be seen to do appreciable harm.

'Mrs. Ormonde, mum,' whispered Bessie, when they were seated in the carriage.

'What is it, Bessie?'

'Would you take us round by the front road? Miss Trent hasn't never seen the sea, and she'd like to as soon as she can; it's only natural.'

Mrs. Ormonde had cast one or two discreet glances at Thyrza. As she did so her smile subdued itself a little; a grave thought seemed to pass through her mind. She at once gave an order to the coachman in compliance with Bessie's request.

'Mr. Grail is quite well, I hope?' she said, feeling a singular embarrassment in addressing Thyrza.

Thyrza replied mechanically. To ride in an open carriage
with a lady, this alone would have been an agitating experience ; the almost painful suspense with which she waited
for the first glimpse of the sea completed her inability to think
or speak with coherence. Her eyes were fixed straight onwards. Mrs. Ormonde continued to observe her, occasionally
saying something in a low voice to the child.

The carriage drove to the esplanade, and turned to pass
along it in the westerly direction. The tide was at full ; a loud
surge broke upon the beach ; no mist troubled the blue line of
horizon. Mrs. Ormonde looked seawards, and her vision found
a renewal in sympathy with the thought she had read on
Thyrza's face.

You and I cannot remember the moment when the sense
of infinity first came upon us ; we have thought so much since
then, and have assimilated so much of others' thoughts, that
those first impressions are become as vague as the memory of
our first love. But Thyrza would not forget this vision of the
illimitable sea, live how long she might. She had scarcely
heretofore been beyond the streets of Lambeth. At a burst
her consciousness expanded in a way we cannot conceive.
You know that she had no religion, yet now her heart could
not contain the new-born worship. Made forgetful of all else
by the passionate instinct which ruled her being, she suddenly
leaned forward and laid her hand on Mrs. Ormonde's. The
latter took and pressed it, smiling kindly.

Bessie, happy in her superior position, looked about her
with a satisfied air. She sat with Mrs. Ormonde on the fore-
seat ; presently she leaned aside to look westward, and informed
Thyrza that the promontory visible before them was Beachy
Head. Thyrza had no response to utter.

The carriage turned inland again. Thyrza lost sight of
the sea. As if she cared to look at nothing else, her eyes fell.

When they arrived at The Chestnuts, Mrs. Ormonde led her
companions to an upper room, where Mrs. Mapper sat talking
with two or three children.

' I think Bessie can have her old bed, can't she ? ' she said,
after introducing Thyrza. ' I wonder whether she knows any
of our children now ?   I dare say Miss Trent would like to rest
a little.'

A few words were spoken to the matron apart, and Mrs.
Ormonde withdrew. Half an hour later, Thyrza, after seeing
the children and all that portion of the house which was theirs,

was led by Mrs. Mapper to the drawing-room. The lady of the house was there alone ; she invited her guest to sit down, and began to talk.

'Are you obliged to be home to-night ? Couldn't you stay with us till to-morrow ? '

Thyrza checked a movement.

'I promised Mr. Grail to be back before dark,' she said.

'Oh, but that will scarcely leave you any time at all. Is there any other need for you to return to-day ? Suppose I telegraphed to say that I was keeping you—wouldn't Mr. Grail forgive me ? '

'I think I might stay, if I could be back to-morrow by tea-time. I must go to work on Monday morning.'

Mrs. Ormonde sighed involuntarily. That work, that work : the consumer of all youth and joy !

'Unfortunately there's no train to-morrow that would help us.'

Thyrza longed to stay ; the other could read her face well enough.

'There's an early train on Monday morning,' she continued doubtfully. 'Do you live with parents ? '

'Oh, no, ma'am. My parents died a long time ago. I live with my sister. We two have a room to ourselves ; it's in the same house where Mr. Grail lives : that's how I got to know him.'

'And is your sister older than yourself ? '

'Yes, ma'am ; four years older. Her name's Lydia. We've always kept together. When I'm married, she's coming to live with us.'

Mrs. Ormonde listened with ever deepening interest. She formed a picture of that elder sister. The words ' We've always kept together,' touched her inexpressibly ; they bore so beautiful a meaning on Thyrza's lips.

'And would your sister Lydia scold me very much if I made you lose your Monday morning's work ? ' she asked, smiling.

'Oh, it's always the other way, ma'am. Lyddy's always glad when I get a holiday. But I never like her to have to go to work alone.'

'Well now, I shall telegraph to Lyddy, and then to-morrow I shall write a letter to her and beg her to forgive me. If I do so, do you think you could stay ? '

'I—I think so, ma'am.'

' And Mr. Grail ? '

' He's just as kind to me as Lyddy is.'

' Then I think we won't be afraid. The telegram shall go at once, so that if there were real need for your return, they would have time to reply.'

The message despatched, they talked till dinner-time. Fulfilment of joy soon put an end to Thyrza's embarrassment; she told all about her life and Lydia's, about their work, about Mr. Boddy, about Gilbert and his books. Mrs. Ormonde led her gently on, soothed by the music.

In the afternoon she decided to drive with Thyrza to the top of Beachy Head; on the morrow the sky might not be so favourable to the view. The children would go out in the usual way; she preferred to be alone with her visitor for a while.

' Will they have the telegraph yet ? ' Thyrza asked, as she again seated herself in the carriage.

' Oh, long since. We could have had an answer before now.'

Thyrza sighed with contentment, for she knew that Lyddy was glad on her behalf.

So now the keen breath of the sea folded her about and made warmth through her whole body; it sang in her ears, the eternal sea music which to infinite generations of mortals has been an inspiring joy. Upward, upward, on the long sweep of the climbing road, whilst landward the horizon retired from curve to curve off the wild Downs, and on the other hand a dark edge against the sky made fearful promise of precipitous shore. The great snow-mountains of heaven moved grandly on before the west wind, ever changing outline, meeting to incorporate mass with mass, sundering with magic softness and silence. The bay of Pevensey spread with graceful line its white fringe of breakers now low upon the strand, far away to the cliffs of Hastings.

' Hastings ! ' Thyrza exclaimed, when Mrs. Ormonde had mentioned the name. ' Is that where the battle of Hastings was ? '

' A little further inland. You have read of that ? '

' Gilbert—Mr. Grail is teaching me history. Yes, I know about Hastings.'

' And what country do you think you would come to, if you went right over the sea yonder ? '

' That must be—really ?— where William the Conqueror came from ? That was Normandy, in France.'

' Yes, France is over there.'

' France ? France ? '

No, it was too hard to believe. She murmured the name to herself. Gilbert had shown it her on the map, but how difficult to transfer that dry symbol into this present reality !

They left the carriage near the Coastguard's house, and walked forward to the brow of the great cliffs. Mrs. Ormonde took Thyrza's hand as they drew near. They stood there for a long time.

Two or three other people were walking about the Head. In talking, Mrs. Ormonde became aware that someone had approached her ; she turned her head, and saw Annabel Newthorpe.

They shook hands quietly. Thyrza drew a little away.

' Are you alone ? ' Mrs. Ormonde asked.

' Yes, I have walked.'

' Who do you think this is ? ' Mrs. Ormonde murmured quickly. ' Mr. Grail's future wife. She has just brought one of my children down ; I am going to keep her till Monday. Come and speak ; the most loveable child ! '

Thyrza and Annabel were presented to each other with the pleasant informality which Mrs. Ormonde so naturally employed. Each was impressed with the other's beauty; Thyrza felt not a little awe, and Annabel could not gaze enough at the lovely face which made such a surprise for her.

' Why did Mr. Egremont give me no suggestion of this ? ' she said to herself.

She had noticed, in drawing near, how intimately her friend and the stranger were talking together. Her arrival had disturbed Thyrza's confidence ; she herself did not feel able to talk quite freely. So in a few minutes she turned and went by the footway along the edge of the height. Just before descending into a hollow which would hide her, she cast a look back, and saw that Thyrza's eyes were following her.

' But how could he speak of her and yet tell me nothing ? '

His delicacy explained it, no doubt. He had not liked to say of the simple girl whom Grail was to marry that she was very beautiful. Annabel felt that most men would have been less scrupulous : it was characteristic of Egremont to feel a subtle propriety of that kind.

Annabel was at all times disposed to interpret Egremont's motives in a higher sense than would apply to the average man.

On her return, Thyrza had tea with Mrs. Mapper and the children, then went with them to the large room upstairs in which evenings were spent till the early bedtime. It was an ideal nursery, with abundant picture-books, with toys, with everything that could please a child's eye and engage a child's mind. There was a piano, and on this Mrs. Mapper sometimes played the kind of music that children would like. She taught them songs, moreover, and a singing evening was always much looked forward to. Saturday was always such; when the little choir had got a song perfect, Mrs. Ormonde was wont to come up and hear them sing it, making them glad with her praise.

It happened that to-night there was to be practising of a new song; Mrs. Mapper had chosen 'Annie Laurie,' and she began by playing over the air. One or two of the children knew it, but not the words; these, it was found, were always very quickly learnt by singing a verse a few times over.

'Do you know "Annie Laurie," Miss Trent?' Mrs. Mapper asked.

It was one of old Mr. Boddy's favourites; Thyrza had sung it to him since she was seven years old.

'Let us sing it together then, will you?'

They began. Thyrza was already thoroughly at home, and this music was an unexpected delight. After a line or two, Mrs. Mapper's voice sank. Thyrza stopped and looked inquiringly, meeting a wonder in the other's eyes. Mrs. Mapper was a woman of much prudence; she merely said:

'I find I've got a little cold. Would you mind singing it alone?'

So Thyrza sang the song through. A moment or two of quietness followed.

'Now I think you'll soon know it, children,' said Mrs. Mapper. 'Lizzie Smith, I see you've got it already. Miss Trent will be kind enough to sing the first verse again; you sing with her, Lizzie—and you too, Mary. That's a clever girl! Now we shall get on.'

The practising went on till all were able to join in fairly well. After that, Mrs. Mapper played the favourite dance tunes, and the children danced merrily. Whilst they were so enjoying themselves, Mrs. Ormonde came into the room. She had dined, and wanted Thyrza to come and sit with her, for she was alone. But first she had five minutes of real laughter and play with the children. They loved her, every one of them, and clung to her desperately when she said she could stay no longer.

'Good-bye!' she said, waving her hand at the door.

'No, no!' cried several voices. 'There's "good-night" yet, Mrs. Ormonde!'

'Why, of course there is,' she laughed; 'but that's no reason why I shouldn't say good-bye.'

She took Thyrza's hand and led her down.

'You shall have some supper with me afterwards,' she said. 'The little ones have theirs now; but it's too early for you.'

If the drawing-room had been a marvel to Thyrza in the daylight, it was yet more so now that she entered it and found two delicately shaded lamps giving a rich uncertainty to all the beautiful forms of furniture and ornaments. She had thought the Grails' parlour luxurious. And the dear old easy-chair, now so familiar to her, how humble it was compared with this in which Mrs. Ormonde seated her! These wonders caused her no envy or uneasy desire. In looking at a glorious altar-piece, one does not feel unhappy because one cannot carry it off from the church and hang it up at home. Thyrza's mood was purely of admiration, and of joy in being deemed worthy to visit such scenes. And all the time she kept saying to herself, 'Another whole day! I shall be by the sea again to-morrow! I shall sleep and wake close by the sea!'

Presently Mrs. Ormonde had to absent herself for a few minutes.

'You heard what the children said about "good-night." I always go and see them as soon as they are tucked up in bed. I don't think they'd sleep if I missed.'

The kind office over, she spoke with Mrs. Mapper about the evening's singing.

'Did you know,' the latter asked, 'what a voice Miss Trent has?'

'She sings? I didn't know.'

'I was so delighted that I had to stop singing myself. I'm sure it's a wonderful voice.'

'Indeed! I must ask her to sing to me.'

She found Thyrza turning over the leaves of a volume of photographs. Without speaking, she sat down at the piano, and began to play gently the air of 'Annie Laurie.' Thyrza looked up, and then came nearer.

'You are fond of music?' said Mrs. Ormonde.

'Very fond.   How beautiful your playing is!'

'To-morrow you shall hear Miss Newthorpe play; hers is much better.   Will you sing this for me?'

When it was sung, she asked what other songs Thyrza knew.   They were all, of course, such as the people sing; some of them Mrs. Ormonde did not know at all, but to others she was able to play an accompaniment.   Her praise was limited to a few kind words.   On leaving the piano, she was thoughtful.

At ten o'clock Mrs. Mapper came to conduct Thyrza to her bedroom.

'We have breakfast at half-past eight to-morrow,' Mrs. Ormonde said.

'If I am up in time,' Thyrza asked, 'may I go out before breakfast?'

'Do just as you like, my dear,' the other answered, with a smile.   'I want you to enjoy your visit.'

In spite of the strangeness of her room, and of the multitude of thoughts and feelings to which the day had given birth, Thyrza was not long awake.   She passed into a dreamland where all she had newly learnt was reproduced and glorified. But the rising sun had not to wait long for the opening of her eyes.   She sprang from bed and to the window, whence, however, she could only see the tall chestnuts and a neighbouring cottage.   The day was again fine; she dressed with nervous speed—there was no Lyddy to do her hair, for the very first time in her life—then went softly forth on to the landing.   No one seemed to be stirring; she had no watch to tell her the time, but doubtless it was very early.   Softly she began to descend the stairs, and at length recognised the door of the drawing-room.   She did not like to enter: it was only Mrs. Ormonde's kindness that had given her a right to sit there the evening before.   But the house-door would not be open yet, she feared.   Just as she was reluctantly turning to go up and wait a little longer in her bedroom, a sound below at once startled and relieved her.   Looking over the banisters, she saw a servant coming from one of the rooms on the ground floor.   She hurried down.   The servant looked at her with surprise.

'Good-morning!' she said.   'Can I get out of the house?'

'I'll open the door for you, Miss.'

'What time is it, please?'

'It isn't quite half-past six, Miss. You're an early riser.'

'Yes, I want to go out before breakfast. Please will you tell me which way goes to the sea?'

The servant gave her good-natured directions, and Thyrza was soon running along with a glimpse of blue horizon for guidance. She ran like a child, ran till the sharp morning air made her breathless, then walked until she was able to run again. And at length she was on the beach, down at length by the very edge of the waves. Here the breeze was so strong that with difficulty she stood against it, but its rude caresses were a joy to her. Each breaker seemed a living thing; now she approached timidly, now ran back with a delicious fear. She filled her hands with the smooth sea-pebbles; a trail of weed with the foam fresh on it was a great discovery. Then her eye caught a far-off line of smoke. That must be a steamer coming from a foreign country; perhaps from France, which was—how believe it?—yonder across the blue vast.

You have watched with interest some close-folded bud; one day all promise is shut within those delicate sepals, and on the next, for the fulness of time has come, you find the very flower with its glow and its perfume. So it sometimes happens that a human soul finds its season, and at a touch expands to wonderful new life.

Mrs. Ormonde perceived at breakfast that Thyrza desired nothing more than to be left to pass her day in freedom. So she gave her visitor a little bag with provision against seaside appetite, and let her go forth till dinner-time; then again till the hour of tea. In the evening Thyrza was again bidden to the drawing-room. She found Miss Newthorpe there.

'Come now, and tell us what you have been doing all day long,' Mrs. Ormonde said. 'Why, the sun and the wind have already touched your cheeks!'

'I have enjoyed myself,' Thyrza replied, quickly, seating herself near her new friend.

She could give little more description than that. Annabel talked with her, and presently, at Mrs. Ormonde's request, went to the piano. When the first notes had sounded, Thyrza let her head droop a little. Music such as this she had not imagined. When Annabel came back to her seat, she gazed at her, admiring and loving.

'Now will you sing us "Annie Laurie"?' said Mrs. Ormonde. 'I'll play for you.'

'What is that child's future ?' Mrs. Ormonde asked of Annabel, when Thyrza had left them together.

'Not a sad one, I think,' said Annabel, musingly. 'Happily, her husband will not be an untaught working man.'

'No, thank goodness for that! I suppose they will be married in two or three weeks. Her voice is a beautiful thing lost.'

'We won't grieve over that. Her own happiness is of more account. I do wish father could have seen her!'

'Oh, she must come to us again some day. Your father would have alarmed her too much. Haven't you felt all the time as if she were something very delicate, something to be carefully guarded against shocks and hazards? As I saw her from my window going out of the garden this morning, I felt a sort of fear; I was on the point of sending a servant to keep watch over her from a distance.

There was a silence, then Mrs. Ormonde murmured:

'I wonder whether she is in love with him?'

Annabel smiled, but said nothing.

'She told me that he is very kind to her. "Just as kind as Lyddy," she said. Indeed, who wouldn't be?'

'We have every reason to think highly of Mr. Grail,' Annabel remarked. 'He must be as exceptional in his class as she is.'

'Yes. But the exceptional people——'

Annabel looked inquiringly.

'Never mind! The world has beautiful things in it, and one of the most beautiful is hope.'

CHAPTER XVII

ADRIFT

IT was partly out of kindness to Thyrza that Totty Nancarrow had changed her mind about going to Eastbourne. Having seen her and mentioned the matter, Totty saw at once how eagerly Thyrza would accept such a chance. But it happened that within the same hour she saw Luke Ackroyd, and Luke had proposed a meeting on Saturday afternoon. Totty had no extreme desire to meet him, and yet—perhaps she might as well. He talked of going up the river to Battersea Park, as the weather was so fine.

So at three on Saturday, Totty stood by the landing-stage at Lambeth. In fact, she was there at least five minutes before the appointed time. But her punctuality was wasted. Ten minutes past three by Lambeth parish church, and no Mr. Ackroyd.

'Well, I call this nice!' Totty exclaimed to herself. 'Let him come now if he likes; he won't find *me* waiting for him. And a lot I care!'

She went off humming a tune and swinging her hands. On the Embankment she met a girl she knew. They went on into Westminster Bridge Road, and there came across another friend. It was decided that they should all go and have tea at Totty's. And before they reached Newport Street, yet another friend joined them. The more the merrier! Totty delighted in packing her tiny room as full as it would hold. She ran into Mrs. Bower's for a pot of jam. Who more mirthful now than Totty Nancarrow!

With subdued gossip and laughter all ran up the narrow staircase and into Totty's room. A fire had first of all to be lit; Totty was a deft hand at that; not a girl in Lambeth could start a blaze and have her kettle boiling in sharper time on a cold dark morning. But, after all, there would not be bread enough. Tilly Roach would be off for that. 'Mind you bring the over-weight!' the others screamed after her, and some current joke seemed to be involved in the injunction, for at once they all laughed as only work-girls can.

Tilly was back in no time. She was a little, slim girl, with the palest and shortest of gold hair, and a pretty face spoilt with freckles. As at all times, she had her pocket full of sweets, and ate them incessantly. As a rule, Tilly cannot have eaten less than a couple of pounds of lollipops every week, and doubtless would have consumed more had her pocket-money allowed it. The second of Totty's guests was Annie West, whom you know already, for she was at the 'friendly lead' when Thyrza sang; she was something of a scapegrace, constantly laughed in a shrill note, and occasionally had to be called to order. The third was a Mrs. Allchin, aged fifteen, a married woman of two months' date; her hair was cut across her forehead, she wore large eardrops, and over her jacket hung a necklace with a silver locket. Mrs. Allchin, called by her intimates 'Loo,' had the air of importance which became her position.

There were only two chairs in the room; the table had to

be placed so that the bed could serve for sitting. Tablecloth there was none; when friends did her the honour of coming to tea, Totty spread a newspaper. The tea-service was, to say the least, primitive; four cups there were, but only two saucers survived, and a couple of teaspoons had to be shared harmoniously. No one ever gave a thought to such trifles at Totty Nancarrow's.

Whilst the kettle boiled, Annie West provided diversion of a literary kind. She had recently purchased a little book in cover of yellow paper, which, for the sum of one penny, purported to give an exhaustive description of 'Charms, Spells, and Incantations;' on the back was the picture of a much-bejewelled Moorish maiden, with eyes thrown up in prophetic ecstasy; above ran the legend, 'Wonderfully mysterious and peculiar.' The work included, moreover, 'a splendid selection of the best love songs.'

'It's cheap at a penny,' was Miss West's opinion.

She began by reading out an infallible charm for the use of maidens who would see in dreams their future husband. It was the 'Nine-key Charm.'

'"Get nine small keys, they must all be your own by begging or purchase (borrowing will not do, nor must you tell what you want them for), plait a three-plaited band of your own hair, and tie them together, fastening the ends with nine knots. Fasten them with one of your garters to your left wrist on going to bed, and bind the other garter round your head; then say:

> St. Peter, take it not amiss,
> To try your favour I've done this.
> You are the ruler of the keys,
> Favour me, then, if you please;
> Let me then your influence prove,
> And see my dear and wedded love.

This must be done on the eve of St. Peter's, and is an old charm used by the maidens of Rome in ancient times, who put great faith in it."'

'When is the eve of St. Peter's?' asked Tilly Roach. Totty, you're a Catholic, you ought to know.'

'Don't bother me with your rubbish!' cried Totty.

'It ain't rubbish at all,' retorted Annie West. 'Now didn't you see your husband, Loo, with a card charm before you'd ever really set eyes on him?'

'Course I did,' assented Mrs. Allchin, aged fifteen.

'Here's another book I'm going to get,' pursued Annie, referring to an advertisement on the cover. 'It tells you no end of things—see here!' "How to bewitch your enemies," "How to render yourself invisible," "How to grow young again," "How to read sealed letters," "How to see at long distances," and heaps more. "Price one and sixpence, or, post free, twenty stamps."'

'Don't be a fool and waste your money!' was Totty's uncompromising advice. 'It's only sillies believes things like that.'

'Totty ain't no need of charms!' piped Tilly, with sweets in her mouth. 'She knows who *she's* going to marry.'

'Do I, miss?' Totty exclaimed, scornfully. 'Do you know as much for yourself, I wonder?'

'Oh, Tilly's a-going to marry the p'liceman with red hair as stands on the Embankment!' came from Mrs. Allchin; whereupon followed inextinguishable laughter.

But they were determined to tease Totty, and began to talk from one to the other about Luke Ackroyd, not mentioning his name, but using signs and symbols.

'If you two wait for husbands till I'm married,' said Totty at length to the laughing girls, ' you've a good chance to die old maids. I prefer to keep my earnings for my own spending, thank you.'

'When's Thyrza Trent going to be married?' asked Mrs. Allchin. 'Do you know, Totty?'

'In about a fortnight, I think.'

'Is the bands puts up?'

'They're going to be married at the Registry Office.'

'Well, I never!' cried Annie West. 'You wouldn't catch me doing without a proper wedding! I suppose that's why Thyrza won't talk about it. But I believe he's a rum sort of man, isn't he?'

Nobody could reply from personal acquaintance with Gilbert Grail. Totty did not choose to give her opinion.

'I say,' she exclaimed, ' we've had enough about marriages. Tilly, make yourself useful, child, and cut some bread.'

For a couple of hours at least gossip was unintermittent. Then Mrs. Allchin declared that her husband would be 'making a row' if she stayed from home any later. Tilly Roach took leave at the same time. Totty and Miss West chatted a little longer, then put on their hats to have a ramble in Lambeth Walk.

o

They had not gone many paces from the house when they were overtaken by some one, who said:

'Totty! I want to speak to you.'

Totty would not look round. It was Ackroyd's voice.

'I say, Totty!'

But she walked on. Ackroyd remained on the edge of the pavement. In a minute or two he saw that Miss Nancarrow was coming towards him unaccompanied.

'Oh, it's you, is it?' she said. 'What do you want, Mr. Ackroyd?'

'Why didn't you come this afternoon?'

'Well, I like that! Why didn't *you* come?'

'I was a bit late. I really couldn't help it, Totty. Did you go away before I came?'

'Why, of course I did. How long was I to wait?'

'I'm very sorry. Let's go somewhere now. I've been waiting about for more than an hour on the chance of seeing you.'

He mentioned the chief music-hall of the neighbourhood.

'I don't mind,' said Totty. 'But I can't go beyond sixpence.'

'Oh, all right! I'll see to that.'

'No, you won't. I pay for myself, or I don't go at all. That's my rule.'

'As you like.'

The place of entertainment was only just open; they went in with a crowd of people and found seats. The prevailing odours of the hall were stale beer and stale tobacco; the latter was speedily freshened by the fumes from pipes. Ackroyd ordered a glass of beer, and deposited it on a little ledge before him, an arrangement similar to that for different purposes in a church pew; Totty would have nothing.

Ackroyd had changed a good deal during the last few months. The coarser elements of his face had acquired a disagreeable prominence, and when he laughed, as he did constantly, the sound lacked the old genuineness. To-night he was evidently trying hard to believe that he enjoyed the music-hall entertainment; in former days he would have dismissed anything of the kind with a few contemptuous words. When the people about him roared at imbecilities unspeakable, he threw back his head and roared with them; when they stamped, he raised as much dust as any one. Totty had no need to affect amusement; her tendency to laughter was such

that very little sufficed to keep her in the carelessly merry frame
of mind which agreed with her, and on the whole it was not
disagreeable to be sitting by Luke Ackroyd ; she glanced at
him surreptitiously at times.

He drank two or three glasses of beer, then felt a need of
stronger beverage. Totty remonstrated with him : he laughed,
and drank on out of boastfulness. At length Totty would
countenance it no longer ; after a useless final warning, she
left her place and pressed through the crowd to the door.
Ackroyd sprang up and followed her. His face was flushed,
and grew more so in the sudden night air.

' What's the matter ? ' he said, putting his arm through
the girl's. ' You're not going to leave me in that way, Totty ?
Well, let's walk about then.'

' Look here, Mr. Ackroyd,' began Totty, ' I'm surprised at
you ! It ain't like a man of your kind to go muddling his head
night after night, in this way.'

' I know that as well as you do, Totty. See ! ' He made
her stop, and added in a lower voice, ' Say you'll marry me,
and I'll stop it from to-night.'

' I've told you already I shan't do nothing of the kind. So
don't be silly ! You can be sensible enough if you like, and
then I can get along well enough with you.'

' Very well, then I'll drink for another week, and then be
off to Canada.'

' You'd better go at once, I should think.'

She had moved a little apart from him. Just then a half-
drunken fellow came along the pavement, and in a freak
caught Totty about the waist. Ackroyd was in the very
mood for an incident of this kind. In an instant he had
planted so direct a blow that the fellow staggered back into
the gutter, Totty with difficulty preventing herself from being
dragged with him. The thoroughfare was crowded, street
urchins ran together with yells of anticipatory delight, and
maturer loafers formed the wonted ring even before the man
assaulted had recovered himself. Then came the play of fists ;
Ackroyd from the first had far the best of it, but the other
managed to hold his ground.

And the result of it was that in something less than a
quarter of an hour from his leaving the music-hall, Ackroyd
found himself on the way to the police-station, his adversary
following in the care of a second constable, all the way loudly
accusing him of being the assailant.

Totty walked in the rear of the crowd; she had been frightened by the scene of violence, and there were marks of tears on her cheeks. She entered the station, eager to get a hearing for a plain story. Ackroyd turned and saw her.

'It's no good saying anything now,' he said to her. 'This blackguard has plenty more lies ready. Go to the house and tell my brother-in-law, will you? I dare say he'll come and be bail.'

She went at once, and ran all the way to Paradise Street, so that when in reply to her knock Mrs. Poole appeared at the door, she had to wait yet a moment before her breath would suffice for speaking. She did not know Mrs. Poole.

'I've got a message from Mr. Ackroyd for Mr. Poole,' she said.

The other was alarmed.

'What's happened now?' she inquired. 'I'm Mrs. Poole, Mr. Ackroyd's sister.'

Totty lowered her voice, and explained rapidly what had come to pass. Mrs. Poole eyed her throughout with something more than suspicion.

'And who may you be, if you please?' she asked at the end.

'I'm Miss Nancarrow.'

'I'm not much wiser. Thank you. I'll let Mr. Poole know.'

She closed the door. Totty, thus unceremoniously shut out, turned away; she felt miserable, and the feeling was so strange to her that before she had gone many steps she again began to cry. She had understood well enough the thought expressed in Mrs. Poole's face; it was gratuitous unkindness, and just now she was not prepared for it. There was much of the child in her still, for all her years of independence in the highways and by-ways of Lambeth, and, finding it needful to cry, she let her tears have free course, only now and then dashing the back of her hand against the corner of her lips as she walked on. Why should the woman be so ready to think evil of her? She had done nothing whatever to deserve it, nothing; she had kept herself a good girl, for all that she lived alone and liked to laugh. At another time most likely she would have cared something less than a straw for Mrs. Poole's opinion of her, but just now—somehow—well, she didn't know quite how it was. Why would Luke keep on drinking in that way, and oblige her to run out of the music-hall ? It was his fault, the foolish fellow. But he had been quick enough to defend her ; a girl would not find it amiss to have that arm always at her service. And in the meantime he was in the police cell.

Mrs. Poole, excessively annoyed, went down to the kitchen. Her husband sat in front of the fire, a long clay pipe at his lips, his feet very wide apart on the fender ; up on the high mantel-piece stood a half finished glass of beer. Though he still held the pipe, he was nodding ; as his wife entered, his head fell very low.

'Jim ! ' exclaimed his wife, as if something had been added to her annoyance.

'Eh ? Well, Jane ?—eh ? '

'Then you *will* set your great feet on the fender ! The minute I turn my back, of course ! If you're too lazy to take your boots off, you must keep your heels under the chair. I won't have my fender scratched, so I tell you ! '

He was a large-headed man, sleepy in appearance at the best of times, but enormously good-natured. He bent down in a startled way to see if his boots had really done any harm.

'Well, well, I won't do it again, Jenny,' he mumbled.

'Of course, I wonder how often you've said that. As it happens, it's as well you have got your boots on still. There's a girl o' some kind just come to say as Luke's locked up for fightin' in the street. He sent for you to bail him out.'

'Why, there ! Tut-tut-tut ! What a fellow that is ! Fightin'? Why now, didn't I tell him this afternoon as he looked like pickin' a quarrel wi' somebody ? But, I say, Jane, it's a low-life kind o' thing for to go a-fightin' in the streets.'

'Of course it is. What'll he come to next, I wonder ? The sooner he gets off to Canada, the better, I sh'd say. But he'll not go ; he talks an' talks, an' it's all just for showin' off.'

Mr. Poole had risen.

'Bail ? Why, I don't know nothin' about bail, Jane ! How d'you do it ? I hadn't never nothing to do with folks as got locked up.'

'I don't suppose you never had, Jim, till now.'

'Nay, hang it, Jenny, I wasn't for alludin' to that ! Give me my coat. How much money have we in the house ? I've sixpence 'apenny i' my pocket.'

'It ain't done with money ; you'll have to sign something. I think.'

'All right. But I'll read it first, though. Who was it as come, did you say?'

'Nay, I don't know. She called herself Miss Nancarrow. I didn't care to have much to say to her.'

Mrs. Poole was a kindly disposed woman, but, like her average sisters, found charity hard when there was ever so slight an appearance against another of her sex. We admire this stalwart virtue, you and I, reverencing public opinion; all the same, charity has something to be said for it.

'Miss Nancarrow, eh?' said Poole, dragging on his big overcoat. 'Don't know her. Kennington Road station, is it?'

'You'd better finish your beer, Jim.'

'So I will. Have a bit o' supper ready for the lad.'

Totty walked as far as the police-station. She could not bring herself to enter and make inquiries; that look of Mrs. Poole's would be hard to bear from men. Her tears were dry now; she stood reading the notices on the board. A man had deserted his wife and left her chargeable to the parish; there was a reward for his apprehension. 'That's the woman's fault,' Totty said to herself. 'She's made his home miserable for him. If I had a husband, I don't think he'd want to run away from *me*. If he did, well, I should say, "good riddance." Catch me setting the p'lice after him!' The body of a child had been found; a woman answering to a certain description was wanted. 'Poor thing!' thought Totty. 'She's more likely to pity than to blame. They shouldn't take her if I could help it.' So she commented on each notice, in accordance with her mood.

It was very cold. She had no gloves on, and her hands were getting quite numb. Would Mr. Poole answer the summons? If not, Luke would, she supposed, remain in the cell all night. It would be cold enough *there*, poor fellow!

She had waited about twenty minutes, when a large-headed man in a big overcoat came up, and, after eyeing the edifice from roof to pavement, ascended the steps and entered.

'I shouldn't wonder if that's him,' murmured Totty. And she waited anxiously.

In a quarter of an hour, the man appeared again, and after him came—oh yes, it was Luke! He had his eyes on the ground. The rescuer put his arm in Luke's, and they walked off together.

He had not seen her, and she was disappointed. She

followed at a short distance behind them. The large-headed man spoke occasionally, but Ackroyd seemed to make brief reply, if any. Their way took them along Walnut Tree Walk; Totty saw that, in passing the house where Lydia and Thyrza lived, Luke cast a glance at the upper windows; probably he knew nothing of Thyrza's absence at Eastbourne. They turned into Lambeth Walk, then again into Paradise Street, Totty still a little distance in the rear. At their house, they paused. Luke seemed to be going further on, and, to the girl's surprise, he did so, whilst Mr. Poole entered.

He turned to the left, this time into Newport Street. Totty felt a strange tightness at her chest, for all at once she guessed what his purpose was.

It was still only half-past ten; people were moving about. Newport Street has only one inhabited side; the other is formed by the railway viaduct, the arches of which are boarded up and made to serve for stables, warehouses, workshops. Moreover, the thoroughfare is very badly lighted; on the railway side one can walk along at night-time without risk of recognition. Totty availed herself of this gloom, and kept nearly opposite to Luke. He stopped before her house, hesitated, was about to approach the door. Then Totty—no stranger being near—called softly across the street:

'Mr. Ackroyd!'

He turned at once, and came over.

'Why, is that you?' he said. 'What are you doing there, Totty?'

'Oh, nothing. So they've let you go?'

She spoke indifferently. It had been on her tongue to say that she had followed from the police-station, but the other words came instead.

'I shall have to turn up on Monday morning,' Luke replied.

'What a shame! Did they keep that man?'

'Yes. They kept us both. He kept swearing I'd an old grudge against him, and that he'd done nothing at all. The blackguard had the impudence to charge me with assault; so I charged him too. Then that constable said he'd had us both in charge before for drunk and disorderly. Altogether, it wasn't a bad lying-match.'

'Why do you run the chance of getting into such rows?'

'Well, I like that, Totty! Was I to let him insult you and just stand by?'

'Oh, I don't mean that. But it wouldn't have happened at all but for you going on drinking—you know that very well, Mr. Ackroyd.'

'I suppose it wouldn't. It doesn't matter. I just wanted to see you'd got home all right. Good-night!'

'Good-night! Mind *you* get home safe, that's all.'

She turned away. He turned away. But he was back before she had crossed the street.

'I say, Totty!'

'What is it?'

'You haven't told me what you were doing, standing here.'

'I don't see as it matters to you, Mr. Ackroyd.'

'No, I suppose it doesn't. Well, good-night!'

'Good-night!'

Each again turned to depart; again Ackroyd came back.

'Totty!'

'What *is* it, Mr. Ackroyd?' she exclaimed, fretfully.

'I can't for the life of me make out what you were doing standing there.'

'I don't see as it's any business of yours, Mr. Ackroyd.'

'Still, I'd rather you told me. I suppose you were waiting for somebody?'

'If you *must* know—yes, I was.'

'H'm, I thought so. Well, I won't stop to be in the way.'

'I say, Mr. Ackroyd!'

'Yes?'

'There's a notice outside the station as says a man has deserted his wife.'

'Is there? How do you know?'

'I read it.'

'Oh, you've been waiting there, have you?'

'And another thing. It wasn't no use you looking up at Thyrza Trent's window. She's away.'

'How do you know I locked up?'

He came nearer, a smile on his face. Totty averted her eyes.

'I suppose it wasn't me you were waiting for, Totty?'

She said nothing.

'Give me a kiss, Totty.'

'I'm sure I shan't, Mr. Ackroyd!'

'Then let me take one.'

She made no resistance.

' When, Totty ? ' he whispered, drawing her near.

' Next Christmas, if you haven't taken a drop too much before then. If I find out you *have*—it's no good you coming after Totty Nancarrow.'

She walked with him to the end of the street, then watched him to his house. She was pleased ; she was ashamed ; she was afraid. Turning to go home, she crossed herself and murmured something.

CHAPTER XVIII

DRAWING NEARER

LYDIA had a little rule of self-discipline which deserved to be, and was, its own reward. If ever personal troubles began to worry her she diligently bent her thoughts upon someone for whose welfare she was anxious, and whom she might possibly aid. The rule had to submit to an emphatic exception ; the person to be thought of must be any one *save* that particular one whose welfare she especially desired, and whom she might perchance have aided if she had made a great endeavour. However, the rule itself had become established long before this exception was dreamt of. Formerly she was wont to occupy her mind with Thyrza. Now that her sister seemed all but beyond need of anxious guarding, and that the necessity for applying the rule was greater than ever before, Lydia gave her attention to Mr. Boddy.

The old man had not borne the winter very well ; looking at him, Lydia could not help observing that he stooped more than was his habit, and that his face was more drawn. He did his best to put a bright aspect on things when he talked with her, but there were signs that he found it increasingly difficult to obtain sufficient work. A few months ago she would have had no scruple in speaking freely on the subject to Mary Bower, or even to Mrs. Bower, and so learning from them whether the old man paid his rent regularly and had enough food. But from Mary she was estranged— it seemed as if hopelessly—and Mrs. Bower had of late been anything but cordial when Lydia went to the shop. The girl observed that Mr. Boddy was now never to be found seated in

the back parlour : she always had to go up to his room.
She could not bring herself to mention this to him, or indeed
to say anything that would suggest her coolness with the
Bowers.   Still, it was all tacitly understood, and it made
things very uncomfortable.

She was still angry with Mary.   Every night she chid herself for doing what she had never done before—for nourishing
unkindness.   She shed many tears in secret.   But forgiveness
would not grow in her heart.   She thought not seldom of the
precepts she had heard at chapel, and—curiously—they by
degrees separated themselves from her individual resentment ;
much she desired to make them her laws, for they seemed
beautiful to her conscience.   Could she but receive that
Christian spirit, it would be easy to go to Mary and say, ' I
have been wrong ; forgive me ! '   The day was not yet come.

So she had to turn over plans for helping the poor old
man who long ago had so helped her and Thyrza.   Of course
she thought of the possibility of his coming to live in Thyrza's
house ; yet how propose that ?   Thyrza had so much to occupy
her ; it was not wonderful that she took for granted Mr.
Boddy's well-being.   And would it be justifiable to impose a
burden of this kind upon the newly-married pair ?   To be sure
she could earn enough to pay for the little that Mr. Boddy
needed.   Thyrza had almost angrily rejected the idea that
her sister should pay rent in the new house ; payment for
board she would only accept because Lydia declared that
if it were not accepted she would live elsewhere.   So there
would remain a margin for the old man's needs.   But his
presence in the house was the difficulty.   It might be very
inconvenient, and in any case such a proposal ought to come
from Gilbert first of all.   The old man, moreover, was very
sensitive on the point involved ; such a change would have to
be brought about with every delicacy.   Still, it must come to
that before long.

Perhaps the best would be to wait until Thyrza was
actually married, and discover how the household arrangements worked.   Thyrza herself would then perhaps notice
the old man's failing strength.

Lydia went to see him on Sunday afternoon.   The bright
day suggested to her that she should take him out for a walk.
She had waited until Mary would be away at the school.   Mr.
Bower lay on the sofa snoring : the after-smell of roast beef
and cabbage was heavy in the air of the room.   Mrs. Bower

would have also slept but for the necessity of having an eye to the shop, which was open on Sunday as on other days; her drowsiness made her irritable, and she only muttered as Lydia went through to the staircase. Lydia had come this way for the sake of appearances; she resolved that on the next occasion she would ring Mr. Boddy's bell at the side door. Upstairs, the old man was reading his thumbed Bible. He never went to a place of worship, but read the Bible on Sunday without fail.

He was delighted to go out into the sunshine.

' And when did the little one get back ? ' he asked, as he drew out his overcoat—the Christmas gift—from a drawer in which it was carefully folded.

' Why, what do you think ? She won't be back till to-morrow. Yesterday, when I got back from work, there was a telegraph waiting for me. It was from the lady at Eastbourne, Mrs. Ormonde, and just said she was going to keep Thyrza till Monday, because it would do her good. How she will be enjoying herself! '

They left the house by the private door and went in the direction of the river. Lydia ordinarily walked at a good pace; now she accommodated her steps to those of her companion. Her tall shapely figure made that of the old man look very decrepit. When he had anything of importance to say, Mr. Boddy came to a stand, and Lydia would bend a little forward, listening to him so attentively that she was quite unaware of the glances of those who passed by. So they got to the foot of Lambeth Bridge.

' We mustn't go too far,' Lydia said, ' or you'll be tired, grandad. Suppose we walk a little way along the Embankment. It's too cold, I'm afraid, to sit down. But isn't it nice to have sunshine ? How that child must be enjoying herself, to be sure ! She was almost crazy yesterday morning before she got off; I'm certain she didn't sleep not two hours in the night. It's very kind of that lady to keep her, isn't it ? But everybody *is* kind to Thyrza, they can't help being.'

' No more they can, Lyddy; no more they can. But there's somebody else as I want to see enjoying herself a little. When 'll your turn come for a bit of a holiday, my dear ? You work year in year out, and you're so quiet over it any one 'ud forget as you wanted a rest just like other people.'

' We shall see, grandad. Wait till the summer comes, and

Thyrza's well settled down, and then who knows but you and me may run away together for a day at the seaside! I'm going to be rich, because they won't let me pay anything for my room. We'll keep that as a secret to ourselves.'

'Well, well,' said the old man, chuckling from sheer pleasure in her affection, 'there's no knowin'. I'd like to go to the seaside once more, and I'd rather you was with me than any one else. We always find something to talk about, I think, Lyddy. And 'taint with everybody I care to talk nowadays. It's hard to find people as has the same thoughts. But you and me, we remember together, don't we, Lyddy? Now, do *you* remember one night as there come a soldier into the shop, a soldier as wanted to buy——'

'A looking-glass!' Lydia exclaimed. 'I know! I remember!'

'A looking-glass! And when he'd paid for it, he took up his stick an' smashed the glass right in the middle, then walked off with it under his arm!'

'Why, what years it must be since I thought of that, grandad! And I ran away, frightened!'

'I was frightened myself too. And we never could understand it! Last night, when I was lying awake, that soldier came back to me, and I laughed so; and I thought, I'll ask Lyddy to-morrow if she remembers that.'

They both laughed, then pursued their walk.

'Why look,' said Mr. Boddy presently, 'here's Mr. Ackroyd a-comin' along!'

Lydia had already seen him; that was why she had become silent.

'You're not going to stop, are you, grandad?' she asked, under her breath.

'Why no, my dear? Not if you don't wish.'

'I'd rather not.'

Ackroyd was walking with his hands in his pockets, looking carelessly about him. He recognised the two at a little distance, and drew one hand forth. Till he got quite near he affected not to have seen them; then, without a smile, he raised his hat, and walked past, his pace accelerated. Lydia, also with indifferent face, just bent to the greeting. Mr. Boddy had given a friendly nod.

There was silence between the companions, then Lydia said:

'I've thought it better, grandad, not to—not to be quite the same with Mr. Ackroyd as I used to be.'

'Yes, yes, Lyddy; I understand. There's a deal of talk about him. I'm sorry. He's done me more than one good turn, and I hope he'll get straight again yet. I'm afraid, my dear, as—you know—the disappointment——'

Lydia interrupted with firmness.

'That's no excuse at all—not a bit! If he really felt the disappointment so much he ought to have borne it like a man. Other people have as much to bear. I never thought he was a man of that kind, never! We won't say anything more about him.'

Their conversation so lightened the way that they reached Westminster Bridge, and returned by the road which runs along the rear of the hospital.

'You won't come in, Lyddy?' said the old man, when they were near the shop again.

'Not to-day, grandad. I'm going to tea with Mrs. Grail and Gilbert, because Thyrza's away.'

He acquiesced, trying to conceal the sadness he felt. Lydia kissed his cheek, and left him.

All through tea in the Grails' parlour the talk was of Thyrza. How was she passing her time? Was it as fine at Eastbourne as here in London? What sort of a lady was Mrs. Ormonde? And when the three drew chairs about the fire, Gilbert had something of moment to communicate, something upon which he had resolved since Thyrza's departure.

'Lyddy,' he began, 'mother and I think Thyrza had better not go to work again. As she is going to miss to-morrow morning, it'll be a good opportunity for making the change. Isn't it better?'

Lydia did not reply at once. Such a decided step as this reminded her how near the day was when, though they would still be near to each other, Thyrza and she must in a sense part. The thought was always a heavy one; she did not willingly entertain it.

'Do you think,' she asked at length, 'that Thyrza will feel she ought to stay at home?'

'I think she will, when I've spoken to her about it. We want you both to have your meals with us. Thyrza can help mother, and she'll have more time for her reading. Of course you must be just as much together as you like, but it would be pleasant if you would come down here to meals. Will you do us that kindness, Lyddy?'

'But,' Lydia began, doubtfully. Mrs. Grail interrupted her;

'Now I know what you're going to say, my dear. It isn't nice of you, Lyddy, if you spoil this little plan we've made. Just for the next three weeks! After that you can be as independent as you please; yes, my dear, just as proud as you please. There's a great deal of pride in you, you know, and I don't like you the worse for it.'

'I don't think I'm proud at all,' said Lydia, smiling and reddening a little. 'If Thyrza agrees, then I will. Though I——'

'There now, that's all we want,' interposed the old lady. 'That's very good of you.'

By the first post in the morning arrived a letter addressed to 'Miss Trent,' bearing the Eastbourne post-mark. Lydia for a moment had a great fear, but, when she had torn the envelope open, the first lines put her at rest. It was Mrs. Ormonde who wrote, and in words which made Lydia feel very happy. With the exception of a line once or twice from Mary Bower, she had never received a letter in her life; she was very proud of the honour. Gilbert had just come home for breakfast, and all rejoiced over the news of Thyrza.

It was hard for Lydia to sit through her morning at the workroom. Thyrza was to be at home by twelve o'clock. As soon as the dinner-hour struck, Lydia flung her work aside, and was in Walnut Tree Walk in less time than it had ever before taken her. Instinct told her that the child would be waiting upstairs alone, and not in the Grails' room. She flew up. Thyrza rose from a chair and met her.

Not, however, with the outburst of childish rapture which Lydia had anticipated. Their parts were reversed. When the elder sister sprang forward, breathless with her haste, unable to utter anything but broken terms ef endearment, Thyrza folded her in her arms, and, without a spoken word, kissed her with grave tenderness. Her cheeks had the most unwonted colour; her eyes gleamed, and as Lydia's caresses continued, glistened with moisture.

'Dear Lyddy!' she murmured. A tear formed upon her eyelashes, and her voice made trembled music. 'Dear sister! You're glad to see me again?'

'It seems an age, my own darling! You can't think what Sunday was like to me without you. And how well you look, my beautiful! See what a letter I've had from Mrs. Ormonde. Do tell me what she's like! How did she come to ask you if you'd stay! To think of you saying I should be cross with her! But of course that was only fun. My dear one! And what's the sea like? Were you on the shore again this morning?'

'How many questions does that make, I wonder, Lyddy?' Thyrza said, with a smile still much graver than of wont. 'I shan't tell you anything till you've had dinner. It's all ready for you downstairs.'

'You know what they want us to do?'

'Oh, I've talked it all over with Mrs. Grail. I don't think we ought to refuse, Lyddy. And so I'm not to go to work any more? I wish it was the same for you, dear. Shall you find it very hard to go alone?'

'Hard? Not I! Why, whatever should I do with myself if I stayed at home? It's different with you; you must learn all you can, so as to be able to talk to Gilbert.'

'Come to dinner!'

Lydia paused at the door,

'What has come to you, Thyrza?' she asked, looking in her sister's face. 'You're not the same, somehow. Oh, how *did* you manage to do your own hair? But there's something different in you, Blue-eyes.'

'Is there? Yes, perhaps. Oh, we've a deal to talk about to-night, Lyddy!'

'But Gilbert 'll want you to-night.'

'No. That must be to-morrow.'

And so it was. When all had sat together for an hour at Gilbert's late meal, the sisters went up to their room. Gilbert understood this perfectly well. The next evening would be his.

When it came, Mrs. Grail made an excuse to go and sit with Lydia. Thyrza had her easy-chair; Gilbert was at a little distance. The privileges he asked were very few. Sometimes, when Thyrza and he were alone, he would hold her hand for a minute, and at parting he kissed her, but more of acted tenderness than that he did not allow himself. To-night, whilst she was speaking, he gazed at her continuously. He too observed the change of which Lydia had at once become aware. Thyrza seemed to have grown older in those two days. Her very way of sitting was marked by a maturer dignity, and in her speech it was impossible not to be struck with the self-restraint, the thoughtful choice of words, which had taken the place of her former impulsiveness.

She dwelt much upon the delight she had received from

Miss Newthorpe's playing. That had clearly made a great impression upon her.

'There was something she played, Gilbert, that told just what I felt when I first saw the sea. Do you know what I mean? Does music ever seem to speak to you in that way? It's really as if it spoke words.'

'I understand you very well, Thyrza,' he answered, in a subdued voice. And he added, his eyes brightening: 'Shall I take you some night to a concert, a really good concert, at one of the large halls?'

'Will you?'

'Yes, I will. I'll find out from the newspaper, and we'll go together.'

She looked at him gratefully, but did not speak. As she remained silent, he drew his chair nearer and held his hand for hers. She gave it, without meeting his look.

'Thyrza, I heard from Mr. Egremont this morning. He wants to know if I can be ready to begin at the library on May 7, that's a Monday. It won't be opened then, but we shall be able to begin arranging the books. The house will be ready before the end of this month. Will you come and be married to me three weeks from to-day?'

'Yes, Gilbert, I will.'

No flush, but an extreme pallor came upon her face.

He felt a coldness in her hand.

'Then we shall go for a week to the seaside again,' he continued, his voice uncertain, 'and be back in time to get our house in order before the 7th of May.'

'Yes, Gilbert.'

She still did not look at him. He released her hand, and went on in a more natural tone:

'I had a letter from my brother this morning, as well. He'll have to come to London on business in about a month, he says; so I hope we shall be able to have him stay with us.'

'I hope so.'

She spoke mechanically, and then followed a rather long silence. Both were lost in thought. Nor did the conversation renew itself after this, for Thyrza seemed to have no more to tell of her Eastbourne experiences, and Gilbert found it enough to sit near her at times searching her face for the meaning which was new-born in it.

She rose at length, and, when they had exchanged a few words with regard to her occupations now that she would

remain at home, Thyrza approached him to say good-night.
Instead of bending to kiss her at once, he held her hand in
both his and said :

'Thyrza, look at me.'

She did so. His hands were trembling, and his features
worked nervously.

'You have never said you love me,' he continued, just
above a whisper. 'Will you say that now ? '

For an instant she looked down, then raised her eyes again,
and breathed :

'I love you, Gilbert.'

'I don't think words were ever spoken that sounded
sweeter than those ! '

She spoke again, with an earnestness unlike anything he
had ever seen in her, quite different from that which had inspired similar words when first she pledged herself to him.

'Gilbert, I will try with all my strength to be a good wife
to you ! I will ! '

'And I hope, Thyrza, that the day when I fail in perfect
love and kindness to you may be the last of my life ! '

She raised her face. For the first time he put his arms
about her and kissed her passionately.

Mrs. Grail said good-night and went downstairs as soon as
Thyrza appeared. Thyrza seated herself and pressed a hand
against her side ; her heart beat painfully.

'Why there ! ' Lydia exclaimed of a sudden. 'She's left
the photographs ! '

'What photographs ? ' Thyrza asked.

Lydia took from the table an envelope which contained
some dozen cartes-de-visite. They were all the portraits
which Mrs. Grail and her son possessed, and the old lady was
very fond of looking over them and gossiping about them.
She had brought them up to-night because she anticipated an
evening of especial intimacy with Lydia.

Thyrza held out her hand for them. She knew them
all, including the latest addition, which was a photograph of
Walter Egremont. Egremont had given it to Grail about
three weeks ago ; it was two years old. She turned them out
upon her lap.

'I think I'd better take them down now, hadn't I ? ' said
Lydia.

P

'I wouldn't trouble till morning,' Thyrza answered, in a tired voice.

Two lay exposed before her: that of Gilbert, taken six years ago, and that of Egremont. Lydia, looking over her shoulder, remarked:

'What a boy Mr. Egremont looks, compared with Gilbert!

Thyrza said nothing.

'Come, dear, put them in the envelope, and let me take them down.'

'Oh, never mind till morning, Lyddy!'

The voice was rather impatient.

'But I'm afraid Mrs. Grail 'll remember, and have the trouble of coming up.'

'She won't think it worth while. And I want to look at them.'

'Oh, very well, dear.'

The two unlike faces continued to lie uppermost.

CHAPTER XIX

A SONG WITHOUT WORDS

WHILST the repairs were going on in the house behind the school, the old caretaker still lived there. Egremont found that she had in truth nowhere else to go, and as it was desirable that someone should remain upon the premises, he engaged her to do so until the Grails entered into possession.

As soon as painters, plasterers, and paperhangers were out of the way, Grail and Thyrza went to the house to decide what furniture it would be necessary to buy. The outlay was to be as little as possible, for indeed there was but little money to spend. Mrs. Butterfield—that was the old woman's name—admitted them, but without speaking; when Gilbert made some kindly-meant remark about its being disagreeable for her to live in such a strong odour of paint, she muttered inarticulately and withdrew into the kitchen. Thyrza presently peeped into that room. The old woman was sitting on a low stool by the fire, her knees up to her chin, her grizzled hair unkempt; she looked so remarkably like a witch, and, on Thyrza's appearance, turned with a gaze of such extreme malignity, that the girl drew back in fear.

' I suppose she takes it ill that the old state of things has been disturbed,' Gilbert said. ' Mr. Egremont tells me he has found that she is to have a small weekly allowance from the chapel people, so I don't suppose she'll fall into want, and we know he wouldn't send her off to starve ; that isn't his way.'

The removal of such things as were to be brought from Walnut Tree Walk, and the housing of the new furniture, would take only a couple of days. This was to be done immediately before the wedding ; then Lydia and Mrs. Grail would live in the house whilst the husband and wife were away.

Egremont found that the large school-room would be ready sooner than he had anticipated. When it was cleaned out, there was nothing to do save to fix shelves, a small counter, and two long tables. For some time he had been making extensive purchases of books, for the most part from a second-hand dealer, who warehoused his volumes for him till the library should be prepared to receive them. He had drawn up, too, a skeleton catalogue, but this could not be proceeded with before the books were in some sort of order upon the shelves. He was nervously impatient to reach this stage. Since his last visit to Eastbourne he had seen no friends in civilised London, and now that he had no longer lectures to write, his state of mind grew ever more unsatisfactory. Loneliness, though to so great an extent self-imposed, weighed upon him intolerably. He believed that he was going through the dreariest time of his life.

How often he thought with envy of the little parlour in Walnut Tree Walk ! To toil oneself weary through a long day in a candle factory, and then come back to the evening meal, with the certainty that a sweet young face would be there to meet one with its smile, sweet lips to give affectionate welcome—that would be better than this life which he led. He wished to go there again, but feared to do so without invitation. The memory of his evening there made drawing-rooms distasteful to him.

He had a letter from Mrs. Ormonde, in which a brief mention was made of Thyrza's visit. He replied :

' Why do you not tell me more of the impression made upon you by Miss Trent ? It was a favourable one, of course, as you kept her with you over the Sunday. You do not mention whether Annabel saw her. She is very fond of

music ; it would have been a kindness to ask Annabel to play
to her. But I have Miss Newthorpe's promise that she and
her father will come and see the library as soon as it is open ;
then at all events they will make the acquaintance of Mrs.
Grail.

‘ She interests me very much, as you gather from my way
of writing about her. I hope she will come to think of me as
a friend. It will be delightful to watch her mind grow. I am
sure she has faculties of a very delicate kind ; I believe she
will soon be able to appreciate literature. Has she not a
strange personal charm, and is it not impossible to think
of her becoming anything but a beautiful-natured woman ?
You too, now that you know her, will continue to be her
friend—I earnestly hope so. If she could be for a little time
with you now and then, how it would help to develop the
possibilities that are in her ! ’

To the letter of which this was part, Mrs. Ormonde quickly
responded :

‘ With regard to Miss Trent,’ she said, ‘ I beg you not to
indulge your idealistic habits of thought immoderately. I
found her a pretty and interesting girl, and it is not unlikely
that she may make a good wife for such a man as Mr. Grail—
himself, clearly, quite enough of an idealist to dispense with
the more solid housewifely virtues in his life-mate. But I add
this, Walter : It certainly would not be advisable to fill her
head too suddenly with a kind of thought to which she has
hitherto been a stranger. If I had influence with Mr. Grail,
I should hint to him that he is going to marry a very young
wife, and that, under the circumstances, the balance of
character to be found in sober domestic occupation will, for
some time, be what she most needs to aim at. You see, I
am *not* an idealist, and I think commonplace domestic happiness of more account than aspirations which might not
improbably endanger it. Forgive me for these remarks,
which you will say have a slight odour of the kitchen, or, at
best, of the store-room. Never mind ; both are places without which the study could not exist.’

Egremont bit his lips over this ; for the first time he was
dissatisfied with Mrs. Ormonde. He wondered on what terms
she had received Thyrza. He had imagined the girl as treated
with every indulgence at The Chestnuts, but the tone of this
letter made him fear lest Mrs. Ormonde had deemed it a duty
to refrain from too much kindness. It was very unlike her ;

what had she observed that made her so disagreeably prudent all at once ?

It added to his mental malaise. What change was befalling his life ? Was he about to find himself actually sundered from the friends he had made in the sphere which his birth gave him no claim to enter ? It all meant that he was reverting to the condition wherein he was born. His attempt to become a member of Society (with a capital) was proving itself a failure. Very well, he would find his friends in the working world. When he needed society of an evening, he would find it with Gilbert Grail and his wife. He would pursue his work more earnestly than ever; he would get his club founded, as soon as the library was ready for a rallying-place ; he would seek diligently for the working men of hopeful character, and by force of sincerity win their confidence. Let the wealthy and refined people go their way.

And at this point he veritably experienced a great relief. For two days he went about almost joyously. His task was renewed before him, and his energy at the same time had taken new life. Doubt, he said to himself, was once more vanquished—perchance finally.

Then came another letter from Mrs. Ormonde, asking him to come and drink the air of these delicious spring days by the shore. He replied that it was impossible to leave London. That very day he had despatched seven packing-cases full of volumes to the library, and he was going to begin the work of setting the books on the shelves.

That was a Monday ; a week remained before Thyrza's marriage-day. Thyrza had not been to the new house since she went with Gilbert to see about the furniture. Her curiosity was satisfied ; her interest in the place had strangely lessened. More than that : in walking by herself she never chose that direction, whereas formerly she had always liked to do so. It seemed as if she had some reason for avoiding sight of the building.

This Monday her mind changed again. She frequently went to meet her sister at the dinner-hour, and to-day, having set forth somewhat too early, she went round by way of Brook Street. No positive desire impelled her ; it was rather as if her feet took that turning independently of her thoughts. On drawing near to the library she was surprised to see a van standing before the door ; two men were carrying a wooden box into the building. She crossed to the opposite side of the way, and went forwards slowly. The men came out, mounted to the box-seat of the van, and drove away.

That must be a delivery of books. Who was there to receive them ?

She crossed the street again, and approached the library door. She walked past it, stopped, came back. She tried the handle, and the door opened. There was no harm in looking in.

Amid a number of packing-cases stood Egremont. His head was uncovered, and he had a screw-driver in his hand, as if about to open the chests. At sight of Thyrza he came forward with a look of delight and shook hands with her.

' So you have discovered what I'm about ! I didn't wish anyone to know. You see, the shelves are all ready, and I couldn't resist the temptation of having books brought. Will you keep the secret ? '

' I won't say a word, sir.'

Warmth on Thyrza's cheeks answered the pleasure in his eyes as he looked at her. Perhaps neither had fully felt how glad it would make them to meet again. When Thyrza had given her assurance, Egremont's face showed that he was going to say something in a different tone.

' Miss Trent, will you speak to me in future as you do to your friends ? I want very much to be one of your friends, if you will let me.'

Thyrza kept her eyes upon the ground. She could not find the fitting words for reply. He continued :

' Grail is my friend, and we always talk as friends should. Won't you cease to think of me as a stranger ? '

' I don't think of you in that way, Mr. Egremont.'

' Then let us shake hands again in the new way.'

Thyrza gave hers. She just met his eyes for a moment ; her own had a smile of intense happiness.

' Yes, keep this a secret,' Egremont went on, quickly resuming his ordinary voice. ' I'll surprise Grail in a few days, by bringing him in. Now, how am I to get this lid off ? How tremendously firm it is ! I suppose I ought to have got the men to do it, but I brought a screw-driver in my pocket, thinking it would be easy enough. Ah, there's a beginning ! I ought to have a hammer.'

' Shall I go and ask Mrs. Butterfield if she has one ? '

' Oh no, I'll go myself.'

' I'll run—it won't take me a minute ! '

She went out by the door that led into the house. In the dark passage she was startled by coming in contact with someone.

' Oh, who is that ? '

A muttered reply informed her that it was the old woman. They went forward into the nearest room. There was a disagreeable smile on Mrs. Butterfield's thin lips.

' If you please, have you got a hammer ? ' Thyrza asked. ' Mr. Egremont wants one.'

The old woman went apart, and returned with a hammer which was used for breaking coals.

' Oh, could you just wipe it ? ' Thyrza said. ' The handle 's so very black.'

It was done, ungraciously enough, and Thyrza hastened back. Egremont was standing as she had left him.

' Ah, now I can manage ! Thank you.'

With absorbed interest Thyrza watched the process.

' I saw them bringing the last box in,' she said ; ' that's why I came to look.'

' That was a risk I foresaw—that someone would notice the cart. But perhaps you are the only one.'

' I hope so—as you don't want any one to know.'

She paused, then added :

' I was going to meet Lyddy—my sister. I don't go to work myself now, Mr. Egremont. Perhaps Gilbert has told you ? '

' No, he hasn't mentioned it. But I am glad to hear it.'

' I don't much like my sister going alone, but she doesn't really mind.'

' I hope I shall soon know your sister.'

He had suspended the work, and stood with one foot upon the case. Thyrza reflected, then said :

' I hope you will like her, Mr. Egremont.'

' I am sure I shall. I know that you are very fond of your sister.'

' Yes.' Her voice faltered a little. ' I couldn't have gone to live away from her.'

Egremont bent to his task again, and speedily raised the lid. There was a covering of newspapers, and then the books were revealed.

' Now,' he said, ' it shall be your hand that puts the first on the shelf.'

He took out the first volume of a copy of Gibbon, and walked with it to the wall.

'This shall be its place, and there it shall always stay.'

'Will you tell me what the book is about, Mr. Egremont?' Thyrza asked, timidly taking it from him. 'I should like to remember it.'

He told her, as well as he could. Thyrza stood in thought for a moment, then just opened the pages. Egremont watched her.

'I wonder whether I shall ever be able to read that?' she said, in an under-voice.

'Oh yes, I'm sure you will.'

'And I've to stand it here?'

'Just there. You shall put all the volumes in their place, one after the other. There are eight of them.'

He brought them altogether, and one by one she took them from him. Then they went back to the case again, and there was a short silence.

'Gilbert's going to take me to a concert to-night, Mr. Egremont,' Thyrza said, looking at him shyly.

'Is he? You'll enjoy that. What concert?'

'It's at a place called St. James's Hall.'

'Oh yes! You'll hear admirable music.'

'I've never been to a concert before. But when I was at Eastbourne I heard a lady play the piano. I *did* enjoy that!'

Egremont started.

'Was it Miss Newthorpe?' he asked, looking at her without a smile.

'Yes, that was her name.'

She met his look. Walter half turned away, then bent down to the books again.

'I know her,' he said. 'She plays well.'

He took a couple of volumes, and went with them to the shelves, where he placed them, without thought, next to the Gibbon. But in a moment he noticed the title, and moved them to another place. He had become absent. Thyrza, remaining by the case, followed his movements with her eyes. As he came back, he asked:

'Did you like Mrs. Ormonde?'

'Yes. She was very kind to me.'

To him it seemed an inadequate reply, and strengthened his fear that Mrs. Ormonde had not shown all the warmth he would have desired. Yet, as it proved, she had asked Annabel to play for Thyrza. Thyrza, too, felt that she ought to say more, but all at once she found a difficulty in speaking. Her thoughts had strayed.

'I think I must go now,' she said, 'or I shall miss my sister.'

'In that case, I won't delay you. I shall open one or twc more of these boxes, then go somewhere for lunch. Good-bye!'

Thyrza said good-bye rather hurriedly, and without raising her face.

It happened that just then Mr. Bower was coming along Brook Street. He did not usually leave the works at mid-day, but to-day an exceptional occasion took him to Paradise Street in the dinner-hour. Thyrza came forth from the library just as he neared the corner; she did not see him, but Bower at once observed her. There was nothing singular in her having been there; possibly the furnishing of the house had begun. In passing the windows of the future library, Bower looked up at them with curiosity. Egremont stood there, gazing into the street. He recognised Bower, nodded, and drew back.

Bower did not care to overtake Thyrza. He avoided her by crossing the street. She in the meantime was not going straight to meet her sister; after walking slowly for a little distance, she turned in a direction the opposite of that she ought to have taken. Then she stopped to look into a shop-window.

A clock showed her that by this time Lydia would be at home. Yet still she walked away from her own street. She said to herself that five-and-twenty minutes must pass before Gilbert would leave the house to return to his work. The way in which she now was would bring her by a long compass into Kennington Road. Rain threatened, and she had no umbrella; none the less, she went on.

At home they awaited her in surprise at her unpunctuality. Mrs. Grail could not say when she had left the house. All the morning Thyrza had sat upstairs by herself. Just when Gilbert was on the point of departure, the missing one appeared.

'Where *have* you been, child?' cried Lydia. 'Why, it's begun to rain; you're all wet!'

'I went further than I meant to,' Thyrza replied, throwing off her hat, and at once taking a seat at the table. 'I hope you didn't wait for me. I forgot the time.'

'That was with thinking of the concert to-night,' said Gilbert, laughing.

'I shouldn't wonder,' assented Lydia.

Thyrza smiled, but offered no further excuse. Gilbert and Lydia left the room and the house together. Their directions were opposite, but Gilbert went a few steps Lydia's way.

'I want you to alter your mind and go with us to-night,' he said.

'No, really! It isn't worth the expense, Gilbert. I don't care so much for music.'

'The expense is only a shilling. And Thyrza won't be quite happy without you. I want her to enjoy herself without *any* reserve. You'll come?'

'Well. But——'

'All right. Be ready both of you by half-past six.'

They nodded a good-bye to each other.

Thyrza was making believe to eat her dinner. Mrs. Grail saw what a pretence it was.

'Was there ever such an excitable child!' she said, affectionately. 'Now do eat something more, dear! I shall tell Gilbert he must never let you know beforehand when he's going to take you anywhere.'

But Thyrza had no appetite. She helped the old lady to clear the table, then ran upstairs.

It was an unspeakable relief to be alone. She had never known such a painful feeling of guilt as whilst she sat with Gilbert and Lydia regarding her. Yet why? Her secret, she tried to assure herself, was quite innocent, trivial indeed. But why had she been unable to come straight home? What had held her away, as forcibly as if a hand had lain upon her?

She moved aimlessly about the room. It was true that these last two days she had agitated herself with anticipation of the concert, but it was something quite different which now put confusion into her thought, and every now and then actually caught her breath. She did not feel well. She wished Liddy could have remained at home with her this afternoon, for she had a need of companionship, of a sort of help. There was Mrs. Grail; but no, she had rather not be with Mrs. Grail just now.

On the table were a few articles of clothing which Lydia and she had made during the last fortnight, things she was going to take away with her. This morning she had given them a few finishing touches of needlework, now they could be put away. She went to the chest of drawers. Of the two small drawers at the top, one was hers, one was Lydia's; the two long ones below were divided in the same way. She drew one out and turned over the linen. How some young lady about to be married—Miss Paula Tyrrell, suppose—would have viewed with pitying astonishment the outfit with which Thyrza was more than content. But Thyrza had never viewed marriage as an opportunity of enriching her wardrobe.

Having put her things away, she opened another drawer, and looked over some of Lydia's belongings. She stroked them lightly, and returned each carefully to its place, saying to herself, 'Lyddy wants such and such a thing. She'll have more money to spend on herself soon. And she shall have a really nice present on her next birthday. Gilbert 'll give me money to buy it.'

Then she went to the mantel-piece, and played idly with a little ornament that stood there. The trouble had been lighter for a few minutes, now it weighed again. Her heart beat irregularly. She leaned her elbows on the mantel-piece, and covered her face with her hands. There was a strange heat in her blood, her breath was hot.

Was it raining still? No, the pavement had dried, and there was no very dark cloud in the sky. She could not sit here all through the afternoon. A short walk would perhaps remove the headache which had begun to trouble her.

She descended the stairs very lightly, and hastened almost on tip-toe along the passage; the front door she closed as softly as possible behind her, and went in the direction away from Mrs. Grail's parlour window. To be sure she was free to leave the house as often as she pleased, but for some vague reason she wished just now not to be observed. Perhaps Gilbert would think that she went about too much; but she could not, she could not, sit in the room.

Without express purpose, she again walked towards Brook Street. No, she was not going to the library again; Mr. Egremont might still be there, and it would seem so strange of her. But she went to a point whence she could see the building, and for some minutes stood looking at it. Was he still within—Mr. Egremont? Those books would take him a long time to put on the shelves. As she looked someone came out from the door; Mr. Egremont himself. She turned and almost ran in her desire to escape his notice.

He was going home. Even whilst hurrying, she tried to

imagine how he was going to spend his evening. From Gilbert's description she had made a picture of his room in Great Russell Street. Did he sit there all the evening among his books, reading, writing? Not always, of course. He was a gentleman, he had friends to go and see, people who lived in large houses, very grand people. He talked with ladies, with such as Miss Newthorpe. (Thyrza did not trouble to notice where she was. Her feet hurried her on, her head throbbed. She was thinking, thinking.)

Such as Miss Newthorpe. Yes, he knew that lady; knew her very well, as was evident from the way in which he spoke of her. Of what did they talk, when they met? No doubt she had often played to him, and when she played he would look at her, and she was very beautiful.

She would not think of Miss Newthorpe. Somehow she did not feel to her in the same way as hitherto.

When she was married, she would of course see him very often—Mr. Egremont. He would be at the library constantly, no doubt. Perhaps he would come sometimes and sit in their room. And when he began his lectures in the room upstairs, would it not be possible for her to hear him? She would so like to, just once. She could at all events creep softly up and listen at the door. How beautiful his lectures must be! Gilbert could never speak strongly enough in praise of them. They would be a little hard to understand, perhaps; but then she was going to read books more than ever, and get knowledge.

She was in the part of Lambeth Walk farthest from her own street, having come there by chance, for she had observed nothing on the way. She did not wish to go home yet. One end of Paradise Street joins the Walk, and into that she turned. If only there were a chance of Totty Nancarrow's being at home! But Totty was very regular at work. Still, an inquiry at the door would be no harm.

Little Jack Bunce was standing in the open doorway; he had a rueful countenance, marked with recent tears.

'Do you know whether Miss Nancarrow's in?' Thyrza asked of the little fellow.

He regarded her, and nodded silently.

'Really? She's really in?'

'Yes, she's up in her room,' was the grave answer.

Thyrza ran upstairs. A tap at the door, and Totty's voice

—unmistakable—gave admission. The girl sat sewing; on the bed lay a child, asleep.

Totty, looking delighted at Thyrza's coming, held up her finger to impose quietness. Thyrza took the only other chair there was, and drew it near to her friend.

'That's Nelly Bunce,' Totty said in a low voice, nodding to the bed. 'Just when I was going back to work, what did the child do but tumble head over heels half down stairs, running after me. It's a wonder she don't kill herself. I don't think there's no more harm done except a big bump on the back of the head, but Mrs. Ladds wasn't in, and I didn't like to go and leave the little thing; she cried herself to sleep. So there's half a day lost!'

Thyrza kept silence. She had felt that she would like to talk with Totty, yet now she could find nothing to say.

'How's things going on?' Totty asked, smiling.

'Very well, I think.'

'So the day's coming, Thyrza.'

Thyrza played with the ends of a small boa which was about her neck. She had no reply. Her tongue refused to utter a sound.

'What's the matter?'

Thyrza's hand fell, she touched the sewing that was on Totty's lap. Then she touched Totty's hand.

'Will you tell me about—about Mr. Ackroyd?'

Totty drew in her lips, knitted her brows, then bent to bite off an end of cotton.

'What is there to tell?' she asked.

'Is he doing as he promised?'

'As far as I know,' said the other, in a voice which affected indifference.

'And do you think he'll keep right till Christmas?'

'That's a good deal more than I can say, or anybody else.'

'But you'll do your best to make him?'

'I don't know that I shall bother much. It's his own look-out. I shall know what he means if he goes wrong again.'

'But——'

'Well? What?'

'You hope he'll keep his promise?' Thyrza said, bending a little nearer, and dropping her eyes as soon as she had spoken.

'H'm. Yes. Perhaps I do,' said Totty, putting her head

on one side. And forthwith she began to hum a tune, which however, she checked the next moment, remembering Nelly.

'But you speak in a queer way, Totty.'

'So do you, Thyrza. What are you bothering about?'

Again she searched Thyrza's face, this time with something very curious in her gaze, a kind of suspicion one would have said.

'I—I like to know about you,' Thyrza said, with embarrassment.

'I've told you all there is to tell.'

'But you haven't told me really whether—— Do you,' she sank her voice still lower, 'do you love him, Totty?'

A singular flush came and went upon the other girl's face. She herself was little disposed to use sentimental words, and it was the first time that Thyrza had done so to her. The coarseness she heard from certain of her companions did not abash her, but this word of Thyrza's seemed to do so strangely. She looked up in a moment. Thyrza's face was agitated.

'What does that matter?' Totty said, in a rather hard voice. And she added, drawing herself up awkwardly, 'You've made your own choice, Thyrza.'

For an instant surprise held Thyrza mute; then she exclaimed:

'But, Totty, you don't think——? I was thinking of you, dear; only of you. You never supposed I—— Oh, say you didn't think that, Totty!'

Totty relaxed her muscles a little. She smiled, shook her head, laughed uneasily.

'I meant, dear,' Thyrza continued, 'that I hope you *do* love him, as you're going to marry him. I hope you love him very much, and I hope he loves you. I'm sorry I said that. I thought you wouldn't mind.'

'I don't mind at all, old dear. If you *must* know—I like him pretty well.'

'But it ought to be *more* than that—it ought, Totty— much more than that, dear——'

She was trembling. Totty looked at her in surprise, coldly.

'Don't go on like that,' she said. 'There, you've woke the child, of course! Now there'll be two of you crying. See which can make most noise. Now, Nelly! Well, I call this nice!'

At the sound of the child's voice, Thyrza at once restrained herself and rose from her chair. Totty managed to quieten her little charge, whom she took upon her lap. She did not look at Thyrza.

'Good-bye, Totty!' said the latter, holding out her hand.

'Good-bye!' Totty returned, but without appearing to notice the hand offered. 'I hope you'll be better before next Monday, Thyrza.'

'You're unkind to-day, Totty. I wish I hadn't come in.

There was no reply to this, so Thyrza said another farewell and left the house.

She got back to her room, and, hopeless of otherwise passing the time till Lydia's return, lay down on the bed. Perhaps she could close her eyes for half an hour. But when she had turned restlessly from one side to the other, there came a knock at the door. She knew it must be Mrs. Grail, and made no answer. But the knock was repeated, and the door opened. Mrs. Grail looked in, and, seeing Thyrza, came to the bedside.

'Aren't you well, my dear?' she asked, gently.

Thyrza made pretence of having just awoke.

'I thought I'd try and sleep a little,' she replied, holding her face with one hand. 'No, I don't feel quite well.'

'Lie quiet, then. I won't disturb you. Come down as soon as you'd like some tea.'

It was a weary time till Lydia returned, although she came back nearly half an hour earlier than usual. Thyrza still lay on the bed. When they had exchanged a few words, the latter said :

'I don't think I can go to-night, Lyddy. My head's bad.'

'Oh, what a pity! Can't we do something to make it better?'

Thyrza turned her face away.

'I'd altered my mind,' Lydia continued. 'I meant to go with you.'

'Really? You'll go with us?'

Thyrza felt that this would lessen the strange reluctance with which through the afternoon she had thought of the concert. She at once rose, and consented more cheerfully to try if a cup of tea would help her. She bathed her forehead, smoothed her hair, and went down.

It was not long before Gilbert entered, he too having come away earlier from work. In order to get a seat in the gallery of the concert hall, they must be soon at the doors. Thyrza declared that she felt much better. Her heavy eyes gave little assurance of this, but something of her eagerness had returned, and for the time she had indeed succeeded in subduing the torment within.

An omnibus took the three into Piccadilly. They were not too early at the hall, for the accustomed crowd had already begun to assemble. Thyrza locked her arm in her sister's, Gilbert standing behind them. He whispered a word now and then to one or the other, but Thyrza kept silence; her cheeks were flushed; she inspected all the faces about her. At length, admission was gained and seats secured.

Thyrza sat between the other two, but she still kept her hold on Lydia's arm, until the latter said laughingly :

'You're not afraid of losing me now. I expect we shall be dreadfully hot here soon.'

She withdrew her hand. Gilbert began to talk to her. Had it not been for the circumstances, he must have observed a difference in Thyrza's manner to him. She scarcely ever met his look, and when she spoke it was with none of the usual spontaneity. But she seemed to be absorbed in observation of the people who had begun to seat themselves in other parts of the hall. The toilettes were a wonder to her. Lydia, too, they interested very much ; she frequently whispered a comment on such as seemed to her 'nice' or the contrary. She could not help trying to think how Thyrza would look if 'dressed like a lady.'

Thyrza started, so perceptibly that Lydia asked her what was the matter.

'Nothing,' she answered, moving as if to seat herself more comfortably. But henceforth her eyes were fixed in one direction, on a point down in the body of the hall. She no longer replied to the remarks of either of her companions. The flush remained warm upon her cheeks.

'Thyrza !' whispered Gilbert, when the musicians were in their places, and the preliminary twanging and screeching of instruments under correction had begun. 'There's Mr. Egremont !'

'Is he? Where?'

'Do you see that tall lady in the red cloak? No, more to the left ; there's a bald man on the other side of him.'

'Yes, I see him.'

She waited a moment, then repeated the news to Lydia, with singular indifference. Then she began to gaze in quite other directions. The instrumental uproar continued.

'Oh dear!' said Lydia, with a wry face. 'I'm sure *that* kind of music won't do your head any good. Is it still better?'

'I think so—yes, yes.'

'Grandad doesn't take anything like that time to tune his fiddle,' the other whispered, conscious that she was daring in her criticism.

Thyrza, on an impulse, conveyed the remark to Gilbert, who laughed silently.

The concert began. Thyrza's eyes had again fixed themselves on that point down below, and during the first piece they did not once move. Her breathing was quick. The heart in her bosom seemed to swell, as always when some great emotion possessed her, and with difficulty she kept her vision unclouded. Lydia often looked at her, so did Gilbert; she was unconscious of it.

'Did you like that?' Gilbert asked her when the piece was over.

'Yes, very much.'

She had leaned back. Lydia sought her hand; she received a pressure in return, but the other hand did not remain, as she expected it would.

Gilbert himself was not much disposed to speak. He, too, was moved in the secret places of his being—moved to that ominous tumult of conflicting joy and pain which in the finer natures comes of music intensely heard. He had been at concerts before, but had little anticipated that he would ever attend one in such a mood as was his to-night. It seemed to him that he had not yet realised his happiness, that in his most rapturous moments he had rated it but poorly, unimaginatively. The strong wings of that glorious wordless song bore him into a finer air, where his faculties of mind and heart grew unconditioned. If it were possible to go back into the world endowed as in these moments! To the greatest man has come the same transfiguration, the same woe of foreseen return to limits. But one thing was real and would not fail him. She who sat by him was his—his now and for ever. Why had he yet loved her so little?

The second piece began. Again Thyrza looked down into the hall. After a while there came a piece of vocal music. The singer was not of much reputation, but to Thyrza her voice seemed more than human. In the interval which followed she whispered to Lydia:

Q

'I shall never pretend to sing again.'

Egremont had risen in his place, and was looking about him. Thyrza was yet in some doubt whether he was alone. But he had not yet spoken to that lady next to him, and now, on sitting down, he did not speak. He must be without companion.

CHAPTER XX

RAPIDS

In the crowd with which they mingled on passing out again, Thyrza saw men in evening dress; she looked in every direction for Egremont, but was disappointed. Gilbert had begged her to hold his arm; he moved forward as quickly as possible, and with Lydia following they were soon in the street. Gilbert wished to cross, for the sake of quickly getting out of the throng. Thyrza threw one glance back. A hat was raised by someone going in the opposite direction, who also had turned his head. She had seen him. She was glad he did not come up to speak. Could he discern the flash of joy which passed over her face as she recognised him? She hoped he had, but at once hoped that he had not.

There was waiting for an omnibus. Thyrza still had her arm within Gilbert's; she was unconscious of all the bustle amid which she stood, unconscious of the pressure with which Gilbert drew her nearer to him. When at length bidden, she entered the vehicle, and leaned back with her eyes closed.

How dark and quiet these streets of Lambeth seemed! As she passed the threshold of the house, a sudden chill fell upon her, and she shook. How sombre the passage was, with its dim lamp suspended against the wall! Voices seemed strange; when Mrs. Grail welcomed her in the parlour, she did not recognise the sound.

She could not be persuaded to get to bed immediately. Neither could she sit still, but walked restlessly about the floor.

'How hot it is!' she complained to Lydia. 'Do you mind if I open the window just a little?'

'I don't, but I'm afraid it'll give you cold. Now do undress, there's a dear!'

'Just for a minute.'

She threw the window up, and stood breathing the air. Her thoughts strayed into the darkness. Had Mr. Egremont gone to the concert just because she mentioned that she was going? It was not likely, but perhaps so. When should she see him to speak of it? Would he still be arranging books the next morning?

'Now, Thyrza, you *must* shut the window! I shall be angry. Do as I tell you, and get to bed at once.'

At the voice, Thyrza drew the window down, then turned and stood before her sister, as if she were going to say something. But she did not speak.

'Do you feel ill, dear?' Lydia asked, anxiously.

'Not well, Lyddy. Don't get cross with me. I'll go to bed directly.'

She walked again the length of the room, then began to hum an air. It was the first song of the concert. She took the crumpled programme from her pocket, and glanced over it. Lydia moved impatiently. Thyrza put the programme down on the table, and began to loosen her dress.

'Are you glad you went, Lyddy?' she asked, in a tired voice.

'I shan't be glad we any of us went if it's going to make you ill, Thyrza.'

'I shall be all right to-morrow, I dare say. I wonder whether Mr. Egremont often goes to concerts?'

'Very likely. He can afford it.'

'I mustn't go again for a long time.'

She had seated herself on the bed and was undoing the braid of her hair. She spoke the last words thoughtfully. In a minute or two the light was out.

Lydia soon fell asleep. In the very early morning a movement of her sister's awoke her. She found that Thyrza was sitting up in the bed.

'What is it, dear?' she asked. 'Lie down and go to sleep.'

'I can't, Lyddy, I can't! I *am* so tired, and I haven't closed my eyes. Keep awake with me a minute, will you?'

Lydia took the sleepless girl in her arms.

'The music won't leave me,' Thyrza moaned. 'It's just as if I heard them playing now.'

Lydia nursed her into a fitful sleep.

Though Thyrza had no work to go to, she still always rose together with her sister, and, whilst the latter put the room

in order, went down to assist Mrs. Grail in getting the breakfast. But on the morning after the concert Lydia was glad
to see that the head beside her own was weighed down with
sleep when the hour for rising had come. She dressed as
quietly as possible, leaving the blind drawn, and descended to
say that Thyrza would be a little longer than usual. Gilbert
was in the parlour.

'Has she slept well?' he asked.

'Not very well. She couldn't get the sound of the music
out of her ears. But she's fast now.'

'We shall have to be careful of her, Lyddy,' Gilbert said,
anxiously.

For he had had her face before him all night, with its
pale, wearied look of over-excitement. He knew how delicate
a nature it was that he was going to take into his charge, and
already his love was at times gently mingled with fear.

Lydia went upstairs again, and softly into the room.
Thyrza had just awoke and was sitting with her hands
together upon her face.

'What time is it?' she asked. 'Why did you let me
sleep? Have you been up long?'

Lydia constrained her to lie down again. She was unwilling at first, but in the end fell back with a sigh of relief.

'What day is it, Lyddy? Oh, Tuesday, of course. I
suppose the days 'll go very slow till Saturday. I'm sure I
don't know what I shall do all the time.'

'Don't trouble about it now, dear. Try and sleep a little
more, and I'll bring you up some breakfast just before I go.'

'That'll be like when I was poorly, won't it, Lyddy?'

She lay and laughed quietly.

'You feel better?'

'Oh yes. Is it a fine morning?'

'The pavement's just drying.

'Good-night!'

She drew the clothes over her head. Lydia could hear
her still laughing, and wondered. Thyrza could not have
told what it was that amused her.

She did not sleep again, but had breakfast in bed. Lydia
sat with her as long as possible. Thyrza, as soon as she
heard the front door close behind her sister, sprang on to the
floor and began to dress with nervous rapidity; her hands
were so unsteady that she had all sorts of difficulties with
buttons and hooks and eyes.

'Don't trouble with your hair,' Lydia had said. 'I'll do it at dinner-time.'

But Thyrza could not obey in this. She did the plaiting twice over, being dissatisfied with the first result, and even took a new piece of blue ribbon for the ends.

The sun was shining. That always affected her pleasurably, and this morning, as soon as she was dressed, a gladness altogether without conscious reason made her sing, again the song of the concert. The air, which she could not wholly remember the night before, had grown to completeness in her mind; she longed to know the words, that the whole song might henceforth stay with her. And the sun, so rare in our dull skies, seemed to warm the opposite houses. She threw open the window, and heard the clocks striking nine.

'I'll just make the bed and put things straight, then—oh, then I must really go and do something for Mrs. Grail. I left her alone nearly all yesterday. And then I might go and meet Lyddy. But it's a long time till half-past twelve. Perhaps——'

Having made the bed she sat down to rest for a moment. After all, the headache was certainly not gone, though it had been disguising itself. The moment grew to a quarter of an hour. Her eyes seemed to behold something very clearly, just in front, down there on the floor. But the floor itself had made way for a large hall; among rows of people she saw a tall lady in a red cloak, and a bald-headed gentleman, and between them someone whose face was at an angle which allowed her to see it very well, to note even the look, not quite a smile, of pleasure which made it so interesting. She knew no other face which affected her as that did. She desired it to turn full upon her, to look straight into hers with its clear, gentle eyes, which seemed to be so full of wonderful knowledge. Once or twice, yes, in truth, once or twice it had done so, but never for long enough. It would do so yet again. Oh but not for long enough! A look not of instants, but of minutes, of full minutes ticked to their last second; what would she give for that! One such gaze and she would be satisfied. It was not to ask much, surely not much.

But she was going to live there, behind the library, and he would come often, very often. For a time he would certainly come every day. To be sure, she could not see him daily. Her duties would be in the house; she would be a wife; people would call her 'Mrs. Grail.'

A voice whispered, a very timid, one would have said a guilty, voice, 'Who will be called "Mrs. Egremont"?' Not once; the voice, faint as it was, had an echo, a tingling echo from her heart outwards to the smallest vein. Who will bear that name? Some tall, beautiful, richly-clad lady, such as Miss Newthorpe. Was there any one who at this moment sat alone, longing for one look of his eyes? Did ladies think and feel in that way? or only foolish little work-girls, who all their lives had dreamed dreams of a world that was not theirs? Did ladies ever press down a heart beating almost to anguish and say, half-aloud, to themselves: 'I love you!'

No; a stately life theirs, no weakness, no sense of a measureless need, self-respect ever, and ever respect from all about them. Think of Miss Newthorpe's face. How noble it was! How impossible that it should plead for anything! It might concede with a high, gracious smile, but not beseech anything. That was the part of poor girls who had not been taught, in whom it was no shame to look up to one far above them and long—long for kindness.

The sunlight was creeping along the floor, nearer to her. Oh sun of spring! nearer, nearer! Your warmth upon my hands, upon my face! Your warmth upon my heart, that *something* warm may press there!

The clocks were striking ten. It was unkind to leave Mrs. Grail alone. The girl hired to do rough work was coming to-day, but for all that it behoved her to be attentive to the good old lady, who never spoke to her save with good, motherly words.

Yes, away with it all! She must go down and be company to Gilbert's mother. Had she forgotten that in less than a week she would be Gilbert's wife? A simple test: could she speak out these thoughts of hers to Lyddy? The hot current in her veins was answer enough. And that had been the criterion of right and wrong with her since she was a little child. Lyddy knew the right instinctively, and never failed to act upon her knowledge. What had been Lyddy's thoughts of Luke Ackroyd? Perhaps not very different from these to which she had been listening; for Lyddy too was a work-girl, not a lady. Yet the brave sister had kept it all hidden away; more, had done her very best to bring together Luke and someone else whom he loved. How was it possible to reach that height of unselfishness? But the example should not be without its effect.

Thyrza presented herself in the parlour. The room was in some disorder; a girl was on her knees by the fireplace, cleaning. Thyrza went down to the little back kitchen, which was behind the room where Mr. and Mrs. Jarmey practically lived. It was dark and cold. Mrs. Grail was making a pudding,

'Good-morning, my dear!' she said, nodding several times. 'Better now? I hoped you wouldn't be down yet, but I suppose you couldn't sleep for the sunshine. I don't think you ought to sit here.'

'Oh, but I'm going to help you. Please give me something to do. Shall I clean these knives?'

'The idea! Charlotte 'll be down to do those directly. If you really don't find it too cold here, you may tell me something about the concert.'

'Yes, I'll tell you, but I must work at the same time. I want to, I *must*! Yes, I shall do the knives. Please don't be cross!'

She was bent on it; Mrs. Grail quietly acquiesced. For ten minutes Thyrza wrought strenuously at the knife-board, speaking only a few words. Then the girl Charlotte made her appearance.

'Now, Thyrza,' Mrs. Grail said, 'if you really want something to do, suppose you go and dust upstairs. You haven't dusted yet, have you, Charlotte?'

'No, mum, not yet.'

Thyrza rubbed away for a minute longer, then agreed to go up to the lighter work. Her head had not profited by the violent exercise.

Dusting is an occupation not incompatible with reverie. How hard it was to keep her mind from the subject which she had determined not to think of! As often as her face turned to the sunlight, that longing came back.

Mrs. Grail joined her presently. We know that the old lady had no fondness for domestic bustle. She sat down, and at length persuaded Thyrza to do the same.

At half-past eleven Mrs. Grail said:

'My dear, I think you ought to go out for a little, while it's so bright. I'm not at all sure that the sun 'll last till dinner-time; it's getting rather uncertain. Just go into Kennington Road and back.'

Thyrza shook her head.

'Not this morning. I'm a little tired.'

' Yes, but it'll make you feel more cheerful, and you'll have an appetite for dinner, which I'm sure you haven't had for a week and more. How ever you live on the few mouthfuls you eat is a wonder to me. You ought to have half an hour's walk every day, indeed you ought.'

It was sorely against her will to go forth, yet desire called to her from the sunlit ways. Slowly down the stairs, slowly to the end of Walnut Tree Walk.

Look at that white billow of cloud on its fathomless ocean ! Even now there were clouds like that high up over Eastbourne. One such had hung above her as she drove with Mrs. Ormonde up Beachy Head. At this moment the sea was singing ; this breeze, which swept the path of May, made foam flash upon the pebbled shore. Sky and water met on that line of mystery ; far away and beyond was the coast of France.

More quickly now. Whither was she tending ? She had at first kept southwards, straight along Kennington Road ; now she had crossed, and was turning into a street which might—only might—conduct her round into Brook Street. Desire was in her feet ; she could no longer check them ; she must hasten on whithersoever they led.

Oh, why had she left the house ! Why had Mrs. Grail—a cruel mother—bidden her go forth when her will was to stay, and work, and forget ! Could she not stop, even now, and turn ?

She stopped. Was it likely that he would be there this morning ? No, not very likely. He would finish all the books yesterday. Yet others might have been brought.

If he would give her one long look—the look for which she fainted—then that should be the end. That should be the very end. She would not play with danger after that. For now she knew that it was danger ; that thought of Lyddy had made everything terribly clear. He would never know anything of what had been in her foolish heart, and it would cost him nothing to look once at her with a rich, kind look. He was all kindness. He had done, was doing, things such as no other man in his position ever thought of. She would like to tell him the immeasurable worship with which his nobleness inspired her ; but the right words would never come to her, and the wrong would be so near her lips. No, one look for him, and therewith an end.

The library was within sight ; she had walked very quickly. If he should not be there ! Her hand was on the door ; the bitterness of it if the door proved to be locked.

It was open. She was in the little entrance hall. At the door of the library itself she stood listening.

Was that a sound of someone within ? No, only the beat of her own heart, the throb which seemed as if it must kill her. She *could* not open the door ! She had not the strength to stand. The pain, the pain !

Yet she had turned the handle, and had entered. He was in the act of placing volumes on the shelves. She moved forward and he looked round.

That was not the look she desired. Surprise at first, surprise blent with pleasure; but then a gravity which was all but disapproval.

Yet he gave his hand.

' Good-morning, Miss Trent ! ' The voice was scrupulously subdued, as inflexionless as he could make it. ' I am still at my secret work, you see. When I went away for lunch yesterday something prevented me from returning, so I came down again this morning.'

' You have got them nearly all put up.'

She could not face him, but kept her eyes on the almost empty cases.

' Yes. But I expect some more this afternoon.'

He walked away from her, with books in his hands. Thyrza felt ashamed. What must he think of her ? It was almost rude to come in this way—without shadow of excuse. Doubtless he was punishing her by this cold manner. Yet he could not unsay what he had said yesterday ; and his recognition of her just outside the Hall last night had been so friendly. She felt that her mode of addressing him had been too unceremonious ; the ' Sir ' of their former intercourse seemed demanded again. Yet to use it would be plain disregard of his request.

Must she speak another word and go ? That would be very hard. Shame and embarrassment notwithstanding, it was so sweet to be here ; nay, the shame itself was luxury.

He said :

' I am so sorry I haven't a chair to offer you. If I put the top on this box ? That is a very rude sort of seat, but ——'

Then he wished her to remain a little ? Or was it mere politeness, which modesty should direct her to meet with similar refusal ? It was so hard that she did not know what was proper, how she was expected to behave.

In the meantime, the seat was improvised. He asked her with a smile if she would take it.

'Thank you, Mr. Egremont. I'm afraid I mustn't stay. Or only a minute.'

He glanced at the inner door, leading to the house. Had some sound come thence?

Thyrza seated herself. With one hand she held the edge of the box nervously. Her eyes were bent downwards. Egremont again walked away from her. On returning, he said, in the same almost expressionless tone:

'I hope you enjoyed the concert last night?'

This was what she had wished, that he would speak of the concert.

'I did, so very much,' she replied.

And, as she spoke, her face was lifted. He was regarding her, and did not at once avert his eyes. For an appreciable space of time they looked at each other.

Was she then satisfied? Could she leave him now and draw a hard line between this hour and the future? Less satisfied than ever. His gaze was a mystery; it seemed so cold, and yet, and yet—what did it suggest to her? That just observable tremor on his lip; that slight motion of the forehead, those things spoke to her miraculously sharpened sense, and yet she could not interpret their language. It was very far from the look she had yearned for, yet perhaps it affected her more profoundly than a frank gaze of kindness would have done.

He moved a little, again glancing at the inner door.

'I was there myself,' were his next words.

'Yes, I saw you. In the Hall, I mean; not only afterwards.'

Uttered without forethought she desired to say that and had said it.

'Did you?' he said, more coldly still.

'Gilbert pointed you out to us.'

It was true, and it involved a falsehood. Egremont happened to regard her as she spoke, and at once a blush came to her cheeks. To what was she falling? Why did she tell untruths without the least need? She could not understand the motive which had impelled her to that.

Egremont had a distinct frown on his face. It was as though he read her deceit and despised her for it. Thyrza added, confusedly:

'My sister went with us. She hadn't meant to, but Gilbert persuaded her at last.'

'Do you remember which piece you liked best?'

'No, I couldn't say. It was all so beautiful. I liked the songs so much.'

'But Mr. Grail must take you to hear better singers than those.'

'Weren't they good?' she asked in astonishment.

'Certainly not bad, but not really excellent.'

He mentioned one or two world-echoed names, and spoke in particular of a concert shortly to be given, at which such singers would be heard.

'You have heard them?' Thyrza asked, gazing at him.

'Several times.'

'I should be almost afraid.'

He thought it a wonderful word to come from this untaught girl. Again their eyes met. He laughed.

'Something like my own feeling when I got out at Niagara Station, and began to walk towards the Falls. I dreaded the first sight of them.'

He was purposely turning it to a jest. He durst not reply to her in her own mood. And he saw that she had not understood.

'You have heard of Niagara?'

'No, Mr. Egremont. Will you tell me about it?'

He made a very brief pause, and she noticed it with fear. Did he despise her ignorance, or did he think her troublesome? Yet he began to explain, and was soon speaking much more freely, almost as he had spoken that evening in the Grails' room, when he told of his sea-experiences.

He ended somewhat abruptly, and went to the shelves with books. Thyrza rose and followed him. He looked back, strangely, as if startled.

'May I look at the books I put up yesterday?' she asked, timorously.

'Ah yes! There is old Gibbon, our corner-stone. He hasn't much elbow-room now.'

Again he laughed. The laugh troubled her; she preferred him to be grave.

'And some more books are coming to-day?' she said.

'Yes, this afternoon.'

'Mr. Egremont, may I come and help to put up a few to-morrow morning?'

Again her tongue uttered words in defiance of herself. She could not believe it when the words were spoken.

Egremont perused the floor. The slight frown had returned.

'But perhaps I shall be in your way,' she continued, hastily. 'I didn't think. I am troublesome.'

'Indeed you are not at all, Miss Trent. I should be very glad. If—if you are sure you can spare the time?'

'I can quite well. I do a little work for Mrs. Grail, but that doesn't take anything like all the morning.'

A word was on his tongue. He was about to say that perhaps it would be as well, after all, to tell Grail, and for Thyrza to ask the latter's permission. He even began to speak, but hesitated, ceased.

'Shall I come at this same time?' Thyrza inquired, her voice almost failing her.

'I shall be here at about eleven; certainly by half-past.'

'Then I will come. I shall be so glad to help.'

A pronoun was lost; something prevented its utterance. Egremont made no reply. Thyrza found power to hold her hand out and take leave. How often they seemed to have held each other's hand!

CHAPTER XXI

MISCHIEF AFOOT

IT would have been a remarkable thing if Egremont had succeeded, even for a day or two, in keeping secret his work at the library. The vulgar in Lambeth are not a jot less diligent in prying and gossip than are their kin in Mayfair. And chance is wont to be mischief-making all the world over.

When Mr. Bower passed the library in the dinner-hour on Monday, and, after seeing Thyrza Trent come out, forthwith observed Mr. Egremont standing within at the window, his mind busied itself with the coincidence very much as it might have been expected to do. When he reached home he privately reported the little incident to his wife. They looked at each other, and Mr. Bower lowered first one eyelid, then the other.

'Is Grail still at his work?' Mrs. Bower inquired.

'Safe enough. He goes on till Saturday. Ackroyd told me so yesterday.'

'And her sister's at work too?'

'Safe enough.'

'Is the workmen there still?'

'No, they're all out. Safe enough.'

Mr. Bower seemed to find a satisfaction in repeating the significant phrase. He chuckled disagreeably.

'It looks queer,' remarked his wife, with a certain contemptuousness.

'It looks uncommon queer. I wonder whether old Mrs. Butterfield happened to be safe likewise.' He nodded. 'I'll look in and have a word with the old lady to-night, eh?'

Mrs. Butterfield's husband, some years deceased, had been a fellow-workman with Bower. The latter, prying about the school-building as soon as he heard that Egremont was going to convert it into a library, had discovered that the caretaker was known to him. There seemed at the time no particular profit to be derived from the circumstance, but Mr. Bower regarded it much as he would have done a piece of lumber that might have come into his possession, as a thing just to be kept in mind, if perchance some use for it should some day be discovered. It is this habit of thought that helps the Bower species to become petty capitalists. We call it thrift, and—respecting public opinion—we do not refuse our admiration.

On Monday evening, about eight o'clock, Mr. Bower went up to the house-door in the rear of the building, and knocked. The door was opened about two inches, and an aged voice asked who was there.

'It's me, Mrs. Butterfield—Bower,' was the pleasantly modulated reply.

The door opened a little wider.

'Does Mr. Egremont happen to be here?' the visitor went on to ask.

'No, Mr. Bower, he ain't here, nor likely to come again to-night, I shouldn't think.'

'Never mind. I dare say you'd let me have a look in, just to see how things is goin' on. I saw him at the window as I passed at dinner-time, and we just nodded to each other, but I hadn't time to stop.'

The old woman admitted him. In the house was an exultant savour of frying onions; a hissing sound came from the sitting-room.

'Cooking your supper, eh, Mrs. Butterfield?' said Bower, with genial familiarity. 'Why, that's right · make yourself

comfortable. Don't you fuss about, now ; I'll sit down here ;
I like the smell.'

Mrs. Butterfield was not at all the same woman with this
visitor that she was with strangers. For one thing, he brought
back to her the memory of days when she had possessed a home
of her own, and had not yet been soured by ill-hap; then again,
Bower belonged to her own class, for all his money saved up
and his pomposities of manner. There is a freemasonry
between the members of the pure-blooded proletariat; they are
ever ready in recognition of each other, and their suspicion of
all above them, whether by rank or by nature, is a sense of
the utmost keenness. Mrs. Butterfield varied somewhat from
the type, inasmuch as she did not care to cringe before her
superiors ; but that was an accident ; in essentials of feeling
she and Bower were at one.

The table was half covered with a dirty cloth, on which
stood a loaf of bread (plateless), a small dish ready to receive
the fry, and a jug of beer. In the midst of the newly painted
and papered room, which seemed ready to receive furniture of
a more elegant kind than that of working-class homes, these
things had an incongruity.

'And how does the world use *you*, Mrs. Butterfield,
ma'am ? ' Bower asked, as he settled his bulky body on the
small chair.

'I earn my bed and my victuals, Mr. Bower,' was the
reply, as the old woman stirred her hissing mess with a fork.

'And a thing to be proud of at your age, ma'am.'

From such friendly dialogue, Bower gradually turned the
talk to Egremont, of whom he spoke at first as a respected
intimate. Observation of his collocutor led him shortly to
alter his tone a little. When he had heard that books were
already arriving, he remarked :

'That's as much as to say that you'll soon be turned out,
Mrs. Butterfield. Well, I call it hard at your age, ma'am.
Now if Egremont had acted like a gentleman and had offered
me to be librarian, you'd still have kept your place here. I
don't want to say disagreeable things, but if ever there was a
mean and indecent action, it was when he passed over *me* and
gave the place to a stranger. Why, Mrs. Butterfield, he has
to thank *me* for everything ! But for *me* he'd never have had
a soul to hear his lectures. Well, well, it don't matter. And
what do you think o' the young girl as is coming to keep
house here after you ? '

Mrs. Butterfield was turning out her supper into the dish.
She gave him a peculiar look.

'When's she goin' to be wed?' was her question in reply.

'Next Monday.'

'And does the man as is goin' to marry her know as she
comes here to meet this young gent?'

'She comes to meet him? *Does* she, now? Tut—tut—
tut! But we needn't think harm, Mrs. Butterfield—though
you can tell from her face she'll need a good deal of looking
after. And does she come regular, now?'

The old woman confessed that she only knew of two
meetings, with a very long interval, but she hinted that the
first had taken place under circumstances very suspicious; in
fact, that it was obviously an appointment. And this morning,
as soon as she knew of Thyrza's presence in the library (by
the borrowing of the hammer), she had kept a secret espial
through the key-hole of the inner door, with the result that
she witnessed the two chatting together in a way sufficiently
noteworthy, considering the difference of their stations.

The matter having been made to bear all the fruit it would
in malevolent discussion, Mr. Bower left the old woman at her
supper, and with a candle went to explore the state of the
library. He did not remain long, for the big room was very
cold, and shortly after rejoining the caretaker he bade her the
friendliest good-evening.

'I consider you've done very right to tell me this,' he said,
as she went to let him out. 'In *my* opinion it's something as
Grail ought to know. You keep an eye open to-morrow
morning; depend upon it, you're doing a good work. I
shouldn't wonder if I look in to-morrow night. And I dare
say you could do with a nice bit of cheese, eh? I'll see if I
can pick a bit out of the shop.'

On Tuesday night he repeated his visit, bringing half a
pound of very strong American in his pocket. He heard a
shocking story. Thyrza had again been to the library, and so
secretly that but for her station at the key-hole Mrs. Butterfield
would have known nothing of it.

'Well, well, now! Tut—tut—tut!' commented portly
Mr. Bower. 'To think! You never *can* trust these young
men as have more money than they know what to do with!
But I didn't think it of Egremont. That's the kind of fellow
as comes to preach to the working man and tell him of his
faults! Bah! Well, I'm not one for going about spreading

stories. Grail must take his chance. Perhaps it 'ud be as
well, Mrs. Butterfield, if *you* kept this little affair quiet—just
between you and me, you know. There's no knowing.—Eh ?
A time may come.—Eh ? It's none of our business *just now.*
—Eh ? You understand, Mrs. Butterfield ? It might be as
well to keep an eye open to the end of the week.'

Mr. Bower, on the way home, turned into his club, just to
drink a glass of whisky at the club price. In the reading-room
were a few men occupied with newspapers or in chat. In a
corner, reading his favourite organ of ' free thought,' sat Luke
Ackroyd.

Bower got his glass of spirits, brought it into the reading-
room, and sat down by Ackroyd.

' So our friend Egremont 's begun to get his books together,'
he began.

' Has he ? '

Luke was indifferent. Of late he had entered upon a new
phase of his mental trouble. He was averse from conversation, shrank from his old companions, seemed to have resumed
studious habits. It had got about that he was going to marry
Totty Nancarrow, but he refused to answer questions on the
subject. Banter he met with so grim a countenance that the
facetious soon left him to himself. He no longer drank, that
was evident. But his face was pale, thin, and unwholesome.
One would have said that just now he was more seriously
unhappy than he had been throughout his boisterous period.

Bower, after one or two glances at him, lowered his voice
to say :

' I can't think it's altogether the right thing for Thyrza
Trent to be there every morning helping him. Of course you
and me know as it's all square, but other people might—eh ?
Grail ought to think of that—eh ? '

Now it had seemed to Mr. Bower, in his native wisdom,
that any scandal about Thyrza would tickle Ackroyd im-
mensely. He imagined Luke bearing a deep grudge against
the girl and against Grail—for he knew that the friendship
between Luke and the latter had plainly come to an end. In
his love of gossip, he could not keep the story to himself, and
he thought that Ackroyd would be the safest of confidants.
In fact, though he spoke to Mrs. Butterfield as if he had conceived some deep plan of rascality, the man was not capable
of anything above petty mischief. He liked to pose in secret
as a sort of transpontine schemer ; that flattered his self-

importance; but his ambition did not seriously go beyond making trouble in a legitimate way. He did indeed believe that something scandalous was going on, and it would be all the better fun to have Ackroyd join him with malicious pleasure in a campaign against reputations. Luke was a radical of the reddest; surely it would delight him to have a new cry against the patronising capitalist.

Ackroyd, having heard that whisper, looked up from his paper slowly. And at once Bower knew that he had made a great miscalculation.

'Other people might think *what*?' Luke asked, with gravity passing into anger.

'Well, well; you must take it as I meant it, old man.' Bower was annoyed, and added: 'No doubt Egremont likes to have a pretty gyurl to talk to every morning. I don't blame him. Still, if I was Grail——'

'What the devil do you mean, Bower? What's all this about?'

Ackroyd clearly knew nothing. The other recovered some of his confidence.

'Well, you needn't let it go further. It's no good thinking the worst of people. For all I know Grail sends her to help with the books, just because he can't go himself.'

Luke laid down the paper, and said quietly:

'Will you tell me all about it? It's the first I've heard. What's going on?'

Bower brought out his narrative, even naming the authority for it. He took sips of whisky in between. Ackroyd heard in silence, and seemed to dismiss his indignation.

'There's nothing in all that,' he said at length. 'Of course Grail knows all about it. This Mrs. What's-her-name seems to have too little to do.'

'Well, there's no knowing.'

'And you're going to tell this story all over Lambeth?'

'Why, didn't I ask you to keep it quiet?'

'Yes, Bower, you did. And I mean to. And—look here! If you'd been a man of my own age, for all we've known each other a goodish time, I should have sent you spinning half across the room before now. So that's plain language, and you must make what you like of it!'

Therewith Luke thrust back his chair and walked out of the room.

He did not pause till he was some distance from the club.

His blood was tingling. But it was not in anger that he at length stood still and asked himself whither he should go. His heart had begun to sink with fear.

Had he done wisely in insulting Bower? The fellow would take his revenge in an obvious way. That calumny would be in every one's mouth by the morrow.

And yet, as if that would not have come about in any case! How long was anything likely to remain a secret that was known in Mrs. Bower's shop? No, it made no difference.

Such stories going round with regard to Thyrza Trent! What was the meaning of it? Had there been some impru‑ dence on Grail's part, some thoughtlessness in keeping with his character, which had in it so little of the everyday man? It was a monstrous thing that opportunities should have been given to that lying old woman!

He walked on, in the direction of home. There was a hideous voice at his ear. Suppose Grail in truth knew nothing about those meetings in the library? How explain the first of them, two months ago?

He altered his course, and, without settled purpose, hurried towards Walnut Tree Walk. As he drew near to the house he saw someone about to enter. He ran forward. It was Gilbert.

'How does the library get on?' he asked, with an abrupt‑ ness which surprised Grail.

'Oh, all the carpenter's work is finished.'

'Any books come yet?'

'No, not yet.'

'Ah! Good‑night!'

He passed on, leaving Gilbert still in surprise, for it was perhaps the first word Ackroyd had spoken to him concerning the library.

Luke began to run, and did not cease until he was in Brook Street in front of the library. He tried to look in at the windows, but found that the blinds were drawn. A police‑ man passed and scrutinised him.

'Do you know whether any one lives on these premises?' Luke asked at once.

He excited suspicion, but after a short dialogue the con‑ stable showed him the approach to the caretaker's house. He knocked at the door several times; at length it was barely opened.

' Is that Mrs. Butterfield ? '

' Yes. What may you want ? '

' I want to know, if you please, if Mr. Egremont called here to-day and left a message for Mr. Smith about some books.'

' He's been here, but he left no message.'

' Was he here long ? '

' All the morning.'

' Putting books on the shelves ? '

' Yes.'

' Thank you. If there was no message, it's all right.'

Luke went off. In Kennington Road he again stood still. He felt chilled and wretched to the heart's core. Thyrza ! Thyrza Trent ! Was it possible ?

He moved on. This time it was to Newport Street. Half-past ten had just gone; would Totty be up still ? Whether or no, he must see her. He rang the bell which was a summons to her part of the house. Bunce opened.

' I want to see Miss Nancarrow,' Luke said to him in a low voice. ' Will you please knock at her door ? I must see her.'

Totty came down immediately. She had her hat on and a shawl thrown about her.

' What ever is it ? ' she asked.

' Just come a little way off, Totty; I want to speak to you.'

She accompanied him to the dark side of the street, and, having got her there, he could find no fitting word with which to begin. He had no intention of telling her what he had heard and what he had discovered for himself, but she was a close friend of Thyrza's and might know or suspect something; moreover, she was a good girl, a girl thoroughly to be trusted, he felt sure of her. Perhaps a hint would be enough to induce her to share a secret with him, when she understood what his suspicions pointed to.

' Totty——'

' Yes, you frighten me. What is it ? '

' Have you seen Thyrza Trent lately ? '

' Why ? '

She tried to read his face through the darkness. Her yesterday's conversation with Thyrza was vivid in her mind. Suspicion was irritated at the sound of Thyrza's name on Luke's tongue.

'Totty, I want to ask you something.' He spoke with
deepest earnestness, taking her hand. 'You won't keep anything from me, now? I want to know if Thyrza has talked
to you about—about her marriage.'

'Why do you want to know that?' the girl asked, in a
hard voice.

'I'll speak plainer, Totty. Be a good girl, Totty dear!
Tell me what I want to know! Has she ever said anything
to make you think that—that she liked any one better than
Grail?'

What a coil was here! She had pulled her hand away,
furious with him for his shamelessness. Yet self-respect did
not allow her to speak vehemently.

'It seems to me,' she said, 'you'd better go and ask her.'

He hung in doubt. Totty added, with more show of
feeling:

'Thyrza Trent's a little fool. You may tell her I said so,
if you like. If you know all about it, what do you come
bothering me for at this time o' night? I'm not going to be
mixed up in such things, so I tell you! And there's an end
of it!'

She left him. He stood and saw her re-enter the house.

Then is was true. 'If you know all about it,' . . . 'I'm
not going to be mixed up in such things.' . . . Totty had been
told, either by Thyrza herself or by someone already spreading
the story. The story was true.

He was struck with weakness. Sweat broke out from all
his body. Nothing he had ever heard had seemed to him so
terrible. A girl like Thyrza! He had held her honesty as
sure as the rising of day out of night.

Half an hour later he sat in his bedroom writing:

'Dear Miss Trent,—I want very much to see you. I will
wait in Kennington Road, opposite the end of your street, from
eight o'clock to-morrow night (Wednesday). Please do come.
I *must* see you, and I wish no one to know of our meeting.

                                  'Yours truly,
                                          'LUKE ACKROYD.'

He addressed this to Lydia, 'Miss Lydia Trent,' that there
might be no mistake, and went out to post it. But at the
letter-box he altered his intention. If it was delivered by the
postman, Thyrza would see it; it would lead to questionings.

He determined to deliver it at the hat factory in the morning,
with his own hand.

CHAPTER XXII

GOOD-BYE

LEFT alone, after Thyrza's second visit to him in the library, Egremont had no mind to continue his task. He idled about for a while, read half a page in a volume he took out of the box at hazard, then put on his overcoat and went out by the front door, which he locked behind him with the key he carried for his own convenience.

He was wishing that he had not fallen into this piece of folly. As long as no one but Grail and himself was concerned, it mattered nothing; to have established a secret intercourse with Thyrza was a result of his freak for which he was not at all prepared. And he could not see his way out of the difficulty. He might go and see Grail, and let him know what he was doing, but that would involve deliberate concealment of Thyrza's visits. He could not speak of them; he had no right to do so. If Thyrza on her part told all about it—why, that would make it, for him, still more unpleasant. And Thyrza was not likely to do that; he felt assured of it. Precisely; that meant that henceforth there would be a secret understanding between himself and Gilbert's wife. Most certainly he desired nothing of the kind.

A weak way of putting it. Walter dreaded anything of the kind. Two days—Monday, Tuesday—and in that brief time the whole face of the future had changed for him. On Sunday evening he had sat thinking over his future relations with Grail and Thyrza. The fact that he consciously brought himself to reflect upon the subject of course proved that it involved certain doubts and difficulties for him, but in half an hour he believed that he had put his mind in order. Thyrza interested him—why not say it out, as he was bent on understanding himself? She interested him more vitally than any girl he had ever known. Very possibly he saw her in the light of illusion; should his opportunities grant him a completer knowledge of her, he might not improbably discover that after all she was but a pretty girl of the people, attractive in a great measure owing to her very deficiencies. He would

very likely come to laugh at himself for having thought that
her value was above that of Annabel Newthorpe. But he had
to deal with the present, and in the present Thyrza seemed
to him all gold. Had there existed no Gilbert Grail, he would
have been in love with Thyrza.

The plain truth. But Gilbert Grail did exist, and in
Walter Egremont existed a sense of honour, a sense of shame.
Should he by word or deed throw light upon Gilbert Grail's
future, he felt that all the good of his own life would be at an
end. He could not face man or woman again.

It came to this, then. Henceforth he must remember
that, however near his intimacy with Gilbert, there must be
no playing at friendship with Gilbert's wife. Friendship was
impossible. That golden-haired girl had a power over him
which, if ever so slightly and thoughtlessly exercised, might
drive him into acts of insanity. He had seen her three times
—this is Sunday night, remember—and yet the thought of
Annabel was like a pale ghost beside his thought of her. He
had till now suspected that his nature was not framed for
passion; a few weeks had taught him that, if he allowed
passion to take hold upon him, no part of his soul could
escape the flame.

Two days had passed since then. On two successive
mornings he had been alone with Thyrza; one evening he
had spent at a concert, for the mere sake of being where
Thyrza was, and feeling emotions such as he knew she would
feel. ' No playing at friendship with Gilbert's wife.' And he
had himself held out his hand to her, had asked her to address
him familiarly, had talked of things which brought them into
closer communion, had—yes—had bidden her keep their
interviews a secret from Gilbert. Had insanity begun ?

A piece of folly; nothing else. As he walked towards
Westminster, he viewed the situation, or tried to view it, as
it is put in the second paragraph of this chapter. He had
got into a very disagreeable position; he really must find
some becoming way out of it ; Thyrza was a silly girl to come
a second time ; of course the appointment for the following
morning must not be kept. There was no harm in it all,
none whatever, but——

Bah ! The worst had come about ; the miserable fate had
declared itself ; he was in love with Thyrza Trent !

He entered the Abbey. He seated himself in a shadowed
place. Alone ? Whose then was the voice that spoke to him

unceasingly, and the hand which he was holding, which stirred his blood so with its warmth? 'Put aside every thought of the living fact; say that there is no Gilbert Grail in the world. You and I—you, Thyrza, my sweet-eyed, my beautiful—sit here side by side and hold each other's hands. Your voice has become very low and reverent, as befits the place, as befits the utterance of love such as this you say you bear me. What can I answer you, my golden one? Only, in voice low as your own, breathe that the world is barren but for you, that to the last drop of my heart's blood I love and worship you! A poor girl, a worker with her hands, untaught—you say that? A woman, pure of soul, with loveliness for your heritage, with possibilities imaginable in every ray of your eyes, in every note of the rare music of your voice!'

Even so. In the meantime, this happens to be Westminster Abbey, where a working man, one Gilbert Grail, has often walked and sought solace from the bitterness of his accursed lot, where he has thought of a young girl who lives above him in the house, and who, as often as she passes him, is like a gleam of southern sky somehow slipped into the blank hideousness of a London winter. Hither he has doubtless come to try and realise that fate has been so merciful to him that he longs to thank some unknown deity and cry that all is good. Hither he will come again, with one whom he calls his wife——

Walter rose and went forth, went home.

He had not been ten minutes in his room, when a servant appeared, to tell him that a lady had called and desired to see him, her name Mrs. Ormonde.

She came in, looking bright and noble as ever, giving him both her hands.

'I am glad to see you. I did not expect you to-day. Will you sit down?'

He did not know what he said. Mrs. Ormonde examined him, and for a moment kept silence.

'You have come up to-day?'

'Yes. I have come here direct from the station, because I wished to make use of you. But it seems to me that the doctor would have been a more fitting visitor. What has come to you, Walter?'

'It is true. I am not well. But always well enough to desire to serve you.'

'Though not, seemingly, to bear in mind my first wish.

Why have you not answered my last letter, as I particularly
asked you to ? If you were ill, why have you remained here
alone ? I am angry with you.'

He was reflecting, as absorbedly as if she had not been in
the room. She was his friend, if any man had one ; she was
of the priceless women who own both heart and brain. Should
he speak out and tell her everything ? If he did so, he was
saved. He would leave town. Grail should come back, after
the wedding holiday, and get on with the arrangement of the
library under written directions. Illness would explain such
a step. In a month, all would be right again.

' Walter ! '

Her eyes were searching him. Did she half know ? He
had written so foolishly in the letter about Thyrza. But it
was impossible that she could divine such a thing. The circumstances made it too incredible.

' Tell me,' she went on. ' What has caused your illness ? '

No, he could not. She would scorn him. And he could
not bear to sink in her estimation. He could not seem
childish before her.

' I have no idea,' he answered. ' Perhaps I have so accustomed myself to rambling over land and sea, that a year
without change is proving too much for me. I must have
the library started, and then be off—anywhere—a voyage to
New Zealand ! '

Mrs. Ormonde showed disappointment. She did not
believe that this was the truth, even as he knew it. The truth
was glimmering in the rear of her thoughts, but she would
not allow it to come forward ; in plain daylight it was really
difficult to entertain. Still, as an instinct it was there, instinct
supported even by certain pieces of evidence.

' You wish to go away ? To go a distance—to be away for
some time ? '

' Yes.' He did not meet her look. ' I don't think I shall
get back my health till I do that. Don't let us talk of it.'

' What are you doing at the library ? '

' Putting up books.'

' With Mr. Grail ? '

' No. He doesn't leave the factory till the end of the
week.'

' Then leave the place as it stands, and come to Eastbourne
with me to-morrow.'

' I'm afraid I——'

'And so am *I* afraid,' she interrupted him gravely. 'I wish you to come to Eastbourne. I wish you to!'

'No, not to Eastbourne. I have reasons.'

Her eyes fell.

'But I promise you,' he continued, 'that I will leave town to-morrow. I promise you. Don't think me unkind that I refuse to come with you. I will go to Jersey again; it suits me. I'll stay there till Grail comes back with his wife, and then see if I feel well enough to come and go on with the work.'

'Very well,' Mrs. Ormonde replied, slowly.

'Do you doubt my word?' he asked, moving forward to her.

'We are not so far as that, Walter.'

'And now tell me what I am to do for you.'

She hesitated, but only for a moment.

'I wish you to see Mr. Bunce for me. Do you meet him nowadays?'

'Not just now, but I can see him any time.'

'I want to arrange, if possible, to keep his child with me for some time, for a year or more. It is not impossible that her disease might be checked if she lived at Eastbourne, but in London she will very soon die. I should like to see Mr. Bunce myself, and I thought you might be able to arrange for a meeting between us. My idea is this: I shall tell him that the girl can make herself useful in the house, and that I wish to pay her for her services. The money would of course go to him, and he might use it to get help in his home. Bessie, the child, has explained to me all the difficulties in the way of her remaining with me; they are heightened by her father's character, as you can understand. Now do you think he would see me? He might come to my hotel, or he might come here, or if he allows me, I would go to him.'

'I will arrange it, somehow. Trust me, I will arrange it.'

'You should have said that with a wave of the hand, as omnipotent people do on the stage.'

He laughed.

'There is no feeling miserable with you. Have you not something of that mesmeric power which draws one back into health under a touch?'

'Perhaps. A little. My children sometimes show astonishing improvement, when they get fond of me.'

They talked of various things, but no mention was made of the Newthorpes by either.

'Is Paula back yet ? ' Mrs. Ormonde asked.

'I have no idea. I am not likely ever to see her again.'

'Oh, yes ! When you come back from New Zealand. I shall go and see the Tyrrells this afternoon, I think. I have to dine with friends at Hampstead. When can I have the result of your inquiries ? '

'I will come to you to-morrow morning.'

'At ten, please. I have a great deal to get into the day; and you yourself must be off by noon.'

'By noon I shall be.'

This visit had been happily timed. Sympathy was essential to Egremont as often as he suffered from the caprices of his temperament, and in grave trouble it was a danger for him to be left companionless. He was highly nervous, and the tumult of his imagination affected his bodily state in a degree uncommon in men, though often seen in delicately organised women. When Mrs. Ormonde left him he felt relieved in mind, but physically so brought down that he stretched himself upon the sofa. He remained there for more than an hour.

How much better, he was saying to himself, not to have told Mrs. Ormonde ! That would have been a greater folly than anything yet. No irreparable harm was as yet done ; to confess a mere state of mind would have been to fill his friend with fears wholly groundless, and to fix a lasting torture in his own memory. It would have been to render impossible any future work in Lambeth. Yet upon the continuance of such work practically depended Grail's future. To Gilbert Grail he had solemn duties to perform. Henceforth the scope of his efforts would be lessened ; instead of exerting himself for a vague populace, it would really be for Grail alone that he worked. Grail he must and would aid to the end. It was a task worthy of a man who was not satisfied with average aims. He would crush this tyrannous passion in his heart, cost him what struggle it might, and the reward would be a noble one.

He rose at length with a haggard face. It was long past the hour at which he usually took his mid-day meal, and he had no appetite for food. He went to a restaurant, however, and made pretence of eating ; thence into the smoking-room, where he spent the time till five o'clock, drinking coffee and reading papers. His only object now was to kill time.

At half-past eight he was in Lambeth. He knew Bunce's

address, but had never before been in Newport Street. It was his habit to discover places by the aid of a map alone, and, thus guided, he found the house.

Totty Nancarrow happened to be on the stairs when he knocked; she had just come in. She ran down to the door. Egremont inquired for Bunce, and was told he was not at home, and would not be till very late.

'Do you know when I could be sure to find him here?'

'Yes,' replied Totty, who was able to guess at Egremont's identity, and examined him with some interest. 'He'll be here to-morrow after eight. He's on a job in Hammersmith, working late. But to-morrow's the last day, and he's sure to be back by eight o'clock.'

'He leaves early in the morning, I suppose?'

'At half-past five.'

'Thank you. I will call to-morrow evening. Could you let him know that, from Mr. Egremont? I wish to see him particularly.'

'I'll let him know, sir.'

This was a mishap. It would necessitate another whole day in London.

He called upon Mrs. Ormonde next morning, at the hotel which it was her wont to use when in town for a day or two. At first she was strongly opposed to his waiting just on this account.

'I cannot go till I have done this for you,' he said firmly. 'I shall see Bunce to-night, and go away to-morrow. You must let me have my way in this.'

And he desired to remain for a weightier reason than the apparent one. It was this morning, Wednesday, that Thyrza would expect to find him at the library. She must be disappointed, and he would prove to himself that he was yet strong enough to resist, that he had not so lost self-control that his only safety lay in flight.

The strength was that of a man who combats desperately with some ailment which threatens his life. 'Am I then of those who have no will power? Will is that whereby men raise themselves above the multitude; let me give proofs now that my claims are not those of a charlatan.' He passed six hours in his room.

Thyrza would go to the library at eleven, or a little after. She was there now. She would find the front door closed against her. She would go round to the house, and make inquiry of Mrs. Butterfield. Perhaps she would wait for him.

Yes, she would wait for him. She was sitting in the library, on the chest which he had offered her for a seat, alone, disappointed.

Disappointed. More than that. Why had she come on Tuesday, the second morning? Why had she desired to come yet again? Had he read her face truly?

He knew, he knew with miserable certainty, that she did not love Grail. She had not known what love was; a child, so merely a child! But when love once was born in her, would it not be for life and death?

He was lying on the sofa again, his eyes fixed on the ceiling. Moisture stood upon his forehead, formed into beads and ran off. His torment was that of the rack. He believed that Thyrza had at least begun to love him. Madman that he was, he *hoped* it! Thyrza's love was a thing for which one would dare uttermost perdition, the blind leap once taken. Yes, but that leap he would not take; he was on firm ground; he knew what honour meant; he acknowledged the sanctity of obligations between man and man.

But if she loved *him*, was it right that she should wed Grail? Obligations, forsooth! Was it not his first duty to save her from a terrible self-sacrifice? What could overrule love? There was time to intervene; four days more, and it would be too late for ever—for ever. What hideous things might result from conscientiousness such as he was now striving to preserve.

'Thyrza! She is waiting there, waiting for *me* to come to her. She trembles at every sound, thinking it *my* footstep. If her anguish be but the shadow of mine——'

He sprang up, ghastly. He had not closed his eyes through the night, but had lain, and walked about the room, in torment. Desire, jealousy, frenzy of first passion, the first passion of his life; no pang was spared him. Oh, how had it grown so suddenly! He had imagined love such as this for some stately woman whose walk was upon the heights of mind—some great artist—some glorious sovereign of culture. Instead of that, a simple girl who lived by her needle, who spoke faultily. And he loved her with the love which comes to a man but once.

The evening came at last. Long before it was really time

to start for Lambeth, on his visit to Bunce, he began to walk southwards. He was at Westminster Bridge by half-past seven; probably it would be useless to call in Newport Street for another hour. He went down on to the Lambeth Embankment.

It was his hope that no acquaintance would pass this way. Still blameless in fact, he could not help a fear of being observed; the feeling could not have been stronger if he had come with the express purpose of seeking Thyrza. The air was cold; it blew at moments piercingly from the river. Where the sun had set, there was still a swarthy glow upon the clouds; the gas-lamps gave a haggardness to the banks and the bridges.

He walked at a quick pace; this way, then that. Workmen and women in numbers were hurrying in both directions. Egremont kept his face towards the river, that he might see no one. There was no likelihood that Thyrza would pass. If she did, if she were alone and saw him, he knew she would come up to him and speak.

The bell at Westminster struck out the hour of eight. He turned off the Embankment and went on to Lambeth Bridge, stopping at length to lean on the parapet at the same place where Gilbert had stood and mused one night when his happiness was almost too great to bear. To Egremont the darkening scene was in accord with the wearied misery which made his life one dull pain. London lay beneath the night like a city of hopeless toil, of aimless conflict, of frustration and barrenness. His philosophy was a sham, a spinning of cobwebs for idle hours when the heart is restful and the brain seeks to be amused. He had no more strength to bear the torture of an inassuageable desire than any foolish fellow who knew not the name of culture. He could not look forward to the day of forgetting; he would not allow himself to believe that he ever could forget.

But it was time now to go on to Newport Street. In Paradise Street, just before the railway arch, he glanced at the Bowers' shop, and dreaded lest Bower should meet him. But he saw no one that he knew before reaching Bunce's abode.

The landlady opened the door. Bunce was at home, and in a moment came down. He returned his visitor's greeting awkwardly, much wondering.

'Could I have a few words with you?' Egremont asked. 'I have come on Mrs. Ormonde's behalf—the lady at the

Eastbourne home, you know. I have a message about your little girl.'

'Something happened?' Bunce inquired, in a startled voice.

'No, no; good news, if anything.'

Bunce did not willingly invite Egremont into his poor room, but he felt that he had no choice. He just said: 'Will you come upstairs, sir?' and led the way.

The two children were playing together on the floor; Bunce had been on the point of putting Nelly to bed. In spite of his mood, natural kindness so far prevailed with Egremont that he bent and touched the child's curls. Bunce, with set lips, stood watching; he saw that Egremont had not so much as cast an eye round the room, and that, together with the attention to his child, softened his naturally suspicious frame of mind.

'It's better than coming back to an empty room every night?' Egremont said, looking at the man.

'Yes, sir, it's better—though I don't always think so.'

'These two keep well?'

'Fairly well.'

'There's never nothing the matter with me!' exclaimed young Jack, bluff though shamefaced.

'Nothing except your grammar, you mean, Jack,' replied his father. 'Will you just sit down, sir? I was afraid at first there was something wrong, when you mentioned Mrs. Ormonde.'

Egremont reassured him, and went on to say that Mrs. Ormonde was anxious to see him personally whilst she was in town. He felt it would be better not to explain the nature of the proposal Mrs. Ormonde was going to make, and affected to know nothing more than that she wished to speak of the child's health. Bunce had knitted his brows; his heavy lips took on a fretful sullenness. He knew that it was impossible to meet Egremont with flat refusals, and the prospect of being driven into something he intensely disliked worked him into an inward fume. He gave a great scrape on the floor with one of his heels as if he would have ploughed a track in the boards.

'I'm sorry,' he began, 'I've got no free time worth speaking of. I'm much obliged to the lady. But I don't see how I'm to——'

He wanted to blunder out words of angry impatience; his

rising choler brought him to a full stop in the middle of the sentence.

Egremont addressed himself in earnest to the task of persuasion. More was involved than mere benefit to the child's health; it was easy to see that Bunce's position was a miserable one, and Mrs. Ormonde, if once she could establish direct relations with the man, would doubtless find many a little way of being useful to him. He put it at length as a personal favour. Bunce again ploughed the floor, then blurted out:

'I'll go, Mr. Egremont. I'm not one to talk to ladies, as you can see yourself, but I can't help that. I shall have to go as I am.'

'Mrs. Ormonde will gladly come here, if you will let her.'

'I'd rather not, if you don't mind, sir.'

'Then it will be simplest if you go to my rooms in Great Russell Street, just by the British Museum. I leave town to-morrow; Mrs. Ormonde will be quite alone to meet you. Could you be there at nine o'clock?'

The appointment was made, Egremont leaving one of his cards to insure recollection of the address. Then he spoke a word or two to the children, and Bunce led him down to the door. They shook hands.

'I shall see you at the library soon, I hope,' Egremont said. 'You must give me your best help in making it known.'

The words sounded so hollow in his own ears that, as he turned to go along the dark street, he could have laughed at himself scornfully.

As Bunce reascended, someone met and passed him, hurrying with light feet and woman's garments silently.

'That you, Miss Nancarrow?' he asked, for there was no light on the staircase.

'No,' came a muffled reply. 'Miss Nancarrow isn't in.'

It was the voice of Thyrza Trent. Bunce did not recognise it, for he knew her too slightly.

She had come to the house not long before Egremont. After a day of suffering she wished to speak with Totty. Totty was the only one to whom she *could* speak now; Gilbert, her own Lyddy—them she dreaded. Notwithstanding the terms on which she had parted with her friend on Monday night, she felt an irresistible need of seeing her. It was one way, moreover, of passing a part of the evening

away from Walnut Tree Walk. But Totty was out, had not
yet come home since her work. Thyrza said she would go
upstairs and wait.

She did so. Totty's room was dark and, of course, fire-
less; but she cared neither for the darkness nor the cold.
She groped her way to a chair and sat very still. It was a
blessed relief to be here, to be safe from Gilbert and Lyddy
for ever so short a time, to sit and clasp the darkness like
something loved. She was making up her mind to tell Totty
everything. Someone she must tell—someone. Not Lyddy;
that would be terrible. But Totty had a kind heart, and
would keep the secret, perchance could advise in some way.
Though what advice could anyone give?

What voice was that? She had heard someone knock at
Bunce's door, then heard Bunce go down. He was coming up
again, and someone with him—someone who spoke in a voice
which made her heart leap. She sprang to the door to listen.
Bunce and his companion entered the opposite room, and shut
themselves in. Thyrza opened her door as softly as possible,
leaned forward, listened. Yes, it was *his* voice!

What was he doing here? He had not come to the library,
had not kept his promise. Was it not a promise to her? He
had said that she should see him again, should be in the room
alone with him, talk with him for one hour—one poor, short
hour; and in the end it was denied. Why did he come to see
Mr. Bunce? But he was well; nothing had happened to him,
which all day had been her dread.

She would not try to overhear their conversation. Enough
that he was safe in that next room, never mind for what
purpose he came. She was near to him again.

She threw up her hands against the door, and leaned her
face, her bosom on it. Her throat was so dry that she felt
choking; her heart—poor heart! could it bear this incessant
throbbing pain? She swallowed tears, and had some little
bodily solace.

But if Totty should come! She hoped to be alone as
long as he was there. It was so sweet to be near him, and
alone!

And Totty did not come. Of a sudden the opposite door
opened. He was leaving, going forth again she knew not
whither—only that it was away from her.

Then desire became act. She heard the house-door close,
and on the moment sped from the room. She scarcely knew

what she said to Bunce on the stairs. Now she was in the
street. Which way? There he was, there, at but a little
distance.

But she must not approach him here, in this street. Any
moment Totty might come—one of the Bowers might pass.
She kept at an even remoteness, following him. Into Paradise
Street, into High Street, out into Lambeth Road, with the
bridge in sight. He meant to go along the Embankment.
But it was quieter here. A quickened step, almost a run, and
she was by his side.

'Mr. Egremont!'

He stood.

'Mr. Egremont. I thought it was you. I wanted——'

They were under the church. As Thyrza spoke, the bells
suddenly broke out with their harsh clanging; they had been
ringing for the last twenty minutes, and were now recommencing after a pause.

Egremont glanced towards the tower, startled and seemingly annoyed.

'I'm very sorry I couldn't come to the library this morning, Miss Trent,' he said, very formally. 'I was unexpectedly
kept away.'

What automaton had taken his place and spoke in this
contemptible tone of conventional politeness?

'Those bells are so loud,' Thyrza said, complainingly. 'I
wanted to—to ask you something. May I go with you a little
further—just to the bridge?'

He said nothing, but looked at her and walked on. They
entered the bridge. Egremont still advanced, and Thyrza
kept by him, till they were nearly on the Westminster side of
the river. Very few people passed them, and no vehicles
disturbed the quiet of the dark road along the waterside. On
the one hand was a black mass of wharfs, a few barges
moored in front; on the other, at a little distance, the gloomy
shape of Millbank prison. The jangle of the bells was
softened.

'They certainly might be more musical,' Egremont said,
with a forced laugh. 'I should not care to live in one of the
houses just under the church.'

She was speaking.

'I waited this morning. Oh, it didn't matter; but I was
afraid—I thought you might have had some accident, Mr.
Egremont.'

s

'No. It was business that prevented me from coming. But you wish to ask me something, Miss Trent?'

'If you will be there to-morrow—that was all. I like helping. I like looking at the books, and putting them up—if you would let me.'

The nearest lamp showed him her face. What held him from making that pale loveliness his own? His heart throbbed as terribly as hers; he with difficulty heard when she spoke, so loud was the rush of blood in his ears.

But he had begun the fight with himself. He could not turn away abruptly and leave her standing there; if the victory were to be won, it must be by sheer wrestle with the temptation, for her sake as well as his own. To let her so much as suspect his feeling were as bad as to utter it; nay, infinitely worse, for it would mean that he must not see her after to-night. He and she would then be each other's peril in a far direr sense than now.

He replied to her:

'I'm so sorry; I shall not be there to-morrow. I have to go out of London.'

He looked her in the face unwaveringly. It was the look which tormented her, not that which she yearned for. She could not move away her eyes.

'You are going away, Mr. Egremont?'

'Yes, I am going out of England for a week or two—perhaps for longer.'

It was wrong—all wrong. In spite of himself he could not but admit a note of pathos. The automatic voice of politeness would not come at his bidding. He should have left her on the other side of the bridge, where the harsh bells allowed no delicacies of tone.

'To France?' she asked.

'No. To an island very near France. I must not keep you standing here, Miss Trent. It is very cold.'

Yes, the wind was cold, but perspiration covered his face.

'Please—only a minute. May I go to the library and do some more of the books? Are they all finished?'

'No. There's still one case of them, and more will be coming. Certainly you may go there if you wish.'

Her voice fell.

'But I shan't know how to put them. No, I can't do it alone.'

'I shall write to Mr. Grail, and tell him what I have been doing. You can help him.'

'Yes.'

The monosyllable fell from her like a whisper of despair. But the utterance of Grail's name had brought Egremont the last impulse he needed.

'When I come back,' he said, 'I shall find you in your new home. As I shan't see you again, let me say now how much I hope that you will live there a long time and very happily. Good-bye, Miss Trent.'

Surely that was formal and automatic enough. Not one more word, not one more glance at her face. He had touched her hand, had raised his hat, was gone.

She stood gazing after him until, in a minute or two, he was lost in the dark street behind the wharfs. So suddenly! He had scarcely said good-bye—so poor a good-bye! She had vexed him with her importunities; he wished to show her that she had not behaved in the way that pleased him. Scarcely a good-bye!

She went to the end of the bridge, and there crept into a dark place whither no eye could follow her. Her strength was at an end. She fell to her knees; her head lay against something hard and cold; a sob convulsed her, and then in the very anguish of desolation she wept. The darkness folded her; she could lie here on the ground and abandon herself to misery. She wept her soul from her eyes.

But for Egremont the struggle was not over. He had scarcely passed out of her sight when fear held his steps. Thyrza must not be left there alone. That face of hers, looking like marble, threatened despair. How could he leave her so far from home, in the night, by the river?

He went back. He knew what such return meant. It was defeat after all. He knew what his first word to her would be.

He sought her now, sought her that she might never leave him again. The flood of passion was too strong; that moment of supreme restraint had but massed the waters into overwhelming power. It was the thought of danger to her that had ended all pity for Gilbert.

She was not in sight. Could she have passed the bridge so quickly? He ran forward. True, it must be more than five minutes since he had left her, much more, perhaps, for he could not judge how long he had stood battling with him-self behind the wharfs.

A policeman stood at the end of the bridge. Egremont asked him if a young girl had just passed. Yes, such a one had gone by a minute or two ago.

He ran on, past the church, into High Street. But would she go this way? A girl crossed the road a little way ahead, into Paradise Street. He overtook her, only to be dis-appointed.

At the end of Newport Street a man stood, waiting. It was Gilbert Grail; he had come in the hope of meeting Thyrza, who, Lydia had told him, was gone to see Totty Nancarrow. He was greatly anxious about her.

Egremont, coming up at a swift pace recognised Gilbert and stopped. They shook hands. Grail was silent, Egremont began to stammer words. He had been to see Bunce, just now, for such and such reasons, with such and such results. But he could not stop, he had an engagement. Good-night!

The shame of it! He found himself in Lambeth Walk, no longer searching, anxious only to get away from the sight of men. Thyrza must be home by this time. That speech with Gilbert had chilled him, and now he was hot with self-con-tempt. He made his way out into Westminster Bridge Road, thence walked to his own part of the town.

CHAPTER XXIII

CONFESSION

THIS Wednesday morning Lydia went to her work reluctantly. Thyrza was so strange; it looked as if she was going to have an illness. Again there had been a night of sleeplessness; if the girl fell for a moment into slumber she broke from it with an inarticulate cry as if of fear. It was now nearly a week since Thyrza had really slept through the night, but it was growing worse. She was feverish; she muttered, so that Lydia was terrified lest she had become delirious. And there was no explaining it all. The excitement of the concert, surely, could not have such lasting results; indeed, Thyrza seemed no longer to give a thought to the music. All she begged for was that she might be allowed to remain alone. She did not wish

Mrs. Grail to come up to the room. She said she would go out in the course of the morning, and that would do her good.

So Lydia went forth reluctantly. At the entrance to the factory she met Totty Nancarrow. They just gave each other a good-morning. Totty seemed dull. She did not run up the stairs as usual, but walked with a tired step.

Lydia, following her, broke her habit, and spoke.

' Thyrza isn't at all well.'

' Isn't she ? ' said the other, without turning her head, and in a tone of little interest.

Lydia bit her lip, vexed that she had said anything.

They came into the work-room. There were a number of tables, at which girls and women were beginning to seat themselves. A portion of the room was divided off by a glass partition, and within the little office thus formed sat the fore-woman, surrounded with felt hats, some finished, some waiting for the needle to line them and put the band on. Sitting here, she overlooked the workers, some fifty when all were assembled.

There was much buzzing and tittering and laughing aloud. All belonged to the class of needlewomen who preserve appearances; many of them were becomingly dressed, and none betrayed extreme poverty. Probably a fourth came from homes in which they were not the only wage-earners, and would not starve if work slackened now and then, having fathers or brothers to help them. Whether they liked coming to work or not, all showed much cheerfulness at the commencement of the day. They greeted each other pleasantly, sometimes affectionately, and not one who lacked a story of personal incident to be quickly related to a friend whilst the work was being given out. So much seemed to happen in the hours of freedom.

Lydia was much quieter than usual. It was not her wont to gossip of her own affairs, or to pry into the secrets of her acquaintances ; but with the little group of those with whom she was intimate she had generally some piece of merriment to share, always marked by kindness of feeling. She was a favourite with the most sensible girls of her own age. Thyrza had never been exactly a favourite, though some older than herself always used to pet her, generally causing her annoyance.

About a quarter of an hour had passed, and work was

getting into trim, when a girl, a late arrival, in coming to her place, handed Lydia a letter.

'Someone downstairs asked me to give it you,' she whispered. 'You needn't blush, you know.'

Lydia was too surprised to manifest any such self-consciousness. She murmured thanks, and looked at the address. It was a man's writing, but she had no idea whose. She opened the envelope and found Ackroyd's short note.

What did this mean? It at once flashed across Lydia's mind that there might be some connection between this and Thyrza's strange disorder. Old habit still brought Ackroyd and Thyrza together in her thoughts. Yet how was it possible? Ackroyd was engaged to Totty Nancarrow, and Thyrza had never shown the least interest when she mentioned him of late. Was he going to make trouble, now at the last moment, when everything seemed to have taken the final form?

Since Thyrza's engagement to Gilbert, there was no longer need of subtle self-deceptions, but, though she might now freely think of him, Lydia soon found that Ackroyd was not the same in her eyes. The first rumours of his abandonment to vulgar dissipation she utterly refused to credit, but before long she had to believe them in spite of herself. She saw him one night coming out of a public-house, singing a drunken song. It was a terrible blow to her; she had to question herself much, and to make great efforts to understand a man's nature. She had thought him incapable of such things. The vague stories of earlier wildness she had held no account of. When a woman says 'Oh, that is past,' she means 'It does not exist, and never did exist.'

It surprised her that she still thought of him with heartache. Her quarrel with Mary Bower seemed an encouragement to the love she kept so secret. She found a thousand excuses for him; she pitied him deeply; she longed to go and speak to him. Why could she not do so? Often and often she rehearsed conversations with him, in which she told him how unworthy it was to fall so, and implored him for his own sake to be a man again. She might have realised such a dialogue—though it would have cost her much—but for the news that he had begun to pay attention to Totty Nancarrow.

Then she knew jealousy. Of Thyrza she could not be jealous, but to imagine him giving his affection to a girl like

Totty Nancarrow made her rebellious and scornful. How little could any of her work-room companions know what was passing in Lydia's breast when she had one of her days of quietness and bent with such persistence over her sewing! If spoken to, she raised the same kind, helpful face as ever; you could not imagine that a minute ago a tear had all but come to her eyes, that in thought she had been uttering words of indignant passion. They were rare, those days in which she could not be quite herself. It was not her nature to yield when weakness tempted.

And now he had written to her. Having read the note, she put it into the bosom of her dress, and, whilst her fingers were busy, she turned over every possible explanation in her mind. She knew that he had abandoned his evil habits of late, and she could be just enough not to refuse Totty some credit for the change. Gilbert himself had said that the girl's influence seemed on the whole good. But some mystery was now going to reveal itself. It concerned Thyrza; she was sure it did. The fact that the note was delivered in this way, and the request for secrecy which it contained, made this certain.

At dinner-time, and again in the evening, Thyrza was still in the same state of depression and feverishness. Lydia said nothing of the business which would take her out at eight o'clock. When the time came, and she had to make an excuse, Thyrza said that she too would go out; she wanted to see Totty.

'You'll tell Gilbert?' Lydia replied, afraid to make any opposition herself.

'No. He'd say it wasn't good for me to go out, and I want to go. You won't say anything, Lyddy?'

'I ought to, dear. You're not well enough to go, that's quite certain.'

'I won't be long. I must go just for half an hour.'

'Why do you want to see her?' Lydia asked, masking her curiosity with a half-absent tone.

'Oh, nothing to explain. I feel I want to talk, that's all.'

From time to time—in her more difficult moments—Lydia had felt a little hurt that the course of circumstances made no difference in Thyrza's friendship for Totty. When her truer mind was restored, she knew that the reproach was a foolish one. More likely it was she herself who was to blame for having always nourished a prejudice against Totty.

At present, Thyrza's anxiety to go out was another detail connecting itself with Ackroyd's summons. Something unexplained was in progress between those three, Totty and Ackroyd and Thyrza. Her resentment against the first of them revived.

She would soon know what it all meant. Thyrza and she left the house together and went in opposite directions. Lydia crossed Kennington Road, and found Luke waiting for her. She approached him with veiled eyes.

'I'm so glad you've come,' he began, with signs of disturbance. 'It's kind of you to come. I have a great deal to say, and I can't speak here. Will you come round into Walcot Square?—it'll be quieter.'

She said nothing, but walked beside him. It was a new and strange sensation to be thus accompanying Ackroyd. She was conscious that her pulses quickened. They went on in silence till they reached the spot which Luke had mentioned, an irregular little square, without traffic, dark.

'I don't know how to begin to tell you, Miss Trent,' Ackroyd said, when he stopped and turned towards her. 'It's your sister I have to speak about.'

She had foreseen truly. Her heart sank.

'What can you have to say about my sister, Mr. Ackroyd?' she asked in a hard voice.

'I'm not surprised that you speak in that way. I know that I shall seem a busybody, or perhaps something worse, meddling with things that don't concern me. It would be easier for me to leave it alone, but I couldn't do that, because I can't think of you and your sister as strangers. I've heard something said about Thyrza that you ought to know. Be friendly to me, and believe I'm only telling you this because I think it's my duty.'

Lydia was looking at him in astonishment.

'You've heard something? What? What has anybody to say about my sister?'

'I shall make no secret of anything—it's the only way to prove I'm behaving honestly to you. I was at the club last night, and Bower came and sat down by me, and he began to talk about Thyrza. He said it looked strange that she should be alone with Mr. Egremont in the library every morning. The woman that takes care of the place told him about it, and he's seen Thyrza himself coming away at dinner-time, when Mr. Egremont was there. He says she goes to help

him to put books on the shelves. He spoke of it in a way
that showed he was telling the story to all sorts of people,
and in a way that means harm. I'd sooner bite my tongue
out than repeat such things about your sister, if it wasn't
that you ought to know. I might have told Grail, but I felt
it was better to see you first. I know I'm making trouble
enough any way, but I believe you will give me credit for
acting honestly. Don't think of me as the kind of man I've
seemed since Christmas. You used to think well of me, and
you must do so now, Miss Trent. I'm speaking as a true
friend.'

He hurried out his words of self-justification, for he saw
the anger in her face.

' And you believe this ? ' Lydia exclaimed, when she could
use her voice. ' You believe a man that will go saying things
like this about my sister ? Why is he trying to do us harm ?
Why, there *is* no books to put on the shelves ! No books
have come to the library yet ! '

She laughed scornfully, and, before he could speak, continued with the same vehemence.

' What have we done to Mr. Bower? I suppose it's
because we're not so friendly with them as we were. So
he does his best to take away our good name, and to ruin
Thyrza's life ! Of course, I knew very well what you mean.
I know what *he* means. He's a cruel coward ! It's a lie that
he's seen Thyrza coming out of the library ! Why, I tell you
there *is* no books there ! How could she help to put them on
the shelves ? You shall come with me this minute to the
Bowers' house ! You can't refuse to do that, Mr. Ackroyd :
it's only fair, it's only justice. You shall come and repeat to
them all you've told me, and then see if he'll *dare* to say it
again. I'm glad you didn't tell Gilbert ; you was right to tell
me first. I'm not angry with you ; you mustn't think that ;
though you speak as if you believed his lies. I should have
thought you knew Thyrza better. Come with me, this minute !
You *shall* come, if you're an honest man, as you say you are ! '

She laid her hand upon his arm. Ackroyd took the hand
and held it whilst he compelled her to listen to him.

' Lydia, we can't go till you've heard everything. I've got
more to tell you.'

' More ? What is it ? A man that 'll say so much 'll say
anything. You've told me quite enough, I should think,
considering it's about my own sister.'

'But, Lydia, do listen to me, my poor girl! Try and quiet yourself, and listen to me. There's nothing more of Bower's telling; he didn't say any more; and there was more harm in his way of telling it than in the story itself. But I have something to tell you that I've found out myself.'

She looked him in the face. Her hand she had drawn away.

'And *you* are going to say harm of Thyrza!' she said under her breath, eyeing him as though he were her deadliest enemy.

'Think and say of me what you like, Lydia. I've got something that I must tell you; if I don't, I'd a deal better never have said anything at all. You're not right about the library. There *are* books there, and Mr. Egremont has been busy with them of a morning.'

'But how can *you* know better than Gilbert?' she cried.

'I know, because I went last night to find out. As soon as I'd heard Bower's tale, I went. And I was there again to-day, at dinner-time, and I saw your sister come out of the door.'

She was silent. In spite of her passionate exclamations, a suspicion had whispered within her from the first, a voice to which she would lend no ear. Now she was constrained to think. She remembered Thyrza's lateness at dinner on Monday; she remembered that Thyrza had been from home each morning this week. And if it were true that books had arrived at the library, and that Gilbert knew nothing of it—— Was *this* the explanation of Thyrza's illness, of her inexplicable agitations, of her sleeplessness?

She could not raise her head. Ackroyd too kept silent. She asked at length: 'Have you anything more to tell me?'

'Yes, I *have* something more. It's another thing that I found out last night, after leaving Bower. Say that you don't accuse me of conduct as bad as Bower's!' he added, vehemently. 'I *must* tell you everything, and it makes me seem as if I told it for the sake of telling. Say you believe in my honesty, at all events!'

'I don't accuse you of anything,' she replied, still under her breath. 'What is it you have to say?'

'I went to see Miss Nancarrow. I had no thought of repeating the story to her—you must believe me or not, as you like, but I am telling you the truth. I wanted to see if she had heard anything from the Bowers, and I wanted to try and find out, if I could, whether Thyrza had told her any secret. It wasn't out of a wish to pry into things I'd no concern with, but because I felt afraid for Thyrza, and because I wanted to be sure that there was sufficient reason for it before I came to you to put you on your guard. I said to Totty : "Have you any reason to think that Thyrza cares for somebody else more than for Grail?" She got angry at once, and said she knew all about it, that she'd no patience with Thyrza, and that she wasn't going to have anything more to do with the affair. I've told you plainly, Lydia, told you everything. I hope I've done it for the best.'

She stood as if she heard nothing. Her arms hung down; her eyes were fixed on the ground. She was thinking that now she understood Thyrza's urgency in wishing to see Totty. Now she understood everything.

She moved, as if to go away. Ackroyd could find no word. All he had to say was so much sheer cruelty, and to attempt comfort would be insult. But Lydia faced him again.

'And you think the worst of my sister?'

Again her look was defiant. She had no enemy in the world like the man who could accuse Thyrza of guilt. It was one thing to point out that Thyrza was in danger of being culumniated, another to believe that the evil judgment was merited.

'I *don't* think the worst of her, Lydia,' he replied, firmly. 'I think it likely that she has been doing something very thoughtless, and I am quite sure that that man Egremont has been doing something for which he deserves to be thrashed. But no more than that. More than that I *won't* believe !'

'Thank you, Mr. Ackroyd! A minute ago I hated you, now I know that I have always been right in thinking you had a good heart. Thyrza may have been foolish in keeping things from me, but she's no more to blame than that. You can believe me. I would say it, if it was my life or death!'

He took her hand and pressed it.

'And you think Mr. Bower is telling everyone?' she asked, her voice wonderfully changed, for all at once she became a woman, and felt her need of a strong man's aid.

'I'm afraid so. When he'd done his tale to me last night, I told him that if he hadn't been a man so much older than myself I'd have struck him in face of all in the club. I'd perhaps better not have angered him, but it wouldn't make

much difference. He's got ill feeling against Egremont, I
believe.'

Lydia's eyes flashed when she heard of that speech to
Bower.

'And you think he's doing this more to harm Mr. Egremont than Thyrza ?'

'I do. He's a gossiping fool, but I don't believe he'd
plot to ruin a girl in this way. Still, I'm quite sure the
story 'll have got about, and it comes to the same thing.'

Both stood in thought. Lydia felt as if all the bright
future were blasted before her eyes. Thyrza loved Egremont.
Egremont was the falsest of friends to Gilbert, the most
treacherous of men. Her darling had been artfully drawn by
him into this secret intercourse ; and how was it all to end ?

'I must go home to Thyrza, Mr. Ackroyd. I don't know
what to do, but it will come to me when I see my sister.'

She reflected a moment, then added :

'She went to see Totty Nancarrow, at the same time when
I came out. Perhaps she'll be there still. If I don't find her
at home, I must go to the other house. Good-bye !'

'I do wish I could be some help to you, Lydia !' he said,
holding her hand and looking very kindly at her.

'You can't. Nobody can help. Whatever happens
Thyrza and me will be together, and I shall keep her from
harm. But you've been a good friend to me to-night, Mr.
Ackroyd. I can't do more than say I'm grateful to you. I
shall be that, as long as I live.'

'Lydia—— I don't want to pry into anything between
you and your sister, but if I *can* do anything to be of use to
her—or to you—you'll tell me ? You could easily send a
message to me.'

'Thank you. I *will* ask you if there is anything. Let
me go home alone, Mr. Ackroyd.'

She came to the house, and saw that there was no light in
the window of their room. Still, Thyrza might be sitting
there. She ran upstairs. The room was vacant.

Then she hurried to Newport Street. Mrs. Ladds told her
that Totty had not come in yet, and that Thyrza had been and
was gone away again. She turned on her steps slowly, and
after a short uncertainty went home again, in the hope that
Thyrza might have returned. As she entered, Gilbert met her
in the passage.

'Is Thyrza come back ?' she asked.

' No, she isn't in the house. Where did she go to ? '

' She went just to see Totty Nancarrow.' Nothing was to be gained by concealing this now. ' I've been there, but she's gone away. I dare say she'll be back in a few minutes.'

Lydia went upstairs, not feeling able to talk. Gilbert, who since Monday had fallen into ever deeper trouble, left the house and walked towards Newport Street, hoping to find Thyrza. It was thus that he came to be met by Egremont. He was back in half an hour. Lydia came down when she heard him enter.

' Lydia,' he said, gravely, ' you shouldn't have allowed her to go out. She isn't in a fit state to leave the house.'

' It was wrong, I know,' she said, standing just inside the door of the parlour.

Gilbert mentioned that he had seen Egremont. Before she could check herself, Lydia exclaimed :

' Where ? '

He looked at her in surprise. She turned very pale. Mrs. Grail was also gazing at her.

' It was at the end of Newport Street,' Gilbert replied. ' Why are you so anxious to know where ? '

' I'm sure I don't know. I'm worrying so about that child. I spoke without thinking at all.'

Half an hour more passed, then, as all sat silently together, they heard the front door opening. Lydia started up.

' Don't move, Gilbert ! Let me go up with her. She'll be afraid of being scolded.'

She went out into the passage. The little lamp hung against the wall as usual, and when by its light she saw Thyrza, she was made motionless by alarm. Not only was the girl's face scarcely recognisable; her clothing was stained and in disorder.

' Thyrza ! ' she whispered. ' My darling, what has happened ? '

The other, with a terrified look at the Grails' door, ran past and up the stairs, speaking no word. Her sister followed.

In the room, Thyrza did not sit down, though her whole body trembled. She took off her hat, and tried to undo her jacket.

' What is it ? ' Lydia asked, coming near to her. ' Where have you been ? What's made you like this ? '

She was almost as pale as her sister, and fear pressed on her throat. Knowing what she did, she imagined some dreadful catastrophe. Thyrza seemed unable to speak, and her eyes were so wild, so pain-stricken, that they looked like madness. She tried to smile, and at length said disconnectedly:

'It's nothing, Lyddy—only frightened—somebody—a drunken man—frightened me, and I fell down. Nothing else!'

Lydia could make no reply. She did not believe the story. Silently she helped to remove the jacket, and led Thyrza to a chair. Then she drew the dear head to her and held it close against her breast.

'You are so cold, Thyrza! Where have you been? Tell me, tell Lyddy!'

'Totty wasn't at home. I walked a little way. Gilbert doesn't know? You haven't told him?'

'No, no, dear, it's all right. Come nearer to the fire: oh, how cold you are! Sit on my lap, dearest; rest your head against me. Why have you been crying, Thyrza?'

There was no answer. Held thus in her sister's arms, Thyrza abandoned herself, closed her eyes, let every limb hang as it would, tried to be as though she were dead. Lydia thought at first that she had lost consciousness, but her cry brought an answer. They sat thus for some minutes.

Then Thyrza whispered:

'I'm poorly, Lyddy. Let me go to bed.'

'You shall, dear. I'll sit by you. You'll let me stay by you?'

'Yes.'

As her clothes were removed she shook feverishly.

'They won't come up?' she asked several times. 'Mrs. Grail won't come? Go and tell them I've got a headache, and that it'll be all right in the morning.'

'They won't come, dear. Get into bed, and I'll go and tell them directly.'

She could have wept for misery, but she must be strong for Thyrza's sake. Whatever hope remained depended now upon her own self-command and prudence. When Thyrza had lain down, Lydia succeeded in showing almost a cheerful face.

'I'll just go down and say you're poorly. You won't move till I come back?'

Thyrza shook her head.

Her sister was only away for a minute or two. She re-entered the room panting with the speed she had made. And she sat down at the bedside.

There was no word for a long time. Thyrza's eyes were closed; her lips quivered every now and then with a faint sob. The golden braid, which Lydia had not troubled to undo, lay under her cheek.

Lydia held counsel with herself. Something had happened, something worse, she thought, than a mere fit of wretchedness in the suffering heart. There was no explaining the disordered state in which the girl had come back.

Gilbert said that he had met Mr. Egremont at the end of Newport Street. Was it conceivable that Thyrza had had an appointment with Egremont at Totty's house? No; that was not to be credited, for many reasons. Totty—by Luke's account—was angry with Thyrza, and refused to hear anything of what was going on. Yet it was very strange that he should be going to see Mr. Bunce just at the same time that Thyrza was there, and in Totty's absence too.

What to think of Mr. Egremont? There was the central question. She knew him scarcely at all; had only seen him on that one occasion when she opened the house-door to him. There was Gilbert's constant praise of him, but Lydia knew enough of the world to understand that Gilbert might very easily err in his judgment of a young man in Egremont's position. Ackroyd seemed to have no doubt at all; he had said at once that Egremont deserved to be thrashed. Clearly he believed the worst of Egremont, attributed to him a deliberate plot. If he was right, then what might not have befallen?

She had said to herself that she would not dishonour her sister by fearing more than a pardonable weakness. Now there was a black dread closing in upon her.

How to act with Thyrza? Must she reveal all that Ackroyd told her, and so compel a confession?

Not that, if it could possibly be avoided. It would drive Thyrza to despair. No; it must be kept from her that prying eyes had watched her going and coming. Already it might be too late; the marriage with Gilbert might be impossible, if only because Thyrza would inevitably betray her love for Egremont; but there was all the future to think of, and Thyrza must not be driven to some irreparable folly.

There was one hypothesis which Lydia quite left aside. She did not ask herself whether Egremont might not truly and honestly love her sister. It was natural enough that she should not think of it. Every tradition weighed in favour of

rascality on the young man's part, and Lydia's education did
not suffice to raise her above the common point of view in such
a matter. A gentleman did not fall in love with a work-girl,
not in the honest sense. Lydia had the prejudices of her
class, and her judgment went full against Egremont from the
outset. He had encouraged secret meetings, the kind of
thing to be expected. He must have known perfectly what a
blow he was preparing for Gilbert, if the fact of these meetings should be discovered. What did he care for that? His
selfishness was proof against every scruple, no doubt.

She could not argue as an educated person might have
done. Egremont's zeal in his various undertakings made no
plea for his character, in her mind. To be sure, a more subtle
reasoner might have given it as little weight, but that would
have been the result of conscious wisdom. Lydia could only
argue from her predisposition regarding the class of ' gentlemen.' We know how she had shrunk from meeting Egremont.
Guided by Gilbert and Thyrza, she had taught herself to
think well of him, but, given the least grounds of suspicion,
class-instinct was urgent to condemn.

Only one way recommended itself to her, and that the way
of love. She must lead Thyrza to confide in her, must get at
the secret by constraint of tenderness. She might seem to
suspect, but the grounds of her suspicion must be hidden.

Having resolved this, she leaned nearer and spoke gentle
words such as might soothe. Thyrza made no response, save
that she raised her lids and looked wofully.

'Dear one, what is it you're keeping from me?' Lydia
pleaded. 'Is it kind, Thyrza, is it kind to me? It isn't
enough to tell me you're poorly; there's more than that.
Do you think I can look at you and not see that you have a
secret from me?'

Thyrza had closed her eyes again, and was mute.

'Dear, how can you be afraid of *me*, your old Lyddy?
When there's anything you're glad of, you tell me; oughtn't
I to know far more when you're in trouble? Speak to me,
dear sister! I'll put my head near yours; whisper it to me!
How *can* I go on in this way? Every day I see you getting
worse. I'm miserable when I'm away at work; I haven't a
minute's peace. Be kind to me, and say what has happened.'

There was silence.

'Do you think there's anything in me but love for you,
my dearest, my Thyrza? Do you think I could say a cruel

word, tell me whatever you might? Do you think I shan't love you only the better, the more unhappy you are? Perhaps I half know what it is, perhaps——'

Thyrza started and gazed with the same wildness as when she first came in.

'You know? What do you know? Tell me at once, Lyddy!'

'I don't really know anything, love—it's only that I can't help thinking—I've noticed things.'

Thyrza raised herself upon one arm. She was terror-stricken.

'What have you noticed? Tell me at once! You've no right to say things of that kind! Can't I be poorly without you talking as if I'd done something wrong? What have I done? Nothing, nothing! Leave me alone, Lyddy! Go downstairs, and leave me to myself!'

'But you don't understand me,' pleaded the other. 'I don't think you've done anything, but I know you're in trouble—how can I help knowing it?'

'But you said you've noticed things. What do you mean by that? You'd no right to say it if you don't mean anything! You're trying to frighten me! I can't bear you sitting there! I want to be alone! If you must stay in the room, go away and sit by the fire. Haven't you no sewing to do? You've always got plenty at other times. Oh, you make me feel as if I should go mad!'

Lydia withdrew from the bedside. She sat down in a corner of the room and covered her face with her hands.

Thyrza fell back exhausted. She had wrought herself almost to hysteria, and, though she could not shed tears, the dry sobs seemed as if they would rend her bosom.

Minutes passed. She turned and looked at her sister. Lydia was bent forward, propping her forehead.

'Lyddy, I want you.'

Lydia came forward. She had been crying. She fell on her knees by the bed.

'Lyddy, what did you mean? It's no good denying it, you meant something. You said you'd noticed things. You've no right to say that and say no more.'

'You won't tell me what your secret is without me saying what I've thought?'

'I've got no secret! I don't know what you mean by secret!'

T

'Thyrza—have you—have you seen Mr. Egremont to-night?'

They looked at each other. Thyrza's lips were just parted; she drew herself back, as if to escape scrutiny. The arm with which she supported herself trembled violently.

'Why do you ask that?' she said, faintly.

'That's what I meant, Thyrza,' the other whispered, with a face of fear.

'Have I seen Mr. Egremont? I don't know what you're thinking of? Why should I see Mr. Egremont? What have I to do with him?'

Lydia put her hand forward and touched her sister.

'Thyrza!' she cried, passionately. 'Tell me! Tell me everything! I can't bear it! If you have ever so little love for me in your heart—tell me!'

Thyrza could no longer keep her raised position. She fell back. Then with one hand she caught the railing at the head of the bed and held it convulsively, whilst she buried her face in the pillow.

Lydia bent over her, and said in low, quick tones:

'I think no harm of you! Perhaps you've got to like him too much, and he's persuaded you to go to meet him. It's only what I've thought to myself. Tell me, and let me be a sister to you; let me help you! No one else shall hear a word of it, Thyrza. Only Lyddy! We'll talk about it, and see what can be done. You shall tell me how it began—tell me all there is in your heart, poor child. It'll comfort you to speak of it. The secret is killing you, my darling. There's no harm—none—none! You couldn't help it. Only let us both know, and talk to each other about it, like sisters!'

Thyrza's grasp of the iron loosened, and her hand fell. She turned her face to the light again.

'Lyddy, how do you know this?'

'I thought it. You've been out every morning. You spoke of him in a way——'

'Has any one said anything to you? Has Gilbert?'

'No, no! Gilbert hasn't such a thought. It's all myself. Oh, what has he been saying to you, Thyrza?'

A change was coming about in the sufferer. What had at the first suggestion been a terror now grew upon her as an assuagement of pain. She clung to her sister's hand.

'I don't know how it began,' she whispered. 'It seems so sudden; but I think it's been coming for a long time. Ever since I saw him that day at the library—the first time I ever saw him. Ever since, there hasn't been a day I haven't thought of him. I never saw any one else that made me think like that. Day and night, Lyddy! But it didn't trouble me at first. It was only after I came back from Eastbourne. I seemed to think of everything in a different way after that. I dreamt of him every night, and I did so want to see him. I don't know why. Then I saw him at last—on Monday—at the library.'

'You hadn't met him—alone—before then?'

'No, never since that first time.'

'But why did you go there on Monday?'

'Oh, I can't—can't think! Something seemed to tell me to go there. I found there was some books come, and he was putting them on the shelves. He said he didn't want Gilbert to know—just for fun—and I promised not to say anything.'

'You mean last Monday? This week?'

'Yes. Not before then. And it seems—oh, it seems a month ago, Lyddy!'

She lay back, pressing Lydia's hand against her heart.

'But did he ask you to go again, dear?'

'No, he didn't. It was all myself. Lyddy, I couldn't keep away. I couldn't. Will you believe I'm telling the truth? I tried—I did try so hard! I knew I oughtn't to go, because I wanted to so much. I knew it was wrong. I don't think I should have gone if Mrs. Grail hadn't forced me to go out for a walk, because she said it would take my headache away. I was holding myself back all the morning. And when I got out—I couldn't help it—I was drawn there! And then I asked him if I might come again to-day. He said I might, but I could see he thought it was wrong of me. And, Lyddy, he never came. I stayed there waiting. Oh, do you know what I suffered? I can't tell you!'

'My dearest, I know, I feel with you! But it will be better now you've told me. And to-night? Didn't you see him to-night?'

'How do you know? Who told you?' she asked, nervously.

'No one, dear. I only think it. The way you came in——'

Thyrza suddenly bent forward, listening.

'Can any one hear us?' she whispered. 'Go and see if any one's outside.'

'There's no one, dear.'

'Go and look. I'm afraid.'

Lydia went and opened the door. She closed it again, and came back shaking her head.

'I didn't think I should see him,' Thyrza continued. 'I was waiting in Totty's room, and he came to see Mr. Bunce. I heard his voice. When he went away, I followed him. I couldn't help myself. I would have given my life for a word from him. I wanted to know why he hadn't come this morning. I followed him, and walked with him over the bridge. Then he told me he was going away, somewhere out of England, and I shouldn't see him again till after—after I was married.'

She choked. Lydia soothed her again, and she continued, with growing agitation :

'Then he said good-bye—he went away very quickly, after just saying he hoped I should be happy. Happy! How can I be happy? And when he was gone, I went somewhere and fell down and cried—somewhere where nobody could see me. He's gone, Lyddy! How am I to live without him?'

They held each other. Thyrza sobbed out her anguish until strength failed, then lay in her sister's arms, pale as a corpse.

When there had been utter silence ior a while, Lydia asked :

'And he has never said anything to you that—that he oughtn't to have said!'

'Said? What did you think? You thought he—he loved *me*?'

'I didn't know, dearest.'

'Oh, if he did! He asked me not to call him " sir," and to be his friend—never more than that. You thought he loved me? How could he love a girl like me, Lyddy?'

Lydia had followed the unfolding of the tale with growing surprise. It was impossible to doubt Thyrza's truthfulness. Yet there must be more on Egremont's part than appeared. Why did he exact secrecy about those meetings in the library? There was little doubt that Thyrza had betrayed herself to him. True, he had refrained from keeping the appointment for this morning, and it seemed he was going away till after the marriage. But all this was too late.

Still he was innocent of the guilt she had suspected. Thyrza had not come to the dreaded harm. Though heart-broken, she was saved. Lydia felt almost joyous for an instant. Bower's gossip might yet be deprived of its sting, for Mr. Egremont would be gone, and—Monday was so near.

It was the reaction from her terror. She could think of nothing for the moment but that Thyrza must be preserved from future risk by marriage.

Thyrza was lying exhausted. Lydia, deep in thought, was surprised to see a faint smile on the beautiful pale face.

'You thought he loved me?' was whispered. 'Oh, if he did! If he did!'

Lydia was still kneeling. New fears were making themselves heard. Was it possible for Thyrza to marry Gilbert under such circumstances, and within five days? What if Gilbert heard Bower's story? Nay, in any case, what of the future? Egremont would be constantly at the library.

'Thyrza, do you never think of Gilbert?'

Thyrza raised herself, again the look of wild dread in her eyes.

'Lyddy, I can't marry him! You know now that I can't, don't you? It would be wrong. I shall love *him* as long as ever I live—love him and think of him every minute. I can't marry Gilbert.'

There was silence. Lydia looked up with tearful, appealing eyes.

'My dearest, think—think what that means? How can you break your word to him—now, when the day's almost here? Think what it'll mean to him. You'll have to tell him the reason, and then——'

'I'll tell him everything. I'll bear it. Can I help it, Lyddy? Am I happy?'

'But you haven't thought, Thyrza. It means that Gilbert will have to go on with his work at the factory.'

'Why? His mother will go and live with him at the library.'

Her voice sank. She began to understand.

'Do you suppose he can take that place from Mr. Egremont after he knows this, Thyrza?'

Thyrza was mute for a little. Then she said, under her breath:

'He needn't know the reason. He must think it's something else.'

'That's impossible. What a cruel thing it'll be to him! You know how he's looked forward. And then he loves you; he loves you more than you think. It will be dreadful! Thyrza, I don't think you'll make poor Gilbert suffer in that way. You couldn't do that, dear! You know what love means; have some pity for him!'

'I can't! He shan't know the reason; he shall go to the library just the same. We'll say it's only put off. I can't marry him on Monday! I'd sooner kill myself!'

There was a ring of terrible earnestness in the words. Lydia was afraid to plead any more at present. She affected to admit that there was no help. Yes, the marriage should be postponed; perhaps that would be a way.

The hour was late. After her sister's acquiescence Thyrza had fallen into brooding. She moved constantly. There was fire in her cheeks.

Only a few words were exchanged whilst Lydia undressed and lay down by her sister. Sleep was impossible to either of them. Yet Thyrza had not closed her eyes the night before. She was very feverish, could not lie in one position for more than a few minutes. When neither had spoken for nearly an hour, she said of a sudden:

'Lyddy, I want you to promise me that you'll never tell Gilbert nor Mrs. Grail one word of this. I want you to promise.'

'I promise you, dear. How could I think of doing so without your leave?'

There was a pause, then Thyrza resumed:

'I think you'll do as you say. Kiss me, and promise again.'

'I will keep your secret, dearest. I promise you.'

The other sighed deeply, and after that lay still.

CHAPTER XXIV

THE END OF THE DREAM

GILBERT did not go to work next morning. Though Lydia had disguised her sister's strange condition as well as she could, he knew that something was being kept from him, and his mind, ever ready to doubt the reality of the happiness that had been granted him, was at length so beset with fears that he could no longer pay attention to the day's business. He rose at the usual time, but with a word at his mother's door made known his intention not to go out till after breakfast. Having lit a fire in the parlour, he sat down and tried to read.

He had purposed working till Saturday. To-night and to-morrow night (Thursday and Friday) Thyrza and he were to go and purchase such articles of furniture and the like as would be needed for the new house (the list was long since carefully made out, and the places of purchase decided upon), and these would be taken in by Mrs. Butterfield. On Saturday afternoon the contents of Gilbert's own room were to be removed; on that and the following night he would sleep under the new roof, and by Monday morning would have things in sufficient order to allow of Mrs. Grail and Lydia coming, for these two were to keep each other company whilst he and his wife were away. By this scheme he might work on to the end of the week, and suffer no loss of wages.

But Gilbert was not a machine, unhappily for himself. Even had nothing external occurred to trouble the order he had planned, his own mood would probably have rendered steady work impossible now that he could positively count on his fingers the days before his marriage day—before the day which would make him a free man. It was hard to believe that two such blessings could descend upon a mortal at once. It seemed to him that the very hours, as they went by, looked on him with faces of mysterious menace, foretelling a dread successor. Since Monday he had with difficulty accomplished his tasks ; each time he hastened home it was with unreasoning fear lest something had come to pass in his absence. And now it was no longer only apprehension. Thyrza was changing under his eyes. She was physically ill, and he knew that some agitation possessed her mind. She shrank from him.

The glimmer of early morning at the parlour window was cold and threatening. A faint ray of sunlight showed itself, only to fade upon a low, rain-charged sky. The sounds of labour recommencing were as wearisome to him as they always are to one who has watched through an unending night. The house itself seemed unnaturally silent.

Mrs. Grail came in at length, and looked at him anxiously. Her own eyes lacked the refreshment of sleep.

'I didn't feel able to go, mother,' he said. 'I want to hear how Thyrza is as soon as possible. Perhaps you can go up presently?'

She murmured an assent, and began to lay the table.

In a few minutes she ascended very quietly and listened at the girls' door. Her report was that she could hear no sound; they must both be sleeping.

An hour went by. Mother and son made no pretence of conversing. Gilbert kept an open book before him. Rain had begun to fall, and the sky darkened as the minutes ticked themselves away by the clock on the mantel-piece.

Then there was a sound on the stairs. Lydia came into the room, and with her Thyrza.

Lydia smiled, and tried to draw attention from her sister by lamenting their lateness at the meal.

'We were afraid you'd have gone away again,' she said to Gilbert.

'I don't think I shall go to work this morning,' he replied quietly.

She became silent. Thyrza had drawn a chair to the table. One saw that she had risen with difficulty—that she with difficulty sat upright.

Gilbert, without speaking, went and sat by her. Lydia was dreading questions, but she did injustice to the delicacy of his mind. Mrs. Grail just said: 'You're very pale still, dear,' and nothing more.

The meal was made as short as possible. Then Lydia helped Mrs. Grail to take the things to the kitchen. Thyrza, before coming down, had asked to be left alone with Gilbert for a few minutes.

Grail was at the window, watching the rain. He heard Thyrza approaching him, and turned.

'Gilbert,' she said, without raising her eyes, 'I'm behaving very unkindly to you. Will you forgive me?'

'How are you behaving unkindly, Thyrza?' he asked, with gently expressed surprise.

'I've been keeping away from you. I couldn't help it. I don't feel myself.'

'You are ill, Thyrza. Am I to forgive you for that?'

'Yes, I am ill. Gilbert, is it too late to ask you? Will you put it off for a week, one week?'

He let a minute pass before replying. Seeing that she trembled as she stood, he led her to a chair, the chair in which she always sat.

'Dear,' he said at length, 'I will do whatever you wish.'

'I shall be better by then, I think. But I'll go with you to buy the things just the same.'

' We can leave that for a few days,' he said absently.

' It wouldn't make any difference to you at the library ? '

' None, I am sure. I will write and tell Mr. Egremont. He will be very sorry to hear of your illness.'

She stood up, and looked at the clock.

' I've made you late for your work.'

' I shan't go to-day.'

' You won't go ? ' she asked.

'I can't, Thyrza. I'm too uneasy about you.'

' Don't be that, Gilbert. I promise you to try and get better.'

Another silence, then he asked :

' Will you stay here this morning ? '

She just raised her face ; fear and entreaty were on the features.

' I only came down for breakfast, to ask you that, and— and to tell you I was so sorry.'

' To be sure,' he replied at once. ' You are not well enough to be up. Lyddy will stay with you ? '

' Yes, she is going to stay. I'll come and see you again, if I feel able.'

She offered her hand. He took it, held it a little, then said :

' Thyrza, is there anything on your mind, anything you don't wish to tell me just now, but in a day or two per-haps ? '

' No, Gilbert, no ! If you'll forgive me for behaving unkindly.'

' Dear, how can there be any forgiving, so long as I love you ? There must be blame before there is need of for-giveness, and I love you too well to think a reproachful thought.'

She bent her head and sobbed.

' Thyrza, is it any happiness to you to know that I love you ? '

' Yes, it is. You are very good. I know I am making you suffer.'

' But I shall see the old face again, before long ? '

' Soon. I shall be myself again soon.'

She left him and went upstairs. A minute or two after, Lydia knocked at the door.

' Thyrza has gone up ? ' she asked.

' Yes. Come here, Lydia ! '

He spoke with abruptness. Lydia drew near.

'You know that she has asked me to put off our marriage for a week?'

'I didn't know that she was going to ask you now. I thought perhaps she wished it.'

'I can't ask you to betray your sister's secrets, but— Lyddy, you won't keep anything from me that I *ought* to know?'

He paused, then went on again with a shaking voice.

'There are some things that I *ought* to know, if—— You know that, Lyddy? You owe love to your sister first, but you owe something to me as well. There are some things you would have no right to keep from me. You might be doing both her and me the greatest wrong.'

Lydia could not face him. She tried to speak, but uttered only a meaningless word.

'Thyrza is ill,' he pursued. 'I can't ask her, as I feel I ought to, what has made her ill. Tell me this, as you are a good and a truthful girl. If I marry Thyrza, shall I be taking advantage of her weakness? Does she wish me to free her?'

'She doesn't! Indeed, Gilbert, she doesn't! You are her very best friend. All her life depends upon you. You won't break it off? Perhaps she will even be well enough by the end of the week. Remember how young she is, and how often she has strange fancies.'

'You tell me solemnly that Thyrza still wishes to be my wife?'

'She does. She wishes to be your wife, Gilbert.'

To Lydia her sister's fate hung in the balance. What she uttered was verbally true. Before rising, Thyrza had said: 'I will marry him.' In the possible breaking of this bond Lydia saw such a terrible danger that her instincts of absolute sincerity for once were overridden. If she spoke falsely, it was to save her sister. Thyrza once married, the face of life would be altered for her; this sudden passionate love would fall like a brief flame. Lydia had decided upon a bold step. As soon as it was possible, she would go and see Mr. Egremont, see him herself, and, if he had any heart or any honour, prevail with him that Thyrza might be spared temptation. But the marriage must first be over, and must be brought about at all costs.

In her life she had never spoken an untruth for her own advantage. Now, as she spoke, the sense that her course was

chosen gave her courage. She looked Gilbert at length boldly
in the face. His confidence in her was so great that, his own
desires aiding, he believed her to the full. Thyrza's suffering,
he said to himself, had not the grave meaning he had feared ;
it was something that must be sacred from his search.

So much power was there in Lydia's word, uttered for her
sister's saving.

All day long it rained. Gilbert did not go from the house.
He wrestled with hope, which was still only to be held by
persistent effort. Sunshine would have aided him, but all day
he looked upon a gloomy, wet street. At dinner-time he had
all but made up his mind to go to work ; the thought, however, was too hateful to him. And he felt it would be hard
to meet men's faces. Perhaps there would be comfort by the
morrow.

Thyrza did in fact come down for tea. She spoke only a
few words, but she seemed stronger than in the morning.
Lydia had a brighter face too. They went up again together
after the meal.

Another night passed. Lydia slept. She believed that
the worst was over, and that there might after all be no post-
ponement of the marriage. For Thyrza had become very
quiet ; she seemed worn out with struggle, and resigned.
Her sleep, she said, had been good. Yet her eyelids were
swollen ; no doubt she had cried in the night.

Lydia had no intention of leaving home. Gilbert had
gone to work, reassured by her report the last thing on the
previous evening.

There was no more speech between the sisters on the
subject of their thoughts. Through the morning Thyrza lay
so still that Lydia, thinking her asleep, now and then stepped
lightly and bent over her. Each time, however, she found
the sad eyes gazing fixedly upwards. Thyrza just turned
them to her, but without change of expression.

' Don't look at me like that, dear,' Lydia said once. ' It's
as if you didn't know me.'

The reply was a brief smile.

Thyrza got up in the afternoon. About five o'clock, when
Lydia was making tea, Mrs. Jarmey came with a message. She
said Mr. Boddy had sent word that he wished to see Lydia
particularly ; he begged she would come during the evening.

' Who brought the message ? ' Lydia asked, going outside the door to speak with the landlady.

' A little boy,' was the answer. 'I never see him before, as I know.'

Lydia was disturbed. It might only mean that the old man was anxious at not having seen her for five or six days, or that he was ill; but the fact of his living in the Bowers' house suggested another explanation. An answer was required ; she sent back word that she would come.

' I shan't be more than half an hour away at the very longest,' she said, when she reluctantly prepared to go out after tea. ' Wouldn't you like to go downstairs just for that time, dear ? '

' No, Lyddy, I'll stay.'

Thyrza had left her chair, and stood with her hand resting on the mantel-piece. She did not turn her head.

' How funny you look with your hair like that ! '

Thyrza had declined to have her hair braided, and had coiled it herself in a new way. She made no reply.

' Good-bye, pet !' Lydia said, coming near.

Thyrza did not move. She was looking downwards at the fire. Lydia touched her ; she started, and, with a steady gaze, said, ' Good-bye, Lyddy ! '

' I do wish I hadn't to go. But I shall be very quick.'

' Yes. Good-bye ! '

They kissed each other, and Lydia hastened on her errand.

Her absence did not last much longer than the time she had set. Mr. Boddy had heard from Mrs. Bower all the story about Egremont. He gave no faith to it, but wished to warn Lydia that such gossip was afloat, and to receive from her an authoritative denial. She declared it to be false from beginning to end. Without a moment's hesitation she did this, having determined that there was no middle course. She denied that Thyrza had been to the library. Whoever originated the story had done so in malice. She enjoined upon him to contradict it without reserve.

She felt as if she were being hunted by merciless beasts. To escape them, any means were justifiable. Of the Bowers she thought with bitter hatred. No wrong to herself could have excited all her fiercest emotions as did this attack upon her sister. Running homewards, she felt the will and the strength to take the life of her enemy. She had entered the

Bowers' house, and left it, by the private door ; it was well that she had met no one.

She remembered that Thyrza must not discover her excitement, and went up the stairs slowly, regaining breath, trying to smooth her face. A fable to account for Mr. Boddy's summons was ready on her tongue. She entered, and found an empty room.

So Thyrza had gone down to Mrs. Grail after all. That was good. The poor girl was making a brave struggle, and would conquer herself yet. If only Bower's gossip could be kept from Gilbert. But there was still a long time till Monday, still two whole days, and Bower, determined as he evidently was to work mischief, would not neglect the supreme opportunity. It would have been better if Gilbert had not returned to work.

She took off her things.

What was that lying on the table ? An envelope, a dirty one which had been in the drawer for a long time ; on it was written ' Lyddy.' It was Thyrza's writing. Lydia opened it. Inside was a rough piece of white paper, torn off a sheet in which something had been wrapped. It was written upon, and the writing said this :

' I have gone away. I can't marry Gilbert, and I can't tell him the truth. Remember your promise. Some day I shall come back to you, when everything is different. Remember your promise, so that Gilbert can go to the library just the same. No harm will come to me. Good-bye, my dear, dear sister. If you love me you will say you know nothing, so that it will be all right for Gilbert. Good-bye, Lyddy, darling.'

Crushing the paper in her hand, Lydia, just as she was, ran out into the street. It was not yet dark. Instinctively, after one glance towards Kennington Road, she took the opposite way and made for Newport Street. Thyrza would communicate with Totty Nancarrow, if with any one at all ; she would not go there at once, but Totty must be won over to aid in discovering the child and bringing her back.

It rained, not heavily, but enough to dew Lydia's hair in a few minutes. Little she thought of that. Thyrza wandering alone—straying off into some far part of London ; Thyrza, ill as she was—with at most a few pence to procure lodging for this one night—alone among what dangers ! The thought was fire in her brain.

She was in Paradise Street, and someone stood in her way, speaking.

'Lydia! Where ever are you going like that?'

It was Mary Bower. Lydia glared at her.

'How dare you speak to me! I hate you!'

And with a wild gesture, almost a blow at the girl, she rushed on.

Totty had just come in from work. Lydia scarcely waited for a reply to her knock before she burst into the room.

'Totty! Will you help me? Thyrza has left me—gone away. I was out for half an hour. She left a note for me, to say good-bye. Help me to find her! Do you know anything? Can you think where she'd go?'

Totty was on her knees, lighting a fire. In her amazement she made no effort to rise. A lighted piece of paper was in her hand; forgetting it, she let the flame creep on till it burnt her fingers. Then she stood up.

'What does she say in the note?' she asked with deliberation.

Lydia opened her hand and spread out the crumpled paper. She was going to read aloud, but checked herself and looked at the other piteously.

'You know all about it, don't you? Thyrza told you?'

'I suppose I know pretty well,' Totty replied, in the same deliberate and distant way.

'Has she said anything to you about going away?'

'I don't know as she has.'

'Then look what she's written.'

Totty hesitated, then said:

'Thank you, I'd rather not. It's not my business. If I was you, I'd speak to Mr. Ackroyd. I know nothing about Thyrza.'

'To Mr. Ackroyd?' exclaimed Lydia. 'But I'm sure she won't see him. It's you'll hear from her, if anybody does. Can't you think of any place she'd be likely to go? Hasn't she never said anything in talking? You wouldn't keep it back, just because you don't like me? It's my sister—she's all I have; you know she can't look out for herself like you and me could. And she's been ill since Monday. Won't you help me if you can, just because I'm in trouble?'

'I'd help you if I could,' replied the other, not unmoved by the appeal, but still distant. 'I'm quite sure Thyrza won't

let me know where she is. If you take my advice you'll see
Mr. Ackroyd.'

In her agitation Lydia could not reflect upon the com-
plicated details of the case. She never doubted that Totty
knew the truth; in this, we know, Luke had unintentionally
deceived her. Perhaps the advice to consult Ackroyd was
good; perhaps he had learned something more since Wednesday night, something that Totty also knew but did not care
to communicate herself.

'I'll try and find him,' Lydia said. ' But if you *do* hear
anything you wouldn't keep it from me ? '

' You'll hear just as soon as I do,' was the reply.

Lydia turned away, feeling that the girl's coldness was a
cruelty, wondering at it. She herself could not have behaved
so to one in dire need.

She was going away, but Totty stopped her.

'You can't go back like that, in the rain. Take my
umbrella.'

' What do I care for the rain ! ' Lydia cried. ' I must
find Thyrza. I thought you pretended to be her friend.'

She hastened into the street. Not many yards from the
door she met the man she desired to see. Ackroyd was coming
to ask for Totty, for the first time since Tuesday night. Lydia
drew him to the opposite side of the way, and hurriedly told
him, showing him the scrap of paper.

' I've been to Totty,' she added. ' She didn't seem to
wish to help me ; she spoke as if she didn't care, and said I'd
better ask you. Do you know anything more ? '

He was mute at first. His mind naturally turned to one
thought. Then he said, speaking slowly :

' I know nothing more, except that lots of people have
heard Bower's story. Does Grail know ? '

' Not unless he has heard since this morning.'

' I haven't seen much of him to-day, but I noticed he
looked very queer.'

' That's because Thyrza asked him to put off the wedding
for a week. I never thought she'd leave me. We talked
about everything that night after I left you. I pretended I'd
found it out myself; I durstn't let her know that other people
had noticed anything. She had a dreadful night, but she
seemed better since.'

' And did she tell you—everything ? '

' Everything ! She said he'd never spoken a word to her

that he shouldn't. I'm sure it was the truth ; Thyrza wouldn't have deceived me like that. He's gone away, somewhere out of London.'

Luke stopped her. He looked closely at her through the dusk, and said in a low voice :

' He's gone away ? Did *she* tell you he was going away ? '

' Yes. He said good-bye to her, and hoped she would be happy.'

' But, Lydia—if he's gone away—and now *she's* gone——'

Lydia understood him.

' Oh ! Don't think that ! ' she said, her eyes full of fear. ' No, no ! I'm sure that isn't true ! He'd never said a word to her. He hadn't given her to think he cared for her. She cried because he didn't.'

' But if she's so mad with love of him,' Luke said, dropping his eyes, ' who knows what she might do ? You'd never have thought she could leave you like this.'

The rain was falling more heavily. As Lydia stood, unable to utter any argument against him, Ackroyd saw that her hair was quite wet.

' You mustn't stand out here,' he said. ' Come round into Paradise Street with me, and I'll get you something of my sister's to go home in. Poor girl ! You came out like this as soon as you'd found she was gone ? Come quick, or you'll get your death.'

She accompanied him without speaking. Her mind was working on the suggestion he had uttered. Against her will he compelled her to step into the house whilst he procured a hat and a garment for her. He took care that no one saw her, and when she was clad, he went out with her, carrying an umbrella for her protection.

' Don't come with me,' she said.

' Yes, you must let me. I was going to try and see you to-night, Lydia, to ask what——'

' And I wanted to see you. I felt I must tell you how well everything seemed to be going. Oh, and now—— How shall I tell Gilbert ? How *shall* I tell him ? What ought I to do, Mr. Ackroyd ? Thyrza made me promise faithful I wouldn't tell her secret. She says that, in the note. I'm sure she hasn't gone—gone to him. She couldn't marry Gilbert, and yet she doesn't want him to lose the library. That's why she's gone ; I know it is. She believes I shall keep my promise. But what must I do ? How can I pretend I don't know anything ? '

'I don't think you can.'

'I didn't care for anything as long as it helped her. Mr. Boddy sent for me just now—that was why I had to go out. Mrs. Bower had been telling him. I said it was all a lie from beginning to end. Didn't I do right, Mr. Ackroyd? I'd say and do anything for Thyrza. But how can I keep it from Gilbert now?'

'You can't, Lydia. He's bound to hear from somebody. And if you feel so sure that she hasn't gone——'

'She hasn't! She hasn't! You promised me you wouldn't think harm of her.'

'Indeed I won't. But Grail's bound to know. I can't see that you'll make it a bit better by denying.'

'But my promise to Thyrza! The last thing she ever asked of me. And Gilbert 'll refuse the place; I know he will!'

'Yes, he will. There's no man could take it after this. I'm right down sorry for poor Grail.'

They were in Walnut Tree Walk by this time.

'Don't come any farther,' Lydia said. 'Thank you for being so kind to me. Here, take these things of your sister's; you can just carry them back—or I'll leave them, if you like.'

'No, you shan't have that trouble. If Gilbert's home you ought to tell him now. He'll go to the police station, and ask them to help to find her. Let me know at once if you hear anything. She may come back.'

'No, she won't.'

'Run into the house at once.'

The parlour door opened as she entered the passage. Gilbert came out.

'Where has Thyrza gone to?' he asked, after examining her for an instant.

She could not speak, and could not stir from the place. Her hope had been to have time before she saw him.

'Lydia, where has Thyrza gone?'

She stepped into the room. The piece of paper was still crushed within her hand; she held it closer still.

'She's gone away, Gilbert. I don't know where. I had to go out, and when I came back she was gone. Perhaps she'll come back.'

Mrs. Grail was in the background. She was supporting herself by a chair; her face gave proof of some agitation just experienced. Gilbert was very pale, but when Lydia ended he seemed to master himself and spoke with an unnatural calm.

U

'Have you heard anything,' he asked, 'of a calumny the Bowers have been spreading, about your sister and Mr. Egremont?'

'Yes. I have heard it.'

'When did it first come to your knowledge?'

'On Wednesday night. Mr. Ackroyd told me.'

'And did Thyrza hear of it?'

'No, Gilbert. I think not.'

He moved in surprise.

'You say she has gone? What makes you think she has left us?'

To hide anything now was worse than useless. Without speaking, she held to him the scrap of paper. He, having read, turned to his mother.

'Will you let us be alone, mother?'

The poor old woman went with bowed head from the room. Gilbert's voice dropped to a lower note.

'Lydia, as you have shown me this, you must have decided that you cannot keep the promise which is spoken of here.'

'I can't keep it, Gilbert, because you might think worse of Thyrza if I do.'

'Think worse? Then you suppose I believe what is said about her—about Thyrza?'

'I can't think you believe what Mr. Bower *wishes* people to, but you can't know how little she's been to blame.'

He was silent, then said:

'I came home a few minutes ago, thinking that what Bunce has just told was a mere lie, set afloat by someone who wished us harm. I thought Thyrza knew of the lie, and that it had made her ill—that she could not bring herself to speak to me of it. But I see there's something more.'

She stood before him like one guilty. His calmness was terrible to her. She seemed to feel in herself all the anguish which he was repressing. He continued:

'You told me yesterday morning that Thyrza still wished to marry me. This note shows me why you said that, and in what sense you meant it. I don't blame you, Lydia; you were loyal to your sister. But I must ask you something else now, and your answer must be the simple truth. Does Thyrza love Mr. Egremont?'

'Yes, Gilbert.'

She said it with failing voice, and, as soon as she had spoken, burst into tears.

' Oh, I have broken the promise I made to my dear one !
The last thing she asked, and perhaps I shall never see her
again ! What could I do, Gilbert ? If I kept it back, you'd
have thought there was something worse. She seems to have
behaved cruel to you, but you don't know what she's gone
through. She's so ill; she'll go somewhere and die, and I
shall never hear her speak to me again ! I've been unkind to
her so often; she doesn't know how I love her ! Gilbert,
help me to find her ! I can't live without my sister. Don't
be angry with her, Gilbert; she's suffered dreadful; if you
only knew ! She tried so hard. Her last thought was about
you, and how she could spare you. Forgive her, and bring
her back to me. What shall we do to find her ? Oh, I *can't*
lose her, my little sister, my dear one ! '

One would have thought Gilbert had no grief of his own,
so anxiously did he try to comfort her.

' Lyddy,' he said, when she could listen to him, ' you are
my sister, and will always be. If I could think unkindly of
Thyrza now, I should show that I was never worthy of her.
Don't hurt me by saying such things. We will find her ;
have no fear, we will find her.'

' And you'll do as she wished ? You'll still go to the
library ? '

' I can't think of myself yet, Lyddy. You must have her
back again, and there'll be time enough to think of trifles.'

' But let me tell you all I know, Gilbert. He doesn't love
her; you mustn't think that. There's never been a word
between them. She went to help him with the books, and so
it came on her.'

' It's true, then,' he said gravely, ' that they met there ? '

' He didn't encourage her. She told me again and again
he didn't. She went on Wednesday morning, and he never
came. That was on purpose, I'm sure.'

' But why wasn't I told about the books ? '

' He wanted to surprise you. And now he's gone away,
Gilbert. He told her he wouldn't be back till after her
marriage.'

' He's gone away ? '

She raised her face, and continued eagerly :

' You see why he went, don't you ? I had hard thoughts
of him at first, but now I know I was wrong. You think so
much of him ; you know he wouldn't be so cowardly and
wicked. Thyrza told me the solemn truth ; I would die rather

than doubt her word. You must believe her, Gilbert. It's all
so hard! She couldn't help it. And you mustn't think
harm of him!'

He said under his breath :

' I must try not to.'

She sat down, overcome, yielding herself to voiceless
misery. It was a long time before Gilbert spoke.

' Do you know where he is gone to, Lyddy ? '

' No, I don't.'

Again silence. Then he moved, and looked at the clock.

' Will you sit with my mother ? This is a great blow to
her as well, and it is hard to bear at her age. I will go out
and see what I can do. Don't fear, we'll find her. You
shall soon have her back. Do you feel able to sit with
mother ? '

' Yes, I will, Gilbert.'

' Thank you. It will be kindness. I don't think I shall
be very late.'

In passing her, he just touched her hand.

In the meanwhile, Ackroyd had returned to Newport
Street. He sent up word by the landlady that he wished to
see Totty. The latter sent a reply to him that perhaps she
would be coming out in about an hour, but could not be
certain.

He waited, standing in the rain, over against the house.
Perhaps twenty minutes passed ; then he saw the girl come
forth.

' We can't talk here,' Luke said, joining her. ' Will you
come under the archway yonder ? '

' I don't see that we've got so much to talk about,' Totty
answered, indifferently.

' Yes, I've several things to ask you.'

' All right. But I can't wait out in the cold for long.'

They went in the direction away from Paradise Street, and
found shelter under a black vault of the railway. A train
roared above their heads as they entered.

' I've just seen Lydia Trent,' he began. ' Did you expect
that anything of this kind would happen ? '

' I've told you already that I have nothing to do with
Thyrza and her goings on. I told Lydia she'd better go to
you if she wanted to find her sister. I hope you told her all
you know.'

'What do you mean by that? How should I be able to help her to find Thyrza?'

'Oh, don't bother me!' Totty exclaimed, with impatience. 'I'm sick of it. If you've brought me out to talk in this way, you might as well have let it alone.'

'What are you driving at, Totty? I tell you I don't understand you. Speak plainly, if you please. You think that I know where Thyrza is?'

'I suppose you're as likely to as anybody.'

'Why? Confound it, why?'

She shrugged her shoulders, and turned away. He pressed his question with growing impatience.

'Why, what did you come telling me the other night?' cried Totty at length. 'It was like your impudence.'

'What did I tell you? I didn't tell you anything. I asked if you knew of something, and you said you did. I don't see how I was impudent. After hearing Bower's tale it was likely I should come and speak to you about it.'

'Bower's tale? What tale?'

'You don't know that Bower's found it all out, and is telling everybody?'

'Found all *what* out? I haven't been to the shop for a week. What do you mean?'

Ackroyd checked some impulsive words, and recommenced gravely:

'Look here, Totty. Will you please tell me in plain words what you supposed I was asking you about on Tuesday night?'

'All right. It's nothing to me. You'd found out somehow that Thyrza was foolish enough to want to have you instead of Mr. Grail, and so you was so kind as to come and tell me. I quite understood; there's no need of saying "I beg your pardon." You may go your way, and I go mine.'

'And you mean to say you believed that! Well, I don't wonder at you being in the sulks. And that's why you send Lydia to me to ask about Thyrza? By the Lord, if I ever heard the like of that! Well, I've got a fair lot of cheek, but I couldn't quite manage that.'

'Then what *did* you mean?' she cried angrily.

'Why, nothing at all. But what did *you* mean by saying you knew all about it?'

'About as much as you did,' she answered coldly.

'H'm. Then we both meant nothing. I'll say good-night, Totty.'

'No you won't. You'll please to tell me what you *did*
mean!'

He was about to answer lightly, but altered his intention
and said :

'I can't do that. It's not my business.'

'As you please. I shall go and ask Mrs. Bower what's
going on.'

'I can't prevent you. But listen here, Totty. If you
repeat what they tell you—if you repeat it once—you're
not the girl I thought you. It's more than half a cursed
lie, and you can't tell one half the story without meaning the
other.'

'I shall know what to think when I've heard it, Mr.
Ackroyd. And as to repeating, I shall do as I think fit.'

'Look here! When you've heard that story, you'll just go
and say to everybody that ever mentions it to you that it's a
lie from beginning to end. You understand me?'

'I shall do as I please.'

'No, you'll do as *I* please!'

'Indeed! And who made you my master, Mr. Ackroyd?'

'I've nothing more to say, but you've heard me. And
you'll do it, because your own heart 'll tell you it's the right
thing to do. I don't often use words like that, but I mean it
to-night. Good-bye!'

She allowed him to walk away.

CHAPTER XXV

A BIRD OF THE AIR

WHEN Paula had been three or four days wedded, it occurred
to her to examine her husband's countenance. They were at
breakfast at Biarritz, and certain words that fell from Mr. Dalmaine, as he sat sideways from the table with his newspaper,
led her eyes to rest for a few moments on his face. He was
smiling, but with depressed brows. Paula noted the smile
well, and it occupied her thoughts now and then during the
day. She was rather in want of something to think of just
then, feeling a little lonely, and wishing her mother, or her
brother, or somebody whom she really knew, were at hand to
talk to.

It was with that same peculiar smile—the bushy eyebrows closing together, the lips very tight—that her husband approached her late one evening in the first week of May. They were in their house in Kensington now; there had been a dinner party, the last guest was gone, and Paula sat in the drawing-room, thinking how she had impressed a certain polite old member of Parliament, a man whom it was worth while impressing. Mr. Dalmaine took a seat near her, and leaned forward with his hands clasped between his knees.

He asked : ' What were you saying to Puggerton when I passed and looked at you—you remember ? Something about working men and intelligent voting.'

' Oh, I was telling that tale of yours about the candidate whose name was Beere, and who got in so easily for——'

' I thought so,' he remarked, before she had finished. ' And you went on to say that I thought it a pity that there were not more men on our side with names of similar sound ? '

' Yes, I did. Mr. Puggerton laughed ever so much.'

' H'm. Paula, my dear, I think it won't be amiss if you leave off talking about politics.'

' Why ? I'm sure I've been talking very cleverly all the evening. Mr. Liggs said I was an acquisition to—something, I forget what.'

' No doubt. For all that, I think you had better give your attention to other things. In fact—it's not a polite thing to say—but you're making a fool of yourself.'

Paula's features hardened. She looked very beautiful to-night, and had, in truth, been charming. Her appearance suffered when the delicate curves of her face fell into hard lines. It was noteworthy that the smile her husband now wore always caused this change in her expression.

I'm glad you know that it isn't polite,' she answered, sourly. ' You often need to be told.'

' I hope not. But you try my patience a little now and then. Surely it's better that I should save you from making these ridiculous mistakes. Once or twice this week I've heard most absurd remarks of yours repeated. Please remember that it isn't only yourself you—stultify. Politics may be a joke for you ; for me it is a serious pursuit. I mustn't have people associating my name with all kinds of nonsensical chatter. I have a career before me, Paula.'

He said it with dignity, resting a hand on each knee, and letting his smile fade into a look of ministerial importance.

'Why are you ashamed of having your stories repeated?'

'Well, I told you that when—when I didn't think of the need of measuring my words with you. I've been more cautious lately. If you had any understanding for such things at all, I could explain that a trifle like that might be made to tell heavily against me by some political enemy. Once more—if you are drawn into talk of that kind, you must always speak of working people with the utmost respect—with reverence. No matter how intimate a friend you may be speaking with— even with your mother or your father——'

Paula laughed.

'You think papa would believe me if I told him I reverenced working men, the free and independent electors?'

'There again! That's a phrase you must *not* use; I say it absolutely; you must forget the phrase. Yes, your father must believe you.'

'Do you think he believes *you*?'

Mr. Dalmaine drew himself up.

'I don't know what you mean, Paula.'

'And I don't know what *you* mean. You are ridiculous.'

'Excuse me. That is the word that applies to you. However, I have no wish to wrangle. Let it be understood that you gradually abandon conversation such as this of to-night. For the sake of appearances you must make no sudden and obvious change. If you take my advice, you'll cultivate talk of a light, fashionable kind. Literature you mustn't interfere with; I shouldn't advise you to say much about art, except that of course you may admire the pictures at the Grosvenor Gallery. You'd better read the Society journals carefully. In fact, keep to the sphere which is distinctly womanly.'

'And what about your anxiety to see women take part in politics?'

'There are exceptions to every rule. And the programme of the platform, be good enough to try and understand, doesn't always apply to domestic circumstances. If one happens to have married a very pretty and delightful girl——'

'Oh, of course!'

'I repeat, a very pretty and charming girl, with no turn whatever for seriousness, one can't pretend to offer an instance in one's own house of the political woman. Once more understand—in England politics must be pursued with gravity. We don't fly about and chatter and scream like Frenchmen. No man will succeed with us in politics who has not a reputation for solid earnestness. Therefore, the more stupid a man, the better chance he has. I am naturally fond of a joke, but to get a name for that kind of thing would ruin me. You are clever, Paula, very clever in your way, but you don't, and you never will, understand politics. I beg of you not to damage my prospects. Cultivate a safe habit of speech. You may talk of the events of the season, of pigeon shooting, of horse racing, of the Prince and Princess of Wales, and so on; it's what everybody expects in a fashionable lady. Of course if you *had* been able to take up politics in earnest—but, never mind. I like you very well as you are. How well you look in that dress ! '

' I rather think you're right,' Paula remarked, after a short pause, turning about a bracelet on her wrist. It'll be better if you go your way and I go mine.'

' Precisely; though that's an unkind way of putting it.'

He sat looking at the ground, and a smile of another kind came to his face.

' By-the-by, I've something to tell you—something that'll amuse you very much, and that you *may* talk about, just as much as you like.'

She made no reply.

' Your friend Egremont has come out in a new part—his first appearance in it, absolutely, though he can't be said to have created the *rôle*. He's run away with a girl from Lambeth—in fact, the girl who was just going to be married to his right-hand man, his librarian.'

Paula looked up in astonishment : then, with indignant incredulity, she said :

' What do you mean ? What's your object in talking nonsense of that kind ? '

' Again and again I have to tell you that I never talk nonsense ; I am a politician. I heard the news this morning from Tasker. The man Grail—Egremont's librarian—was to have been married two days ago, Monday. Last Friday night his bride-elect disappeared. She's a very pretty girl, Tasker tells me—wonderfully pretty for one in her position, a work-girl. Egremont seems to have thought it a pity to let her be wasted. He's been meeting her secretly for some time—in the library, of all places, whilst the man Grail was at work, poor fellow ! And at last he carried her off. There's no getting on his track, I'm told. The question is : What will become of

the embryo library ?   The whole thing's about the finest joke
I've heard for some time.'

Paula had reddened.   Her eyes flashed anger.

' I don't know whether you've invented it,' she said, ' or
whether your secretary has, but I know there isn't one word
of truth in it.'

' My dear child, it's no invention at all.   The affair is the
common talk of Lambeth.'

' Then do you mean to say Mr. Egremont has married this
girl ? '

' Well, I don't know that we'll discuss that point,'
Dalmaine replied, twiddling his thumbs.   ' There's no information to hand.'

' I don't believe it !   I tell you I don't believe it !   Mr.
Egremont is engaged to my cousin Annabel ; and besides, he
couldn't do such a thing.   He isn't a man of that kind.'

' Your experience of men is not great, my dear Paula.'

' I don't care !   I know Mr. Egremont.   Even if you said
he'd married her, it isn't true.   You mustn't judge every man
by——'

' You were going to say ? '

She rose and swept her train over a few yards of floor.
Then she came back and stood before him.

' You tell me that people are saying this ? '

' A considerable number of my respected constituents—and
their wives—are saying it.   Tasker shall give you judicial
evidence, if you please.'

' I'm sure I'm not going to talk to Mr. Tasker.   I dislike
him too much to believe a word he says.'

' Of course.   But he is absolutely trustworthy.   I called at
Egremont's this afternoon to make sure that he was away
from home.   Now there is something for you to talk about,
Paula.'

' I shall take very good care that I don't speak a word of
it to anyone.   It's contemptible to make up such a story about
a man just because you dislike him.'

' It seemed to me that you were not remarkably fond of
him two months or so ago.'

' Did it ? ' she said, sarcastically.   ' If I know little of men,
it's certain you don't know much more of women.'

He leaned back and laughed.   And whilst he laughed
Paula quitted the room.

Paula still kept up her habit of letter-writing. After breakfast next morning she sat in her pretty boudoir, writing to Annabel. After sentences referring to Annabel's expected arrival in London for the season, she added this :

' A very shocking story has just come to my ears. I oughtn't really to repeat it to you, dear, and yet in another way it is my duty to. Mr. Egremont has disappeared, and with him the girl who was just going to marry his librarian—the poor man you know of from him. There are no means of knowing whether they have run away together to be married —or not. Everybody knows about it ; it is the talk of Lambeth. My husband heard of it at once. The girl is said to be very good-looking. I wish I could refuse to believe it, but *there is no doubt whatever*. You ought to know at once ; but perhaps you will have heard already. I never knew anything more dreadful, and I can't say what I feel.'

There was not much more in the letter. Having fastened up the envelope, Paula let it lie on her desk, whilst she walked about the room. Each time she passed the desk she looked at the letter, and lingered a little. Once she took it up and seemed about to open it again. Her expression all this time was very strange ; her colour came and went ; she bit her lips, and twisted her fingers together. At length she rang the bell, and when the servant came, gave the letter to be posted immediately.

Five minutes later she was in her bedroom, sitting in a low chair, crying like a very unhappy child.

The letter reached Eastbourne two days before that appointed for the departure of Annabel and her father for London. They had accepted Mrs. Tyrrell's invitation to her house ; Mr. Newthorpe might remain only a fortnight, or might stay through the season—but Annabel would not come back to Eastbourne before August. She said little, but her father saw with what pleasure she anticipated this change. He wondered whether it would do her good or harm. Her books lay almost unused ; of late she had attended chiefly to music, in such hours as were not spent out of doors. Mr. Newthorpe's health was as far improved as he could hope it ever would be. He too looked forward to associating once more with the few friends he had in London.

It was in the evening that Annabel, entering after a long drive with her father, found Paula's letter. She took it from the hall in passing to her room.

At dinner she spoke very little. After the meal she said that she wished to walk over to The Chestnuts. She left her father deep in a French novel—he read much more of the lighter literature now than formerly.

Mrs. Ormonde was upstairs with her children; they were singing to her; Annabel heard the choir of young voices as she entered the garden. The servant who went to announce her brought back a request that she would ascend and hear a song.

She did so. The last song was to be 'Annie Laurie,' in which the children were perfect. Annabel took the offered seat without speaking, and listened.

Bessie Bunce was near Mrs. Ormonde. When the song was over she said:

'I'd like to hear Miss Trent sing that again; wouldn't you, mum?'

'Yes, I should, Bessie. Perhaps we shall have her here again some day.'

Mrs. Ormonde went down with Annabel to the drawing-room. She was in a happy mood to-night, and, as they descended together, she put her arm playfully about the girl's waist.

'I wonder where Mr. Grail has taken her?' she said. 'I can't get any news from Mr. Egremont. I wrote to Jersey, and behold the letter is returned to me, with "Gone and left no address." I wonder whether he's back in town!'

'I have some news of him,' Annabel said quietly.

'Have you?'

There was no reply till they were in the drawing-room; then Annabel held out her cousin's letter.

'Will you read that?'

Mrs. Ormonde complied, Annabel watching her face the while. The girl looked for indignation, for scornful disbelief; she saw something quite different. Mrs. Ormonde's hand trembled, but in a moment she had overcome all weakness.

'Sit down, dear,' she said, calmly. 'You have just received this? Yes, I see the date.'

Annabel remained standing.

'Your letter is returned from Jersey,' she remarked, with steady voice. 'Paula mentions no dates. Did he go to Jersey at all?'

'I have no means of knowing, save his own declaration, when he said good-bye to me on Thursday of last week. And he told me he was going to his old quarters at St. Aubin's.'

'Do you give credit to this, Mrs. Ormonde?'

'Annabel, I can say nothing. Yet, no! I do not believe it until it is confirmed beyond all doubt. I owe that to him, as you also do.'

'But it does not seem to you incredible. I saw that on your face.'

'One thing suggested here *is* incredible, wholly incredible. If there is any truth in the story at all, by this time she is his wife. So much we know, you and I, Annabel.'

'Yes.'

'Remember, it is possible that he is in Jersey. The old rooms may have been occupied.'

'The people would know where he had gone, I think. Though if he—if he was not alone, probably he would go to a new place at once. He may have told you the truth in saying he was going to Jersey.'

'Then it was needless to add the untruth. I did not ask him where he would live. Sit down, dear.'

'Thank you. I shall not stay now. I thought it was better to come to you with this at once. Please destroy the letter.'

Mrs. Ormonde mused.

'Can you still go to your aunt's?' she asked, when Annabel moved for leave-taking.

'You are taking the truth for granted, Mrs. Ormonde.'

'I mean that we have no way of discovering whether it is true or not.'

'It will make no change. I shall not speak of it to father. There will be no change, in any case.'

Again there fell a short silence.

'I can only wait in hope of hearing from him,' Mrs. Ormonde said.

'Of course. If my aunt says anything to me about it, I will write to you. Good-bye.'

'I shall see you to-morrow, as we arranged?'

'Oh yes. But, please, we won't refer again to this.'

They parted as on an ordinary occasion.

But Annabel did not go home at once. She walked down to the shore, and stood for a long time looking upon the dim sea. It was the very spot where Thyrza had stood that Sunday morning when she came out in the early sunlight.

Annabel had often thought how fitting it was that at this period of her life she should leave the calm, voiceless shore of

Ullswater for the neighbourhood of the never-resting waves. The sea had a voice of craving, and her heart responded with desire for completion of her being, with desire for love.

The thought that she would be near Walter Egremont had a great part in her anticipation of London.

She was not hitherto sure that she loved him. It was rather, ' Let me see him again, and discover how his presence affects me.' Yet his manifest coldness at the last meeting had caused her much vague heartache. She blamed herself for being so cold : was it not natural that he should take his tone from her? He would naturally watch to see how she bore herself to him, and, remembering Ullswater, he could not press for more than she seemed ready to give. Yet her reserve had been involuntary; assuredly she was not then moved with a longing to recover what she had rejected.

There was a change after the meeting with Thyrza Trent. It seemed to her very foolish to remember so persistently that Egremont had said nothing of the girl's strange loveliness, yet she could not help thinking of the omission as something significant. She even recollected that, in speaking to her of Thyrza, he had turned his eyes seaward. Such trifles could mean nothing as regarded Egremont, but how in reference to herself? How if she knew that he had given his love to another woman? I think that would be hard to bear.

And it was hard to bear.

Passion had won it over everything. He had taken Thyrza at the eleventh hour, and now she was married to him. She did not doubt it ; she felt that Mrs. Ormonde did not doubt it. It *had* meant something—that failure to speak of the girl's beauty, that evasion with the eyes.

The night was cold, but she sat down by the shore, and let her head droop as she listened to the sea-dirge. She could love him, now that it was in vain. She knew now the warm yearning for his presence which at Ullswater had never troubled her, and it was too late. No tears came to her eyes; she did not even breathe a deeper breath. Most likely it would pass without a single outbreak of grief.

And perhaps the thought of another's misery somewhat dulled the edge of her own. Gilbert Grail was only a name to her, but he lived very vividly in her imagination. Of course she had idealised him, as was natural in a woman thinking of a man who has been represented to her as full of native nobleness. For him, as for herself, her heart was heavy. She knew that he must return to his hated day-labour, and how would it now be embittered! What anguish of resentment! What despair of frustrate passion!

She wished she could know him, and take his hand, and soothe him with a woman's tenderness. His lot was harder than hers; nay, it was mockery to compare them.

Annabel rose, murmuring old words:

' " Therefore I praised the dead which are already dead more than the living which are yet alive. Yea, better is he than both they, which hath not yet been, who hath not seen the evil work which is done under the sun." '

CHAPTER XXVI

THE IDEALIST AND HIS FRIEND

EGREMONT alighted one evening at Charing Cross. He came direct from Paris, and was alone. His absence from England had extended over a fortnight.

He did not look better for his travels; one in the crowd waiting for the arrival of the train might have supposed that he had suffered on the sea-passage and was not yet quite recovered. Having bidden a porter look after the bag which was his only luggage, he walked to the book-stall to buy a periodical that he wished to take home with him. And there he came face to face with two people whom he knew. Mr. Dalmaine was just turning from the stall with an evening paper, and by his side was Paula. Egremont had not seen either since their marriage.

The three pairs of eyes focussed on one point. Egremont saluted—did it nervously, for he was prepared for nothing less than an encounter with acquaintances. He saw a smile come to Paula's face; he saw her on the point of extending her hand; then, to his amazement, he heard a sharp ' Paula ! ' from Dalmaine, and husband and wife turned from him. It was the cut direct, or would have been, but for that little piece of impulsiveness on Paula's part. The two walked towards one of the platforms, and it was plain that Dalmaine was delivering himself in an undertone of a gentlemanly reproof.

He stood disconcerted. What might this mean ? Was it

merely an urbane way of reminding him that he had neglected certain civilities demanded by the social code? Dalmaine would doubtless be punctilious; he was a rising politician. Yet the insult was too pronounced: it suggested some grave ground of offence.

As the cab bore him homewards, he felt that this was an ominous event for the moment of his return to London. He had had no heart to come back; from the steamer he had gazed sadly on the sunny shores of France, and on landing at Dover the island air was hard to breathe. Yet harder the air of London streets. The meeting in the station became a symbol of stiff, awkward, pretentious Anglicism. He had unkind sentiments towards his native country, and asked himself how he was going to live in England henceforth.

His room in Great Russell Street seemed to have suffered neglect during his absence; his return was unexpected; everything seemed unhomely and unwelcoming. The great front of the British Museum frowned, as if to express disapproval of such aimless running hither and thither in one who should be spending his days soberly and strenuously: even the pigeons walked or flew with balance of purpose, with English respectability   It seemed to have rained all day; the evening sky was heavy and featureless.

The landlady presented herself. She was grieved exceedingly that she had not known of Mr. Egremont's coming, but everything should be made comfortable in less than no time. He would have a fire? To be sure; it was a little chilly, though really 'summer has come upon us all at a jump, whilst you've been away, sir.'

'I got your telegram, sir, that I wasn't to send any letters on.   Gentlemen have called and I——'

'Indeed?   Who has called?'

'Why, sir, on the day after you went—I dare say it was nine o'clock in the evening, or a little later—someone came, wishing very much to see you. He wouldn't give a name.   I don't think it was a gentleman; it seemed like somebody coming on business. He was very anxious to have your address. Of course I didn't give it. I just said that any note he liked to leave should be forwarded at once.'

'A dark man, with a beard?   A working man?'

'No doubt the one you're thinking of, sir.   He called again—let me see, four or five days after.'

'Called again?   Then it couldn't be the man I mean.'

He entered into a fuller description of Gilbert Grail. The landlady identified the caller as Grail beyond all doubt.

'What day was it?'

'Why, sir, it 'ud be Wednesday; yes, Wednesday,'

'H'm! And you told him I had left Jersey?'

'Yes, sir. He said he knew that, and that——'

'Said he knew it?' repeated Egremont, astonished.

'Yes, sir, and that he wished to see if you had got home again.'

'Has he been since?'

'No, sir, but—I was coming in a night or two after, sir, and I saw him standing on the opposite side of the way, looking at the house. He hadn't called, however, and he didn't again.'

Egremont bent his eyes on the ground, and delayed a moment before asking:

'Who else has been?'

'A gentleman; I don't know who it was. The servant went to the door. He said he only wished to know if you were in town or not. He wouldn't leave a name.'

Egremont's face changed to annoyance. He did not care to pursue the subject.

'Let me have something to eat, please,' he said.

The landlady having withdrawn, he at once sat down to his desk and wrote a note. It was to Grail, and ran in substance:

'I am just back from the Continent. Am I right in thinking that it is you who have called here twice in my absence? If so, your second call was at a time when I hoped you were out of London. Do let me see you as soon as possible. Of course you received my letter from Jersey? Shall I come to you, or will you come here? I will stay in to-night. I send this by a messenger, as I wish you to receive it immediately.'

The landlady had a son at home, a lad of sixteen. Having discovered that the boy's services were available, Egremont gave him directions. He was to take a cab and drive to the library in Brook Street. If he should not find Grail there, he was to proceed to Walnut Tree Walk. If Grail would come back with him, so much the better.

Walter was left to refresh himself after his journey. He changed his clothes, and presently sat down to a meal. But appetite by this time failed him. He had the table cleared ten minutes after it was laid.

He was in the utmost uneasiness. Could it be Grail who had called? He tried to assure himself that it must be a mistake. How could Grail expect him to be in town, after reading that letter from Jersey? If indeed the visitor were Gilbert, some catastrophe had befallen. But he would not entertain such a fear. Then the second caller; that might be any acquaintance. Still, it was strange that he too had refused his name.

You know the state of mind in which, whatever one thinks of, a pain, a fear, draws the thought another way. It was so with Egremont. The two mysterious callers and the annoying scene at the railway station plagued him successively, and for background to them all was a shadow of indefinite apprehension.

He could scarcely endure his impatience. It seemed as though the messenger would never return. The lad presented himself, however, without undue delay. He had found Mr. Grail, he said, at the second address.

'And whom did you see in Brook Street?'

'A woman, sir; she said Mr. Grail didn't live there.'

'He couldn't come with you?'

'No, sir. But he said he'd come very soon.'

'Thank you. That will do.'

So Grail was *not* at the library. Then of a certainty something had happened. Thyrza was ill; perhaps——

He walked about the room. That dread physical pain which clutches at all the inner parts when one is waiting in agonised impatience for that which will be misery when it comes, racked him so that at moments he had to lean for support. He felt how the suffering of the last fortnight, in vain fled from hither and thither, had reduced his strength. Since he took leave of Thyrza, he had not known one moment of calm. When passion was merciful for a time, fear had taken its turn to torment him. It had not availed to demonstrate to himself that fear *must* be groundless. Love from of old has had a comrade superstition; if he awoke from a wretched dream, he interpreted it as sympathy with Thyrza in some dreadful trial. And behold! he had been right. His flight had profited nothing; woe had come upon her he loved, and upon the man he most desired to befriend.

Half an hour after the return of the messenger, the servant came to the door and said that ' Mr. Grail' was below.

' Yes. I'll see him.'

He spoke the words with difficulty. He advanced to the middle of the room. Gilbert came in, and the door was closed behind him.

The man looked as if he had risen from his death-bed to obey this summons. The flesh of his face had shrunk, and left the lines of his countenance sharp. His eye-sockets were cavernous; the dark eyes had an unnatural lustre. His hair and beard were abandoned to neglect. His garments hung with strange looseness about him. He stood there, just within the door, his gaze fixed on Egremont, a gaze wherein suspicion and reproach and all unutterable woe were blended.

Walter took a step forward, vainly holding out his hand.

' Grail, what has happened? You are ill. What does it mean?'

' Why have you sent for me, Mr. Egremont?'

The question was uttered with some sternness, but bodily weakness subdued the voice, which shook. And when he had spoken, his eyes fell.

' Because I want to know what is the matter,' Egremont replied, in quick, unnerved tones. 'Have you been here to try and see me?'

' Yes, I have.'

' Why? you knew I was away. What has happened, Grail?'

' I thought you knew, Mr. Egremont.'

' How should I know? I have heard nothing from London for a fortnight. You speak to me in an unfriendly way. Tell me at once what you mean.'

Gilbert looked up for a moment, looked indignantly, bitterly. But his eyes drooped again as he spoke.

' A fortnight ago Miss Trent left her home, and we can hear nothing of her. I tried to find you, because I had reason to think that you knew where she was.'

Walter felt it as a relief. He had waited for something worse. Only after-thought could occupy itself with the charge distinctly made against him. He said, as soon as he could command his voice:

' You were wrong in thinking so. I know nothing of Miss Trent. I have no idea where she can have gone.'

It was only when he found Grail's eyes fixed upon him that he added, after a pause :

'What were the reasons that led you to think so ? '

'You know nothing?' Gilbert said, slowly.

'Nothing whatever. How could you think I did ? I don't understand you.'

Walter was not used to speak untruthfully. He knew all this time that a man upon whom a charge such as this had come as a sheer surprise would have met it with quite other face and accent. Remembering all that had passed between Thyrza and himself, remembering all that he had undergone, all that he had at one moment proposed, he could not express the astonishment which would have given evidence on his behalf. As yet he had not even tried to affect indignation, for it was against his nature to play the hypocrite. He knew that his manner was all but a tacit admission that appearances were against him. But agitation drove him to the brink of anger, and when Gilbert stood mute, with veiled eyes, he continued impetuously:

'I tell you that you have amazed me by your news. Are you accusing me of something ? You must speak more plainly. Do you mean that suspicion has fallen upon me ? How ? I don't—I can't understand you ! '

'I thought you would understand me,' Gilbert replied, gravely, not offensively, with far more dignity than the other had been able to preserve. 'Several things compelled me to believe that you knew of her leaving us. I was told of your meetings with her at the library.'

He paused. Like Egremont, he could not speak his whole thought. Whilst there remained a possibility that Egremont indeed knew nothing of Thyrza's disappearance, he might not strengthen his case by making use of the girl's confession to her sister. He could only make use of outward circumstances.

'The meetings at the library ? ' Egremont repeated. ' But do you think they had any meaning that I can't at once and freely explain to you ? It was the idlest folly on my part. I had a plan that I would get books on to the shelves that week, and at the end of it take you there and surprise you. Didn't I imply that in my letter to you from Jersey ? It was childish, of course. On the Monday, Miss Trent surprised me at work. She had happened to see a box being brought in, and naturally came to see what was going on. I was unthinking enough to ask her to keep the secret. By allowing her to help me, **I** encouraged her to come again the next day. So much was wholly my fault, but surely not a very grave one. Do you imagine, Grail, that anything passed between us on those two mornings which you might not have heard ? How is it possible for you, for *you*, to pass from the fact of that foolish secret to such suspicions as these ? '

In the pause Gilbert offered no word.

' And who told you about it ? Evidently someone bent on mischief.'

Again a pause. Gilbert stood unmoving.

' You still suspect me ? You think I am lying to you ? Do you know me no better than that ? '

It rang false, it rang false. His own voice sounded to him as that of an actor, who does his poor best to be forcible and pathetic. Yet what lie had he told ? Could he say all he thought he had read in Thyrza's eyes ? There was the parting that night beyond Lambeth Bridge ; how could he speak of that ? Was he himself not absolutely innocent ? Had he not by a desperate struggle avoided as much as a glance of tenderness at the girl for whom he was mad with love ?

Gilbert spoke at length.

'I find it very hard to believe that you know nothing more. There are other things. As soon as we knew that she was gone, that Friday night, I came here to ask for you.'

' And why ? Why to me ? '

' Because she had been seen with you at the library, and people had begun to talk. They told me you were gone, and I asked for your address. They wouldn't give it me.'

' That meant nothing whatever. It was merely my landlady's idea of her responsibility to me.'

' Yes, that may be. On Saturday night a letter came from you, from Jersey.'

' Well ? Was that the kind of letter I could have written if I had been such a traitor to you ? '

' I don't know what the letter would have seemed to me if I had been able to judge it with my ordinary mind. I couldn't : I was going through too much. I believed it false. On Monday I went to Southampton, and from there at night to Jersey ; it was the earliest that I could get there.'

' You went to Jersey ? '

'I had no choice. I had to see you. And I found you had gone away on Saturday morning, gone to France. It was only Saturday night that I got your letter. There was no word in

it about going to France ; instead of that, you said plainly that
you would be in Jersey for a week or more.'

' It is true.   I see how I have made evidence against myself.'

He said it with impatience, but at once added in a steadier
voice :

' I wrote the letter and posted it on Friday night, when I
had only been at St. Aubin's half a day.   The very next morning I was compelled by restlessness to give up my idea of remaining there.   When I wrote to you I had no thought of
leaving the island.'

How pleasant it was to be able to speak with unshadowed
veracity !   Walter all but smiled, and, when the other made
no reply, he went on in a voice almost of pleading:

' You believe this ?   Is your mind so set against me that
you will accuse me of any cowardice rather than credit my
word ? '

A change came over Gilbert's face.   It was wrung with
pain, and as he looked up it seemed to cost him a horrible
effort to speak.

' If,' he said, ' in a moment of temptation you did her the
greatest wrong that a man can do to a woman, you would perhaps say and do anything rather than confess it.'

Walter tried to meet those eyes steadily, but failed.   He
broke forth into passionate self-defence.

' That means you think the worst of me that one man can
think of another.   You are wrong !   You are basely wrong !
You speak of a moment of temptation.   Suppose me to have
suffered that ; what sort of temptation do you suppose would
have assailed me ?   A man is tempted according to his fibre.
Do you class me with those who can only be tempted by base
suggestions ?   What reason have I ever given you to think of
me so ?   Suppose me to have been tempted.   You conclude
that I must have aimed at stealing the girl from you solely to
gratify myself, heedless of her, heedless of you.   Such a
motive as that is to outweigh every higher instinct I possess,
to blind me to past and future, to make me all at once a
heartless, unimaginative brute.   That is your view of my
character, Grail ! '

Gilbert had not the appearance of a man who listens.
Since entering the room, he had not moved from the spot
where he stood, and now, with his head again drooping, he
seemed sunk in a reverie of the profoundest sadness.   But he

heard, and he strove to believe. A fortnight ago he would not have thought it possible for Walter Egremont to speak a word of which the sincerity would seem doubtful. Since then he had spent days and nights such as sap the foundations of a man's moral being and shake convictions which appeared impregnable. The catastrophe which had come upon him was proportionate in its effects to the immeasurable happiness which preceded it. Remember that it was not only the imaginary wrong from which his mind suffered; the fact that Thyrza loved Egremont was in itself an agony almost enough to threaten his reason. His love was not demonstrative; perhaps he did not himself know all its force until jealousy taught him. How, think you, did he spend that night on the Channel, voyaging from Southampton to Jersey? What sort of companions were the winds and waves as he paced the deck in the dim light before dawn, straining his eyes for the first sight of land? To the end of all things that night would remain with him, a ghastly memory. And since then he had not known one full hour of forgetfulness. The days and the nights had succeeded each other as in a torture-chamber. His body had wasted; his mind ever renewed its capability of anguish. With all appearances against Egremont, could he preserve the nice balance of his judgment through an experience such as this?

Had he seen Egremont at once, after Thyrza's disappearance, it would not have been so hard for him to credit the denial. The blow was not felt to its full until the night had passed. Thyrza's exculpation of Egremont would then have been strong upon the latter's side. But the fruitless journey frenzied him. It was impossible for him to avoid the belief that the letter had been contrived to deceive him. All the suspicions he had entertained grew darker as his suffering increased. His meeting with Egremont at the end of Newport Street on the Wednesday night seemed to him beyond doubt condemnatory. He remembered the young man's haste and obvious agitation. Then Thyrza's words ceased to have weight; he thought them due to her desire to avert suspicion from her lover. And now that he was at length face to face with the man whom in his lonely woe he had cursed as the falsest friend, his ear was keen to detect every note of treachery, his eyes read Egremont's countenance with preternatural keenness. Walter could not sustain such proof; his agitation spoke against him. Only when he

at length passed from uncertain argument and pleading to
scornful repudiation of the charge, did his utterances awake
in the hearer the old associations of sincerity and nobleness.
How many a night Gilbert had hung on every word that fell
from him ! Could he speak thus and be no more than a contemptible hypocrite ?

Walter paused for a few moments. When no reply came
he continued with the same warmth :

'I have told you that, on those two mornings, when she
was with me in the library, no word passed between us that
you might not have heard. It is true. But one thing I did
say to her which doubtless would not have been said in your
presence. She was speaking to me as if to a superior ; I
begged her to let there be an end of that, and to allow me to
call myself her friend. I meant it in the purest sense, and
in that sense she understood it. If I was wrong in taking
that freedom with her, at least there was no thought of wrong
in my mind.'

'You met her on Wednesday night in that week,' Gilbert
said, speaking with uncertain voice. 'The night that you
saw me and said you had been to Bunce.'

' Do you know of that from some spy, her enemy and
mine—or how ? '

' I know it. I can't tell you how.'

' Yes, I met her that night. Not by appointment, as you
suppose. It was by mere chance, as I came away from
Bunce's house. I told her I was leaving town next day,
and I said good-bye to her. Again, not a syllable was uttered
that any one might not have heard.'

' Were you coming away from her, then, when I saw
you ? ' Gilbert asked, in a hard voice.

' No, not straight from her.'

As is wont to be the case with us when we have recourse
to equivocation, Egremont thought that he read in his rival's
countenance a scornful surmise of the truth. As is also wont
to happen, this sense of detection heated his blood, and for a
moment he could have found pleasure in flinging out an angry
defiance. But as he looked Grail in the face, the latter's eyes
fell, and something, some slight movement of feature, touching once more Walter's sense of compassion, shamed him
from unworthy utterance. He said, in a lower voice :

' If I *had* yielded to temptation, if I had so far lost control
of myself as to speak a word to her which at once and for ever

altered our relations, do you think I should have tried to keep secret what had happened ? Do you think I could have conceived a desire which had *her* suffering for its end ? Are you so embittered that you can imagine of me nothing better than that ? You think I could have made *her* my victim ? '

Grail read his face. The emphasis of this speech was deliberate, could not be misunderstood. For the first time Gilbert turned and moved a little apart.

Walter had not the exclusive privilege of being an idealist. When at length he spoke out of his deepest feeling, when he revealed, though but indirectly, the meaning of his agitation, of his evasions, and doubtful behaviour, he had found the way of convincing his hearer. It was a new blow to Gilbert, but it put an end to his darkest fears and to the misery of his misjudgment. In the silence that followed all the details of the story passed before him with a new significance. The greatness of his own love—a love which drew into its service every noblest element of his nature, enabled him, once the obscuring mists dispelled, to interpret his rival's mind with justice. Regarding Egremont again, he could read aright the signs of suffering that were on his face. It was with a strange bitter joy that he recovered his faith in the man who had been so much to him. Yet his first words seemed to express more of passionate resentment than any he had yet spoken.

' Then you acted wrongly ! ' he exclaimed, in a firm, clear voice. ' You were wrong in allowing her to stay and help you in the library. You were wrong in speaking to her as you did, in asking her to address you as an equal, and to let you be her friend. You must have known then what your real meaning was. It is only half a truth that you said and did nothing to disturb her mind. You were not honest with yourself, and you had no just regard for me. You *did* yield to temptation, and all you have said in defence of yourself has only been true in sound.'

' No ! You go too far, Grail. You accused me of baseness, and I have never had a base thought.'

Then came a long silence. Gilbert stood motionless, Egremont walked slowly from place to place. The point at issue between the two men was changed ; anger and suspicion were at an end, but so was all hope of restoring the old union.

Then Egremont said :

' You must tell me one thing plainly. Do you still doubt

my word when I say that I knew nothing of her flight from
you, and know nothing of where she now is ? '

'I believe you,' was answered, simply.

'And more than that. Do you think me capable of wrong-
ing her and you in the way you suspected ? '

'I was wrong. I was unjust to you.'

Grail could suffer jealousy, but was incapable of malice.
The stab of the revelation that had been made might go
through and through his heart, but the wound would breed
no evil humours. He made his admission with the relief
which comes of recovered self-respect.

'Thank you for that, Grail,' Walter replied, moved as a
gentle nature always is by magnanimity.

After another pause, he said :

'May I ask you anything more about her ? Had she
money ? Could she have gone far ? '

'At most she had a few pence.'

'Did she leave no written word ? '

'Yes. She wrote something for her sister.'

Walter hesitated. Grail, after a struggle with himself, repeated the substance of Thyrza's note.

A few more words were interchanged, then Gilbert said :

'I will leave you now, Mr. Egremont.'

Walter dreaded this parting. Could he let Grail go from
him and say no word about the library ? Yet what was to be
said ? Everything was hopelessly at an end ; the hint of
favour from him to the other was henceforth insult. Gilbert
was moving towards him, but he could not look up. Forcing
himself to speak :

'If you find her—if you hear anything—will you tell me ?
I mean only, will you let me know the fact that you have
news ? '

'Yes, I will.'

At length their eyes met. Then Grail held out his hand,
and Egremont clasped it firmly.

'This is not the end between us,' he said, huskily. 'You
must wish that you had never seen me, but I can never lose the
hope that we may some day be friends again.'

The haggard man went his way in silence. Egremont,
throwing himself upon a seat in utter weariness, felt more
alone than ever yet in his life. . . .

Who or what was left to him now ? A little while ago,
when he had felt that his connection with the world of wealth

and refinement was practically at an end, it seemed more than a substitute to look forward to intimacy with that one household in Lambeth, and to associations that would arise thence. He believed that it would henceforth content him to have friends in the sphere to which he belonged by birth, and, for the needs of his mind, to find companionship among his books. He saw before him a career of practical usefulness such as only a man in his peculiar position could pursue with unwavering zeal. What now was to become of his future ? Where were his friends ?

Grail had said that in Lambeth people were gossiping evil of him. Such gossip, he understood too well, would have its lasting effect. No contradiction could avail against it. Even if Thyrza returned, it would be impossible for her to resume her life in the old places ; the truth could never be so spread as to counteract the harm already done. Lambeth had lost its free library. How long would it wait before another man was found able and willing to do so much on its behalf ?

Looking in the other direction, he could now explain that scene at Charing Cross. Dalmaine, through his connection with Lambeth, had already heard the story. He took this way of showing that he was informed of everything, and of manifesting his august disapproval. It needed only a word of admonition to Paula, and she at once recognised how improper it would be to hold further relations with so unprincipled a man. So they turned away, and, in the vulgar phrase, ' cut ' him.

The Dalmaines knowing, of course their relatives and their friends knew. The Tyrrells would by this time have discussed the whole shocking affair, doubtless with the decision that they could no longer be ' at home ' to Mr. Egremont.

And if the Tyrrells—then Annabel Newthorpe.

Would Annabel give faith to such a charge against him ? Perhaps such evidence would be adduced to her that she could have no choice but to judge and condemn him. Gilbert Grail had thought him infamous ; perhaps Annabel would hesitate as little. She would have remarked a strangeness in his manner to her, explicable now. Believing, how she must scorn him ! How those beautiful eyes of hers would speak in one glance of cold contempt, if ever he passed beneath them ! She *might* take the nobler part ; she *might* hold it incredible till she had a confession from his very lips. But were women magnanimous ? And Annabel, very clear in thought, very pure in soul—was she after all so far above her sisters as to face all hazard of human weakness in defence of an ideal?

Annabel, now in London, would write the news to Mrs. Ormonde. Would it receive credence from her—his dearest friend? Assuredly not, if she had known nothing to give the calumny startling support. But there was that letter he wrote to her about Thyrza; there was her recollection of the interview in Great Russell Street, when it might be that he had betrayed himself. She had found him in a state of perturbation which he could not conceal; it was on the eve of his own departure from London—of Thyrza's disappearance. Well, she too must form her own judgment. If she wrote to him and asked plainly for information, he would know how to reply. Till she wrote, he must keep silence.

So there was the bead-roll of his friends. No, he had omitted Annabel's father. Mr. Newthorpe was a student, and apt to be humorously cynical in his judgment of men. To him the story would not appear incredible. Youth, human nature, a passionate temperament; these explain so much to the unprejudiced mind. Mr. Newthorpe must go with the rest.

For other acquaintances he cared nothing.

So his fate at last had declared itself. Even though the all but impossible should befall, and Grail should still marry Thyrza, how could the schemes for common activity survive this shock? Say what he might, he had no longer even the desire to work personally for the old aims. How hard to believe that he was the same man who had lectured to that little band of hearers on English Literature, who had uttered with such vehemence the 'Thoughts for the Present!' That period of his life was gone by like smoke; the heart in which such enthusiasms were nourished had been swept by an all-consuming fire. Henceforth he must live for himself, the vainest of all lives. To such a one the world was a sorry place. He had no mind to taste such pleasures as it offered to a rich man with no ideal save physical enjoyment; he no longer cared to search out its beautiful things, to probe its mysteries. To what end, since all pleasure and all knowledge must end in himself? . . .

Where at this moment was Thyrza? The thought had mingled with all those others. Did she then love him so much that marriage with Grail had become impossible—that she would rather face every hardship and peril of a hidden life in some dark corner of London ? For she lived; proof of it seemed to be in the refusal of his mind to contemplate a fatal issue of her trial. She lived, and held him in her heart—the strong, passionate heart, source of music and of love. And he—could he foresee the day when he should no longer love her ?

But of that she knew nothing, and must never know of it. The one outlook for his life lay yonder, where love was beckoning; grant him leave to follow, and what limitless prospect opened in place of the barren hills which now enclosed him ! But follow he must not. In that respect nothing was altered. When he thought of Thyrza, it must still be with the hope that she would return and fulfil her promise to Gilbert Grail.

At a late hour he went to his bedroom. He lay down with a weary brain, and, in trying to ask himself what he should do on the morrow, fell asleep.

CHAPTER XXVII

FOUND

Mrs. Ormonde waited anxiously for Annabel's first letter from London. Neither of them had spoken of Egremont after Annabel's visit with the news from Paula. The girl gave no sign of trouble; she appeared to continue her preparations with the same enjoyment as before. It was doubtful whether, in writing, she would make any reference to Egremont, but Mrs. Ormonde hoped there would be some word.

The letter came five days after Annabel's arrival in London, and was short. It mentioned visits to the Academy and the Grosvenor, made a few comments, spoke of this and that old acquaintance reseen ; then came a concluding paragraph :

'Father called at Mr. Egremont's two days ago, but did not see him. He learnt that Mr. Egremont had been at home for one day, but was gone out of town again. My aunt, as I gather from a chance word, takes the least charitable view ; I fear that was to be expected. We, however, *know* the truth—do we not ? It is sad, but not shameful. I have no means of hearing anything about the library. I believe father has been to Lambeth, but he and I do not speak on the subject. Paula, for some reason, avoids me.'

It was one of several letters that arrived that morning. After opening two appeals from charitable institutions, Mrs. Ormonde found an envelope which, from the handwriting upon it, she judged to be a similar communication from a private source. The address was laboriously scrawled, and ill-spelt; the postage stamp was badly affixed; there were finger-marks on the back. Such envelopes generally came from the parents of children who had been in the Home, and frequently— dirtiness announced such cases—made appeal for temporary assistance. The present missive, however, was misleading; its contents proved to be these:

'Madam,—We have a young girl with us as lies very bad. She come to us not more than three week ago and asked for ployment, and me and my husband wasn't unwilling for to give her a chance, seeing she looked respectable, though we thought it wasn't unlikely as there might be something wrong, because of her looks and her clothing, which wasn't neither of them like the girl out of work, and then it's true she couldn't give no reference. And now she's had fainting fits, and lies very bad, having broke two dishes with falling, and which of course she couldn't help, and we don't say as she could. My husband told me as I ought for to look in her pocket, and which I did, and there I found a envelope as had wrote your name and address on it. So I take the liberty of writing, and which I am not much of a scholar, because she do lie very bad, and if so be she has friends, they had ought to know. I do what I can for her, but I have the customers to tend to, because we keep a coffee-shop, which you'll find it at Number seventeen, Bank Street, off the Caledonian Road. And I beg to end. From yours obedient,

'SARAH GANDLE.'

There could be little doubt who this young girl was. Bad spelling and worse writing rendered the letter difficult to translate into English, but from the first sentence Mrs. Ormonde thought of Thyrza Trent. The description would apply to Thyrza, and Thyrza might by some chance have kept in her pocket the address which, as Mrs. Ormonde knew, Bunce had given her when she brought Bessie to Eastbourne.

Her first emotion was of joy. This was quickly succeeded

by doubts and fears in plenty, for it was difficult to explain Thyrza's taking such a step as this letter suggested. But the course to be pursued was clear. She took the first train to London.

Caledonian Road is a great channel of traffic running directly north from King's Cross to Holloway. It is doubtful whether London can show any thoroughfare of importance more offensive to eye and ear and nostril. You stand at the entrance to it, and gaze into a region of supreme ugliness; every house front is marked with meanness and inveterate grime; every shop seems breaking forth with mould or dry-rot; the people who walk here appear one and all to be employed in labour that soils body and spirit. Journey on the top of a tram-car from King's Cross to Holloway, and civilisation has taught you its ultimate achievement in ig-noble hideousness. You look off into narrow side-channels where unconscious degradation has made its inexpugnable home, and sits veiled with refuse. You pass above lines of railway, which cleave the region with black-breathing fissure. You see the pavements half occupied with the paltriest and most sordid wares; the sign of the pawnbroker is on every hand; the public-houses look and reek more intolerably than in other places. The population is dense, the poverty is un-disguised. All this northward-bearing tract, between Cam-den Town on the one hand and Islington on the other, is the valley of the shadow of vilest servitude. Its public monu-ment is a cyclopean prison: save for the desert around the Great Northern Goods Depôt, its only open ground is a malodorous cattle-market. In comparison, Lambeth is pic-turesque and venerable, St. Giles's is romantic, Hoxton is clean and suggestive of domesticity, Whitechapel is full of poetry, Limehouse is sweet with sea-breathings.

Hither Mrs. Ormonde drove from Victoria Station. The neighbourhood was unknown to her save by name. On entering the Caledonian Road, her cabman had to make in-quiries for Bank Street, which he at length found not far from the prison. He drew up before a small coffee-shop, on the window whereof was pasted this advertisement: 'Dine here! Best quality. Largest quantity! Lowest price.' Over the door was the name 'Gandle.'

Mrs. Ormonde bade the driver wait, and entered. It was the dinner-hour of this part of the world. Every available place was occupied by men, some in their shirt-sleeves, who were doing ample justice to the fare set before them by Mrs. Gandle and her daughter.   Beyond the space assigned to the public was a partition of wood, four feet high, with a door in the middle; this concealed the kitchen, whence came clouds of steam, and the sound of frying, and odours manifold.   At the entrance of a lady—a lady without qualification—such of the feeders as happened to look from their plates stared in wonderment.   It was an embarrassing position.   Mrs. Ormonde walked quickly down the narrow gangway, and to the door in the partition.   A young woman was just coming forth, with steaming plates on a tray.

'Can I see Mrs. Gandle?' the visitor asked.

The girl cried out: 'Mother, you're wanted!' and pushed past, with grins bestowed on either side.

Above the partition appeared a face like a harvest moon.

'I have come in reply to your letter,' Mrs. Ormonde said, 'the letter about the girl who is ill.'

'Oh, you've come, have you, mum!' was the reply, in a voice at once respectful and surprised.   'Would you be so good as step inside, mum?   Please push the door.'

Mrs. Ormonde was relieved to pass into the privacy of the kitchen.   It was a room of some ten feet square, insufferably hot, very dirty, a factory for the production of human fodder. On a side table stood a great red dripping mass, whence Mrs. Gandle severed portions to be supplied as roast beef.   Vessels on the range held a green substance which was called cabbage, and yellow lumps doled forth as potatoes.   Before the fire, bacon and sausages were frizzling; above it was spluttering a beef-steak.   On a sink in one corner were piled eating utensils which awaited the wipe of a very loathsome rag hanging hard by.   Other objects lay about in indescribable confusion.

Mrs. Gandle was a very stout woman, with bare arms. She perspired freely, and was not a little disconcerted by the appearance of her visitor.   Her moon-face had a simple and not disagreeable look.

'You won't mind me a-getting on with my work the whiles I talk, mum?' she said.   'The men's tied to time, most of em, and I've often lost a customer by keepin' him waitin'.   They're not too sweet-tempered in these parts.   I was born and bred in Peckham myself, and only come here when I married my second husband, which he's a plumber by trade.   I can't so much as ask you for to sit down, mum.   You

see, we have to 'conomize room, as my husband says. But I
can talk and work, both; only I've got to keep one ear
open——'

A shrill voice cried from the shop:

'Two beefs, 'taters an' greens! One steak-pie, 'taters!
Two cups o' tea!'

'Right!' cried Mrs. Gandle, and proceeded to execute the
orders.

'What is this poor girl's name?' Mrs. Ormonde asked.
'You didn't mention it.'

'Well, mum, she calls herself Mary Wood. Do you know
any one o' that name?'

'I think not.'

'Now come along, 'Lizabeth!' screamed the woman of a
sudden, at the top of her voice. 'Don't stand a-talkin' there!
Two beefs, 'taters and greens.'

'That's right, Mrs. Gandle!' roared some man. 'You
give it her. It's the usial Bow-bells with her an' Sandy Dick
'ere!'

There was laughter, and 'Lizabeth came running for her
orders. Mrs. Gandle, with endless interruptions, proceeded
thus:

'Between you and me, mum, I don t believe as that *is* her
name. But she give it at first, and she's stuck to it. No, I
don't think she's worse to-day, though she talked a lot in the
night. Yes, we've had a doctor. She wouldn't have me send
for nobody, and said as there was nothing ailed her, but then
it come as she couldn't stand on her feet. She's a littlish girl,
may be seventeen or eighteen, with yellow-like hair. I haven't
knowed well what to do; I thought I'd ought to send her to
the 'orspital, but then I found the henvelope in her pocket,
an' we thought we'd just wait a day to see if anybody answered us. And I didn't like to act heartless with her,
neither; she's a motherless thing, so she says, an' only wants
for to earn her keep and her sleep; an' I don't think there's no
harm in her, s'far as I can see. She come into the shop last
night was three weeks, just after eleven o'clock, and she says,
"If you please, mum," she says, speakin' very nice, "can you
give me a bed for sevenpence?" "Why, I don't know about
that," says I, "I haven't a bedroom as I let usial under a
shilling." Then she was for goin' straight away, without
another word. And she was so quiet like, it took me as I
couldn't send her off without asking her something about

Y

herself. And she said she hadn't got no 'ome in London, and only sevenpence in her pocket, and as how she wanted to find work. And she must have walked about a deal, she looked that dead beat.

'Well, I just went in and spoke a word to Mr. Gandle. It's true as we wanted someone to help me 'an 'Lizabeth ; we've wanted someone bad for a long time. And this young girl wouldn't be amiss, we thought, for waitin' in the shop ; the men likes to see a noo face, you know, mum, an' all the more if it's a good-looking 'un. If she'd been a orn'ary lookin' girl, of course I couldn't have not so much as thought of it, as things was. She told me plain an' straightforward as she couldn't say who she was and where she come from. And it was something in her way o' speakin', a kind o' quiet-ness like, as you don't hoften get in young girls nowadays. They're so for'ard, as their parents ain't got the same 'old on 'em as they had when I was young. I shouldn't wonder if you've noticed the same thing with your servants, mum. An' so I said as I'd let her have a bed for sevenpence ; and if you'd a' seen how thankful she looked. She wasn't the kind to go an' sleep anywhere, an' goodness only knows what might a' come to her at that hour o' the night. And the next mornin' she did look that white an' poorly, when I met her a-comin' down the stairs. " Well," says I, " an' what about breakfast, eh ? " She went a bit red like, an' said as it didn't matter ; she'd go out an' find work. " Well, look here now," says I, " suppose you wash up them things there to pay for a cup o' tea and two slices ? " An' then she looked at me thankful again, an' says as it was kind o' me. Well, of course, you may say as it isn't everybody 'ud a' took her in for sevenpence, but then, as I was a-sayin', we did want some-body to help me an' 'Lizabeth, an' I don't take much to myself for what I did.'

'You acted well and kindly, Mrs. Gandle,' said Mrs. Ormonde.

So the long story went on. The girl had been only too glad to stay as general servant, and worked well, worked as hard as any one could expect, Mrs. Gandle said. But she was far from well, and every day, after the first week, her strength fell off. At length she had a fainting fit, falling with two dishes in her hands. Her work had to be lightened. But the fainting was several times repeated, and, now three days ago, illness it was impossible to struggle against kept her to her bed.

'Well, I begged an' I prayed of her as she'd tell me where she belonged, and where her friends was. But she could only cry an' say as she'd go away, and wouldn't be a burden. "Don't talk silly, child," I kep' sayin'. "How can you go away in this state? Unless you're goin' to your friends?" But she said no, as she hadn't no friends to go to. An' she cried so, it fair went to my heart, the poor thing! An' I begun to be that afraid as she'd die. I am that glad as you've come, mum. If you don't mind waitin' another ten minutes, the worst o' this 'll be over, an' then I can leave 'Lizabeth to it, and go upstairs with you.'

'Is she conscious at present?'

'She was, a little while ago. It is the nights is worst, of course. Last night she talked an' talked: it's easy to see she has some trouble on her mind. I haven't got nobody as can sit with her when we have the shop full. But I was with her up to three o'clock this morning; then 'Lizabeth took my place till the shop was opened for the early corfee. I don't think she's no worse, and the doctor he don't think so. He's a clever man, I believe; at all events he has that name, as I may say, and he lives just round here in Winter Street, a house with green-painted railing, and "'Spensary" wrote up on the window.'

'Will he call again to-day?'

'I don't suppose as he *would*, but he's sure to be at 'ome in an hour, and, if you'd like, mum, I'd just send 'Lizabeth round.'

'Thank you; I think I'll go and see him.'

At last the burden of the dinner-hour was over, and 'Lizabeth could be left alone for a little. Mrs. Gandle washed her hands, in a perfunctory way, and guided her visitor to a dark flight of stairs. They ascended. On the top floor the woman stopped and whispered:

'That's the room. Should I just look in first, mum?'

'Please.'

Mrs. Gandle entered and came forth again.

'She seems to me to be asleep, mum. She lays very still, and her eyes is shut.'

'I'll go in. I shall sit with her for an hour and then go to see the doctor.'

Mrs. Ormonde passed in. It was a mean little room, not as tidy as it might have been, and far from as clean. There on the low pillow was a pale face, with golden hair disordered

about the brow; a face so wasted that it was not easy in the
first moment to identify it with that which had been so
wonderful in its spell-bound beauty by the sea-shore. But it
was Thyrza.

Her eyes were only half closed, and it was not a natural
sleep that held her. Mrs. Ormonde examined her for several
moments, then just touched her forehead. Thyrza stirred and
muttered something, but gave no sign of consciousness.

The hour went by very slowly. The traffic in the street
was incessant and noisy; two men, who were selling coals
from a cart, for a long time vied with each other in the utterance of roars drawn out in afflicting cadence. Mrs. Ormonde
now sat by the bed, regarding Thyrza, now went to the window
and looked at the grimy houses opposite. The prescribed
interval had almost elapsed, when Thyrza suddenly raised
herself and said with distinctness :

'You promised me, Lyddy; you know you promised!'

Mrs. Ormonde was standing at the foot of the bed. She
drew nearer, and, as the sick girl regarded her, asked :

'Do you know me, Thyrza?'

Thyrza fell back, fear-stricken. She spoke a few discon-
nected words, then her eyes half-closed again, and the lethargy
returned upon her.

In a few minutes Mrs. Ormonde left the room and sought
her acquaintance in the cooking department. Mrs. Gandle
gave her the exact address of the medical man, and she found
the house without difficulty.

She had to wait for a quarter of an hour in a bare, dusty,
drug-smelling ante-chamber, where also sat a woman who
coughed without ceasing, and a boy who had a formidable
bandage athwart his face. The practitioner, when he presented
himself, failed to inspire her with confidence. He expressed
himself so ambiguously about Thyrza's condition and gave on
the whole such scanty proof of intelligence that Mrs. Ormonde
felt it unsafe to leave him in charge of a case such as this. She
easily obtained his permission to summon a doctor with whom
she was acquainted.

She drove to the latter's abode, and was fortunate enough
to find him at luncheon. She was on terms of intimacy with
the family, and accepted very willingly an invitation to join
them at their meal. But the doctor could not get to Caledonian Road before the evening. Having made an appointment with him for seven o'clock, she next drove to the east

side of Regent's Park, where, in a street of small houses, she knocked at a door and made inquiries for 'Mrs. Emerson.' This lady was at home, the servant said. Mrs. Ormonde went up the first floor and entered a sitting-room.

Its one occupant was a young woman, probably of six-and-twenty, who sat in out-of-doors attire. Her look suggested that she had come home too weary even to take her bonnet off before resting. She had the air of an educated person ; her dress, which was plain and decent in the same rather depressing way as the appointment of her room, put it beyond doubt that she spent her days in some one of the manifold kinds of teaching ; a roll upon her lap plainly consisted of music. She could not lay claim to good looks, save in the sense that her features were impressed with agreeable womanliness ; the smile which followed speedily upon her expression of surprise when Mrs. Ormonde appeared, was natural, homely, and sweet. She threw the roll away, and sprang up with a joyous exclamation :

'To think that you should come just on this day and at this time, Mrs. Ormonde ! It's just by chance that I'm at home. I've only this moment come back from Notting Hill, where I found a pupil too unwell to have her lesson. And in half an hour I have to go to St. John's Wood. Just by a chance that I'm here. How vexed I should have been if I'd heard of you coming whilst I was away ! *Isn't* it annoying for people to call whilst one's away ? I mean, of course, people one really wants to see.'

'Certainly, things don't often happen so well. I'm in town on very doleful business, and have come to see if you can help me.'

'Help you ? How ? I do hope I can.'

'Have you still your spare room ? '

'Oh, yes.'

'Then I may perhaps ask you to let me have it in a few days. I must tell you how it is. A poor girl, in whom I have a great interest, has fallen ill in very dreary lodgings. I don't think it would be possible to move her at present ; I don't in fact yet know the nature of her illness exactly, and, of course, if it's anything to be afraid of, I shouldn't bring her. But that is scarcely likely ; I fancy she will want only careful nursing. Dr. Lambe is going to see her this evening, and he's just promised me to send a nurse from some institution where he has to call. If we can safely move her presently, may I bring her here?'

'Of course you may, Mrs. Ormonde! I'll get everything ready to night. Will you come up and tell me of anything you'd like me to do?'

'Not now. You look tired, and must rest before you go out again. I'll come and see you again to-morrow.'

'To-morrow? Let me see; I shall be here at twelve, but only for a few minutes; then I shan't be home again till half-past nine. Could you come after then, Mrs. Ormonde?'

'Yes. But what a long day that is! I hope your're not often so late?'

'Oh, I don't mind it a bit,' said the other, cheerfully. 'It's a pupil at Sevenoaks, piano and singing. Indeed I'm very glad. The more the better. They keep me out of mischief.'

Mrs. Ormonde smiled moderately in reply to the laugh with which Mrs. Emerson completed her jest.

'How is your husband?'

'Still far from well. I'm so sorry he isn't in now. I think ne's—no, I'm not quite sure where he is; he had to go somewhere on business.'

'He is able to get to business again?' Mrs. Ormonde asked, without looking at the other.

'Not to his regular business. Oh no, that wouldn't be safe yet. He begins to look better, but he's very weak still. It must be very hard for a man of his age to be compelled to guard against all sorts of little things that other people think nothing of, mustn't it it?'

'Yes, it must be trying,' Mrs. Ormonde replied, quietly.

Mr. Emerson was a young gentleman of leisurely habits and precarious income. Mrs. Ormonde suspected, and with reason, that he nurtured a feeble constitution at the expense of his wife's labour; he was seldom at home, and the persons interested in Mrs. Emerson had a difficulty in making his nearer acquaintance.

'And I can't think there's another man in the world who would bear it so uncomplainingly. But you know,' she added, laughing again, 'that I'm very proud of my husband. I always make you smile at me, Mrs. Ormonde. But now, I am so very, very sorry, but I'm obliged to go. I manage to catch a 'bus just at the top of the street; if I missed it, I should be half an hour late, and these are very particular people. Oh, I've such a laughable story to tell you about them, but it must wait till to-morrow. Harold says I tell it so well; he's sure I could write a novel if I tried. I think I will try some day;

I believe people make a great deal of money out of novels, don't they, Mrs. Ormonde ? '

' I have heard of one or two who tried to, but didn't.'

' I do hope the poor girl will soon be well enough to come. I'll get the room thoroughly in order to-night.'

They left the house together. Mrs. Emerson ran in the direction of the omnibus she wished to catch ; the other shortly found a vehicle, and drove back again to Bank Street, Caledonian Road.

Thyrza still lay in the same condition. In a little more than half an hour came the trained nurse of Dr. Lambe's sending, and forthwith the sick-room was got into a more tolerable condition, Mrs. Ormonde procuring whatever the nurse desired. Much private talk passed downstairs between Mrs. Gandle and 'Lizabeth, who were greatly astonished at the fuss made over the girl they had supposed friendless.

' Now let this be a lesson to you, 'Lizabeth.' said the good woman, several times. ' It ain't often as you'll lose by doin' a bit o' kindness, and the chance always is as it'll be paid back to you more than you'd never think. Any one can see as this Mrs. Ormonde's a real lady, and when it comes to settlin' up, you'll see if she doesn't know how to behave *like* a lady.'

Mrs. Ormonde took a room at a private hotel near King's Cross, whither her travelling bag was brought from Victoria. She avoided the part of the town in which acquaintances might hear of her, for her business had to be kept secret. A necessary letter despatched to Mrs. Mapper at The Chestnuts, she went once more to Bank Street and met her friend Dr. Lambe.

She told him, in general terms, all she knew of the circumstances which might have led to Thyrza's illness. At first she had been in doubt whether or not to go to Lambeth and see Lydia Trent, but on the whole it seemed better to take no steps in that direction for the present. Should the case be declared dangerous, Lydia of course must be sent for, but that was a dark possibility from which her thoughts willingly averted themselves. The sister could doubtless throw some light on Thyrza's strange calamity. What did the child's ' You know you promised me ' mean? But that would be no aid to the physician, upon whom for the present most depended. Nor did Dr. Lambe exhibit much curiosity. He seemed quickly to gather all it was really necessary for him to know, and, though he admitted that the disorder was likely to be troublesome, he gave an assurance that there was no occasion for alarm.

'You are not associated in her mind with anything distressing?' he asked of Mrs. Ormonde.

'I believe, the opposite.'

'Good. Then be by her side as often as you can, so that she may recognise you as soon as possible.' He added with a smile: 'I needn't inform Mrs. Ormonde how to behave when she *is* recognised!'

They were at a little distance from the bed, and both looked at the unconscious face.

'A very beautiful girl,' the doctor murmured.

'But you should see her in health.'

'No. I am a trifle susceptible. Well, well, we shall have her through it, no doubt.'

We have to jest a little in the presence of suffering, or how should we live our lives?

The recognition came late on the following afternoon. Thyrza had lain for a time with eyes open, watching the movements of the nurse, but seemingly with no desire to speak. Then Mrs. Ormonde came in. The watchful look at once turned upon her; for a moment that former fear showed itself, and Thyrza made an effort to rise from the pillow. Her strength was too far wasted. But as Mrs. Ormonde drew near, she was plainly known.

'Thyrza, you know me now?'

'Mrs. Ormonde,' was whispered, still with look of alarm and troubled inability to comprehend.

'You have been ill, dear, and I have come to sit with you,' the other went on, in a soothing voice. 'Shall I stay?'

There was no answer for a little, then Thyrza, with sudden revival of memory like a light kindled in her eyes, said painfully:

'Lyddy?—does Lyddy know?'

'Not yet. Do you wish her to?'

'No!—Don't tell Lyddy!—I shall be better——'

'No one shall know, Thyrza. Don't speak now. I am going to sit by you.'

Much mental disturbance was evident on the pale face for some time after this, but Thyrza did not speak again, and presently she appeared to sleep. Mrs. Ormonde left the house at midnight and was back again before nine the next morning. Thyrza had been perfectly conscious since daybreak, and had several times asked for the absent friend. She smiled when Mrs. Ormonde came at length and kissed her forehead.

'Better this morning?'

'Much better, I think, Mrs. Ormonde. But I can't lift my arm—it's so heavy.'

The doctor came late in the morning. He was agreeably surprised at the course things were taking. But Thyrza was forbidden to speak, and for much of the day she relapsed into an apathetic, scarcely conscious state. Mrs. Ormonde had preferred not to leave her the evening before, and had explained by telegram her failure to keep her appointment with Mrs. Emerson. To-night she visited her friends by Regent's Park. On looking in at the eating-house before going to her hotel for the night, she found the patient feverish and excited.

'She has been asking for you ever since you went away,' whispered the nurse.

Thyrza inquired anxiously, as if the thought were newly come to her:

'How did you know where I was, Mrs. Ormonde?'

'Mrs. Gandle found my name and address in your pocket, and wrote to me.'

'In my pocket? Why should she look in my pocket?'

'She was anxious to have a friend come to you, Thyrza.'

'Does any one else know? Lyddy doesn't—nor anybody?'

'Nobody.'

'Yes, it was in my pocket. I kept it from that time when I went to—to—oh, I can't remember!'

'To Eastbourne, dear.'

'Yes—Eastbourne!'

The only way of quieting her was for Mrs. Ormonde to sit holding her hand. It was nearly dawn when the fit of fever was allayed and sleep came.

A week passed before it was possible to think of removing her from these miserable quarters to the other room which awaited her. Mrs. Ormonde's presence had doubtless been a great aid to the sufferer in her struggle with intermittent fever and mental pain. As Thyrza recovered her power of continuous thought, she showed less disposition to talk; the trouble which still hung above her seemed to impose silence. She was never quite still save when Mrs. Ormonde sat by her, but at those times she generally kept her face averted, closing her eyes if either of her nurses seemed to watch her. She asked no questions. Mrs. Gandle came up occasionally, and to her Thyrza spoke very gently and gratefully. She asked to see 'Lizabeth, and that damsel made an elaborate toilette for the ceremony of introduction to the transformed sick-room.

'I don't believe as she's a workin' girl at all,' 'Lizabeth remarked mysteriously to her mother, afterwards. She's Mrs. Ormind's daughter, as has runned away from her 'ome, an' that's the truth of it.'

'Don't be silly, 'Lizabeth! Why, there ain't no more likeness than in that there cabbage!'

'I don't care. That's what I think, an' think it I always shall, choose what!'

'You always was obstinit!'

'Dessay I was, an' it's good as some people is. It wouldn't do for us all to think the same way; it 'ud spoil our appetites.'

One day of the week Mrs. Ormonde spent at Eastbourne. During her absence from home no letter had come from Egremont; she expected daily to hear from Mrs. Mapper that he had called at The Chestnuts, but nothing was seen of him. She preferred to keep silence, though her anxiety was constant. Out of the disparaging rumours which had found ready credence in the circle of the Tyrrells, and the facts which she had under her own eyes, it was not difficult for her to construct a story whereby this catastrophe could be explained without attributing anything more than misfortune to either Egremont or Thyrza. Her suppositions came very near to the truth. A natural, inevitable, error was that she imagined a scene of mutual declaration between the two. She could only conjecture that in some way they had frequently met, with the result which, the characters of both being understood, might have been foreseen. Possibly Egremont had thrown aside every consideration and had asked Thyrza to abandon Grail for his sake; in that case, it might be that Thyrza had fled from what she regarded as dishonourable selfishness, unable to keep her promise to Grail, alike unable to find her own happiness at his expense.

This was supposing the best. But, as a woman who knew the world, she could not altogether deny approach to fears which, in speaking with Annabel, she would not glance at. It was unlike Egremont to pass through a crisis such as this without having recourse to her sympathy, which had so long been to him as that of a mother. Perhaps he could not speak to her.

In any case, the immediate future was full of difficulties. It was a simple matter to take Thyrza to the Emersons' lodgings and get her restored to health, but what must then become of her? The best hope was that even yet she might marry Grail. Between the latter and Egremont doubtless everything was at an end; all the better, if there remained a possibility of Thyrza's forgetting this trial and some day fulfilling her promise. But in the meantime—a period, perhaps, of years—what must be done? The sisters might of course live together as hitherto and earn their living in the accustomed way, but Mrs. Ormonde understood too well the dangers of an attempt to patch together old and new. There was no foreseeing the effect of her sufferings on Thyrza's character; in spite of idealisms, suffering more often does harm than good.

In fact, she must become acquainted with the truth of the case before she could reasonably advise or help. It had seemed wise as yet to keep the discovery of Thyrza a secret, even though by disclosing it she might have alleviated others' pain. When Lydia should at length be told, perhaps difficulties would in one way or another be lessened.

Mrs. Ormonde at length spoke to the invalid of the plan for removing her. Tyyrza made no reply, but, when her friend went on to speak of the people in whose care she would be, averted her eyes as if in trouble. Mrs. Ormonde was silent for a while, then asked:

'Would you like your sister to come, when you are in the other house?'

Thyrza shook her head. She would have spoken, but instead sobbed.

'But she must be in dreadful trouble, Thyrza.'

'Will you write to her, please, Mrs. Ormonde? Don't tell her where I am, but say that I am well again. I can't see her yet—not till I have begun to work again. Do you think I can soon go and find work?'

'Do you wish, then, to live by yourself?' Mrs. Ormonde asked, hoping that the conversation might lead Thyrza to reveal her story.

'Yes, I must live by myself. I mustn't see any one for a long time. I can earn as much as I need. If I can't find anything else, Mrs. Gandle will let me stay with her.'

There was silence. Then she turned her face to Mrs. Ormonde, and, with drooping eyelids, asked in a low voice:

'Do you know why I left home, Mrs. Ormonde?'

'No, I don't, Thyrza,' the other replied gently. 'I have not seen any of your friends. I think very likely you are the only one that could tell me the truth.'

'Lyddy knows,' was spoken presently, after the shedding of a few quiet tears. 'I left a letter for her. Besides, she knew before—knew that——'

The voice faltered and ceased.

'Can you tell me what it was, Thyrza?'

'I didn't do anything wrong, Mrs. Ormonde. But I was going to be married—do you remember about Mr. Grail?'

'Yes, dear.'

'I couldn't marry him—I didn't love him.'

She turned her face upon the pillow. Mrs. Ormonde touched her with kind hand, and, when she saw that the girl could tell no more, tried to soothe her.

'I understand now, Thyrza. I know it must have been a great trouble that drove you to this. I will do nothing that you don't wish. But we must let Lyddy know that you are in safety. Suppose you write a letter and tell her that you have been ill, but that you are quite well again, and with friends. You needn't put any address on it, and you had better not mention my name. It will be enough for the present to relieve her mind.'

'Yes, I'll do that, Mrs. Ormonde, if I can write.'

'You will be able to, very soon. It would frighten Lyddy, if the letter came to her written in a strange hand.'

Mrs. Ormonde made up her mind not to let it be known that she was in communication with Thyrza. Much was still dubious, but clearly it would be the wise course to avoid the possibility of Egremont's discovering Thyrza's place of abode. For the sake of the long future, a little more must be borne in the present. She had more than Thyrza's interests to keep in mind. Egremont's happiness was also at stake, and that, after all, was the first concern with her. By prudent management, perhaps the lives of both could be saved from this seeming wreck, and sped upon their several ways—ways surely very diverse.

But Thyrza was troubled with desire to ask something. When tears had heightened the relief of having told as much as she might, she asked timidly:

'Do you know if Mr. Grail has gone to the library—
Mr. Egremont's library?'

'I have not heard. Could he go after this happening,
Thyrza?'

'Yes,' she replied eagerly, 'he would go just the same.
Why shouldn't he? It wouldn't prevent that, just because I
didn't marry him. He would go and live there with Mrs.
Grail, his mother. I said, when I wrote to Lyddy, that he'd
go to the library just the same. There was no reason why
he shouldn't, Mrs. Ormonde.'

She grew so agitated that Mrs. Ormonde, whilst asking
herself what further light this threw on the matter, endeavoured to remove her trouble.

'Then no doubt he has gone, Thyrza. We shall hear all
about it very soon.'

'You think he really has? We were to have been away
for a week, and then have gone to live at the library.
Haven't you heard anything from——'

'From whom, dear?'

'Anything from Mr. Egremont? He was beginning to
put the books on the shelves—I was told about that. It was
all ready for Gilbert to go and begin. Haven't you heard
about it, Mrs. Ormonde?'

'I've been away from home, you see. No doubt there are
letters for me.'

'I shall be so glad when I know, Mrs. Ormonde. You'll
tell me, when you've heard, won't you, please? I've been
thinking about it a long time—before I was ill, and again
since I got my thoughts back. I want to be sure of that,
more than anything. I'm sure he must have gone. Mr.
Egremont was going away somewhere, and when he came
back of course he would be told about—about me, and he
wouldn't let that make any difference to Gilbert. And then
I told Lyddy in the letter that I should come back some day.
I'm quite sure it wouldn't keep him from going to the library.'

Mrs. Ormonde was herself very desirous of knowing what
turn things had taken in Lambeth. She had no ready means
of inquiry. But doubtless Mr. Newthorpe would have intelligence; it was only too certain that the affair was being
discussed to its minutest details among the people who knew
Egremont. She determined to see Mr. Newthorpe as soon as
Thyrza was transported to the house by Regent's Park.

This took place on the following day, with care which

could not have been exceeded had the invalid been a person
as important and precious as even the late Miss Paula Tyrrell.
Mrs. Gandle was adequately recompensed ; her conviction
that Mrs. Ormonde was a real lady suffered no shock under
this most delicate of tests. Mrs. Ormonde bade farewell to
Bank Street and Caledonian Road with a great hope that duty
or necessity might never lead her thither again.

Thyrza still, of course, needed the nurse's attendance, and
accommodation was found for that person under the same
roof. When the party arrived, at mid-day, Mrs. Emerson was
at home by appointment. She assisted in carrying the invalid upstairs, where a bright warm room was in readiness—
as pleasant a change after the garret in Bank Street as any
one could have desired.

CHAPTER XXVIII

HOPE SURPRISED

MRS. TYRRELL and Annabel were lunching with friends somewhere : Mr. Newthorpe had just taken a solitary meal in the
room which he used for a study. Thither Mrs. Ormonde was
conducted.

She noticed that he looked by no means so well as he had
done before leaving Eastbourne. His greeting was nervous.
He would not sit down, preferring to move restlessly from one
position to another.

' I was about to write to you,' he said. ' What news do
you bring ? '

' I have come to you for news.'

' But you have seen Egremont ? '

' Neither seen nor heard from him.'

' Then I suppose that settles the matter. I went to his
place once, but could hear nothing of him, and since then I
have just waited till the muddy water should strain itself
clear again.'

' But I am in ignorance yet of the state of things in
Lambeth,' said Mrs. Ormonde. ' Do you know anything
about the library ? '

' Dalmaine keeps our world supplied with the latest information,' Mr. Newthorpe replied, with cold sarcasm. ' The

library scheme, I suppose, is at an end. The man Grail, we are told, pursues his old occupation.'

Mrs. Ormonde kept silence. The other continued, assuming a tone of cheerful impartiality :

' Really it is very instructive, an affair of this kind. One knows very well, theoretically, how average humanity fears and hates a nature superior to itself; but one has not often an opportunity of seeing it so well illustrated in practice. Tyrrell's attitude has especially amused me ; his lungs begin to crow like chanticleer as often as the story comes up for discussion. He has a good deal of personal liking for Egremont, but to see "the idealist " in the mud he finds altogether too delicious. His wife feels exactly in the same way, though she expresses her feeling differently. And Dalmaine—if I were an able-bodied man I rather think I should have kicked Dalmaine downstairs before this. " Lo you, what comes of lofty priggishness ! "—that is his text, and he enlarges on it in a manner worthy of himself. And the amazing thing is that it never occurs to these people to explain what has happened on any but the least charitable hypothesis.'

' What of Annabel ?' Mrs. Ormonde asked.

' She seems to have no interest in the matter. So far so good, perhaps.' He added, with a smile, ' She is revenging herself for her years of retirement.'

' I supposed so. And really seems to be enjoying herself ? '

' Astonishingly. I don't see much of her. She came in the other night to tell me that a Captain Somebody had proposed to her after six minutes of acquaintance, and laughed more gaily over it than I ever saw her. It's part of her education, of course ; probably it was wise to postpone it no longer. I wait with curiosity to hear her opinion of this world at the end of July.'

Mrs. Ormonde mused. Mr. Newthorpe walked about a little, then asked :

' What do you prophesy of their future ? '

' Of whose future ? '

' Egremont's and his wife.'

' You are premature. He is not married.'

' Oh, then you are not altogether without news ? '

' I shall take you into my confidence. I find the responsibility a little too burdensome. The fact is, this girl, Thyrza Trent, is at present in my care.'

She gave a succinct account of the recent events, and

explained them as far as her information allowed. The all-important point still remained obscure, but she showed her reasons for believing that something had passed between Egremont and Thyrza which could lead to but one result if they met again, now that the old objections were at an end.

'My desire is,' she pursued, 'to prevent that meeting. I have racked my brains over the matter, with no better result than Mrs. Grundy would at once have arrived at by noble intuition. It would be a grave mistake for Walter to marry this girl.'

'On general grounds, or from your special knowledge of her character?'

'Both. A third reason is—that I have long ago made up my mind whom he is to marry.'

'Yes,' said Mr. Newthorpe, gravely, the worry he no longer cared to conceal making him look old and feeble, 'yes, but that project has hardly become more hopeful during the last few weeks.'

'We have to think of a lifetime. I have by no means lost hope. I fear the atmosphere in which you are living has some effect upon you. The case stands thus: Walter has done nothing in the least dishonourable, but he has been carried away, as any imaginative young fellow would probably have been under the circumstances. The girl is very beautiful, wonderfully sweet and lovable; if a man ruined himself to obtain her I dare say it would be a long time before he repented.'

'At least six months.'

'No, I can't joke about Thyrza. I love her myself, and if I can by any means guide her life into a smooth channel it will make me very happy. But she must not marry Walter; that would assuredly *not* be for her happiness. The prospect before her was ideal, too good, of course, to be realised. We must devise some other future for her.'

'You think of taking her definitively from her former sphere?'

'There is no choice. She can't go and work for her living in the old way; I foresee too well what the end of *that* would be. She must either be raised or fall into the black gulfs—so beautifully is our society constructed. For the present she has to recover her health; the doctor tells me her constitution is very delicate. She must come to the sea-side as soon as she is well enough. I mustn't have her in my house, because Walter may come any day; but it will have to be Eastbourne,

I fancy, as I don't know how to make plans for her elsewhere. And in the meantime we must think.'

'A question occurs to me. Is it quite certain that she won't of her own motion communicate with Egremont ?'

'It is a question, of course. But I can't do more than take all reasonable precautions. I have a hope, though, that before long she will confide in me completely. The poor child knows nothing of this scandal; she even believes that Mr. Grail will take the librarianship as if nothing had happened. I can't with certainty foresee what effect it will have upon her when she hears the truth. Of course she must see her sister before very long. In the meantime, I have to tell her that things are going on quite smoothly ; it is the only way to keep her calm.'

'What of the sister? Is she a person to be trusted ?'

'I don't know her; but from the way in which Thyrza always speaks of her, I should think she is very trustworthy. She is some years older.'

After some further conversation, Mr. Newthorpe asked :

'What is Egremont doing, then, do you suppose ?'

'I can form no idea.'

'Won't you write to him ?'

'I think not. The poor fellow is, no doubt, going through his "everlasting Nay," as he used to say a few years ago; I fear it has come in earnest this time. He will come to me when I can really be of use to him. If I see him just now I shall have to act too much—I am bad at that.'

'Had I better try to find him ?'

'Write, if you like, and see what answer you get.'

'A gloomy business for that poor fellow in Lambeth.'

'Yes, it's hard that one can give so little thought to him. If I speak the very truth, I still have a secret hope that she may marry him. But all in good time. What a blessed thing Time is ! It makes everything easy.'

'It does. Most of all, when it destroys itself.'

He said it with a sad smile. Mrs. Ormonde turned again to the subject of Annabel. They decided that it was better to say nothing to her as yet.

In a fortnight Thyrza went to Eastbourne. She had written a letter to Lydia a few days after her establishment with Mrs. Emerson—a letter without any address at the head of it. Mrs. Emerson posted it in a remote district, that the

z

office stamp might give no clue. Mrs. Ormonde provided her with lodgings at the side of Eastbourne farthest from The Chestnuts, in the house of a decent woman who did sewing for the Home. That her days might not become wearisome for lack of occupation, it was arranged that Thyrza should give her landlady occasional help with the needle.

Her main task, however, was to recover health and strength. The sea air helped her a little, but the heaviness of her heart kept her frame languid. At first she could walk only the shortest distances; as soon as she reached the sands, she would sit down wearily and fix her eyes seawards, gazing with what other thoughts than when that horizon met her vision for the first time! She had great need of uttering all her sorrow, but could not do so to Mrs. Ormonde; it seemed to her that it would be an unpardonable presumption to speak of Mr. Egremont as she thought of him, and perhaps she could not have brought herself to tell such a secret, whoever had been involved in it, to one who, kind as she was, remained in many senses a stranger. To Lyddy, and to her alone, she could have poured out all her heart. The longing for her sister was now ceaseless. She grieved that she had left London without seeing her. In the night she sometimes cried for hours because Lyddy was so far from her.

Mrs. Ormonde came to see her every other day. Though nothing had been said on the point, Thyrza understood that, for some reason, she was not expected to go to The Chestnuts. And, indeed, it was too far for her to walk in her present weak state.

But one evening she was drawn in that direction. Her landlady had gone to Hastings, and would be absent till the next day. It was not the day for Mrs. Ormonde's visit, and rain since morning had made it impossible to leave the house; the hours had dragged wearily. After tea the clouds broke, and soon there were warm rays from the westering sun. Thyrza was glad to leave her room. She walked into the main street of the town, for her solitude was become a pain, and she felt a desire to be among people, even though she could speak to no one. She came to the tree-shadowed road which, as she well remembered, led to Mrs. Ormonde's house. It tempted her on: she would like to look at the house. A friend lived there, and her heart ached to be near someone who cared for her. The prime need of her life was love, and love alone could restore her strength and give her courage to live.

It was nearer than she thought. Though troubled by the consciousness that she ought not to have come so far in this direction, and that perhaps her strength would be overtaxed before she could reach home again, she went still on and on, until, reaching the point where another road joined that by which she had come, she found The Chestnuts just before her. Beyond the house, the hill rose darkly and hid the setting sun. As she stood, a man issued from the adjoining road and walked straight towards the entrance of the garden. Her eyes followed him, and, though for a moment she did not believe their evidence, they told her that Egremont had passed so near to her that a whisper would have drawn his attention.

She was in the shade of thick trees ; perhaps that circumstance, and the dark colour of her dress, accounted for his not observing her. He was walking quickly, too, and was looking fixedly at the house.

She followed. Had her voice been at her command, in that instant of recognition she would have called to him. But all her powers seemed to desert her, and she was rather borne onwards than advanced by any effort of her own.

He had passed through the gate when she reached the end of the garden wall. Losing him from sight, she understood what she was doing, and stayed her steps. A sense of having escaped a great danger made her tremble so that she feared she must fall to the ground if she could not find some place in which to rest. A few steps brought her into a piece of common ground, which lay in the rear of the garden, and here, at the foot of the wall, were some pieces of timber, the severed limbs of a tree that had fallen in the past winter. Here she could sit, leaning against the brickwork and letting her heart throb itself into quietness.

The wall was a low one, and above it in this place rose a screen of trellis, overgrown with creepers, making the rear of a spacious summer-house, which Mrs. Ormonde had had constructed for the use of children who had to be sheltered from too much either of sun or breeze when they were brought out of doors. Thyrza had not been resting for more than a minute or two, when a voice spoke from the other side of the wall, so plainly that she started, thinking she was observed and addressed. The voice was Mrs. Ormonde's.

' So at last,' she said, ' you have come.'

There was a brief silence, then the tones for which she waited once more fell upon her ear.

' You are alone to-night ? ' asked Egremont.

' Quite. I have been reading and thinking. Shall we go into the house ? '

' If you will let me, I had rather sit with you here.'

Again there was silence. When Mrs. Ormonde spoke, it was in a lower voice, and such as one uses in reply to a look of affection.

' Why have you kept me in anxiety about you for so long, Walter ? '

' I have had no mind to speak to any one, not even to you. I had nothing to tell you that would please you to hear. Often I have resolved to leave England for good, and give no account of myself to any one. It seemed unkind of you not to write. I waited till I knew you must have heard all that people had to say of me, and then every day I expected your letter. You could only be silent for one reason.'

' Why, then, have you come now ? '

'Because I am ill and can be alone no longer.'

Thyrza scarcely breathed. It was as though all her senses had merged in one—that of hearing. Her eyes beheld nothing, and she was conscious of no more bodily pain. She listened for the very breathing of the two, who were so close to her that she might almost have touched them.

' How do you know that people are occupying themselves with your concerns at all ? '

' From Jersey I went to France. When I reached London again, knowing nothing of what had happened whilst I was away, I met Dalmaine and his wife at Charing Cross station. They turned away, and refused to speak to me. When I got home, I found what it meant. Grail told me plainly what the general opinion was.'

' You saw Grail ? '

' Of course. You think, naturally, that I should have hidden my face from him.'

' Don't be so harsh with me. You forget that I have still to learn everything.'

' Yes, I will tell you ; I will explain ; I will defend myself. I want your sympathy, and I will do my best to prove that I am not contemptible.'

' Hush ! Be quiet for a moment. I have not written to you because I thought it needless to make conjectures, and ask questions, and give assurances, when you were sure, sooner or later, to come and tell me the whole story. I won't pretend that I have not had my moments of uneasiness. For instance, I wrote to you to Jersey, and the letter was returned to me; that came disagreeably, in connection with news I just then had from London; it was only human to suppose that for some reason you had talked of going to Jersey, and then had not gone there at all.'

'Grail followed me there, and, failing to find me, of course had the same thought.'

'And yet, you know, I could think more calmly than was possible for him. Now tell me all that you wish. What had happened, that this suspicion fell upon you?'

Thyrza heard a complete and truthful account of all that had passed between herself and Egremont, from the first meeting in the library to their parting near Lambeth Bridge.

Then Mrs. Ormonde asked :

'And where is she?'

'If only I knew! She has written to her sister, but without saying where she is, only that she has been ill, and is safe with people who are kind to her.'

'And what is your explanation of her disappearance?'

'I believe she could not marry Grail, loving another man.'

The silence that followed seemed very long to the listener. She dreaded lest they should end their conversation here. In that story of those meetings and partings, as told by Egremont, there had now and then been a word, a tone, that seemed to bear meaning yet incredible to her. By degrees she was realising all that her flight had entailed upon those she left, things undreamt of hitherto. But the last word of explanation was still to come. She did not dare to anticipate it, yet her life seemed to depend upon his saying something more.

'Have you made efforts to find her?' Mrs. Ormonde at length asked.

'Every possible effort.'

'With what purpose?'

'Need I tell you?'

'You think it is your duty to offer her reparation for what she has suffered, because you were unwillingly the cause of it?'

'Yes, if that is the same thing as saying that I love her, and that I wish to make her my wife.'

'In a sense I suppose it is the same thing. You have been compelled to think so much of her, that pity and a desire to do your best for an unhappy girl have come to seem love. Remember that, by your own admission, you are ill; you

cannot judge soundly of anything, even of your own feelings.
You have done a good deal of harm, Walter, though unintentionally ; do you wish to do yet more ? '

  ' How ? '

  ' By binding yourself for life to a poor girl who can never
by any possibility be a fit companion for you. I have seen
such marriages ; I have seen the beginning of them and the
end. You, least of all men, should fall into such an error.
Oh yes, I know ; you are not brutal ; you would never as
much as speak an unkind word. No, but you would do what
in this case would be worse. Brutally treated, Thyrza would
die and be out of her misery ; with you, she would drag
through years of increasing wretchedness. Your thwarted
life would be her long torture. Remember how often I have
told you that you have much that is feminine in your character. You have little real energy ; you are passive in great
trials; it is easier to you to suffer than to act. Your idealism
is often noble, but never heroic. You have talked to me of
your natural nearness to people of the working class, and I
firmly believe that you are further from them—for any such
purpose as this in question—than many a man who counts
kindred among the peerage. You have a great deal of spiritual pride, and it will increase as your mind matures. You
think you *are* mature ; tell me in ten years (if I am alive, old
woman that I am !) how you look back on your present self.
Walter Egremont, if ever you ask Thyrza to marry you, you
will be acting with cruel selfishness—yes, selfishness, for all
that you would pay bitterly for it in the end. You will be
acting in a way utterly unworthy of a man who has studied
and reflected.'

  Thyrza heard Egremont laugh.

  ' To hear all this from you,' he said, ' surprises me very
much.'

  ' You credit me with so little power of mind ? '

  ' I thought you were the last to talk the common talk of
the world that has outlived its generous instincts.'

  'Pray believe that there is such a thing as outliving youthful passion, and yet retaining all the generous feeling that you
speak of. I am not an ignoble schemer, and you know that I
am not. Think over my arguments before you scorn me.'

  ' You think me so boyish and weak-minded that I cannot
distinguish between pure love and base ? One thing I left out
of my narrative just now. I ought to have said that I was *not*

wholly without blame in that intercourse. I strove with myself to seem nothing more than friendly to her, and yet I know that at times I spoke as no mere friend would have done, and simply because I could not help it. I loved Thyrza even then with more intensity of pure feeling than I had ever before known, and now I love her with a love which lasts a lifetime. You have no right to pronounce so confidently upon her fitness or unfitness to mate with me; your knowledge of her is very slight. I know her as a woman can only be known by the man who loves her. You cannot judge for me in this case; no one could judge for me. I shall act on my conviction; it is poor waste of life to do otherwise.'

A pause, whereof the seconds were to one ear beaten out in heart-throbs. Then Mrs. Ormonde said, very quietly:

'You have told Mr. Grail of this intention?'

'Yes.'

'It has never occurred to you that the great wrongs this man has suffered might yet be repaired, perchance, if you were willing to let them be?'

'I have suffered on his account more than I can say. But it is certain that he and Thyrza would never marry after this.'

'I see no such certainty.'

'Then it merely comes to this, that he and I love the same woman, and must abide by her decision.'

'The library?'

'Gone. I can give no thought to it, for I am suffering a greater loss. Be human! Be honest! Would you not despise me if, loving her as I do, I came to you and puled about the overthrow of my schemes for founding a public library? Let it go! Let the people rust and rot in ignorance! I am a man of flesh and blood, and the one woman that the world contains is lost to me!'

Mrs. Ormonde seemed to think long over this passionate outcry. Egremont broke the silence.

'Once more, be human! She writes to her sister that she has been ill, but is now taken care of by friends. What friends? You are not ignorant of the world. How small a chance it is that she has fallen among people who will protect her! A girl with her beauty, and so simple, so trustful—friends, indeed! I am all but frenzied to think of the dangers that may surround her. She is more to me than my life's blood, and perhaps even now she is in terrible need of some honest man to protect her. And you can talk coldly about prudence, about what we shall think and say years hence! Well, I can talk no more. To-morrow morning I shall go back to London and go on searching for her, walking about the streets day and night, wearing my life away in longing for her. I have done with the past, and all those I used to call my friends. There is no room in my thought for anything but her memory and the desire to find her. Let us say good-bye, Mrs. Ormonde. If I am wrong and selfish as you say, then it is beyond my power to conquer the faults.'

The listener heard a deep sigh. Then :

' Walter, sit down ; you are not going from me like that.'

' I can't stay ; I can't talk as you wish to! I am so utterably miserable, and I came to you because I had always known you gentle and sympathetic.'

' I would never be anything else with you. But listen ; have you entirely forgotten Annabel ? '

' She is as little to me as if I had never seen her. You cannot say that I have any obligation to her. I asked her to be my wife, and she refused me; that was the end. There indeed, if you like, I was misled. I admired and respected her, and made myself believe that it was love. Again and again I doubted myself, even then. Since I first knew that I loved Thyrza, I have never doubted one moment. You, for all your subtle analysis of my character, do not know me. You think I must have a woman of fine intellect for my companion. You are wrong. What I need, I have seen in one face, and one only.'

Mrs. Ormonde spoke in a changed voice.

' On one point I can set your mind at rest, and I will, for I cannot bear to see you suffering. It is true that Thyrza is with friends. I know the people with whom she is living.'

' You know them ? You know where Thyrza is ? '

' I found her where she lay ill ; the chance of her having my address in her possession led the people of the house to send for me. I took her away, and put her in good care.'

' And you could keep this from me ? '

' You see why I did. Can I trust you not to abuse my kindness ? '

' You mean—— ? '

' That it will be wholly dishonourable if you make any attempt to discover her after this. Do so, and we are friends no longer.'

How can you exact any such promise as that ? '

' Because I am within my right in exacting it. I make a bargain with you, Walter. For two years from now Thyrza remains under my guardianship. At the end of that time, you are at liberty to see her. I give you my word that neither directly nor indirectly will I seek to influence her affections as regards either you or Grail ; I shall never speak to her on such subjects, nor will any one with whom I have authority. Is it agreed ? '

Poor heart, again beating out the seconds !

' Will Grail know where she is living ? '

' He will not. She must see her sister from time to time, but it shall be away from her ordinary dwelling, and Thyrza will understand the conditions. I shall offer her no explanation ; it shall merely be my desire, and if she prove untrustworthy in this small matter, I think you will admit that no harm has been done—you and I will only have a new light on her character. It is very simple, provided that we two can trust each other, and that Thyrza is what you think her. I need not say, by-the-by, that she will not be living here ; you can freely come to me as often as you please.'

Would he never reply ?

' For two years ? That is a long time.'

' Not at all, the circumstances considered. Are you afraid of submitting your love to the test ? '

' You asked me to trust you implicitly. It is a great thing, you being my enemy to begin with.'

' Your enemy ? Well, then, your enemy ; and still I ask you to trust me. I have never yet betrayed man or woman, Walter.'

' Never ; that I know well ! Forgive me. On this day, this day of the month, two years hence, I may go to her ? '

' On this day of the month, two years hence. Is it a bargain ? '

' I agree. Thyrza could not be in safer keeping.'

He went on :

' What a load you have lifted from me ! If that suspense had continued much longer, I don't know how I should have borne it. And you were with her in her illness ? Tell me about her. Was she gravely ill ? Tell me where you found her.'

' No ; it is needless. I am a bad one to hear love confidences ; I get impatient, and am apt to be satirical. I shall never talk to you of Thyrza.'

' But if she falls ill again, I must know.'

' I hope for better things. Tell me just one thing, before we change the subject. What is your opinion of her sister? What do you really know of her? '

' I know nothing save what I have gathered from Thyrza's talk, and from Grail's. I never saw her. But there can be little doubt that she is of sterling character.'

' Well, let it be. Now come in with me. I suppose you have had no thought for such a foolish ceremony as dinner? '

Their voices passed into silence. By this time it was dark, and the tall chestnuts beyond the house rustled in a cool breeze from the sea. Thyrza did not move for several minutes; when at length she endeavoured to rise, her numbed limbs would scarcely sustain her. She looked up and saw the yellow crescent of a young moon sailing in a sky of delicate pearl hue.

One glance at the upper windows of the house, and then, with strength which seemed to pass into her limbs from the sharp air, she set out for the cottage which was her present home.

CHAPTER XXIX

TOGETHER AGAIN

LYDIA held desperately to hope through the days and the nights. From all others Thyrza might hide away, but could she persist in cruelty to her sister? Surely in some way a message, if only a message, would be delivered; at least there would come a word to relieve this unendurable suspense. Every added day of silence was an added fear.

Unable to associate with acquaintances to whom Thyrza's name had become an unfailing source of vulgar gossip, she changed her place of work. Work had still to be done, be her heart ever so sore; the meals must be earned, though now they were eaten in solitude. And she worked harder than ever, for it was her dread that at any moment she might hear of Thyrza in distress or danger, and she must have money laid by for such an emergency. All means of inquiry were used, save that of going to the police-court and having the event made public through the newspapers. Neither Lydia nor

Gilbert could bear to do that, even after they felt assured that the child was somewhere wandering alone.

Totty Nancarrow was an active ally in the search, though Lydia did not know it. Totty, as soon as that unfortunate game of cross-purposes with Luke Ackroyd had come to an end, experienced a revival of all her kindness for Thyrza. Privately she was of opinion that no faith whatever should be given to Egremont's self-defence. In concert with Ackroyd, she even planned an elaborate scheme for tracking Egremont in his goings hither and thither. They discovered that he was very seldom at his rooms in Great Russell Street, but their resources did not allow them to keep a watch upon him when he was away from town, which appeared to be very frequently the case. Circumstances of a darkly suggestive kind they accumulated in abundance, and for weeks constantly believed themselves on the point of discovering something. Bunce was taken into their confidence, but he, poor fellow, had occupation enough for his leisure at home, since Bessie was at Eastbourne. Little Nelly Bunce often fretted in vain for the attentions of 'Miss Nanco,' upon whom she had begun to feel a claim. 'Miss Nanco,' for the nonce a female detective, had little time for nursing.

And Gilbert Grail was once more going to his daily labour, not at the same factory, however, for he too could not mix with men who knew him. About a fortnight after the day on which he should have been married, he got a place at candle-works in Battersea. He could not leave the house in Walnut Tree Walk, for he, as persistently as Lydia, clung to the hope that Thyrza might reappear in her home some night. To go away would be to say good-bye for ever to that dream which had so glorified a few months of his life, and in spite of all he could not do that.

In comparison with his own, the suffering of others seemed trifling. When his mother went about in silence, bending more than she had done, all interest in the things of life and in her studies of Swedenborg at an end, he thought that much of it was due to her wish to show sympathy with him. When Lydia sat through an hour with her face hidden in her hands, he knew that the day had been very dark and weary with her, but said in himself that a sister's love was little compared with such as his. He would not reason on what had happened, save when to do so with Lydia brought him comfort; alone, he brooded over his hope. It was the only way to save himself from madness.

On the day after seeing Egremont he received a long letter from him. Egremont wrote from his heart, and with a force of sincerity which must have swept away any doubts, had such still lingered with the reader. The inevitable antagonism of the personal interview was a pain in his memory; if the intercourse of friendship was for ever at an end for them, he could not bear to part in this way, with hesitating words, with doubts and reticences. 'In your bitter misery,' he said, 'you may accuse me of affecting sympathy which I do not feel, and may scorn my expressions of grief as a cheap way of saving my self-respect. I will not compare my suffering with yours, but none the less it is intense. This is the first great sorrow of my life, and I do not think a keener one will ever befall me. Keep this letter by you ; do not be content to read it once and throw it aside, for I have spoken to you out of my deepest feeling, and in time you will do me more justice than you can now.' And further on : 'As to that which has parted us, there must be no ambiguity, no pretence of superhuman generosity. I should lie if I said that I do not wish to find Thyrza for my own sake. If I find her, I shall ask her to be my wife. I wanted to say this when we spoke together, but could not ; neither was I calm enough to express this rightly, nor you rightly to hear it.'

Gilbert allowed a day or two to go by, then made answer. He wrote briefly, but enough to show Egremont that the man's natural nobility could triumph over his natural resentment. It was a moving letter, its pathos lying in the fact that its writer shunned all attempt to be pathetic. 'Now that I know the truth,' he said, 'I can only ask your pardon for the thoughts I had of you ; you have not wronged me, and I can have no ill-feeling against you. If Thyrza is ever your wife, I hope your happiness may be hers. As for the other things, do not reproach yourself. You wished to befriend me, and I think I was not unworthy of it. Few things in life turn out as we desire ; to have done one's best with a good intention is much to look back upon—very few have more.'

Gilbert did not show this letter to Lydia, nor had he told her of what he had learnt in the conversation with Egremont. The fear would have seemed more intolerable if he had uttered it. But the hope which supported him was proof against even such a danger as this. To his mind there was something unnatural in a union between Egremont and Thyrza ; try as he would, he could not realise it as having come to pass. The two were parted by so vast a social distinction, and, let Nature say what it will, the artificialities of life are wont to prevail. He could imagine an unpermitted bond between them, with the necessary end in Thyrza's sacrifice to the world's injustice; but their marriage appeared to him among the things so unlikely as to be in practice impossible. Of course the wish was father to the thought. But he reasoned upon the hope which would not abandon him. Thyrza had again and again proved the extreme sensitiveness of her nature; she could not bear to inflict pain. He remembered how she had once come back after saying good-night, because it seemed to her that she had spoken with insufficient kindness. The instance was typical. And now, though tempted by every motive that can tempt a woman, she had abandoned herself to unimagined trials rather than seek her own welfare at another's expense. To fulfil her promise had been beyond her power, but, if there must be suffering, she would share it. And now, in that wretched exile, he knew that self-pity could not absorb her. She would think of him constantly, and of such thought would come compassion and repentance. Those feelings might bring her back. If only she came back, it was enough. She could not undo what she had done, but neither could she forbid him to live with eyes on the future.

Reasoning so, he did his daily work and lived waiting.

Then came the day which put a term to the mere blank of desolation, and excited new hopes, new fears. Thyrza's letter arrived. It was delivered in the afternoon, and Lydia found it pushed under her door when she returned from work. She listened for Gilbert's coming home, then ran down to the sitting-room, and, without speaking, put the letter into his hand. Mrs. Grail was present.

'I knew it had come,' she said, in her low voice, which of late had begun to quaver with the feebleness of age. 'Mrs. Jarmey brought it here to show me, because she guessed who it was from.'

Gilbert said very few words, and when he returned the letter, Lydia went upstairs with it, to nurse the treasure in solitude. It lay on her lap, and again and again she read it through. Every word she probed for meanings, every stroke of the pen she dwelt on as possibly revealing something. 'I have been poorly, dear, but I am quite well again now.' That sentence was the one her eye always turned to. The writing was not quite the same as Thyrza's used to be; it showed weakness, she thought. She had foreseen this, that Thyrza would fall ill; in fear of that she had deprived herself of all save the barest necessaries, that she might save a little money. But strangers had tended her sister, and with her gladness at receiving news mingled jealousy of the hands that had been preferred to her own. Only now the bitterness of separation seemed to be tasted to the full.

At half-past nine she went downstairs again, knowing that she would find Gilbert alone. He was sitting unoccupied, as always now in the evenings, for his books gathered dust on the unregarded shelves. Seeing that she had the letter with her, he held out his hand for it in silence.

'There's one thing I'm afraid of,' Lydia began, when she had glanced at him once or twice. 'Do you think it's friends of *his* that she's with?'

He shook his head.

'He would have told me if he'd found her.'

'Are you quite sure?'

'Yes, I am sure. He wouldn't have said where she was, very likely, but he'd tell us that she was found.'

Gilbert had reason to think of Lydia as a great power on his side. The girl was now implacable against Egremont. She had ceased to utter her thoughts about him, since she knew that they pained her friend, but in her heart she kept a determined enmity. The fact of Thyrza's love in no way influenced her: her imagination was not strong enough to enable her to put herself in Thyrza's place and see Egremont as her sister saw him. With the narrowness of view which is common enough in good and warm-hearted women, she could only regard him as the disturber of happiness, the ruin of Thyrza's prospects. Lydia was not ambitious; she had never been enthusiastic about Gilbert's promotion to the librarianship, and doubtless it would have pleased her just as well for Thyrza to marry Grail if the latter had had no thought of quitting his familiar work. Consequently it was no difficulty to her to leave altogether out of sight Egremont's purposed benefits to Gilbert. She no longer believed that he was innocent of designs in his intercourse with Thyrza. This change was a natural enough consequence of Lydia's character, just as it had been perfectly natural for her to think and speak as she had done under the first shock of her sister's flight. Since then she had suffered terribly, and the suffering turned her against him who was the plain cause of it.

'What is the post-mark on the envelope?' Gilbert asked, Lydia continuing to brood over her jealousies and dreads.

The stamp was 'Charing Cross.' Small help derivable from that.

'She doesn't even say whether she'll write again,' Lydia murmured.

Gilbert said presently: 'I shall write to Mr. Egremont, and tell him that we have heard.'

'Oh no!' Lydia protested, indignantly. 'Why should you tell him? You mustn't do that, Gilbert; I don't want him to know.'

'I promised him, Lyddy. Of course I shouldn't tell him where she was, if we knew, but I promised to let him hear if we had any news.'

'Then I don't see why you promised such a thing. It doesn't concern him.'

Gilbert was troubled by this persistence. Lydia spoke with earnest disapproval. He could not do as he wished in defiance of her, yet he must certainly keep his promise to Egremont.

'You must remember,' he said gently, 'that he has reason to be anxious, as well as we.'

'What have we to do with that?' she replied, stubbornly. 'He has no right to think anything about her.'

'I mean, Lyddy, that he is troubled because of our trouble. All I want to do is to tell him that a letter has come from Thyrza, without address, and that she says she has found friends. Won't you consent to that?'

After a short silence, Lydia replied:

'I won't say any more, Gilbert. As you like.'

'No, that's not enough. I must have your full agreement. It's either right or wrong to do it, and you must make up your mind clearly.'

'I shouldn't wonder if he knows,' she said briefly.

'He doesn't know. I shall not distrust him again. He would have told me.'

'Then you had better write.'

'You see that I ought to?'

'Yes, as you promised. But I can't see why you did.'

This form of consent had to suffice, feminine as it was. But Gilbert knew Lydia well by this time, and no trifling fault could touch his deep affection and respect for her.

She was very lonely in these days, Lydia. Of her own

sex, she had now no friend, unless it were poor old Mrs. Grail.
By changing her place of employment, she had lost even the
satisfaction of being among familiar faces, and her new work-
mates thought her dull. The jokes and gossip of each morning were things of the past; she plied her needle every moment
of the working day, her thoughts fixed on one unchanging
subject. Yes, for she could not really think even of Ackroyd;
he was always, it is true, a presence in her mind, but there
was no more pondering about him. Every stitch at the lining
of a hat meant a fraction of a coin, and each day's result was
to have earned something towards the money saved for Thyrza's
assistance.

With Mary Bower she spoke no longer, not even formal
words. That insult on the miserable night had been a blow
Mary could not soon forgive, for it came just at the moment
when, having heard her parents' talk about Thyrza, she was
sincerely anxious to reunite herself to her former friend and
be what comfort to her she might. So now, whenever Lydia
went to see Mr. Boddy, she gave a private signal at the side
door, and the old man descended to admit her. Then, Totty
Nancarrow. Strangely, Lydia could now have been almost
friends with Totty; she did not know why. She met her by
chance occasionally, and nodded, or at most spoke a brief
greeting, yet each time she would have liked to stop and talk
a little. Totty had been Thyrza's close friend; that formerly
had been a source of jealous feeling, now it seemed to have
become an attraction. Totty gave looks that were not unkind,
but did not make advances; she was a little ashamed of the
way she had behaved when Lydia came to her for help.

Lydia did not think it necessary to tell Gilbert that she
too wanted to let someone know that there was news from
Thyrza. After leaving the parlour, she ran out to a little
shop in Kennington Road and purchased a sheet of note-paper
and an envelope. Writing a letter was by no means a simple
thing to Lyddy; it was after midnight before she had schemed
the sentences—or rather, the one long hyper-Attic sentence
—in which she should convey her intelligence to Ackroyd.
Several things were to be considered in this composition.
First, it must be as brief as possible; then, it must be very
formal in its mode of address. Both these necessities came
of the consideration that the letter would of course be shown
to Totty Nancarrow, and Totty must have no cause of complaint. ' Dear Mr. Ackroyd '—that was written, but might it

stand ? It meant so much, so much. But how else to begin?
Did not everybody begin letters in that way ? She really
could not say 'Dear Sir.' Then—for the letter *must* be
finished, the hour was getting so late—'Yours truly, Lydia
Trent.' Surely that was commonplace enough. Yes, but to
say 'yours;' that too meant so much. Was she not indeed his?
And might not Totty suspect something in that 'yours ?'
You see that Lyddy was made a very philosopher by love;
she had acquired all at once the power of seeing through the
outward show of things, of perceiving what really lies below our
conventional forms. Well, the letter had to stand; she had
no second sheet of note-paper, and she had no more time, for
the weary eyes and hands must get their rest for to-morrow's
toil. She closed the envelope and addressed it; then, the ink
being dry, she put the written name just for an instant to her
lips. Totty could not divine that, and it was not so great a
wrong. Perhaps Lydia would not have done it, but that the
great burden upon her was for the moment lightened, and she
longed to tell someone how thankful she was.

Would he reply by letter ? Or would he make an opportunity of seeing her? Since the forming of that sudden
intimacy under the pressure of misery, he and she had not
seen each other often. They always spoke if they met, and
Lydia was very grateful to him for the invariable kindness of
his voice and his look, but of course it was not to be expected,
not to be desired, that they should sustain the habit of conversing together as close friends. Ackroyd had evidently remembered that it was unwise; perhaps he had reported the
matter to Totty, with the result that Totty had pronounced a
quiet opinion, which it was only becoming in him to respect.

He wrote back; the letter came as speedily as could have
been expected. 'Dear Miss Trent,' and 'Yours truly'—even
as she had written. How can one write such words and mean
nothing by them ? But he said, 'Believe me, yours truly;'
ah, she would never have ventured upon that! To be sure, it
meant nothing, nothing; but she liked that 'Believe me.' He
said he was very glad indeed that Thyrza had written, and he
hoped earnestly that more satisfactory news would come before
long. Very short. Lydia put away the note with that she
had received from the same writer one sad morning in the
work-room. How long ago that seemed !

More than a month of summer went by, and Lydia waited
still for another word from her sister. After each day's

disappointment, she closed her eyes saying, 'It will come to-morrow.' During the hours she spent at home the only event that interested her was the passing of the postman. She watched constantly from the window at the times when letters were delivered, and if, a rare chance, the man in uniform stopped at the door below, she sprang to the top of the stairs and hung there breathless, to see if someone would come up. No, the letter was never for her. On coming home from work she always threw open her door eagerly, for perhaps she would see the white envelope lying on the floor again. The defeat of hope always made the whole room seem barren and cold. Sunday was of all days in the week the longest and gloomiest; on that day there was no postman.

But at length came the evening when, looking down by mere dull habit as she opened her room door, behold the white envelope lay there. She could not believe that at last it was really in her hand. As she took the letter out, there fell from it a light slip of paper; with surprise she saw that it was a post-office order. This time a full address stood at the head of the page.

'Eastbourne!' she uttered. 'Then she is with Mrs. Ormonde, and Mrs. Ormonde is *his* friend.'

Hastily her eyes sought the sense of what was written. Thyrza said that she was well, but could not live longer without seeing her sister. Lydia was to come by as early a train as possible on the following morning; money was enclosed to provide for her expenses. No news could be sent, but in a few hours they would talk to each other. Finally, the address was to be kept a secret, to be kept even from Gilbert; she depended upon Lydia to obey her in this. A postscript added: ' You will easily find the house. I would come to the station and meet every train, but I couldn't bear to see you there first.'

Lydia had deep misgivings, but they did not occupy her mind for long. She was going to see Thyrza; that, as she realised it, rang a peal of joy in her ears and made her forget all else. But the money she would not use; she had enough to pay her fare, and in any case she would somehow have obtained it rather than spend this, which came she knew not from whom. It might be that Thyrza had earned it, but perhaps it was given to her by an enemy—under this name Lydia had come to think of Egremont.

She told Gilbert in private. The concealment from him

of Thyrza's address he seemed to accept as something quite natural. He drew a sigh of relief, and, as Lydia left him, gave her a look whose meaning was not hard to understand.

The new day did come at last, and at last Lydia was in the train ; she had remembered that by which Thyrza went with Bessie, and she took the same. A strange feeling she had as, instead of going to the work-room, she set off through the sunshine to the railway station ; a holiday feeling, had she known what holiday meant. That she was going for the first time to the sea-side was nothing ; her anticipation was only of Thyrza's look and Thyrza's first kiss. Why were all the other people who went by the same train so joyous and so full of hope ? Were they too going to meet someone very dear to them ?

She had copied the address on to a piece of paper, which she kept inside her glove ; impossible that she should forget, but even impossibilities must be provided for. When she descended at Eastbourne, she was so agitated and so perplexed by the novelty of the experience that with difficulty she found her way into the street. She hurried on a little way, then remembered that the first thing was to ask a direction. On inquiring from a woman who stood in a shop-door, she at once had her course clearly indicated. Forwards then, as quickly as she could walk. How astonishingly clean the streets were! What great green trees grew everywhere! How bright and hot was the sunshine !—Yes, this turn ; but to make quite sure she would ask again. A policeman, in an unfamiliar uniform, reassured her. Now a turn to the right— and of a sudden everything ceased; there seemed to be nothing but blue sky before her. Ah, that was the sea, then; its breath came with wondrous sweetness on her heated face. But what was the sea to her ! Along here to the left again. She must be very near now. Again she asked, and in so uncertain a voice that she had to repeat her question before it was under- stood. Number so-and-so ; why, it was just over yonder ; the cottage that seemed to be built of some glistening white stone. And so she stood at the door.

A child opened, and, without questioning, laughed and said, ' Come in, please.' She found herself at once in a com- fortable kitchen. The child pointed to an inner door, which, in the same moment, softly opened.

' Lyddy ! '

So it had come at last. Once again they were heart to

heart. Lydia cried as though something dreadful had befallen her; Thyrza sobbed once or twice, but she had shed so many tears for misery that none would come at the bidding of joy.

They were in a little room which looked through a diamond-paned lattice upon the flat beach which lies at this side of Eastbourne. In front was a black, tar-smeared house of wood for the keeping of fishers' nets, and fishing boats lay about it. When Lydia's emotion had spent itself, Thyrza drew her to the window, threw back the lattice, and said 'Look!'

'I can't look at anything but you, dearest,' was the answer.

'But let us look together, just for a minute, then we shall come fresh again to each other's faces. The sea, Lyddy! I love it; it seems to me the best friend I ever had.'

'You're very pale still, darling. You've been ill, and you wouldn't send for me. How cruel that was of you, Thyrza! You might have got so bad you couldn't send; you might have died before I could know anything. Dear, you don't love me as I love you. I couldn't have given you that pain, no, not for any one, not for any one in the world. Oh, why didn't you let me go away with you? I'd have gone anywhere; I'd have done anything you asked me. Are you sure you're well again? Do you feel strong?—What is it?'

Thyrza had let herself sink upon a chair, and her face, which had indeed been strangely colourless, was for a moment touched with pain. But she laughed.

'It's only with exciting myself so, Lyddy. I haven't stood or sat still a minute since I got up. Oh, I'm as well as ever I was, better than ever I was in my life. Don't I look happy? I only wanted you; that was the only thing. I never felt so well and happy.'

Somebody knocked at the door.

'That's something for you to eat after your journey,' said Thyrza. 'It's too early for dinner yet, but you must have just a mouthful.'

She went out and came back with a tray, on which was milk and cake.

Lydia shook her head.

'I can't eat, Thyrza. I want you to tell me everything.'

'I shan't tell you anything at all till you've had a glass of milk. Let me take your things off. You're going to stay with me to-night, you know. Sit still, and let me take them off.

Dear, good old Lyddy! Oh, will you do my hair for me to-morrow morning? Think of doing my hair again! Poor old Lyddy, you always did cry when you were glad, and never for anything else. Shall I sit on your lap, like I used to do after I'd been naughty, years and years ago? Oh, years and years; you don't know how old I am, Lyddy. You don't think you're still older than me, do you? No, that's all altered. Mrs. Guest here asked me how old I was the other day, and I wouldn't tell her, because the truth wasn't true. I was so ill, Lyddy dear; I did think I should die, and I should have wished to, but for you. I couldn't send for you: I was ashamed to. I'd behaved too bad to you and to everybody. But people were kind, much kinder than they'd need have been. Some day I'll go and see Mrs. Gandle and tell her I haven't forgotten her kindness. You shall go with me, Lyddy. But no, no; you wouldn't like. We'll forget all about that.'

' Where was that, Thyrza?'

' A place where I got work. Do you know where the Caledonian Road is?'

Lydia tightened her embrace, as if shame and hardship still threatened her dear one and she would guard her from them.

' But how did you get better? What happened then?'

' When I was very bad, Mrs. Gandle one night looked in my pocket to see if I'd anything about me to show where I belonged. And she found that bit of paper with Mrs. Ormonde's name and address. But wait, Lyddy; I've something to say. Did you do as I asked, about not telling any one where I was?'

' I didn't tell any one, Thyrza. Nobody knew where I was going. I mean, of course I told Gilbert that I was going to you, but not where you were.'

Thyrza, after a short pause, asked very quietly:

' How is Gilbert, Lyddy?'

' He seems pretty well, dear.'

' Has he—has he felt it very hard?'

She kept her eyes veiled, and pressed her head closer to Lydia's shoulder.

' He's had a great deal to go through, dear.'

The touch of severity in Lydia's voice came of her thoughts turning to Egremont. But Thyrza felt herself judged and rebuked; she trembled.

' What is he doing?' she asked, in a voice barely audible.

'He goes to work, as usual. It's a new place.'

'Poor Gilbert! Oh, I'm sorry for him! He never deserved this of me. Lyddy,' she added in a whisper, 'it makes you so cruel to other people when you love any one.'

Lydia found no answer. She was gazing through the open window, but saw nothing of sea or sky. She, then, did not know what it was to love? Well, love is of many kinds.

'But I was going to say something, Lyddy,' Thyrza pursued, when a kiss upon her hair assured her that from one at all events there was no need to ask forgiveness. 'It's Mrs. Ormonde that has done everything for me, and she doesn't want anybody to know—nobody except you. She's very kind, but—she's a little hard in some things, and she thinks—I can't quite explain it all. Will you promise not to tell any one when you go back?'

'But are you going to stay here, Thyrza?'

'No, dear; I'm going to London. Mrs. Ormonde is going to send me to some friends of hers. I'm not allowed to tell you where it is, and you won't be able to come and see me there; but we shall see each other somewhere sometimes. You'll keep it secret?'

'Then we're going to be parted always?' Lydia asked, slowly.

'No, no; not always, dear sister. Just for a time; oh, not long. I told Mrs. Ormonde that I knew you'd do as I asked.'

'Thyrza,' said the other gravely, 'I broke the other promise. I showed Gilbert the letter you left for me, and I told him all you'd told me.'

'Yes,' Thyrza uttered mechanically.

'It couldn't be helped. People had begun to talk, and Gilbert had heard about—about the library, you know. Mrs. Bower got to know somehow.'

'Lyddy, I told you all the truth; I told you every word of the truth!'

'I'm sure you did, Thyrza—all you knew.'

'Everything! What did people say about me? No, I don't want to hear; don't tell me. That's all over now. And you couldn't help telling Gilbert; I understand how it was. But will you promise me this other thing, Lyddy?'

She raised herself, and looked solemnly into her sister's face.

'It'll mean more to me than you think, if you refuse, or if

you break your promise. I don't think you would do me harm, Lyddy ? '

The answer was long in coming. At last Lydia made inquiry :

' Why does Mrs. Ormonde want to hide you ? '

Thyrza grew agitated.

' She means it for my good. She believes she's doing the best. She's been kind to me, and I can't say a word against her. I think I ought to do as she wants. She seems to like me, only—I can't tell you how it is, Lyddy ; I can't tell any one ; no, not even you ! '

' Don't worry yourself so, dearest.'

' Lyddy, you might promise me ! ' Thyrza went on, shaken with emotion, one would have said, with fear. ' I've done wrong to you and to Gilbert, but do try and forgive me. Why are you so quiet ? Haven't you love enough for me to do just this ? '

She stood up, flushed and with wild eyes.

' Be quiet, Thyrza dearest ! ' pleaded her sister.

' Then answer me, Lyddy ! Promise me ! '

' I want to know one thing first. Have you seen Mr. Egremont ? '

' I haven't spoken to him since that night when I said good-bye to him by the river. Can't you believe me ? '

' I don't think you'd tell me an untruth.'

' If I'd spoken to him, Lyddy, I'd tell you at once ; I would ! I'd tell you everything ! '

' I must say what I mean, Thyrza ; it's no good doing anything else. Tell me this : does Mrs. Ormonde want you to marry him ? '

Thyrza laughed strangely. Then she exclaimed :

' She doesn't ! She wouldn't hear of such a thing, not for the world ! She wants to be kind to me in her own way, but not that ; not that ! How you distrust me ! Are *you* against me, then ? What are you thinking about ? I hoped you would be kind to me in everything. You don't look like my Lyddy now.'

' It's because I don't understand you,' said the other, in a subdued voice, her eyes on the ground. ' You're not open with me, Thyrza. If it's true that Mrs. Ormonde thinks in that way, why do you——'

She broke off.

' I can't talk about it ! It's very hard to bear. We shall

never be what we were to each other, Thyrza. Something's come between us, and it always will be between us. You must take your own way, dear. Yes, I promise, and there's an end of it.'

Thyrza sprang forward.

'What is it you're afraid of?' she pleaded. 'Why do you speak like this? What are you thinking?'

'I think that Mr. Egremont 'll know where you are.'

'Lyddy, he won't know! I give you my solemn word he won't know.'

'Do you write to him? Perhaps you meant that, when you said you hadn't *spoken* to him?'

'I meant what I said, that I've neither written nor spoken, nor him to me. He won't know where I am; I shall have nothing to do with him in any way. But of course if you refuse to believe me, what's the use of saying it!'

There was a strange intonation in Thyrza's voice as she added these words. She looked and spoke with a certain pride, which Lydia had never before remarked in her. Lydia mused a little, then said:

'I don't doubt the truth of your words, Thyrza. I promise not to tell any one anything about you, and I'll keep my promise. But can't you tell me what you're going to do?'

'I don't really know myself. Mrs. Ormonde took me to her house the day before yesterday, and there was a lady there that I had to sing to. I think she wanted to see what sort of a voice I had. She played a sound on the piano, and asked me to sing the same, if I could. She seemed satisfied, I thought, though she didn't say anything. Then Mrs. Ormonde brought me back in her carriage, but she didn't say anything about the singing. She's very strange in some things, you know.'

Lydia asked presently:

'Then was it Mrs. Ormonde gave you this money?'

And she took the post-office order from her pocket.

'What! you didn't use it?'

'No; I had enough of my own. Please give it back.'

'Oh, Lyddy, how proud you are! You never would take any help from anybody, and yet you went on so about grandad when he made bother. Oh, how is poor grandad?'

'The same as usual, dear.'

'And you go to work every day just the same? My poor Lyddy!'

The contention was over, and the tenderness came back.

'Speak something for me to Gilbert, Lyddy! Say I— what can I say? I do feel for him; I can never forget his goodness as long as I live. Tell him to forget all about me. How wrong I was ever to say that I loved him!'

Then again, in a whisper:

'What about Mr. Ackroyd, dearest?'

'The same. They're not married yet. I dare say they will be soon.'

They spent long hours together by the ebb and flow of the tide. Lydia almost forgot her troubles now and then. As for Thyrza, she seemed to drink ecstasy from the live air.

'It's a good friend to me,' she said several times, looking out upon the grey old deep. 'It's made me well again, Lyddy. I shall always love the sound of it, and the salt taste on my lips!'

CHAPTER XXX

MOVEMENTS

'WE are going first of all to the Pilkingtons', in Warwickshire,' said Annabel, talking with Mrs. Ormonde at the latter's hotel in the last week of July. 'Mr. Lanyard—the poet, you know —will be there; I am curious to see him. Father remembers him a "scrubby starveling"—to use his phrase—a reviewer of novels for some literary paper. He has just married Lady Emily Quell—you heard of it? How paltry it is for people to laugh and sneer whenever a poor man marries a rich woman! I know nothing of him except from his poetry, but that convinces me that he is above sordid motives.'

'Then you do still retain some of your idealism, Bell?'

'All that I ever had, I hope. Why? You have feared for me?'

'Pitch! Pitch!'

'Yes, I know,' Annabel answered, rather absently, letting her eyes stray. 'Never mind. You had something particular to say to me, Mrs. Ormonde.'

'Yes, I have a good-bye for you from an old acquaintance.'

Annabel's complexion had not borne the season as well as those of women whose whole and sole preoccupation it is to combat Nature in the matter of their personal appearance.

Her tint was, as they say, a little fatigued. Fatigued, too, were her eyes, which seemed ever looking for something lost; that gaze she had in sitting by Ullswater with ' Sesame and Lilies ' on her lap would not be easily recovered. Her beauty was of rarer quality and infinitely more suggestive than on that day something more than a year ago; to the modern mind nothing is complete that has not an element of morbidity. At Mrs. Ormonde's words she turned with grave interest.

' Where, then, is he going ? ' she asked, just smiling.

' To a small manufacturing town in Pennsylvania. His firm has just opened works there, and he has it in view to prepare himself for superintending them.'

' You are serious ? '

' Quite. I think it was chiefly my persuasion that decided him. I have no doubt that in a year or two he will thank me, though he is not very ardent about it at present.'

' But surely he—— No, I think you are right.'

' I have not advised him to become an American,' Mrs. Ormonde continued, smiling, when Annabel abandoned an apparent intention of saying more. ' No doubt he will come to England now and then, and probably, with his disposition, he will some day make his home here again. I hardly expect to see him for some two years.'

' I hope it is right. I think it is.'

Annabel paused a little, then made an unforced transition to other matters. She rose to leave before long. Whilst her hand was in Mrs. Ormonde's, she asked :

' May I know anything more than father told me ? '

She had said it with a little difficulty, but without confusion of face.

' What did your father tell you ? '

' Only that she is in your care, and that you think her voice can be cultivated, so as to serve her.'

' Yes, I will tell you more than that, dear. He is absolutely without bond as regards her. They have never met since her flight from home, and, more, she has no suspicion that he ever took an interest in her save as Mr. Grail's future wife.'

' She does not know that ? '

' She has no idea of it. They have never exchanged a more than friendly word. He believed, when absent from England, that she was already married, and of *his* movements since then she is wholly ignorant.'

She listened with frank surprise; her face showed nothing more than that.

'But,' she said, hesitatingly, 'I cannot quite understand. He holds himself quite without responsibility? He leaves England without troubling about her future?'

'Not at all. He knows I have her in my care. She being my ward, I have a perfect right to demand that the child's fate shall not be trifled with, that she shall be allowed to grow older and wiser before any one asks her to take an irrevocable step—say for the space of two years. Mr. Egremont grants my right, and I have never yet had real grounds for doubting his honour.'

'I never doubted it, even on seeming grounds,' said Annabel, quietly.

'You are justified, Bell. Well, as you asked me, I thought it better to tell you thus much. He leaves England morally as free as if he had never heard her name.'

'One more question. How do you *know* that she has no assurance of his—affection?'

'He has himself told me that there has been not a word of that between them. The only other possible source was her sister, who has seen her. I did not see Lydia before the interview, because it was repugnant to me to do so; their love for each other is something very sacred, and a stranger had no right to come between them before they met. But I subsequently saw Lydia in London. She soon spoke to me very freely, and I found that she almost hated me because she thought I was planning to marry her sister to Mr. Egremont. I also found out—I am old, you know, Bell, and can be very deceitful—that Lydia, no more than her sister, suspects serious feeling on his part. She scorned the suggestion of such a possibility. It is her greatest hope that Thyrza may yet marry Mr. Grail.'

'And what can you tell me of Thyrza herself?'

'She has been ill, but seems now in very fair health. The day she spent with Lydia evidently did her a vast amount of good. That natural affection is an invaluable resource to her, and, if I am not mistaken, it will be the means of recovering happiness for me. She is quiet, but not seriously depressed—sometimes she is even bright. The singing lessons have begun, and she enjoys them; I think a new interest has been given her.'

'Then I hope a very sad beautiful face will no longer haunt me.'

Thus did two ladies transact the most weighty part of their business after shaking hands for good-bye—an analogy to the proverbial postscript, perhaps.

The same evening there was a dinner-party at the Tyrrells'. Mr. Newthorpe had, as usual, kept to his own room. Annabel went thither to sit with him for a while after the visitors were gone.

He had a poem that he wished to read to her; there was generally some scrap of prose or verse waiting for her when she went into the study. To-night Annabel could not give the usual attention. Mr. Newthorpe noticed this, and, laying the book aside, made one or two inquiries about the company of the evening. She replied briefly, then, after hesitation, asked:

'Do you very much want to go to the Pilkingtons', father?'

He regarded her with amazement.

'I? Since when have I had a passionate desire to camp in strangers' houses and eat strange flesh?'

'Then you do *not* greatly care about it—even for the sake of meeting Mr. Lanyard?'

'Lanyard? Great Heavens! The fellow has done some fine things, but spiritual converse with him is quite enough for me.'

'Then will you please to discover all at once that you are really not so well as you thought, and that, after your season's dancing and theatre-going, you feel obliged to get back either to Eastbourne or Ullswater as soon as possible?'

'The fact is, Bell, I haven't felt by any means up to the mark these last few days.'

'Dear father, don't say that! I am wrong to speak lightly of such things.'

'I only say it because you ask me to, sweet-and-twenty. In truth I feel very comfortable, but I shall be far more sure of remaining so at Eastbourne than at the Pilkingtons'.'

'Eastbourne, you think?'

'Nay, as you please, Bell.'

'Yes, Eastbourne again.' She came to her father and took his hands. 'I'm tired, tired, tired of it all, dear; tired and weary unutterably! If ever we come to London again, let us tell nobody, and take quiet rooms in some shabby quarter, and go to the National Gallery, and to the marbles at the Museum, and all places where we are sure of never meeting a soul who belongs to the fashionable world. If we go to a concert, we'll sit in the gallery, among people who come because they really want to hear music——'

'*Eheu !* The stairs are portentous, Bell ! '

'Never mind the stairs ! Nay then, we won't go to public concerts at all, but I will play for you and myself, beginning when we like, and leaving off when we like, and using imagination—thank goodness, we both have some!—to make up for the defects. We'll go back to our books—oh ! *you* have never left them ; but I, poor sinner that I am——! Give me my Dante, and let me feel him between my hands ! Where is Virgil ?

> Heu ! fuge crudeles terras, fuge litus avarum.

Is it quoted right ? Is it apropos ? '

'Savonarola's word of fate.'

'Then mine too! How have you been so patient with me ? A London season—and I still have Homer to read ! Still have Sophocles for an unknown land ! My father, I have gone far, very far, astray, and you did not so much as rebuke me.'

'My dearest, it is infinitely better to hear you rebuke yourself. Nor that, either. A chapter in your education was lacking ; now you can go on smoothly.'

'Now read the poem over again, father. I can hear it now.'

Paula came to the house next morning. She and Annabel had seen very little of each other throughout the season, but, on the last two or three occasions of their meeting, Paula had betrayed a sort of timid desire to speak with more intimacy than was her wont. Annabel was not eager in response, but, in spite of that letter which you remember, she had always judged her cousin with much tolerance, and a suspicion that Paula Dalmaine was not quite so happy a person as Paula Tyrrell had been, inclined her to speak with gentleness. They were alone together this morning in the drawing-room.

'So you're going to the Pilkingtons',' Paula said, when she had fluttered about a good deal.

'No. We have changed our minds. We go back to Eastbourne.'

'Ah ! How's that, Bell ? '

'We are a little tired of society, and father needs quietness again. Where do you go ? '

' To Scotland, with the Scalpers. Lord Glenroich is going
down with us. He's promised to teach me to shoot.'

Paula spoke of these arrangements with less gusto than
might have been expected of her. She was fidgety and
absent. Suddenly she asked:

' What has become of Mr. Egremont, Bell?'

' He has either gone, or is just going, to America, to live
there, I believe, for some time.'

' Oh, indeed!—*with* anybody, I wonder?'

' He has not told me anything of his affairs, Paula.'

' Then you have seen him?'

' No, I haven't.'

' Don't be cross with me, Bell. I don't mean anything.
I only wanted to know something true about him; I can hear
lies enough whenever I choose.'

It was pathetic enough, because, for once, evidently sincere. Annabel smiled and made no reply. Then, with abrupt
change of subject, Paula remarked:

' I think I shall come and see you at Eastbourne, if you'll
let me.'

' I shall be glad.'

' No, you won't exactly be glad, Bell—but, of course, I
know you couldn't say you'll be sorry. Still, I shall come, for
a day or two, all by myself.'

' Come, and heartily welcome, Paula.'

' Well now, that does sound a little different. I don't often
hear people speak like that.'

She nodded a careless good-bye, and at once left the
house. She went straight home. Mr. Dalmaine was absent
at luncheon-time; Paula ate nothing and talked fretfully to
the servant about the provision that was made for her—
though she never took the least trouble to see that her
domestic concerns went properly. She idled about the
drawing-room till three o'clock. A visitor came; her instruc-
tions were: ' Not at home.' At half-past three she ordered a
hansom to be summoned, instead of her own carriage, and,
having dressed with nervous rapidity, she ran downstairs and
entered the vehicle. ' Drive to the British Museum,' she
spoke up to the cabman through the trap.

But just as the horse was starting, it stopped again.
Looking about her in annoyance, she found that her husband
had bidden the driver pull up, and that he was standing by
the wheel.

'Where are you going?' he asked, smilingly.

'To see a friend. Why do you stop me when I'm in a hurry? Tell him to drive on at once.'

She was obeyed, and, as the vehicle rolled on, she leaned back, suffering a little from palpitation. It was a long drive to Great Russell Street, and once or twice she all but altered her direction to the man. However, she was on the pavement by the Museum gates at last. When the cab had driven away, she crossed the street. She went to the house where Egremont had his rooms.

'Yes, Mr. Egremont was at home.'

'Then please to give him this card, and ask if he is at liberty.'

She was guided up to the first floor; she entered a room, and found Egremont standing in the midst of packing-cases. He affected to be in no way surprised at the visit, and shook hands naturally.

'You find me in a state of disorder, Mrs. Dalmaine,' he said. 'Pray excuse it; I start on a long journey to-morrow morning.'

Paula murmured phrases. She was hot, and wished in her heart that she had not done this crazy thing; really she could not quite say why she had done it.

'So you're going to America again, Mr. Egremont?'

'Yes.'

'I heard so. I knew you wouldn't come to say good-bye to me, so I came to you.'

She was looking about for signs of female occupation; none whatever were discoverable.

'You are kind.'

'I won't stay, of course. You are very busy——'

'I hope you will let me give you a cup of tea?'

'Oh no, thank you. It was only just to speak a word—and to ask you to forget some very bad behaviour of mine. You know what I mean, of course. I was ashamed of myself, but I couldn't help it. I'm so glad I came just in time to see you; I should have been awfully vexed if I—if I couldn't have asked you to forgive me.'

'I have nothing whatever to forgive, but I think it very kind of you to have come.'

'You'll come back again—some day?'

'Very likely, I think.'

'Then I'll say good-bye.'

He looked into her face, and saw how pretty and sweet it was, and felt sorry for her—he did not know why. Their hands held together a moment or two.

'There's no—no message I can deliver for you, Mr. Egremont? I'm to be trusted—I am, indeed.'

'I'm very sure you are, Miss Tyrrell—Oh, pardon me!'

'No, no! I shan't forgive you.' She was laughing, yet almost crying at the same time. 'You must ask me to do something for you, in return for that. How strange that did seem! It was like having been dead and coming to life again, wasn't it?'

'I have no message whatever for anybody, Mrs. Dalmaine; thank you very much.'

'Good-bye, then. No, no, don't come down. Good-bye!'

She drove back home.

She had been sitting for an hour in her boudoir, when Dalmaine came in. He smiled, but looked rather grim for all that. Seating himself opposite her, he asked:

'Paula, what was your business in Great Russell Street this afternoon?'

She trembled, but returned his gaze scornfully.

'So you followed me?'

'I followed you. It is not exactly usual, I believe, for young married ladies to visit men in their rooms; if I have misunderstood the social rules in this matter, you will of course correct me.'

Mr. Dalmaine was to the core a politician. He was fond of Paula in a way, but he had discovered since his marriage that she had a certain individuality very distinct from his own, and till this was crushed he could not be satisfied. It was his home policy, at present, to crush Paula's will. He practised upon her the faculties which he would have liked to use in terrorizing a people. Since she had given up talking politics, her drawing-room had been full of people whom Dalmaine regarded with contempt—mere butterflies of the season. She had aggressively emphasised the difference between his social tastes and hers. He bore with it temporarily, till he could elaborate a plan of campaign. Now the plan had formed itself in most unhoped completeness, and he was happy.

'What did you want with that fellow?' he asked, coldly.

'Mr. Egremont is going to America, and I wanted to say good-bye to him. He was my friend long before I knew you.'

She rose, and would have gone; but he stopped her with a gentle hand.

'Paula, this is very unsatisfactory.'

'What do you want? What am I to do?'

' To sit down and listen. As I have such very grave grounds for distrusting you, I can only pursue one course. I must claim your entire obedience to certain commands I am now going to detail. Refusal will, of course, drive me to the most painful extremities.'

'What do you want?'

'To-morrow you were to give your last dinner-party. You will at once send a notice to all your guests that you are ill and cannot receive them.'

'Absurd! How can I do such a thing?'

'You will do it. We spoke of going to Scotland with the Scalpers. Instead of that, you accompany me to Manchester when Parliament rises, and you live with me there in retirement whilst I am occupied with my study of the factory questions which immediately interest me.'

Paula was silent.

'These are my commands. The alternative to obedience is—you know what. Pray let me know your decision.'

'Why do you behave to me in this way? What have I done to be treated like this?'

'Pray do not ask me. I wait for your answer.'

'I can only give in to you, and you're coward enough to take advantage of it.'

'You undertake to obey me?'

'I want to go to my room. Can I do so without asking?'

'You are mistress of my house, Paula, as long as you obey me in essential matters.'

Paula disappeared, and Mr. Dalmaine sat reflecting with much self-approbation on the firmness and suavity he had displayed.

CHAPTER XXXI

AN OLD MAN'S REST

IT was not without much reluctance, much debate with conscience, that Bunce allowed his child to remain at Eastbourne. He could not, of course, have finally refused consent to a plan which might be the means of saving Bessie's life, and to be relieved of the cost of her support, receiving into the bargain a small monthly sum which Mrs. Ormonde represented as the value to her of Bessie's services at The Chestnuts, was a great consideration to a man in his perpetual state of struggle to make ends meet. But he had a suspicion that Mrs. Ormonde desired to get the girl away from him that Bessie might be, as he would have phrased it, perverted to the debasing superstition of Christianity.

Mrs. Ormonde had interviews with him, and it helped her to understand the man. She soon found out what it was that troubled him, and went directly to the point with an assurance that no attempt whatever should be made to prejudice Bessie against her father's views. Any printed matter he chose to send her would be uninterfered with. Another woman would have thought Bunce a mere bear when she parted with him, but Mrs. Ormonde had that blessed gift of divination which comes of vast charity ; she did not misjudge him. And he in turn, though he went away with his face still set in the look of half-aggressive pride which it had assumed when he entered, found in a day or two that Mrs. Ormonde's tones made a memory as pleasant as any he had. He felt a little uncomfortable in remembering how ungraciously he had borne himself.

Another woman there was who had begun to exercise influence of an indefinable kind on the rugged fellow, a woman whom he saw a good deal of, and to whom he had grown accustomed to look for a good deal of help. This was Miss Totty Nancarrow. Totty was no slight help with little Nelly, and even with Jack. For the former she ceased to be ' Miss Nanco,' and became ' Totty ' simply ; to Jack she was a most estimable acquaintance, who never grudged flattering wonder at his school achievements, even though they involved no more than a mastery of compound multiplication, and occasionally he felt a wish that some one of his schoolfellows would call Miss Nancarrow names, that he might punch the rascal's head. But in the father's mind there was an obstacle to complete appreciation. Totty was a Roman Catholic. She often went to St. George's Cathedral, in Southwark, and even for the purpose of confession. When this fact was strongly before Bunce's consciousness, he was inclined to scorn Totty and to feel an uneasiness about her associating with his children. Somehow, the scorn and the mistrust would not hold out in Totty's presence. He found himself taking more pains to be

polite to her than to any other person. When she had had
Nelly in her room, and brought the child to him on his coming
home, he invented excuses to get her to talk for a few
moments. Unfortunately, Totty appeared little disposed to
talk.

Luke Ackroyd was not infrequently in Bunce's room.
These two discussed religion and politics together, and their
remarks on these subjects lacked neither vigour nor per-
spicuity. Ye gods! how they went to the root of things!
Ackroyd had persevered in his pronounced Antinomianism;
he did not take life as 'hard' as his companion, and consequently was not as sincere in his revolt, but he represented
very fairly the modern type of brain-endowed workman, who
is from birth at issue with the lingering old world. That is,
he represented it intellectually; there was, however, much in
his character which does not mark the proletarian as such.
Essentially his nature was very gentle and ductile, and he had
strong affections. Probably he could not have told you, with
any approach to accuracy, how often he had been in love, or
fancied himself so, and for Ackroyd being in love was, to tell
the truth, a matter of vastly more importance than all the
political and social and religious questions in the world.

He and Totty were still on the terms of that compact
which had Christmas in view. His own part was discharged
conscientiously; he visited no public-houses and was steady
at his work. In fact, he had never had those tastes which
bring a man to hopeless sottishness. More than half his dissipation had come of that kind of vanity whereof young gentlemen of the best families have by no means the monopoly.
He liked people to talk about him; he liked to know that it
was deemed a pity for such a clever young fellow to go to the
dogs. Even in his recklessness after the loss of Thyrza there
was much of this element; disappointment in love is known to
make one interesting, and if Luke could have brought on a
mild fever, so that people could say he was in danger of dying,
it would probably not have displeased him. That was over
now. He persuaded himself that he was in love with Totty,
and he told himself daily how glad he was in the thought of
marrying her shortly after Christmas.

For all that, they quarrelled, he and she. It would not be
easy to say how many times they quarrelled and made it up
again during the latter half of the year. There was a certain
unlikeness of temperament, which perpetually made them

think more of their difficulties in getting on together than of the pleasure they received from each other's society. Ackroyd frequently pondered on the question of how this matter would arrange itself after they were married; at times he was secretly not a little alarmed. As his wont was, he talked over the question exhaustively with his sister, Mrs. Poole. The latter for a time refused to converse on the subject at all. She was by no means sure that Miss Nancarrow was in any sense a desirable acquisition to the family, having conceived a great prejudice against her from the night when Ackroyd had dealings with the police. A hint to this effect led to a furious outbreak on Luke's part; he was insulted, he would leave the house and find quarters elsewhere, his sister was a narrow-minded, calumniating woman. He was bidden to take his departure as soon as he liked, but somehow he did not do so. Then Mrs. Poole got her husband to make private inquiries about Miss Nancarrow. Good-natured Jim obeyed her, and had to confess that the report was tolerable enough; the girl was perhaps a little harum-scarum, no worse.

'Oh, you're always so soft when there's talk about women!' exclaimed his wife, disappointed. 'I declare you're as bad as Luke himself. I shall see what I can find out for myself.'

She too found that no evil report was current about Totty, save that she was a Roman Catholic. To be sure, this was bad enough, but could not perhaps be made a ground of serious objection to the girl. So Mrs. Poole fell back on an old line of argument.

'I'm tired of hearing about your girls!' she exclaimed, when Luke next broached the subject. 'When it ain't one, it's another. You must find somebody else to talk to. One thing I *do* know—if I was a girl, I wouldn't marry you, no, not if you'd a fortune.'

But in the end she yielded, for she saw that the matter was serious.

'I want to bring Totty here,' Luke said one night. 'I can't always see her in the street, and there's no other handy place. What do you say, Jane?'

'You must do as you like. There's the parlour you're welcome to. But you mustn't go bringing her down here, mind. I've an idea her and me won't quite hit it. You're welcome to the parlour.'

Further quarrels and reconcilements led to a modification

of this standpoint; Mrs. Poole at length said that she was willing to be introduced to Totty, and sent an invitation to tea for Sunday evening.

'Let him get married, and have done with it,' she said to her husband. 'I shall have no peace till he does. He worrits my life out.'

'He'll worrit you a good deal more afterwards, if I'm not mistook,' remarked Jim, with a dry chuckle.

But an unforeseen difficulty presented itself. Totty positively declined to visit Mrs. Poole at present. There was plenty of time for that, she said; wait till Christmas was nearer.

So Ackroyd and Totty once more fell out, and this time very gravely. For a fortnight they did not see each other. And even when the inevitable renewal of kindness came about, Totty made it a condition that she must not be asked to visit Mrs. Poole. Time enough for that.

Mrs. Poole was, of course, offended. It took her longer than a fortnight before she could hear any reference to Totty.

Early in December Totty had a bit of news to impart which gave Ackroyd a good deal of anxiety. She had been talking with Mrs. Bower, and that lady had as good as said that she could no longer keep old Mr. Boddy in her house.

'He's three weeks behind with his rent,' Totty said, 'and he's sold everything he had to sell, except his fiddle, to pay even so long.'

'But do you think Lydia Trent knows that?'

'I can't say. I should think most likely she doesn't. She's nothing to do with none of the Bowers, and hasn't had for a long time; and you may be quite sure Mr. Boddy wouldn't be the first to tell her how things was. Thyrza often said what work they had to get him to take anything from them.'

'He's got no work then?'

'Only a shilling now and then. Mrs. Bower says he's getting too slow for the people as employed him. I shouldn't wonder if he's as good as starved most days.'

'What brutes those Bowers are! And now, I suppose, they're going to turn the old man into the street. That's the Christianity that their girl has taught them. I tell you what, I'll see if I can't find a bit of something for him to do. But then, what's the good? It'll only keep him a day or two. Lydia 'll have to be told about it.'

'It's all very well,' remarked Totty, 'but I don't see how she's to keep him. Besides, I think she might have found out for herself how things was going before now.'

'You may depend upon it, it's only because the old man's hidden it from her so that she couldn't have an idea. I don't like to hear you speak like that of Lydia, Totty.'

'I don't see that there's any harm in what I said.'

'Well, I know you didn't mean it to be unkind, but it sounded so.'

'You're always very sharp about Lydia.'

'I know I am. She's a good girl, and she's a great deal to bear. I think everybody ought to respect her.'

It was perilously near a misunderstanding, but Totty was not altogether in earnest, and had good sense enough to refrain from unworthy suggestions on such a subject. Ackroyd had sometimes half suspected that she quarrelled on trivial grounds of set purpose, for he was well aware of her native sincerity and honest plainness of dealing.

Her bad news was unfortunately true enough. For half a year Mr. Boddy had been breaking up; the process began very suddenly, and was all the harder to bear. Under any circumstances he could not have held his own in the battle with society much longer—the battle for the day's food of which society does its best to rob each individual,—and the catastrophe in the home of the girls who were dear to him as though they had been his own children, sounded the note of retreat. Thyrza was not so much to him as Lydia, but still was very much, and the sorrow which darkened Lydia's life was to him the beginning of the end of all things.

Yes, he hid the state of things very skilfully from Lydia's eyes. He told her that he was working, when he had no work to do; he laughed at her questions as to whether he had comfortable meals, when he had had no meal at all. The Bowers never invited him to come to the parlour now and sit at their table; they were so indifferent about him, so long as he paid his rent, that for a long time they did not know how hard bestead he was. Lydia had ventured to ask him if he would change his lodgings, provided she found him a room in a house where she could visit him without unpleasantness; but the old man avoided her request. If he moved, all sorts of things would become known to Lydia which at present he was able to conceal.

One thing he could not hide. His hand had become so

unsteady that the bow would no longer strike true notes from the violin; so he ceased to play to the girl when she came. Lydia did not press him, thinking that probably it was too painful for him to revive memories of the old days. When hardships thickened, he would have sold the instrument, in spite of every pang, but for the certainty that Lydia would miss it from his room.

He lived more and more to himself. Till the beginning of November he was able just to keep body and soul together after paying his rent, then the rent was no longer forthcoming. Not one article remained to him for which he could obtain money, not one save the violin. He durst not sell it. In spite of everything, he clung to a vague hope that someone would find work for him. To Ackroyd he could not go ; that would be the same as telling Lydia, for he could trust no one in the state of mind which he had reached ; even to strangers he was afraid to appeal with overmuch earnestness, lest stories should get about. Still an odd shilling came to him now and then. Poor old fellow, he did sad things. One morning he took the old blacking-brushes which he had used for years for his one boot, and a little pot of blacking, and an old box, and walked far away across the river, to a place where no one could know him, and there tried to earn a little by rivalling with the shoeblacks. It was useless ; in three days he had earned but as many pence ; he could not waste time thus. It was a terrible moment when he had first to tell Mrs. Bower that he could not discharge his due to her. He tried to put on a half-jesting air, to make out that his difficulty was of the most passing kind. Mrs. Bower ungraciously bade him not to trouble himself, to pay as soon as he could. But when the second day of default came, the landlady was even less gracious.

'I ain't an unreasonable woman, Mr. Boddy,' she said, ' and nobody could never say I was. But then I've a 'ome to keep up, as you know. Isn't it time as you thought things over a bit ? I dessay there's them as 'll see you don't want, if only you'll speak a word. I don't want to be disagreeable to a old lodger, but then reason *is* reason, ain't it ? '

That Saturday night hunger drove him out. He stumped painfully into the busy region on the south side of London Bridge, and there, at midnight, he succeeded in begging a handful of fried potatoes from a fish-shop that was just closing. It was all he could do, after a dozen vain efforts to earn a copper.

But, when he got home in the early morning, a strange thing had happened. On his table lay half a loaf of bread, a piece of butter, and some tea twisted up in paper. How came these things here? He was in anguish lest Lydia had left them, lest Lydia had somehow discovered his condition and had come in his absence.

But it was not so. Lydia came, as usual, on Sunday afternoon, and clearly knew nothing of that gift. He had eaten, and was able once more to talk so cheerfully—in his great relief—that the girl went away happy in the thought that he had got over a turn of ill-health. They had talked, as always, of Thyrza. With Thyrza it was well, outwardly at all events; Lydia had just seen her, and could report that she seemed even happy. Mr. Boddy rejoiced at this. Might not *he* see the little one some day? Yes, surely he should; Lydia would try for that.

Who had left him the food, then? No one entered his room to do anything for him, save at intervals of a fortnight, when Mrs. Bower sent up a charwoman; otherwise he had always waited upon himself. Two days went by, then the offering was renewed, just in the same way, and this time with the addition of some sugar. The giver could be but one person. Mary Bower knew of his need, and was doing what she could for him. He knew it in meeting her on the stairs the morning after; she said a kind 'Good-day,' and reddened, and went by with her head bent.

But it was bitter to receive such help. He could not refuse it, for otherwise he must have lain down in helplessness, and he trusted yet that there would come a turn in things. The winter cold began. Mrs. Bower had not refused coals; he always burned so little that fuel was allowed to be covered by the rent. But now he scarcely ventured to keep his fire alight long enough to boil his kettle; he still had a little supply for burning, and felt that he durst not go down to the cellar for more, when that was done.

Then came the day when his landlady told him with decisive brevity that she could trust him no longer. He must not be a foolish old man, but must ask help from those whose duty it was to give it him.

That was in the afternoon. Mrs. Bower had come up to his room and had asked for the rent. He waited until it was dark, then stole out of the house, carrying his violin.

He would not sell it, only borrow a sum at the pawnbroker's, then he could some day recover the instrument. Nor must he go to a pawn-shop in this neighbourhood, whence tales would spread. He stumped over into Southwark, and found a quiet street where the three brass balls hung above an illuminated shop front. The entrance to the pawning department was beneath a dark archway. At the door he stopped; there was a great lump in his throat, and suddenly, with great physical anguish, tears broke from his eyes. He stood away from the door until he could master the flow of tears; then he went in, carefully selected a box which was empty, and pledged the violin for ten shillings. The man refused to lend him more, and he could not argue.

That fit of weeping seemed to have affected him for ill; going forth again into the cold, he trembled violently, and by no effort could recover himself. He had to sit down upon a door-step. The chillness of his blood, which yet beat feverishly at his temples, affected him with a dread lest he should not have strength to reach home. His thoughts would not obey his will; again and again he fell into torment of apprehension, asking himself how to find money for the rent that was due, and only with a painful effort of mind remembering the ten shillings in his pocket. The door beneath which he was sitting suddenly opened; he staggered up and onwards.

But the cold and the weakness and the anguish of dread grew upon him. He could not remember the streets by which he had come. He stumped on, fancying that he recognised this and that object, and at length knew that he had reached Westminster Bridge Road. The joy of drawing near home supported him. He had only to go the length of Hercules Buildings, and then he would be close to the end of Paradise Street. He reached the grave-yard, walking for the most part as in a terrible dream, among strange distorted shapes of men and women, the houses tottering black on either hand, and ever that anvil-beat of the blood at his temples. Then of a sudden his wooden limb slipped, and he fell to the ground.

He was precisely in front of the Pooles' house. A woman just passing, who happened to know Mrs. Poole, ran up to the door and knocked, and, when Mrs. Poole came, asked for some water to throw over a poor old man who was in a fit on the pavement. Jane, going in for the water, spoke to her brother, who was sitting in the kitchen. Ackroyd went forth to see what could be done.

'Why, it's Boddy!' he exclaimed. 'We must carry him in. Jane, go and tell Jim to come here.'

Of course a crowd had already collected, dark as the street was.

'Hadn't we better take him over to the Bowers'?' asked Jim.

'Yes, it's old Mr. Boddy!' cried a voice. 'He lives at Mrs. Bower's.'

'I know that very well,' said Ackroyd, 'but it's no good taking him there. Lend a hand, Jim; see, he's coming round a bit.' And he added, muttering, 'I expect he's starved to death, that's about it.'

Only the night before, Totty had told him of the old man's position, and he had been casting about for a way of giving help. He did not like to tell Lydia what was going on, yet the inquiries he had made of the men who occasionally employed Mr. Boddy convinced him that there was no hope of the latter's continuing to support himself. In his present state, the old man must at least have friends about him, and not cold-blooded pinchers and parers, who had come to dislike him because of his relation to the Trent girls. With characteristic impulsiveness, Luke made up his mind that Mr. Boddy should be brought into the house and kept there; if need be he would provide for him out of his own pocket.

Mrs. Poole was no grumbler when a fellow-creature needed her kindness. In a moment a match was put to the fire in the parlour; thither Jim and Ackroyd bore the old man, and laid him upon the couch.

He did not seem wholly unconscious, for his eyes regarded first one, then the other, of those who were ministering to him, but he made no effort to speak; spoken to, he gave no sign of understanding. It was found that there was blood upon his head; he must have injured himself in falling. For a quarter of an hour the attempts at restoring him were vain. Then Luke said:

'I shall have to run round for the doctor. For all we know, he may be dying, for want of the proper things.'

'Aye, go, lad,' assented Jim. 'I don't like the look of his face. Do you, Jane?'

Husband and wife whispered together during Luke's absence. They knew from the latter into what a miserable state the old man had sunk, and Jane was vigorous in reprobation of the Bowers. Ackroyd returned, saying that the doctor would be at hand in a minute or two.

' Oughtn't you to go and tell Miss Trent ? ' Jane asked him, as all three stood helpless, waiting.

' I've thought of it, but I'd rather not, if it can be helped. Wait till the doctor comes.'

The old man lay quite still, breathing heavily. His eyes were yet open, but had fixed themselves in one direction.

The doctor came. He directed that the sufferer should at once be put into a warm bed.

' My room, then,' said Luke. ' Come and help, Jim.'

The directions were soon carried out, and the doctor went off, asking someone to follow for medicine.

The wound proved to be of no moment ; graver causes must have led to the state of coma in which the old man lay. When Luke returned from the doctor's, he reported that the latter had spoken rather seriously.

' I must go and see Lydia,' he said to his sister. ' You don't mind this bother, Jane, eh ? You'll sit by him ? '

' Of course I will. Go and fetch her ; it's my belief he hasn't very long to live.'

It seemed to Ackroyd a long time since he had knocked at the door in Walnut Tree Walk ; very much had come about since then. Impatient, he had to repeat his knock before any one came. Then Mr. Jarmey appeared. No, he knew Miss Trent was not in ; she had gone out with his wife half an hour ago, but it was getting late, and they were sure to be soon back.

' Is Mr. Grail in ? '

' I think so. I'll just knock and see.'

Gilbert was at home, and Ackroyd went into the parlour. The two were very friendly whenever they met, but that was seldom ; Grail was surprised at the visit. He was sitting with his mother ; they seemed to have been talking, for no book lay on the table. Luke explained why he had come to the house.

' Will you let me sit here till she comes in, Grail ? '

A chair was at once brought forward, with quiet readiness. One chair there was in the room which no one ever used, though at evening it was always put in a particular position, between the table and the fireplace. Gilbert kept his hand on the back of it as he talked.

Ackroyd railed against the Bowers. Gilbert did not seem able to express very strong feeling, even when he had heard all that the other knew and suspected ; his brows darkened, however, and he was anxious on Lydia's account.

An oppressive silence had fallen upon the three, when at length they heard the front-door open.

'Would you like mother to go upstairs to her and tell her?' Gilbert asked.

'I should. It would be kind of you, Mrs. Grail. But only just speak as if it was an accident; I wouldn't say anything else.'

Mrs. Grail left the room without speaking. She returned in a few minutes, and, leaving the door a little open, said in her very low, tremulous voice, that Lydia was waiting in the passage. Ackroyd shook hands with the two, and went out.

Lydia looked eagerly into his face.

'Is he very bad, Mr. Ackroyd?' she whispered.

'I hope he's come round by this time,' was his reply. 'My sister's attending to him, and we've got things for him from the doctor.'

They passed into the street, and walked quickly side by side.

'It was very good of you to take him in,' Lydia said. 'It would have been very hard to ask Mrs. Bower for help.'

'Yes, yes. We don't want them.'

Lydia and Mrs. Poole had never met. They looked with interest at each other. Ackroyd went down into the kitchen, leaving them together in the room with the old man.

The night went on. Ackroyd and his brother-in-law smoked innumerable pipes by the kitchen fire. Jim often nodded, but Luke was far from sleep; the sad still half-hour spent with the Grails had troubled his imagination, and thoughts of Thyrza had been revived in him. Yes, he had loved Thyrza; all folly put aside, he knew that the memory of the sweet-voiced, golden-haired girl would for ever remain with him. And all this night he did not once think of Totty Nancarrow.

Fortunately, as it was Saturday, they had no need to think of work next morning. Jim would not go to bed; he kept up the most determined struggle with sleep, subduer of mortals. His wife came down now and then, and was angry with him for his useless obstinacy, so plain it was that he could scarcely hold up his great thick head. There was nothing good to report of the patient; he had not recovered consciousness.

At five o'clock, when, in spite of fire and lamp, the little kitchen looked haggard, Mrs. Poole entered hurriedly.

' Do you think the doctor 'ud come, Luke, if you went for him ? He can't get breath. Lydia does want the doctor fetching.'

Luke was off in an instant.

Lydia stood by the bed, pale, anguished. Happily, that struggle, which seemed of death, did not last very long. The worn old face, almost venerable at length in spite of the grotesqueness of its features, fell into calm. Then, almost as in a natural waking from sleep, the eyes opened and were aware of things.

' Are you feeling better, grandad dear ? ' Lydia asked.

He looked surprised, tried to speak ; but there was no voice.

Luke was long.

The two women stood side by side. The old man kept endeavouring to utter words ; his powerlessness was dreadful to him, his face showed. But at length he spoke.

' Lyddy !—Thyrza ! '

' She shall come and see you, grandad. She shall come very soon.'

Again a vain endeavour to speak. His face altered ; it expressed Lydia knew not what. A supreme effort, and he again spoke.

' Mary Bower gave me all I wanted. Be friends with her, Lyddy ! '

No more than that. Gradually, an end of struggle, an end of pain, an end of all things.

The doctor came. He said that no doubt there would have to be an inquest.

They left Lydia alone in the room. When it was midway through the winter morning, Mrs. Poole came down and told Luke that the girl wished to speak to him ; he would find her in the parlour.

She had swollen eyes, but spoke with perfect calmness.

' Mr. Ackroyd, what did he mean ? The last thing he said was, " Mary Bower gave me all I wanted." I don't know what he meant. Your sister says you'll tell me.'

Luke could only guess at the sense of the words, but he told her all he knew.

' I only heard it on Friday night, from Totty,' he said. ' I was thinking of every way I could to help him.'

' Oh, but to think that you never told me ! ' she exclaimed.

' You'd no right to keep such a thing from me. It wasn't kindness; it wasn't kindness at all. See what's come of it ! '

' I do wish I had told you.'

Early in the afternoon Lydia went home. But before leaving, she searched in the poor old garments to see if, indeed, he had been penniless. The discovery of the money at first astonished her, but immediately after she found the pawn ticket. It was proof enough.

She was sitting in her room, at nightfall, when someone knocked. She went to the door. Mary Bower was there.

' May I come in, Lydia ? ' Mary asked, with eyes downcast.

Lydia had started. She drew back, leaving the door open. Mary entered, closed the door behind her, and stood in agitation.

' I know you hate me more than ever, Lydia,' she began, tremulously ; ' but I did what I could for him. I want to tell you that I did what I could for him, and I'd never have let mother give him notice. I told her last night that, if she did, I'd leave home. I put food in his room, and nobody knew about it. Perhaps you don't believe me ; if he could speak, he'd tell you someone did, and it was me.'

Lydia covered her face and wept. Mary, drawing nearer, went on with broken voice :

' I've been very much to blame, Lydia. I've been hard and unforgiving. But that night when you told me you hated me, I wanted to say how sorry I was for you. I never spoke a word against Thyrza, not a word. And now I couldn't help coming to you. I want to be friends again, Lyddy dear. Don't send me away ! I've been to blame in everything ; I've been bad-hearted. You might well not believe my religion when you saw me acting as I did.'

She ceased, drawn to Lydia's heart and kissed with more than the old affection.

' I know what you did for him, Mary. He told me—the last words he spoke. He asked me to be friends with you again. I do want a friend, Mary ; I'm very lonely. I'll love you as long as I live for being kind to him.'

They lit no light, but sat together by the glow of the fire, speaking in very low voices, often with long intervals of silence. Two poor girls, the one as ignorant as the other, but speaking with awed spirit of death and the hope that is thereafter.

CHAPTER XXXII

TOTTY'S LUCK

' THE Little Shop with the Large Heart' had suffered a
grave loss : Miss Totty Nancarrow had withdrawn her custom
from it.

Totty had patronised Mrs. Bower very steadily for some
five years. It was true that the large-hearted shop put a
rather large price on certain things, in comparison with what
they *could* be bought for in Lambeth. If you wanted a pot
of marmalade, for instance, Mrs. Bower sold it for sixpence,
whereas it was notoriously purchasable for fivepence-half-
penny at grocers in Lambeth Walk. If you went for a
quarter of a pound of butter, you had no choice of quality,
and paid fourpence three farthings, whilst in Lambeth Walk
you obtained a better article for the even fourpence. Totty,
however, had a principle that one ought to deal rather with
acquaintances than with strangers, and another principle
that it was better to pay a halfpenny more for an article to
be had by crossing the street than a halfpenny less and go a
whole street's length for it. True girl of the people was
Totty, herein as in other respects. It was a simple fact that
Mrs. Bower's business depended on the indolence and indifference to small economies of those women who lived in
her immediate neighbourhood. It is the same kind of thing
that leads working people to pay for having meat badly
cooked at the baker's instead of cooking it cheaply and well
themselves ; that leads them to buy expensive, ready-pre-
pared suppers at the pork butcher's and the fried-fish shop,
instead of tossing up an equally good and very cheap supper
for themselves.

Considering her income, Totty had spent a great deal
with Mrs. Bower, as you remember that lady once remarking.
Totty had a mind to live on luxuries ; if she had not money
enough for both bread and marmalade, she chose to have the
marmalade alone ; if she could not buy meat and pickles at
the same time, she would have pickles and go without meat.
Marmalade and pickles she deemed the indispensables of life ;
if you could not get those—well, it was no uncommon thing

for poor creatures to be driven to the workhouse. And the strange thing was that she looked so well on such diet. Since the age of fifteen, when, in truth, she had been a little peaked and terribly tenuous at the waist, her personal appearance had steadily improved. Her spirits had, by degrees, reached their present point of perpetual effervescence. But Totty could be grave, and, if occasion were, sad.

She had been both grave and sad many a time since Thyrza had gone away. She reproached herself in secret for her 'nastiness' to the little one at their last meeting, nastiness for which, as it proved, there was no justification whatever. Now she was sad for poor old Mr. Boddy's death. She knew that it was another hard blow to Lydia, and, as you are aware, in her heart she respected Lydia profoundly. Her sorrow led to that one practical result—no more marmalade and pickles from Mrs. Bower. The Bowers had behaved vilely; from every point of view, that was demonstrable. Under the circumstances, they ought to have done without their rent, if need were, till Doomsday when, as Totty understood, all such arrears are made good to one with the utmost accuracy—nay, with interest to boot. She had not seen any reason for quarrelling with the Bowers on the score of the scandal they spread about Thyrza, since there really seemed ground for their stories; and it was right that 'goings on' of that kind should be put a stop to. Totty would always—that is, as often as she could—be scrupulously just. But this last affair was beyond endurance. Not another penny went from her pocket to 'The Little Shop with the Large Heart.'

Her income this past year had fallen short of what she usually counted upon; not to a great extent, but the sum deducted had been wont to come to her as a pure grace, and she felt the loss of it. Her uncle had omitted to send his usual present on her birthday. Nor had he visited her to renew the proposal that she should surrender her liberty in return for being housed and dressed respectably. What did this mean? Had he—it was probable enough—grown tired of her, and said to himself that, as she wished to go her own way, go her own way she should? He was a crusty old fellow. Totty had often wondered that he 'stood her cheek' so good-humouredly. Yet somehow she did not think it likely that he would break off intercourse with her in this abrupt way; no, it was not like him. He would have, at all events, seen her for a last time, and have given her a well-understood last chance. Was he dead? Possible enough; his age must be nearer seventy than sixty. If dead, well, there was an end of it. No more birthday presents; no more offers to 'be made a lady of.'

It did not greatly matter, of course. Totty could not be expected to nurture an affection for her crusty uncle with his ∴hop in Tottenham Court Road; in fact, he had behaved badly to her branch of the family, and such behaviour cannot always be made up for. As to the offer, she had declined it in perfect good faith. Yes, she preferred her liberty, her innocent nights at the Canterbury Music Hall, her scampering about the streets at all hours, her marmalade and pickles eaten off a table covered with a newspaper in company with half a dozen friends as harum-scarum as herself. Deliberately, she preferred these joys to anything she could imagine as entering into the life of a 'lady.'

However, it was a fact that Christmas was very near, also a fact that she stood pledged to marry Luke Ackroyd any day after Christmas that he chose to claim her. She was a little sorry that she could not inform her uncle in Tottenham Court Road of the change she was about to make in her life; there was no knowing how he might have behaved on such an occasion. Luke had been saving a little money of late, but it was naturally a very little; he, foolish fellow, had a way of buying her things which she did not in the least want, but which she could not refuse since it gave him such enormous pleasure to offer them. Luke was very generous, whatever his faults might be. Certain presents of his she had returned to him, in wrath, probably once a fortnight, and when, in the course of things, she had to take them back again, some object was always added. The presents cost little, it is true; Totty did not ask the price of them, but liked the kindness which suggested their purchase. She liked many things about Luke Ackroyd; whether she really liked him himself, liked him in 'the proper way'—well, that was a question she asked herself often enough without any very definite answer.

No matter, she had promised to marry him, and she was not the girl to break her word. Now, if her uncle had still been in communication with her, was it not a very likely thing that he would have felt a desire to—in fact, to do something for them? It was not nice to begin married life in furnished lodgings, especially if prudence dictated the living in a single room, as such numbers of her acquaintances did. Totty had discovered that couples who wedded and went to live in one furnished room seldom got along well together. It was well if the wife did not shortly go about with ugly-looking bruises on her face, or with her arm in a sling. No, to be sure, Luke Ackroyd was not a man of that kind; it was inconceivable that he should ever be harsh to her, let alone brutal. Still, it was *not* nice to begin in furnished lodgings. And perhaps her uncle in Tottenham Court Road—he was, in fact, a furniture dealer—would have seen his way to garnish for them a modest couple of rooms, by way of wedding present. But, he having drawn back from communication, Totty could not bring herself to his notice again, not she.

She was thinking over all these things a week before Christmas. It was Sunday afternoon, and, for a wonder, she was sitting alone in her room. Mr. Bunce was at home, or she would have had little Nelly to keep her company. Still, she said to herself that she was not sorry to have a minute or two to put certain things straight in her mind. What a mind it was, Totty Nancarrow's !

The landlady looked in at the door.

' Here's a gemman wants to see you, Miss Nancarrow.'

' Oh ? What sort of a gentleman ? '

' Why, oldish—five-an'-forty, I dessay. Greyish beard and a big nose. Speaks very loud and important like.'

Not her uncle; he had no beard and a very small nose, and could not thus have altered since she last saw him.

' All right. I'll go and ask him what he wants.'

Totty gave a glance at her six square inches of looking-glass, made a movement with her hand which was like a box on each ear, then went downstairs in her usual way, swinging by the banisters down three steps at a time. At the door she found a person answering very fairly to the landlady's graphic description. The experienced eye would have perceived that he was not, in the restricted sense of the word, a gentleman ; still, he wore good clothing, and had of a truth an important air.

' You want me, sir ? ' Totty asked, coming to a sudden stand in front of him, and examining him with steady eye.

He returned the gaze with equal steadiness. Both hands rested on the top of his umbrella, and his attitude was very much that of a man who views a horse he has thoughts of purchasing.

'You are Miss Nancarrow, I think?' he said, clearing his throat. 'Christian name, Totty.'

'That's me, I believe.'

'Jusso! I should like to have a word with you, Miss Nancarrow, if you will allow me.'

'You can't say it here, sir?'

'Why, no, I can't. If you could——'

Totty did not wait for him to finish, but ran away to get permission to use the landlady's parlour. To this she introduced her visitor, who seated himself without invitation, and, after gazing about the room, said:

'Pray sit down, Miss Nancarrow. I've come to see you on a matter of some importance. I am Mr. Barlow, an old friend of your uncle's. You have possibly heard of me?'

'No, I haven't,' Totty replied.

As she spoke, it struck her that there was a broad black band round Mr. Barlow's shiny hat.

'Ah, you haven't; jusso!'

Mr. Barlow again cleared his throat, looking about the floor as if he were in the habit of living near a spittoon. And then he paused a little, elevating and sinking his bushy eyebrows. Totty, who had taken the edge of a chair, moved her feet impatiently.

'Well, Miss Totty Nancarrow,' resumed her visitor, using his umbrella to prop his chin, and rolling out his words with evident enjoyment of his task, 'I have the unpleasant duty of informing you that your late uncle is dead.'

The phrase might have excited a smile. Totty kept an even countenance and said she was sorry to hear it.

'Jusso! He has been dead nearly a month, and he was ill nearly six. I am appointed one of the executors by his will—me and a friend of mine, Mr. Higgins. I dare say you haven't heard of him. We've been putting your late uncle's affairs in order.'

'Have you?' said Totty, because she had nothing else to say.

'We have. I have come to see you, Miss Nancarrow, because you are interested in the will.'

'Oh, am I?'

It was said with a kind of disinterested curiosity. Mr. Barlow, having regarded her fixedly for a moment, bent his head till his forehead rested upon the umbrella, and seemed to brood.

'Don't you feel well, sir?' Totty asked, with a *naïveté* which betrayed her impatience.

'Quite well, quite well.'

'You was saying something about my uncle's will.'

'Jusso! Your name is in the will, Miss Nancarrow. Your uncle has bequeathed to you the sum of two hundred and fifty pounds.'

'Have you brought it with you, sir?'

'The will?'

'No, the money.'

'My dear Miss Nancarrow, things are not done in that way,' remarked Mr. Barlow, smiling at her ingenuousness.

'How then, sir?'

'There are conditions attached to this bequest. It is my duty to explain them to you. I shall avoid the terms of the law, out of consideration to you, Miss Nancarrow, and try to express myself very simply. I hope you'll be able to follow me.'

Totty regarded him with wide eyes and smiled.

'I'll do my best, sir.'

'Now please listen.' He rested one elbow on his umbrella, and with the other hand made demonstrations in the air as he proceeded. Throughout he spoke as one who addresses a person partly imbecile.

'This sum of two hundred and fifty pounds, Miss Nancarrow, is not—you follow me?—is not to be given to you at once—you grasp that?—I am trustee for the money; that means—attend, please—it lies in my hands until the time and the occasion comes for—mind—for giving it to you. You understand so far?'

'I shouldn't mind a harder word now and then, sir, if it makes it easier for you.'

Mr. Barlow examined her, but Totty's face was very placid. She cast down her eyes, and watched her toes tapping together.

'Well, well; I think you follow me. Now the conditions are these. The money is payable to you—payable, you see—on your marriage.'

'Oh!'

'I beg you not to interrupt me. Is payable to you on your marriage, and then—now pray attend—*not* unless you obtain the approval of myself and of Mr. Higgins—unless you obtain *our* approval of the man you propose to marry.'

'Oh!'

'You have understood, I hope?'

'I shall marry who I like, sir,' observed Totty, quietly.

Mr. Barlow looked at her with surprise.

'My dear Miss Nancarrow, nobody ever said you shouldn't. It isn't a question of your marrying, but of two hundred and fifty pounds.'

'I don't see what it's got to do with anybody who I choose to marry.'

'Jusso, jusso! nothing could be truer. It's only a question of two hundred and fifty pounds.'

Totty was about to make another indignant remark, but she checked herself. Her toes were tapping together very rapidly; she watched them for half a minute, then asked:

'And suppose I don't choose to marry anybody at all?'

'I see you are capable of following these things,' said Mr. Barlow, smiling. 'If you reach the age of five-and-twenty without marrying, the money goes to another purpose, of which it is not necessary to speak.'

'Oh! I don't see why my uncle bothered himself so much about me marrying.'

'No doubt your late uncle had some good reason for these provisions, Miss Nancarrow,' said the other, gravely. 'We should speak respectfully of those who are no more. It seems to me your late uncle took very kind thought for you.'

Totty considered that, but neither assented nor differed.

'Will you tell me,' she asked after a silence, speaking with a good deal of hauteur, 'what sort of a man you'd approve of?'

'With pleasure, Miss Nancarrow; with very great pleasure. Mr. Higgins and me have thought over the subject, have given it our best attention. We think that by laying down three conditions we shall meet the case.'

He stared at the ceiling, till Totty asked:

'Well, and what are they, sir?'

'Pray do not interrupt me; I was about to tell you. First, then, this man's age must be at least three-and-twenty. You understand?'

'I think I do.'

'Secondly, he must have a recognised profession, business, trade, or handicraft, and must satisfy me and Mr. Higgins that he is able to support a wife.'

'And then?'

' And then, as you say, Miss Nancarrow, he must be able to prove to me and Mr. Higgins that he has lived in one and the same house for a year previous to his marriage with you.'

Mr. Barlow delivered this with slow emphasis, as if such a test of respectability were the finest fruit of administrative wisdom.

Totty laughed. She had expected something quite different.

' You smile, Miss Nancarrow ? ' remarked Mr. Barlow, with a slightly offended air.

' No, I was laughing.'

' And at what, pray ? '

' Nothing.'

' H'm. Well, I hope I have made everything clear to you.

' All the same, sir, I shall marry whoever I like.'

' I've no doubt whatever you will. I shall leave you my address, Miss Nancarrow, so that you can communicate with me at any moment.'

' Thank you, sir.' She took the offered card and thrust it into her pocket. ' And if I don't want to marry at all, I shan't.'

' It is at your option, Miss Nancarrow. Now I'll say good-morning to you. Perhaps you'll allow me to shake hands with you and congratulate you upon this—this little fortune.'

' Oh, yes.'

Totty gave Mr. Barlow's fat hand a jerk. He drew himself up, cleared his throat, and stalked to the door, regarding with lofty patronage the signs of poverty about him. At the door he took off his hat, bowed, departed.

Totty returned to her room. She resumed her former seat, and began to hum a slow air. Then she tilted her chair back against the wall, and turned her face upwards musing.

It was not easy for her to realise the meaning of two hundred and fifty pounds. Reckon it up, for instance, in marmalade and pickles ; it became confusing very soon. Reckon it up in tables and chairs ; ah, that was more to the point. But even then, what a stupendous margin ! For twenty pounds you could furnish a couple of rooms in a way to make all your neighbours envious. It was like attempting to comprehend infinity by making clear to one's mind the distance to the moon.

The three conditions ; Luke Ackroyd could satisfy them all. How often he had said that what he wanted was a little capital to establish a comfortable home of his own, when he would feel settled for life. No thought now of furnished lodgings. Fancy making one's husband a present of two hundred and fifty pounds! Much better that than receiving presents oneself.

She was to meet Luke to-night, and it was time that a definite arrangement was made as to their marriage. Somehow, Totty did not feel quite so joyous as she ought to have done; she could not fix her mind on the two hundred and fifty pounds, but it wandered off to other things which had nothing to do with money. 'Come now,' she said to herself at length, 'do I care for anybody more than for him? No; it's quite certain I don't. Do I care much for him himself? Do I care for him properly?' Suddenly she thought of Thyrza; she remembered Thyrza's question: 'Do you love him, Totty?'

No, she did not love him. She had known it for a good many weeks. And, what was more, she had known perfectly well that he did not love her.

There it was, no doubt. 'If he loved me, I should love him. I could; I think I could. Not like Thyrza loved Mr. Egremont, to go mad about him; that isn't my style; I wouldn't be so foolish about *any* man, not I! But I could be very fond of him. And—there's no hiding it—I'm not—I shouldn't grieve a bit if we said good-bye to-night and never saw each other again.'

How did she know he didn't love her? 'As if I couldn't tell! Just listen when he speaks about Thyrza; he'd never speak about me like that, if I ran away from him. And how he speaks about Lydia; why, even about Lydia he thinks a good deal more than he does about me. He often talks to me as if I was a man; he wouldn't if he—if he loved me.'

Totty found it difficult to say that word even to herself. 'The fact of the matter is, I don't think as I shall ever care proper for anybody. I've a good mind not to marry at all, as I always said I wouldn't. I was right enough as long as I kept to that. The girls 'll only make fun of me.'

Yes, but her promise?—She began to feel gloomy. Perhaps nightfall had something to do with it. Should she make tea? No, she didn't care for it. She would go out—somewhere.

She walked from Newport Street to Lambeth Road, passed Bethlehem Hospital (Bedlam), and came to St. George's

Cathedral. It is a long, vast, ugly building, unfinished, for it still lacks towers ; in the dark it looked very cold and forbidding, but Totty had a sense that there was warmth within, warmth and shelter of a kind that she needed just now.

She entered, and, at the proper place, dropped to her knees and crossed herself. Then she stood looking about. Near her, hanging against a pillar, was a box with the super·scription : ' For the Souls in Purgatory.' She always put a penny into this box, and did so now.

Then she walked softly to an image of the Virgin, at whose feet someone had laid hothouse flowers. A poor woman was kneeling there, a woman in rags ; her head was bent in prayer, her hands clasped against her breast. Totty knelt beside her, bent her own head and clasped her hands.

Yes, it was good to be here. All was very still ; but few lights were burning. When Totty needed a mother's counsel, a mother's love, she was wont to come here and whisper humble thoughts to the image which looked down so soothingly upon all who made appeal. To Totty her religion was a purely private interest. It would never, for instance, have occurred to her to demand that her husband should be a Catholic, not even that he should view her faith with sympathetic tolerance. No word on this subject would ever pass her lips. What was it to any one else if she had in secret a mother to whom she breathed her troubles and her difficulties? Could any one grudge her that ? The consolation was too sacred to speak of. Her thoughts did not rise to a Deity ; she thought but seldom of the story which told her that Deity had taken man's form. The Madonna was enough, the mother whose gentle heart was full of sorrows and who had power to aid the sorrowful.

The poor ragged woman sighed deeply, rose and went forth with humble step—went forth to who knows what miseries, what cruelties and despairs. But in her sigh there had been consolation. ·

Even so with Totty. When at length she left the church, her way was by no means clear of all obstacles, but the trouble which had come upon her with unwonted force was much simplified. It was plain to her that she *could* give herself to Ackroyd, and that to give him the two hundred and fifty pounds would be a very substantial pleasure. Growing accustomed to the thought of her wealth, she derived from it a quiet pride, which made her walk homewards more staidly than usual. Luke could never forget that she had been a great help to him.

She would let him settle everything to-night, then would tell him.

These winter nights were troublesome to an unfortunate pair who wished to talk in a leisurely way together, yet had no shelter save that of a place of public entertainment, or an archway under the line. And to-night it was particularly cold ; there had even fallen a little snow. Totty and Ackroyd met, as usual, at the end of Paradise Street. It being Sunday, they could not go to the music-hall, and it was really impossible to stand about in the open air.

'Look here, Totty,' said Ackroyd, 'you *must* come into the house. You needn't see any one, unless you like. We can have the sitting-room to ourselves. The others always sit downstairs.'

Totty hesitated, but at length assented. If the truth were known, her two hundred and fifty pounds had probably something to do with her yielding on this point. At present she could face Mrs. Poole on equal terms.

So they entered the house, and Luke, having left his companion in the parlour, went down to apprise his sister. Jane came up, and gave the girl a civil greeting. It was not cordial, nor did Totty affect warmth of feeling. Mrs. Poole speedily left the two to themselves.

Totty sat in her chair rather stiffly. She was not accustomed to take her ease in rooms even as well appointed as this. Luke tried to be merry, to show that he was delighted, to be affectionate ; he did not succeed very well. Presently they were sitting at a little distance from each other, each waiting for the other to speak.

'When is it to be ?' Ackroyd said at length, bending forward.

'I don't know. Is it *really* to be ?'

'Why not ? Of course it is.'

Totty had felt colder to him than ever before, since she had entered this room. The strangeness of the surroundings affected her disagreeably. She wished they had walked about in the snowy streets.

'Of course you know we shall always be quarrelling,' she said, with a laugh.

'No, we shan't. It'll be different then. At all events, it'll be your fault if we do.'

Silence came again.

'What day?' Luke asked.

'When you like. If you really mean it.'

'Now what's the use of talking in that way? Why *shouldn't* I mean it?'

'If I ask you a question will you answer me honest?'

She was leaning forward, with a touch of colour on her cheeks, and a sudden curious light in her eyes; she seemed ashamed at something, and both eager and reluctant.

'What is it? Yes, I'll answer you the truth.'

'The very truth? No, I shan't ask you. What day do you want it to be?'

'Nonsense! What was the question? I won't listen to anything till you've told me.'

'It was a silly question. I don't really want to ask you. I forget what it was.'

Totty was strangely unlike herself, hesitating, diffident, ashamed. He insisted; she refused to speak. He got vexed, turned mute.

'Well then, I *will* ask you,' Totty exclaimed of a sudden. 'And mind, I shall know if you're honest or not. Suppose both Thyrza Trent and me was in this room, and you had your choice between us, which would it be?'

Ackroyd flushed, then looked seriously offended.

'Won't you answer?'

'I don't like to joke about such things.'

'And I don't either, that's the truth; that's why such a thing came into my head. You needn't answer; I'd rather you didn't. Of course I know what you'd have to say.'

'You are talking nonsense. There couldn't be a choice, because I've *made* my choice. Will you marry me or not?'

'Yes, I will. Any day you like.'

'Yes, and afterwards keep asking me questions like this.'

'It wasn't right, I know. But you're wrong when you say I should ever speak of it again.'

'I don't know what to think, Totty. It looks very much as if *you* didn't want to have *me*. Now look, here's a question for *you*. Suppose I'd never asked you before to-night, and now I came and asked you to marry me, what would you say? Now, honest.'

'You've not answered me.'

'I have.'

He spoke it significantly, and she understood him.

'Now, what *would* you say, Totty?'

'I should say, that I couldn't say neither yes nor no for certain, and I wanted to wait.'

'You're an honest girl. Shake hands, and let us wait another six months.'

Totty reddened, and inwardly reproached herself with complete meanness. But she was glad—and Luke Ackroyd was glad.

CHAPTER XXXIII

THE HEART AND ITS SECRET

THYRZA was not to be a boarder with the Emersons, nor did Mrs. Ormonde request them to make a friend of her. Nothing more was proposed than that she should rent from them their spare room, which was tolerably spacious and could be used both as bed-chamber and parlour. Her meals were to be supplied to her by the landlady of the house. The only stipulation with the Emersons was that she should receive her singing-lessons in their sitting-room, where there was a piano.

Thyrza herself specially desired of Mrs. Ormonde that she might live as much alone as possible. She declared that it would be no hardship whatever to her to be without companionship. Her day's occupation would be chiefly sewing, for Mrs. Ormonde had made arrangements that she should have regular employment for her needle from a certain charitable 'Home' at Hampstead. For this work she received payment, which—Mrs. Ormonde made it appear—would suffice to discharge her obligations to the Emersons and her landlady. Moreover, two days of the week she was to spend at the said Home, where certain, not too exacting, duties were assigned to her.

All this was very neatly contrived, and Mrs. Ormonde felt rather proud of her success in so far meeting the requirements of a very difficult case. A competent judge had reported so favourably of Thyrza's voice, that there was a strong probability of its some day enabling her to earn a living—should that be necessary—in one of the many paths which our musical time opens to those thus happily endowed; no stress was laid on that, however, for it was far from desirable that

Thyrza should be nursed into expectation of a golden future.
Mrs. Ormonde had determined that, if her exertion would
accomplish it, Thyrza should yet have as large a share of
happiness as a sober hope may claim for a girl of passionate
instincts, of rare beauty, and, it might be, of latent genius.
To be sure, such claim cannot be extravagant. The happy
people of the world are the dull, unimaginative beings from
whom the gods, in their kindness, have veiled all vision of the
rising and the setting day, of sea-limits, and of the stars of the
night, whose ears are thickened against the voice of music,
whose thought finds nowhere mystery. Thyrza Trent was
not of those. What joys were to be hers she must pluck out
of the fire, and there are but few of her kind whom in the end
the fire does not consume.

But for the present things seemed to be set going on a
smooth track. And to be sure, though she had thought it better
to ask no such kindness, Mrs. Ormonde knew that her friend
Clara Emerson would very shortly make a companion of
Thyrza. It was Clara's nature to make a friend of any
' nice ' person who gave a sign of readiness for friendly intercourse ; the fact of Thyrza's being untaught, and a needle-
plier, would make no difference to her when she had discovered
the girl's sweetness of disposition.

Thyrza wondered much at the way in which her singing-
master proceeded with her instruction. She had looked forward to learning new songs, and she was allowed to sing
nothing but mere uninteresting scales of notes. A timid
question at length elicited one or two abrupt remarks which
humbled, but at the same time informed, her. The teacher,
like most of his kind, was a poor creature of routine, un-
burdened by imagination ; he had only a larynx to deal with,
and was at no pains to realise that the fountain of its notes was
a soul. To be sure, that was a thought which he was not
accustomed to have forced upon him.

Humbled and informed, Thyrza took her lessons with
faultless patience, and with the hopeful zeal which makes
light of every difficulty. She felt her voice improving, and
when she sang to herself the old songs she was no longer
satisfied with the old degree of accuracy. A world of which
she had had no suspicion was opening to her ; music began
to mean something quite different from the bird-warble which
was all that she had known. Moreover, she began to have an
inkling of the value of her voice. Mrs. Ormonde had scarcely

with a word commended her singing, and had spoken of the lessons as something that might be useful, with no more emphasis. The master, of course, had only praise or blame for the individual exercise. But there was someone in the house who felt bound by no considerations of prudence; Clara, hearing Thyrza's notes, was entranced by them, and of course took the first opportunity of saying so.

' You really think I have a good voice ? ' Thyrza asked once, when they had grown accustomed to each other.

' You have a splendid voice, Miss Trent ! ' replied Clara, who delighted in bestowing praise.

' Do you think I shall really be able to sing some day—I mean, to people ? '

' Why not ? I fancy people will be only too anxious to get you to sing.'

' In—in places like St. James's Hall ? ' Thyrza asked, her ears tingling at her audacity.

' Some day, I've no doubt whatever.'

Thyrza sewed, as a rule, for six hours a day, save of course on the days when she went to the Home. For her leisure she had found so much occupation that she seldom went to bed before midnight. In her walk to the omnibus which took her to Hampstead, she had to pass a second-hand book-shop, and it became her habit to put aside sixpence a week—more she could not—for the purchasing of books. With no one to guide her choice, and restricted as she was in the matter of price, she sometimes made strange acquisitions. She avoided story books, and bought only such as seemed to her to contain solid matter—history by preference, having learned from Gilbert that history was the best thing to study. Over these accumulating volumes she spent many a laborious hour. At first it was very hard to keep awake much after ten o'clock ; eyelids *would* grow so heavy, and the coil of golden hair (she no longer wore the long plait with the blue ribbon) seemed such a burden on the brain. But she strove with her drowsiness, and, like other students, soon made the grand discovery that, the fit once over, one is wider awake than ever. What hard, hard things she read ! ' Tytler's Universal History,' in one fat little small-typed volume, very much spoilt by rain, she made a vade-mecum ; the ' Annals of the Orient, of Greece, of Rome '—with difficulty not easily estimated she worked her way through them. An English Dictionary became a necessity ; she had to wait three weeks before she had money enough to purchase the cheapest she could find. At the very beginning of Tytler were such terrible words: *chronological*, and *epitome*, and *disquisitions*, and *exemplification*.

'If I had someone to ask, what time it would save me! Wouldn't *he* help me? Wouldn't *he* be glad to tell me what long words mean?'

Never mind, she would do it by herself. She had brains. Poor Gilbert had so often said that she could learn anything in time. So the lamp burned on till midnight. Compendious old Tytler! In his grave it should have given him both joy and sorrow that so sweet a face grew paler over his long hard words.

Had she not her reward before her? Two years; in one way it would be all too short a time. Not an hour must be lost. And when the two years had come full circle, and some morning she was told that someone wished to see her, and she went down into the sitting-room, and he, he stood before her, then she would say, ' This and this I have done, thus hard have I striven, for your sake, because I love you better than my own soul!'

That secret: no one must suspect it; no, not even Lyddy. After a hard night's work she would wake up feeling yet weary, her brain dull, and a strange pain at her heart—the pain that came so often; but, whilst her thoughts were struggling to consciousness, she felt that there was some joy beyond the present pain. And, behold! with sense of the new day came ever renewed hope. She rose, and a bright angel circled her with protecting, comforting arms. Dark or sunny, for her the morning had its golden rays.

How near he sometimes might be to her! She knew nothing of Egremont's having left England; Lydia did not, and would scarcely have mentioned the name even if she had known. Thyrza thought of himself as always very near. There was a possibility that she might by chance see him. It would have been very dear to her to see him at a distance, but she dreaded lest he should see her. That would spoil all. No, it was a sacred compact. Two years—two whole years—had to be lived through, and then no one could say a word against their meeting.

She would be able to sing to him then. If her voice proved good enough for her to sing in a concert, like *the* concert at St James's Hall, would he not be proud of her?

Artist's soul that she had, she never gave it a thought that, if she became his wife, he might prefer that she should not sing in public. She imagined herself before a great hall of people, singing, yet singing in truth to one only. But all the others must hear and praise, that he might have joy of her power.

Yet there would be the hour, also, for singing to him alone—they two alone together. Would not her song be then the most glorious? Not with her own voice, but with the voice of very love, would she utter her hymn of gladness and worship. And he would praise her in few words—more with looks than with words. And again she would say: ' So I can sing, and no one can sing like me; but only because I sing for you, and with my soul I love you! '

She could not often be sorrowful, and never for long together, even in thinking of the past. Yes, one day there was of unbroken grief, the day on which she received, through Mrs. Ormonde as always, the letter wherein Lydia told her of Mr. Boddy's death. On that day she shed bitter tears. Lydia spared her all that was most painful. She said that the old man had fallen insensible by the Pooles' house, had been taken in by them, and had died. She said that just before the end he uttered Thyrza's name. And Thyrza had thought too seldom of Mr. Boddy, to whom she and her sister owed so much. Had she hastened his death— she now asked herself—by bringing upon him a great grief? The common remorse, the common vain longings, assailed her. Even in the old days she had somewhat slighted him; she had never shown him such love and care as Lydia always did. And the poor old man was buried, with so much of her past.

Only one little shadow there was that fell upon her at times when she thought of Egremont. What was that question of Mrs. Ormonde's—a question asked in the over-heard conversation? ' Have you altogether forgotten Anna-bel? ' And Walter's reply had shown that he did once love someone named Annabel. He had asked her to marry him, and she — strange beyond thought! — had refused him. Thyrza believed — she could not be quite sure, but she believed—that she had heard Mrs. Ormonde address Miss Newthorpe by that name. She remembered Miss Newthorpe very distinctly, her refined beauty, her delightful playing; strangely, too, she had associated Egremont with that lady

in the thoughts she had after her return from Eastbourne.
If that were Annabel, did there remain no fear ? If he had
once loved her, might not the love revive ? He and she
would meet—doubtless, would meet. Her beauty, her ac-
complishments, would be present, and was there no danger
to the newer love if that memory were frequently brought
back ?

If he had not loved Annabel, be she who she might ! If
this love for herself had been his first love, how thankful she
would have been ! The love she gave him was her first;
never had she loved Gilbert Grail, though she had thought
her friendship for him deserved the dearer name. Her first
love, truly, and would it not be her last ?

Very often, when she had sat down to her book, thoughts
of this kind would come and distract her. What to her were
the kings of old Eastern lands, the conquests of Rome, the
long chronicles dense with forgotten battle and woe ? So
easily she could have yielded to her former habits, and have
passed hour after hour in reverie. What—she wondered
now—had she dreamed of in those far-off days ? Was it not
foresight of the mystery one day to rule her life ? Had she
not visioned these sorrows and these priceless joys, when as
yet unable to understand them ? Indeed, sometimes there
seemed no break between then and now. She longed unconsciously for what was now come, that was all. Everything
had befallen so naturally, so inevitably, step by step, a rising
from vision to vision.

Would the future perfect her life's progress ?

But Lydia was not forgotten. To her she wrote long
letters, telling all that she might tell. The one thing of
which she would most gladly have spoken to her sister must
never be touched upon. For in one respect Lydia was
against her—fixedly against her ; she had come to know that
too well. Lydia bitterly resented Egremont's coming between
her sister and Gilbert ; she hoped his name would never
again be spoken, and that all remembrance of him would
pass away. This made no difference to Thyrza's love. When
she met Lydia it was always with the same passionate joy.
Their meetings took place in a private room at the hotel Mrs.
Ormonde always used. Lydia never made any inquiry ;
whatever she might tell about herself, Thyrza had to tell
unasked. It would have made a great difference had there
been no secret to keep beyond that comparatively unimportant

one of where Thyrza was living. But Thyrza resolved to breathe no word till the two years were gone by. Would it, then, make a coldness between her and her sister? It should not; her happiness should not have that great flaw.

When the spring came, Thyrza knew a falling off in her health. The pain at her heart gave her more trouble, and she had days of such physical weakness that she could do little work. With the reviving year her passion became a yearning of such intensity that it seemed to exhaust her frame. For all her endeavours it was seldom during these weeks that she could give attention to her books; even her voice failed for a time, and when she resumed the suspended lessons, she terrified her teacher by fainting just as he was taking leave of her. Mrs. Ormonde came, and there was a very grave conversation between her and Dr. Lambe, who was again attending Thyrza. It was declared that the latter had been over-exerting herself; work of all kind was prohibited for a season. And when a week or two brought about little, if any, improvement, Thyrza was taken to Eastbourne, to her old quarters in Mrs. Guest's house.

There Lydia spent two days with her.

The elder sister could not give herself to full enjoyment of these days. Much as she delighted to be with Thyrza, there was always one and the same drawback to her pleasure in the meetings. Thyrza was so unfeignedly cheerful that Lydia could by no effort get rid of her suspicion that she was being deceived. She shrank from reopening the subject, because it was so disagreeable to her to pronounce Egremont's name; because, too, she could not betray doubt without offending Thyrza. It was hard to distrust Thyrza, yet how account for the girl's most strange apparent happiness? Even now, though under troubled health, her sister's spirits were good. Far more easily Lydia could have suspected Mrs. Ormonde of some duplicity, yet here she was checked by instincts of gratitude, and by a sense of shame. Mrs. Ormonde did not certainly impress her as likely to be deceitful. Still, though she would not specify accusation, Lydia felt, was convinced indeed, that something very material was being kept from her. It was a cruel interference with the completeness of her sympathy in all the conversation between Thyrza and herself.

'So you are friends again with Mary Bower,' Thyrza said,

D D

soon after they had met. 'Do you go and have tea with her on Sundays sometimes?'

'No, she comes to me.'

'And you go to chapel?'

Thyrza laughed, seeing Lydia look down.

'Poor Lyddy, what a trial it always was to you! Do you mind it so much now?'

They were sitting on the beach. Lydia picked up pebbles and threw them away.

'I don't think about it as I used to, Thyrza,' she replied, quietly, after a short pause. 'I go now because I like to go.'

'Do you, dear?' Thyrza said, doubtfully, feeling there was a change and not understanding it. 'You always liked the singing, you know.'

'Yes, I like the singing. But there's more than that. I like it all now.'

'Do you?' said Thyrza, in yet a more uncertain voice.

Lydia looked up and smiled brightly.

'We won't talk about it now, dearest. Some day we will, though—a good long talk. When we are again together. If we ever shall be together again, Thyrza.'

'I think so, Lyddy. I hope so. At all events, we shall see each other very often.'

'Very often? Not always together?'

Thyrza was silent, but said presently:

'Perhaps. We can't tell, Lyddy.'

'But you don't *think* we shall. You don't *hope* we shall.'

Thyrza did not speak.

'No,' Lydia went on, very sadly, 'that's all over and gone. There's something between us, and now there always will be, always. It's very hard for me to lose you like this.'

'Don't speak about it now, Lyddy,' her sister murmured. 'It isn't true that there'll always be something between us. You'll see. But don't speak about it now, dear.'

Lydia brightened, and found other subjects. Then Thyrza said:

'You never told me, Lyddy, what it was that first made you break off with Mary. You know you never would tell me. Is it still a secret?'

'No. I can tell you if you like.'

'Please, do.'

'It was because Mary spoke against Mr. Ackroyd. I still don't think that she ought to have spoken as she did, and Mary owns she was unkind; but I understand better now what she meant.'

' What was it she said ? '

' It was about his having no religion, and that, because he had none, he did things he couldn't have done if he'd felt in the right way.'

' Yes, I understand,' Thyrza mused. She added : ' He's still not married ? '

' No.'

᾿ Why not ?—Lyddy, I don't believe they ever will be married.'

' And I don't either, dear.'

Thyrza looked quickly at her sister. Lydia was again playing with pebbles, not quite smiling, but nearly.

' You don't. Then what has happened ? Won't you tell me ? '

' I don't think they suit each other.'

' But there's something else, I'm sure there is. You said, " And I don't either," in such a queer way. How do you know they don't suit each other ? '

' Since grandad's death, you know, I've often been to Mrs. Poole's. She tells me things sometimes. You mustn't think I ever ask, Thyrza. You know that isn't my way. But Mrs. Poole often speaks about her brother. Only two days ago, she told me he wasn't going to marry Totty.'

' Really ? And I don't think you'd have said a word about it if I hadn't made you ! It's broken off for good ? '

' I believe it is.'

Neither spoke for a while. Then Thyrza said :

' I suppose you see Mr. Ackroyd sometimes at the house ? '

' Sometimes,' the other replied, heedlessly.

' Does he talk to you, Lyddy ? '

' A little. Just a little, sometimes.'

' But *why* has he broken off with Totty ? What does Totty say about it ? '

' I believe she was the first to ask him to break off. I met her a week ago, and she looked very jolly, as if something good had happened to her. I suppose she's glad to be free again.'

' How queer it all is, Lyddy ! Now you might mention things like this in your letters. If there's anything else of the same kind happens, remember you tell me.'

'I don't see how there can be. Unless they begin over again.'

'Well, mind you tell me if they do—and if they don't.'

On the second day of Lydia's visit, they heard from The Chestnuts that Bessie Bunce was dead. She had died suddenly, and just when she seemed to be in better health than for years.

Thyrza, speaking of the event with Lydia, said gravely :

'I can't feel sorry. It's a good thing to die like that, with no pain and no looking forward.'

'Oh, do you think so, Thyrza? There's something dreadful in the suddenness to me.'

'To me it's just the opposite. I'm afraid of death. I don't think I could sit by anybody that was dying. I hope, I hope I may die in that way ! '

Lydia was shocked, and wondered grieving.

CHAPTER XXXIV

A LOAN ON SECURITY

YET again it was summer-time, the second summer since the parting between Lydia and her sister, all but the end of the second twelvemonth since the day when Thyrza had heard something that was not meant for her ears. In Walnut Tree Walk the evening was clear and warm. A man was going along the street selling flowers in pots ; his donkey-cart was covered with leaf and bloom, and with a geranium under each arm, he trudged onwards, bellowing. Children were playing at five-stones on the pavement ; you heard an organ away in Kennington Road.

Lydia was having tea and trimming a bonnet at the same time ; the bonnet belonged to Mrs. Poole, and the work on it was for friendship's sake. Only on that understanding had Lydia consented to do it. Mrs. Poole had frequently wished to give her an odd job at needlework for which she herself either had not time or lacked the skill, and to pay for it as she would have had to pay any one else. For some reason, Lydia declined to do anything for her on those conditions ; she would help as a friend, but not otherwise.

She was hurrying, for she wanted to take the bonnet to Paradise Street by eight o'clock, and it was now half-past seven. Her face had the air of thoughtful contentment which best became it. Her window was open, and, as in the old days, there were flower-pots on the sill. Her eye now and then rested for a moment on the little patches of colour; she did not think of the flowers, but they helped pleasantly to tone her mind. Even so will a strain of music sometimes pass through the memory, unmarked by us, yet completing the happiness of some peaceful hour.

She drank her last drop of tea, and, almost simultaneously, put her last touch to the bonnet. Then she prepared herself for going out, hummed a tune whilst she carefully packed the piece of head-gear in its bandbox, and went on her way.

When Mrs. Poole answered her knock at the house-door, Lydia said:

'I hope you'll like it. I shall see you on Sunday, and you'll tell me then.'

'But where are you going? Why won't you come in?'

'Oh, I have to buy something.'

'Come in for a minute, then.'

'No, thank you; not to-night.'

'Do as I tell you!' said the other, with good-natured persistence. 'I believe you're ashamed of your work, and that's why you're running away. Come in at once.'

Lydia yielded, though seemingly with reluctance. They went down into the kitchen, where the two young Pooles were at an uproarious game.

'Now there's been just about enough of that!' exclaimed their mother, raising her voice to be heard. 'Miss Trent 'll think we have a bear-garden down here. You must play quietly, or off you go to bed—I mean it!'

The bonnet was taken forth and examined, with many ejaculations of delight from its owner. The only article of attire upon which Mrs. Poole ever spent a thought was her bonnet, a noteworthy instance of the inconsequence of human nature, seeing that it was the rarest thing for her to leave the house, save when she ran out at night to make purchases, and then she always donned an object of straw, whose utility was its only merit. Though as happy a woman as you could have found in Lambeth, she seldom had a moment of leisure from getting-up to bedtime. Her kind are very numerous. Such women pass through a whole summer without an hour of rest in the sunshine, and often through a married lifetime without going beyond the circle of neighbouring streets.

But the bonnet delighted her. She tried it on, and, having placed a looking-glass on the table, went through the wonderful feat in which women are so skilled, that of seeing the back of her head. Then, having constrained Lydia to sit down, she pursued multifarious occupations, talking the while.

'I hope you don't notice any bad smells in the house,' she said; 'there's Luke at his usual work, upstairs. What pleasure he can find in that is more than I can understand. I know he's ruined my table with his chemicals. There's Jacky with him, too. If I was Mr. Bunce I should be afraid to have the boy taught such things. He'll set the house on fire some day, will Master Jack, and burn himself and his little sister to death.'

'But you see,' said Lydia, 'Mr. Ackroyd does keep to it. You didn't think he'd persevere more than a week or two, and now it must be a good three months.'

'Well, yes, it *does* look as if it was going to be different from the other things,' Mrs. Poole admitted, with a grudging laugh. 'Well, he always had a liking for reading books of that kind. Let's hope he knows his own mind at last. But then he can't never do anything in moderation, can't Luke. He's got an idea into his head that he's going to invent a new kind of candle—if you ever heard such a thing! "Well," says I to him, last night, when he come talking to me about it, "it's what I call a come-down. Here a while ago you wasn't content with nothing but setting the world upside down; now you'll be satisfied if you can invent a new candle, and make money out of it. Well," I says, "I'd be above candles, Luke!" My! you should have seen how angry he got! Who said he wanted to make money? Who'd ever heard him mentioning money, he'd like to know? If people had low minds, that wasn't his fault! And then he went off grumbling to himself.'

'But,' ventured Lydia, with diffidence, 'I don't see there's any harm even if he did think of making money—do you, Mrs. Poole?'

'Not I, child! I only talked so just to tease him. I do so like to tease Luke; he puts on such airs. Let him make money of course, if he can; all the better for him. I'd a deal rather have him doing this than spending all his nights at that club in Westminster Bridge Road, talking nonsense, and worse. Why, he's ever so much better to live with now than he used to be. He really does talk sensible sometimes, and he isn't such a great baby about—about some things.'

Mrs. Poole smiled and held her tongue.

'And what's the last news from your sister?' was her next question.

'Oh, I had a letter yesterday,' Lydia replied, her face lighting up. 'It was all about the concert next Wednesday.'

'Well, well! She must be full of it, mustn't she, now? It must be a trying thing, to sing for the first time.'

'But it isn't so bad as if she had to sing alone, you know.'

'No, to be sure; but it must be bad enough even in a choir. Shan't you see her before the night?'

'No. And I shan't be able to speak to her on Wednesday, either. But the next day we shall have all the evening together. She sent me my ticket. Look, I've brought it to show you.'

It was a ticket for a concert in one of the suburbs of London. Lydia kept it in an envelope, and handled it with care. Mrs. Poole, before taking it, wiped her hands on her apron, and then held the card between the tips of her thumb and middle finger.

'Will her name be on the programme?' she asked.

'No. They're called Mr. Redfern's choir, that's all.'

'Well, I'm sure it's very nice, and something to be proud of. And she still keeps her health?'

'She says she is very well indeed.'

'Mrs. Poole,' added Lydia, lowering her voice, 'you haven't said anything about it?'

'No, no, my dear; not I.'

'It's better not, I think. Of course it doesn't really matter, but still——'

'Bless you, I understand very well, Lydia. There's no occasion to talk about such things at all. I suppose Mary Bower knows?'

'Oh yes, I told Mary.'

'Wouldn't she have liked to go with you?'

'Yes, I'm sure she would. But I think I'd rather be alone. There'll be another concert before long, I dare say, and then she shall go. It's just this first time, you know.'

It was a cosy kitchen, and Lydia, once seated here, seemed to forget about the shopping of which she had spoken. Mrs. Poole's stream of talk was intimate and soothing; plenty of good sense, no scandal, and no lack of blitheness. But at length it was declared to be the children's bed time, and Lydia made this the signal for rising to take her leave.

'Now do sit still !' urged Mrs. Poole. 'You're such a restless body. I've got lots of things I want to talk about yet, if only I could think of them.'

'I really must go,' Lydia pleaded.

'No, you mustn't now, I shan't be a minute getting these children off to bed, and then we'll have just five minutes' comfortable talk. Just sew me a new tape into that apron, there's a good girl. You know where the cotton is—on the dresser up there.'

Lydia took up the task cheerfully, and by when it was completed the youngsters were stripped and night-gowned, and ready to say their reluctant good-night. Their mother carried them upstairs, one on her back and one in her arms— good strong mother.

And the chat was renewed, till the next event of the evening, supper, had to be prepared for. Lydia seemed to have given up the struggle ; she consented to stay for the meal without much pressing. When the table was laid Mrs. Poole went upstairs to her brother's bedroom. On opening the door she was met with a very strong odour of chemical experimentalising. Despite the warmth of the season, there was a fire, with two or three singular pots boiling upon it. A table was covered with jars and phials, and test-tubes and retorts. Here Ackroyd was bending to explain something to a sharp-eyed little lad, Jacky Bunce. Luke had allowed his beard to grow of late, and it improved his appearance ; he looked more self-reliant than formerly. He was in his shirt-sleeves.

'Now, Jacky,' began Mrs. Poole, 'what'll your father say to you staying out till these hours ? He'll think you're blowed up. Why, it's half-past nine.'

'All right, Jane,' said Ackroyd. 'Jack and I have had a deal of talk about the compounds of hydrogen.'

'And if I was his mother, him and I would have a deal of talk about waistcoats,' rejoined Mrs. Poole, shrewdly.

'I declare, Luke, you ought to tie an apron over him, if he's going to make that mess of himself.'

'It's an old waistcoat, Mrs. Poole,' protested Jack. 'I keep it on purpose.'

'Oh, you do ! Well, mind it don't go through to your shirt, that's all. Now run away home, Jacky, there's a good boy.

'He shan't be five minutes more,' interposed Luke. 'I'm coming down myself in five minutes.'

'Well, supper's waiting. And here's Miss Trent here, too. Not that that'll make you come any quicker; perhaps I'd better not have mentioned it.'

Jane pressed her lips together after speaking, and withdrew.

'Don't you like Miss Trent, Mr. Ackroyd?' Jack inquired, when they were left alone. He was, as I have said, a sharp-eyed boy, and Luke could have given wonderful reports of his keenness of brain. It is often thus. The father has faculties which never ripen in himself, and which, as likely as not, cause him a life's struggle and unrest; they come to maturity and efficiency in the son. What more pathetic, rightly considered, than the story of those fathers whose lives are but a preparation for the richer lives of their sons? Poor Bunce, fighting with his ignorance and his passions, unable to overcome either, obstinate in holding on to a half-truth, catching momentary glimpses of a far-away ideal—what did it all mean, but that his boy should stand where *he* had been thrown, should see light where *his* eyes had striven vainly against the fog! Perhaps there is compensation to the parent if he live to see the lad conquering; but what of those who fall into silence when all is still uncertain, when they recognise in their offspring an hereditary weakness and danger as often as a rare gleam of new promise? One would bow reverently and sadly by the graves of such men.

It was a happy thought of Ackroyd's to give the boy lessons in chemistry. To teach is often the surest way of learning. In explaining simple things, Luke often enough discovered for the first time his own ignorance. In very fact, the greater part of the past two years had been spent by him in making discoveries of that nature—long before he thought of new combinations of oleaginous matter. By degrees he had come to suspect that, as regarded the employment of his leisure hours, he was very decidedly on the wrong track. Curiously, for Ackroyd as well as for Bunce, there had arisen a measure of evil from Walter Egremont's aspiring work. Luke, though not to such a violent degree as Bunce, was led to offer opposition to everything savouring of idealism—that is to say, of idealism as Egremont had presented it. He had heard but one of Walter's lectures, yet that was enough to realise for him the kind of thing which henceforth he disliked and distrusted. Egremont, it seemed to him, had sought to make working men priggish and effeminate, whereas what they wanted was back-bone and consciousness of the hard facts of life. Ackroyd had never cared much for literature proper; his intellectual progress was henceforth to be in the direction of hostility to literature. When his various love difficulties ceased to absorb all his attention, he went back to his scientific books, and found that his appetite for such studies was keener than ever. At length he converted his bedroom into a laboratory, resolved to pursue certain investigations seriously. When his heart—or diaphragm, or whatever else it may be—left him at peace, his brain could work to sufficient purpose. And of late he had worked most vigorously. He ceased to trouble himself about politics, and religion, and social matters. His views thereon, he declared, had undergone no change whatever, but he had no time to talk at present.

But a question of Jack's waited for an answer.

'That's only my sister's fun,' Luke replied, with a smile. 'There's no reason why I shouldn't like her.'

'I think she don't look bad,' Jack remarked, as if allowing himself to stray from chemistry to a matter of trivial interest. He added: 'But she don't come up to Miss Nancarrow. I like *her*; she's the right kind of girl, don't you think so?'

'First-rate.'

'I say, Mr. Ackroyd, why don't you never come now and call for her, like you used to?'

'Used to? When?'

'Why, you know well enough. Not long ago.'

'Oh, years ago!'

'No, not more than a year ago.'

'Yes, Jack; a year and a half.'

'Well it didn't seem so long. I say, why don't you? I've only just thought of it.'

'There's no need to call. I see her sometimes, and that's enough for friends, isn't it?'

'I believe you was going to marry Miss Nancarrow, wasn't you?'

'Hollo! Who told you such a thing as that?'

'Nobody. I thought of it myself. It looks like it, when I think. I'm older now, you see, than I was then; I see more into things.'

Ackroyd laughed heartily.

'It seems you do.'

' Well but, tell me, Mr. Ackroyd.'

' No, I shan't. When you get a bit older still, you'll know that men have no business to talk about such things. Understand that, Jack. Never get into the way of talking about things that aren't your business ; there's been a deal of harm done by that.'

' Has there ? '

Luke was silent. The boy continued :

' You're sure you *are* friends with Miss Nancarrow ? '

' Of course I am, capital friends. Why, we were both of us on the Greenwich boat last Sunday, and we laughed and talked no end of time.'

But Luke was ready to leave the room. He appointed another evening when Jack should come, and the lad scampered off.

Leaving Ackroyd to go down and have supper with his sister and Lydia, and with Mr. Poole, who had just come home from a late job, let us go after Jack into Newport Street. As he reached the house, his father was just coming out.

' You're too late,' said the latter, with a shake of the head. ' Tell Mr. Ackroyd you must be back by nine. What about your lessons, eh ? '

' Lessons ! ' exclaimed Jack, scornfully. ' Do them in half a crack before breakfast. Why, there's nothing but a bit of jography, and some kings, and three proportion sums, and a page of——'

' All right. Go to bed quietly. Nelly's asleep long ago. I shall be back in half an hour.'

Jack went very softly upstairs. In the one room which was still the entire home of his father and himself and his little sister, he found a lamp burning low. The child was in her small cot, sleeping peacefully. Jack began to unbutton his acid-stained waistcoat, having seized a piece of bread and butter that lay waiting for him, when his thoughts intervened to suspend the operation of undressing. He left the room again, and looked at the door on the opposite side of the landing. He saw a light beneath it. He advanced and rapped softly.

' Who's that ? ' was asked from within.

' You ain't in bed yet, Miss Nancarrow, are you ? ' Jack asked, with the frankness of expression which became his age.

The door opened, and Totty appeared, able to receive visitors still with perfect propriety.

' What is it, Jacky? '

The lad was munching his bread and butter.

' You haven't got a spoonful of that jam left, have you, Miss Nancarrow?' he asked, with a mixture of confidence and shamefacedness.

Totty laughed.

' I dare say I have. But this is a nice time to come asking for jam. Isn't your father in? '

' Gone out. Says he'll be half an hour. Plenty of time, Miss Nancarrow.'

' Come in then.'

Totty closed the door, and produced from her cupboard— a receptacle regarded with profound interest both by Nelly and the maturer Jack—a pot of black currant preserve. She spread some with a liberal hand on the lad's bread, then watched him as he ate, her enjoyment equalling his own. The bread finished, she offered a spoonful of jam pure and simple; it was swallowed with gusto.

' I say, Miss Nancarrow,' remarked Jack, ' I don't half-like going to a new house. I can't see what father wants to move for ; we're well enough off here.'

' Why don't you want to go? '

' Well, there's a good many things. I shouldn't mind so much, you know, if you was coming as well.'

Again she laughed.

' That's as much as to say, Jack, you'll be sorry when there's no jam. It isn't *me*, not it! '

' Don't be so sure. I shall come and see you often enough, and not for jam, either. You're always jolly with me. And I don't see why you can't come as well. Father 'ud like you to.'

Totty regarded him with a smile for an instant, then asked, carelessly :

' How do you know that? As if it made any difference to your father! '

' But he's said he wished you was coming. He said so day before yesterday.'

' Nonsense! Now get off to bed. He'll be back, and we shall both get scolded.'

Jack drew to the door, but Totty recalled him.

' What an idea, for your father to say he wished I was coming! Tell me how he said it.'

'Why, it was about Nelly. We was talking and saying Nelly 'ud miss you. And father said, half to himself like, "Nelly wouldn't be sorry if Miss Nancarrow 'ud come and be with her always, and I dare say somebody else wouldn't be sorry, either."'

'Why, you silly boy, he meant you, of course.'

'Oh no, he didn't. Think I can't tell what he meant!'

'Run off to bed! I think I hear your father coming in.'

Jack made a rush, and in one minute and a half was under the bed-clothes.

The removal which Bunce was about to effect signified an improvement of circumstances. It was time for his luck to turn. Year after year he had found himself still at grip with poverty. The shadow of his evil domestic experiences lengthened as he drew further away, and it seemed as if he would never get beyond it. To a man of any native delicacy, the memory of bondage to a hateful woman clings like a long disease which impoverishes the blood; there is only one way of eradicating it, and that is with the aid of a strong, wholesome, new emotion. And at length Bunce began to feel that the past was really past; one sign of it was the better fortune which enabled him to earn more money. One of his children was dead, but the other two were growing in health of mind and body, and he could clothe them better, could look forward to their future, at last, without that sinking of the heart which at times had made him pause by night on one of the river bridges and long for a moment's madness that he might plunge and have done with everything. Few men had come out of darkness into the light of a sober working day with less help than he had had. It was his nature to keep silence on his difficulties. He did not much care to hold continuous friendship with any man, for, like all who have the habit of talking to themselves, he was conscious that his companionship lacked attraction. Moreover—a thing which superficial observers do not realise—like all who are most genuinely at odds with the world, the first head of his quarrel was with himself. He was only too well aware of his own defects and errors. He felt himself to be unamiable, often gross of understanding, always ready to fall into a blunder which other men would avoid. He had stood in his own way as often as he had been balked by others, perhaps oftener.

Now he was going to risk a step forward, was going to leave his single room lodging and take two rooms in a brighter street some distance away. They would be vacant for him a fortnight hence, and he had money enough to buy furniture. Yet he did not look forward to the change as cheerfully as might have been expected.

For one reason, and for one only, the old abode was preferable to him; it was a reason of such weight that it cost him no little exertion of common sense to put it aside. At the same time, it *had* to be put aside, and most resolutely, for, whenever it occupied his mind, he soon found himself uttering contemptuous remarks upon his own thick-headed folly. He would sometimes blurt out such words as 'fool—idiot—blockhead,' as he walked along the street, astonishing passers-by who could not be supposed to know that the speaker was applying these epithets to himself.

On Sunday evening, a day or two after the conversation just reported between Jack and Totty, Bunce took his children to Battersea Park. When there, he did not walk about among the people, but sought a retired piece of lawn and sat down to enjoy a pipe. Nelly had brought a doll with her, and found delectable occupation in explaining to it all the various objects which might reasonably excite its curiosity in such a place. Jack talked with his father of chemistry, of his school teachers, of what he would be when he was a man. Their conversation was interrupted by Nelly's exclaiming:

'See, there's Miss Nancarrow!'

Totty was coming over the grass at a little distance, between two companions, girls dressed with an emphasis of Sunday elegance which made her look rather brown and and plain by contrast. Totty never cared to spend much on clothes, a singular feature of her character. When the three were passing at a distance of twenty yards, Nelly cried out with shrill voice:

'Miss Nancarrow!'

'Hush, child!' said her father, more annoyed than seemed necessary. 'Don't scream at people in that way.'

Nelly was abashed, but her cry had caught Totty's ear. The latter nodded, laughed, and went on with her friends.

'I say, father,' Jack began, 'do you know what I think?'

'What, boy?'

'Why, I think if you asked Miss Nancarrow to come and take a room in the new house, she would.'

'Why on earth should I ask her to do such a thing?' inquired Bunce, laying down his pipe on the grass; it had gone out since Totty's passing. He looked at his son with bent brows, and rather fiercely.

'Well, I know I'd like her to, and so would Nelly. I can get on with Miss Nancarrow, 'cause she's got so much sense. I don't think much of other women.'

Bunce grubbed up roots of grass with his hard, blunt fingers. Then he took up his pipe again and turned the stem about between his teeth. And the while he cast glances at Jack, side glances, half savage.

'What makes you think she'd come?' he inquired at length, with a blundering attempt at indifference of tone.

'I talked to her about it the other night.'

'Oh, you did, did you? And what business had you to talk about such things, I'd like to know?'

'I don't see no harm. I told her we'd all be glad if she'd come.'

'What the confusion! And who told you to say any such thing?'

Jack was amazed at the outburst of wrath he had provoked.

'Well, father,' he muttered, 'I've heard you say yourself that you'd be glad if she was coming.'

'Then I'll thank you not to repeat what I say. Leave Miss Nancarrow alone. If I find you've talked to her in that way again, you and me 'll quarrel, Jack.'

The boy fell into a fit of sulks, and drew to a little distance, where he lay flat, beating the earth vigorously with a stick.

Then it strangely happened that someone came round the bushes, in the shadow of which the three were reposing, and that it was no other than Miss Nancarrow, this time unaccompanied. Bunce did not notice her till she stood before him, then he jumped to his feet.

'Don't disturb yourself, Mr. Bunce,' said Totty, with her usual self-command. 'I'm only going to have a talk with Nelly, that's all.'

She sat down on the grass by the little one, and began a grave dialogue on the subject of certain ailments from which the doll had recently recovered.

It had been nursed through measles—Nelly having had them not long ago—and its face still showed signs of the disease.

Jack was not disposed to talk. His discretion had been

impugned, and at Jack's age one feels anything of that kind shrewdly. Letting his eyes wander about the portion of park that lay before them, he saw at a little distance the nucleus of a religious meeting. At any other time he would have scorned to pay attention to such a phenomenon; at present he was glad of any opportunity of asserting his independence. He knew his father ridiculed prayer-meetings, consequently he rose and began to walk in the direction of the group of people.

'Where are you going, Jack?' cried Bunce.

'Only for a walk. I'll come back.'

His father acquiesced. Totty suspended her talk and gazed after him for a moment. Then she turned to Bunce.

'So you've found rooms, Mr. Bunce?' she said, with a piece of sorrel between her lips.

'Yes, I've got two that'll suit us, I think.'

He mentioned where they were, and made a few remarks about them.

'If there's anything I can do to help you,' said Totty, looking at Jack's distant figure, 'you'll tell me, I know. There might be some sewing. I've got plenty of time. Window blinds, and those things.'

'Well, I've made arrangements about all that with the landlady,' Bunce replied, in some embarrassment. 'I thank you very much, Miss Nancarrow, all the same.'

'That's too bad of you. You knew very well I'd have been glad to help. Tell your father he's very soon forgetting his old friends, Nelly.'

She drew the child to her as she spoke, and kissed her cheek.

'You know very well I shan't do that, Miss Nancarrow,' said Bunce, glancing at her. 'Whoever else, I'm not likely to forget you.'

'I'm not so sure of that. Are you, Nelly?'

He said nothing. Totty let her eyes catch a glimpse of his face. He was looking down, and again grubbing up grass.

'I shall be very sorry if you don't come and see the children sometimes,' he mumbled. 'Or at all events, I hope they can come and see you.'

'Shall you still work at the same shop?' Totty asked, paying no attention to the last remark.

'Yes, for a bit at all events.'

'Why don't you start a shop of your own, Mr. Bunce?' she next inquired, as if a happy idea had struck her.

'I shouldn't mind doing that,' he answered, with a hard laugh. 'But shops can't be had for the wishing.'

'You don't need a big one. Now like that shop in Duke Street, you know. What's the rent of a place like that?'

'I'm sure I don't know. I suppose it goes with the house.'

'Then what's the rent of the house likely to be? You could let all you didn't want, you know, and that 'ud almost pay the rent, I should think.'

He laughed again.

'What's the good of talking about it? Why there's a little locksmith's and ironmonger's shop to let in that street just off the far end of Lambeth Walk. They're selling off now; I'm going to buy a few things to-morrow. But what's the good of thinking about it?'

'I don't know. What's the rent?'

'Not more than forty pounds, house and all, I dare say. A mate of mine was talking about it. He said he wished he'd a couple of hundred pounds to take it and start. The man's dead, and his wife wanted to sell the business, but she can't get an offer.'

The meeting which Jack was attending had begun to sing a hymn. The voices, harmonised by distance, sounded pleasantly.

'I like that hymn-tune, Mr. Bunce,' said Totty, 'don't you?'

'I don't think much about hymns, Miss Nancarrow.'

'Well, you might say you like it.'

'I do, to tell the truth—so long as I can't hear the words.'

'I don't care nothing about the words, either. So we agree about something, at all events.'

'I don't think we've differed about many things, have we?'

She looked at him frankly, and smiled. Then she said:

'Oh, you used to be a bit afraid of me, I know. Shall I tell you what it was made us real friends? It was when you burnt your hand, and I did it up for you.'

Bunce now returned her look, and his swarthy cheeks reddened. His eyes fell again.

'You behaved very kindly,' he said in a half-ashamed way. 'I don't forget, and I'm not likely ever to. And I shan't forget all you've done for the children, either. I don't think there's any one living I've more to thank for than you.'

'The idea.'

'Well, it's true.'

'But look here, Mr. Bunce. About that shop. Suppose

E E

you had two hundred and fifty pounds ; could you make a start, do you think ? '

' I rather suppose I could.   And where's two hundred and fifty pound to come from, Miss Nancarrow ? '

' I'll lend it you if you like.'

He gazed at her with so strange a face that Totty broke into hearty laughter. Bunce joined, appreciating the joke.

' I mean it, Mr. Bunce. I've got two hundred and fifty pounds—at all events I can have, whenever I like.'

He gazed again, wondering at her tone.

' Now I see you don't believe me, so I shall have to explain.'

She told him the story of her legacy, only forbearing to speak of the condition attached to it.

' Will you let me lend it you, Mr. Bunce ? '

' No, I'm sure I shan't, Miss Nancarrow.   You'll have plenty of use for that yourself.'

' Look here, Nelly ! '   The child was listening to this remarkable dialogue, and trying to understand. ' Tell your father he's to do just what I want. If he doesn't, I'll never speak again neither to you nor Jacky. Now, I mean it.'

' Please father,' said Nelly, ' do what Miss Nancarrow wants.'

Bunce kept his face half averted.   He was at a dire pass.

' Well, Mr. Bunce ? '

' That's all nonsense ! ' he exclaimed.   ' How can I tell that I should ever be able to pay you back ? '

' So you won't ? '

' Of course I can't. It's just like you to offer, but of course I can't.'

' Very well, I can't help it.'   She lowered her voice.   ' I forgot to tell you that I can't get the money till I'm married. It doesn't matter, I've offered it.'

Bunce stared at her.

' Good-bye, Nelly,' Totty went on. ' I can't be friends with you after this.   Your father's told me to go about my business.'

' No, he hasn't,' protested the child, dolorously. ' You haven't, have you, father ? '

' Yes, he has. It doesn't matter, I'm off.'

She jumped up. Bunce sprang to his feet at the same time, and caught her up in a moment. She turned, looked at him reddened, laughed.

'Why did you say anything about that money?' he began, able to speak without restraint at length. 'If I hadn't known about that!'

'I don't see what the money's got to do with it.'

'I do. Look, I should have felt like making a fool of myself—a man of my age and with two children—but I do believe when I'd got into those new rooms I couldn't have helped some day asking you if—well, I can't say it. I'm ashamed of myself, that's the truth.'

'And what does that matter, Mr. Bunce, so long as I'm not ashamed of you?'

'When you might do so well? A man like me—and the children?'

'How you talk! Don't you think I'm fond of the children?'

'Come and sit down again and talk a bit.'

'No. Will you have the money, Mr. Bunce, or won't you?'

'I'd very much rather have you without it, Totty, and that's the honest truth.'

'Yes, but you can't, you see. Now, you'll have a rare tale to tell of me some day, when you're tired of me. And it's all come of your changing your lodgings.'

'I know.'

'No, you don't know. Come and sit down, and I'll tell you.'

Totty went back, and fondled Nelly against her side, and explained why the threatened change of abode had made her act with such independence—characteristic to the end.

CHAPTER XXXV

THREE LETTERS

Walter Egremont to Mrs. Ormonde.

'WERE I to spend the rest of my natural life in this country —which assuredly I have no intention of doing—I think I should never settle down to an hour's indulgence of those tastes which were born in me, and which, in spite of all neglect, are in fact as strong as ever. I cannot read the books I wish to read; I cannot even think the thoughts I wish to think. As I have told you, the volumes I brought out with me lay in their packing-cases for more than six months after my arrival, and for all the use I have made of them in this second six months they might be still there. The shelves in the room which I call my library are furnished, but I dare not look how much dust they have accumulated.

'I read scarcely anything but newspapers—it is I who write the words! Newspapers at morning, newspapers at night. Yes, one exception; I have spent a good deal of time of late over Walt Whitman (you know him, of course, by name, though I dare say you have never looked into his works), and I expect that I shall spend a good deal more ; I suspect, indeed, that he will in the end come to mean much to me. But I cannot write of him yet; I am struggling with him, struggling with myself as regards him; in a month or so I shall have more to say. It is perfectly true, then, that till quite recently I have read but newspapers. The people about me scarcely by any chance read anything else, and the influence of surroundings has from the first been very strong upon me. You have complained frequently that I say nothing to you about my *self* ; it is one of the signs of my condition that with difficulty I think of that self, and to pen words about it has been quite impossible. I long constantly for the old world and the old moods, but I cannot imagine myself back into them. I would give anything to lock my door at night, and take down my Euripides ; if I get as far as the shelf, my hand drops.

' I begin to see a meaning in this phase of my life. I have been learning something about the latter end of the nineteenth century, its civilisation, its possibilities, and the subject has a keen interest for me. Is it new, then ? you will ask. To tell you the truth, I knew nothing whatever about it until I came and began to work in America. I am in the mood for frankness, and I won't spare myself. All my so-called study of modern life in former days was the merest dilettantism, mere conceit and boyish pedantry. I travelled, and the fact that wherever I went I took a small classical library with me was symbolical of my state of mind. I saw everything through old-world spectacles. Even in America I could not get rid of my pedantry, as you will recognise clearly enough if you look back to the letters I wrote you at that time. I came then with theories in my head of what American civilisation must be, and everything that I saw I made fit in with my preconceptions.

This time I came with my mind a blank. I was ill, and had not a theory left in me on any subject in the universe. For the first time in my life I was suffering all that a man can suffer; when the Atlantic roared about me, I scarcely cared whether it engulfed me or not. Getting back my health, I began to see with new eyes, and have since been looking my hardest. And I have still not a theory on any subject in the universe.

'In fact, I believe that for me the day of theories has gone by. I note phenomena, and muse about them, and not a few interest me extremely. The interest is enough. I am not a practical man; I am not a philosopher. I may, indeed, have a good deal of the poet's mind, but the poet's faculty is denied to me. It only remains to me to study the word in its relations to my personality, that I may henceforth avoid the absurdities to which I have such a deplorable leaning.

'Do you know what I ought to have been?—a schoolmaster. That is to say, if I wished to do any work of direct good to my fellows in the world. I could have taught boys well, better than I shall ever do anything else. I could not only have taught them—the "gerund-grinding" of Thomas Carlyle—but could have inspired them with love of learning, at all events such as were capable of being so inspired. My class of working men in Lambeth exercised this faculty to some extent. When I was teaching them English Literature, I was doing, as far as it went, good and sound work. When I drifted into "Thoughts for the Present"—Heaven forgive me!—I made an ass of myself, that's the long and short of it. My ears tingle as I remember those evenings.

'I am infinitely more human than I was; I can even laugh heartily at American humour, and that I take to be a sign of health. Health is what I have gained. The devotion of eight or ten hours a day to the work of the factory has been the best medicine any one could have prescribed to me. It was you who prescribed it, and it was your crowning act of kindness to me, dear Mrs. Ormonde. It is possible that I have grown coarser; indeed, I know that I associate on terms of equality and friendliness with men from whom I should formerly have shrunk. I can get angry, and stand on my rights, and bluster if need be, and on the whole I think I am no worse for that. My ear is not offended if I hear myself called "boss;" why should it be? it is a word as well as another. Nay, I have even felt something like excitement when listening to political speeches, in which frequent mention was made of "the great State of Pennsylvania." Well, it *is* a great State, or the phrase has no meaning in any application. Will not this early life of the New World some day be studied with reverence and enthusiasm? I try to see things as they are.

'Social problems are here in plenty. Indeed, it looks very much as if America would sooner have reached an acute stage of social conflict than the old countries; naturally, as it is the refuge of those who abandon the old world in disgust. American equality is a mere phrase; there is as much brutal injustice here as elsewhere. But I can no longer rave on the subject; the injustice is a *fact*, and only other facts will replace it; I concern myself only with facts. And the great fact of all is the contemptibleness of average humanity. I will submit for your reverent consideration the name of a great American philanthropist—Cornelius Vanderbilt. Personally he was a disgusting brute; ignorant, base, a boor in his manners, a blackguard in his language; he had little if any natural affection, and to those who offended him he was a relentless barbarian. Yet the man was a great philanthropist, and became so by the piling up of millions of dollars. Of course he did that for his own vulgar satisfaction, though personally he could not use the money when he had it; no matter, he has aided civilisation enormously. He as good as created the steamship industry in America; he reorganised the railway system with admirable results; by adding so much to the circulating capital of the country, he provided well-paid employment for unnumbered men. Thousands of homes should bless the name of Vanderbilt—and what is the state of a world in which such a man can do such good by such means? Well, I have nothing to say to it. It is merely part of the tremendous present, which interests me.

'And I once stood up in my pulpit, and with mild assurance addressed myself to the task of improving the world! Do not make fun of me when we meet again, dear friend; I am too bitterly ashamed of myself.

'It seems a long time since you told me anything of Thyrza. I do not like to receive a letter from you in which there is no mention of her name. Does she still find a resource in her music? Are you still kind to her? Yes, kind I know you are, but are you gentle and affectionate, doing your utmost to make her forget that she is alone? You do not see her very frequently, I fear. I beg you to write to her often, the helpful letters you can write to those whom you love. She can repay you for all trouble with one look of gratitude.'

(Three months later.)

'I am sending you Whitman's "Leaves of Grass." I see from your last letter that you have not yet got the book, and have it you must. It is idle to say that you cannot take up new things, that you doubt whether he has any significance for *you*, and so on. You have heart and brain, therefore his significance for you will be profound.

'I would not write much about him hitherto; for I dreaded the smile on your face at a new enthusiasm. I wished, too, to test this influence upon myself thoroughly; I assure you that it is easier for me now to be sceptical than to open my heart generously to any one who in our day declares himself a message-bringer to mankind. You know how cautiously I have proceeded with this American *vates*. At first I found so much to repel me, yet from the first also I was conscious of a new music, and then the clamour of the vulgar against the man was quite enough to oblige me to give him careful attention. If one goes on the assumption that the ill word of the mob is equivalent to high praise, one will not, as a rule, be far wrong, in matters of literature. I have studied Whitman, enjoyed him, felt his force and his value. And, speaking with all seriousness, I believe that he has helped me, and will help me, inestimably, in my endeavour to become a sound and mature man.

'For in him I have met with one who is, first and foremost, a man, a large, healthy, simple, powerful, full-developed man. Read his poem called "A Song of Joys"—what glorious energy of delight, what boundless sympathy, what *sense*, what *spirit*! He knows the truth of the life that is in all things. From joy in a railway train—" the laughing locomotive! To push with resistless way and speed off in the distance "—to joy in fields and hillsides, joy in " the dropping of rain-drops in a song," joy in the fighter's strength, joy in the life of the fisherman, in every form of active being—aye, and

Joys of the free and lonesome heart, the tender, gloomy heart,
Joys of the solitary work, the spirit bow'd yet proud, the suffering and the struggle;
The agonistic throes, the ecstasies, joys of the solemn musings day or night;
Joys of the thought of Death, the great spheres Time and Space!

What would not I give to know the completeness of manhood implied in all that? Such an ideal of course is not a new-created thing for me, but I never *felt* it as in Whitman's work. It is so foreign to my own habits of thought. I have always been so narrow, in a sense so provincial. And indeed I doubt whether Whitman would have appealed to me as he now does had I read him for the first time in England and under the old conditions. These fifteen months of practical business life in America has swept my brain of much that was mere prejudice, even when I thought it worship. I was a pedantic starveling; now, at all events, I *see* the world about me, and all the goodliness of it. Then I am far healthier in body than I was, which goes for much. It would be no hardship to me to take an axe and go off to labour on the Pacific coast; nay, a year so spent would do me a vast amount of good.

' I wonder whether you have read any of the twaddle that is written about Whitman's grossness, his materialism, and so forth? If so, read his poems now, and tell me how they impress you. Is he not *all* spirit, rightly understood? For to him the body with its energies is but manifestation of that something invisible which we call human soul. And so pure is the soul in him, so mighty, so tender, so infinitely sympathetic, that it may stand for Humanity itself. I am often moved profoundly by his words. He makes me feel that I am a very part of the universe, and that in health I can deny kinship with nothing that exists. I believe that he for the first time has spoken with the very voice of nature; forests and seas sing to us through him, and through him the healthy, unconscious man, " the average man," utters what before he had no voice to tell of, his secret aspirations, his mute love and praise.

' Look you! I write a sort of essay, and in doing so prove that I am myself still. Were it not that I have mercy on you, I could preach on even as I used to do to my class in Lambeth. Ha, if I had known Whitman then! I believe that by per-suading those men to read him, and helping them to under-stand him, I should really have done an honest day's work. There were some who could have relished his meaning, and whose lives he would have helped. For there it is; Whitman helps one; he is a tonic beyond all to be found in the drug-gist's shop. I image that to live with the man himself for a few days would be the best thing that could befall an invalid; surely vital force would come out of him.

' He makes one ashamed to groan at anything. Whatever comes to us is in the order of things, and the sound man accepts it as his lot. Yes, even Death—of which he says noble things. The old melodious weeping of the poets—Moschus over his mallows, and Catullus with his " *Soles occidere et redire possunt* "—Whitman has no touch of that. Noble grief there is in him, and noble melancholy can come upon him, but acquiescence is his last word. He holds that all is good, because it exists, for everything plays its part in the scheme of nature. When his day comes, he will die, as the greatest have done before him, and there will be no puny repining at the order of things.

' Has he then made me a thorough-going optimist? Scarcely, for the willow cannot become the oak. Your old name for me was " The Idealist," and I suppose in a measure I deserved it; I know I did in the most foolish sense of the word. And in my idealism was of course implied a good deal of optimism. But shall I tell you what was there in a yet larger measure? That which is termed self-conceit. An enemy speaking of me now—Dalmaine for example, if he chose to tell the truth—would say that a business life in America has taken a great deal of the humbug out of me. I shall always be rather a weak mortal, shall always be marked by that blend of pessimism and optimism which necessarily marks the man to whom, in his heart, the beautiful is of supreme import, shall always be prone to accesses of morbid feeling, and in them, I dare say, find after all my highest pleasure. Nay, it is certain that Moschus and Catullus will always be more loved by me than Whitman. For all this, I am not what I was, and I am a completer man than I was. I shall remain here yet nine months, and who can say what further change may go on in me?

' Now to another subject. It gladdens me to hear what you say of Thyrza, that she seems both well and happy. I envy you the delight of hearing her sing. It is a beautiful thing that in this way she has found expression for that poetry which I always read in her face. By-the-by, does she still meet her sister away from the place where she lives? Is that still necessary? However, all these details are in your judgment. The great thing is that she is happy in her life, that she has found a great interest.

' I wish to know—I beg you to answer me—whether she has ever spoken of me. When I used to press you to speak on this subject, you always ignored that part of my letter. Need you still do so? Will you not tell me whether she has asked about me, has spoken in any way of me? To be sure you must betray no confidences; yet perhaps it will not be doing so.

'Read Whitman; try to sympathise with me as I now am. You know that I am anything but low-spirited, yet in very truth I have no single companion here to whom I can speak of intimate things, and, except on business, I write absolutely to no one in England save to you. And intellectual sympathy I do need; I scarcely think I could live on through my life without it.

'Another thing, and the last. You have never once spoken of Miss Newthorpe, nor have I, in all this long time. I pray you tell me something of her. It is very likely that she's married—to whom, now? Her husband should be an interesting man, one I should like some day to know. Or is she another example of the unaccountable things women will do in marriage? Pray Heaven not!'

(*Eight months after the last.*)

'I have just been reading a leader in the *New York Herald* wherein there is mention of Dalmaine's factory bill. Dalmaine is spoken of with extreme respect; his measure is one of those which "largely testify to the practical wisdom and beneficence of the spirit which prevails in British legislation." This kind of thing it is, says the writer, which keeps England in such freedom from the social disturbance so rife on the continent of Europe, and from which America has so much to fear. Seriously, this is all very right and just: Dalmaine is deserving well of his country. But the amazing fact is that *such* a man comes forward to perform such services. However, it is only the Vanderbilt business over again. These men are the practical philanthropists, and to sneer at them is very much the same as to speak contemptuously of the rain-shower which aids the growth of the corn.

'I have written very short letters lately. Business has claimed me night and day. We have had sundry difficulties of late, which you certainly would not thank me for explaining, and I am only just beginning to feel that if I take my due sleep at night I am doing nothing wrong. For months I have been the man of business, pure and simple. I have exerted myself to over-reach people, and have fumed because others

all but succeeded in over-reaching me. I have lived the life
of a cunning and laborious animal. Well, I have my profit of
it in several ways, but I think I have had about enough of it
for the present.

'I shall be in England in a month.

'Whether I shall remain there long, is uncertain. But at
all events I shall not be back here again for some time. One
of our London men is coming to take my place. I have
compliments from my fellows in the firm;—it makes me feel
that I must have sunk low.

'And now to the subject which I really took up my pen to
write about. I am very glad that you speak of letting Lydia
visit her sister before long. I remember well how much they
are to each other. It has been no less than heroism in Thyrza
to submit to practical separation for so long a time, at your
mere bidding, without explanation asked or given.

'Shall you speak of me to Thyrza before my return? No,
I suppose you will take no such responsibility. I don't know
what your mind is now on this matter, but in any case you
have performed your part right generously and nobly, and it
is a very pleasant thought to me that through her life Thyrza
will regard you as her dearest friend, the one to whom she
owes most. It will be a never-failing source of sympathy
between her and myself.

'Do you think she *expects* my coming before long? Does
such expectation explain her constant cheerfulness?—otherwise, I do not quite understand her, and have long felt it a
difficulty. I put absolute faith in all you tell me of her—need
I say that? But, if indeed she looks forward to seeing me, in
what manner has she conceived that hope? I confess I did
not think that her nature was of the kind which can derive
sufficient support from hope alone, hope which comes of mere
wish. It would be so very different if any word had even
passed between us which her memory could store up as
encouragement. In that case she would hope on for years,
her own fidelity making it impossible for her to suspect me of
unfaithfulness. That, I believe, *is* in her character. You
remember that, in my raving, I accused myself to you and said
that I was conscious of having allowed her to read my thoughts.
I cannot now be sure whether that was true or not; I heartily
wish I could. Still, I am sure that I did not purposely lead
her to think I was in love with her. And, as things turned
out, nothing subsequently happened to give her that idea; at

all events, nothing I ever knew of. True, I made confession to Grail, but he would not have spoken of it to Thyrza, even if he had had opportunity, which you are convinced he has not. And you say it is equally certain that Lydia Trent would not help her to such knowledge. We can only conclude that the fact of your adopting her, as it were, makes her hope that she is being prepared for something in the future.

'Well, I know it is not impossible that she has forgotten me, in the lover's sense. I am not so conceited as to believe that a girl who has once conceived a liking for me must necessarily hold me in her heart for ever. There would be nothing strange, certainly nothing unworthy, in her putting away all thought of one who, for anything she knew, had never dreamed of loving her. I wonder what your own belief is? But do not write about this. I shall see you very soon. I mean to be in England just before the appointed day, and to come to you at once.

'The future puzzles me a little at times, and yet after all it will be very simple. When a man marries the duties of life are suddenly made very plain. Formerly it was my incessant question: What ought I to do with myself, with my time, with my money? And of course, being what I am and living in our age, I drove on the rocks of philanthropic enterprise. No more risk of that. The one task before me is to make a woman as happy as by all endeavour I may; to think of nothing in this world until her heart is at rest; to sacrifice everything to her advancement; and therein, easily enough, to find my own happiness. The circumstances of my marriage will give me more opportunity of making this aim predominant than men usually have. Thyrza will need to be taught much, and will be eager to learn. I think I shall take a house not far from London, and live there quietly for two or three years. It has occurred to me to bring her here, but I had rather she developed her intellectual life in England. It is scarcely probable that, after once quitting it, I shall return to this humdrum business; I have vast arrears to make up in all my natural pursuits, and with Thyrza to bear me company in the fields, I am not very likely to go back of my own will to a factory. So that, after all, the future is clear enough; more peaceful and more fruitful than ever the past was. You will often come to us, will you not? It will be a joy to open our door to you, and to seat you at our table. And in the evenings Thyrza shall sing to us.

'By-the-by, suppose when I offer myself to her, she refuses to marry me!—Is it possible? Is it impossible? Of course, if her contentment has nothing to do with hope of seeing me again, then my appearance will only surprise and alarm and trouble her.

'Things must rest till I see you. I will cable from New York when I am starting for Europe. I shall be glad to see England again, glad to leave trade behind me, thrice glad to hold your hand.'

CHAPTER XXXVI

THYRZA WAITS

'I CAN'T promise, Mrs. Emerson, that my sister will come down and have tea with you. Please don't make any preparations; it's only perhaps.'

Thyrza had looked into the sitting-room to say this late in the evening.

'Oh, but she must!' Clara pleaded. 'Why not, dear? Won't you let me see her at all, then?'

Thyrza closed the door, which she had been holding open, and advanced into the room. She wore a dress of light hue, and had some flowers in her girdle. The past year had added a trifle to her stature; it could not add to her natural grace, but her manner of entering showed that diffidence had been overcome by habit. There was very little now to distinguish her from the young lady who has always walked on carpets.

'You won't mind if I ask you to come up to my room instead, Mrs. Emerson?' she said, standing before the sofa on which Clara sat sewing. 'I don't know that it will be necessary, but, if it should be——'

'Oh, I will gladly come. It's only that I didn't like to think of not making her acquaintance at all.'

'There's no reason why I shouldn't explain it to you,' Thyrza said, holding her hands together. 'My sister has never been with any except working people, and it is quite natural that she should feel a little afraid of meeting strangers. I'm sure she needn't be; but of course I must do what she wishes.'

'But, my dear, surely nobody in the world could be afraid of *us*! And, as you say, I feel certain that *your* sister needn't be afraid of any one. I'll come up and see her, and we'll talk a little, and she'll get used to me.'

'Yes. I am so glad she is coming!'

'I'm sure you are. And how well you look to-night, dear! It's so seldom you have any colour in your cheeks. There now! If I was another sort of person, you'd go away thinking I'd said that on purpose to hurt you.'

'How could I?' Thyrza uttered in surprise. 'What sort of people would have that thought?'

'Oh, very many that I know.'

'Surely not, Mrs. Emerson! But it's quite true; my cheeks feel a little hot to-night. They generally do when I've been making myself very happy about anything.'

'But you're always so happy.'

'Not more than you are,' Thyrza replied, laughing.

'Well, I think you show it more. When I'm happiest, I sit very quiet, and look very dull. Now you sing, and your eyes get so bright and large, you don't know how large your eyes look sometimes.'

Thyrza laughed and shook her head.

'I sing too much,' she said. 'If I don't mind I shall be hurting my voice. But it's late; I must be off to bed. And I know I shan't sleep all night. To tell the truth, it isn't often I sleep more than three or four hours. Good-night, Mrs. Emerson!'

'Good-night, happy girl!'

She went away, laughing in pure, liquid notes. Her light step could not be heard as she ran up the stairs.

It wanted but a week of the day to which Thyrza's life had pointed for two years. That day of the month had stood long since marked upon her calendar; and now the long months had annihilated themselves; it wanted but seven days.

External changes of some importance had come to her of late. Since her admission to Mr. Redfern's choir she no longer wrought with her needle. More than that, every other day there came a lady who read with her and taught her. The time of weary toil without assistance was over. She had never been able to seek help of Mrs. Emerson; it was repugnant to her to speak of what she was doing in secret. To tell of her efforts would have seemed to Thyrza like half revealing her motives, so closely connected in her own mind were the endeavour and its hope. Mrs. Ormonde had known, but hitherto had offered no direct assistance.

To the latter Thyrza's relation was a strange one. As her mind matured, as her dreaming gave way more frequently to conscious reflection, she often asked herself how, knowing Mrs. Ormonde's thoughts, she could accept from her so much and repay her with such sincere affection. Told to her of another, she could with difficulty have believed it. Yet the simple truth remained that she had never shrunk from Mrs. Ormonde's offers of kindness, had never felt humiliated in receiving anything at her hands. This could not have been but for the sincerity of affection on Mrs. Ormonde's side. A dialogue such as that which Thyrza had overheard at Eastbourne would have inspired hatred in a nature less pure than hers. She had wondered, had at times thought that Mrs. Ormonde misjudged her; yet such was the simple candour of her mind that, instead of fostering evil, that secret knowledge had wrought upon her in the most beneficial way. 'She thinks that I am no fit wife for him; but that isn't all. She thinks of me, too, and believes that he could not make me happy. Though speaking in private, she did not say a word that could truly offend me. I know her to be good. I remember what she was by my bedside when I was ill; and I have seen numberless things that prove how impossible it is for her to deceive any one who puts trust in her.' And from that Thyrza derived both comfort and guidance. 'I will not fear her. Perhaps she has acted in the wisest and kindest way. To him who loves me two years will be nothing : and cannot *I* use the time to prove to her that I am worthy to be his wife ? If his love is still the same—how can it not be ?— and my worthiness is put beyond doubt, she can have no further reason for opposing our marriage ; nay, she will be glad in my happiness and in his. She shall see that I can bear trial, that I can work quietly and perseveringly, above all that I am faithful.'

And time made the affection between them stronger. Thyrza believed that Mrs. Ormonde's opposition to the marriage was weakening ; when at length, as the time drew to an end, menial work was put aside and she was encouraged to spend her days in improving her mind, it seemed to her a declaration that she was found fit for a higher standing than that to which she was born. The joy which filled her became almost too great to bear. She no longer strove to conceal it in Mrs. Ormonde's presence. There was a touching little scene between them on the afternoon before the concert at

which Thyrza was to sing for the first time, Mrs. Ormonde
came to Thyrza's room unannounced ; the latter was laying
out the dress she was to wear in the evening—a simple white
dress, but far more beautiful than any she had ever put on.
Seeing her friend enter, she turned, looked in her face, and
burst into tears. When she could utter words, they were a
passionate expression of gratitude. Mrs. Ormonde believed in
that moment that her two years' anxiety had found its end.

Very shortly after came the permission for Lydia to visit
her. It was new assurance that Mrs. Ormonde was reconciled
to what she had tried to prevent. A week, and there would
come another visitor, one who was more to her even than her
sister.

In looking back, the time seemed very brief, for, whatever
change had been made in her, the love which was her life's
life had known no shadow of change. Had it perhaps
strengthened ? It was hard to believe that she could love
more than in that day of her darkest misery, when it had seemed
that she must die of longing for him to whom she had given
her soul. Yet she was stronger now, her life was richer in a
multitude of ways, and every gain she had achieved paid
tribute to her life's motive. Her singing she valued most as
a way of uttering the emotion she must not speak of to anyone ; in music she could ease herself of passion, yet fear no
surprisal of her secret. Nothing was a joy save in reference to
that one end that was before her. If she felt happy in a piece
of knowledge attained, it was because she would so soon speak
of it to him, and hear him praise her for it. Everything and
all people about her seemed to conspire for her happiness.
Even the bodily pain which had often tried her so was no
longer troublesome, or very seldom indeed. Mrs. Emerson
might well call her ' happy girl.'

In him she could imagine no change. His face was as
present to her as if she had seen him an hour ago, and she
never asked herself whether two years would have made any
alteration even in his appearance. His voice was the voice in
which he had spoken to Mrs. Ormonde, when he uttered the
golden words that said he loved her. He would speak now in
the same way, with those inflections which she knew so well,
dearer music than any she had learnt or could learn. In the
beginning she had known a few fears ; time then was so long
—so long before her ; but what had she to do with fear now ?
Was he not Walter Egremont, the man of all men—the good,

wise, steadfast? She had heard much praise of him in the old days, but never praise enough. No one knew him well enough; no one the half as well as she did. Should she not know him who dwelt in her heart?

His life had always been strange to her, but by ceaseless imagining she had pictured it to herself so completely that she believed she could follow him day by day. Gilbert Grail had told her that he dwelt in a room full of books, near the British Museum, which also was full of books. Most of his time was spent in study; she understood what that meant. He did not give lectures now; that had come miserably to an end. He had a few friends, one or two men like himself, who thought and talked of high and wonderful things, and one or two ladies, of course—Mrs. Ormonde, and, perhaps, Miss Newthorpe. But probably Miss Newthorpe was married now. And, indeed, he did not care much to talk with ladies. He would go occasionally out of London, as he used to; perhaps would go abroad. If he crossed the sea, he must think much of her, for the sea always brings thoughts of those one loves. And so he lived, only wishing for the time to go by.

Lydia's visit was on Sunday. She was to come immediately after dinner; and, perhaps, though it remained uncertain—for she had not ventured to speak of it in her letter—they would have tea with the Emersons.

Concerning Thyrza's sister Mrs. Emerson had much curiosity, but she was not ill-bred. She made no attempt to get a glimpse of Lydia as the latter went upstairs to Thyrza's room. Thyrza stood just within her open door. She had put a flower in her hair for the welcoming.

'So this is where you have lived all this time,' Lydia said, looking about the room. 'How pretty it is, Thyrza! But of course it's a lady's room.'

The other stood with her hands together before her, and, a little timidly, said:

'Do I look like a lady? Suppose you didn't know me, Lyddy, should you think I was a lady?'

'Of course I should,' her sister answered, though in a way which showed that she did not care to dwell on the subject.

Still, Thyrza laughed with pleasure.

'And do you think I love my sister a bit the less?'

'Of course I don't.'

Lydia was not quite at her ease.

'I'm not at all sure of that. Take your things off[1] and sit

F F

down in that chair, and talk to me as if we were in the old room at home. I must see our room again, Lyddy. I must see it before long.'

Lydia always had to overcome feelings of suspicion and remoteness at the beginning of her meetings with Thyrza; time had not changed her in this respect; she still feared that something was being concealed from her. And to-day it was long before she grew sufficiently accustomed to the room to talk with freedom. Thyrza lost all hope of persuading her to have tea with the Emersons. She was obliged to broach the subject, however, and it excited no less opposition than she had looked for. Lydia shrank from the thought. Yet, when Thyrza ceased to urge, and even exerted herself to make her sister forget all about it, Lydia said all at once :

' Do you always have tea with them on Sundays ? '

' Yes. But it doesn't make the least difference. I have it here by myself other days, and I can do just as I like about it. Don't trouble, dear.'

' There won't be anybody except those two ? '

' Oh no. There never is.'

Lydia changed her mind. Much as she disliked meeting strangers and sitting at their table, she felt a wish to see these people with whom Thyrza lived, that she might form her own opinion of them. Thyrza, much delighted, ran down at once to tell Mrs. Emerson.

Having made up her mind to face the trial, Lydia went through it as might have been expected, sensibly and becomingly. Clara made much of her ; Mr. Emerson—at home for once—was languidly polite. After tea Thyrza was asked to sing, but she excused herself as having no voice to-day. Her real reason was that she could only sing ' week-day ' songs, and, though not certain, she thought it just possible that Lydia might dislike that kind of thing on Sunday. However, the good Lyddy had not quite reached that pass.

The sisters went upstairs again. Lydia had found Mrs. Emerson very different from her expectation, and was feeling a relief. She talked naturally once more. A subject of much interest to both was the approaching marriage of Totty Nancarrow.

' But is it *quite* certain this time, Lyddy ? '

' Oh, quite, dear. The names are up in the registry-office.'

Lydia knew nothing of Totty's fortune, nor did any one else

in Lambeth. To this day Totty and her husband have kept that a secret.

'Well, what a girl Totty is!' Thyrza exclaimed. 'And she used to declare that she wouldn't be married on any account. Of course I always knew that was all nonsense. I shall go and see her some day, Lyddy, before long.'

Lydia noticed the frequency with which Thyrza spoke of shortly seeing old places and old friends. It puzzled her, but she asked for no explanation. Perhaps all these mysteries would be at an end in time.

Thyrza found it very hard to part to-night. She found numberless excuses for detaining Lydia from moment to moment, when it was really time for her to go. She was agitated, and as if with some great joy.

'Next Sunday, at the same time, Lyddy!' she repeated again and again.

'But is there any fear of me forgetting it, dearest?' urged her sister.

'No, no! But I am so glad for you to come here. You like coming? I don't think I shall write to you in the week; but of course you'll write, if there's anything. I *might* send a line; but no, I don't think I shall. It'll be such a short time till Sunday, won't it? Does the week go quickly with you? Oh, we *must* say good-bye; it's getting too late. Good-bye, my own, my dearest, my old Lyddy! Think of me every hour—I'm always the same to you, whatever kind of dress I wear; you know that, don't you? Good-bye, dear Lyddy!'

She clung to Lydia and kissed her. They went downstairs together, then, before opening the door, again embraced and kissed each other silently.

When a few yards away, Lydia turned. Thyrza stood on the door-step; light from within the house shone on her golden hair and just made her face visible. She was kissing her hand. . . .

It was Saturday. The week had been neither long nor short; Thyrza could not distinguish the days in looking back upon them. She had not lived in time, but in the eternity of a rapturous anticipation. Her daily duties had been performed as usual, but with as little consciousness as if she had done all in sleep. She rose, and it was Saturday morning.

What time to-day? That he would let one day pass had never occurred to her as a possibility. But perhaps he would be at Eastbourne in the morning, and in that case she must wait many hours. Happily, she had nothing to attend to; to-day she could not even have pretended to live her wonted life.

Mrs. Emerson would be out till evening. No one would come upstairs to disturb about trifles.

She pretended to breakfast, then sat down by the window. She was fearful now, not for the event, but of her own courage when the time came. Could she stand before him? In what words could she speak to him? Yet she must not let him doubt what her two years had been. Would it be right to tell him that he came not unexpected, to confess that she had heard him when he spoke to Mrs. Ormonde? Not at once, not to-day. He must know, but not to-day.

How short a time, two years; how long, how endlessly long each hour on this day of waiting!

For the morning passed, and he did not come. He was at Eastbourne; he had not even asked Mrs. Ormonde to keep her word till the very day came.

Her dinner was brought up, and was sent down again untouched. She sat still at the window. Every wheel that approached made her heart leap; its dull rumbling into the distance sickened her with disappointment. But most likely he would walk to the house, and then she would not know till the servant came up to tell her.

Why had she not thought to get a railway-guide, that she might know all the trains from Eastbourne? She could not now go out to purchase one; he would come in her absence.

It drew to evening. Thyrza knew neither hunger nor thirst; she did not even feel weary. Dread was creeping upon her. She fought with it resolutely. She would be no traitor to herself, to him her other self. He might very well leave it till evening, to make sure of her being at home.

Her mind racked her with absurd doubts. Had she mistaken? *Was* this the day?

Pale and cold as marble, whilst the evening twilight died upon her face. She did not move. Better to sit so still that she forgot impatience, perchance forgot time. The vehicles in the street were fewer now; her heart-throbs as each drew near were the more violent. Nor would the inward pulse recover its quietness when there was silence. She heard it always; she felt it as an unceasing pain.

Why should she rise and light the lamp? If he did not come, what matter if she sat in darkness and pain for ever?

And the long summer evening did in truth become night. The street grew yet more quiet. She saw the moon, very clear and beautiful.

There sounded a loud double-knock at the street door. She sprang up and stood listening. It was a visitor to the Emersons. Even when assured of that, something in her would not believe it, hoped against conviction. But at length she went back to her chair. No tears; but the pain harder to bear than ever.

She awoke at very early morning; she was lying on her bed, fully clad. There was a dread in her mind at waking, and in a few moments she recognised it. Lydia was coming to-day. Would it be possible to sit and talk with her?

Only by clinging with stern determination to the last hope. Something had rendered it impossible for him to come yesterday, and to-day he was not likely to come; no, not to-day. But there was always the morrow. By refusing to think of anything but the morrow she might bear Lydia's presence.

Sunday, Monday; and now it was Tuesday at dawn. Thyrza had but one thought in her mind. Mrs. Ormonde was treacherous. She had broken her promise. He was wishing to come to her, and knew not where she was—Lydia would not tell him. Lydia too was pitiless.

She had sat still in her room since Sunday night. She had pleaded illness to avoid all visits and all occupation. Whether really ill or no, she could not say. Yes, there was the pain, but she had become so used to that. She only knew that the days and the nights were endless, that she no longer needed to eat, that the sunlight was burdensome to her eyes.

Clara had been troublesome with her solicitude; it had needed an almost angry word to secure privacy.

At mid-day Thyrza took up the railway-guide which she had procured and sought for something in its pages. Then she began to attire herself for going out. She looked into her purse. In a few minutes she went quietly down the stairs, as if for an ordinary walk, and left the house.

CHAPTER XXXVII

A FRIENDLY OFFICE

ON the Friday when Thyrza, in her happiness, had said 'To-morrow he comes,' Mrs. Ormonde also was thinking of a visitor, who might arrive at any hour, Nine days ago she had received a telegram from New York, informing her that Walter Egremont was there and about to embark for England. She, too, avoided leaving the house. Her impatience and nervousness were greater than she had thought such an event as this could cause her. But it was years now since she had begun to accept Walter in the place of her own dead son, and in that spirit she desired his return from the exile of twice twelve months. It was with joy that she expected him, though with one uncertainty which would give her trouble now and then, a doubt which was, she felt, shadowy, which the first five minutes of talk would put away.

She had dined, and was thinking that it was now too late to expect an arrival, when the arrival itself was announced.

'A gentleman asks if you will see him,' said the servant, 'Mr. Egremont.'

'I will see him.'

He came quickly to her over the carpet, and they clasped hands. Then, as he heard the door close, Walter kissed the hand he held, kissed it twice with affection. They did not speak at first, but looked at each other. Mrs. Ormonde's eyes shone.

'How strong and well you look!' were her first words. You bring a breath from the Atlantic.'

'Rather from a pestilent English railroad car!'

'We say "railway" and "carriage," Walter.'

'Ah! I confused a cabman at Liverpool by talking about the "depôt."'

He laughed merrily, a stronger and deeper laugh than of old. Personally he was not, however, much changed. He was still shaven, still stood in the same attitude; his smile was still the same inscrutable movement of the features. But his natural wiriness had become somewhat more pronounced, and the sea-tan on his cheeks prepared one for a robuster kind of speech from him than formerly.

'Of course you have not dined. Let me go away for one moment.'

'I thank you. Foreseeing this, I dined at the station.'

'Then you behaved with much unkindness. Stand with your face rather more to the light. Yes, you are strong and well. I shall not say how glad I am to see you; perhaps I should have done, if you had waited to break bread under my roof.'

'I shall sit down if I may. This journey from Liverpool has tired me much. Oh yes, I was glad as I came through the Midlands; it was poetry again, even amid smoke and ashes.'

'But you must not deny your gods.'

'Ah, poetry of a different kind. From Whitman to Tennyson.

And one an English home; grey twilight poured—

No, I deny nothing; one's moods alter with the scene.'

'I find that Mr. Newthorpe has good words for your Whitman.'

'Of course he has. What man of literary judgment has not? He is here still?'

'Not at present. They went a fortnight ago to Ullswater.'

'To stay there till winter, I suppose?'

'Or till late in autumn.'

Walter did not keep his seat, in spite of the fatigue he had spoken of. In a minute or two he was moving about the room, glancing at a picture or an ornament.

'That photograph is new, I think,' he said. 'A Raphael?'

'Andrea del Sarto.'

'Barbarian that I am! I should have known Lucrezia's face. And your poor little girls? I was grieved to hear of the death of Bunce's child. I always think of poor Bunce as a heavily-burdened man.'

'He came a month ago to see Bessie's grave. He talked to me in a very human way. And things are better with him. Pray sit down! No, there is nothing else new in the room.'

He seemed to obey with reluctance; his eyes still strayed. Mrs. Ormonde kept a subdued smile, and did her best to talk with ease of matters connected with his voyage, and the like. Walter's replies grew briefer. He said at last:

'The two years come to an end to-morrow.'

'They do.'

Mrs. Ormonde joined her hands upon her lap. She avoided his look.

'What have you to tell me of Thyrza?' he went on to ask, his voice becoming grave. 'When did you see her?'

'Quite recently. She is well and very cheerful.'

'Always so cheerful?'

'Yes.'

'And you will tell me now where she is?'

She looked him steadily in the face.

'You wish to know, Walter?'

'I have come to England to ask it.'

'Yes, I will tell you.'

And she named the address. Walter made a note of it in his pocket-book.

'And now will you also tell me fully about her life since I went away? I should like to know with whom she has been living, exactly how she has spent her time——'

'Man of business!'

Mrs. Ormonde tried to jest, but did it nervously.

'Do I seem to you coarser-grained than I used to be?'

'More a man of the world, at all events. No, not fallen off in the way you mean. But I think you judge more soberly about grave matters. I think you know yourself better.'

'Much better, if I am not mistaken.'

'But still can have la tête montée, on occasion? Still think of many things in the idealist's fashion?'

'I sincerely hope so. Of everything, I trust.'

'Could make great sacrifices for an imaginary obligation?'

He left his seat again. Mrs. Ormonde was agitated, and both kept silence for some moments.

'It grieves me that you say that,' Walter spoke at length, earnestly. 'This obligation of mine is far from imaginary. That is not very like yourself, Mrs. Ormonde.'

'I cannot speak so clearly as I should like to, Walter. I, too, have my troublesome thoughts.'

'Let us go back to my questioning. Tell me everything about her, from the day when you decided what to do. Will you?'

'Freely, and hide nothing whatever that I know.'

For a long time her narrative, broken by questioning, continued. Egremont listened with earnest countenance, often looking pleased. At the end, he said:

'You have done a good work. I thank you with all my heart.'

'Yes, you owe me thanks,' Mrs. Ormonde returned, quietly. 'But perhaps you give them for a mistaken reason.'

'In what you have told me of the growth of her character, there is nothing that I did not foresee. It is good to know that, even then, I was under no foolish illusion. But the circumstances were needed, and you have supplied them. How can I be mistaken in thanking you for having so tended her who is to be my wife?'

'Wait, Walter. You foresaw into what she might develop; it is true, and it enables us to regard the past without too much sadness. Did you foresee her perfect equanimity, when once she had settled down to a new life?'

He said hesitatingly, 'No.'

'Believing that she had taken such a desperate step purely through love of you, you thought it more than likely that she would live on in great unhappiness?'

'Her cheerfulness surprises me. But it isn't impossible to offer an explanation. She has foreseen what is now going to happen. She knows you are my friend; she sees that you are giving great pains to raise her from her former standing in life; what more likely than that she explains it all by guessing the truth? And so her cheerfulness is the the most hopeful sign for me.'

'That is plausible; but you are mistaken. Long ago I talked to her with much seriousness of all her future. I spoke of the chances of her being able to earn a living with her voice, and purposely discouraged any great hope in that direction. Her needlework, and what she had been trained to at the Home, were, I showed her, likely to be her chief resources. I have even tested her on the subject of her returning to live with her sister.'

'Hope has overcome all these considerations. You kept her sister from knowing where she was. Why, if there was not some idea of severing her from her old associations?'

'I explained it to her in one of our talks. I showed her that her rashness had made it very difficult to aid her.'

'You spoke of me to her?'

'Never, as I have told you. Nor has she ever mentioned you. I pointed out to her that of course I could not explain the state of things to the Emersons, and therefore Lydia had better not visit her for some time.'

Egremont sat down at a distance, and brooded.

'But a contradiction is involved!' he exclaimed presently.

'How can a girl of her character have forgotten so quickly such profound emotion?'

'You must not forget that weeks passed between my finding her and her going to live with the Emersons. During all that time the poor girl was wretched enough.'

'Weeks!'

'Her cheerfulness only came with time, after that.'

'And it is your conviction that she has absolutely put me out of her mind? That she has found sufficient happiness in the progress she has felt herself to be making?'

'That is my firm belief. Her character is not so easy to read as to-day's newspaper. She can suffer, I think, even more than most women, but she has, too, far more strength than most women, a mind of a higher order, purer consolations. And she has art to aid her, a resource you and I cannot judge of with assurance.'

Walter looked up and said:

'You are describing a woman who might be the most refined man's ideal.'

'I think so.'

'You admit that Thyrza is in every way more than fit to be my wife.'

'I will admit that, Walter.'

'Then I am astonished at your tone in speaking of what I mean to do.'

'You have asked me two questions,' said Mrs. Ormonde, her face alight with conviction. 'Please answer two of mine. Is this woman worthy of a man's entire love?'

He hesitated, but answered affirmatively.

'And have you that entire love to give her? Walter, the truth, for she is very dear to me.'

(In her room in London Thyrza sat, and said to herself, 'To-morrow he comes!')

He answered: 'I have not.'

'Then,' Mrs. Ormonde said, a slight flush in her cheeks, 'how can you express surprise at what I do?'

A long silence fell. Walter brooded, something of shame on his face from that confession. Then he came to Mrs. Ormonde's side, and took her hand.

'You are incapable,' he said gently, 'of conscious injustice. Had you said nothing of this to me, I should have gone to Thyrza to-morrow, and have asked her to marry me. She would not have refused; even granting that her passion has gone, you know she would not refuse me, and you know too that I could enrich her life abundantly. My passion, too, is over, but I know well that love for such a woman as she is would soon awake in me. I do not think I should do her any injustice if I asked her to be my wife : shall I be unjust to her if I withhold ? '

Mrs. Ormonde did not answer at once. She retained his hand, and her own showed how strongly she felt.

' Walter, I think it would be unjust to her if you asked her—remembering her present mind. It is not only that your passion for her is dead ; you think of another woman.'

' It is true. But I do not love her.'

She smiled.

' You are not ready to behave crazily about her ; no. But I believe that you love her in a truer sense than you ever loved Thyrza. You love her mind.'

' Has not Thyrza a mind ? '

' You do not know it, Walter. I doubt whether you would ever know it. Recall a letter you wrote to me, in which you dissected your own character. It was frank and in a very great measure true. You are not the husband for Thyrza.'

' You place Thyrza above Annabel Newthorpe ? '

It was asked almost indignantly, so that Mrs. Ormonde smiled and raised her hand.

' You, it is clear, resent it.'

He reddened. Mrs. Ormonde continued :

' I compare them merely. I don't think Thyrza will find the husband who is worthy of her, but I think it likely that she will win more love than you could ever give her. I have told you that she is dear to me. To you I would give a daughter of my own with entire confidence, for you are human and of noble impulses. But I do not wish you to marry Thyrza. Yes, you read my thought. It is not solely the question of love. I wish you—I have so long wished you—to marry Annabel. To Thyrza you do not the least injustice by withholding your offer ; she is happy without you. You are entirely free to consult your own highest interests. If I counsel wrongly, the blame is mine. But, Walter, you must after all decide for yourself. It is a most hazardous part this that I am playing ; at least, it would be, if I did not see the facts of the case so clearly. Rest till to-morrow ; then let us speak again. Shall it be so ? '

Egremont left The Chestnuts and walked along the shore

in moonlight. His mind had received a shock, and the sense of disturbance affected him physically. He was obliged to move rapidly, to breathe the air.

He had left America with fixity of purpose. His plain duty was to go to Thyrza and ask her to marry him. Be her position what it might, his own was clear enough. He looked forward with a certain pleasure to the mere discharge of so plain an obligation.

Mrs. Ormonde had studiously refrained from expressing any thought with regard to the future in her letters. He quite expected that she would repeat to him with a certain emphasis the fact of Thyrza's present cheerfulness; but he did not anticipate serious opposition to the course he had decided upon. Practically Thyrza had lived in preparation for a life of refinement; Mrs. Ormonde, he concluded, knew that he could act but in one way, and, though refusing to do so ostensibly, had in fact been removing the rougher difficulties. Her attitude now surprised him, made him uneasy.

Yet he knew his own inability to resist her. He knew that she spoke on the side of his secret hope. He knew that a debate which had long gone on within himself, to himself unavowed, had at length to find its plain-spoken issue.

His passion for Thyrza was dead; he even wondered how it could ever have been so violent. It seemed to him that he scarcely knew her; could he not count on his fingers the number of times that he had seen her? So much had intervened between him and her, between himself as he was then and his present self. It was with apprehension that he thought of marrying her. He knew what miseries had again and again resulted from marriages such as this, and he feared for her quite as much as for himself. For there was no more passion.

Neither on her side, it seemed. Was not Mrs. Ormonde right? Was it not to incur a wholly needless risk? And suppose the risk were found to be an imaginary one, what was the profit likely to be, to each of them?

But as often as he accepted what he held to be the common sense of the case, something unsettled him again. The one passion of his life had been for Thyrza. He called it dead; does not one mourn over such a death? He would not have recourse to the old dishonesty, and say that his love had been folly. Was it not rather the one golden memory he had? Was it not of infinite significance?

One loves a woman madly, and she gives proof of such unworthiness that love is killed. Why, even then the dead thing was inestimably precious ; one would not forget it. And Thyrza was no woman of this kind. She had developed since he knew her ; Mrs. Ormonde spoke of her as few can be justly spoken of. Was it good to let the love for such a woman pass away, when perchance the sight of her would revive it and make it lasting ?

The stars and the night wind and the breaking of the sea— the sea which Thyrza loved—spoke to him. Could he not understand their language ? . . .

On Monday morning he took the train to London, thence northwards. A visit to the Newthorpes after two years of absence was natural enough.

CHAPTER XXXVIII

THE TRUTH

MRS. ORMONDE was successful, but success did not bring her unmixed content. She was persuaded that what she had done was wholly prudent, that in years to come she would look back on this chapter of her life with satisfaction. Yet for the present she could not get rid of a shapeless misgiving. This little centre of trouble in the mind was easily enough accounted for. Granted that Thyrza could live quite well without Walter Egremont, it was none the less true that, in losing him, she lost a certainty of happiness—and does happiness grow on every thicket, that one can afford to pass it lightly ? The fear lest Egremont should reap misery from such a marriage, and cause misery in turn, was no longer seriously to be entertained ; it could not now have justified interference, had there been nothing else that did so. Mrs. Ormonde could not rob Thyrza thus without grieving.

But it was the happiness of two against that of one ; and, however monstrous the dogma that one should be sacrificed even to a million, such a consideration is wont to have weight with us when we are arguing with our conscience and getting somewhat the worst of it. Mrs. Ormonde felt sure that Annabel Newthorpe would not now reject Walter if he again offered himself ; many things had given proof of that. Annabel knew that Thyrza had thoroughly outlived her trouble ; she knew, moreover, that Egremont had never in reality compromised himself in regard to her. In her eyes, then, the latter was rather the victim of misfortune than himself culpable. If Walter eventually—of course, some time must pass—again sought to win her, without doubt he would tell her everything, and Annabel would find nothing in the story to make a perpetual barrier between them. The marrirge which Mrs. Ormonde so strongly desired would still come about.

On the other hand, in spite of arguments that seemed irresistible, she could not dismiss the question : Does Thyrza know anything of Egremont's by-gone passion ? That she could know anything of the compact which had run its two years, was of course impossible ; but Walter's persistence in urging that, if once she had learnt his love for her, that, together with the circumstances of her life, would make sufficient ground for hope—this persistence had impressed Mrs. Ormonde. In a second long conversation the subject had been gone over, point by point, for a second time. ' If harm come,' Mrs. Ormonde said to herself, ' I am indeed to blame, for, though his wishes oppose it, I had but to show doubt and he would have taken the manly part and have gone to Thyrza.' She did not seek to defend herself by saying—as she might well have done—that throughout he encouraged her in her resistance. He was of firmer substance than two years ago, yet had not become, nor ever would, a vigorously independent man. In her hands the decision had lain—and the affair was decided.

On Tuesday, the day after Egremont's departure for the North of England, she was still thinking these thoughts. At four o'clock in the afternoon, having seen her children come in from the garden and gather for tea, she went with a book to spend an hour in the arbour where she had had that fateful conversation with Walter on the summer night. As she drew near to the covered spot, it seemed to her that there was a footfall behind on the grass. She turned her head, and with surprise saw Thyrza.

With something more than surprise. As she looked in Thyrza's face, that slight uneasiness in her mind changed to a dark misgiving, and from that to the certainty of fear. Thyrza had never regarded her thus ; and she herself had never seen features so passionately woe-stricken. The book fell from her hand ; she could not utter a greeting.

'I want to speak to you, Mrs. Ormonde.'

'Come in here, Thyrza. Why have you come? What has happened?'

She drew back under the shelter of leaf-twined trellis, and Thyrza followed. Mrs. Ormonde met the searching eyes, and compassion helped her to self-command. She could not doubt what the first words spoken would be, yet the mystery of the scene was inscrutable to her.

'I want to ask you about Mr. Egremont,' Thyrza said, resting her trembling hand on the little rustic table. 'I want to know where he is.'

Prepared as she had been, the words, really spoken, struck Mrs. Ormonde with new consternation. The voice was not Thyrza's; it had no sweetness, but was like the voice of one who had suffered long exhaustion, who speaks with difficulty.

'Yes, I will tell you where he is, Thyrza,' the other replied, her own accents shaken with sympathy. 'Why do you wish to hear of Mr. Egremont?'

'I think you needn't ask me that, Mrs. Ormonde.'

'Yes, I must ask. I can't understand why you should come like this, Thyrza. I can't understand what has happened to make this change in you since I saw you last.'

'Mrs. Ormonde, you do understand! Why should you pretend with me? You know that I have been waiting— waiting since Saturday.'

Thyrza spoke as if there were no mystery in her having attached a hope to that particular day. All but distraught as she was, she made no distinction between the mere fact of her abiding love, which she could not conceive that Mrs. Ormonde was ignorant of, and the incident of her having surprised a secret.

'Since Saturday?' Mrs. Ormonde repeated. 'What did you wait for on Saturday?'

She had a wretched suspicion. From Egremont alone that information could have come to Thyrza. Had he played detestably false, having by some means, at the height of his passion, communicated with the girl? But the thought could only pass through her mind; it would not bear the light of .reason for a moment. Impossible for him to speak and act so during these past days, knowing that his dishonesty was certain of being discovered. Impossible to attach such suspicion to him at all.

'I expected to see him,' Thyrza replied. 'I knew he was

to come in two years. I have waited all the time ; and now
he has not come. I heard——'

She checked herself, and looked at the trellis at the back
of the summer-house. She understood now that it was needful to explain her knowledge.

' You heard, Thyrza——? '

' That night that he was here. I had walked to look at
your house. I was going home again when he passed me—he
didn't see me—and went into the garden. I couldn't go back
at once ; I had to sit down and rest. It was on the other side
of the leaves.' She pointed. ' I sat down there without
knowing he would be here and I should hear him talking to
you. I heard all you said—about the two years. I have been
waiting for him to come.'

Mrs. Ormonde could not reply ; what words would express
what she felt in learning this ? Thyrza's eyes were still fixed
upon her.

' I want you to tell me where he is, Mrs. Ormonde.'

It was a summons that could not be avoided.

' Sit here, Thyrza. I will tell you. Sit down and let me
speak to you.'

' No, no ! Tell me now ! Why not ? Why should I sit
down ? What is there to say ? '

The words were not weakly complaining, but of passionate
insistence. Thyrza believed that Mrs. Ormonde was preparing
to elude her, was shaping excuses. Her eyes watched the
other's every movement keenly, with fear and hostility. She
felt within reach of her desire, yet held back by this woman
from attaining it. Every instant of silence heightened the
maddening tumult of her heart and brain. She had suffered
so terribly since Saturday. It seemed as if her gentleness, her
patience, were converted into their opposites, which now ruled
her tyrannously.

' Mr. Egremont is not in London,' Mrs. Ormonde said at
last. She dreaded the result of any word she might say. She
was asking herself whether Walter ought not to be summoned
back at once. Was it too late for that ?

' Not in London ? Then where ? You saw him on
Saturday ? '

' Yes, I saw him.'

' And you would not tell him where I was, Mrs. Ormonde ?
You spoke like you did that night. You persuaded him not
to come to me—when I was waiting. I forgave you for what

you said before, but now you have done something that I shall never forgive——'

'Thyrza——'

'There's nothing you can say will make me forgive you! Your kindness to me hasn't been kindness at all. It was all to separate me from him. What have you told him about me? You have said I don't think of him any more. You made him believe I wasn't fit for him. And now you will refuse to tell me where he is.'

'Thyrza!'

Mrs. Ormonde took the girl's hands forcibly in her own, and held them against her breast. She was pale and overcome with emotion.

'Thyrza, you don't know what you are saying! Do force yourself to be calmer, so that you can listen to me.'

'Don't hold my hands, Mrs. Ormonde! I have loved you, but I can't pretend to, now that you have done this against me. I will listen to you, but how shall I believe what you say? I didn't think one woman could be so cruel to another as you have been to me. You don't know what it means, to wait as I have waited; if you knew, you'd never have done this; you wouldn't have had the heart to do this to me.'

'My poor child, think, think—*how* could I know that you were waiting? You forget that you have only just told me your secret for the first time. I have seen you always so full of life and gladness, and how was I to dream of this sudden change?'

Thyrza listened, and, as if imperfectly comprehending, examined the speaker's face in silence.

'I am not the cruel woman you call me,' Mrs. Ormonde went on. 'I had no idea that your happiness depended upon meeting with Mr. Egremont again.'

'You had no idea of that?' Thyrza asked, slowly, wonderingly. 'You say that you didn't know I loved him?'

'Not that you still loved him. Two years ago—I knew it was so then. But I fancied——'

'You thought I had forgotten all about him? How could you think that? Is it possible to love any one and forget so soon, and live as if nothing had happened? That cannot be true, Mrs. Ormonde. I know you *wished* me to forget him. And that is what you told him when you saw him on Saturday! You said I thought no more of him, and that it was better he shouldn't see me! Oh, what right had you to say that? Where is he now? You say you are not cruel; let me know where I can find him.'

There was but one answer to make, yet Mrs. Ormonde dreaded to utter it. The girl's state was such that it might be fatal to tell her the truth. Passion such as this, nursed to this through two years in a heart which could affect calm, must be very near madness. Yet what help but to tell the truth? Unless she feigned that Egremont's failure to come on Saturday was her fault, in the sense Thyrza believed, and then send for him, that this terrible mischief might be undone?

If only she could have time to reflect. Whatever she did now, in this agitation, she might bitterly repent. Only under stress of the direst necessity could she summon Egremont back; there was something repugnant to her instinct, something impossible, in the thought of undoing all she had done. Egremont's position would be ignoble. Impossible to retrace her steps!

'I have no wish to prevent you from seeing him, Thyrza,' she said, making her resolve even as she spoke. 'He is not in London now, but he will be back before long, I think.'

'Is he in England?'

'Yes; in the North. He has gone to see friends. You don't know that he has been in America during these two years?'

Something was gained if Thyrza could be brought to listen with interest to details.

'In America? But he came back at the time. How could you refuse to keep your promise? What did he say to you? How could he go away again and let you break your word to him in that way?'

Mrs. Ormonde said, as gently as she could:

'I didn't break my word, Thyrza. I gave him your address. He had it on Friday night.'

She, whose nature it was to trust implicitly, now dreaded a deceit in every word. She gazed at Mrs. Ormonde, without change of countenance.

'And,' she said, slowly, 'you persuaded him not to come.'

Mrs. Ormonde paused before replying.

'Thyrza, is all your faith in me at an end? Cannot I speak to you like I used to, and be sure that you trust my kindness to you, that you trust my love?'

'Your love?' Thyrza repeated, more coldly than she had spoken yet. 'And you persuaded him not to come to me.'

'It is true, I did.'

Mrs. Ormonde had never spoken to any one with a feeling of humiliation like this which made her bend her head. Thyrza still looked at her, but no longer with hostility. She gazed with wonder, with doubt.

'Why did you do that to me, Mrs. Ormonde?'

There was heart-breaking pathos in the simple words. Tears rushed to the listener's eyes.

'My child, if I had known the truth, I should have said not a word to prevent his going. I did not know that you still loved him, hard as it is for you to believe that. I was deceived by your face. I have watched you month after month, and, as I knew nothing of your reason for hope, I thought you had found comfort in other things. Cannot you believe me, Thyrza?'

'And you told him that?'

'Yes, I told him what I thought was the truth. Thyrza, I *have* been cruel to you, but I had no thought that I was so.'

Thyrza asked, after a silence:

'But you told him where I was living?'

'I told him; he asked me, and I told him, as I had promised I would.'

Thyrza stood in deep thought. Mrs. Ormonde again took her hands.

'Dear, come and sit down. You are worn out with your trouble. Don't repel me, Thyrza. I have done you a great wrong, and I know you cannot feel to me as you did; but I am not so hard-hearted that your suffering does not pierce me through. Only sit here and rest.'

She allowed herself to be led to the seat. Her eyes rested on the ground for a while, then strayed to the leaves about her, which were golden with the sunlight they intercepted, then turned again to Mrs. Ormonde's face.

'He knew where I lived. How could you be sure he wouldn't come to me?'

Mrs. Ormonde sunk her eyes and made no reply.

'Did he promise you that he would never come?'

'He made me no promise, Thyrza.'

'No promise? Then how do you know that he won't come?'

A gleam shot to her eyes. But upon the moments of hope followed a revival of suspicion.

'You say you can't prevent me from seeing him. Tell me where he is—the place. You won't tell me?'

'And if I did, how would it help you?'

'Cannot I go there? Or can't I write and say that I wish to speak to him.'

'Thyrza, I asked no promise from him that he wouldn't go to you. I don't think you would really try to see him, knowing that he has your address.'

'You asked no promise, Mrs. Ormonde, but you persuaded him! You spoke as you did two years ago. You told him I could never make a fit wife for him, that he couldn't be happy with me, nor I with him.'

'No; I did not speak as I did two years ago. I know you much better than I did then, and I told him all that I have since learnt. No one could speak in higher words of a woman than I did of you, and I spoke from my heart, for I love you, Thyrza, and your praise is dear to me.'

That fixed, half-conscious gaze of the blue eyes was hard to bear, so unutterably piteous was it, so wofully it revealed the mind's anguish. Mrs. Ormonde waited for some reply, but none came.

'You do not doubt this, Thyrza?'

Still no answer.

'Suppose I give you the address, do you feel able to write, before he has—— ?'

There was a change in the listener's face. Mrs. Ormonde sprang to her, and saved her from falling. Nature had been tried at last beyond its powers.

Mrs. Ormonde could not leave the unconscious form; her voice would not be heard if she called for help. But the fainting fit lasted a long time. Thyrza lay as one who is dead; her features calm, all the disfiguring anguish passed from her beauty. Her companion had a moment of terror. She was on the point of hastening to the house, when a sign of revival checked her. She supported Thyrza in her arms.

'Thank you, Mrs. Ormonde,' was the latter's first whisper, the tone as gentle and grateful as it was always wont to be.

'Can you sit alone for a minute, dear, while I fetch something?'

'I am well, quite well again, thank you.'

Mrs. Ormonde went and speedily returned. Thyrza was sitting with her eyes closed. They spoke only broken words. But at length Mrs. Ormonde said:

'You must come into the house now, Thyrza. You shall be quite alone; you must lie down.'

'No, I can't stay here, Mrs. Ormonde. I must go back before it gets too late. I must go to the station.'

Even had Thyrza's condition allowed of this, her friend would have dreaded to lose sight of her now, to let her travel to London and thereafter be alone. After trying every appeal, she refused to allow her to go.

'You must stay here for the night, Thyrza. You must. I have much more to say to you. But first you must rest. Come with me.'

Her will was the stronger. Thyrza at length suffered herself to be taken into the house, and to a room where she could have perfect quietness. Mrs. Ormonde alone waited upon her, brought her food, did everything to soothe body and mind. By sunset, the weary one was lying with her head on the pillow. On a table within her reach was a bell, whose sound would at once summon her attendant from the next room.

At ten o'clock Mrs. Ormonde entered silently. Three nights of watching, and the effects of all she had endured this afternoon, were weighing heavily on Thyrza's eyelids, though as yet she could not sleep. Foreseeing this, Mrs. Ormonde had brought a draught, which would be the good ally of Nature striving for repose. Thyrza asked no question, but drank what was offered like a child.

'Now you will soon rest, dear. I must not ask you to kiss me, Thyrza?'

The lips were offered. They were cold, for passion lay dead upon them. She did not speak, but sank back with a sigh and closed her eyes.

Again at midnight Mrs. Ormonde entered. The small taper which burnt in the room showed faintly the sleeping face. Standing by the bed, she felt her heart so wrung with sorrow that she wept.

In the morning Thyrza declared that she did not suffer. She rose and sat by the open window. She fancied she could hear the sea.

'You said you had more to tell me, Mrs. Ormonde,' she began, when the latter sat silently by her.

'To speak with you and to try to help you, my child, that was all.'

'But you told me very little yesterday. I am not sure

that I understood. You need not be afraid to tell me any-thing. I can bear anything.'

' Will you ask me what you wish to know, Thyrza ? '

' You say you persuaded him—and yet that you said good of me.'

The other waited.

' Didn't he come from America to see me ? '

' He did.'

' You mean that he came because he thought it was right to. I understand. And when you told him that I was not thinking of him, he—he felt himself free ? '

' Yes.'

' Do you think—is it likely that he will ever wish to see me now ? '

' If he knew that you had suffered because he did not come, he would be with you in a few hours.'

Thyrza gazed thoughtfully.

' And he would ask me to marry him ? '

' Doubtless he would.'

' So when you persuaded him not to see me, he was glad to know that he *need* not come ? '

It was a former question repeated in another way. Mrs. Ormonde kept silence. It was several minutes before Thyrza spoke again.

' I don't know whether you will tell me, but did he think of any one else as well as of me when he came back to Eng-land ? '

' I am not sure, Thyrza.'

' Will you tell me what friends he has gone to see ? '

' Their name is Newthorpe.'

' Miss Newthorpe—the same I once saw here ? '

' Yes.'

' What is Miss Newthorpe's name, Mrs. Ormonde ? '

' Annabel.'

Thyrza moved her lips as if they felt parched. She asked nothing further, seemed indeed to forget that she had been conversing. She watched the waving branches of a tree in the garden.

Mrs. Ormonde had followed the working of the girl's mind with intense observation. She knew not whether to fear or to be glad of the strange tranquillity that had succeeded upon such uncontrolled vehemence. What she seemed to gather from Thyrza's words she scarcely ventured to believe. It was a satisfaction to her that she had avoided naming Egremont's address, yet a satisfaction that caused her some shame. Indeed, it was the sense of shame that perhaps distressed her most in Thyrza's presence. Egremont's perishable love, her own prudential forecasts and schemings, were stamped poor, worldly, ignoble, in comparison with this sacred and extinguishable ardour. As a woman she felt herself rebuked by the ideal of womanly fidelity; she was made to feel the inferiority of her nature to that which fate had chosen for this supreme martyrdom. In her glances at Thyrza's face she felt, with new force, how spiritual was its beauty. For in soulless features, however regular and attractive, suffering reveals the flesh; this girl, stricken with deadly pallor, led the thoughts to the purest ideals of womanhood transfigured by woe in the pictures of old time.

'I will go by the train at twelve o'clock,' Thyrza said, moving at length.

'I want you to stay with me till to-morrow—just till to-morrow morning, Thyrza. If my presence pains you, I will keep away. But stay till to-morrow.'

'If you wish it, Mrs. Ormonde.'

'Will you go out? Into the garden? To the shore?'

'I had rather stay here.'

She kept her place by the window through the whole day, as she had sat in her own room in London. She could not have borne to see the waves white on the beach and the blue horizon; the sea that she had loved so, that she had called her friend, would break her heart with its song of memories. She must not think of anything now, only, if it might be, put her soul to sleep and let the sobbing waters of oblivion bear it onwards through the desolate hours. She had no pain; her faculties were numbed; her will had spent itself.

Mrs. Ormonde brought her meals, speaking only a word of gentleness. In the evening Thyrza said to her:

'Will you stay a few minutes?'

She sat down and took Thyrza's hand. The latter continued:

'I shall be glad if they would give me the sewing to do again, and the work at the Home. Do you think they will, Mrs. Ormonde?'

'Don't you wish to go on with your lessons?'

'No. I can't stay there if I don't earn enough to pay for everything. I shall try to keep on with the singing.'

It was perhaps wiser to yield every point for the present.

'It shall be as you wish, Thyrza,' Mrs. Ormonde replied. After a pause :

'Mrs. Emerson will wonder where I am. Will you write to her, so that I needn't explain when I get back to-morrow?'

'I have just had an anxious letter from her, and I have already answered it.'

Thyrza withdrew her hand gently.

'I was wrong when I spoke in that way to you yesterday, Mrs. Ormonde,' she said, meeting the other's eyes. 'You haven't done me harm intentionally; I know that now. But if you had let him come to me, I don't think he would have been sorry—afterwards—when he knew I loved him. I don't think any one will love him more. I was very different two years ago, and he thinks of me as I was then. Perhaps, if he had seen me now, and spoken to me—I know I am still without education, and I am not a lady, but I could have worked very hard, so that he shouldn't be ashamed of me.'

Mrs. Ormonde turned her face away and sobbed.

'I won't speak of it again,' Thyrza said. 'You couldn't help it. And he didn't really wish to come, so it was better. I am very sorry for what I said to you, Mrs. Ormonde.'

But the other could not bear it. She kissed Thyrza's hands, her tears falling upon them, and went away.

CHAPTER XXXIX

HER RETURN

IT was a rainy autumn, and to Thyrza the rain was welcome. A dark, weeping sky helped her to forget that there was joy somewhere in the world, that there were some whom golden evenings of the declining year called forth to wander together and to look in each other's faces with the sadness born of too much bliss. When a beam of sunlight on the wall of her chamber greeted her as she awoke, she turned her face upon the pillow and wished that night were eternal. If she looked out upon the flaming heights and hollows of a sunset between rain and rain, it seemed strange that such a scene had ever been to her the symbol of hope ; it was cold now and very distant ; what were the splendours of heaven to a heart that perished for lack of earth's kindly dew ?

To the eyes of those who observed her, she was altered indeed, but not more so than would be accounted for by troubles of health, consequent upon a sort of fever—they said —which had come upon her in the hot summer days. In spite of her desire this weakness had obliged her to give up her singing-practice for the present ; Dr. Lambe, Mrs. Ormonde's acquaintance, had said that the exertion was too much for her. What else that gentleman said, in private to Mrs. Ormonde, it is not necessary to report ; it was a graver repetition of something that he had hinted formerly. Mrs. Ormonde had been urgent in her entreaty that Thyrza would come to Eastbourne for a time, but could not prevail. Mrs. Emerson refused to believe that the illness was anything serious. ' I assure you,' she said to Mrs. Ormonde, ' Thyrza is in anything but low spirits as a rule. She doesn't laugh quite so much as she used to, but I can always make her as bright as possible by chatting with her in my foolish way for a few minutes. And when her sister comes on Sunday, there's not a trace of gloom discoverable. I've noticed it's been the same with her the last two autumns ; she'll be all right by winter.'

It was true that she disguised her mood with almost entire success during Lydia's visits. Lydia herself, for some cause, was very cheerful throughout this season ; she believed with more readiness than usual when Thyrza spoke of her ailments as trifling. Every Sunday she brought a present of fruit ; Thyrza knew well with how much care the little bunch of grapes or the sweet pears had been picked out on Saturday night at the fruit-shop in Lambeth Walk.

' You're a foolish old Lyddy, to spend your money on me in this way,' she said once. ' As if I hadn't everything I want.'

' Yes, but,' said Lydia, laughing, ' if I don't give you something now and then, you'll forget I'm your elder sister. And I shall forget it too, I think. I've begun to think of you as if you was older than me, Thyrza.'

' So I am, dear, as I told you a long time ago.'

' Oh, you can talk properly, which I can't, and you can write well, and read hard books, but I used to nurse you on my lap for all that. And I remember you crying for something I couldn't let you have, quite well.'

Thyrza laughed in her turn, a laugh from a heart that mocked itself. Crying for something she might not have— was she then so much older ?

To Lydia nothing was told of the cessation of lessons, and on Sunday all signs of needlework were hidden away. Mrs. Emerson of course knew the change that had been made, but it was explained to her as all being on the score of health, and Thyrza had begged her to make no allusion to the subject on the occasional evenings when Lydia had tea in Clara's room. And Clara was of opinion that it was very wise to rest for a while from books. ' Depend upon it, it's your brain-work that brought about all this mischief,' she said.

And after bidding her sister good-bye with a merry face, Thyrza would go up to her room, and sink down in weariness of body and soul, and weep her fill of bitter tears.

The nights were so long. She never lay down before twèlve o'clock, knowing that it was useless ; then she would hear the heavy-tongued bells tolling each hour till nearly dawn. It was like the voice of a remorseless enemy. ' I am striking the hour of Two. You think that you will not hear me when I strike next ; you weep and pray that sleep may close your ears against me. But wait and see ! ' She would sometimes, in extremity of suffering, fling her body down, and let her arms fall straight, and whisper to herself : ' I look now so like death, that perchance death will come and take me.' That she might die soon was her constant longing.

There were times when her youth asserted itself and bade her strive, bade her put away the vain misery and look out again into the world of which she had seen so little. A few weeks ago she had rejoiced in the acquiring of knowledge, and longed to make the chambers of her mind rich from the fields to which she had been guided, and which lay so sunny-flowered before her. But that was when she had looked forward to sharing all with her second and dearer self. Now, when her thoughts strayed, it was to gather the flowers of deadly fragrance which grow in the garden of despair. The brief glimpses of health made the woe which followed only darker.

A strange, unreal hope, an illusion of her tortured mind, even now sometimes visited her. It was certain that Egremont knew where she lived ; it might be that even yet he would come. Perhaps Miss Newthorpe would not receive him as he hoped. Perhaps Mrs. Ormonde would have pity, and would tell him the truth, and then he could not let her perish of vain longing. What other could love him as she did? Who else thought of him: 'You are all to me; in life or death there is nothing for me but you?' If he knew that, he would come to her.

She had read a story somewhere of someone being drawn to her who loved him by the very force of her passionate longing. In the dread nights she wondered if such a thing were possible. She would lie still, and fix her mind on him, till all of her seemed to have passed away save that one thought. She was back again in the library, helping to put books on the shelves. Oh, that was no two years ago; it was yesterday, this morning! Not a tone of his voice had escaped her memory. She had only to think of the moment when he held his hand to her and said, 'Let us be friends,' and her heart leaped now as it had leaped then. Could not her passion reach him, wherever he was? Could he sleep peacefully through nights which for her were one long anguish?

So it went on to winter, and now she had more rest; her brain was dulled with the foul black atmosphere; she slept more, though a sleep which seemed to weigh her down, an unhealthful torpor. The passion of her misery had burned itself out.

Lydia came and spent Christmas Day with her. They talked of their memories, and Thyrza asked questions about Gilbert Grail, as she had several times done of late. Lydia had no very cheerful news to give of him.

'Mrs. Grail can't do any work now. She sits by the fire all day, and at night she won't let him do anything but talk to her. It isn't at all a good servant they've got. She's expected to come at eight in the morning, but it's almost always nine before she gets there.'

'Couldn't you find someone better, Lyddy?'

'I'm trying to, but it isn't easy. I do what I can myself. Mrs. Grail sometimes seems as if she doesn't like me to come about. She wouldn't speak to me this morning; I'm sure I don't know why. She's changed a great deal from what she was when you knew her. And she can't bear to have things moved in the room for cleaning; she gets angry with the servant about it, and then the girl talks to her as she shouldn't, and it makes her cry.'

'Is she impatient with Gilbert?' Thyrza asked.

'No, I don't think so. But she always wants him to be by

her. If he's a few minutes late, she knows it, and begins to fret and worry.'

'So he sits all the evening just keeping her company?'

'Yes. He reads to her a good deal, generally out of those religious books—you remember? I feel sorry for her; I'm so sure there's other things he might read would give her a deal more comfort. And you'd think he never got a bit tired, he's that kind and good to her, Thyrza.'

'Yes, I know he must be. Does Mr. Ackroyd ever come to see him?'

'Not to the house, no. Nobody comes.'

Thyrza was very silent after this.

Two weeks later, when the new year was frost-bound, Lydia received this letter from her sister:

'I want to come and see you in the old room, as I said I should, and at the same time I want to see Gilbert. But I must see him alone. I could come at night, and you could be at the door to let me in, couldn't you, dear? You said that Mrs. Grail goes to bed early; I could see Gilbert after that. You may tell him that I am coming, and ask him if he will see me. I hope he won't refuse. Write and let me know when I shall be at the door—to-morrow night, if possible. You will be able to send a letter that I shall get by the first post in the morning.'

Had the visit proposed been a secret one, to herself alone, Lydia would not have been much surprised, as Thyrza had several times of late said that she wished to come. But the desire to see Gilbert was something of which no hint had been given till now. Strange fancies ran through her head. She doubted so much on the subject, that she resolved to say nothing to Gilbert; if Thyrza persisted in her wish, it would be possible to arrange the interview when she was in the house. She wrote in reply that she would be standing at the front door at half-past eight on the following evening.

Exactly at the moment appointed, a closely-wrapped figure hurried through the darkness out of Kennington Road to the door where Lydia had been waiting for several minutes. The door was at once opened. Thyrza ran silently up the stairs; her sister followed; and they stood together in their old home.

Thyrza threw off her outer garments. She was panting from haste and agitation; she fixed her eyes on Lydia, but neither spoke nor smiled.

'Are you sure you did right to come, dearest?' Lydia said in a low voice.

'Yes, Lyddy, quite sure,' was the grave answer.

'You look worse to-night—you look ill, Thyrza.'

'No, no, I am quite well. I am glad to be here.'

Thyrza seated herself where she had been used to sit, by the fireside. Lydia had made the room as bright as she could. But to Thyrza how bare and comfortless it seemed! Here her sister had lived, whilst she herself had had so many comforts about her, so many luxuries. That poor, narrow bed—there she had slept with Lyddy; there, too, she had longed vainly for sleep, and had shed her first tears of secret sorrow. Nothing whatever seemed altered. But yes, there was something new; above the bed's head hung on the wall a picture of a cross, with flowers twined about it, and something written underneath. Noticing that, Thyrza at once took her eyes away.

'It's a bitter night,' Lydia said, approaching her and examining her face anxiously. 'You must be very careful in going back; you seem to have got a chill now, dear; you tremble so. I'll stir the fire, and put more coals on.'

'You told Gilbert?' Thyrza asked, suddenly. 'You didn't mention it in your letter. He'll see me, won't he?'

'No, I haven't spoken to him yet, dear. I thought it better to leave it till you were here. I'm sure he'll see you, if you really wish.'

'I do wish, Lyddy. I'm sorry you left it till now. Why did you think it better to leave it?'

'I don't quite know,' the other said, with embarrassment. 'It seemed strange that you wanted to see him.'

'Yes, I wish to.'

'Then I'll go down in a few minutes and tell him.'

They ceased speaking. Lydia had knelt by her sister, her arm about her. Thyrza still trembled a little, but was growing more composed. Presently she bent and kissed Lydia's hair.

'You didn't believe me when I said I should come,' she whispered, smiling for the first time.

'Are you sure you ought to have come? Would Mrs. Ormonde mind?'

'I am quite free, Lyddy. I can do as I like. I would come in daylight, only perhaps it would be disagreeable for you, if people saw me. I know they have given me a bad name.'

'No one that we need to care about, Thyrza.'

'Gilbert has no such thoughts now?'

'Oh, no!'

'Shall I see much change in him?'

'Not as much as he will in you, dearest.'

They were silent again for a long time, then Lydia went to speak with Gilbert. Alone, Thyrza tried to recall the mind with which she had gone down to have tea with the Grails on a Sunday evening. It used to cause her excitement, but that was another heart-throb than this which now pained her. In those days Gilbert Grail was a mystery to her, inspiring awe and reverence. How would he meet her now? Would he have bitter words for her? No, that would be unlike him. She *must* stand before him, and say something which had been growing in her since the dark days of winter began. Only the utterance of those words would bring her peace. No happiness; happiness and she had nothing to do with each other. She thought she would not live very long; she must waste no more of the days that remained to her. There was need of her here at all events. The parting from her sister would be at an end; Lydia would rejoice. He too, yes, *he* would be glad, for he would know nothing of the truth. It might be that his whole future life would be made lighter by this act of hers. Mrs. Ormonde alone would understand; it would give her pleasure to know that Gilbert Grail's sorrow was at an end.

So many people to be benefited, and the act itself so simple, so merely a piece of right-doing, the reparation of so great an injury. Strange that her whole mind had undergone this renewal. Half a year ago, death would have been chosen before this.

Lydia returned.

'Mrs. Grail will be gone in half an hour. He will see you then, Thyrza.'

Very few words were interchanged as the time passed. They held each other by the hand. At length Lydia, hearing a sound below, went to the door.

'You can go now,' she said, returning. 'Shall I come down with you?'

'No, Lyddy.'

'Oh, can you bear this, Thyrza?'

The other smiled, made a motion with her hand, and went out with a quick step.

The parlour door—entrance so familiar to her—was half

open. She entered, and closed it. Gilbert came forward. His face was not at all what she had feared; he smiled pleasantly, and offered his hand.

'So you have come to see me as well as Lydia. It is kind of you.'

The words might have borne a very different meaning from that which his voice and look gave them. He spoke with perfect simplicity, as though no painful thought could be excited by the meeting. Thyrza saw, in the instant for which her eyes read his countenance, that he did not often smile thus. He was noticeably an older man than when she abandoned him; his beard was partly grizzled, his eyes were yet more sunken. There was some change, too, in his voice; its sound did not recall the past quite as she had expected.

But the change in her was so great that he could not move his eyes from her. When she looked up again, he still seemed to be endeavouring to recognise her.

'I didn't know whether you would see me,' she said with hurried breath.

'I am very, very glad to see you.'

He seemed about to ask her to sit down. His eyes fell on the chair which was always called hers. Thyrza noticed it at the same time. From it she looked to him. Gilbert averted his eyes.

'I did not come to see Lyddy,' Thyrza said, forcing her voice to steadiness. 'It was to speak to you. I didn't dare to hope you would be so——'

'Don't say what it pains you to say,' Gilbert spoke, when her words failed. 'It will pain me even more. Speak to me like an old friend, Miss Trent.'

'Can you still feel like a friend to me?'

'I don't change much,' he said. 'And it would be a great change that would make me have any but friendly thoughts of you.'

She raised her face.

'I behaved so cruelly to you. If I could hope that you would forgive that——'

A sob broke her voice.

'Don't talk of forgiveness!' Gilbert replied, with less self-control. 'I have never thought a hard thought of you. I can't bear to hear *you* speak in that voice to me.'

The tenderness he had concealed found expression in the last words. Her wonderful new beauty, the humility of her bowed head, her tears, overcame the show he had made of easy friendliness. He saw her eyes turned to him again, and this time he met their gaze.

'Do you know all of my life since I left you?' Thyrza asked. 'Lyddy knows how I have lived all the time, from that day to this. Has she told you?'

'Yes, she has told me.'

'Will you let me fulfil the promise I made to you? Can you forget what I have done? Will you let me be your companion—do all I can to make your home a happy one? I have no right to ask, but if—if not now—if some day I could be a help to you! I will come to live with Lyddy. We will find a room somewhere else. I will work with Lyddy, till you can let me come——'

Her pallor turned to a deep flush. She spoke brokenly, till her lips became mute, the last word dying in a whisper. She had not known what it would cost her to say this. A deadly shame enfolded her; she could have sunk to the ground before him after the first sentence.

Gilbert listened and was shaken. He knew that this was no confession of love for him, but of the sincerity of what she had said he could have no doubt. There was not disgrace upon her; she humbled herself solely in grief for the suffering she had caused him. He loved her, loved her the more for the awe her matured beauty inspired in him. That Thyrza should come and speak thus, was more like a dream than simple reality. And for all his longing, he durst not touch her hand.

'What you offer me,' he said, in low, tremulous accents, 'I should never have dared to ask, for it is the greatest gift I can imagine. You are so far above me now, Thyrza. I should take you into a life that you are no longer fit for. My home must always be a very poor one; it would shame me to give you nothing better than that.'

'I want nothing more than to be with you, Gilbert. I am not above you; you are better in everything. I broke a promise which ought to have been sacred. If you let me share your life, that is your forgiveness. I want you to forgive me; I want to be a help to you still; I wish to forget all that came between us. You won't reject me?'

'Oh, Thyrza, I love you too much! I am too selfish to act as I ought to! Thyrza! That you can be my wife still, when no spark of hope was left to me!' . . .

It did not seem to Lydia that she had waited long when she heard her sister's step on the stairs again.

'I mustn't stay another minute,' Thyrza said, going at once to where her hat and cloak lay. 'It will be late before I get home.'

'I shall come with you as far as the 'bus.'

Lydia would have asked no question, though agitated with wonder and a surmise she scarcely dared to entertain. When they were both ready to go out, Thyrza turned to her.

'Gilbert has been very good to me, Lyddy. He will forget all the harm I have done him, and I shall be his wife.'

The other could find no word for a moment.

'Are you glad of this, Lyddy?'

'I don't know what to think or say,' her sister replied, looking at her with half-tearful earnestness. 'Did you always mean this, when you said you were coming here soon?'

'No, not always. But I was able to do it at last. Now I shall rest, dear sister.'

'You are sure that this is right? It isn't only a fancy, that you'll be sorry for, that'll make everything worse in the end?'

'I shall never be sorry, and everything will be better, Lyddy.'

They kissed each other.

'Come, dear, I mustn't wait.'

They walked quickly and without speaking as far as the lights and noise of Westminster Bridge Road. For them the everyday movement of the street had no meaning; such things were the mere husk of life; each was absorbed in her own being.

'I shall come again on Saturday night,' Thyrza said hurriedly, as they parted. 'And perhaps I shall stay over Sunday. May I?'

'Do!'

'Be at the door again at the same time.'

CHAPTER XL

HER REWARD

THIS was on Thursday. The two days which followed were
such as come very rarely in a London winter. Fog had
vanished ; the ways were clean and hard ; between the house-
tops and the zenith gleamed one clear blue track of frosty sky.
The sun—the very sun of heaven—made new the outline of
every street, flashed on windows, gave beauty to spires and
domes, revealed whiteness in untrodden places where the
snow still lingered. The air was like a spirit of joyous life,
tingling the blood to warmth and with a breath freeing the
brain from sluggish vapours. Such a day London sees but
once in half a dozen winters.

Thyrza felt the influence of the change. She breathed
more easily ; her body was no longer the weary weight she
had failed under. When she rose and saw such marvellous
daylight at her window, involuntarily she let her voice run
over a few notes. The power of song was still in her ; ah, if
health and happiness had companioned with her, would she
not have sung as few ever did !

But henceforth that was part of the past, part of what she
must forget and renounce. When she said to Mrs. Ormonde
that she would still try to keep up her singing, there was a
thought in her mind worthy of a woman cast in such a mould
as hers. She had a vision of herself, on some day not far off,
sending forth her voice in glorious song, and knowing that
among the crowd before her *he* sat and listened. He would
know her then. To him her voice would say what no one else
understood, and for a moment—she wished it to be for no
more than a moment—he would scorn himself for having forgotten her.

It was all gone into the past, buried for ever out of sight.
She would no longer even sigh over the memory. If the sky
were always as to-day, if there were always sunlight to stand
in and the living air to drink. she might find the life before
her in truth as little of a burden as it seemed this morning
But the days would again be wrapped in nether fumes, the
foul air would stifle her, her blood would go stagnant, her
eyes would weep with the desolate rain. Why should Gilbert

remain in England ?   Were there no countries where the sun shone that would give a man and a woman toil whereby to support themselves ?   Luke Ackroyd had spoken of going to Canada.   He said it cost so little to get there, and that life was better than in England.   Could not Gilbert take her yonder ?   But there was his mother, old, weary ;   no such change was possible for her.   And the thought of her reminded Thyrza of one of the first duties she must take upon herself. It mattered little where she lived—mattered little if the sundawn never broke again.   Her life was to be in a narrow circle, and to that she would accustom herself.

What of to-morrow ?   To-day she was full of courage, even of a kind of hope.   Never should Gilbert feel that she was not wholly his ;   never would she wrong his faithfulness by slighting the claims of his love.   In her misery she had said that there were things she could not do—could not bear ; as if a woman cannot take up any burden that she wills, and carry it faithfully even as far as the gates of death !   And this duty before her she would not even think of as a burden.   There are some women who never know what love is, who marry a man because they respect and like him, and are good wives their life long.   She would be even as one of these.   Suppose love to be something she had outgrown ;   the idleness of girls. Now was the season of her womanhood, and the realities of life left no room for folly.

How long since she had felt so well !   She sewed through the morning, and had but little trouble to keep her thoughts always forward-looking.   She sang a little to herself, for who but must sing when there is sunlight ?   She ate when dinner was brought to her.   Then she prepared to go out for half an hour.

Clara just then came up.

' Ah, you are going out !   Do come with us into the park, will you ?   You haven't to go anywhere.   My husband has taken a half-holiday on purpose to skate.   Reckless man !   He says you don't get skating weather like this every day.   Can you skate ? '

Thyrza shook her head, smiling.

' No more can I.   Harold wants to teach me, but it seems absurd to bruise oneself all over, and make oneself ridiculous too, to learn an amusement you can't practise once in five years.   But do come with us.   It really is nice to watch them skating.'

'Yes, I will come, gladly,' Thyrza said.

And so they went to the ice in Regent's Park, and Mr. Emerson put on his skates, and was speedily exhibiting his skill amid the gliding crowd. Clara and her companion walked along the edge. Thyrza, regarding this assembly of people who had come forth to enjoy themselves, marvelled inwardly. It was so hard to understand how any one could enter with such seriousness into mere amusement. How many happy people the world contained ! Of all this black-coated swarm, not one with a trouble that could not be flung away at the summons of a hard frost ! They sped about as if on wings, they shouted to friends, they had catastrophes and laughed aloud over them. And, as she looked on, the scene grew so unreal that it frightened her. These did not seem to be human beings. How came it that they were exempt from the sorrow that goes about the world, blighting lives and breaking hearts ? Or was it she that lived in a dream, while these were really awake ? She was not sorrowful now, but light-hearted pastime such as this was unintelligible to her.

Clara chatted and ran, and thoroughly enjoyed herself. At one spot she came at length to a pause, having lost sight of her husband, fretting that she could not find him. Her eye discovered him at length, however, and just as she spoke her satisfaction she was surprised by a laugh from Thyrza—a real laugh, sweet and clear as it used to be.

'What is it ? ' she asked in wonder.

'Oh, look ! Do look ! '

Just before them, on the ice, a little troop of ducks was going by, fowl dispossessed of their wonted swimming-ground by the all-hardening frost. Of every two steps the waddlers took, one was a hopeless slip, and the spectacle presented by the unhappy birds in their effort to get along at a good round pace was ludicrous beyond resistance. They sprawled and fell, they staggered up again with indignant wagging of head and tail, they rushed forward only to slip more desperately ; now one leg failed them, now the other, now both at once. And all the time they kept up a cackle of annoyance ; they looked about them with foolish eyes of amazement and indignation ; they wondered, doubtless, what the world was coming to, when an honest duck's piece of water was suddenly stolen from him, and he was subjected to insult on the top of injury.

Thyrza gazed at them, and the longer she gazed the more merrily she laughed.

'Poor ducks! I never saw anything so ridiculous. There, look! The one with the neck all bright colours! He'll be down again; there, I said he would! Why *will* they try to go so quickly? They wouldn't stumble half so much if they walked gently.'

Thyrza had thought that nothing in the world could move her to unfeigned laughter. Yet as often as she thought of the ducks it was with revival of mirth. She laughed at them long after, alone in her room.

It was as bright a day on the morrow, and still she knew that lightness of heart, that freedom of the breath which is physical happiness. Had she by the mere act of redeeming her faith to Gilbert brought upon herself this reward? It was so strangely easy to keep dark thoughts at a distance. She had not lain awake in the night, for her a wonderful experience. Could it last?

There was a letter this morning from Gilbert. She did not open it at once, for she knew that there would be more pain than content in reading it. Yet, when she had read it, she found that it was not out of harmony with her mood. He wrote because he could say things in this silent way which would not come to his lips so well. The gratitude he expressed —simply, powerfully—moved Thyrza; not as the words of one she loved would have moved her, but to a feeling of calm thankfulness that she had it in her power to give so much joy. And perhaps some day she could give him affection. She had, in her belief, spoken truly when she said that he was above her. He was no ignorant man, without a thought save of his day's earnings. She could respect his mind, as she had always done, and his character she could reverence. It was well.

She told Mrs. Emerson that she was going to see her sister again, and that probably she would not return till Sunday night.

On setting forth, she had a letter to post. It was to Mrs. Ormonde. Purposely she had delayed writing this till Saturday afternoon; she wished to show that there had been a couple of days for thought since the step was taken, and that she could speak with calm consciousness of what she had done. The posting of this letter was like saying a last good-bye.

Lydia was again waiting just at the door, and again they reached the room without having been observed.

'I shall go down at once,' Thyrza said. 'Gilbert expects me. I am going to speak to Mrs. Grail.'

Lydia was pleased to see that the pale face had not that terrible look to-night. To-night there were smiles for her, and many affectionate words. During Thyrza's absence of half an hour, she sat puzzling over the mystery, as she had puzzled since Thursday night. Would all indeed be well? It was so sudden, so unthought of, so hard to believe. For Lydia had by degrees come to think of her sister as raised quite above this humble station. Though she could not reconcile herself to it, though she would above all things have chosen that Thyrza should still marry Gilbert, yet there was a contradictory sort of pride in knowing that her sister was a lady. Lyddy, we are aware, was little given to logical processes of thought; her feelings often got her into troublesome perplexities.

Thyrza came up again. Mrs. Grail had received her with tears and silence at first, but soon with something of the gratitude which Gilbert felt.

'I told them I was going to stay till to-morrow. I shall have tea with them then. You'll spare me for an hour, Lyddy?'

There was no talk between them as yet on the main subject of their thoughts. Something that was said caused Lydia to go to her cupboard and bring forth an object which Thyrza at once recognised. It was Mr. Boddy's violin.

'I shall always keep it,' she said. 'I have had offers to buy it, but I shall have to be badly in want before it goes.'

She had redeemed it from the pawnbroker's, and no one had opposed her claim to possess it. The expenses of the old man's burial had been defrayed by a subscription Ackroyd got up among those who remembered Mr. Boddy with kindness.

Thyrza touched the strings, and shrank back frightened at the sound. The ghost of dead music, it evoked the ghost of her dead self.

They fell into solemn talk. Thyrza had resolved that she would not tell her sister the truth of everything for a long time; some day she would do so, when the new life had become old habit. But, as they sat by the fire and spoke in low voices, she was impelled to make all known. Why should there any longer be a secret between Lyddy and herself? It would be yet another help to her if she told Lyddy; she felt at length that she must.

So the story was whispered. Lydia could only hold her sister in her arms, and shed tears of love and pity.

'We will never speak of it again, dearest,' Thyrza said ; 'never, as long as we live !'

'No, never as long as we live !'

'It's all very long ago, already,' Thyrza added. 'I don't suffer now, dear one. I have borne so much, that I think I can't feel pain any more. With you, here in our home, I am happy, and, wherever I am, I don't think I shall ever be *un*-happy. I have written to Mrs. Ormonde, and she will let him know. He will think I came back because I had long forgotten him, and was sorry that I ever left Gilbert. You see, that's what I wish him to believe. Now there'll be nothing to prevent him from marrying who he likes. No one can say that he has done harm which can never be undone, can they ? I shall rest now, and life will seem easy. So little will be asked of me ; I shall do my best so willingly.'

In the morning Thyrza said :

'I have a fancy, Lyddy. I want you to do my hair for me again.'

'Like you wear it now ?'

'No, I mean in the old way. Will it make me look a child again ? Never mind, that is what I should like. I'll have it so when I go downstairs to tea.'

And whilst Lydia was busy with the golden tresses, Thyrza laughed suddenly. She had only just thought again of the ducks in the park. She told all about them, and they laughed together.

'I wonder whether Mrs. Jarmey knows I'm here,' Thyrza said. 'You think not ? Won't someone be coming to see you ? Won't Mary ?'

'Yes. She always calls for me to go to chapel. Would you rather not see her ?'

'Not to-day, Lyddy. Not till I'm in my own home.'

'But I may tell her you're here ? I'll go down in time to meet her, and I won't go to chapel this morning. No, I'll stay with you this morning, dear.'

So it was arranged. And they cooked their dinner as they used to ; only Thyrza declared that Lydia had been extravagant in providing.

'I see how you indulge yourself, now that I'm away ! Oh yes, of course you pretend it's only for me.'

How could she be so merry? Lydia thought. But this smile was not always on her face.

The day passed very quickly. Lydia said she would go out whilst Thyrza was with the Grails; she had promised to see someone. Thyrza did not ask who it was.

When she came upstairs again the other had not yet returned. She was yet a quarter of an hour away. Then she appeared with signs of haste.

' I was afraid you'd be here alone,' she said.

' But have you had tea, Lyddy?'

' Yes.'

This 'yes' was said rather mysteriously. And Lydia's subsequent behaviour was also mysterious. She took her hat off and stood with it in her hand, as if not knowing where to put it. Then she sat down, forgetting that she still wore her jacket. Reminded of this, she stood about the room, undecidedly.

' What are you thinking of, Lyddy?'

'Nothing.'

She sat down at last, but had so singular a countenance that Thyrza was obliged to remark on it.

' What have you been doing? Never mind, if you'd rather not tell me.'

Two or three minutes passed before Lydia could make up her mind to tell. She began by saying:

' You know when I went down to see Mary this morning?'

' Yes,'

' She said she'd seen—that she'd seen Mrs. Poole, and that I was to be sure to go round to Mrs. Poole's some time in the afternoon, as she wanted to see me, particular.'

' Yes. And that's where you went?'

Lydia seemed to have no more to say. Thyrza looked at her searchingly.

' Well, Lyddy, there's nothing in that. What else? I know there's something else.'

' Yes, there is. I went to the house, and, when I knocked at the door, Mr. Ackroyd opened it.'

Thyrza had begun to tremble. Her eyes watched her sister's face eagerly; she read something in the heightened colour it showed.

' And then, Lyddy? And then?'

' He asked me to come into the sitting-room. And then he—he said he wanted me to marry him, Thyrza.'

'Lyddy! It is true? At last?'

Thyrza could scarcely contain herself for joy. She had longed for this. No happiness of her own would have been in truth complete until there came like happiness to her sister. She knew how long, how patiently, with what self-sacrifice, Lydia had been faithful to this her first love. Again and again the love had seemed for ever hopeless; yet Lydia gave no sign of sorrow. The sisters were unlike each other in this. Lydia's nature, fortunately for herself, was not passionate; but its tenderness none knew as Thyrza did, its tenderness and its steadfast faith.

'Thyrza, any one would think you are more glad of it than I am.'

'There are no words to tell my gladness, dearest! Good Lyddy! At last, at last!'

Her face changed from moment to moment; it was now flushed, now again pale. Once or twice she put her hand against her side.

'How excitable you always were, little one!' Lydia said. 'Come and sit quietly. It's bad luck when any one makes so much of a thing.'

Thyrza grew calmer. Her face showed that she was suppressing pain. In a few minutes she said:

'I'll just lie down, Lyddy. I shall be better directly. Don't trouble, it's nothing. Come and sit by me. How glad I am! Look pleased, just to please me, will you?'

Both were quiet. Thyrza said it had only been a feeling of faintness; it was gone now.

The fire was getting low. Lydia went to stir it. She had done so and was turning to the bed again, when Thyrza half rose, crying in a smothered voice:

'Lyddy! Come!'

Then she fell back. Her sister was bending over her in an instant, was loosening her dress, doing all that may restore one who has fainted. But for Thyrza there was no awaking.

Had she not herself desired it? And what gift more blessed, of all that man may pray for?

She was at rest, the pure, the gentle, at rest in her maidenhood. The joy that had strength to kill her was not of her own; of the two great loves between which her soul was divided, that which was lifelong triumphed in her life's last moment.

She who wept there through the night would have lain dead if that cold face could in exchange have been touched by the dawn to waking. She felt that her life was desolate; she mourned as for one on whom the extremity of fate has fallen. Mourn she must, in the anguish of her loss; she could not know the cruelty that was in her longing to bring the sleeper back to consciousness. The heart that had ached so wearily would ache no more; for the tired brain there was no more doubt. Had existence been to her but one song of thanks-giving, even then to lie thus had been more desirable. For to sleep is better than to wake, and how should we who live bear the day's burden but for the promise of death.

On Monday at noon there arrived a telegram, addressed to 'Miss Thyrza Trent.' Gilbert received it from Mrs. Jarmey, and he took it upstairs to Lydia, who opened it. It was from Mrs. Ormonde; she was at the Emersons', and wished to know when Thyrza would return; she desired to see her.

'Will you write to her, Gilbert?' Lydia asked.

'Wouldn't it be better if I went to see her?'

Yes, that was felt to be better. It was known that Thyrza had written to Mrs. Ormonde on Saturday, so that nothing needed to be explained; Gilbert had only to bear his simple news.

Arrived at the house, he had to wait. Mrs. Ormonde was gone out for an hour, and neither Mr. Emerson nor his wife was at home. He sat in the Emersons' parlour, seldom stirring, his eyes unobservant. For Gilbert Grail there was little left in the world that he cared to look at.

Mrs. Ormonde came in. She regarded Gilbert with uncertainty, having been told that someone waited for her, but nothing more. Gilbert rose and made himself known to her. Then, marking his expression, she was fearful.

'You have come from Miss Trent—from Thyrza,' she said, giving him her hand.

'She could not come herself, Mrs. Ormonde.'

'Thyrza is ill?'

He hesitated. His face had told her the truth before he uttered:

'She is dead!'

It is seldom that we experience a simple emotion. When the words, incredible at first, had established their meaning in her mind, Mrs. Ormonde knew that with her human grief there blended an awe-struck thankfulness. She stood on other ground than Lydia's, on other than Gilbert's; her heart had been wrung by the short unaffected letter she had received from Thyrza, and, though she could only acquiesce, the future had looked grey and joyless. To hear it said of Thyrza, ' She is dead!' chilled her; the world of her affections was beyond measure poorer by the loss of that sweet and noble being. But could she by a word have reversed the decision of fate, love would not have suffered her to speak it.

They talked together, and at the end she said:

'If Lydia will let me come and see her, I shall be very grateful. Will you ask her, and send word to me speedily?'

The permission was granted. Mrs. Ormonde went to Walnut Tree Walk that evening, and Gilbert conducted her to the door of the room. The lamp gave its ordinary stinted light. There was nothing unusual in the appearance of the chamber. In the bed one lay asleep.

Mrs. Ormonde took Lydia's hands and without speaking kissed her. Then Lydia raised the lamp from the table, and held it so that the light fell on her sister's face. No remnant of pain was there, only calm, unblemished beauty; the lips were as naturally composed as if they might still part to give utterance to song; the brow showed its lines of high imaginativeness even more clearly than in life. The golden braid rested by her neck as in childhood.

'Have you any picture of her?' Mrs. Ormonde asked.

'No.'

'Will you let me have one made—drawn from her face now, but looking as she did in life? It shall be done by a good artist; I think it can be done successfully.'

Lydia was in doubt. The thought of introducing a stranger to this room to sit and pore upon the dead face with cold interest was repugnant to her. Yet if Thyrza's face really could be preserved, to look at her, for others dear to her to look at, that would be much. She gave her assent.

Mary Bower came frequently; her silent presence was a help to Lydia through the miseries of the next few days.

One other there was who asked timidly to be allowed to see Thyrza once more—her friend Totty. She sought Mary Bower, and said how much she wished it, though she feared Lydia would not grant her wish. But it was granted readily, Totty had her sad pleasure, and her solemn memory.

Mrs. Ormonde knew that it was better for her not to attend

the funeral. On the evening before, she left at the house a small wreath of white flowers. Lydia, Gilbert, Mary Bower, Luke Ackroyd and his sister, these only went to the cemetery. He whom Thyrza would have wished to follow her, in thought at least, to the grave, was too far away to know of her death till later.

The next day, Lydia sat for an hour with Ackroyd. They did not speak much. But before she left him, Lydia looked into his face and said :

'Do you wish me to believe, Luke, that I shall never see my sister again ? '

He bent his face and kept silence.

'Do you think that I could live if I believed that she was gone for ever ? That I should never meet Thyrza after this, never again ?'

'I shall never wish you to think in that way, Lyddy, he answered, kindly. 'I've often talked as if I knew things for certain, when I know nothing. You're better in yourself than I am, and you may feel more of the truth.'

The next morning, Lydia went to her work as usual. Gilbert had already returned to his. The clear winter sunshine was already a thing of the far past; in the streets was the slush of thaw, and darkness fell early from the obscured sky.

CHAPTER XLI

THE LIVING

THIS winter the Newthorpes spent abroad. Mr. Newthorpe was in very doubtful health when he went to Ullswater, just before Egremont's return to England, and by the end of the autumn his condition was such as to cause a renewal of Annabel's former fears. On a quick decision, they departed for Cannes, and remained there till early in the following April.

'There's a sort of absurdity,' Mr. Newthorpe remarked, ' in living when you can think of nothing but how you're to save your life. Better have done with it, I think. It strikes me as an impiety, too, to go playing at hide-and-seek with the gods.'

They came back to Eastbourne, which, on the whole, seemed to suit the invalid during these summer months. He did little now but muse over a few favourite books and listen to his daughter's conversation. Comparatively a young man, his energies were spent, his life was behind him. To Annabel it was infinitely sorrowful to have observed this rapid process of decay. She could not be persuaded that the failure of his powers was anything more than temporary. But her father lost no opportunity of warning her that she deceived herself. He had his reasons for doing so.

His temper was perfect: his outlook on the world remained that of a genial pessimist, a type of man common enough in our day. He seemed to find a pleasure in urbanely mocking at his own futility.

' I am the sort of man,' he once said, ' of whom Tourguéneff would make an admirable study. There's tragedy in me, if you have the eyes to see it. I don't think any one can help feeling kindly towards me. I don't think any one can altogether despise me. Yet my life is a mere inefficacy.'

' You have had much enjoyment in your life, father,' Annabel replied, ' and enjoyment of the purest kind. In our age of the world I think that must be a sufficient content.'

' Why, there you've hit it, Bell. 'Tis the age. There's somebody else I know who had better take warning by me. But I think he has done.'

They were talking thus as they sat alone in one of the places of shelter on the Parade. Other people had departed on the serious business of dining; but the evening was beautiful, and these two were tempted to remain and watch the sea.

' You mean Mr. Egremont,' Annabel said.

' Yes. I wonder very much what he will be at my age. He won't be anything particular, of course.'

' No, I don't suppose he will do anything remarkable,' the girl assented impartially.

' Yet he might have done,' recommenced her father, with some annoyance, as if his remark had not elicited the answer he looked for. ' This mill-work of his I consider mere discipline. I should have thought two years of it enough ; three certainly ought to be. A fourth, and he will never do anything else.'

' What else should he do ? '

Mr. Newthorpe laughed a little.

'There's only one thing for such a fellow to do nowadays. Let him write something.'

'Write?' Annabel mused. 'Yes, I suppose there is nothing else. Yet he happens to have sufficient means.'

'Do you mean it for an epigram? Well, it will pass. True, there's the hardship of his position. There's nothing for him to do but to write, yet he is handicapped by his money. I should have done something worth the doing, if I had had to write for bread and cheese. Let him show that he has something in him, in spite of the fact that he has never gone without his dinner. Yes, but that would prove him an extraordinary man, and we agree that he is nothing of the kind.'

'Haven't you ever felt a sort of uneasy shame when you have heard of another acquaintance taking up the pen?'

'Of course I have. I've felt the same when I've heard of someone being born.'

'Suppose I announced to you that I was writing a novel?'

'I am a philosopher, Bell.'

'Precisely. It would be disagreeable to me if I heard that Mr. Egremont was writing a novel. If he published anything very good, it wouldn't trouble one so much after the event. I don't see why he should write. I think he'd better continue to give half his day to something practical, and the other half to the pleasures of a man of culture. It will preserve his balance.'

'Bella mia, you are greatly disillusioned for a young girl.'

'I don't feel that the term is applicable to me. I am disillusioned, father, because I am getting reasonably old.'

'You live too much alone.'

'I prefer it.'

Mr. Newthorpe seemed to be turning over a thought.

'I suppose,' he said at length, with a glance at his daughter, 'that what you have just said explains our friend's return to his oil-cloth.'

'Not entirely, I think.'

'H'm. You sent him about his business, however.

Annabel looked straight before her at the sea; her lips barely smiled.

'You are mistaken. He gave me no right to do so.'

'Oh? Then I have been on a wrong tack.'

'Shall we walk homewards?'

Towards the end of August, Mr. and Mrs. Dalmaine were at Eastbourne for a few days. Paula spent one hour with her cousin in private, no more. The two had drifted further apart than ever. But in that one hour Paula had matter enough for talk. There had been a General Election during the summer, and Mr. Dalmaine had victoriously retained his seat for Vauxhall. His wife could speak of nothing else.

'What I would have given if you could have seen me canvassing, Bell! Now I've found the one thing that I can do really well. I wish Parliaments were annual!'

'My dear Paula, what has made you so misanthropic?'

'I don't understand. You know I never do understand your clever remarks, Bell; please speak quite simply, will you? Oh, but the canvassing! Of course I didn't get on with people's wives as well as with people themselves; women never do, you know. You should have heard me arguing questions with working men and shopkeepers! Mr. Dalmaine once told me I'd better keep out of politics, as I only made a bungle of it; but I've learnt a great deal since then. He admits now that I really do understand the main questions. Of course it's all his teaching. He puts things so clearly, you know. I suppose there's no one in the House who makes such clear speeches as he does.'

'The result of your work was very satisfactory.'

'Wasn't it! Fifteen hundred majority! Then we drove all about the borough, and I had to bow nicely to people who waved their hats and shouted. It was a new sensation; I think I never enjoyed anything so much in my life. He is enormously popular, my husband. And everybody says he is doing an enormous lot of good. You know, Bell, it was a mere chance that he isn't in the Ministry! His name was mentioned; we know it for a fact. There's no doubt whatever he'll be in next time, if the Liberal Government keeps up. It is so annoying that Parliaments generally last so long! Think what that will be, when he is a Minister! I shouldn't wonder if you come to see me some day in Downing Street, Bell.'

'I should be afraid, Paula.'

'Nonsense! Your husband will bring you. Don't you think Mr. Dalmaine's looking remarkably well? I'm so sorry I haven't got my little boy here for you to see. We've decided that *he's* to be Prime Minister! I hope you read Mr. Dalmaine's speeches, Bell?'

'Frequently.'

'That's good of you! He's thinking of publishing a volume of those that deal with factory legislation. You should have heard what they said about him, at the election time!'

Paula was still charming, but it must be confessed a trifle vulgarised. Formerly she had not been vulgar at all; at present one discerned unmistakably the influence of her husband, and of the world in which she lived. In person, she showed the matron somewhat prematurely; one saw that in another ten years she would be portly; her round fair face would become too round and too pinky. Mentally, she was at length formed, and to Mr. Dalmaine was due the credit of having formed her.

This gentleman did his kinsfolk the honour of calling upon them. He had grown a little stouter; he bore himself with conscious dignity; you saw that he had not much time, nor much attention, to bestow upon unpolitical people. He was suave and abrupt by turns; he used his hands freely in conversing. Mr. Newthorpe smiled much during the interview with him, and, a few hours later, when alone with Annabel, he suddenly exclaimed:

'What an ignorant pretentious numskull that fellow is!'

'Of whom do you speak?'

'Why, of Dalmaine, of course.'

'My dear father!—A philanthropist! One of the forces of the time!'

Mr. Newthorpe leaned back and laughed.

'Perfectly true,' he said presently. 'Whence we may arrive at certain conclusions with regard to mankind at large and our time in particular. That poor pretty girl! It's too bad.'

'She is happy.'

'True again. And it would be foolish to wish her miserable. Bell, let us join hands and go to the old ferryman's boat together.'

'It would cost me no pang, father. Still we will walk a little longer on the sea-shore.'

And whilst this conversation was going on, Mr. and Mrs. Dalmaine sat after dinner on the balcony of their hotel, talking occasionally. Dalmaine smoked a cigar: his eyes betrayed the pleasures of digestion and thought on high matters of State.

He said all at once:

'By-the-by, Lady Wigger is at the Queen's Hotel, I see. You will call to-morrow.'

'Lady Wigger ? But really 1 don't think I can, dear,' Paula replied, timidly.

'Why not ?'

'Why, you know she was so shockingly rude to me at the Huntleys' ball. You said it was abominable, yourself.'

'So it was, but you'd better call.'

'I'd much rather not.'

Dalmaine looked at her with Olympian surprise.

'But, my dear,' he said with suave firmness, 'I said that you had better call. The people must not be neglected ; they will be useful. Do you understand me ?'

'Yes, love.'

Paula was quiet for a few moments, then talked as brightly as ever. . . . .

One day close upon the end of September, Mrs. Ormonde had to pay a visit to the little village of West Dean, which is some four miles distant from Eastbourne, inland and westward. Business of a domestic nature took her thither ; she wished to visit a cottage for the purpose of seeing a girl whom she thought of engaging as a servant. The day was very beautiful ; she asked the Newthorpes to accompany her on the drive. Mr. Newthorpe preferred to remain at home; Annabel accepted the invitation.

The road was uphill, until the level of the Downs was reached ; then it went winding along, with fair stretches of scenery on either hand, between fields fragrant of Autumn, overhead the broad soft purple sky. First East Dean was passed, a few rustic houses nestling, as the name implies, in its gentle hollow. After that, another gradual ascent, and presently the carriage paused at a point of the road immediately above the village to which they were going.

The desire to stop was simultaneous in Mrs. Ormonde and her companion ; their eyes rested on as sweet a bit of landscape as can be found in England, one of those scenes which are typical of the Southern counties. It was a broad valley, at the lowest point of which lay West Dean. The hamlet consists of very few houses, all so compactly grouped about the old church that from this distance it seemed as if the hand could cover them. The roofs were overgrown with lichen, yellow on slate, red on tiles. In the farmyards were haystacks with yellow conical coverings of thatch. And around all closed dense masses of chestnut foliage, the green just touched with gold. The little group of houses had mellowed with age ;

I I

their guarded peacefulness was soothing to the eye and the spirit. Along the stretch of the hollow the land was parcelled into meadows and tilth of varied hue. Here was a great patch of warm grey soil, where horses were drawing the harrow; yonder the same work was being done by sleek black oxen. Where there was pasture, its chalky-brown colour told of the nature of the earth which produced it. A vast oblong running right athwart the far side of the valley had just been strewn with loam; it was the darkest purple. The bright yellow of the 'kelk' spread in several directions; and here and there rose thin wreaths of white smoke, where a pile of uprooted couch-grass was burning; the scent was borne hither by a breeze that could be scarcely felt.

The clock of the old church struck four.

'A kindness, Mrs. Ormonde!' said Annabel. 'Let me stay here whilst you drive down into the village. I don't wish to see the people there just now. To sit here and look down on that picture will do me good.'

'By all means. But I dare say I shall be half an hour. It will take ten minutes to drive down.'

'Never mind. I shall sit here on the bank, and enjoy myself.'

Now it happened that on this same September day a young man left Brighton and started to walk eastward along the coast. He had come into Brighton from London the evening before, having to pay a visit to the family of an acquaintance of his who had recently died in Pennsylvania, and who, when dying, had asked him to perform this office on his return to England. He was no stranger to Brighton; he knew that, if one is obliged to visit the place, it is well to be there under cover of the night and to depart as speedily as possible from amid its vulgar hideousness. So, not later than eight on the following morning, he had left the abomination behind him, and was approaching Rottingdean.

His destination was Eastbourne; the thought of going thither on foot came to him as he glanced at a map of the coast whilst at breakfast. The weather was perfect, and the walk would be full of interest.

One would have said that he had a mind very free from care. For the most part he stepped on at a good round pace, observing well; sometimes he paused, as if merely to enjoy the air. He was in excellent health; he smiled readily.

At Rottingdean he lingered for awhile. A soft mist hung

all around; sky and sea were of a delicate blurred blue-grey, the former mottled in places. The sun was not visible, but its light lay in one long gleaming line out on the level water; beyond, all was vapour-veiled. There were no breakers; now and then a larger ripple than usual splashed on the beach, and that was the only sound the sea gave. It was full tide; the water at the foot of the cliffs was of a wonderful green, pellucid, delicate, through which the chalk was visible, with dark masses of weed here and there. Swallows in great numbers flew about the edge, and thistle-down floated everywhere. From the fields came a tinkle of sheep-bells.

The pedestrian sighed when he rose to continue his progress. It was noticeable that, as he went on, he lost something of his cheerfulness of manner; probably the early rising and the first taste of exercise had had their effect upon him, and now he was returning to his more wonted self. The autumn air, the sun-stained mist, the silent sea, would naturally incline to pensiveness one who knew that mood.

The air was unimaginably calm; the thistle-down gave proof that only the faintest breath was stirring. On the Downs beyond Rottingdean lay two or three bird-catchers, prone as they watched the semicircle of call-birds in cages, and held their hand on the string which closed the nets. The young man spoke a few words with one of these, curious about his craft.

He came down upon Newhaven, and halted in the town for refreshment; then, having loitered a little to look at the shipping, he climbed the opposite side of the valley, and made his way as far as Seaford. Thence another climb, and a bend inland, for the next indentation of the coast was Cuckmere Haven, and the water could only be crossed at some distance from the sea. The country through which the Cuckmere flowed had a melancholy picturesqueness. It was a great reach of level meadows, very marshy, with red-brown rushes growing in every ditch, and low trees in places, their trunks wrapped in bright yellow lichen; nor only their trunks, but the very smallest of their twigs was so clad. All over the flats were cows pasturing, black cows, contrasting with flocks of white sheep, which were gathered together, bleating. The coarse grass was sun-scorched; the slope of the Downs on either side showed the customary chalky green. The mist had now all but dispersed, yet there was still only blurred
I I 2

sunshine. Rooks hovered beneath the sky, heavily, lazily, and uttered their long caws.

The Cuckmere was crossed, and another ascent began. The sea was now hidden; the road would run inland, cutting off the great angle made by Beachy Head. The pedestrian had made notes of his track; he knew that he was now approaching a village called West Dean. He had lingered by the Cuckmere; now he braced himself. And he came in sight of West Dean as the church clock struck four.

He wished now to make speed to Eastbourne, but the loveliness of the hollow above which the road ran perforce checked him; he paced forward very slowly, his eyes bent upon the hamlet. Something moved, near to him. He looked round. A lady was standing in the road, and, of all strange things, a lady of whom at that moment he was thinking.

By what inconceivable chance does this happen, Miss Newthorpe ?' he said, taking her offered hand.

'Surely the question would come with even more force from me,' Annabel made answer. ' You might have presumed me to be in England, Mr. Egremont; I, on the other hand, certainly imagined that you were beyond the Atlantic.'

'I have been in England a day or two.'

'But here ? Looking down upon West Dean ?'

'I have walked from Brighton—one of the most delightful walks I ever took.'

'A long one, surely. I am waiting for Mrs. Ormonde. She is with the carriage below. I chose to wait here, to feast my eyes.'

Both turned again to the picture. The two did not sort ill together. Annabel was very womanly, of fair, thoughtful countenance, and she stood with no less grace, though maturer, than by the ripples of Ullswater, four years ago. She had the visage of a woman whose intellect is highly trained, a face sensitive to every note of the soul's music, yet impressed with the sober consciousness which comes of self-study and experience. A woman, one would have said, who could act as nobly as she could speak, yet who would prefer both to live and to express herself in a minor key. And Egremont was not unlike her in some essential points. The turn for irony was more pronounced on his features, yet he had the eyes of an idealist. He, too, would choose restraint in preference to outbreak of emotion : he too could be forcible if occasion of sufficient pressure lay upon him. And the probability remained, that both one and the other would choose a path of life where there was small risk of their stronger faculties being demanded.

They talked of the landscape, of that exclusively, until Mrs. Ormonde's carriage was seen reascending the hill. Then they became silent, and stood so as their common friend drew near. Her astonishment was not slight, but she gave it only momentary expression, then passed on to general talk.

'I always regard you as reasonably emancipated, Annabel,' she said, 'but none the less I felt a certain surprise in noticing you intimately conversing with a chance wayfarer. Mr. Egremont, be good enough to seat yourself opposite to us.'

They drove back to Eastbourne. All conversed on the way with as much ease as if they had this afternoon set forth in company from The Chestnuts.

'This is what, at school, we used to call a "lift,"' said Egremont.

'A welcome one, too, I should think,' Mrs. Ormonde replied. 'But you always calculated distances by "walks," I remember, when others measure by the carriage or the railway. Annabel, you too are an excellent walker; you have often brought me to extremities in the lakes, though I wouldn't confess it. And pray, Mr. Egremont, for whom was your visit intended? Shall I put you down at Mr. Newthorpe's door, or had you my humble house in view?'

'It is natural to me to count upon The Chestnuts as a place of rest, at all events,' Walter replied. 'I should not have ventured to disturb Mr. Newthorpe this evening.'

'We will wait at the door, Mrs. Ormonde,' put in Annabel. 'Father will come out as he always does.'

Accordingly the carriage was stopped at the Newthorpes' house, and, as Annabel had predicted, her father sauntered forth.

'Ah, how do you do, Egremont?' he said, after a scarcely appreciable hesitation, giving his hand with perfect self-possession. 'Turned up on the road, have you?'

The ladies laughed. Annabel left the carriage, and the other two drove on to The Chestnuts.

Egremont dined and spent the evening with Mrs. Ormonde. Their conversation was long and intimate, yet it was some time before reference was made to the subject both had most distinctly in mind.

'I went to see Grail as soon as I got to London,' Egremont said at length.

'I am glad of that. But how did you know where to find him?'

'They gave me his address at the old house. He seems comfortably lodged with his friend Ackroyd. Mrs. Ackroyd opened the door to me; of course I didn't know her, and she wouldn't know me; Grail told me who it was afterwards. I could recall no likeness to her sister.'

'There is very little. The poor girl is in calm water at last, I hope. She was to have been married on Midsummer Day, and, the night before, Mrs. Grail died; so they put it off. And what of Mr. Grail?'

'He behaved admirably to me; he did not let me feel for a moment that I excited any trouble in his memory.'

'But does his life seem bitter to him—his employment, I mean?'

'I can't think he finds it so. He spoke very frankly, and assured me that he has all the leisure time he cared to use. He says he is not so eager after knowledge as formerly; it is enough for him to read the books he likes. I went with the intention of asking him to let me be of some use, if I could. But it was a delicate matter, in any case, and I found that he understood me without plain speech: he conveyed his answer distinctly enough. No, I sincerely think that he has reached that point of resignation at which a man dreads to be disturbed. He spoke with emotion of Mrs. Ackroyd; she is invaluable to him, I saw.'

'She is a true-hearted woman.'

Egremont let a minute pass, then said:

'You will show me the portrait?'

'Certainly. It hangs in my bedroom; I will fetch it.'

She went and returned quickly, carrying a red crayon drawing framed in plain oak. In the corner was a well-known signature, that of one of the few living artists to whom one would appeal with confidence for the execution of a task such as this, a man whom success has not vulgarised, and who is still of opinion that the true artist will oftener find his inspiration in a London garret than amid the banality of the pluto-crat's drawing-room. The work was of course masterly in execution; it was no less admirable as a portrait. In those few lines of chalk, Thyrza lived. He had divined the secret of the girl's soul, that gift of passionate imagination which in her early years sunk her in hour-long reverie, and later burned her life away. The mood embodied was one so characteristic of Thyrza that one marvelled at the insight which had evoked it from a dead face; she was not happy, she was not downcast; her eyes *saw* something, something which stirred her being, something for which she yearned, passionately, yet with knowledge that it was for ever forbidden to her. A face of infinite pathos, which drew tears to the eyes, yet was unutterably sweet to gaze upon.

Holding the picture, Egremont turned to his companion, and said in a subdued voice:

' This was Thyrza?'

' Her very self.'

' He knew her story?'

' The bare facts, of course without names, without details. He would take nothing for the original drawing—Lydia has it—and nothing for this copy which he made me. He said I had done him a great kindness.'

' Oh, if one could be a man like that!'

The words answered to his thoughts, yet implied something more than their plain meaning. They uttered more than one regret, more than one aspiration.

' Let me take it, Walter.'

' One moment!—This was Thyrza?'

' Let me take it.'

' Tell me—has Miss Newthorpe seen it?'

' Yes.'

Mrs. Ormonde bore the picture away. In a few minutes Egremont took his leave, and went to the hotel to which he had sent his travelling-bag from Brighton. It was long before he slept. He was thinking of a night a little more than a year ago, when he had walked by the shore and held debate with himself. . . . .

On the following evening, shortly before sunset, Annabel and he walked on the short dry grass of the Down that rises to Beachy Head. There had been another day of supreme tranquillity, of blurred sunshine, of soothing autumnal warmth. And this was the crowning hour. The mist had drifted from the land and the sea; as the two continued their ascent, the view became lovelier. They regarded it, but spoke of other things.

' I have no wish to go back to America,' Egremont was saying, ' but, if I do, I shall very likely settle there for good.

I don't think I am ideally adapted to a pursuit of that kind, but habit makes it quite tolerable.'

'What should you do if you remained in England?' Annabel asked, her voice implying no more than friendly interest.

'I might say that I don't know, but it wouldn't be true. I know well enough I should live the life of a student, and of a man who looks on contemporary things with an artistic interest, though he lacks the artistic power to use his observations. In time I should marry. I should have pleasure in my house, should make it as beautiful as might be, should gather a very few friends about me. I should not become morbid; the danger of that is over. Every opportunity I saw of helping those less fortunate than myself I should gladly seize; it is not impossible that I might seek opportunities, that I might found some institution—of quite commonplace aims, be assured. For instance, I should like to see other Homes like Mrs. Ormonde's; many women could conduct them, if the means were supplied. And so on.'

'Yes, that is all very reasonable. It lies with yourself to decide whether you might not have a breezier existence in America.'

'True. But not with myself to decide whether I remain here or go back again. I ask you to help me in determining that.'

Annabel stood as one who reflects gravely yet collectedly. Egremont fixed his eyes upon her, until she looked at him; then his gaze questioned silently.

'Let us understand each other,' said Annabel. 'Do you say this because of anything that has been in the past?'

'Not *because* of it; in continuance of it.'

'Yet we are both very different from what we were when that happened.'

'Both, I think. I do not speak now as I did then, yet the wish I have is far more real.'

They were more than half-way up the ascent; it was after sunset, and the mood of the season was changing.

The plain of Pevensey lay like a vision of fairyland, the colouring indescribably delicate, unreal; bands of dark green alternated with the palest and most translucent emeralds. The long stretch of the coast was a faint outline, yet so clear that every tongue of sand, every smallest headland was distinguishable. The sky that rested on the eastern semicircle of horizon was rather neutral tint than blue, and in it hung long clouds of the colour of faded daffodils. A glance overhead gave the reason of this wondrous effect of light; there, and away to the west, brooded a vast black storm-cloud, ragged at the edge, yet seeming motionless; the western sea was very night, its gloom intensified by one slip of silver shimmer, wherein a sail was revealed. The hillside immediately in front of those who stood here was so deeply shadowed that its contrast threw the vision of unearthly light into distance immeasurable. A wind was rising, but, though its low whistling sound was very audible, it seemed to be in the upper air; here scarcely a breath was felt.

Annabel said:

'Have you seen Thyrza's portrait?'

'Yes.'

She raised her eyes; they were sad, compassionate, yet smiled.

'She could not have lived. But you are conscious now of what that face means?'

'I know nothing of her history from the day when I last saw her, except the mere outward circumstances.'

'Nor do I. But I saw her once, here, and I have seen her portrait. The crisis of your life was there. There was your one great opportunity, and you let it pass. She could not have lived; but that is no matter. You were tried, Mr. Egremont, and found wanting.'

'Her love for me did not continue. It was already too late at the end of those two years.'

'Was it?'

'What secret knowledge have you?'

'None whatever, as you mean it. But it was not too late.'

They were silent. And as they stood thus the sky was again transformed. A steady yet soft wind from the north-west was propelling the great black cloud seaward, over to France; it moved in a solid mass, its ragged edges little by little broken off, its bulk detached from the night which lay behind it. And in the sky which it disclosed rose as it were a pale dawn, the restored twilight. Thereamid glimmered the pole-star.

Eastward on the coast, at the far end of Pevensey Bay, the lights of Hastings began to twinkle; out at sea was visible a single gleam, appearing and disappearing, the lightship on the Sovereign Shoals.

Annabel continued speaking :

'We have both missed something, something that will never again be offered us. When you asked me to be your wife, four years ago at Ullswater, I did not love you. I admired you ; I liked you ; it would have been very possible to me to marry you. But I had my ideal of love, and I hoped to give my husband something more than I felt for you at that time. A year after, I loved you. I suffered when you were suffering. I was envious of the love you gave to another woman, and I said to myself that the moment I hoped for had come only in vain. Since then I have changed more than I changed in those twelve months. I am not in love with you now ; I can talk of these things without a flutter of the pulse. Is it not true ?'

She held her hand to him, baring the wrist. Egremont retained the hand in both his own.

'I can tell you, you see,' she went on, 'what I know to be the truth, that you missed the great opportunity of your life when you abandoned Thyrza. Her love would have made of you what mine never could, even though she herself had been taken from you very soon. I can tell you the mere truth, you see. Dare you still ask for me ?'

'I don't ask, Annabel. I have your hand and I keep it.'

'You may. I don't think I should ever give it to any other man.'

The night was thickening about them.

'Shall we go up to the Head ?' Egremont asked.

'No higher.'

She said it with a significant look, and he understood her.

THE END.

Notes to the Text

p.1:
Ullswater. Gissing had spent some time there with Frederic Harrison's family in August, 1884, visiting most of the places mentioned in this chapter. On August 12, 1884, he wrote to his brother, Algernon: "Yesterday I mounted Helvellyn. Bernard and Austin were with me. . . . A steamer runs from Pooley Bridge, at one end of Ullswater, to Patterdale at the other, and it calls at Howtown, a little bay close by us. This steamer we took to Patterdale, getting there at 9.30. From Patterdale the ascent begins immediately . . ." The area is, of course, associated with Wordsworth, and two days later Gissing made an excursion to Grasmere, the village where Wordsworth had lived, again taking the steamer to Patterdale from Howtown.

p.5:
Ruskin's "Sesame and Lilies." The second edition (1868) contained three lectures dealing with the value of literature, the role of women in society, and the subject of mystery in art and religion.

p.16:
Egremont's plan of lecturing to workingmen is one which Gissing himself had thought of during his early years in London. On January 19, 1879, he wrote to Algernon: "I have got an idea which I fancy is by no means a bad one. It is, in short, to give *public readings.* . . . You see, it would be a step in the direction of lecturing." On January 26th: "If I succeed in my scheme of delivering lectures, one of my first will be entitled 'Intellectual Emancipation.' It will review at length the present situation of our but moderately educated classes with regard to the highest thought and effort of the age." But he was aware of the difficulties, and said in the same letter: "We are too apt to forget the deplorable state of the intellect of 999 out of every 1,000 men, that utter absence of receptivity, that absolute lack of formulative power which renders the assault of a new idea as little effective as that of a cannon-ball against a feather bed."

p.23:
Chapter III A Corner of Lambeth. In preparing to write *Thyrza*, Gissing spent much time in Lambeth, and his observations are reflected in this

chapter and elsewhere. On July 31, 1886, he wrote to his sister Margaret: "I am living at present in Lambeth, doing my best to get at the meaning of that strange world, so remote from our civilization." On the same day he wrote to his other sister, Ellen: "I am again day after day in Lambeth; this morning I got home only at 2 o'clock. Ah, but you will see the result, I have a book in my head which no one else can write, a book which will contain the very spirit of London working-class life."

p.25:
Lambeth Bridge. The old suspension bridge, where Gilbert Grail walks in a later scene, was built in 1862. *Paradise Street*: this, like all the place-names, is authentic.

p.59:
Swedenborg ... the Church of the New Jerusalem. Emanuel Swedenborg (1688–1772) based his beliefs on special interpretations of the Scripture, in accordance with mystical revelations granted to him. The first London churches belonging to his sect were founded in 1784.

p.69:
The "Might have been." etc. Gissing is using the language of the first two lines of Dante Gabriel Rossetti's sonnet, "A Superscription," No. XCVII of *The House of Life.* It begins: Look in my face; my name is Might-have-been; I am also called No-more, Too-late, Farewell;

p.75:
Eastbourne. In September, 1886, while working on *Thyrza*, Gissing found himself unable to continue, and abruptly left London to go to Brighton. In a letter to his sister Margaret dated September 27, he says that he walked from Brighton to Eastbourne, along the route taken by Egremont in the last chapter of *Thyrza.* When he reached Eastbourne, "... here at last was rest. Surely there is no more beautiful watering place. ...." His letter mentions most of the places he put to use in the Eastbourne scenes.

p.86:
a Carlylean editor. An allusion to the supposed editor of *Sartor Resartus*, who has excerpted the confused manuscripts of Teufelsdrockh.

p.88:
"He beginneth not ...". From Sir Philip Sidney's *Apology for Poetry.*

p.90
"A free library ... with a good reading-room." Not long after his return from America, on November 9, 1878, Gissing wrote to Algernon: "What a scandalous condition England is in with regard to public libraries. ... There is not a town of the least pretensions in the States, which has not its excellent Free Library. ... It is a disgrace that London possesses nothing to compare with all this."

p.146:
Dominie Sampson A character in Scott's Guy Mannering.

p.173:
It dealt with Religion. Gissing carried out his intention of lecturing, as Egremont does, only to the extent of giving one lecture before a club of workingmen on the subject of religion. On March 23, 1879, he wrote to Algernon: "Last night I lectured at Paddington on 'Faith and Reason.' It was an immense success! I spoke (not read) for an hour and a half, and at the end received the enthusiastic thanks of the meeting." Another lecture on religion for a similar audience was proposed, but never delivered.

p.303:
"Therefore I praised the dead . . ." Ecclesiastes, 4:2—3.

p.365:
Heu! fuge crudeles terras, fuge litus avarum. Aeneid, III, 44. "Alas! flee from this cruel land, this greedy shore." The words are spoken by the spirit of Polydorus, who has been killed for gold, to Aeneas, who has stopped in Thrace, and is planning to build his city there. *Savonarola* The fifteenth-century Florentine priest of course denounced the acquisition of wealth and worldly values in general.

p.419:
Chapter XXXV. Egremont's intellectual development during his stay in America reflects, to some extent, Gissing's own reactions during his own visit in 1876—77, but they are by no means the same. The part played in them by Walt Whitman, if it is relevant to Gissing's own ideas, belongs to a later date. In his introduction for the 1927 edition of *Thyrza,* Morley Roberts, who was one of Gissing's closest friends, claimed that he had first introduced him to *Leaves of Grass.* Gissing was at first reluctant to give Whitman a hearing, according to Roberts, but relented on listening to some of his verse. On the whole, the effect of Whitman on Egremont, who finds him bracing, healthy and inspiriting is not really favourable, in spite of his praise.

p.425
Moschus and Catullus. The elegant Sicilian pastoral poet of the second century B.C., and the Latin writer of notoriously free love poems and epithalamia who lived 84—54 B.C. are far more specialized in their appeal than Whitman.

p.439:
And one an English home; grey twilight poured —. From Tennyson's "Palace of Art." It begins a stanza describing one of the scenes pictured in a room of the palace: And one, an English home—grey twilight pour'd/On dewy pastures, dewy trees,/Softer than sleep—all things in order stored,/A haunt of ancient Peace.

Bibliography

Allen, Walter, *The English Novel*, New York, 1958.

Blench, J.W., "George Gissing's *Thyrza*," *Durham University Journal*, March, 1972,85—114.

Coustillas, Pierre, ed., *Collected Articles on George Gissing*, London, 1968.

Coustillas, Pierre, and Colin Partridge, eds., *Gissing: The Critical Heritage*, London and Boston, 1972.

Donnelly, Mabel Collins, *George Gissing, Grave Comedian*, Cambridge, Mass., 1954.

Francis, C.J., "The Revision of *Thyrza*," *The Gissing Newsletter*, October, 1971, (VII, 4),7—9.

Gapp, Samuel Vogt, *George Gissing, Classicist*, Philadelphia, 1936.

Gissing, George, *George Gissing's Commonplace Book*, ed. Jacob Korg; New York, 1962.

Gissing, George, *The Letters of George Gissing to Eduard Bertz*, 1887—1903 ed. Arthur C. Young; New Brunswick, New Jersey, 1961.

Gissing, George, *The Letters of George Gissing to Gabrielle Fleury*, ed. Pierre Coustillas; New York, 1964.

Gissing, George, *The Private Papers of Henry Ryecroft*, 1903.

Keating, P.J., *The Working Classes in Victorian Fiction*, London 1971.

Koike, Shigeru, "The Education of George Gissing," *English Criticism in Japan*, ed. Earl Miner, Tokyo, 1972.

Korg, Jacob, *George Gissing: A Critical Biography*, Seattle, 1963.

Roberts, Morley, *The Private Life of Henry Maitland*, New and revised ed. London, 1923. New ed. by Morchard Bishop, 1958.

Rosengarten, Herbert, "The Theme of Alienation in *Thyrza*," *The Gissing Newsletter*, December, 1966 (II, 4),1—3.

Sherif, Nur, "The Victorian Sunday in *Little Dorrit* and *Thyrza*," *Cairo Studies in English*, 1960,155—165.

Swinnerton, Frank, *George Gissing, A Critical Study*, London, 1912.

Bibliography